1916.

Amidst the harrowing chaos of World War I, a dedicated team of American volunteer nurses, led by Lydia Blackwell, find themselves stationed at a French casualty clearing station, near the front lines.

Supporting a remarkable team of surgeons and serving countless wounded, they navigate the relentless trials of war. Drawing strength from their unwavering convictions of faith and duty, and the steadfast support they offer one another, their journey explores the enduring forces of healing, love, and faith, even in unimaginably dark times.

The Meuse

THE MEUSE

Book I of *The River Series*
by
Rachael Hiatt

URBAN BOHEMIIA INC

For permission requests, contact:
Urban Bohemia, Inc.
23890 Copper Hill Dr., ste. 187
Valencia, CA 91354 USA.
info@urbanbohemia.com
rachaelhiatt.com

Library of Congress Cataloging-in-Publication Data is available.

ISBN 979-8-9914213-2-4
ISBN 979-8-9914213-0-0 (ebook)

Second Edition, 2024

This is a work of fiction dedicated to the volunteer nurses
who served with the Allied armies of
"The Great War", WWI.

Also with gratitude to my mother, who read the pages faster than
I could write at times, kept me on task,
and who also fell in love with the characters, as deeply as I did.

To Marilyn Downing

my mother, loyal critic, confidant
& a literary force of nature

Contents

... celebrations of life
with prayers, hymns, and homilies,
We brought our memories and regrets,
vain wishes we had spent
more time in laughter and the dance.

"There is
    a time to be born and a time to die..."

But the 'time to love' goes on into eternity.

-Marilyn M. Downing
"Beyond Time Marked on Calendars", *Samples From a Private Cask*

Prologue

Welcome to The River Series

These novels rely heavily on the art of written dialogue. In modern times, the telling of stories, the sharing of life experiences, the simple art of verbal communication is often superceded by handheld electronic devices, the distractions of television, computers, and the general bedlam of noise in our fast-paced world.

In contrast, *The River Series* novels rely on interpersonal dialogue for expression of feelings, emotions, thoughts, hopes, and expectations. The benefit of this type of dialogue is that the reader becomes an intimate part of the characters' experiences. A challenge, of this style of writing, is the risk that the reader may be drawn so far into the characters' lives that it feels very real. Reader be warned. You may laugh, you may cry.

I personally wept through the last half of book three, *Fishing Creek*, even while writing it.

But then again, I wept through half of *Tributary* as well, so, there you have it.

- Rachael Hiatt

Introduction

Lydia jumped out of the way of two men hurriedly carrying a soldier toward the temporary surgical tent. Stumbling backward, she found herself by the outside tables where surgeons were also hard at work under lantern light. Terrified, Lydia recognized Simon, being lifted onto one of the outer tables. A surgeon was bending over him, saw in hand. Lydia pushed past an orderly, knocking him off balance in her haste to intervene. "Stop!" she screamed, seeing Simon prostrate on the table. "Stop!"

The surgeon, someone unknown to her, paused, his hand raised above Simon's knee. Lydia sprinted to them, grabbing the man's arm. He shook her off sharply. "What are you doing, Nurse!" he demanded.

"Stop, please!" Lydia begged the doctor.

He pushed her to the ground. "You're hysterical. I'm trying to save this man's life!" he barked.

Lydia, summoning all of her remaining strength, screamed into the night, "Marcus!!!"

Inside the tent, Marcus heard the scream. He knew her voice. He heard the terror. He dropped everything, running toward the sound.

Jumping back up to her feet, Lydia threw herself over Simon's body, a medic attempted to pry her loose as she gripped the edge of the table. From the corner of her eye, she saw Marcus running toward them. "Marcus! Stop them!" she implored. "It's Simon!"

Marcus immediately assessed the situation, focused in on the bone saw and stayed the surgeon's hand, pushing the saw away from Simon.

"This is my patient!" the man barked at Marcus in confused disbelief. "For God's sake, let me save his life. The leg has to come off."

Marcus whipped around the table, grabbed the man, and in one swift move, placed the saw to his neck. "If you touch this man, I will cut your throat," Marcus pronounced coldly.

.... Chapter 10: Schism ....

The Meuse

Chapter 1
South of Verdun

1916

Lydia absent-mindedly stirred a spoon of sugar into the tin mug in front of her. It was the best way to tolerate the French army's version of coffee. She stretched her lower back, took a swig, grimaced and then hunched over the mess tent table where her best efforts to write an update, a summary to the American Red Cross, were failing her. How to describe what was happening here? How to explain what the small group of nurses were doing at the casualty clearance station along the Western Front? Would the people in Philadelphia even believe her? She was fairly certain that they would disapprove on some level. The nurses here in France were doing things that hadn't been taught in the two-year nurse training program back in the States. But then, in war, many things were not included in the manual. Adding a bit of descriptive language about the nurses' talents to the report wouldn't hurt its reception back home. Perhaps the leadership in Philadelphia wouldn't pick up on just how far these nurses were overstepping boundaries under the extreme circumstances of war.

The table shook abruptly as two men, carrying trays, plopped themselves down on the bench opposite her. Her coffee splashed slightly so she blotted the drops which had landed on her papers with the hem of her shirt. Brown on olive, drab. No one would even notice the spots. Usually, any blotches were blood, so what was a little coffee? Anyway, the powers that be, here, were not as big on uniform and propriety as they were on military bases placed anywhere other than eastern France. She regarded her damp papers and sighed as her companions enthusiastically dug into their meals, driven by a hunger born from spending most of the morning on their feet in surgery.

"Writing your memoirs, Nurse Blackwell? Life story?" one man asked the nurse. "Can I read the juicy parts? You know I'm quite interested!"

She shook her head and smiled. "No, Doctor Lovell. I am trying to find the right words to describe you to our liaison with the Red Cross."

The other man appraised his companion. "How about irreverent, rebellious, but a really good surgeon?" he offered between bites of potatoes and canned meat which were loaded onto the metal tray in front of him.

"Thanks, Doctor Finney," Marcus Lovell nodded. "Well said. But you forgot persistent, charming... and irresistible to women... am I not irresistible, Nurse Blackwell?"

Lydia raised her hand. "Irresistible. But stop there, Doctor... I got it back with 'irreverent'. I actually don't think the Red Cross cares about your skill outside of the surgery, as personable as you certainly can be. In fact, not to burst your bubble, but they might not be interested in you doctors at all. I'm including you primarily to let them know that the surgeons here seem to respect what we're doing. The Red Cross is more interested in how we nurses are faring."

Marcus nodded while chewing. "Then we have a lot in common, Nurse Blackwell, the Red Cross and I... I also have a personal and intense interest in you nurses..."

"Oh, good grief," Lydia sighed and finished off the coffee in her cup in two short swigs. It was even more bitter, now cold.

"What kind of report are they looking for?" Doctor Simon Finney asked with interest. "You've been with us almost three months now and know the lay of the land. What are you going to tell them about the work you ladies are doing here?"

Lydia sighed and placed her pen carefully by the report. "Something that does not get us sent home. I can't tell them where we are, exactly, because the French army won't allow it. And I can't tell them too much about the wounded men; that's also not allowed. And I can't tell them about what we need because that's army information. So, that leaves how many bedpans we empty, how many hours we work in a shift, how many dressings we change every day... things like that."

Simon shook his head regretfully. "Then you really can't tell them anything at all. You nurses are the heart and soul of the medical team. You should be able to report on how you look into a wound and tell us there's a bleed or how you knock on the tent at night and wake us up because one of the soldiers is bottoming out. Or how you put a clamp in our hands in the surgery before we even ask for it..."

Marcus took in the nurse sitting across from him as he considered the impact she had made, even on him alone, since her arrival. "Or how you nurses brighten our day, just walking into the surgery, when we're ready to throw in the proverbial towel because too many young soldiers were carried out in tarps the day before?" his teasing had shifted to a welcome sincerity.

The nurse once again raised her pen. "Definitely not that! No mortality figures."

"No, I expect not," Simon agreed. "We don't even want to dwell on that... we never count bodies."

The three of them fell silent, thinking of the death which they all witnessed daily.

Marcus, slightly smiling, teased, "Promise me you will tell them about my finer attributes, Nurse Blackwell." He then looked to Simon, "What are you going to say about my friend here? Have you noticed his finer attributes, too? Or just mine..."

Lydia twirled the pen slowly between her fingers for a moment, taking in the young doctor, Simon Finney, sitting just opposite of her. "Hmm," she started—

"No, don't say anything!" he exclaimed. Instantly embarrassed, Simon flushed beneath his beard. "I'm not sure I want to know!"

Lydia proceeded thoughtfully. "How about how Doctor Finney always says 'thank you' at the end of a case in the surgery. When we're on duty, he always asks if we need anything, before he leaves the recovery..." She said nothing about his calm, reserved disposition, or his thoughtful brown eyes. He was so steady... so dedicated...

Marcus poked his companion in the side. "Ah, you are the stuff of legend, my friend." He stood up, disentangling himself from the bench, picking up his empty tray and nodding to the two remaining. "Hate to eat and run, but I am off to recovery to round on the patients, and I will be most certain to ask the nurses on duty if they need anything at all before I leave the tent. Can't have Doctor Finney one-up me with manners now, can I?"

Simon stood as well, meal inhaled and plate clean. "And I am off to the shower and to sleep... my feet are killing me."

Lydia absently waved off the both of them, alone once again at the mess tent's long table. She readied her pen to complete the intentionally abbreviated report of what the volunteer Red Cross nurses had actually been doing since their arrival.

When the dozen nurses had arrived at the medical triage near the battle zone, the station's three surgeons had been waiting to greet their truck with anticipation. The decision to bring volunteer nurses from the Red Cross had been discussed at length, both the pros and cons of having women in the mobile camp... for certain, there were considerable benefits, but also serious challenges. The doctors did not like that these women would be so close to such real danger. They also knew that the surgical team was severely hampered by not having skilled nurses to assist them with the volume of wounded coming through their camp daily. Why these nurses had volunteered was anyone's guess. The surgeons had watched in measured gratitude as the truck pulled in and the women jumped out of the back, dressed in army trousers and shirts, ready for work. The nurses had quickly surveyed the small camp of tents and smiled at each other—a good sign that they weren't intimidated by the austere conditions of the camp. One of them had stepped forward to speak for the group.

"I'm Lydia Blackwell," she had told the doctors. "We're hungry and need to freshen up... long drive in a hot truck."

"I'm Doctor Harold Stockton, and these are doctors Marcus Lovell and Simon Finney. We're the surgeons for this station. You're most welcome here. We've been looking forward to your arrival at camp," he had replied.

They had regarded the brunette who was looking back at them steadily; she was sizing them up in return. Her introduction had been bold, direct, and then she had immediately introduced the other eleven. "We're here to make a difference and are all looking forward to working with you."

Then with impressive efficiency, they had settled into camp.

Clouds drifted over and past the summer sun. Lydia knew there was a gentle breeze outside the canvas walls, but it offered only mild relief from the stagnant heat inside the tents. The light wind attempted, ineffectively, to dry the sweat which rolled down her neck and between her shoulder blades. A lone leaf fell from the singular tree just outside the door of the surgical tent... one leaf, responding to an unspoken command to let go and drift down to die in the dry, brown grass. Lydia breathed out deeply, clearing her nose of the various smells which had barely been held at bay by the cloth mask she had just removed. It too was dripping wet. She turned her face up to the sky and felt the air move over her damp skin as she sank down onto a stack of tires, waiting for assignment. Immediately, the heat of the rubber seared through her trousers, so she sought out a patch of dry grass instead. A long shadow reached across her, dimming the sun, as someone drew closer. Shielding her eyes, she looked up.

"Mind if I join you?" Simon said tiredly, pulling the mask from his own face and using it as a damp towel to wipe his forehead. His brown curls were plastered to his forehead. He was concerned about her after their long hours in surgery.

"Please do. Free grass, compliments of the French," she replied. "Such as it is... well trampled and a bit downtrodden, what's left of it... like France."

Plopping down beside her on the ground, he gladly stretched out his legs – there was precious little time to get to know her better. "My feet are killing me."

"Pull off your boots," Lydia told him. "Let me have a look."

He obliged, not apologizing for the sweat-soaked socks. She got up on her knees as she pulled off his socks, laying them on the grass to dry. Peering at the bottom of his feet and between his toes, she sighed.

"No wonder," she said ruefully. "You should know better! You need to change your socks more often... you've got a couple of blisters. Wait here while I get some dry socks and some foot powder."

As she started to get to her feet, Simon grabbed her arm to stay her. "Don't, Lydia," he insisted, happy they were now on a first-name basis. "You're as tired as I am. I'll go to my tent, myself. Please sit back down and rest... in fact, let me check your feet as well!"

"My feet are fine," she assured him. "It's every other part of me... I'm just plain worn out. What a grueling day."

Simon nodded, but didn't say a word, knowing already what was in her mind—the damaged bodies they had just tried to put back together—young French and British men, all too far from home. Two days prior, the distant rumbling of cannon fire had been their warning of the casualties to come, the echoes reached the casualty clearing station, or CCS, as some called it, faster than messages sent over military radio. The medical team had worked through the night, litter bearers bringing them wounded, pulled from the back of horse-drawn carts or wheezing trucks, as fast as the doctors and nurses could tend to them—their weary compatriots sleeping wherever a blanket found them. He was concerned about the toll this was taking on the nurses, particularly this one.

"I've got to get over to recovery," Lydia broke the silence. "Check on them. Give one of the girls a break. They've all been at it for two solid days."

He stayed her again, lightly pressing her hand into the dry grass. "Look who's talking about adequate self-care now! You've been putting in just as many hours as they have. Stay a minute. You need a break too."

"What I need is..." she faltered, "to make a difference, Simon."

The doctor looked up to the sky scuttled with clouds. "Good grief, Lydia!" he blurted out. "What do you think you just did in there? What did we do all night in there?" he added, as a small reconnaissance plane droned off somewhere in the distance as they fell into another moment of silence.

"Half of them will still die—you know it as well as I do, Simon, and don't say you don't because you'd be lying." She looked down at the ground and the yellow grass beneath her fingers. It was dying, too.

"Probably so." He nodded, wishing he could hold and comfort her. "But they would have had no chance at all if we hadn't spent the night doing our best to give them a shot of making it home to their families. You've been at this station almost three months now. Think of all the young men we've saved in just three months by being out here, close to where they're getting hit... all those who made it back to the field hospitals because of what we do here. You volunteered for this, right? And why? Because you believed it would matter. And it does. I hope your reports include all of this."

She retrieved her hand from his, rested her elbows on her knees and perched her chin on balled-up fists. "I couldn't tell Philadelphia that most of these boys don't even have beards... haven't even had their first date yet." There was more than a hint of anger in her voice.

He looked compassionately at her, his brown eyes filled with kindness and reassurance. "With hearts of lions..." Then he saw her eyes tearing above her sun-dried cheeks and awkwardly shifted closer to her, wrapping a sweaty arm around her shoulders. He had wanted to add "like you", but couldn't bring himself to say it. The friendship that had been growing between them since her arrival, did however permit the expression of at least a little bit of comfort. "Look, Lydia," Simon thoughtfully offered, "I see how those wounded men look up at you nurses when you walk into the recovery, how their eyes light up at your touch. You make a difference every time you minister to one of those young men, and you shouldn't doubt it for a second. When they go to the field hospital, they'll remember there was that one nurse out there—"

She pulled away immediately. "Don't, Simon," she whispered, her voice tired, but not resentful of his gesture. "If I stop and think about it anymore, I'll lose it completely. And I must, must go to the recovery to check on them and relieve one of the girls. You know me, Simon. I need to stay on task."

Indeed, Simon was getting to know her. There was something about Lydia in particular that had conquered his shyness with the opposite sex enough to try to talk with her. She had caught his eye instantly. From the minute she'd arrived, he had wanted to welcome her, to express his appreciation for the dedication that compelled her to come into an active war zone.

Now, Simon squeezed her hand again, trying to infuse her with some of his strength. "Go do what you have to. I'll be over at the recovery in a little bit, if Marcus doesn't beat me to it. I need a quick wash and a cup of coffee."

"Bring me one?," she asked as she stood.

"Which? The wash or the cup of coffee?" he teased, looking up at her and squinting against the sun.

"The coffee and..."

"I know," Simon interrupted her with a small smile. "Black with one sugar, if there is any."

Nodding, Lydia turned away toward the adjacent tent that was lined within by two rows of cots filled with injured soldiers. The door and flaps of the large tent were tied open to allow air to blow in over the hot bodies, lying listless in their medical triage. Bending her head slightly and dodging a pole, she entered. Immediately Lydia saw that very few of the men were awake; only an isolated moan escaped from one man's lips. In a few hours, when the ether wore off and the laudanum rounds were due, there would be many more moans. Ether, the standby for half a century of medicine, still hung sweetly over the men. Lydia could smell it in the air as she moved between the boys, looking at their faces for signs of fever, cheeks flushed from more than warm air, dry skin where it should be perspiring. The nurses and orderlies could never get enough water into these men without running an intravenous.

Lydia stopped by one of the other women who were, like her, part of the early Red Cross volunteer nurses. Her friend and tentmate Nancy Mitchell bent over a young man as she attempted to see under his shoulder where a thick bandage had been secured using layers of cloth.

"What is it, Nancy?" Lydia pressed, noting her look of concern. Following her gaze, Lydia saw the small pool of blood on the ground under the man's cot. "Let me help you," she added, quickly grasping his torso to roll him up onto his side. Worriedly, they saw the extent of the blood-soaked cloth underneath. Catching the attention of another nurse across the tent, Lydia called over, "Charlotte, go speed up Doctor Lovell. He should be heading this way. Let's get this bandage off, Nancy, and see what's going on..."

Together, the two nurses pulled at the long string of now sticky cloth, letting it pile in a heap on the ground by the cot. Blood was dripping, bright red and warm, from the newly sutured bayonet gash, just below the man's scapula. Lydia wadded the remaining end of the bandage into a ball against the wound, putting her weight against the man's back as he groaned.

"Go tell Gretha to get a table cleaned off next door and wash some instruments, quickly," she told the other nurse. "He's losing blood and we have none to replace it."

Nancy nodded, wiping her hands on her trousers, hurrying off in the direction of the operating tent to give Gretha the message to make ready a table for Doctor Lovell.

Lydia called out, to no one in particular, "Ordonné!" until a weary soul near the recovery tent came into view. "Help me, please," Lydia urged the young man, who was stumbling from fatigue, but still on his feet in these morning hours. "Get a litter for him." The orderly nodded, finding the energy to pick up his pace once again, in search of the nearest empty litter, while Lydia kept her hold on the back of the bleeding man.

"And you, young man," she whispered to his closed eyes and pale face, "Ne lâche pas... don't you let go! Just think of your mother and your girl back home. They're going to need you to come back in one piece, safe and sound. You just think of them and hold on."

In just a few minutes, Marcus rushed into the tent, Nancy on his heels, as she informed him that Gretha had already completed her task; a table was clean and ready.

"Keep the pressure on while we get him on the litter, Nurse Blackwell," Marcus said quickly as Lydia pressed with both hands, one against the man's scapula and the other against the front of his chest wall. Others lifted the man onto a litter, carrying him the twenty feet into the next tent where the assembled team would take over. Inside the surgery, Lydia stayed briefly, watching as Doctor Lovell cut the sutures, only recently applied, to locate the bleeding artery in the man's shoulder and tie it off. He wouldn't suture the wound shut again so they could watch for infection. The young soldier just might make it, Lydia thought before backing out of the tent wearily. Maybe Simon was right. Maybe they were making a difference... just one soldier at a time.

Simon was outside waiting. "Finally," he said, waving a cup of coffee in one hand. "I heard what happened... you're a bit of a mess."

Lydia looked down at her blood-soaked clothes. "Yes. It would appear that I am," she conceded.

"Just can't stop saving life, can you?" he gently teased. "C'mon." Simon led her away from the surgery to where he knew the shower tent was currently empty. "Saved you a room at the inn. Get in," he commanded... Lydia complied without protest. A shower was a welcome relief, and she was glad he'd kept it available on her behalf.

Stepping obediently into the tiny shower, Lydia pulled off her sticky shirt and trousers, hanging them on a hook to wash later. A bucket sat on a stand next to a large tank of tepid water with a metal spigot. Lydia turned the valve, filling the bucket with clear water and pouring it over her head, willing the sweat and stains of the last two days to wash away. Taking a cake of soap from the stand, she scrubbed every last inch of her body before refilling the bucket to pour it over her face and hair, letting it run into the ground trough where it rolled away, a mix of soap, blood, and fatigue. Filling the bucket several more times, she let the water slowly trickle down her skin, finally enjoying the relief cleanliness offered, the rejuvenation it brought.

"This was a good idea," she called out gratefully to Simon. The flap of the tent opened slightly, letting in a wedge of sunshine.

"Done?" Simon asked cheerfully. "Feel a little better?" He extended a set of clean clothes to her and looked appreciatively for a fleeting second at the nurse glistening now from fresh wash water instead of sweat. For him, it was an incredibly bold move... just to look. She was beautiful.

Knowing that the man was testing the waters, Lydia turned to take the towel and met Simon's gaze, not attempting to hide her vulnerability. "What do you see, Simon?" she asked him, as she started drying off, curious how he would respond, and hoping he would be pleased.

He paused before answering, dispensing a flippant answer he knew his best friend Marcus would have used. "I see a very beautiful nurse," he finally replied, his heart pounding in his chest... closing the tent flap again he allowed her to dry herself and get dressed behind the privacy of the canvas.

But is that all you see, I wonder...? she asked without speaking aloud. *Is there nothing more?*

The evening came quickly. As many as could, slept while the sun moved high overhead and then began its descent into the west, before starting their work in the cooler evening air. There had been no more rumors of battle casualties en route to their station near the front lines, south of Verdun. The small French contingent of soldiers who protected, translated, and helped to relocate the mobile unit were milling about the camp. It was not travaux légers, or light duty, as the casualty clearing station moved often and was never far from the front line with the Germans. Among those stationed at the CCS, there was a shared "sigh of relief" that tonight would be quiet. This evening, it was almost cool enough to cover the wounded with more than just a thin army blanket. There were still three doctors, but now only eleven nurses in the compound tending to the wounded. One of the nurses had already been sent out to a field hospital after suffering from a bout of pneumonia that persisted, exhausting her beyond her ability to return to duty.

All of the nurses were volunteers answering the call of the "Edith Clavell" of their day to try to ease suffering and rescue the maimed and injured wherever possible. They all knew Nurse Clavell had been imprisoned and shot to death by the Germans for her role in the war. They knew and volunteered anyway, some over the objections of family and friends back home, across the ocean. Others had no family to speak of and came just because it seemed the right thing to do. This group of nurses, in particular, hailed from all over the United States. Only Gretha Bernstein spoke German fluently due to a strong family lineage, but all of them kept practicing basic French from the infantry manual provided by the War Department to help them with the French soldiers. Their bedside manner, though, needed no translation. Easing suffering was universally understood.

After they had eaten some supper, some of those not tending to the wounded sat around a small campfire sheltered from early evening breeze by the encircling tents. Overhead, a few stars came out, sparkling brilliantly against a sky growing dim. Their chief medical officer, Harold Stockton, went off to catch a few hours of sleep in his tent, expecting any number of possible emergencies would arise during the night. He was a Hopkins doctor, one of the very best in setting shattered bones and restoring blood flow to starved limbs. The Hopkins doctors were known for forming highly specialized units for mobile triage and evacuation near the battle lines. Harold was lanky with fine, strong hands and a wife-to-be waiting for his return home to Maryland. Marcus and

Simon, the other two doctors, sat near the fire talking about past, and future, fishing adventures in the lakes of upstate New York, where apparently salmon could be found at the right time of year by those willing to wade icy streams with rod and hook, which sounded quite inviting in the summer heat.

Off duty nurses, orderlies and French soldiers lay on blankets or sat on makeshift benches from planks of wood, a few staring into the glowing coals of the dying fire as if they were reading their fortunes... Lydia watched her companions, busy in their own thoughts or in conversation, then turned her attention to an outdated letter she had received several days ago. It had been waiting in the small footlocker by the cot in her tent until the next lull in the surgery. She had intentionally avoided reading it till now, almost certain she knew what it contained. So, in the quiet between storms, she pulled it out of her trouser pocket and carefully tore it open along the top, trying not to rip the delicate sheets within. As expected, it was a letter from home, from Greensburg, Pennsylvania, where the northern Appalachian mountains lifted the landscape into folded valleys and running creeks.

"*Dear Lydia,*" she read, "*I hope this finds you well. I cannot imagine the things you are seeing and doing over there... or even where you might be right now.*

No one here seems to know anything about the war, if there is victory or defeat. Perhaps you are rolling bandages, as you did here. What a mountain of bandages you girls rolled and boxed up. Can't imagine anyone needing so many rolled-up bandages as that. By the way, the high school girls still roll them up now and ship them off to God knows where.

We're all rationing and supporting the war effort in every conceivable way. There are newsreels that come through occasionally, but it's always old news. An oxymoron that, old news... Say, did you know that they think they can figure out how to make talking movies? Just imagine that! Whatever will the organ players do? Maybe they will go join the Army now – ha ha!

Well, I know I'm just running on here. I thought you may have heard by now that I'm heading out west. I've accepted a terrific post at a small college in Utah needing a professor in math and science. They found me from an editorial I wrote about science changing societal values if not applied properly and figured I would fit right into their group out there. It's reasonable pay, and what it lacks monetarily will be made up for in some research opportunities and free room and board.

I suspect your mother has informed you of this already and that I will be taking Linda with me. You remember Linda, don't you? The woman from the school who helps in the financial office? Well, I'm sure you've been told that we've become close friends, and she is excited about the opportunity to see Utah. I know you will understand that I need someone able to be with me during this exciting transition. And really, who knows how long you will be away and if it would be realistic for us to try again upon your return. I know you will wish me well and I remain fondly yours, Derrick"

Lydia only read the letter one time. She took a deep breath and let it out slowly. Derrick had thought Lydia made an excellent teller at the bank where she had worked and where she had met him through the bars of her teller window, carefully counting his transactions. Then she went on to nursing training. When she told Derrick she was volunteering for the Red Cross and the war, he started pulling away almost immediately. He had not even asked her to accompany him to his college Christmas dance, claiming that with the war on it was frivolous to even hold such an event. Perhaps he had taken Linda. Lydia realized he would never be able to comprehend why she had chosen to leave for Europe and war.

But no, Derrick, Lydia thought now, *Mother did not share your news with me. Nor does it matter to me, now. We are more than just miles apart at this point... and have been for some time.*

Lydia stood in the twilight, letter in hand, deliberating. Conversation around the fire was softening as night fell. She heard the breeze rustle the remaining leaves on the singular tree. She could hear faint murmurings from patients in the recovery tent. There was the sound of the horses shuffling and snorting quietly along the rope line where they were tethered. The fire crackled. She took a few steps closer to where the few flickering flames ate away at the dried wood underneath them... they always wanted more to eat. So, she took the letter in her hand and allowed the pages to fall into the red, hot coals, where they quickly caught, curled and blackened as they burned. And after a short pause, Lydia turned and walked across the grass, slipping into her tent without saying goodnight to anyone... not even a nod to Simon and Marcus.

Simon looked up from where he lay stretched out on a blanket and saw her move close to the embers. He watched her let the pages of the letter catch fire to be consumed and then turn immediately away from the gathering.

"Curious", Marcus had seen it, too. "Hm. Wonder what that's all about?"

Simon watched Lydia turn and disappear into her tent. She hadn't, as was usual, gone to the recovery to check on the others before retiring... instead leaving the other nurses to the task. That, more than the burning of the letter, told Simon she must be upset by whatever news had finally reached her. Simon considered his somewhat limited options. He was better with a scalpel than delicate conversation, well suited to being a surgeon where orders were clear and the focus was the patient. Surgery had come easily to him, whereas relationships had not. So, Simon didn't answer Marcus' question about the pages in the fire. He remained on the blanket and berated himself lightly for his insecurities. The man sighed, wondering if Lydia was even interested in a relationship.

Would she even want any emotional support? he wondered. *Still, earlier, hadn't she allowed him a rather provocative invitation to draw closer?* He looked over at the nurses' tents.

Simon's mother had been taken to a sanitorium when he was just twelve. His father had died of consumption years before that, his older brother and sister were sent to relatives to work on their farms or in their homes, to help with childcare. They never did move back home. After his mother's illness took her from him, Simon, who had shown an aptitude for medicine, had been taken under tutelage by Dr. Dwayne Albright, the local doctor, surgeon and veterinarian in the mountains which curved around Sutton, West Virginia. Doc Albright had ensured that young Simon finished his eighth-grade exams, continued his education and applied for his medical training straightaway.

As a boy, Simon had come to love the old man who had been his mentor and a father figure as he grew into adulthood. The country doctor remained a bachelor, devoting his entire life to being a rural physician instead of pursuing a wife or family. Doc Albright had been adept at diagnosing illnesses, from smallpox to a ruptured appendix, a capable teacher for Simon in those matters. He could not teach the young man the social graces of caring for a woman or how to appreciate the concerns of the opposite sex, beyond helping them to birth a baby of course.

Watching Lydia go to her tent, Simon wished he knew the right thing to do or say, to show his concern for her... and before Marcus beat him to it. Lydia intrigued Simon with her technical skill and uncanny ability to anticipate when a patient was "getting into trouble" before there were any obvious signs of infection or complication from surgery. If truth be known, he found her intuitions a bit frightening, as he was often left wondering if she could sense his lack of experience in relationships just as easily as she could sense one of his patients failing. He was always glad when she was elbow to elbow with him at his table. He knew that he wanted her beside him in surgery, a given, but there was so much more he wanted to share with her.

More disconcerting though, he had also begun to recognize a certain anticipation if she merely sat beside him in the mess tent. And although he had seen his share of the female anatomy, his reaction to her was rather remarkable. This morning's move to hand her clean trousers and a shirt in the shower was something more properly carried out by one of the nurses. He had hoped not to offend Lydia, but he hadn't expected her to have been so openly comfortable about him seeing her. Now Simon was even entertaining the idea that Lydia might want his attention and, with the incident in the shower, maybe had extended an invitation to... something more than just their professional relationship.

It was so much easier to diagnose a broken bone or ruptured spleen!

Rising from the ground by the fireside, Simon shook out his blanket and carefully folded it. "I'll make the rounds, Marcus," he told his friend beside him. "You take the night off... and may it be quiet tomorrow!"

Marcus nodded and looked gratefully in the direction of his own cot. "Good enough, but I'm afraid any lull we have will be short-lived."

"What've you heard?" Simon returned quickly.

"Only a rumor that our wounded will be carted off to the field hospital within twenty-four hours and we will be moving to follow the companies nearest the front." Marcus sighed deeply. Overhearing, the others around the fire turned to listen. "I'm afraid we won't be staying in any one place very long, people. And we are short of surgical supplies. We need... everything. Lieutenant Aubert sent a telegram to Major d'Espèrey yesterday during the surgery... told him we are depleted."

Simon nodded. "Hope we have enough for tomorrow, at least. Sometimes, the army approaches the locals. They do have apothecaries."

"They have little more than bandage rolls made from clothing from their own dead," Marcus replied. "And there is plenty of that."

Simon nodded. "I'm sure the French will find supplies for us. If nothing else happens in war, they expect casualties and plan for it. Armies will run out of everything else before they run out of care for the wounded who end up going home as heroes, carrying their scars and wounds that win more support than politics."

Marcus also rose to his feet. "You're probably right. We also must add to the supply list something to treat those exposed to the trench gases, to improve their breathing. Maybe the heroin the Germans use. We're going to see more gas injuries as we move north."

Simon nodded. "We need to talk to Aubert about how to get some to try it. We don't even have basic suction out here, let alone up-to-date gas treatment information." He moved off thoughtfully toward the recovery, now distracted from his earlier relationship dilemma by this new information that the station might move again so soon. Stooping, he entered the recovery where the sides had been rolled down for the night. He made rounds by the light of lanterns softly shining throughout, illuminating the drawn faces of the men within. The duty nurse, Alice Miller, quietly and efficiently moved from bed to bed, offering the men drops of laudanum and tucking in sheets, some of which had been supplied by locals who had compassion on the French soldiers lying in the French countryside.

"How are the men doing, Nurse Miller?" he asked her quietly. "Any you're concerned about?"

"Most are as well as I can hope for," the nurse replied. "Their pain seems to be under control. Everyone is breathing. We've been vigilant in washing and airing out the tent as often as possible to stop the spread of germs and to keep the lice from jumping from litters as they arrive. I think we have a better success rate containing germs out here than in the hospital, if truth be told. But the lice do seem to love us."

"Hm, perhaps..." the doctor mused. "Infection rates are high everywhere. Of course, we haven't had as many patients all at one time, out here near the front, as they do at the field hospitals where sometimes patients spend months recovering. We just don't keep them here very long. Whatever bugs they have here probably leave with them when we truck them out. No doubt even the pesky ones. We probably ship them on."

Alice paused after leading him down to stop at the side of one young man lying still on a cot. "The hospitals should have less infection because they have a lot more resources than we do, like running water, so no excuse, I say. But there is this one soldier worrying me, Doctor. He hasn't woken up to ask for pain medication, not even once, and he was one of the first on the table this morning. Doctor Lovell saw him earlier, but he still hasn't stirred."

Simon looked closely at the man. "Fred Howser," he read, taking a quick glance at the metal identification tag hanging around his neck. Lifting the man's eyelids, he peered into his pupils by the light of the lamp. He took note of their width, seeing in the dim light that one was now much larger than the other. He listened carefully to the soldier's chest, to the beat of his heart, and then shook him roughly by the shoulder and called, "Frederick! Can you hear me?"

The soldier didn't stir. His chest moved in slow, shallow breaths.

Simon turned to Alice. "Not even once... not even a moan?"

She shook her head.

"Understood. I'll be back shortly." He saw the immediate need.

Simon left the tent, crossing the short distance to where he knew Lydia lay on her cot, probably asleep, but perhaps not. What she needed the most was to make a difference; she had told him as much earlier that day. And burr holes were always a risky procedure. He wanted her by his side as another set of eyes and ears. He wanted her intuition next to him. He wanted her to feel valued. He also wanted an excuse to make sure that she was alright. He knocked softly at the strut to the nurses' tent and called inside. "Nurse Blackwell?"

Her prostrate form on the cot did not respond. He pushed back the tent flap, went to her cot, and sat on the footlocker beside it. Resisting the temptation to touch her hair, he instead took her hand.

"Lydia," he said again, softly.

She rolled over, waking from the deep escape of sleep. "Simon?" she started. "What on earth?"

"One of the young soldiers, Howser, no doubt has an intracranial bleed. He needs a burr hole. Will you assist me?"

Opening her eyes, she felt his hand around her own and didn't immediately pull it away. "Of course," she said. "You don't ever need to ask."

He nodded, his face dim in the light from the embers of the fire making its way through the screens. He pulled her to a sitting position on her cot. "I thought, of course, you might be too tired to help me…"

She shook her head, her eyes dark in the early night. "No, I wasn't really tired. I just… I just needed to clear my thoughts for a while and sleep. I'm fine now."

"I saw," Simon started awkwardly, "I mean, earlier, I thought I saw you put a letter in the fire? I just wondered if you were… if you are alright? If you received bad news from home?"

Lydia squeezed his hand lightly. "It was old news," she replied quickly. Then she paused, deciding to be honest with him. "No, that's not true, actually. Yes, it was old news. But it was from a friend who wrote that he was moving on... to go to Utah... to, to a new life, with someone new to share that life..."

Simon squeezed her hand firmly. "Lydia, I am truly sorry," he started.

Lydia interrupted him. "Don't be. It's alright, Simon. He and I drifted apart long ago when I left for nursing training in Philadelphia. He never thought I should be a nurse. He never thought it was a good idea for me to train for something like war, let alone go be part of an actual conflict. He felt that changing dirty bandages and washing sick bodies was distasteful... was beneath me."

This time, Simon boldly reached up and touched her cheek in the twilight. "He was profoundly wrong. What you do for your patients only adds to an already beautiful spirit. I think you're a remarkable woman, Lydia."

The woman beside him sighed. "I think I have just a typical, average spirit, Simon. But in answer to your first question, no, I'm not tired. I'll help you fix up that young soldier."

"If I can."

"You can. Your hands are so steady. If there is a chance, you'll give it to him," she said matter-of-factly.

Simon felt his own hands in the darkness, rubbing his thumbs against his palms thoughtfully. "Using my hands for surgery was the only goal I ever had in life, Lydia. I never aspired to run a hospital, or travel, or even serve in war. I only wanted to help patients wherever I was called. A very old friend of mine, my mentor, told me once that whether a patient was a horse, a child, or an elderly man trying to get up off the floor, the patient deserved the best these hands could give."

She nodded, which was barely discernible in the darkness. "Then that man would be proud of you, Simon. I've watched you work in the surgery for three months now, and your dedication to your patients is the same no matter what you are attempting to do. I'm sure the ones you left behind in the States must miss you terribly. I think you're a fine doctor... and a really good man."

He laughed dryly. "After my own training, when I was a country doctor, I did surgeries in the most unlikely places at times—kitchen tables, barns, a horse drawn cart. Never knew what would come through the door or where I would be called in the middle of the night."

Lydia grew curious. "Who assisted you then, mister Country Doctor?"

"Oh, it varied," he laughed again. "Sometimes a farmer's wife or a nosey cow. And when I was lucky, a nurse in training for country medicine would come out, usually a Catholic nun from Pittsburgh or one of the other convents. Like the ones who sent women to serve back in the Civil War and still do in the hills of Appalachia. They came to me and asked me to give them some field experience meeting the needs of those, shall we say, less advantaged. Wonderful people live in those hills in West Virginia."

Lydia wished she could see his face and the expression it wore while describing these memories. She had read about the nuns who had served in Gettysburg, Vicksburg, and other dreadful battlegrounds where too many people had died. Even her own great-great grandmother was supposedly a midwife of sorts out on the prairies of the newly explored west.

"I'd better help you then, since I don't see any cows or nuns lurking in the shadows," she stated, rising to follow him to the recovery. They stopped for a surgical drill, antiseptics, and bandages and took the supplies into the recovery tent.

Alice was still attending to her other patients, but now, upon the return of the doctor, she approached them at the soldier's cot. "Need any help, Doctor?" she asked, seeing Lydia come in behind the man.

"No, thanks, Nurse Miller. This is going to be guesswork at best," Simon told her. "Since we don't even know where the bleed is."

Alice nodded at her friend Lydia and moved on, but glanced anxiously from time to time at the two huddling over the stricken young soldier.

After laying out their supplies, Simon carefully checked the man's reflexes, muscle tone, and his pupils once more. He poured antiseptic on the left side of his scalp, and Lydia quickly shaved away a circle of soft dark hair, leaving a bare patch resembling a bull's eye on a marksman's post. She briefly wondered if she should save the curl for a girlfriend that he might have back home... but pushed the thought away not wanting to attract any bad luck.

Adjusting the light of the lantern to where she could watch the patient's limbs for twitch or tremor, Lydia sat at the top of the cot where she could hold his head still and see into his eyes. She watched Simon carefully press the drill against the man's exposed skull. The broken skin bled slightly, the drill crunching against the bone as Lydia held a bandage underneath to catch the bleed to come. Simon's hands worked steadily, boring into the skull, finally just breaking through and pulling it back to see if a flow of clot or hemorrhage would follow. There was nothing. She took her razor to another patch of hair, choosing an area two inches farther back along the left temporal ridge, watching Simon apply the drill bit slowly to penetrate the new area. A drop of blood seeped out around the tip.

"I think you've found it," she said quietly.

The doctor nodded, "I think actually that you found it!" He pulled the drill bit out slowly, inserted a scalpel into the hole, and made a very small incision. He was gratified to see an issue of dark blood beginning to ooze out from the opening of the skull. "Give me a little more..." he started, but she had already adjusted the lamp to shine on the new hole as he wiped away an emerging black clot.

"Here's the real trick of the thing, isn't it? As long as I didn't drill too deep and damage his brain... if tissue doesn't follow..." Simon watched carefully. "Or a fresh bleed..."

Lydia peered into the soldier's eyes intently as the two of them waited. Their patient began to breathe more deeply. She reached down, pinching the soldier's right arm just below the elbow, and felt the arm withdraw slightly. "We've got a little responsive movement," she reassured the doctor waiting beside her.

Simon pulled out the large clot carefully. There was no overtly fresh blood following it from the open tract leading into the young man's injured brain. Simon looked up and saw a threaded needle gleaming in the lamp light, already extended in his direction.

"I suspect you want me to close up these holes?" he teased her.

"Indeed," she replied, dabbing antiseptic on both open wounds again. "We'll watch him for swelling."

"I have no doubt," he stated, stitching the scalp closed, over both burr holes, to keep any infection at bay.

Then, the soldier involuntarily drew in a deep, ragged breath as the pressure on his brain eased. Simon took his stethoscope and listened through the chest wall, hearing the steady regularity of the heartbeat underneath. He looked up as Alice hurried over to check on their progress. "I think this is going to work, Nurse Miller... Just let me know if you see any seizure activity."

Alice nodded gratefully. "Of course, Doctor Finney. I have a cousin named Fred..."

"Over here?" he asked her with concern, wiping his hands on a towel.

"No, Cincinnati. He's only fourteen, thank goodness. This one doesn't look to be much more than that though..."

Simon nodded at the woman with understanding. "I'm glad he's safe. No opiates for this one for a while. Let's get him awake first. Just call me if anything changes."

She nodded, bending down to check young Fred's eyes for herself as his one large pupil began to shrink in size. She peered at him, satisfied. The doctor heard her whisper as he turned away. "Good. This is very good..."

Simon exited into the darkness, the campfire extinguished for the nightly black-out, with Lydia right behind him. Their location was far from secret, but the army was understandably cautious. "I'm famished," he told Lydia as they made their way to the benches under the empty mess tent. There was never foodstuff left out in the open for rodents to find during the night.

"You're always hungry," she said, looking around. "Day-old bread sound appetizing? We could probably locate that much."

He smiled. "Not really. I can wait till the cook starts breakfast. It's only six hours from now for dried eggs and canned meat. Ah well, at least the air has cooled off. Anyway, you'd better get back to your tent to finish the nap I so rudely interrupted. We'll have another long day tomorrow, no doubt."

She smiled. "It's okay, I'm awake now." She sat down on one of the benches and leaned back against the wooden table, stretching her legs, wishing he would join her. "I'm glad you came and got me, Simon."

"Marcus says he heard we're moving out soon," he informed her, changing the subject, as he stood nearby.

"Do we know where?" she asked, quickly looking up at him.

He shook his head. "Closer to the trenches, above Verdun, I'd guess. Harold and Marcus want to know how to treat gas exposure, so I expect we're heading farther north where more of that is happening."

Lydia's voice dropped. "Those poor men. Struggling to breathe. Their lungs just filling with fluid."

"Have you seen it?" Simon asked, surprised.

She nodded. "Not immediately, but after the fact. Those masks only help a little. The gas lingers in the air, and some of the soldiers take the masks off too soon, thinking they're through the worst of it... just breathe it right in. They said it's chlorine gas."

"Dear God," Simon exclaimed. "Where were you?"

"Ypres... I came over with a group of British nurses and worked with them for a while before I asked to be assigned to a medical clearing station. The poor men, hiding from the bullets in the trenches, but not able to hide from the gas. And where do you run if you're in a crowded trench? How do you get away from a poison filling every inch of breathable air, in a trench? You get your head blown off if you rise up to find clean air. Men were panic-stricken when they got to us. They were difficult to assess because their French was confused and difficult to translate. I can't imagine how so many survived. The ones above ground just pulled in more gas by running, gulping in more air. Better to hunch down and breathe less."

Shaking his head, Simon contemplated, "The ways men find to kill each other... never ceases to baffle me..." Now he lowered himself onto the plank bench beside her, stretching one arm along the table, close, barely touching her back, feeling again that incredible anticipation she awoke in him... and the uncertainty of where she might set the limits for his attention.

Lydia turned her head and looked at his profile, his eyes catching the smallest glitter of night, seeing the beard on his chin. *He has a nice profile*, she thought. *Is he ever going to make an overture to deepen whatever this is?* "Simon," she started, suddenly thinking there was a reason why he held himself back with her. "Are you married?"

He gave a short laugh. "After three months working side by side, you ask me if I am married? No, none of the nuns wanted me."

She elbowed him lightly in the ribs. "Don't tease. I never asked because it's none of my business. But you asked me earlier about my... the letter I got from home and I told you. So now I'm asking about you."

He sighed into the night. "Nope, never married. My aspirations never got quite that far. And that man I told you about earlier, the guy who mentored me, he stepped in after my mother was taken to a sanitorium when I was a kid. His entire life was medicine. He taught me well, got me to medical school, trained me afterward in the field... sometimes in a literal countryside field... but he wasn't the kind who could make sure I was schooled in the social graces."

Lydia nodded, now understanding his hesitance with her. "I see. But surely there were scads of nurses in the hospitals where you trained, surely someone who turned your head?" she offered helpfully.

"There were scads of student nurses," he nodded, teasing. "But none that turned my head. After all, I was in the operating theater a lot of the time at the hospitals, and the nurses, if there were any, were all covered from head to toe and never spoke. Not a very good way to get to know someone."

Her voice was quiet and serious in the darkness. "Are you sorry about that now? That there is no young woman waiting for you back home, waiting for that next letter to come telling her how much you miss her? To give you a reason to want to get home from... all of this?"

Simon paused before answering, so out of his element and feeling it acutely. He deflected. "I could ask you the same question. After your... the... letter you got, if he is no longer there waiting for you to join him, do you have a reason to want to... are you anxious to get back home?"

"You dodged the bullet, Simon," she observed dryly, lightly patting his knee for emphasis.

He then turned to the woman beside him on the rough bench and took her hand in his own. "I'm lousy at this, Lydia, truly I am. I enlisted voluntarily for this... well, you volunteered, too. But all

I can tell you is that I am glad I'm right here, right now, even with war all around us... and I'm grateful that you are here, even with the war all around us. And as far as that man back home in the States... in my mind, he wasn't ever worthy of you."

"Well then!" she softly exclaimed. "I'm glad I'm right here with you, too." And they sat quietly in the darkness as Simon kept his arm around her, happily holding her hand, until they both decided to get some sleep before the night was totally spent.

Chapter 2
The Call of Duty

The hooves of the horses clopped along the hardened dirt road, pulling wagons filled with tents, litters, medical supplies, water collectors, the canteen and more. The unit's few trucks and ambulances wheezed along behind the horses, carrying most of the personnel: the nurses, doctors, and orderlies. Along the road, they had passed civilians walking south against traffic—people leading livestock, carrying heavy bundles on their backs, the local French... mostly those displaced by war, heading away from the worst of the fighting. The mobile clearing station was instead heading north, closer to a place none of them had ever heard of before the war, Verdun. This is where there had been heavy fighting since February. There, the French were holding the line against the Germans with only incremental gains, while even further north, fighting was comparably intense at a place called Somme. The battle line was extensive, casualties were reported to be very heavy and the Allied Army was in dire need of surgeons.

The Red Cross and the army commanders had assured the nurses that they were in no way required to go to the triage outposts at the front. After all, they were not commissioned by the army. There was ample need for nursing care back in field hospitals which were scattered across France, away from the front lines... a respectable option for service. Only nurses who volunteered to do so went closer to the dangerous Red Zone.

The mobile clearing station had been steadily moving along the road for most of the morning, passed by faster, less burdened army vehicles heading north along the Western Front. French soldiers, who had been assigned to the CCS, marched alongside with rifles at the ready and the medical team in the trucks were committed to moving forward right along with them. As they witnessed refugees trudging southbound, war-weary with, too often, vacant eyes, the eleven nurses and three doctors in the truck frequently fell silent, considering the gravity of this somber retreat. These eleven American nurses had, like Lydia, started out with British forces before asking the powers-that-be to go forward where the need was the greatest.

Officially, back home in the States, the Red Cross was actively recruiting and providing appropriate war training for nurses, as was the American Army Nurse Corps. They were preparing nurses for the ordeal yet to come overseas if America engaged in the war, but these small groups of nurses, in the field, were already seasoned and doing work which those yet in training could not even imagine. These women were highly skilled, being taught by the doctors who relied on them here and learning from each other what it means to be part of a clearing station.

With each human they passed, their resolve to make any necessary sacrifices only deepened.

After a long period of travel, the motorcade finally halted for fuel and a break along a tributary to the Meuse River. Grateful for the reprieve, the medical staff disembarked from their truck and rested under the shade of a stand of trees, near the road, on the edge of a village they were passing. Some of the team stretched out on the grass, glad to be away from the jostling of the truck. Others quietly opened tin cans of food they'd carried with them, eating it cold. No one watching the little group would have recognized the nurses. These women wore the same green-brown, drab trousers and shirts just like the men, apparel more suited for the field than the white dresses and head scarfs of the field hospitals where nurses officially practiced. As they rested, the medical team watched the unit soldiers water the horses and refuel the truck engines.

Lydia was one of their group who dropped down under the trees, stretching herself out flat, easing leg and back muscles that had grown stiff and tired from being bent over and bounced along the rutted roadways. After a short, quiet rest, the nurse regarded her companions. She did not know why the other women had dubbed her their unspoken leader. Perhaps it was just her stubborn persistence. Lydia saw what a subdued lot they were as they traveled, all surely wondering what lay ahead of them. She would need to find time to collect them all for a quick talk as they set up a new camp. She glanced over at the doctors—Simon, Marcus, and Harold— who stood in their own small group talking with an army sergeant, crisply uniformed and carrying a rifle slung over one shoulder by its leather strap. Lydia wondered what they were discussing so earnestly. For a minute, she closed her eyes in the shade. The early morning conversation she had had with Simon before their unit took to the road was still on her mind.

"Are you absolutely sure you want to do this?" Simon had pressed her as soldiers were breaking down their tents and helping to load the medical equipment, carefully packed by the nurses, onto the trucks.

Lydia nodded. "I'm sure," she had told him.

His eyes were troubled. "We've been told there is heavy artillery fire up there, lots of armament... it's been a back-and-forth lobbying of shells, of advancing and falling back for both the French and Germans... the line changing all the time. Very uncertain... and dangerous."

"Don't you think," she had countered, "there will be even more wounded than ever who need us then, Simon? Those boys need your skill... and you need ours. Why should the nurses pull back when the need has never been greater?"

"I'm ordered to go. I won't pull back, but I think maybe you nurses should consider it, Lydia. Go to one of the field hospitals and be of service there. It's just as valuable to help the wounded where shells are not falling around you. You could make a difference there just as well as you could anywhere else, and much more safely."

Lydia had laid her hand on his arm in reassurance. "No, I couldn't, Simon. You forget that I started out at a field hospital and soon asked to join up with a clearing station. It was my choice from the beginning to come out here. The trained nurses in field hospitals don't see the volunteer nurses in the same light as you do. They don't realize what we do. The ability to document our kind of work doesn't exist in nursing yet, but we do it anyway, and the girls here look to me for steady leadership. I wouldn't have the same freedom to work like I do here if I were at some field hospital working a shift in the wards, taking direction from a French or British nurse."

He had pulled her aside, behind the only tent that remained standing, the one covering the latrine, only minimally out of sight from the others who were preparing to leave. There, he dared to grasp both of her arms and made her look straight into his face. "I don't want you to be killed by a shell, Lydia, either a stray one or one aimed deliberately at us. This is going to get a lot worse and a lot more dangerous. You have become... very important to me... and I'm worried."

Lydia had looked up into his face. "Nor do I want to be killed by a falling shell. And I'd wonder every day if you've fallen into the same fate, Simon. If I leave the station, I would never know. No, I belong with you, with our group, in the surgery helping you doctors, being a positive force for our team of nurses."

"Oh, Lydia," he had started, "I just don't know about this..."

The anxiety in his face was unmistakable.

Lydia then reached up with both of her hands, taking his bearded face into them. Drawing him down, she had gazed intently into his worried brown eyes. She lifted her lips up to his, and to his great surprise, she had softly kissed his mouth, lingering for a moment past a mere casual gesture. "I don't want to leave you. And I don't intend to."

"I..." he had faltered, not wanting to continue to try to change her mind, but feeling it was imperative that he do so.

She then stopped him once more, repeating, "I belong here... this is where I make a difference. You cannot make me change my mind, Doctor Finney." Again, drawing his face to hers, she had kissed his lips, more firmly this time as if to seal her commitment.

Then she turned and walked determinedly over to where the other nurses were getting ready to board one of the waiting army trucks.

Simon had stared after her as she walked away, the feel of her soft mouth against his, lingering. A cascade of emotion washed over him... fear and surprise... longing and relief. She wanted to be with him... Lydia wanted to be with him, Simon Finney. He just might have found the woman he wanted to have in the center of his life at the very time and place where he stood the greatest risk of losing her.

Now, Lydia lay on the grass, remembering her earlier interaction with Simon. That man had certainly been right when he'd said he was unaccustomed to relationships with someone, beyond those while holding a scalpel in one hand and a stethoscope in the other. She hoped she hadn't been too bold kissing him. She opened her eyes and sat up, looking over at the three doctors and their military companion. The soldier had taken out a gas mask and was apparently trying to bring something to their attention. This intrigued her, so she jumped to her feet and crossed the clearing to listen in.

"C'est un nouvel appareil, new device, the M2," the French soldier was telling the doctors. "More efficient at protecting us from gas... chlorine, mustard or whatever l'enfer the Germans wish to, to drop on us. All will have one, je m'en assurerai. Fits this way, but ils offrent plus de protection, more safety. Most people survive the gas bombs avec ces, at least do not die, like they did at first. Nous devon... we must have them where we're going." The sergeant looked up as Lydia joined them.

"Mademoiselle," he said directly, "vous, les infirmières, should think again where we are headed. Many men dying there. Ce n'est pas un endroit pour une femme… not a place for a woman… is all I have to say."

Lydia didn't mince words. "We've all discussed it, Sergeant. Nous sommes l'infirmières… and nurses go where we're needed most. Every one of these women knows the dangers ahead and has decided to stay with our doctors and help you boys. It wasn't a decision we made lightly."

The young man looked exhausted. "I do not wish to see you die, mademoiselle. Bad enough when soldiers die, but worse when it is a woman."

Lydia avoided Simon's face echoing the same anxieties without words. "Nor do I wish to see anything happen to you. Now, teach me how to put this thing on so we can show the other nurses." She directed him away from the doctors, abruptly ending the discussion and redirecting him to teach her the benefits of the new M2 gas mask.

Harold looked at the other two doctors as Lydia and the soldier headed for the group of nurses waiting along the road. "I suppose maybe I could tell the French Command we don't want them?"

The three pondered this for a moment. Then Marcus spoke for them all, "But we do… want them… and so do the wounded. And we don't have orderlies who can do what these nurses do."

"They could be taught," Harold assured him. "Probably. In time…"

Simon nodded, fighting with his own ambivalence. "Yes, of course. But if what we're hearing is correct, that thousands of casualties are coming off the battlefield daily, then all the clearing stations need teams that can function efficiently the minute they arrive near the front. There won't be time to train others to meet that kind of demand. We already have that kind of team. That means keeping our nurses close to us."

Marcus said quietly, "Yesterday, I would have wondered at you saying that, my friend. I'd have thought you'd want to send them as far away as possible—even back to the States if you could. And I think I would have agreed with you, but today, as we're getting closer, I think you're right. I also think if we try to force our nurses to leave us, we'll have a different kind of fight on our hands."

Simon remembered his own dismal attempt at persuasion. "And I'm sure we would lose it."

Harold stroked his beard and looked over at the women now surrounding the sergeant, who was demonstrating the mask in his hands. "It's true we have a well-developed team. We do need them in the surgery and doing the triage. And the patients respond well to a female touch. So, here's what I suggest. We're going to arrive by nightfall and set up camp in the dark. There will be less fighting then and we'll have a chance to more clearly assess the situation. But in the morning, when the wounded start coming in, and at the first sign that our own station will be the focus of bombardment, we'll get the nurses on a truck out... even if we have to put ether masks over their faces to get it done."

The other two doctors nodded. Given the parameters of the situation ahead of them, it seemed reasonable enough.

Nightfall was closing in again, but now everything was different as they set up the new camp. So much closer to the Western Front, there was no small campfire in the midst of their tents.

The lanterns were shuttered, allowing only a sliver of light to filter through so that they could organize their supplies. Tent flaps were to be drawn if a lantern was shining, even dimly, inside... and the air inside was stifling. The nurses sat on a row of cots in their new recovery tent. There, they spoke together, softly, about the day ahead of them.

Alice Miller spoke for them all. "It's not going to be pretty, for sure. Listen to all that rumbling. Must be a lot of cannons out there somewhere, maybe even those new tanks blowing stuff to bits... people, too. How will we ever know between one patient and the next who has the best chance of making it... if we can even get to them fast enough?"

Lydia looked at her companions. "We won't. We're going to do a lot of things absolutely right and the boys will die anyway. And we're going to do a lot of things wrong... and boys will live."

"Well, then what's the point of triage out here anyway?" Nancy Mitchell wondered. "If it's as arbitrary as that?"

Lydia smiled softly. "I didn't say it was arbitrary. It's just that it isn't up to us who's going to make it and who is not. All we do is the best we can and trust that the rest isn't in our hands. We can't mess with God's territory."

Susannah Boyton shook her head. "I don't think there's a god who has much to do with this war, Lydia. If he did, and if he wanted to, he'd stop it here and now... but on it goes... year one, year two, soon three years of this struggle already. Maybe he doesn't really care all that much who wins, and the Germans and the French are carrying on regardless."

"Okay," Lydia returned. "Assume that's true for a minute, that God doesn't care who wins. Then why are we all here on the side of the Allies instead of with the Germans?"

Sally Winfield shifted on her cot. "That's easy," she answered with her southern drawl. "We're here because a patient is a patient, is a patient, regardless of where he is born or who wins or loses. If someone's hurt, we take care of them just the same. It's what we do. And I think God does care about who wins because the Germans shouldn't want to take over the world. They've got enough land of their own already. It's being greedy to want to own the whole world."

Susannah spoke again. "Well, if there is a god, who does care, then I wish he'd put an end to all this so everyone could go home still having two arms and legs. Because we've seen too many guys already who've gone home leaving a big part of themselves in the dirt, in some crater on the field, from a shell."

Gretha Bernstein's voice was very quiet. "We're going to see a lot of missing arms and legs now... and worse than that, I think..."

Lydia stopped her. "A lot of these boys are going to die right here. And we're going to have to be their mothers and their sisters and their girlfriends and tell them they are loved until they take that last breath. Remember the Civil War? What did nurses do? Feed the men broth, give them whisky for pain and change bloody stump dressings. And close their eyes when they died. We're going to see a lot of death, but we can give them dignity even in death... we can make their crossing as good a crossing as possible. We'll focus on each singular soldier, not the long line waiting in the wings. Each one is our focus. It's easier to take it one at a time."

Alice nodded at Linda in the silence that followed Lydia's admonition. "We used to keep count of how many we saved and lost. I don't think we should do that anymore. Let the army do that."

One of the nurses named Mary Atkins, a southern nurse from Georgia who had been quietly listening so far, spoke up in agreement. "No counting... we'll let the army do that. If we start counting how many we lose tomorrow, we'll lose our minds. No death counts. No life counts. Just each one counts."

"Don't forget our doctors," added Marlene Sullivan, another of their group. "My family is full of doctors, and the Sullivans have never backed away from a challenge. We're also here for our doctors. We know how hard they take it when patients die. We have good surgeons and we need to have their backs."

"I couldn't agree more, Marlene," Lydia replied heartily. "Our doctors are braver than the generals out on the battlefield. The powers that be send men out whole. Our doctors pick up the pieces. It takes a lot of courage to do that. So, let's be their comfort, too, when we can." She paused, taking in the group of women before her, " I think that you all are the bravest women I've ever met... to be here, right now. I've never been with a stronger, more skilled group of women at any time in my life. It's a privilege to be here. Now, all of us should get some sleep. Doctor Stockton says the war starts at dawn with the first light of day. We can expect casualties as soon as we wake up. So! Everyone sleeps whenever they can grab a cot, eats whenever they can eat, and works as long as they can work. If you're exhausted, tell someone. We're more likely to make mistakes when we're exhausted. If you need to go to bed, tell someone and we'll trade off as often as we can, to recharge."

Charlotte Stein chimed in. "I could use a nice bed, soft mattress, comfy pillow…"

Laura Bertolli added to that thought, "… and maybe a warm body next to me saying sweet things in my ear."

Susannah continued to lighten the mood. "Does it matter which gender we alert? That we need to go to bed?"

"Oh, Suzie," Mary Atkins retorted with her sultry drawl. "Make it easier on yourself. Try to make it female. It gets so complicated with the other."

Susannah retorted quickly, "But the opposite sex is so much more fun! Just you try telling one of the men here, soldier or doctor, that you need to go to bed and watch what happens! You'll get your warm body for sure!"

The women looked at each other and laughed knowingly, drawing strength from the bonds they had formed over the past many months. They rose from the cots which would soon support more patients than they had ever seen before. With some walking arm in arm, the nurses headed to their tents for the night.

Lydia decided to make one last round to check the readiness of the recovery, then crossed over to do the same in the surgery, where a corpsman was stacking litters outside of the tent. "Merci, Jorge," she told the man. "Can always count on you to have things ready and waiting." Jorge was one of the French men who had been with them since the beginning.

"Oui, mademoiselle, I try," he replied.

Lydia was not ready for sleep yet, though she knew she should be. The rumbling had quieted a bit. The only glow in the sky was from starlight. She looked up and caught sight of the Dipper in the north sky. It always amazed her that it hung in the same direction here, as it did back home. *Did her mother ever look up at the Dipper? Did her sister Peggy stand outside on a summer night in Pennsylvania and look at the stars between washing clothes for the little niece and nephew Lydia was missing grow up?* she wondered. And her father... *would he approve of what she was doing now?* He had agreed with her going to Philadelphia for the Red Cross training, but she had informed her parents of setting sail for England by writing them a letter, not wanting to see the worry in their eyes during a tearful goodbye, had it been done face to face. She'd mailed it just before boarding the ship to depart.

Simon found her deep in thought, in the blackout of their first night here, her profile barely discernible in the starlight. "I was looking for you, Lydia. Just wanted to... to check on you before getting some sleep," he said quietly, knowing what was coming against them. Marcus and he had been at Verdun when that terrible battle had started.

She did not turn, clasping her arms across her chest, against the relatively cooler night air. "I'm glad you did, Simon. I was just looking at the stars and wondering how it is that they look just the same up there as they do at home..."

He stood next to her and looked up at the night. "Sure do," he agreed. "Same North Star and Dipper overhead. Same dragon."

"Dragon?" she asked.

"Yes, that arc of stars around that way, around the North Star... there... I guess you have to have a good imagination."

She nodded. "The Greeks and Romans certainly did... making stars into animals and gods... I'm really glad we stayed and that I'm here, Simon."

His shoulder brushed hers. "I'm not... not glad you're in danger, I admit it. But at the same time... oh, Lydia..."

Lydia reached out in the darkness and found him. She put her arms around his waist, and he pulled her close to him, emboldened by her earlier behavior and drawn by a need for a caring touch ahead of the brutality ahead of them. She whispered, "Simon, before... when I kissed you..."

"When we kissed, you mean," he corrected her quickly.

"No, I kissed you and you were shocked!" she said emphatically. "I could tell you didn't expect it. And... I just want to explain that I—"

Simon found her face in the darkness and, finding her lips, prevented her saying anything more. His kiss slowed time, exploring her mouth softly while holding her tight in his arms. When he stopped, he whispered, "You were saying, when we kissed..."

"Okay," she breathed, accepting his correction. "When... we... kissed, I just wanted to explain, to let you know it wasn't because of the letter."

"The letter?" He was caught up in the moment, genuinely confused, thinking now only of the feel of her in his arms, her lips on his lips.

She nodded her head against his chin. "The burned-up letter. I didn't want you to think that just because that man from back home moved on, that I needed someone to fill in some gap. I was afraid you'd think... and I don't want you to think that."

He laughed lightly. "Oh, *that* letter! Well, I'd forgotten about that. Actually, Lydia, I was just amazed that you'd ever find me worthy of your attention. In terms of starting a relationship with a woman, I'm at a disadvantage, you might recall... it's rather undiagnosed territory for me."

Lydia lifted her hands in the darkness, finding his face, tracing the mustache around his mouth, and caressing the beard on his chin. "Is that what we're doing now, Simon? Are we starting a relationship?"

"Almighty God, I certainly do hope so," he breathed the prayer aloud and kissed her again, both of them getting lost in each other, under the stars... he did not want her to leave his arms, while knowing that tomorrow would come all too soon.

"Ordonné, over here!" Nancy shouted amid the din from where she perched over a body on the ground. "Take this man... emporté cet homme... out of here, he's already gone." She moved to the next man, who clutched her arm with his remaining hand. His eyes were wide with fear and pain.

"Aidez-moi, l'infirmière," he pleaded, "I cannot feel my legs, I cannot feel my arm... am I dying?"

Nancy gripped his shaking hand and firmly pried the grasping fingers from her arm. "Your legs are still there, soldier," she said kindly, allaying the depth of fear in his eyes, "and the doctors are taking you into surgery, in just a couple of minutes. N'ayez pas peur... do not be afraid." She looked at the tourniquet, it was wrapped too tightly around his upper right arm and the skin beyond it had a bluish cast. Quickly, she released the device and saw blood spurt out between the exposed muscles in the gash of his upper arm. Nancy pressed hard on the bleeding artery, staying its flow, but now saw that some blood could pass through other intact, open vessels to his lower arm. The skin lightened a little.

"Ordonné!" she shouted again. "Get someone on the other end of this litter. This man goes in next."

Haggard eyes met hers in return, as more shouting followed. The man on the litter was soon lifted from the ground and Nancy held her position as they carried him into the surgery. Doctor Stockton took one look at the arm. "Let me wash my hands and get a clamp on it Nurse, and then you can let go."

"Thank you, Doctor," she quickly replied, scanning the surgery tent where the doctors were all at their posts working steadily on the line of wounded, trying to focus through a stream of commands, orders, and directions, while anesthetists managed the gases at the head of each patient.

Gretha circulated through the tables, passing out clean clamps, sutures, saws, drills, bandages and anything else the doctors needed, or that others were requesting. The clatter of the metal tools on trays collided with the groans of the wounded before the blessed sleep of ether overtook them. "Anesthesia," Gretha called out. "Get this man asleep, please."

The anesthesia mask dropped into place as if by magic as Doctor Stockton returned from the wash. The clamp he held found its place in between the man's arm muscles, even as the soldier fell limp from the ether; Harold stayed the artery from spurting. Relieved of her responsibility, Nancy backed away and rinsed her hands quickly at the spigot just outside the tent door. She looked along the extensive row of litters on the ground, men moaning and crying, soldiers milling in between them and she searched for where the other nurses were located and where the unmet needs were... which was virtually everywhere.

Susannah appeared at her shoulder, carrying bottles of laudanum toward the recovery tent. "How ya' doin', girl?" she asked the other in passing, a cheerful smile on her face.

Nancy pushed a stray, sweaty lock of hair out of her eyes and tucked it back behind her ear. "One man at a time," she reminded her friend. "Remember, one man at a time. Could you trade me a spell? Take triage and let me go in recovery? I've got to get out of the sun for a bit."

Susannah dropped the bottles of laudanum into the arms of the other nurse. "You bet. Where were ya?"

Nancy looked at the rows of men lying in the summer heat. "It doesn't matter where you start, Suzie... Four of us in surgery, three out here, and whoever is in recovery... against this, this tsunami of patients coming in..."

The other nurse followed her gaze and nodded understanding. Then she simply started making her way down the litters, joining Laura Bertolli and Mary Atkins, the two others tending the wounded to see which ones still breathed, still moaned, still bled... and which no longer waited for medical care.

Nancy slipped under the shade of the recovery tent gratefully. Groans of pain assailed her, but at least she had an answer for them, in the bottles she carefully carried. Inside, she saw two nurses and corpsmen assisting the casualties.

Marlene Sullivan was working her way down the rows of cots, systematically doling out pain relief and issuing directives to orderlies to reinforce bandages where needed and give water and broth to the select patients ready to tolerate liquids. Raised in a medical family, Marlene felt foreheads for fever with the back of her hand and listened for the confusion of delirium. She valued her honed sense of smell, the difference between blood and infection or sweat and urine, alerting her to someone's needs.

Nancy thought Alice Miller looked like a policeman directing traffic in downtown New York… the flow of litters moving in and out, as some patients died, while others were stabilized and taken out to the trucks headed for one of the field hospitals… and immediately, another patient from the surgery would take up the newly vacant spot.

Nancy jumped in behind Marlene administering the pain relief and started checking dressings that needed reinforcement, watching hands and feet for signs of gangrene and pus.

In the surgical tent, Lydia remained beside Simon at his operating table. The doctor, hunched over a patient's open abdomen, pulled out shreds of shrapnel from an explosion that had torn through the man's stomach. He probed inside the organs with his bloodied fingers, feeling for hidden hard edges. "This is taking too long," Simon muttered to Lydia. "I need to get him closed. He's losing too much fluid being open this long."

Lydia tried to adjust the light for him to see if a gleam of metal would reflect from within. "Any better?"

"I need you to reach in there, under his liver and try to lift it up for me…"

She slid her hand under the warm, wet organ and gently raised it higher. "Say when," she offered.

"When," he answered tersely. Using both sight and touch, he pulled out a small foreign body, not shrapnel, but a rock lodged in the open tissues. "Rinse him—"

She was already squirting Dakin's solution throughout the wide opening and suctioning it back out again with a bulb syringe, listening for any small pings of metal or stone against the glass bottle where it was deposited. Lydia looked at the fluid collecting in the glass. "Looks clear," she breathed. "We'll hope for the best against infection." She quickly handed him forceps with needle and suture, and Simon began closing the hole in the man's stomach.

"Tie the suture like this," he showed Lydia. "Loop it, then knot it like this."

She watched intently, then tried some of her own, Simon cutting the ends of the knots as fast as she tied them, until they were finished.

"Well done, Nurse Blackwell. Pack his abdomen and let's hope I found all of the holes," he said, stretching his back muscles. Then, Simon stepped away from the table. "I need a minute," he said quietly and backed out of the surgery to the latrine and then to find something to drink.

Lydia quickly changed her surgical apron and washed her hands thoroughly. She greeted the corpsmen already bringing in another patient on a litter, hoisting him up onto the empty table. Mentally surveying the tangled mess of a human before her, she took in the extent of the head damage the young soldier had received. She grabbed a stethoscope from the anesthetist and listened carefully to the very slow and irregular heart, its rhythm counting down the moments until death. Calling back the corpsmen before they could leave, she directed them to take the boy back outside, where the dying had been assembled on the ground. None of their doctors could have saved him, she knew this without a doubt. Not even Doctor Finney, who was so adept at head wounds. Fighting back tears, she watched the men carry this soldier out to the nearby field where the collected rows of bodies beneath tarps were growing longer under the afternoon sun.

By the time Simon returned to the surgery, Lydia had a new casualty waiting. The man's left leg was barely connected. She had already cut off the trousers, washed the skin around the improvised tourniquet, and administered ether to put the man to sleep. Without a word, Simon removed the remainder of the tattered limb, leaving a loose flap over the remaining stump, and sighed tiredly. "Let's leave it unsutured... just wrap it." Then he added, "How many—"

Lydia flashed a warning glance his way over her mask. "Don't do that, Doctor," she advised him. "No numbers here."

He glanced up at her, only his brown eyes visible, quickly clearing sweat from his brow, with his sleeve, to prevent it from falling into the open wound. "How many," he started again, "stars are there in the sky?"

Her hand stopped in midair... a clamp suspended there. "What?" she asked, suddenly confused.

His eyes twinkled at her, over his mask. "How many stars are there in the sky?" he repeated.

Her cheeks flushed. "It depends I suppose," she retorted, "on if it is day or night."

"I knew you didn't know," he teased her. "If you count one per second, it would take you a hundred years to count them. On a semi-clear night, of course."

The anesthetist looked up, curious, listening in on this sudden turn of conversation.

"And I suppose someone who lived to be one hundred and twenty stayed up 24/7, counting, to confirm this little-known fact," she declared as the man on the table was removed and carried away to recovery, the table washed for a new patient to be carried in from triage.

Simon nodded, "Of course. But then you have to subtract the ones that fall out of the sky, also." He started washing his hands again.

"That's too much math for me," she exclaimed as the new patient was settled onto the table. She peered at a hole in the young man's rib cage where bones were jagged and broken. "Besides, I rarely see them fall out of the sky, so that number is likely insignificant."

"Watch his breathing, we're removing those two bottom ribs," Simon told the anesthetist, looking over at the splintered bones, "they'll puncture his lung. He can live without two ribs."

Lydia nodded in unspoken agreement, handing him a saw. "Adam lived without one."

She almost felt his smile through the mask when he answered her. "Ah, but you see, he didn't really lose his rib. It just took another form in the shape of a beautiful woman. It was given right back to him by God."

"What on Earth did you have to drink out there on your break?" she wondered aloud, watching him drop the multitude of bone fragments onto a tray.

"Nurse," he said then, "catch that bleeder, please."

Lydia snatched up a clamp and secured it over a small artery spurting blood, silently rebuking herself for not having noticed the injury before he called it to her attention. She was, however, gratified to see the patient's lungs expanding and contracting, unhindered and out of danger.

"Coffee... black with one sugar," he replied with a soft chuckle.

Finally, there was an end in the line... a period at the end of the sentence, at least for this day. Those who had died had been collected away in trucks. The mobile wounded were driven off over bumpy terrain to the nearest field hospital where they would receive more care. The surgery was quiet, hosed down... instruments cleaned. Only recovery was busy, the nurses working in shifts to tend to the wounded who were unable to tolerate the ride over the French countryside. They would have to hope that by morning, the recovery could be emptied and readied for the next wave of patients to arrive. Doctors, nurses, orderlies and litter bearers slept anywhere they could, wanting sleep more than food, but requiring both. Some of the soldiers who had assisted with rescuing the casualties were from different French and even British units, and they took advantage of the intermingling to inquire about family and friends. In the morning, some would try to rejoin their own units, if they knew where they were located along the front. Others, whose units had been decimated, would work their way to the army field headquarters to be reassigned. The nurses heard the quiet conversations, usually in French, coming in from the darkness outside the tents..

In the doctors' tent, the flaps were pulled down and a dim lantern light was allowed to shine, only inside. The chief medical officer, Harold, appraised their situation carefully. "Well, we all know it took the entire team to do what we did yesterday and today. The lieutenant tells me that Command reports the Germans were pushed back a few yards, and the French advanced a little farther east of the city. That makes us farther from the front. So, the question is..."

"Do we move again?" Marcus finished his thought. "How far would we have to go? Is it worth packing everything up again already? I mean, how mobile is mobile, this close to the fighting? There are still patients in recovery who shouldn't be moved if possible. They should be shipped out first."

Harold nodded, "I know. We might not have a choice about that; have to hope they can tolerate the trip." The three men considered this carefully.

Then Simon spoke up. "There is no question in my mind that most of these boys, who have pulled through so far, did so because we got to them so quickly. The loss of life increases exponentially with every mile they have to be carried to get to us. Some of those who came in yesterday were being carried on the backs of others who were barely able to walk themselves. We can't ask them to do much more of that."

Silence filled the small doctors' tent. "But the closer we get to the line," Marcus said, laying back on his cot while tossing a baseball, a treasured relic from normal life, repeatedly into the air, "the more risk of a bombardment landing right on top of us. Then, who do we help? Save the soldiers just to get them blown up in our own recovery? And for all we know, the Germans could take back the ground they lost, and then we could end up behind enemy lines."

Harold said, "French Army Command is giving us some say in this decision, actually. They have acknowledged that only we can determine where the invisible line is between saving lives and losing our own... the acuity of the patients we're seeing... the resources close at hand. According to Aubert, Major d'Espèrey asked for an answer... by morning."

Simon looked down at his hands. "Then there are the nurses."

"Yes," Harold replied. "Then there are the nurses."

"Remarkable, really," Marcus added, catching the ball deftly in his hands. "So many lives would have been lost without them here. I'm not willing to risk setting up camp right on top of the damned front line if the Germans overrun us and take it back... as they will most certainly be planning to do."

"I'm also concerned about getting caught behind the line," Harold agreed. "As prisoners of war, we'd likely be kept alive, patching up soldiers and prisoners from both sides. It is unlikely we would be shot... at least not right away. The battle lines are being continually redrawn, around Verdun. No one in command can predict a single yard of relative safety. But if we are overrun, and the nurses become prisoners of war..."

He didn't have to finish this thought; they all knew what was at stake.

Simon spoke, his voice measured as he thought out loud. "I want to be as close to the wounded as possible, to save as many of these boys as we can. And yet... and yet we save no one at all if we are caught up in the bombardment ourselves or become caught behind enemy lines. There, we may help save German soldiers, but we won't be saving any Allies. If we stay just far enough behind the front that they can get the wounded to us, then the nurses have some relative safety as well. Truth be known, they are probably saving more lives than we are. Certainly, we do our part in the surgery, but they're the ones keeping the wounded alive before and after that."

Harold nodded. "So... what are we telling Lieutenant Aubert in the morning? Do we move closer?"

Marcus spoke for all of them. "Tell him we'll stay within five, maybe six miles, of the front but not closer for all of the reasons above. However, I think we should ask the French for more ambulances and drivers to get the wounded off the line and back to us as quickly as possible... eliminate those walking and carrying the wounded on their own backs. We can go and get them as the front line ebbs and flows around the trenches."

"An ambulance can't drive over the trenches, Marcus. The trenches stretch for miles and prove a real barrier if the front moves beyond them," Harold corrected him.

"Well, if a new front line is well established on the other side of the trenches, then and only then, we can move to the other side as well!" Marcus exclaimed. "But let's not be caught sitting right on top of those hell holes."

Harold straightened up then, hands firmly planted on his knees. "Then five or six miles it is. I'll speak to Aubert first thing in the morning and give him our decision. Get some rest. And, gentlemen, I appreciate your opinions. Like the Major, it was not a decision I wanted to make on my own, either."

Now in need of some companionship, Marcus looked out toward the darkness. "I'm going to the mess to fill my canteen," he said and slipped out through the tent flap into the night. He didn't come back until after the others were well asleep, and neither did one of the nurses he had set out to find. Laura and he had already heard the sound of bombs falling and both needed some reassurance and comfort they could only find in each other.

In the morning, Harold stood in front of the nurses, the other two doctors flanking him under the shelter of the mess tent, where they had assembled. He had explained the situation as the battle for Verdun continued. As he reviewed the logic of their decision, he was gratified to see the nurses nodding in agreement. It was obvious they were willing to go forward and were also willing to remain with the station, as the options to pack up the unit and move were reviewed. There was a great deal of support for the suggestion Marcus had had for more ambulances, to go and retrieve the injured. And once again, Harold offered the nurses the option of leaving the unit… to fall back to a field hospital, well behind the lines of battle. Not one of the women had changed her mind about staying, despite the weariness and turmoil of the last siege. With one voice, they expressed their intent to continue their work right here, with these patients.

"Is there anything that you can think of after the last battle," Harold asked them, "that the French army could get you nurses, to make things easier?"

The eleven looked at one another, uncertain, then as one, they glanced over to Lydia. Obviously, they had been discussing this… making a wish list.

"Go ahead," Harold prompted her when Lydia hesitated. "Whatever you need. You name it."

Then Lydia spoke for all of them. "We each need our own stethoscope," she said. "It makes no sense at all to call one of you from the surgery to see if one of the patients still has a heartbeat or is having difficulty breathing."

"And we each need a pair of heavy-duty scissors," Laura spoke up timidly. "It's hard to cut off the uniforms with bandage scissors. It takes too much time."

Alice chimed in. "Flashlights for each of us would be nice," she said brightly. "So, we don't have to balance the lantern on a cot while we're doing other things. And it would make it easier to see inside wounds."

"Rubber tourniquets," Nancy sighed. "Instead of having to find sticks and twist ropes."

Harold felt tears sting his eyes. He had expected them to request some sort of creature comforts that the women certainly deserved. He was ashamed of himself for having had such low expectations, especially of these particular nurses. "I'll speak to Lieutenant Aubert immediately and put in your request, ladies. Is there anything else?"

Lydia nodded. "One more thing, Doctor Stockton," she said softly. "We don't have chaplains up here this close to the front. See if we can have some rosaries, or small crosses, for the men to hold while they are dying. It might give them comfort in their last hours."

Harold nodded and turned away so no one would see him wipe his eyes. "That is all," he said gruffly, in a perfunctory army manner. It was all he could come up with at the moment.

The group broke up, some back to the recovery, others to their cots for sleep. Some lingered at the mess table over their tin cup coffee, still warm from the heat of the summer day. Off in the distance, the rumble of bombardment could be heard, muffled by the surrounding hills. The three women looked up at a small set of dots in formation in the sky to the northeast.

"They're at it again," Gretha murmured as she took a drink, raising her mug at the planes in the sky. "Cheers."

Lydia nodded, "Better pour out that coffee and try to sleep. Sounds like we're going to be up tonight."

Gretha put the tin cup down, after draining it first. "I can sleep even with the caffeine," she said dryly. "How about you?"

"I'm going to the recovery to empty out the beds. Doctor Lovell is already there making rounds and deciding who is leaving us. Hopefully, all of them. The trucks have to get back in time for the next wave."

Alice stood up and stretched. "The young British boy with both his legs gone, he left, didn't he?" she asked anxiously.

"Last truckload, Alice," Lydia said. "He's on his way to hospital."

Alice nodded, "Good. I'm glad he has a chance. He spoke before he left, you know."

Lydia looked up in surprise. "Did he now! What did he say?"

"He asked if I knew where his mother was."

Lydia nodded. "What did you tell him?"

"That she was waiting for him to come home. Making him apple pie and the best meatloaf he'd ever eaten."

"Bet he liked that!"

"He said she didn't like meatloaf. Said she couldn't understand why anyone wouldn't just want a good cut of beef on a plate instead of something all smashed up together like that."

Lydia laughed. "That soldier is going to make it, Alice. That was a good answer."

"I may never eat meatloaf again!" the other exclaimed. "Good night, Lydia."

Chapter 3

Into the Night

Each day seemed a clone of the one before. Men piled up in rows, a never-ending stream of litter bearers coming and going. This time though, the nurses decided to place a numbered card on each man for priority, from one to three, as they triaged the rows of wounded. One was for immediate surgery, two was for waiting, and three was to be moved off with a rosary in hand, if there was one. The numbers changed quickly as circumstances changed. Some men who were numbered a two were more seriously wounded, but with the least likely chance of survival. In triage, the doctors' skills could not be tethered too long to one case while the others lay waiting... and weakening. Lydia had insisted tarps be erected over the triage groups of the men dying in the nearby grass. They should not have to endure the fire of the sun above after enduring the fires of hell behind them.

Additionally, the tarps distracted the buzzards soaring high overhead, ever watchful. They had also acquired a sheepdog from a nearby French farm, one that paced around the wounded and fended off stray animals, opportunists seeking an easy approach. The unit adopted the dog as its own and named it Abril, inspired by the French word for shelter. The animal was welcomed by all, not the least by those lying vulnerable, in rows along the ground.

Trucks had returned from a field hospital, stocked with supplies. With great satisfaction, Harold presented each of the nurses with a small haversack containing a stethoscope, a flashlight, many rubber tourniquets, and their own heavy-duty scissors, as requested. He also made sure a new hairbrush was hidden away in each, along with clean headscarves, which arrived in muted army colors, but were in good condition. The doctor received profuse thanks from the nurses, but he again noted that those were more for the medical tools than the personal items. Nevertheless, he noted the new head scarves were employed immediately as the women moved among the patients doing their work... the nurses' long hair tied back out of the way and off their necks in the summer heat... hopefully keeping lice out of their hair as well.

Wounded continued to arrive throughout the day and into the evening as twilight fell. The bombardment they heard rumbling throughout the day sometimes shook the ground beneath the tents. When this happened, everyone outside anxiously looked up, except for those on the medical staff who were from far-away California and repeatedly told the others not to worry about small earthquakes because "they happen all the time." The wounded, though, always scanned the sky in fear; they could no longer run for cover. Though as the dusk of evening took hold overhead, even their haunted eyes began to drift closed as they waited for care.

Growing in confidence, the nurses assigned to triage systematically placed some of the wounded next to waiting trucks, certain enough in their assessments that these patients could tolerate the trip to a field hospital immediately, instead of needing surgical care on-site. They had developed a perfunctory criterion for transport readiness: ensure breathing in both lungs, a steady heartbeat and well contained bleeding, without need of tourniquet. The women became adept at splinting broken bones still below the skin. Before each convoy departed, one of the surgeons stepped out of the surgery tent just long enough to do a quick check of those that had been triaged in this manner. It was rare that they pulled a man back and into the line to be issued a number for a surgery table. Head traumas were more difficult to assess when there were no open wounds, men sitting and staring vacantly from possible internal bleeds or concussions, or even sudden blindness. These patients sometimes went to recovery for observation for a time, before chancing the long, bumpy ride to the field hospital... or until the recovery was overrun by the need for more cots.

As standard routine, during the day, the nurses took turns out in the heat of the sun. When dusk approached though, and the air cooled, they actually preferred open-air triage duty outside of the tents, knowing that the flaps would soon be drawn tight to hide the light of lanterns from shining out across the open fields where enemy eyes might see.

The orderlies of the medical corps were adept at stepping in to watch over the wounded while a nurse rested, ate or attempted to wash off the blood and dirt which accumulated as they worked. Occasionally, a medic came in from the battlefield and helped in the surgery or set bones that were waiting to be tended. Everyone on the team was grateful when a medic appeared. It was always a good day when the nurses had a bit of time to regroup.

Lydia was taking her turn outside in the summer heat with the triage group. Her hair was matted under her headscarf. Beads of sweat stung her eyes as they dripped down her forehead. It was turning early evening and, mercifully, the sun was slipping into the west to bestow its heat somewhere across the ocean. As she squatted down, number cards in her hand, moving from man to man down the row of litters, one of the men prevented her from trying to give him a drink of water from the canteen slung over her shoulder.

"Mademoiselle, pas pour moi," he groaned. "Je n'en veux pas..."

"S'il te plaît, laisse-moi t'aider... let me help you," she urged him, lifting his head slightly and putting the cup to his parched lips. "You must drink."

"I do not deserve to live," he breathed as he gripped his chest and coughed violently.

"Pour quoi pas? Why not?" she insisted, letting the precious water drip over his lips.

"André, mon ami," the man groaned. "I could not find..."

Lydia looked around her at the other men. "Is he here? Where is André?" she pressed him, hoping to find and reassure this young soldier that he must try to hang on to life, even for the sake of his friend.

Another soldier sat nearby on the ground near his companion. His arm was in a sling and he had a bloody bandage around his forehead.

"We had to leave André behind, mademoiselle, there was... no room on the cart or a cheval. I would have walked, but they would not let me."

"D'où venez-vous? Where – where were you?" Lydia pressed the sitting man.

He pointed northeast, where plumes of black smoke still drifted ominously in contrast against the darkening sky.

"How far..." she began, "à quelle distance?"

"Quatre, cinq kilomètres," he said sadly.

"I will see what I can do," she said. "André... his last name?"

"André Besimont, mademoiselle, merci, merci beaucoup," the sitting man replied.

"Je vous en prie and explain to your friend here, that he must stay alive to welcome André when he arrives," she replied. *You have given so much more than I ever will,* she thought.

She stood, legs aching from the strain of standing after crouching for so long and looked toward the wispy plumes of black smoke on the horizon. It would be night soon. Any hope of finding André Besimont on the battlefield was drifting away as fast as the smoke that marked the site where these men had had to leave their comrade behind. Lydia set her mind to the task ahead. She had her haversack on her back already, crammed with bandages to treat the wounded on litters. Quickly, she broke her own rule and counted the men needing to be seen who were remaining on the ground. With the three tables still running in the surgery, these men would be tended to within an hour. She could be spared.

Lydia ducked into recovery and pulled Laura aside, ignoring the curious look Marcus sent her way as he rounded on the wounded in the tent. Briefly, she informed the other nurse what she intended to do; Laura's eyes widened. After grabbing a small vial from the supply shelf, Lydia left the recovery just as quickly as she had entered, in search of an ambulance driver. Most had been pressed into service helping the wounded. But one of the corpsmen, Jorge, was sitting for a quick break in the mess and she called him to her. "Jorge, I need you to drive an ambulance."

Then, one of the French soldiers also sitting in the mess noticed her urgency, left his seat at the bench and approached them. "What is it you mean to do, mademoiselle l'infirmière?"

"We must go find an injured soldier still out there," she said hastily. "Night is coming and we must be quick. Y a-t-il un chemin de traverse?"

"The shortest way is straight toward the smoke," he replied. "This man, ici, he is no soldier. He has no gun, un fusil."

"No," she admitted, noting the look of fatigue, and relief, on Jorge's face at what he hoped the soldier was suggesting... to go in his place.

"Je suis prêt," the Frenchman said. "I will go. Je vais te montrer où nous étions. I will show you where we were. I was there. He is my countryman, also."

"Je vous serais reconnaissant... would be most grateful. Allons-y vite, we must go quickly," Lydia insisted and they headed for one of the ambulances parked behind the tents.

"What is your name? Comment t'appelles-tu?" she asked him as he got behind the grimy wheel and took off over the bouncy French countryside just south of Verdun, at the center of battle.

"Cédric Marcielle, mademoiselle," the Frenchman replied, staring ahead in the dimming light, doing his level best to dodge debris littering the ground.

They bounced in silence, eyes trained on the path ahead. "We will have to hope, Cédric, that he can still hear us call to him," Lydia mused.

"I know where he probably lay, mademoiselle," he said grimly. "We do not choose to leave men. We are forced to. Je vais te montrer... I will... show you."

Simon washed his hands and left the surgery, grateful for the reprieve. His back hurt and his legs were stiff from standing for hours by the operating table. There were no men left waiting for entry to the surgery. The sun was low on the horizon, he noted. The hours had slipped past him unnoticed. The sounds of bombardment had ceased for now, the silence as unnerving as it was welcomed. He grabbed a bit of water and went in search of Lydia. He knew she had been doing triage, but triage was finished... for now. Outside of the surgery, there were no longer lines of men to be tended to, so the doctor walked over to the mess where a few of his team were catching a quick bite of supper with the French soldiers; she might be there. Men milled around, getting ready to move out for their next command or heading off for their cots to rest. Lydia wasn't part of the group at the mess tent either. Recovery... she would be checking on the wounded post-op, he was now certain. He headed over.

The doctor passed through the open door of the recovery tent, the flaps kept open to let in much needed fresh air until the sun retired and blackout was mandatory. Once inside, seeing the row upon row of wounded stopped him in his tracks. He hadn't realized how many men they had treated. The nurses moved between the men efficiently. Nurses were always in motion, he observed. Scanning the rows, where over fifty patients were lined up, like sardines in a can, he still did not see the one face he was looking for. Simon crossed over to Laura as she lifted a patient to help him drink some broth.

"Nurse Bertolli," he said, "have you seen Nurse Blackwell anywhere? I can't find her."

She looked up, frightened. Laura finished the ministration underway and then stood, pulling the doctor away to the end of the cot. "She went out, Doctor Finney…" Laura whispered so no one else could hear.

Simon looked confused. "Out where?" he asked. "Out with the dying? Out to the shower? Out to the mess tent?"

Laura nodded her head toward the door of the tent. "Out in an ambulance to get a wounded man," was all she said.

He wanted to shake information out of the woman, but forced restraint. "She did what?" he demanded under his breath. "What wounded man?"

Laura's eyes were huge and tears began to well within them. "Out on the battlefield, Doctor Finney. Someone left behind out there. She went for him."

Simon circled her in agitation, nearly tripping over a cot where a wounded man lay. "Alone?" He ran his fingers through his hair.

"No, a French soldier went with her."

"A French what? When? How long ago?"

"About an hour ago, Doctor. She told me not to tell anyone—"

"Oh, God watch over them!" He prayed under his breath, fear wrenching at his heart. Then he strode back outside the recovery, where he stood looking northeast to where the wisps of black smoke were barely discernible, having drifted on the changing breezes of early night. There were the recognizable residual smells of battle, but he couldn't see into the falling darkness. *What on hell's earth were you thinking going out there, Lydia?*

When the Frenchman stopped the ambulance on the battlefield, he turned to Lydia cautiously. "Restez en bas," he said in a whisper. "Stay down." He reached down to a body lying on the damp ground, where he retrieved a helmet no longer required by its owner and placed it on her head. "Suis-moi," he added tersely, motioning for her to stay right behind him in the darkness. There was no need to tell her twice. Trying to avoid the dead, piled haphazardly on the field, he picked his way through the bodies to where he recalled their unit had fallen. He carried a small light, heavily wrapped in cloth, allowing only the faintest glimmer to escape when he lifted his palm away to peer into the faces of the dead men, otherwise mere shadows beneath them.

Lydia was overwhelmed. It was unnaturally still except for the buzz of insects. The number of dead strewn about, through which they were picking their way, sickened her viscerally. These were the ones who did not make it to a casualty clearing station. These are the ones who never had a chance at returning home. She stepped carefully, trying to avoid any human remains as they made their way. It seemed to her as though time slowed to a crawl as they crossed the grassy knoll... the open, but unseeing eyes of the dead following their progress in the darkness. Staying as close to the Frenchman as she could, Lydia tried not to trample on his heels or stumble over the debris of battle. The air was acrid with smoke and reeked of both blood... and futility. Finally, Cédric stopped. He bent low to the ground, looked carefully at several faces with his muted light, then knelt, Lydia following suit.

Cédric peered into a young soldier's face with his dim light. "Ah, mon ami..." he breathed. "Peux-tu m'entendre? Can you hear me? André?"

Lydia's heart caught in her throat at hearing a small groan in response.

"Très bien," the soldier went on. "Nous sommes ici. We have come for you, to take you to safety, mon ami."

The nurse knelt at his side, pushing away debris while realizing somewhere in the back of her mind that it was something soft and gooey. She forced herself to focus on the task at hand and ignore the obvious. Lydia felt her way along the young soldier's body in the darkness, down the stricken man's neck, his arms, his legs. At his abdomen, she found the insult he had suffered. A large piece of shell fragment protruded awkwardly from the left side where it met her probing fingers. It was wedged in place. She pulled the stethoscope out of her backpack and listened quickly to the man's heartbeat and breathing. Remarkably, both were steady and even. "I think we can safely move him," she whispered.

"If we cannot," the soldier replied, "then we have come into great danger for nothing."

"I must stabilize him, wrap his belly, mettre un pansement," Lydia whispered urgently.

Cédric nodded in the darkness. Together, the nurse and soldier started to roll the fallen man slightly onto his side so they could work a long cloth wrap under his waist. His groan was sharp in contrast to the stillness of the battlefield. Immediately, a long, crackling burst of rifle fire whizzed around their heads... summoned by the sound of the injured man. Cédric and Lydia dropped flat to the ground, faces in the damp dirt as Cédric clamped his hand over the injured man's mouth. There was a loud ping as one of the bullets ricocheted off Cédric's helmet. They froze, holding their breath until the shooting stopped.

"Are you alright?" she whispered to Cédric.

"Oui, mademoiselle," he replied. "Et toi?"

"Oui," she breathed, her heart pounding in terror.

With trembling hands, Lydia steadied her breathing and pulled a cloth and the small vial from her sack. She squeezed a few drops of ether onto the bandage and pressed it over André's nose until he went limp. They heard German voices in the distance, fading slightly as they moved off in the darkness, apparently now convinced there was no threat to them from the dying men just over the knoll. Peering out from beneath his helmet, Cédric whispered, "They, too, are just looking for their comrades."

With their own comrade quieted from the ether, the two were able to wrap bandage cloths around André's belly several times, Lydia weaving the long strip in a figure eight around the shrapnel from both directions, securing the piece of metal in place.

"It is no wonder they chose to leave him," Cédric whispered. "Impossible... that he lives..."

"The shrapnel is staunching the blood. It must not move," she whispered anxiously. "He will bleed. Il va saigner, si ça bouge..."

Cédric reached into his pack retrieving a poncho with which they could make a litter to carry André down the knoll to the ambulance below. He dragged a body out of the way to make room. Then, without warning, he slammed Lydia face down into the dirt again and threw himself over the helpless man. She heard then what he had already heard... the sound of missiles whistling through the air above their heads, followed by muffled thumps, then tremendous explosions of dirt and debris raining down on top of them. Terrified, Lydia gripped her helmet to her head, her ears ringing. Planes circled and left, then more arrived to deliver whistling shells that landed close nearby, shattering the earth beneath them. Lydia tried to curl herself into a ball. But to her utter astonishment, she heard Cédric chuckle.

"Mon Dieu!" he exclaimed. "Dieu est bon. God is good, mademoiselle... mon amis, they are sending... un message to the Germans to keep them from taking back the land pendant la nuit... this night. They will retreat and not see us carry André ou entendre le son... or hear the motor of ambulance..."

When the dirt and rocks, and God knows what else, stopped falling around them, Cédric opened his poncho, laying it out on the ground and they carefully rolled André onto it. Then Cédric pulled his rifle strap up over the man's legs, positioning the stock of the gun under his knees, using the strap as a sling. "Take the strap, lift his legs," he said. "I take his chest."

Lydia nodded, grasping the strap of the rifle as the soldier grunted, hoisting up the injured man by the poncho. André was not nearly as heavy as she thought he might be... but of course, Cédric carried most of his weight in this makeshift litter. Still, her shoulders burned and she marveled that any soldier could march carrying heavy packs for miles on their backs, the way they did.

Another overhead volley of bombardment, this time not from planes, but from a faraway land source, forced them to lower their burden once again to the ground and wait under the shower of debris until it settled... and for Lydia's heart, which had been lodged in her throat, to return to her chest where it belonged. It took a long time to retrace their steps, between barrages, through the bodies of the fallen. At least there was no rifle fire chasing them down the knoll to the ambulance. Cédric had been correct.

Finally, the dark silhouette of the vehicle took shape in front of them. After sliding the wounded man into the back, Cédric and Lydia hastily climbed into the front seats. In the darkness, Cédric fumbled to start the motor then edged them down the hill away from the deterring bombardment of the Allies. He stopped and got back out once to clear the hood of the ambulance of clods of dirt and bits of human remains that had been showered down on them. Lydia drove the thought away from her conscious awareness. As they moved forward again, she forced herself not to think of what caused the bumps beneath the wheels as the ambulance lurched and slid forward into the night. She couldn't bear the thought of the dead under their wheels. *Think of André,* she repeated over and over to herself; *count the one.*

"C'était très dangereux," Cédric only said once, glancing over at her sitting silently on the seat beside him. "Pour qui fais-tu ça? Why would any l'infirmière wish to do this?"

"I had to," she said quietly, wondering at how calm Cédric seemed, "for the sake of his friends."

"Merci. André cannot thank you for himself," Cédric offered. They did not speak again until they rolled into the camp behind the tents of the mobile unit, sentries posted there raising rifles against them in alarm until they saw, even in the dark, that it was one of their own ambulances returning.

Lydia opened the door while calling out to the first soldier in sight. "Rapidement! Get a litter bearer and alert the doctors. There is a soldier here who must immediately go to surgery," she said in a commanding voice.

"Oui, mademoiselle!" he exclaimed, astonished to hear the nurse, even as he called for help.

Cédric disappeared. André was carried away with alacrity. Alone, Lydia leaned against the ambulance, willing the pounding of her heart to calm itself and the nausea now welling up in her stomach to subside. She was grateful that the night was black, with only the barest sliver of moon in the sky. Out of danger, she began to tremble in earnest now, her teeth chattering and her knees shaking. Only the sturdy wall of the ambulance kept her on her feet. Her mouth filled with salty saliva. Bending over, she vomited next to the vehicle, glad she was hidden by the night. Feeling a hand grip her shoulder, she started in terror, before realizing who had found her in this moment of overwhelming weakness.

Simon had not left his post, waiting instead for her return in the darkness. He took her into his arms without a word and simply gripped her, pressing her tight against his body as she shook violently.

"Don't let go," she begged Simon. She didn't have to ask.

After a moment, he looked at her, his voice was ragged with emotion. "Thank God, thank God... Lydia, what in God's name possessed you..."

She pressed her head against the security of his chest, grateful for his strength, beginning to realize with regret how much fear she had caused him. "I'm not sorry," she whispered, "not sorry we went and found that boy. But I am sorry I worried you."

"Oh Lydia," he breathed, "if anything had happened to you, I don't think that I could—"

She stopped him, raising her arms to wrap around his neck, pulling herself even closer to him, then cried out in pain.

"What is it?" he began. Only then did he feel in the dark that his right hand was sticky. "Are you... are you bleeding?" He sounded incredulous.

She shook her head, "I don't think so…"

"Let's get you into the recovery." He led her, stumbling, to the double flaps of the tent where most of the patients were quiet after being sedated. Nurse Bertolli looked up in surprise and intense relief as the inside flap of the tent opened to reveal the doctor helping Lydia through the opening.

"What happened?" she demanded, quickly setting up a cot at the end of a row in the far corner of the tent.

Simon shook his head, "Don't know yet." Quickly, they pulled off the grimy shirt sticking to Lydia's right shoulder, where a blood stain steadily grew. They laid Lydia face down on the cot as Simon felt the wound. "There's a bullet in there. Say nothing to anyone!" he barked, swearing Laura to secrecy for the second time in one day. "Go get…" but she had already turned and disappeared into the surgery next door.

Running into the quiet surgery tent, Laura quickly collected a scalpel, sutures and forceps. When she returned to recovery, she found that the doctor had already squirted drops of laudanum into Lydia's mouth. Unaccustomed to the analgesic, her friend slipped rapidly into sleep. Quickly, Laura washed Lydia's back and shoulder with antiseptic and waited with bandages while Simon made the smallest incision possible into the nurse's skin, staunching the bleeding as the incision opened.

"There is a bullet in there lodged against the scapula," he muttered. "It's movable… It didn't penetrate the bone, thank God for that. We can get it out right here. No need for the surgery."

He used his fingers to widen the incision and probed with the forceps until the tip hit the hard, offending lead object. Gently, he pulled the bullet back out through its entry track, then peered at the dent in it. "Thank God, this hit something else first," he breathed, "lessening the impact."

Laura rinsed Lydia's wound and staunched a bleeder until Simon could tie it off, allowing her to clean the wound more thoroughly. He wove sutures through the skin of Lydia's back carefully, trying to line up the smooth edges of the incision, hoping to minimize the resulting scar.

Then Simon looked up to Laura. "Let's get a clean shirt on her, Nurse, and keep this well wrapped. You must not tell anyone what you just saw. Lieutenant Aubert and Doctor Stockton are already teetering on sending all of you nurses away. This would tip the balance against you, I'm afraid... although maybe, I don't know, maybe they're right. Maybe this is proof you should all leave."

She nodded wide-eyed. "We don't want to leave. Lydia won't either. Even with this. No one will know but us, Doctor," she promised, as much to him as to herself.

"Well, let's keep her here for the night. Tomorrow will bring some difficult questions about our newest patient, which she'll have to answer for Aubert," Simon sighed heavily.

"Very good, Doctor Finney," Laura nodded. She reluctantly made her way to tend to the other wounded in the tent while Simon remained seated on a box at Lydia's side. Laura saw the doctor gently move the brown wavy curls from her friend's face, lean over, kiss her on the forehead and again on her closed eyes and the edge of her mouth. *No one will know that either, but me,* she thought as she turned away to her other duties... *third time's a charm, for secrets tonight.*

In the morning, as she had expected, Lydia was summoned to the mess tent by Lieutenant Aubert and Doctor Stockton where they were gathered with Simon and Marcus. She'd already thought about what she was going to tell them. But now, sitting on the bench by the table for support, her only concern was that they might see her tremble. Laura had given Lydia a few drops of laudanum before she left the recovery so that her pain was masked. Certainly, the other surgeons would notice if she winced... and ask unwanted questions about her injury. As the group sat, a few scattered soldiers and workers picked up their breakfast trays, moving to the end of the wooden table somewhat, but not quite, out of earshot. Patients in the recovery were already whispering about "l'infirmière des Etats-Unis," the nurse from America, who had been willing to retrieve one of their own.

Harold stood over Lydia, looking as stern as he could with his arms folded across his chest. "What could you possibly have been thinking Nurse Blackwell, pulling such a stunt as that?"

"But isn't that exactly why we requested the army bring additional ambulances here, Doctor?" Lydia questioned him in return. "To retrieve the wounded who couldn't make it back to us?"

He nodded. "Yes, but not you!" He admonished her firmly. "The nurses are to remain in the camp at all times."

"I truly don't remember hearing that directive, Doctor Stockton. And everyone else was tied up in surgery, or recovery, and not expendable," she replied evenly, carefully avoiding Simon's eyes as he stood with arms crossed over his chest, near their chief medical officer, watching and listening intently.

Harold frowned at her, his voice rising slightly with emotion. "Apparently, Nurse Blackwell, you consider yourself expendable to this station?" he demanded. "That we can get by in this war with one less nurse on hand?"

She nodded. "Relatively speaking, yes, Doctor, I do. But also, the Frenchman who took me had solid knowledge of the battlefield and where the soldier had been left behind. He gave us an excellent advantage."

"This kind of stunt makes me think it was a mistake to let any of you nurses remain with this station," Lieutenant Aubert said gruffly. "Tell us exactly what happened."

Lydia, gathering her strength behind a calm, reserved demeanor, recounted the event in detail: searching through the fallen on the field, the actions of the Germans, the repelling mortar fire of the Allies, Cédric's intimate knowledge of the battle location. "The Allied covering bombardment made it possible to retrieve the patient, who safely survived the surgery, thanks to Doctor Stockton."

"Don't deflect this on me, Nurse Blackwell," Harold scolded her. "It was a dangerous—"

Marcus quickly interjected. "I can't say it was a stupid thing to do because it was so damned gutsy. Where did you learn how to tie off the shrapnel to secure the wound like that Nurse Blackwell?" he asked her with a hint of admiration in his voice as he listened from across the table. Lydia had surprised him. "It was a good intervention on your part."

"It just made sense, Doctor," she replied, just wishing this would be over quickly and they would let her go, and rest.

"You'll teach that technique to the medics, corpsmen and nurses," Harold insisted. "It was very effective to use the figure eight to prevent the tamponade of bleeding that would have resulted if the shrapnel had shifted," he begrudgingly admitted.

Lieutenant Aubert shook his head, pondering his next move. "As far as your decision to go out there, I think you already appreciate the gravity of what you did. Let there be no future misunderstanding, I order you nurses to remain in the station. I will ask the French soldier - Cédric Marcielle, you said? - to explain the field advantage to us as we look at options for the next battle. At night, perhaps we can have ambulances waiting for stragglers just behind the bombardment, if it is the custom of the Allies to maintain the lines in this way."

Lydia felt her face flush, as she replied, "Yes, sir."

"And neither you nor the French soldier were injured in any way?" Marcus pressed her, looking at her very closely.

Lydia shook her head. "No, Doctor," she replied faintly. The flush was not leaving her cheeks and Marcus had seen it immediately.

Then Simon, also growing concerned at the color rising in her face, interjected, "Nurse Blackwell has eaten nothing since arriving back. Perhaps we should allow her a break for some breakfast?"

The others nodded and, to Lydia's intense relief, moved off, carrying on their discussion as they left the tent. Marcus glanced back once as if changing his mind about leaving, but Simon had remained with Lydia.

He saw the flush in her cheeks replaced by a pale sheen. Lydia looked ready to faint. He quickly took a seat beside her at the table and pushed a cup of coffee toward her that he had been holding in his hand. It was cold.

"Drink it right down," he ordered her quietly. "You need fluids."

"Are they gone? I believe I am about to pass out..."

They were indeed gone. Simon quickly laid her back on the bench and elevated her feet. One of the litter bearers at the end of the long table jumped up from where he was seated and hurried over.

"What can I do, Doc?" he asked quickly.

The doctor looked up at the man. "It was a long night, Bill," he replied evenly. "I think Nurse Blackwell really needs some sleep. Let's get her to her tent in a minute here." As the color slowly returned to her face, they helped her sit, then stand, before walking her over behind the surgery to the tent where her own cot was situated amid a few of the other nurses'.

Simon nodded at the corpsman as they lowered Lydia onto her bedding, adding, "Thanks for your help, Bill."

"Mais bien sûr, Doctor. The wounded are calling her 'ange de la miséricorde'," the orderly shared.

"Angel of mercy," Simon repeated. "Are they indeed..."

Bill nodded, leaving the small tent, as Lydia sank back in pain.

"I must remember what a superb liar you can be," Simon remarked dryly as she closed her eyes. "I need to check your incision."

She shook her head. "Don't bother," she replied tiredly, glad to be lying down and out of sight of the other doctors who might see through her facade. "Laura said she would do it later."

He laughed softly, but his eyes showed concern. "That's not what you would tell one of the patients, Mademoiselle Ange."

She put a hand on his arm as he sat on her trunk beside her cot. "Don't call me that," she begged him. "All of us are the same... Susannah, Mary, Laura, Charlotte, Linda... any one of them would have gone."

"Maybe to the next batch of wounded, you are all the same," he agreed. "But not to this batch. No, my dear, you have a reputation now with this bunch of men that they will not forget. Now, let me help you roll onto your side so I can look at your incision. The bullet did not penetrate your scapula, which is amazing... lodged right up against it like that. It was dented."

"It ricocheted off Cédric's helmet, so I didn't get the brunt of it. I didn't even know it hit me," she admitted.

Simon pulled the shirt off her shoulder and lifted the bandage covering the incision. "You conveniently left that out of your story back in the mess tent, you know. Yet still, you helped carry that patient to the ambulance... don't know how you managed it, Lydia."

"I didn't think about it, actually," she said quietly. "I'm so sorry I worried you."

He peered at his handiwork, mentally noting the wound looked clean, not inflamed, the sutures holding. He rewrapped her shoulder gently to hold the bandage in place and pulled the shirt back over the dressing, to conceal it. Then he spoke again. "Harold asked you what on earth you were thinking, Lydia. I think I already know the answer as far as that goes. You wouldn't have been able to live with yourself if you'd let that man die out there alone... though I wish to God that you'd come and gotten me to go with you. But what are you thinking about now?"

She remained on her side, avoiding all pressure on the injury, and did not answer him at first. He remained beside her and gently stroked her hair, hoping no one was peering into the nurses' tent. Finally, the tears fell unbidden, streaming down her face, landing on the rough army blanket beneath her. She didn't sob; there was no need, her grief was so near the surface it could not help but spill from her. She simply allowed the tears to fall, as the doctor's heart ached for her having to endure what she had been through.

"Try to tell me," Simon urged her again quietly, not pushing too hard, but encouraging her to speak it out loud, all too aware of the dangers of holding such matters inside for too long, where they would fester worse than any infection.

"In the dark," she faltered, "we stepped on human beings... in the ambulance, we drove over bodies making slippery bumps under us. These were just boys, Simon, just someone's son, someone's brother... and none of them made it to one of the clearing stations... we didn't save any of them. They all laid there until death took them. There were so many dead soldiers... in pieces."

Simon bowed his head, listening. "That is true," he said simply. He wiped the tears from her cheeks, but they were immediately replenished.

Finally, she continued. "And you know what, Simon? The German soldiers were out looking for their wounded, just like we were. And they are just boys, too, just someone's son, someone's brother... and... they probably said their prayers the same way the French boys did yesterday morning... to the same God in Heaven... asking for victory and protection, on both sides."

Simon nodded, watching her carefully, sensing there was more.

"All those mangled boys... on both sides..." she whispered. "Laying in the dark."

"And they all died," Simon finished for her. "Except the one that you brought in."

There was a deep agony in her eyes as she looked up at him. "Maybe, Simon, maybe. But I have to wonder how many more were still alive, dying alone out there, like André? Dying in the field, in pain, in darkness? How many more were still alive when the ambulance rolled over them... and we finished the job with the wheels of the ambulance..." Her voice dropped to the barest whisper. "I can't live with that thought... that the bumps we were rolling over were the wheels catching on the bodies..."

Simon studied her face for a long while. He longed to take her in his arms, to hold her so tightly, pushing away the pain in her soul, but the sides of the tent were open to the screen, and people who might see were walking past outside. He did not want to subject her to gossip.

When at last he answered her, he trusted his voice to carry his conviction. "There are times, Lydia, when we let the boys lay under that tarp out there right in our own station, some clutching a rosary, knowing we can't save them. They, too, are waiting to die, maybe under better circumstances by having a kind word passed their way from time to time, a gentle touch from you nurses, opium for pain and, on a rare occasion, a chaplain coming through... but dying, nonetheless..." He had her attention now, and he knew it as he continued. "And I think that in the darkness of the battlefield, there really are angels moving among the soldiers laying there, sent by the God of both sides, gathering their souls to take them home. And the ambulance you were in may have made that happen quicker for a few, rather than them lingering through the night... but the outcome is the same. There are more souls in heaven today than there were yesterday... and so it will be until the end of time, Lydia. Those souls are not held in some spiritual prison out on the battlefield at night."

Lydia hung on every word Simon spoke. She grew quiet as some little sliver of peace stole over her. Then she reached for his hand and pulled it to her, kissing his palm, sending a jolt through his entire body, then kissing the fingers that had saved so many lives in the months she had known him. Then she curled his fingers shut as if to hold her kiss inside his hand... as if it would flutter away were it not so restrained.

"Merci, mon amour," she whispered in French as he reluctantly left her, headed for the surgery.

Over the following week, while treating heavy casualties, Simon pondered the near-miss of losing Lydia on the battlefield. He wanted to make her his, before the war had a chance to part them forever. He also had become aware that Marcus was increasingly more interested in Lydia himself, and so Simon had a plan forming in his mind to create some time alone with her. So, when he found an opportunity to head over to Lieutenant Aubert's command post, he took it. The man was sitting at a cluttered, makeshift desk reviewing a myriad of memos, orders, and requisitions; he looked up briefly as Simon entered.

"Have a seat," he offered, preoccupied with other things.

"Thank you, sir," Simon replied crisply and took his place on a folding chair.

The lieutenant waited. "Something on your mind, Doctor?" he asked wearily in English, in deference to the American sitting in front of him.

Simon nodded. "You know we'll be low on supplies after so many patients have come through."

The lieutenant sat back and sighed. "Yes, I am aware. The perpetual problem of supplies. Doctor Stockton has already informed me of how quickly we are depleted... again. It cannot be helped. It takes time for things to come from Paris, from the command centers."

Simon nodded in agreement. "We have heard that heroin can help the boys exposed to the trench gases, help them to breathe. We might be able to avert pneumonia if we can stop the incessant coughing from gas exposure. And the coughing at night is a beacon to the enemy as surely as any lantern lights."

Lieutenant Aubert leaned forward over his desk. "What are you suggesting we do, Doctor Finney?"

Simon hesitated. "If there is a lull you can foresee from Command, even twenty-four to forty-eight hours, I would like to take a truck and see if I can obtain some heroin and supplies from the locals close by, in towns well behind the lines. The Germans have to be getting it from somewhere close by on their side, and Metz is not that far from the German border. I'd like to pick up all the medicine and any other needed items we can find. Some of the locals in these rural areas even know more about plant remedies than we do in the States."

Aubert nodded. "But, of course, you realize the trucks will eventually bring supplies from the field hospitals to us as well."

"Not heroin."

"No, not that." Aubert nodded. "Bien, emmène un soldat... take a soldier... avec toi. I do not want to risk losing a doctor by you going alone, even if it is away from the front, not toward it."

Simon cleared his throat. "I do believe a nurse should go. As rumors fly quickly, we may have an advantage of, shall we say, a period of goodwill from the local French... of increased trust, perhaps even... generosity."

"Oh, that matter of the rescue of that soldier Besimont, you mean," the lieutenant replied. "Yes, that kind of thing spreads quickly in my somewhat superstitious country. It was a foolish move, however well meant. People die in war, Doctor Finney. It's an inescapable truth. It is simply a matter of who has the most soldiers left standing at the end that decides who wins. N'est-ce pas?"

Simon bristled, internally, at the man's comment, but kept his voice even and cordial. "Yes, but more Allies will still be standing in the end if we do not run out of antiseptic or bandages... and can possibly obtain some heroin for the wounded."

"True. Very well, I will advise you, Doctor, when you may leave for a short – and I do mean very short – trip through the local towns. If you must take that nurse with you, then go ahead." The lieutenant dropped his eyes back down to the orders on his desk and added, "Dismissed," as if he'd been the one who had summoned Simon to the tent in the first place.

As they ate supper in the mess tent, Marcus and Simon looked at the food tentatively.

"Looks a bit like what we had for breakfast," Marcus observed.

"And supper last night," Simon agreed. "I guess medical supplies aren't the only thing we're running short on."

Marcus picked up his fork. "Ah, well. Man does not live on bread alone... So... what do you think about our nurses now, Simon?"

"What do you mean?" Simon asked, starting in on the food, hunger winning out over taste.

"Well, they're smart, they're quick, they are gifted," Marcus observed. "Lovely creatures. Aren't you glad we didn't ship them out, after all?"

Simon nodded. "Actually, I am, even though it is far from safe for them to be here."

Marcus looked down at the end of the table where many of the nurses had congregated. "I don't see Nurse Blackwell down there..."

"No doubt in recovery," Simon said between bites.

Marcus looked at the nurses thoughtfully. "You know, she intrigues me no end, Simon," Marcus admitted. "She's one brave woman going out into the battlefield like that... I think I'll ask her out."

"I thought you were interested in Nurse Bertolli... after it didn't work out with Nurse Trent, I believe."

"It was Bertolli and that isn't going to last either," Marcus sighed.

Simon looked up. He reached for his tin cup of coffee. "So, you're thinking of Nurse Blackwell now? Going to ask her to the movies? Dinner at a fancy hotel?"

Marcus paused. "No, perhaps just a midnight stroll along the banks of the Meuse, under the starlight. Give her a chance to get to know my finer qualities a little better. She's one of the nurses I haven't had a minute alone with so far. Must rectify that. Have you considered asking one of the nurses for a... stroll in the night, my friend? I've noticed Nurse Blackwell spends more than a little time in the surgery with us when she gets the chance. And then there was that whole letter-in-the-fire business a while ago. I wonder if she's available?"

Simon cleared his throat. "I think you'd have to ask her that," he said evenly, his heart starting to pound against the inside surfaces of his rib cage. Marcus was so much better with women than he was. *Why can't I just tell Marcus that I've fallen for her?*

Marcus pushed his finished tray to the side. "I believe I will," he said decidedly. "After all, didn't she say I have irresistible charm? I think she did! And I really admire what she tried to do saving that soldier. She's a really remarkable woman, and beautiful... won't hurt to at least find out if I have a chance with her."

Chapter 4
Nancy

Lydia's recovery was quick, thanks to the immediate attention to her wound, and the absence of infection. She had returned to her duties straight away, despite Simon's protestations, not wanting anyone to suspect the injury she had sustained. The wounded men who had been aware of young André's rescue had all been moved out to field hospitals. New arrivals came rapidly in their places, many having been exposed to gas in the trenches.

Those new M2 gas masks had improved the men's protection against the deadly canisters volleyed at the soldiers. Though, while their physical recovery had improved, the mental anguish of the bombardments continued to wreak havoc on them. Lydia's compassion ran deep for these men. She accepted, but did not forget her night close to the trenches... realizing firsthand what the soldiers heard and saw as they fought... the images that wouldn't leave them quickly, if ever. They certainly hadn't left her own memory, not in the least.

The weather would soon be changing; cooler days would arrive with September. The ever-present risk of dehydration would be less of a problem as soldiers waited outdoors until their turn in the surgery and afterward in the recovery tents. It was much less oppressive to have the flaps closed tightly each night. Rain came, though, and keeping the wounded dry was a new challenge. More tents were needed, and more cots arrived to get patients off of the soggy, and muddy, grass. When the rain fell steadily, everything in the tents seemed to leak, and every cot seemed to get wet. Wounded soldiers slept with ponchos over them, covering their faces and bodies in an effort to stay dry. The nurses had to make rounds, lifting the ponchos, peering beneath with their flashlights to check wounds and skin, while administering pain medication to those underneath. In the mess hall, hot coffee disappeared more quickly and people learned to ignore the large drops of rain watering down their eggs and biscuits.

Many of the wounded now arrived with severe coughs, not as much from gas exposure, but pneumonia or tuberculosis. To contain the spread, the doctors and nurses decided to set up a recovery tent just for those with respiratory symptoms. The nurses used scarves to cover their nose and mouth when caring for the men lying there. Buckets, filled with disinfectant, were kept close so they could wash their hands as often as possible, especially when coming and going from the tent. Men coughing up bloody phlegm were encouraged to cough into a cloth instead of spitting onto the ground beside their cots. Nights were longer now and the damp air did no favors for those with pneumonia and suspected tuberculosis. Often on the same day of arrival, infected men were trucked out to field hospitals as quickly as possible; the nurses always endeavored to fill a truck with those afflicted, keeping the regular surgical patients apart, and teaching the truck drivers to throw a bucket of disinfectant over the floor before they headed back, empty, on the return trip to camp.

The three doctors met regularly with the nurses to discuss what they called "best practice" for managing the wounded with respiratory afflictions. Harold Stockton was pleased to see the nurses using their stethoscopes regularly to listen for irregularities and bubbling inside the chest which indicated the development of a more serious condition. At one of the meetings, the nurses expressed their frustrations.

"Doctor," Susannah said in one of the meetings. "We must move the respiratory recovery tents every few days. We cannot keep walking on the soiled ground and then into the surgical recovery without spreading the germs."

"The camp will move soon anyway, Nurse Boyton. The worst loss of life, now, is north of Verdun at Somme, farther up the front," he informed them all. "Since engaging the Germans there in July, the British and French have experienced massive losses. They've only been able to estimate the number of dead and wounded. We'll be moving out soon, the entire station, with Verdun now holding its own."

Linda Trent, ever timid, spoke her mind. "It'll be easier to move now than it will be in winter when the stoves have to be set up with every move. And of course, we should go where we're needed the most."

Marcus glanced over at her and agreed. "True. And we also have more soldiers helping us relocate, now that we're closer to the line. It would be an undertaking, though, if we have to get past the trenches. If we go northeast any farther, we'll have to either build some bridges or take the long way around."

Susannah asked, "How much farther are the casualties being trucked to the field hospitals since the Verdun hospital was destroyed? If the patients also have a much longer route to get around the trenches, then we'll need to be absolutely sure they are stable enough for such a move before we let them leave us."

Marcus hesitated before answering. "I'm not sure, really. The railroad station at Verdun was also hit. So, the wounded can't be transported by trains from Verdun either, until it's repaired. You're right... patients might need to stay longer in clearing stations in the field, longer than we're used to. We could be easily overrun and not be able to... I wonder what other stations are doing to handle the flow..."

Lydia spoke in the pause that followed. "There is something else to consider if the station moves closer to more intense activity..."

They waited, turning to her as she hesitated.

Simon caught the haunted look in her eyes. He'd seen it occasionally in her gaze. "What is it, Nurse Blackwell?"

"Well," she started. "I know that we don't count numbers."

They all nodded.

"But I know..." she started again, "but we know from the wounded themselves... that tens of... thousands have died around Verdun alone. Near Somme, if the casualties are even worse, and... the dead are even greater in number... there may not be any fields on either side of the trenches clear enough of certain kinds of debris..."

Interrupting, to help her, Simon said, "You mean we would be crossing fields strewn with the remnants of both sides, which have yet to be recovered, Allies and Germans alike. Nurse Blackwell is correct, I'm afraid. Many bodies have never been buried or weapons retrieved, and the ground along the trenches is full of barbed wire, craters, damaged vehicles and pits from the bombs.

It would be untenable ground for a camp like ours to cross, let alone set up."

This thought provided a chilling image for all of them to consider. They all realized the station couldn't be established just anywhere near the carnage of an active battlefield. It would only become more challenging to find a clear patch of ground to set up their surgical station.

Too easily, Lydia was pulled back into her memory of the piles of bodies strewn over the ground. They would rapidly turn to skeletons, picked clean of all but fragments of uniforms... which was perhaps a worse image than the vivid nightmare of the dead from the night of André's rescue, with their unseeing eyes, staring off into the dark ravages of war. Her mind drifted to the Civil War. Battles were often refought over the same ground of prior skirmishes, and the unburied dead had sometimes remained just where they had fallen, bones bleached and left to be tripped upon or stepped over by a new company, as they attempted to advance against the foe of the day... nuns had served the wounded then.

Marcus studied Lydia's face carefully, seeing something there that drew his concern. The nurse seemed to have left the meeting without leaving the tent. What had it really been like out there for her during her night run in the ambulance? And now, still volunteering to stand by their tables in the surgery, sewing people back together? He wanted to find time to ask her, privately.

Harold cleared his throat. "The French army will have to find a way for us to advance our station and a suitable location along the front, so we aren't treating patients on top of a cemetery. We'll have to trust their forward scouts to find both a route and an empty field maybe near Reims, nearer the heavy fighting, up closer to Somme. Doctor Finney, will you join me? We need to report to Aubert and discuss it with the higher ups." Simon nodded and stood, joining him as they left the mess tent.

As the cook rapped a spoon against a pot announcing lunch, Marcus left his seat to work his way around one of the tables. In passing, he lightly rested a hand on Lydia's shoulder, bringing her back to the present. Lydia shot a quick look of gratitude to him. She also looked over at the retreating chief medical officer, knowing that Simon and Doctor Stockton at least had understood what she had been trying to say with her halting words. She watched Simon, hands in his pockets... he walked slowly beside the other doctor as they crossed the little camp, deep in conversation. They were both such good men. Taking one last look toward Simon, she cleared her head and rose up with the other nurses, the group milling around, trying to lighten their spirits. The cook had prepared lunch during the meeting, but it was too hot to eat in the mess tent. Taking the small plate of food extended to her, Lydia wandered out behind the mess to a knoll where, only yesterday, lines of men had been waiting for care. She sat down and took a bite of what the cook had been able to create, from what was available, which was limited, at best.

The sunshine was suddenly interrupted by Doctor Lovell who rounded the tent looking for her, approaching with a cup of coffee in his hand and a baguette. "Can I sit with you, Nurse Blackwell?" he asked casually.

"Certainly, Doctor," she smiled up at him, shading her eyes from the late morning glare.

He plopped himself on the grass near a tent peg, its long anchor rope, a launching pad for dragonflies which had perched with wings outspread, waiting for takeoff.

"Damn disgusting bugs," he muttered, swatting at a fly.

"I'm sure they find you delicious," she teased him.

He laughed shortly. "It's not the bugs that I want finding me delicious."

"Hm, I think I'll let that one pass," Lydia murmured.

He took a long sip of coffee. "I wish I could find a delicious cup of coffee, that's for sure. Can I ask you something, Nurse Blackwell?"

She nodded. "Of course, Doctor."

He looked at her. "You can skip the doctor thing if you want, when it's just us," he suggested. "We've been working together for what five, six months now? Marcus is fine."

"It's a very good name, indeed," Lydia agreed. "But I think 'doctor' is also respectable."

He chuckled. "I'll have to check my birth certificate back home... but I don't think it reads 'Doctor' Marcus Lucius Lovell."

Lydia took a bite of her food and looked over at him curiously. "Why did you become a doctor, Doctor Lovell?" she wondered out loud.

He looked up to the sky, where a dozen dragonflies zoomed overhead. "Well, now, good question. First, of course, there was all the money that comes with the job." He pointed around them. "All this opulence, you know. Second was the prestige of being asked to share my wealth of knowledge with student doctors and the community... if they speak any English, that is. Third was the opportunity to advance medical science for situations just like this. And…"

Lydia waited, then prompted him, "Is there a fourth?"

He looked at her quickly. "Oh, of course. Fourth was the adoring eyes of the nurses following me every time I walked down a hall at the hospital."

"Worshiping the very floor that you walk upon?" she suggested.

"Something like that," he said, draining his cup then laying it on the grass. "But recounting my formative years isn't why I wanted to talk to you, Ly—Nurse Blackwell."

"What can I do for you, Doctor?" she pressed.

He looked at her blue eyes, long, wavy chestnut brown hair and her unwavering gaze. "You intrigue me. You aren't like the others," he said matter-of-factly.

The color in her cheeks rose slightly. "Is that so?" she asked. "I don't see much difference in any of us."

Marcus rested his arms on his bent knees and studied her. "Yes, it's so," he declared. "You're different. You're different in the surgery. You're different with the wounded. The nurses all like and respect you… and, well, so do the doctors, of course," he added, including himself in the general mix. "But none of the other nurses would have gone out to retrieve that kid on the field, in the night, like you did. You're beautiful and you're brave, Lydia."

Lydia looked down and carefully placed her unfinished plate of food on the ground. "It was—"

He stopped her. "Don't say 'nothing'. Don't say it was 'nothing' because it wasn't. I think you're quite remarkable, Lydia."

She looked at him, that far-away cloud behind her eyes that he'd noted moments ago forming again. "It was just..." she said, "necessary."

"Necessary? To risk your life and the life of the driver for one person?" he asked quietly. "When there were so many others needing care already? Necessary to put yourself at risk... necessary to see what you saw?"

She nodded, recalling the agonized despair of André's friends who had had to leave him behind and were unwilling to live without him. "Yes," she repeated. "It was. His friends were giving up from the guilt of leaving him..."

Marcus saw she was tripping suddenly over the images in her mind and did not want her to fall. He took her hand, linking her to the present, but she was suddenly so far away, somewhere else, on that dark night; he grew concerned. He squeezed her fingers, intertwined his own.

His voice was very soft, "You're seeing it now... aren't you?"

She nodded. "Comes back so quickly..."

"What do you see?" he gently pressed, hoping her ghosts would leave her if she described it out loud. "You shouldn't have to carry this, Lydia."

Lydia stared into that night, in her mind's eye. "I see," she started, "I see the eyes of the dead watching us trying to find our way through the piles of bodies, wondering why we are there, why the living would walk on the dead... only..."

He waited patiently, then prompted, "Only..."

"... only they aren't all dead. We had to find André..."

"You did find André." He led her, "Where was he?"

"Against a small bank of dead men," she whispered. "The Germans heard him crying out in pain... when we first tried to move him..."

"When you tried to carry him out to safety..." Marcus reminded her.

"... bullets flew at us... I didn't even feel it... hitting me... off the helmet... I didn't feel a thing..."

"You were hit?" Marcus said very softly and evenly, hiding his surprise.

"I didn't feel it... my shoulder stinging... and the shells started falling. Dirt and parts of bodies dropping all over us... those poor boys' bodies sliding underneath the wheels... rolling over them... felt like they were rolling over me..." Lydia went pale under the sun. She leaned over and vomited into the grass as Marcus held her long hair out of the way. As she bent her head over the ground, her shirt gaped, her skin slightly exposed. He saw the sutured incision on her back, just under her shoulder. He recognized the suture style, neat and tight. Marcus wiped her mouth with the corner of his shirt and smoothed the wavy brown curls away from her pale face. His empathy taking control.

"Look at me, Lydia," he commanded her. "Look at me." She turned her face to him, at first not seeing him until the specters receded into the distant recesses where such things are best contained.

"You got André back safely, all the way to the station..." he led her to the end—the getting out and the end. "You saved him for his friends."

Finally, her eyes focused, she drew in a deep breath, and she brightened as the color returned to her cheeks... she had returned to the here-and-now.

"Oh," she said simply. "Yes. Well. Nothing anyone else wouldn't have done."

He pulled her to her feet, turning her away from her plate and vomit. Marcus led her away, toward the nurses' tent, through dragonflies which continued to dive-bomb them. "As I was saying, I think you are a most remarkable woman, Lydia Blackwell."

Lydia laughed shakily. "You say that to all of the nurses!" she exclaimed, removing his hand from her elbow. "Now behave yourself, Doctor."

"Yes, ma'am, I will." He nodded like a disobedient child being corrected and winked at her. "But only for now. Get some rest while you can; doctor's orders!... And I really would like to get to know you better, Lydia. Truly, I would." He smiled and turned to head for the doctors' tent with a spring in his step.

Only moments earlier, Lieutenant Aubert had told Doctor Finney to wait a moment, after Stockton had departed the command tent. "We expect a lull in the fighting for a few days, hopefully. The Germans are regrouping to the northwest and east. Before we move this unit, go south to the towns below Verdun to check on the medicines and supplies you spoke to me about. Do not go farther than Nancy. Do you know enough French to converse with the locals or do you need a translator?"

Simon shook his head. "Nurse Blackwell knows a considerable amount of French, it will be sufficient," he said. "She also has the goodwill of the people."

The lieutenant looked up. "She shouldn't have taken off to the Red Zone without orders."

"The nurses are volunteers, sir," Simon reminded him, "despite them wearing our uniforms."

"Indeed," the unit commander replied. "Well, if you still think it's best, and she is willing to go with you, let her spread all that goodwill with our countrymen once more. Come back with as many supplies as you can gather. Don't get shot. Don't get taken prisoner."

"Thank you, sir," Simon replied and left, eagerly.

Marcus crossed the camp and entered the doctors' tent. He stretched out on his cot and found the baseball he always kept nearby, tossing it up in the air and catching it over and over again. Not for the first time, he wondered if they had made a mistake keeping the nurses with them. It was asking too much. But then, they kept refusing the offers to leave. Damn! Lydia Blackwell intrigued him considerably. Why was she holding herself back from his overtures?

The flap of the tent opened, and Simon came inside and plopped down on his cot for a minute, enjoying the feeling of freedom that came with a lull in the day's fighting. No artillery thudding in the distance. No bugles calling them to surgery. They could breathe today.

Marcus looked over at Simon, who seemed happy after his exchange with Aubert. "What did Aubert say?" Marcus questioned, throwing the ball up in the air again and catching it one-handed, preventing it from hitting his nose on the return.

"The army understands we need a clean field and more supplies. No question about it," Simon replied, preoccupied. He rummaged in his small trunk of belongings. Then he felt the whack of the ball as it hit his back.

Simon swung around to look at Marcus as the ball bounced off his cot and rolled to the floor. "What the devil, Marc!"

"I thought we were friends," Marcus said simply. "You should have told me."

"Told you what?" Simon asked, irritated. "You were in the briefing. You know as much as I do."

"I meant," Marcus said, deliberately slowing his words. "You should have told me that Nurse Blackwell took a bullet."

Simon paused. He raised one eyebrow. "And just what makes you think that Nurse Blackwell was shot?" he said quietly, retrieving and tossing the ball, none too gently, back to its owner.

"I saw the suture line... your handiwork. Your name is all over it."

Simon stared at the man.

"As she was puking her guts out behind the mess."

Simon jumped to his feet, but Marcus waved him back down. "Simmer down," he added. "She's okay. She was reliving the memory... I helped her through it. Why didn't you tell me one of our nurses got shot? Especially her?"

Simon reached back into his trunk and pulled out a spare pair of trousers, boxers, and a shirt. "I didn't tell anyone, Marcus, because Aubert is this close to shipping them all out, and you know it. She will heal well."

Marcus sat up on the edge of his cot, tossing the ball from hand to hand, Simon eyeing it warily in case the thing headed his way again.

"Maybe so... probably so... that one. Her commitment is strong as iron," Marcus admitted. "But if we're going to make it through this, you should tell me things like this, that affect our nurses. I would have taken it out for her, too, if I'd known."

Simon nodded, but didn't say anything. "If it happens again," he said gruffly, "you'll be the second to know." He threw a few belongings in a haversack and swung it up on his shoulder.

Marcus stood too, noticing. "Going somewhere, I see?"

Simon turned at the flap of the tent and nodded. "I am taking Nurse Blackwell with me to the quaint little towns of Metz and Nancy to get heroin, bandages, and anything else we can find to fill our empty shelves. And stopping along the way for a nice bottle of red wine and dinner at a pub somewhere. Aubert just authorized two days."

"Son of a bitch!" Marcus exclaimed softly. "Two days away from here with that woman? Alone? I can go for you! I hadn't even known that was an option."

"It wasn't," Simon said evenly as he left the tent with his friend right behind him. And he thought as he strode away, *I at least want a fair shot, to see if I have a chance with her... and if not, then he can try, with my blessing.*

Leaving the tent with heightened anticipation, Simon went in search of Lydia. He had longed for time alone with her for more than a month now, as their friendship had grown. He thought it would also be good for her to get away from the stress of the station, even if just for a short reprieve. Simon felt a wave of anticipation wash over him—it was a good feeling. Perhaps he also needed a break from the surgery to just go to a French village and see normal people trying to live normal lives... even if it was under very abnormal circumstances. At least, mercifully, it did not look like it was going to rain. He wanted to leave as quickly as possible. After the disconcerting exchange with Marcus, Simon was more anxious than ever to find Lydia and get her away from the war for the couple of days they had been given. He found her, as expected, in the recovery, speaking with Gretha Bernstein, Nancy Mitchell, and Alice Miller.

Simon entered the tent with a bounce in his step and quickly appraised Lydia's color, her poise, her demeanor. Nothing seemed amiss, despite Marcus' earlier assessment.

"You look happy, Doctor Finney!" Gretha exclaimed. "Did you get some good news from home or something?"

He shook his head. "No, better than that!"

"Better than good news from home?" Gretha replied. "We cannot wait to hear."

The four stood, expectantly, eight eyes fixed on his own.

Simon quickly exclaimed. "I must borrow Nurse Blackwell from you for a short time. Lieutenant Aubert has graciously authorized me to purchase medicines and supplies from the locals, and I mean to try to collect as much as possible, in a short time. He is sending along Nurse Blackwell as an ambassador of goodwill in the expectation she will help us return with bandages, fruits, vegetables, and any other good thing that the locals wish to bestow upon our station."

"Well, that is very good news!" Alice declared. She looked at Lydia. "Find us fresh apples and I will give you my firstborn child, if I ever have one."

Gretha laughed, "I can top that! Find us green vegetables and you may have the first calf I get from my cow once we're back home... if she is still calving!"

Lydia smiled at the other nurses. "You may keep your baby and your calf," she assured them. She turned to Simon, expressing her surprise at this turn of events. "Did the lieutenant really give permission, Doctor Finney? You aren't teasing us, are you?"

Simon hoisted the haversack on his shoulder. "I'm already packed. How long will it take you to throw together a change of clothes?" he countered, encouraging her with a look to be quick.

Lydia returned the look evenly. "I haven't unpacked since I arrived!" she declared, turning on her heels and heading to the nurses' tent to gather a few overnight belongings.

Simon watched her go. "Can you spare her?" he asked the other nurses.

"We are green with envy," Nancy told them. "And not just because you're visiting a town with my name!"

He nodded. "Why yes, we are! And thank you all for covering everything here."

"Make sure she comes back in one piece, Doctor Finney," Alice added dryly.

"You can count on it," Simon assured her, turning from the recovery as quickly as he had arrived.

Nancy looked at Alice. "A dollar says—"

"You're on, but I will lose," the other retorted as they both resumed their tasks.

Gretha followed behind, asking the other two nurses, "A dollar for what?" But the other women just laughed and returned to work.

Their truck bounced down the road, away from Verdun, briefly following the Meuse River before the road forked—one way slightly west, toward Metz, the other in a more southerly direction, to the little town of Nancy. The red cross on the side of their truck afforded them a measure of safety in their movement across the Argonne. They had been quickly permitted to pass at checkpoints. Overhead, the sky was blue, with scattered white clouds. Lydia allowed her hair to flow freely, the wind passing through the open windows of the vehicle. Fresh and invigorating, without any of the smells associated with sickness and death, it rejuvenated her spirit. After they had been traveling for forty minutes or so, the nurse looked ahead through the flimsy front window seeing a wooded embankment near the edge of a small tributary to the river. She put a hand on Simon's arm to get his attention.

"Can we stop over there for a minute?" she called out over the grinding of the motor. She pointed to the wood.

Simon nodded and steered the truck off the dirt road and toward the copse of trees. The leaves were turning slightly yellow, messaging the soon to come change of seasons. They both got out and stretched, taking in the fresh air.

"Give me a minute," she asked him.

He nodded. "Don't go too far."

Lydia moved off to the privacy afforded her by the trees and took care of her needs. Soon enough, she reemerged wandering over to the stream to wash her hands. The water sparkled as it ran beneath her fingers, catching the rays of sunlight like glittering jewels. She bent over and took a small drink. "Think it's safe?" she asked him. "It looks clean enough. And it's cold!"

"I expect it's cleaner than what's in the camp," Simon assured her, standing on the bank above her, watching the sunlight bounce off her chestnut brown hair. "Anyway, you already drank it, so if you didn't swallow a minnow, and you don't keel over suddenly, you'll get your answer!"

She smiled up at him innocently and patted the soft mossy grass beside her, so he dropped down next to her after washing his own hands and face in the running stream. "That's the clearest looking water we've seen in months, except for the minnows," he agreed. "Icy."

Lydia laid back on the bank and reveled in the calm. A loosely formed vee of geese traveled southbound against the clouds, then honking, they banked and headed west, following some instinctive directive to change course. Small birds sang occasionally overhead, hidden in the summer trees. Leaves rustled in the breeze offering a soothing rhythmic distraction from thought.

"Where did the war go?" she wondered aloud. "It is beautiful out here."

His voice was low next to her, "Still back there, waiting for us to return. Or maybe it can go on without us for a little while. Take off your shirt."

She looked up at him, surprised. "Simon?"

"I want to take the sutures out of your back."

"Oh," she said. "Of course..." She unbuttoned her shirt and dropped it down, soft hairs lifting as the breeze touched her bare skin. Simon knelt behind her, and it was then that she saw he had brought with him his medical box from the truck. He knelt behind her, took out the scissors, gently cut the sutures one by one, and tugged the threads free from her skin. When he finished, only a thin remnant of the incision was left behind. He touched it gently with his fingers, probing for swelling or discharge.

"Any pain when I press it here? Or here? Pain in the bone?" he asked, his fingers lingering over her back. "Move your shoulder for me…"

"None whatsoever," she replied, obeying his prompts… his touch making her shiver as he manipulated her shoulder while she rotated it.

"Are you cold?" he asked gently, raising and lowering her arm.

"No," she said, her breath catching.

He appraised her slowly and lowered her to the ground, her shirt still open. "God above, you are a beautiful woman," he said gazing at her. "I'm glad you have healed."

Lydia closed her eyes and listened to the wind and the songs of nature overhead. The war seemed very, very far away in this singular moment. She felt Simon brush away a wisp of hair from her face. He leaned over her suddenly and gathered her into his arms. For the past three months, they had not been alone except in stolen moments of darkness at the station… and now, there were no inquisitive eyes watching them. Simon lowered her to the mossy bank, as they allowed themselves the uninterrupted pleasure of freedom.

Suddenly, he stopped, his body hovering above hers, his hand caressing her bare skin and he cleared his throat. "I don't know if I've communicated this very well, Lydia, but I am thoroughly in love with you."

She returned the look he had given her. "I don't know if I've communicated this very well either, Simon... what with everything going on back there. But just in case I haven't... I am very much in love with you as well."

Simon felt the rush of permissive confirmation... and a new confidence in a chance of a happy life with this woman, found in the most unlikely of places, at this most singular time in their lives. He lost himself in the knowledge of that, as he covered her with assurances, there on the water's edge. Then, abruptly containing his urgency, he stopped. "Lydia, when we actually come together, tell me if I... do anything that you don't like. Don't leave me guessing."

She smiled at him. "You couldn't do anything that I would not like, Simon," she whispered. "Nothing at all. I don't know what strings you pulled to make this happen... but I'm so glad you did." She reached for him again, this freedom a long time coming, glad for the feel of his body against her own.

Simon propped himself up on one elbow, gazing down at her and tracing the line from her throat to her navel with his finger. "I don't want us to ever be separated, Lydia," he stated. "I was terrified when you disappeared that night, in the ambulance. Terrified that I'd lose you before I had the chance to make you mine."

"I am so sorry about scaring you, Simon. I don't want to be separated from you either," she answered, breathless at what he was suggesting.

"I don't want anything or anyone to ever come between us," he added, thinking back briefly to the morning with Marcus and the man's seemingly insatiable appetite for a challenge like this woman.

Lydia looked up at him. "Nothing and no one, will ever come between us," she reassured him. "I want this too, Simon."

He sat up and pulled her to a sitting position on the bank, her hands in his own. "Then this is sudden, I know, but Lydia, will you be my wife?"

She gazed steadily into his brown eyes. "Yes," she said without hesitation. "But do you mean someday? Or now? Because if you mean someday, then it will be very hard. I want to be your wife now. I don't want to wait until we go home, Simon."

He nodded as he shook out fallen leaves from her shirt, pulled it over her shoulders, and began to button it shut for her as he spoke hurriedly, his mouth barely keeping up with his thoughts. "I've been struggling with this for a while. It's incredibly challenging to be around you day after day like we have been, at the station, and to have to pretend we're nothing more than part of the larger team. But I don't think Lieutenant Aubert would look favorably on a married couple in his camp, and I'm committed to France through next November..."

She ran her fingers through his hair to tame his tousled brown locks. "Are you suggesting waiting, then? Or getting married, but—surely you can't mean to suggest—one of us serving in another clearing station until you are discharged?"

"Far from it!" he exclaimed. "I told you I don't ever want to be separated from you. Ever. I'm just trying to figure out how we can get married now and get past the military red tape to be together."

She looked down at her hands. "I'm not under any command," she started, "to stay or go. The Red Cross advised us not to enter into any nurse-patient relationships... the ethical prohibition of something like that, of course. But they did acknowledge that nurse-soldier relationships might happen... I don't think I have to tell them. I mean, you know I send a very limited update to the States every month, never personal information. They wouldn't even know if one of us nurses married until we were already back home, unless we made a point of sending a separate communiqué."

"But I am under command," Simon sighed. "We are American Army doctors, serving under the French unless the Americans decide to fully support the Allies in this fight. I suppose the French Command could order me to leave, if we married now... if Aubert told them, that is."

"Then I would leave with you," she insisted. "I am not bound."

"It could be worse, Lydia... they could keep me and forbid you to stay. They've often entertained the idea of sending the nurses further from the front. They could use this as the rationale for putting you all on the next truck out."

Lydia rose to her knees and positioned herself in front of him between his legs. Simon leaned his head against her breast, as she ran her fingers through his hair. "Then we won't tell them!" she declared. "We will marry, and we'll go back to the station and we will continue with our work and be together as often as we can discreetly. And we'll know that we belong to one another, heart and soul."

He lifted his head, looked up into her face, and saw that she was pleased with the idea. "Do you realize," he began, "how hard it will be, once we come together, to have you at my side in the surgery or sleeping in a cot in one of the nurses' tents ten feet from the doctors' tent, and yet not be able to go to you?"

She laughed lightly. "Simon, don't you realize that several of the nurses already find ways to, shall we say, interact with others discretely? No one draws attention to it."

The man looked incredulous. "Really? Who...?"

She leaned down and kissed the top of his head. "Oh, Simon," she laughed softly. "Doctor Lovell has been known to steal off, with a few of the nurses, from time to time. Susannah is his love interest for the moment, I think, and no one says a word."

"Marc is with Susannah now?" Simon exclaimed. "I had no idea."

"Of course not, my love," she said. "Because you don't think like the others."

"I certainly do when it comes to you!" he declared. "I just assume what others do is none of my business, but I really did not know Marcus and Nurse Boyton have been seeing each other. I thought it was Laura Bertolli. And Harold? Is he..."

She shook her head, "No, as far as I know, Doctor Stockton is still saving himself for that girl, Tess, waiting for him back home."

"But you, would you be willing to... wait for me, if waiting is the only way this works out for us?" He paused, as he thought better of what he was about to ask, "Lydia, have you... not that it's any of my business if you and your former companion did... I mean, if you have already..." he stopped awkwardly, both wanting and not wanting to know about her past.

She lifted his head and kissed him softly. "I have never been with a man in that way, Simon," she told him. "Of course, I know the mechanics of it. But you will be the only man who ever touches me intimately, whether sooner or... much later. And of this, I'm certain—together, we will figure out what I do or do not like."

He rolled her back onto the grass. "I cannot wait to find out with you."

She pulled away from him and jumped up, walking straight back over to the truck, calling over her shoulder, "Well, you will have to wait; I'm heading to Nancy. You coming?"

He jumped to his feet, grabbed his medical box, taking a long, deep breath as he ran to catch up to her.

The French town of Nancy was very old, known for its love of art and beauty, its bergamot candies and macarons. They arrived at the central plaza surveying with regret the many bombed-out structures, centuries old, but now scarred and spattered with heaps of rubble, which had been pushed back from the street so that vehicles like theirs might safely pass those on bicycles or in horse-drawn carts. Finding an out-of-the-way place to leave the truck with its prominent Red Cross markings, they started to walk, looking for an apothecary amid the shops that remained functional. The Germans had brought the war here many months back, but the French wouldn't give up the city, returning a fierce defense which had ultimately won the day, but at a great cost. It had survived. It would be rebuilt.

Across the plaza, there was a towering, bell-adorned cathedral, undoubtedly Catholic, that had survived the assault of war. The beautiful Baroque structure rose above its surrounding neighbors... remarkably, unscathed from the war. Lydia remembered that their wounded needed rosaries. Hand in hand, Lydia and Simon crossed the plaza and entered the quiet narthex. A nun stood, tending the flickering rows of candles on a table, lit perhaps by desperate petitioners seeking an answer to their prayers.

Supremely conscious of her drab military attire and absence of a head covering, Lydia approached the sister tending the votives. "Bonsoir pouvez-vous me dire si ce soir il y a un... service, a mass, tonight?" Lydia whispered. "We have come from the front and wish to make prayers, but we don't want to interrupt..."

"You are American?" the nun replied, smiling.

"Oui," Lydia said. "We are from a medical station, un docteur, le chirurgien... et je suis infirmière."

The nun nodded in understanding. "There is no Mass tonight. You may enter to pray."

But Simon turned impulsively and took Lydia's hands in his own, right there, in the narthex to the majestic nave ahead of them. "Lydia," he said earnestly. "Let's not wait! Perhaps a priest will marry us."

She looked up at him despondently. "Simon, I am not Catholic. A priest will not marry us if we are not Catholic."

He touched her cheek tenderly. "Then, we can stand before God Almighty and make our oaths before Him, right here, right now, just the two of us... surely God would hear that kind of prayer, in any church."

Lydia looked over at the nun, watching her intently, waiting, hopefully, for her to answer, yet unsure how much she understood of their English. She looked up again at Simon, "I want nothing more than to be your wife, Simon..." she assured him, reaching up to caress his face. "You know that..."

He nodded. "And I want nothing more than to be your husband," he declared with a conviction in his voice that she had never heard from him. "And this is the only church we have been able to walk into in the last six months, Lydia. The great God above only knows when this war will let us find another."

"Pledge our vows? Right now?" she asked. "Are you certain?"

"More than you could ever imagine," he assured her. "No matter what the consequences are when we get back to the front. Even if it means waiting for only a few stolen moments to be with you when there is a lull in the fighting."

Finally, her eyes shining, Lydia decided. She nodded her head and smiled, meeting Simon's brown and gold-flecked eyes which looked intently into her own. "You did say it won't be easy... I may have to remind you of your own words. But yes! Let's go up to the altar and let God Himself hear our promises... if He is not too busy hearing all the prayers of the wounded. And if He is, we will wait in line... theirs come first."

"You truly are the ange de la miséricorde. The French soldiers were right to give you that name." Simon wrapped her arm in his as he led her up the very long and quiet stone aisle, between rows of pews. He turned to the nun as they left her and whispered, "Merci. Merci beaucoup. Thank you for letting us come in, Sister."

The couple walked arm in arm, slowly up an aisle which for centuries had witnessed liturgical processions, led by revered golden crucifixes, burning candles and swinging thuribles, filling the air with the fragrant smoke of incense. This evening, the pews were largely empty, Vespers having not yet begun. Beneath the vast vaulted ceiling, they walked slowly forward, taking in the detailed stained-glass windows towering around them as they passed... then looking back to each other with growing anticipation.

Scattered in ones and twos, a few other faithful were kneeling in the pews, crossing themselves, lips moving in silent prayer, paying the couple no mind. As the two approached the apse, they stopped before the grand altar and the breathtaking organ pipes which stood quietly waiting for skilled fingers to bring them to life. Lydia hesitated, understanding now why the parishioners held to the rear of the cathedral. It was overwhelming to gaze up at the enormous cross suspended overhead from the buttresses far above them. She saw a single red glow from a candle flickering with the sign of the Presence in a small alcove in the stone wall to their right, near an ornately carved wooden lectern. She suddenly felt incredibly small in the cathedral and not just a little insignificant. She led Simon over to the right edge of the railing, nearest to the towering lectern and under the red candle. She did not feel bold enough to kneel at the center-front, before the grand altar.

She knelt down, Simon following her, and closed her eyes in prayer, beseeching the God of the universe to find her in this grand place, thankful that the two of them had been led here and allowed to enter. Simon followed suit, drawing spiritually closer to the One who could inhabit such a masterpiece as this cathedral, just as much as He made his presence known in the rough medical tent where they tried to save the lives of the soldiers in their care. In Simon's theology this was the same God who sanctified all marriages wherever they were being made on Earth. After a time, certain that God had heard him and was listening, he opened his eyes; still kneeling, he took Lydia's hands into his own. She waited for him.

"Before you came to me, Lydia," Simon began, "I was asleep, like Adam. Knowing something was missing, but not knowing what it was. Then you came to the station and, before long, as I began to know you, I realized it was you I had been missing all this time. I've come to love you more each day, as I watch you tend to the wounded, tend to the nurses, and whether or not you were aware of it, you began to tend to me as well." Simon stopped for a moment and cleared his throat before continuing. "I don't know if we'll survive the front, survive this war, or ever make it back to the States. But, Lydia, it doesn't matter to me now because you are my everything. My heart has found a home in you. And before the Lord God and the angels, I promise you… I promise I will never leave you or forsake you, as they say in the real service. I will protect you with all my strength. I am yours for all of time, into eternity, from right here, right now, before God." Bending his head and lightly kissing her empty ring finger. "And one day, I will put a ring worthy of you on this finger."

Lydia lifted his face from her hand and looked at him steadily, her eyes wet with tears. "And for you, Simon Finney," she returned softly, "I have waited my entire life for a man like you to enter it. I didn't know that God would take me across an ocean, into battle, into the struggle with life and death and sorrow and pain, just to find you. I could never have known that in the middle of the greatest heartache, God would also give me the greatest joy. You are the joy of my soul. If we never make it out of the war, I will be your wife for whatever days we have remaining. And if the war ends and God lets us return home, I will be the wife you come home to, the mother of your children if we're ever so blessed, and I will walk beside you in the countryside or a hospital or wherever you are called to serve… I will never leave you in doubt of my love for you. I promise to try not to worry you again, to try not to be too strong-minded. I promise to give all that I am to be a wife you can be proud of until the day that death separates us, for a time.

And may God in heaven let me be with you, not just in this life, but also in the next, so that we can tell others how very, very blessed we have been by Him. I pledge all of my mind, my heart and my body to you, my husband."

Simon couldn't speak. He gently took her face in his hands and kissed her reverently, right there at the edge of the altar rail beneath the red glow of the single ensconced candle. And he knew with every fiber of his being that God had heard. But at that moment, he also heard a throat being cleared from the other side of the lectern. The two of them looked up, startled, to see the nun from the portico and, with her, a robed priest standing above them on the other side of the altar railing.

"C'est la guerre," the priest said softly, shrugging his shoulders as if this fact explained it all. "Many things must... adjust in times of war... the Church also..." The priest lowered his ringed hands to rest one hand on each of their heads. "Père Céleste, écoutez notre prière, que ton nom soit sanctifié, unis ces enfants... in the sight of your Holy Trinity, in the Holy state of matrimony. You have heard these promises of their hearts. Donnez-nous aujourd'hui, divine blessing on this union today... let the two to have truly become one in Thy divine sight. Deliver them from evil, Père céleste, mais délivre-nous du mal. Ta volonté soit faite, thy will... be done. In the name of the Father, and of the Son, and of the Holy Spirit, I acknowledge your vows as man and wife. Amen."

Simon and Lydia raised their heads as the priest finished his blessing and released his hands from them.

"Merci, Father, thank you, merci..." Simon said softly over and over, bowing slightly before the man enrobed in black and white vestments before them.

The nun leaned over the railing and kissed Lydia on both cheeks, then turned to Simon and kissed him as well on both cheeks. But Lydia, eyes wet with tears, reached over and gathered the nun in a long hug, heedless of their surroundings and any impropriety in her actions.

"And where must you go, return to?" the nun asked Lydia under her breath.

"A field station, Verdun," Lydia whispered in reply.

"Mon Dieu," the nun breathed. "Then it is true? You are that same ange de la miséricorde! God go with you, mon cher. God keep you and your husband safe."

"Sister, one thing I must ask..." Lydia hesitated.

"What is it, mon enfant?"

"Rosaries, sister," Lydia said. "I must find rosaries for the dying soldiers."

The nun nodded her head. "You come tomorrow, here," she said. "I give you rosaries."

Lydia hugged her again quickly, gratefully. "Merci, tu es très gentille. Merci."

Simon was waiting for her. He took her arm in his own and walked her back down the long aisle, whispering, "My wife," he was grinning from ear to ear, "what were you asking her for?"

She looked up at him happily. "Rosaries. Another mission accomplished."

Chapter 5

Coming Home

The evening air was fresh and breezy as they stepped out of the cathedral, "How are you feeling, Simon?" Lydia asked curiously as he looked down the street for an inn or tavern.

"I am famished!" Simon exclaimed.

Lydia laughed out loud, marveling at their freedom to do so in the heart of the city. As if in celebration of their union, small sparkling lamps began to appear in the windows surrounding the plaza.

"I meant," she started again, "do you feel any different now that you are my husband, even if only in the eyes of one Catholic priest?"

"I feel... incredibly fortunate," he murmured, wrapping an arm around her waist, "Mrs. Lydia Finney."

"Madame Lydia Blackwell-Finney, for now," she murmured. "at least, for a little longer... but the priest did bless our vows."

Simon laughed. "It's the 'madame' I am enjoying the most. And how about you? Do you feel any different?" he returned, as they headed in the direction of a tavern abutting the plaza, a swinging wooden horse over the door and a light in a paned window that had miraculously survived the bombings of the previous year.

She looked up at him, her eyes suddenly more serious. "Yes, Simon, I do. Something very real happened in there. It was not what I expected it to be."

He smiled gently. "What did you expect it to be, my dear wife... I can't believe I get to call you that. My dear wife..." he repeated, loving the sound of it.

"It was different because, I think we're different, Simon. I will never forget the promises you made in the church," she admitted. "It was so much more than the recited phrases of a traditional service, like when I stood with my sister, when she married, she repeated what the preacher told her to say. And her husband repeated what he told him to say. But, this was real—"

"Even without a ring?"

"Even without a ring."

He pushed open the heavy wooden door of the tavern as she entered in front of him. Simon approached the counter to speak to the man tending bar while Lydia looked around at the paintings on the walls... beautiful artwork where she had not expected to find any remaining art, unaware that the city of Nancy had treasure troves of masterpieces which had been protected, with great determination.

"S'il vous plaît," Simon said, putting several francs on the bartop "she is my wife, cette femme est ma femme... nous venons de nous marier."

"Oui, Monsieur," the tavern owner replied, glancing over at Lydia, and smiling respectfully, yet fully knowing the meaning behind Simon's implied request.

Simon led Lydia toward a wooden staircase with a newel post intricately carved into the shape of a horse's head, in keeping with the tavern's theme. They ascended the stairs and went to an unadorned door, save for a number IV carved into the wooden surface. Simon turned the knob and Lydia entered, immediately charmed by what welcomed them inside. In the center of the room, sat a four-poster bed covered with a fine quilt. A small wooden table and chairs were placed in the corner beneath a window that, in the light of day, would look out over the stone plaza. A dresser with a faded mirror was placed along a wall, with lamp sconces adorning either side. Lace doilies graced the backs of the wooden chairs, a long, crocheted runner covering the bureau top. It was not fancy, but it was a palace compared to the tents of the clearing station they had left behind.

"Oh, Simon," Lydia breathed. "It's just charming."

A knock at the door caused Simon to start a bit. Opening the door, he was met with a simple, but well crafted tray of bread rolls, cheese, and apples presented by a woman who motioned as if there was more to come. She darted off, but returned quickly with a bottle of dark red wine and two glasses. "Bon appetit," she bowed slightly and smiled as Simon closed the door behind her retreating figure.

"Let's eat then and satisfy that never-ending appetite of yours," Lydia teased him. "Nothing out of a can for us tonight!"

He took her in his arms and said softly, "I said I was famished... I didn't say it was for food."

Lydia looked at him, in anticipation, unwavering. "Then let's just eat," she said.

Simon pulled off his shirt and, turning, began unbuttoning hers. Soon, they stood before one another, clothed only in the newness of marital promise. Lydia pulled the quilt down off the bed, and to her surprise, Simon lifted her off her feet, laying her gently onto the bed, resting her head on the pillows. He climbed onto the bed next to her and stroked her hair, her face, kissing her lips softly before letting himself travel down her neck.

Lydia sighed, feeling him awaken her body with something she had never experienced before. He touched her, not just knowing where he could quicken her senses, but with the anticipation of consecrating this long-awaited aspect of their relationship. Savoring the moment was complicated by a rising need she was very much aware could consume them both quickly. "Are you absolutely certain you haven't done this before?" she breathed once.

"Absolutely certain," he murmured. Then Simon repeated what he had told her before, "Lydia, you promised to tell me if there is anything, anything at all, that you don't like. You already have my heart and soul. But I want all of you so much that I may not do this exactly right..."

She felt her body reaching for his touch, inviting them to come together in a language as old as time itself. "I think if you just go slowly—"

"Dear Lord," the man exclaimed softly. "I was afraid that's what you would say."

Simon moved to hover over her, waiting... fighting the urge to quickly unite them. She pulled his face down to her own and wrapped her legs around him. "Just kiss me while you do it," she whispered, wrapping her fingers in his hair and seeking out the warmth of his mouth. She remembered the wives' tales that the first time might be painful, and she did not want any pain to be connected to this... with Simon. She let out a small cry at first, then immediately reassured him, "It's okay, it's okay, don't stop..." He did hesitate, but she pulled him to her. They explored this newfound freedom until their mutual need became more urgent because something else was happening. And then, together, they found the oneness they had both been wondering about and longing for... they held each other tightly as it washed over them both.

Resting on top of her, Simon kept himself joined to her. He was afraid to move, hesitant to withdraw, and unable to stop caressing the woman beneath him. He searched her eyes anxiously for any sign of uncertainty and saw a dreamy peacefulness within their depths. "Are you... are you alright, my beloved?"

She kept her legs wrapped around him and smiled. "So, that's what all the fuss is about," she whispered.

Relief washed over Simon like a crashing wave. "It didn't hurt too much?" he questioned. "The first time?"

She shook her head and traced his lips with her fingertips. "It didn't hurt too much," she said. "And what followed after, more than made up for it."

He gently pulled away from her, briefly disconcerted by the touch of blood that seemed so very out of place in this room, on this bed, with this woman. He felt as though he should tend to her wound, but she curled up next to him as he lay beside her, pondering this. "Would a cold, wet cloth help—"

"Probably," she smiled. "But a glass of wine would be even better."

Simon sat up on the edge of the bed. "Ah, the food..." he said. "Wait here."

"Wild horses..." she replied, not bothering to finish the old saying.

He got up and carried a chair over to the side of the bed, where he perched the tray of food and bottle of wine carefully atop the seat. Handing her a glass, he watched her as she savored the wine, the moment... his own cup remained, for the moment, untouched.

"What are you thinking, Simon?" Lydia asked as she sensed the change in his mood and tone.

"That obey was not included in our promises," he replied quietly.

"Well, they usually only ask the woman to do that," she returned evenly. "I would never ask you to obey me, Simon." She raised a curious eyebrow.

He sat back down on the edge of the bed and took her hand in his own. "Nor I, you. But after what's just happened between us..." he hesitated, trying to piece together his thoughts. "You see, you were right earlier when you asked if I felt different now. And I do. Especially now that I know what it is like to become one with you. So, I ask only that you don't take undue risks when we get back to the front. Give me a little time to know that you'll be safe beside me, tomorrow, and the next day, and the day after that—as safe as the camp can afford, at least."

Lydia sat up in the bed, got on her knees behind him and wrapped her arms around his chest. He leaned his head back against her as he finally tried the wine. "Simon," she thought carefully before continuing. "I promised you before God that I would try not to worry you—that means that I won't take unnecessary risks. Don't you think that I also want to hold onto this, what we've found together, same as you? How could it possibly be otherwise? I'll obey you, not because you tell me to, but because I want it as much as you do."

"Ah, Lydia," he said gruffly, hiding his emotion from her at the memory of the what-might-have-been only a few weeks ago. "I remember saying recently that a different man was not worthy of you, but at this moment, I don't think I am either."

"God brought the two of us together, Simon," she reassured him, "us, this, was meant to be. He'll protect us on this journey. Eat something with me, and then come back to bed. I want you to hold me while we have the time and place to do so."

They ate silently; the reality of their tomorrow crashing in on the bliss of today.

Not sure of the time, Lydia startled into wakefulness. She got out of bed and silently washed herself in the basin in the corner of the room. Standing over the bed, she gazed down at Simon sleeping, in the light of the waxing moon outside the window. He was a surgeon who had become her friend... and now her husband and lover. For a moment, she longed for her mother and sister, wishing she could tell them about her marriage yet knowing she could not. Lydia recalled her very foolish words to Simon, declaring that they would simply get married and then be discrete back at the station. She had spoken about things which she was not able to foresee. Now, she took the water basin, tepid in the summer night, and laid it where their dinner tray had been earlier. She took the cloth, thinking of the countless number of men she had washed before—caring, yes... but dispassionate.

She looked at Simon's body touched with moonlight. He now belonged to her as much as she belonged to him. "Now," she whispered very softly, "it is time for you to tell me what you like and don't like..." She began to wash off the remnants of their earlier lovemaking. His body immediately began to respond to her ministrations. It woke beneath the gentle strokes of the wet rag. Earlier, she had allowed him to guide her through this new thing they had shared. This time, it was she who saw how he awoke to her touch. She leaned over and kissed his body, memorizing the feel of his skin as she brushed her lips against him. When she heard his breathing grow heavy, she looked up and knew, even in the darkness, that he was watching her, giving her the freedom to explore him at her own pace, in her own way, that he was as fully surrendered to her as she had been to him. Finally, she lay on top of him and he wrapped her in his arms. He allowed her to guide him past any soreness before he began to move inside of her. She waited for that peculiar feeling he had awakened earlier in the evening, the abandonment of caution, the desire to surrender. And then he rolled her over and pushed deeper into the secret places she had not even known she possessed. Suddenly, she could hold back no longer, and she cried out softly into the night against him... but Simon was not done. He pursued her, enticing her ever closer to his own needs until he was certain she could not turn back. And only then, as she cried out a second time, did he release himself into her passion until they both lay panting and clinging tightly to each other.

When Simon finally resigned himself to rolling off to lay next to her, he saw that tears were quietly slipping down her cheeks. He leaned over her and kissed them away. Morning would come all too soon. "It will be alright, Lydia," he reassured her quietly. "We belong to each other. We'll find a way."

Morning came. A little sadly, Lydia looked around their little room at the inn, knowing they would never be back this way again. She wanted to preserve the memory, tucking it into the cabinet of her mind labeled "important things". She turned to Simon as he pulled up his boots and looked up at her.

"All set?" he asked her.

She nodded, but her eyes filled... and Simon saw.

Simon pulled her to him by the door before motioning to the little room behind them. "Everything that matters is going with us," he told her matter-of-factly, kissing her forehead before picking up his haversack.

Lydia was not prepared to feel this vulnerable. She followed him down the stairs and out into the plaza, and he took her hand in his own as they returned to the cathedral. Reentering the lofty edifice, they were not the same people who had walked in, the day before. Lydia searched through the small crowd of parishioners gathering for morning Mass. Meanwhile the nun from the previous evening, having spotted the two faces she had hoped to see among the congregation, excitedly approached them.

She held out a small bundle to Lydia, who gladly received it. The nun said, "They are not many, but what we found... are yours. The nuns... in the convent... they give you their own. For soldiers."

Lydia kissed her on both cheeks. "Tell them that that was so very kind. They will be remembered."

The nun nodded and slipped her hands inside the front fold of her habit. She looked at the congregants and whispered, "Now I go. God bless and keep you."

"Thank you," Lydia replied, slipping the small bundle into her haversack.

Simon led her back out into the warm September sunshine of the plaza. "Now, for the apothecary," he told her. "The innkeeper told me where we might try finding medicine." They walked for a little while down the center street of the city, heading back to where the army truck adorned with its protective red cross waited. When they drew near, Lydia cried out and pointed at the truck in astonishment.

"What on earth!" Simon started as they picked up their pace.

Next to the truck, in piles on the ground, people of the town of Nancy had left their donations. There were some bushels of squash and cucumbers. There were a couple of bolts of fabric. A sack of rolled bandages rested on top. Several blankets were rolled up, tied and perched on top of the pile with some bundled sheep's wool. A small basket filled with bottles of wine was beneath the backboard of the truck with a bushel of apples, two wheels of goat cheese, and a feed sack of potatoes. Simon and Lydia looked at each other, amazed. They glanced around them on the street and saw no one in particular watching them or the truck. A few passersby nodded, but did not stop as they went about their personal affairs.

Lydia fingered the fabric bolts, one ream of blue and one of brown flecked with black. "Who did all of this?" She marveled out loud, "and during the night?"

Simon began loading the articles into the back of the truck. "The nun, I expect," he grunted, hoisting a bushel of apples up onto the floor of the vehicle.

Lydia placed the bolts of fabric inside the truck as well. "Why would she do such a thing?" She was in awe of the kindness bestowed on them.

He looked over at her, two large cheese wheels, one in each of his arms. "Probably because of the rosaries for the wounded Frenchmen," he replied. "I imagine she spread the word and the people responded."

"Oh, Simon," Lydia said. "They have so little, though."

He nodded. "Makes the gift even bigger."

Lydia thought back to the nun remarking, '*So you are the one…the ange…*'

"Yes, I suppose you're right," she replied thoughtfully. The sadness she had felt earlier, as they left the tavern, had now vanished.

Simon had been right. Everything that mattered would be going with them as they prepared to find an apothecary and leave Nancy behind.

It was already late afternoon when they finally left the city to head north again. Simon had procured this new medicine, heroin, used to relieve coughing from consumption, pneumonia, and canister gases. They were going to see if they could lessen the inflammation of the hacking coughs, which were the enemy of wounded men desperately needing sleep. As the truck bounced along the road, Simon noticed a checkpoint looming ahead of them, with a troop of French soldiers coming to attention on their arrival. He shifted gears to slow the truck and steered it over to the edge of the road... the soldiers secured the barricade, rifles at the ready.

"What's this all about?" Lydia said under her breath as she looked ahead. "We didn't run into this coming the other way."

Simon kept his hands where the soldiers could see them on the steering wheel of the truck. "Don't worry," he said evenly. "I expect the fighting has intensified up north and they are just on a heightened security alert."

Lydia reached her arm out and rested a hand on top of his thigh. He kept his hands in plain sight on the wheel, and they waited in silence.

When the soldiers drew near, they motioned for the two to get out of the truck. "Allez," one said. "Restez là-bas." He pointed with the tip of his rifle to the edge of the road, near the barricade. Lydia let herself out of the truck and one of the soldiers pulled her away, preventing her from joining Simon. Lydia willed her heart to be steady and made no sudden moves. They could not see what the soldiers were looking for in the back of the vehicle, but it appeared they were removing all of the sacks given to them by the civilians in town.

Under her breath, Lydia asked herself, *what could they possibly want?*

One of the soldiers pulled their haversacks out of the truck and threw one in front of each of them on the ground where they stood. "Videz ces sacs," he ordered them. "Où sont tes armes... les fusils?"

They each complied, knowing the soldiers would find no weapons, no guns... dumping their changes of clothing, the bottles of heroin, and the package containing the rosaries out onto the grass while Simon looked up at the soldier nearest him. "Nous n'avons pas d'armes. Je suis médecin, chirurgien... la femme est mon infirmière. We are with the medical corps near Verdun."

"Qu'est-ce que c'est?" one of the soldiers said to Simon, poking the rifle at the bottles of heroin.

"Medicine," Simon answered evenly. "For the French soldiers that we treat at the casualty clearing station, at the front."

"You are medical, from the front lines?" the soldier asked him, disbelieving.

Then, another soldier strode over, pulling Lydia to her feet. "Donnez-moi, vite!" the soldier ordered her, the contents of her haversack still strewn out on the ground. He grabbed her by the arm, pulling her farther away from Simon toward a military truck. Simon immediately moved to follow her and found the way blocked by the point of a rifle at his chest, the soldier sending a clear message, insisting that he not move from his position by the side of the road.

Lydia could not release her arm from the man's iron grip. "Comment puis-je t'aider... what can I do to help you?" Lydia said to him, her heart pounding in her throat with fear as she was pushed toward the truck.

"Donnez-moi," he repeated. He forced her into the truck where a driver was already waiting, turning over the coughing engine.

"Non, non, attendez, s'il vous plaît, please listen to me!" she begged him. "Je suis l'infirmière! Is someone sick? Does someone need help? Écoutez-moi, cet homme, that man over there is a good doctor... I need him if someone is sick."

The driver was sweating heavily from some recent activity... more than just driving a military vehicle. He looked across, over to

Simon next to the barricade, soldiers milling around him. "That man, he does not hold you prisoner, mademoiselle?" he demanded. "He does not take you against your will?"

"No, no!" she said vehemently. "That man is my husband. Cet homme est mon mari!"

"Mari? And a doctor... médecin?" he questioned. Then, finally, the look in her eyes convinced him. After Lydia waited an agonizing moment, he relented. "Monsieur, allez, allez!" he called out through the open window, and Lydia slid into the truck's middle seat next to the driver to make room for Simon to get in.

The soldiers blocking him moved aside and Simon sprinted the distance to the truck. He swung open the door, climbed in next to Lydia, and slammed it shut behind him. He pressed his body next to hers as the driver plunged the truck gears into reverse, shifted again, and tore off across an open field toward a distant stand of trees where several small smoke trails rose from within. Trying not to hit her head on the roof of the truck, Lydia tried once more.

"Comment pouvons-nous vous aider?" she almost shouted over the roar of the ancient vehicle bouncing them across the grass. "Who needs help? What happened here?"

The driver looked grim. "Last night, la nuit dernière, German soldiers... came through the trees to le village. Ils ont attaqué sans sommation. No warning. They were not dressed as soldiers, but as civilians; they disappeared in the night."

"How many injured," Lydia pressed, "combien sont blessés? How many need help?"

"Trop... too many," he said angrily. "Excusez-nous, we had to be sure you, monsieur, were not one of the German soldiers, that you did not take this woman. That you hid no enemy inside your truck."

Lydia felt Simon's body release some tension. She put a hand on the driver's arm and said again, "C'est un homme bon! He is a good man, a good doctor."

"I understand. We want to help!" Simon added, shouting as the whining truck made its way up a small rise closer to the wooded area, relief flooding him now that there was a valid reason for the disconcerting stop.

"Je l'espère... I hope so," the man returned. "They shot my wife."

When the truck pulled into the village, Lydia and Simon saw that the villagers were in hiding. The cottages were drawn tightly closed, but occasional rifle barrels extended just out of the corner of several windows.

"Où sont les blessés?" Lydia pressed the man as he applied the brakes, working his heavy body out from behind the wheel of the truck. "Where are the wounded?"

"Tu verras... you will see," he replied, leading them over to one of the larger cottages tucked into the trees. As they opened the door, a muffled scream rose up to meet them. A woman writhed on a bed.

The driver of the truck went immediately to her side. "Mon cher, do not scream so... I have brought you help," he pleaded with the woman. Simon was right behind. He immediately saw that she had been shot in the arm, but a quick exam told him it was a clean wound and not the source of her misery. Lydia was right behind, took in the state of the woman and turned to Simon. "I've got this one," she told him.

He met her eyes and nodded, then said to the man, "Take me to the others."

"But my wife—" the driver pleaded.

Lydia grabbed his arm and made him look at her. "The baby is coming too soon," she told him quickly. "I can help her. The doctor must look at the others."

"Oui, mademoiselle," the man said, still hesitating, but obeying her direction.

Lydia scanned the cottage and found a bucket of water and extra bedding. She leaned over the woman and felt her belly rise in a contraction. "I must check you... Je dois t'examiner..."

The woman fiercely clutched Lydia's hand as another contraction washed over her, but she nodded.

Lydia quickly washed her hands, praying the water was somewhat clean. She reached her fingers in between the woman's legs and felt for the baby's head. Mercifully, the head was down and fuzzy hair met Lydia's fingertips. She measured the opening with her fingers. "Thank God," she breathed; it was not a premature breech. This baby would come too soon, into a dangerous world. She made the woman look her straight in the eyes. "Votre bébé arrive bientôt... soon, you will be holding your little one." Quickly, Lydia washed the woman's arm where the bullet had penetrated, she tore off part of a bed cloth to secure it. Washing her hands again and asked the woman to lift her hips to put a sheet underneath her, but the woman shook her head and pointed to the clean, swept dirt floor where a cat slunk out of sight under the bed.

Reluctantly, Lydia complied, spreading out the blanket on the floor where the woman could crouch down, holding onto the wooden legs of the bed for support. She got into position and prayed the baby would be able to breathe.

Simon, meanwhile, had followed the man to another house where a dozen or so injured had collected. Many had already practiced their home-spun medicine on wounds where bullets had flown through windows and doors. He felt that he had suddenly been transported back into the rural hills of West Virginia, just using a different language to ask if anyone had anything resembling an antiseptic or basic soap and clean water from a nearby well. He put the driver to work to distract the man from the intermittent outbursts coming from the cottage next door. Cries from the man's wife were coming more frequently, and Simon knew the baby would soon emerge. He had little time to wonder how far along the woman was in her pregnancy... fervently wishing he had even a few of the basic tools that were available to him back at the station.

He moved from person to person, reassuring and dressing wounds with his limited resources. There were no life-threatening injuries, for which he was grateful. These people were more frightened than physically damaged, though the fear would be harder and take longer to heal. In the back of his mind, he remembered the soldier saying that the enemy was loose and not in uniform. Where the Germans had moved off to next was anyone's guess. Simon decided, right then, that he would not risk driving alone with Lydia through the night.

Suddenly, a final wail came through the walls. Simon paused and listened carefully... he waited, but did not hear what he hoped for. Turning to the man who had driven them there, he pulled him aside. "Excusez-moi," he said. "Wait here, s'il vous plaît."

Simon hurried out of the cottage of the collected wounded and around the corner of the next one. He pushed open the wooden door and saw Lydia on the floor of the structure with the woman whose labor was over. Automatically, he noted the debris, the wet placenta, the amount of blood on the blanket, the pallor and sweat on the new mother's face as she clutched the bed frame for support. His Lydia was still on the floor as well. She ministered to the tiny infant in her arms as it lay limp and quiet. She was turning it onto its side, patting its back, and flicking the small feet to get it to breathe. Then he saw her place her mouth over the infant's mouth and nose and puff into the tiny orifices. She paused and repeated a little puff of air again... and again... and then again. And suddenly, the tiny baby issued a thin cry, began to pink up and waved its minuscule hands.

Lydia tucked the premature baby, naked, between the woman's breasts, skin to skin. She took a bed cloth and wrapped them together as if in a cocoon. "Keep the baby right next to you," she told the woman in French. "He was not ready to come out yet. He must hear your heart beating and feel your love and warmth at all times. Keep him at your breast. Make him think he still lives within you until he is ready for this world."

The woman looked up at Lydia, her face was wet with tears. From under the wrap, only the top of the baby's dark curls showed above. "I will do what you say, l'infirmière," the woman whispered. "I puff, too? If he needs puff?"

"Yes," Lydia said. "If he does not breathe, you puff a tiny bit of air into him."

"I have no milk," the woman said sorrowfully, looking down at her small breasts.

Lydia stroked her hair. "They were not ready. Keep him at your breast, mon cher, it will make the milk come."

In the doorway, Simon moved aside to allow the woman's husband to push past him. The man fell to his knees beside his wife, and as they held their new son, Lydia backed away to give them privacy. She leaned against Simon, who put his arms around her and whispered into her ear, "How did you learn to do that?"

She gazed dreamily at the mother and baby... "It just made sense," she replied.

"Now, where have I heard that before?" he held her close to him.

Chapter 6

En Route to Reims

The piercing call of the bugle echoed through the station. It was an order to move out, quickly. Lieutenant Aubert's troops reflexively jumped to action, collapsing tents and pulling up support poles from the ground. Those designated to it, surrounded the mess tent, filling canteens, packing supplies, and efficiently collapsing the tarp. The station's doctors and nurses had been prepared for this; the wounded having been trucked out the day before. Orderlies had already stacked empty cots and litters in piles, and men had been assigned to help the nurses pack delicate equipment from the surgery into trunks, for transport. The women needed only seconds to pack their personals, living out of their small military lockers at the foot of their cots.

Harold and Marcus stood together, supervising the dismantling of the surgery. Marcus glanced south, toward the horizon.

"I wish they'd come back already," he muttered, his irritation a thin veil over the deep well of worry in his chest. *What if Simon and Lydia had been captured?*

Harold nodded. "Me too. It's the damnedest thing not to be able to communicate with anyone out here. They should have taken soldiers with them."

Marcus looked to his superior. "I totally agree, but Aubert said they were going south, away from the line of fire. Knowing we were going north, Simon must have assumed we'd need the soldiers more."

Harold crossed his arms in his usual manner. "I expect so. Either way, we're down a surgeon and a nurse, and are feeling it. Medics will fill in the gap until they get back, but I'm sure we're all going to be needed immediately when we arrive... Aubert says the intel from Somme is that the battle is intense."

"Damned war," Marcus snapped.

Harold nodded in agreement. "Damned war."

Marcus thought of their missing surgeon. Simon was more than a doctor, having become a good friend over the months they'd been serving together in the Allied effort. They'd not met until they both arrived in London, then went on together to Paris, continuing through the French countryside where they reported for duty at the small casualty clearing station. Haggard doctors, having already served from '14 to '16, had been reluctant to talk, but more than ready to leave and go home. Marcus remembered Simon asking one of the departing doctors if he had any words of advice for them. The short, balding man had only replied, "Do your best... it will never be good enough," before turning away unceremoniously to board a transport truck.

Again, Marcus looked south over the countryside, emptied now of the tents which had been whisked away into the little caravan assembling along the road. He hoped Simon and Lydia were safe, but wondered at Simon's choice to take her with him. Good to have a nurse along if they accidentally ran into wounded, that was certain. But he could have taken a corpsman. And she was still recovering from her injury. Marcus noted Susannah who was pointing at one of the trucks beside a man bearing medical supplies. Her blonde hair shone in the August sunlight. It was good to have someone to appreciate at the end of a long siege in the surgery. He thought Simon was a fool not to take advantage of the presence of the nurses... not all units had them. Marcus turned his attention away from the southern road. It was time to leave.

The camp was now cleared of everything, but buried waste. They all boarded the trucks and the little convoy began to head north. Soldiers, rifles at the ready, sat on the back of the truck beds, hanging their feet down and watching for danger. This medical group would not be crossing the trenches. The army had directed them to skirt Verdun to the west and head closer to Reims, to the northwest, as they'd first thought. It was a strategic point where the French were keeping the German advance at bay, but at tremendous cost. The British were there as well. It would be good to talk to some of the British and see if any new advances were available in the medical field and to share ideas without the hindrance of translation. Winter would be coming soon, perhaps slowing the pace of war with the cold and snow. They would likely stay put outside of Reims through the season.

As they bounced along the road, Marcus thought enviously about his two colleagues, off by themselves. Marcus had no illusions about his own intermittent relationships with the nurses. He knew them for what they were—two people in difficult circumstances, just trying to hold themselves together... by holding onto each other. Marcus had been with Mary... and once with Linda Trent on her arrival at the camp, but she had been too timid to want his attention beyond that. Laura also had held his interest for a time. But Marcus hadn't yet convinced Lydia of how much she needed him. *Damn good nurse*, he thought. *Shouldn't have run off to the front that one night, but what it took for her to do that!* He admired her. She was good for morale... and not just for the wounded. *Damn it!* he exclaimed again in his mind. Simon should have told him she'd been wounded. He wished Aubert had sent Marcus away with Lydia instead of Simon. Alone with her, he would have convinced her that he could be good for her.

In silence, the nurses bounced along inside their truck, as well. They knew what was ahead of them. It had been a tremendous relief to know they would be avoiding the trenches. But even so, as the unit traveled along the road, the signs of war were all around them: craters in the fields, damaged tanks at distorted angles with machine guns now pointed jaggedly at the clouds, vultures, crows circling... ever circling... landing on the hills in sight. The scavengers were constant reminders of what they knew all too well. Occasionally, they could catch sight of a few living humans moving across the hills, pulling hand-drawn carts or leading a heavily laden mule. Nothing was wasted on the field that could be repurposed for the living.

"She didn't make it back in time," Gretha sighed. "We're down another one. Twelve to ten."

Nancy removed the helmet that had been provided to her and let her sweat-soaked hair dry in the breeze. Her voice was cheerful. "She's coming back. They'll follow us along the way."

Mary shook her head. "If she was going to be shot, it would've been with us, back there, a couple weeks ago. Not just gathering supplies from Nancy or Metz."

Alice lurched as the truck hit a hole, tumbling into Nancy. "I think they just wanted to be alone."

Gretha peered out at her from under her helmet. "Alone? Who? Lydia and Doctor Finney? Why?"

"Oh, girl!" Alice exclaimed. "You need to get back home to your cows."

Gretha reddened, "You don't think?"

Alice laughed. "Of course, I think!"

The other woman slowly shook her head. "I don't think so..."

Nancy patted Alice's arm conspiratorially. "That's why she didn't join the bet."

"What bet?" Susannah raised her voice to call over. "Did I miss out on something?"

"Only if you're blind," Alice exclaimed. "Or more interested in livestock like Gretha. Just kidding, Gretha, you know we love you. Anyway, I think they planned this so the good doctor and nurse could get away from us all for a little while."

Mary chimed in. "Not Doctor Finney. He isn't interested in us like..."

Susannah spoke up, "You can say it, Mary. Like Doctor Lovell. That man is a good tonic for a bad day!"

Mary flushed red under her helmet, as the others laughed.

Susannah took her hand. "Not a big deal," she said, lightly squeezing her friend's hand. "There is more than enough of that doctor to go around. It's very soothing, actually, after we've been at it for hours in triage. I, for one, am glad he's available."

"I don't know..." Linda started. "Aren't you afraid you'll get..."

"What?" Susannah declared. "Diseases from a doctor? Not likely!"

"No," Linda continued. "Pregnant."

She was met by a round of laughter for her naivety. "And you're a nurse! You should know enough to find ways to avoid that!"

"I do!" Linda declared, insulted by the insinuation. "I just..."

Susannah looked at her, her face taking a somber expression. "Well, I hope this war ends soon enough for you to have a chance to have a nice long relationship with a man," she said. "You go home and find someone with all of his arms and legs still attached, one who isn't waking up terrified in the middle of the night calling out for us, and then you can live your happy life."

Linda added, "I just want Doctor Finney and Lydia to make it back to us in one piece."

The trucks rolled on and, by nightfall, they had come to their new location where the tents would be quickly set up again, just as before, and made ready for the wounded to start arriving.

Having decided to stay in the village till morning, Simon spread a blanket over a bed of straw in a stable. The rafters overhead rustled with the sound of small animals moving in the night. The couple was certain that the renegade German soldiers would not return, believing there was little in this poor village for which they would risk reigniting the wrath of the French countryfolk. Lydia lay with her head against Simon's shoulder, as he caressed her hair in the darkness... she was thinking of the world into which that tiny, new soul had been born. A cow chewed in a stall nearby. The chickens were quiet. Their, now calm and conciliatory, driver had gone back to the checkpoint and returned with their truck, contents repacked—minus some bottles of wine—but including the haversacks, which contained their military papers. Simon was relieved to have everything back.

"We can make it to the others by noon tomorrow," he said thoughtfully. "If they are still there."

"And if not..." she countered.

He sighed. "We just follow the sound of the shelling."

Lydia unbuttoned her shirt in the darkness, found Simon's hand, and slid it inside. "Are mine too small?" she asked, thinking of the new mother's comment earlier in the night.

He squeezed her gently. "I think they're magnificent," he disagreed. "I'm amazed by you."

"Some would say they aren't good for much unless there's a new little life in need of them."

Simon rolled up onto his side. "I need them," he teased, leaning over to caress her.

Lydia feigned horror as she heard the rustle of his movements, knowing he was undoing his trousers. "In a stable? With the cow?" she whispered.

"In a stable with the cow..." he whispered, now unbuttoning her trousers. "In the tavern in the town... in the woods... or in a palace..." he finished, slipping them over her feet, her legs now bare against the rough woolen blanket.

She lay there, tingling, feeling the straw shift beneath them as he caressed her. "And anywhere else in the sight of God where we are able to find each other," she heard him add. But this time, he was very slow and methodical... knowing her body was not used to this much attention in such a short length of time. He made certain she was ready for him and, even so, advancing very gently when his need would no longer be denied. Lydia's head swam, overcome with electrifying sensations. When Simon had finished meeting his own needs, Lydia still drifted on the edge of awareness... languishing in this thing called love, in the deep, undeniable trust she felt with this man... he continued to minister to her until her breath came quickly, a pure bliss washing over her, she cried out softly in the darkness.

The stable's cow chewed its cud, without comment.

In the morning, they made ready to head out again after checking the wounded, the new mother, and the fragile infant one more time before leaving. One of the villagers supplied them with an ample breakfast of fresh eggs, warm bread, and goat milk. Lydia praised the older woman profusely. As the woman bustled around her hearth, she told the nurse, "Je suis la grand-mère."

"Toutes nos félicitations!" Lydia exclaimed warmly.

"Non, l'infirmière," the woman disagreed softly, wiping her eyes with the corner of an apron. "In war, we wait until l'enfant is at least one year. Then celebrate."

Lydia rose from her seat at the woman's table and hugged her. "In one year, you will be celebrating," she told her, praying that God would keep them safe. Then Lydia rejoined Simon, where he sat at the table gathering scattered breadcrumbs to clear the table. She rested her palms on his shoulders; he placed a hand over hers and gave a loving squeeze.

The village woman saw this as she served them hammered pewter plates of delicious food. "You sit," she ordered, "you eat. Es-tu marié, you two are married?"

They nodded in unison, enjoying the homemade breakfast before them.

"Why you do this war? For not you?" the woman placed her hands on her ample hips. "Why you do this? You should be home—make babies too!"

Lydia blushed. "We were only married yesterday... in Nancy, at the cathedral."

"Non, non! Hier?" the woman exclaimed, agitated. "Only yesterday? Now you go back to fight. Non!"

"It is très important that we return, madame," Simon explained for both of them. "But we do not return to fight. We go to heal—death, sickness, malaise... to help the French."

"Ah, mon Dieu," the woman breathed. "You wait, here. No go yet."

Simon and Lydia looked at her, confused.

"Okay," Simon told her. "We wait here, but only for a short time... peu de temps."

The woman rushed out of her simple cottage. Simon and Lydia finished eating their meal, washed the cups and plates in a bucket and returned them to a place in the cupboard by the hearth.

"How long are we supposed to wait, do you think?" Lydia asked curiously.

"Not a clue," Simon replied. "But we need to get going. I want to make the trip during the busiest time of day when it's less likely a disguised German will jump out of the trees to shoot us."

Lydia turned to him and wrapped her arms around his waist, leaning against him. She tucked her head under his chin and felt his lean body hard against hers. "You know," she said, her voice muffled in his shirt, "for as much as I want another night in a stable, I'm anxious to get back to the unit. Surely, they have needed us by now. I can't imagine how hard it has been for them with fewer hands."

He unwrapped her arms from his waist and entwined his fingers between her own. They kissed slowly, then he gazed at her. "I didn't give you the wedding or the honeymoon you deserve, Lydia," he said regretfully.

She smiled at him. "You gave me more than I ever wanted, Simon," she declared. "I never knew what it was between a husband and wife."

He laughed lightly. "You mean the nurses at camp didn't share any stories?—And no! I do not want to hear about any exploits with Marcus now that I know he's been keeping that from Harold and me. None of the nurses in training...? Not even your mom or sister?"

Lydia brushed his lips with her fingers. "What we have found can't be told with words, anyway," she said.

Simon leaned in and kissed her longingly. "What does that say?" he teased her, his brown eyes fixed on her own light blue ones.

"I think," she started, "that it says there could be a bank along a stream somewhere for us... since the back of the truck is already full."

He held her close. "I have to figure this out, Lydia, with Lieutenant Aubert. I refuse to be apart from you for long and then come together some clandestine way on a table of the surgery or something."

"I think they use the mess tent, actually," Lydia informed him. "When it's too dark for anyone to see."

Simon laughed out loud. "I will never say 'I'm famished' in the mess tent again!"

The door of the cottage swung open, and its owner hurried back across the room. She was beaming. A man smelling of horses followed closely behind. He also looked very pleased.

"Est-ce le couple?" he questioned.

"Mais oui ! Mais bien sûr!" she exclaimed. "Or are you blind!"

The man held out one dirty hand and opened it. Two small pewter rings, one slightly larger than the other, lay in his weathered palm. "It is not much," he explained. "But Madame d'Bounette says you have no ring for wedding... pour votre mariage. So, we do this, for you, help l'enfant... Sois béni..."

Lydia turned to Simon, and overcome with emotion, buried her face in his shoulder. He held her in a reassuring embrace, gratefully receiving the gifts. The smithy looked anxious, but Simon pushed Lydia slightly away just to take her hands in his own. He placed the smaller ring on the middle finger of her right hand, where it slid on snugly. "Avec cette bague, je t'épouse... again," he said softly.

Lydia wiped her eyes and took the larger ring from his hand, sliding it over the fourth finger of his left hand, where it fit comfortably. "Avec cette bague, je t'épouse... again," she repeated, her eyes shining up at him.

The older woman clapped her hands. "Très bien! Très bien!" she exclaimed heartily and kissed Lydia on both cheeks.

Simon shook hands with the smithy, who in turn clapped Simon on the back and kissed both of his cheeks. "You have happy life!" he exclaimed, pleased that his gift had been well received.

Lydia gazed down at the hammered pewter on her third finger, its many facets, from the pounding of the hammer, reflected symbolically how their marriage had arisen out of the pounding of war on this beautiful countryside. "It is perfect," she murmured.

The older woman dabbed her eyes with her apron. "Now you go?" she asked.

Simon nodded. "Now, we must go."

They climbed into the truck. Simon pushed the grinding gears into position, forcing the vehicle to lurch forward. Some of the villagers stood and watched them depart, growing smaller and smaller in the widening distance between them. Lydia looked back once through the window and waved before settling into her seat for the trip ahead of them. "Good people..." she thought aloud.

"Indeed, they are," Simon concurred as the truck headed through the trees. They fell silent under the protests coming from the engine as they swerved around logs and climbed the rise into the open field. Soon, the road was again in sight. Simon saw the familiar checkpoint come into view. This time, though, the soldiers raised their rifles in the air and cheered as they passed right through an open barricade and down the dirt road.

"I guess they finally figured out we were okay," Lydia said in relief.

Simon nodded in agreement, swerving slightly to miss a rather impressive crater in the road. They continued in silence for the better part of two hours, avoiding a myriad of obstacles while praying the tires would hold. As the sun rose high overhead, Simon grew concerned. The casualty station should come into view within half an hour; they had just come around a bend, where the road began to closely follow the Meuse River again. With them safely on their way, he started looking for a place where they could stop to refill their canteens and take a quick break.

A curious battle had begun to rage within Simon as they drove. The incident at the checkpoint, from the day before, came back into his mind to replay again and again. The memory of the soldiers pulling Lydia away toward the truck, rifles pointed at him... the feeling of being utterly powerless as he watched Lydia being dragged away from him. What could she have thought of him at that moment? He hadn't tried to stop the soldiers. He hadn't tried to disarm one of them and grab a rifle. He probably would have gotten shot, but what on Earth had compelled him to stand there and simply watch her be dragged away? Too soon, the dangers of the world were coming against them. He had just found Lydia and was angry with himself for not defending her properly... and the anger was growing.

Finally, just past noon, he found a spot to pull over that seemed relatively secure. Looking ahead, he saw a grouping of trees where a tributary flowed down into the Meuse. On the other side of the river, the hills climbed quickly into the western sky. Water flowed around sandy shoals. A small cluster of egrets waded with delicately splayed feet in the shallows near the bank, snapping their long beaks at the minnows darting past them. They raised their great white wings and fluttered at the sound of the truck, then settled further downstream when he cut the engine.

Simon and Lydia climbed out of the vehicle, listening cautiously for any sounds of war. They were met with stillness, marred only by the sound of running water and intermittent bird song in the trees. Lydia found a protective screen of brush and wondered at her modesty. Hadn't Simon already seen every part of her intimately? So much was the same as they headed back... and so much was... very different.

Finished taking care of her own needs, she found Simon at the water's edge staring silently down at the ripples of light on the river. He squatted down at the edge of the bank and reached into the eddies, where a smooth white stone glittered in the light. He retrieved it and looked at it carefully before slipping it into the pocket of his trousers. Then he filled their canteens, turning his head as Lydia came up behind him to wash while he screwed the caps back on securely.

"Are you ready?" he said abruptly. There was a roughness, in his voice, that he had not intended, as if she had taken too long to finish what she had been doing to get back to him.

Lydia nodded, immediately noticing the change in his mood, the hardness in his voice.

"I'm sorry, Simon," she offered softly... not knowing what to apologize for, but willing to extend an olive branch.

Simon rose up and swung around, his eyes glittering with frustration, at himself... angry at the threats of this world as much as the thoughts in his own head. He dropped the canteens. Pushing her firmly, but not unkindly, by the shoulders down onto the riverbank, he opened her trousers at the buttons before pulling down his own. He held himself over her, one arm on either side of her body, staring down at her. And Lydia met his gaze, her eyes wide as saucers, but willing to trust this man to whom she had consecrated everything.

As intense as he had been getting her to the ground, he was just as gentle entering her. "I will..." he started, his voice with measured emphasis matching the movement of his body, "never allow... anyone... to pull you... away from me... ever again..." The power of his declaration to defend her at any cost sped throughout his frame, and he consummated his oath with that same strength, channeling it through him and into the woman beneath him.

There on the riverbank, returning to the Western Front with this man taking total command of her body, Lydia understood his anger. And she had never felt more safe.

"I wonder how long ago they left," Lydia pondered, surveying the remnants of their triage camp.

Simon also looked around. "Couldn't have been that long," he reasoned. "Probably yesterday. This is only the third day we've been gone."

Three days ricocheted through Lydia's mind. Had it been so few hours since they had started out? It seemed a lifetime ago. They noted the heavy tracks of the trucks, one following another, across the grassy slope.

"At least they left breadcrumbs," she remarked dryly.

They jumped into the truck and set out in pursuit of their comrades, bouncing along the same rutted trail, heading northwest. "We're headed toward Reims," Simon said with certainty. "That's the last place Aubert spoke of as our probable destination if we moved."

"Reims," Lydia nodded. "Midway to Paris?"

"More like midway from here to the coast, but yes," Simon replied. He reached over and took her hand. "We'll find them."

They passed troops on the road marching in both directions, north and south. The men looked haggard and exhausted. Some were bandaged, but still walking.

"Must be getting close," Simon muttered. From time to time, he stopped the truck and asked if anyone had seen a casualty clearing station, also asking, "Est-ce la route de Reims?" Then, reassured that this was indeed the only road to Reims, they inched ahead, parting the troops like the bowhead of a ship would the waters of the sea.

One group of soldiers tried to stop them. "Turn around," they called over. "Go back. There is fighting ahead."

Simon called back, "Where are they taking the wounded? Je suis chirurgien."

One of the soldiers pointed. "Just over that hill, you will find the war." Then, looking overhead, he pointed to a small cluster of planes heading eastward. And moments later, the wounded earth seemed to roll and groan, rattling the truck.

"We're close, Lydia," Simon muttered, steering the vehicle off the road and over the hill.

And find the war they did. Driving into the new station, they saw the familiar tents of the triage... familiar tarps over the wounded and the dying, Abril chasing away great black birds, trucks flowing steadily in and out, ambulances arriving, litter bearers quickly retrieving the men within, before they sped off again toward the plumes of black smoke rising in the near distance.

Simon pulled up to the edge of the camp, the brakes on the truck tearing up the grass as he screeched to a halt. They jumped from the vehicle, leaving everything in it behind, and headed into the melee. Finding Charlotte running the triage, Lydia ran up to her. "Where do you need me?" Lydia called out, catching her attention.

"Surgery!" Charlotte called out over the bodies of the wounded. "There are too many to keep up with. We're backlogged."

Lydia turned and ran.

Simon was already in the surgery tent, having headed there as soon as his feet hit the ground. He stopped at the door of the tent just long enough to scrub in and don a mask and surgical apron. Rolling up his sleeves, he slid between a pair of litter bearers exiting with a wounded man. Harold looked up quickly and nodded at Simon, but remained focused on the patient in front of him. Simon turned sideways to get through two tables to another where a medic was attempting to sew up a bayonet gash on one of the precious surgery tables. "Take it outside," Simon ordered the man. "Corpsman, get me a patient," he called out. Before he could finish the words, the bayonet gash was taken outside and a new wounded man was carried in with a gaping belly wound.

Simon saw Marcus look up from the table where he was amputating a man's arm. "Nice vacation?" He asked. "Nurse, staunch that bleed..."

"The best," Simon replied.

"Welcome back," Marcus remained focused on the job before him. "Thought they got you."

"And leave all of this to you?" Simon demanded. "Not a chance. How long have you been on your feet?"

"They started coming in about nine o'clock."

Simon looked around quickly as an anesthetist sat down at the head of the table and began sedating the writhing man lying in front of him. Almost immediately, to his profound relief, he saw Lydia arrive beside him. He could focus now... and he did. In almost record time, Simon secured the bleeders, closed a hole in the man's intestines, searched for shrapnel, and told Lydia to pack the wound; there was too much damage to close it.

Lydia waved at the corpsman at the door and called for a litter bearer. She quickly brushed past Charlotte circulating and plunged her hands under the spigot of the water reservoir by the door.

"We missed you," Charlotte said in passing.

Lydia nodded. "I missed you too!"

"I'll bet," Charlotte said, winking and lifting a tray of clean instruments high over the head of a litter bearer on his way out of the surgery. She carried the tray in this manner like a French waiter, keeping it clean, over to where Marcus evaluated a man's arm which was fractured, with long spears of sharp bone pushing out through the skin. At the last minute, he decided to try to save the arm instead of amputating it, cutting open the skin, cleaning out the fragments, and realigning the bones as close as possible. "Nurse, splint," he called out. Charlotte was already on her way.

This surgical dance continued for hours. Harold took a break and went to his tent for ten minutes of shut eye to clear his head. It seemed that only a minute had passed when he felt a corpsman shaking him awake and forcing a hot cup of coffee into his hands. Harold reentered the surgery, saw a man brought in with a wedge of metal secured in his left flank, and called over to Lydia. "Nurse Blackwell," he said, "please assist. This one is right up your alley."

"Yes, doctor," she replied, calling for a corpsman to relieve her at Simon's table. She washed her hands and hurried over to Harold.

"Thought you might want to see this, Nurse Blackwell," he pointed toward the wound.

She did; it was her figure eight bandage twist securing the wedged metal in place.

"It got him here to us without bleeding out," he told her. "Now, we will slowly withdraw the shrapnel, tying off the bleeders as we go... this soldier will go home."

Lydia assisted him as they painstakingly withdrew the metal intrusion, her fingers flying as she helped him tie off bleeders with small, tight sutures. "Did Doctor Finney teach you to suture, Nurse Blackwell?" he asked her, pleasantly surprised. She nodded.

"Well," he stated. "You learned it well. Pretty soon, we surgeons won't be needed if the nurses can all do it as well as you can."

"No, Doctor," she disagreed. "We are just nurses. We will never be able to do what you do. But we do love when the doctors teach us something useful..."

"Well said," he returned. "So, you think you'll keep us around?"

"Will you keep us around, Doctor?" she countered quietly.

He looked straight at her. "If I have any say in the matter... yes, but if I ever hear you call yourselves 'just nurses' again, I'll boot you out of camp myself."

"Understood," she said simply and went to wash her hands.

Through the following day, the pile of bodies under the tarp only grew. There were so many casualties that the nurses in triage began sending trucks of non-life-threatening wounded out to the field hospitals without the surgeons coming out to clear them first. As evening drew in, consumed with fatigue, Marcus announced, "Can't do another one, buddy," to no one in particular—there were no more litter bearers coming through the surgery tent opening. A collective sigh ran through the group. Marcus added to his earlier comment, saying to them all, "I'm out of here," stripped off his face mask and headed for the showers and some much-needed sleep. Harold told the corpsman assisting him, "Pack the wound and get him to recovery." He also left his table where he had been standing for these many hours, heading for the mess before hitting his cot in the doctors' tent.

Simon finished up with the last head wound patient. He knew that he finally had to face the moment he had been dreading the most. He leaned on the surgery table, watching the others move around, cleaning-up... Charlotte was gathering instruments to sanitize. He was relieved that Lydia and he had returned in time to help their friends and companions in this last dreadful effort. He hit the shower and, in the darkness that had fallen on the station, he washed, dried himself, got dressed and stepped back outside... wondering what to do next. This moment, when he could not take Lydia into his arms, when he could not help her wash away the sorrows of the day or share the joys... this was the moment he had not wanted to face, the one they'd recognized when they were back in the French tavern. He glanced over to the doctors' tent, where Harold and Marcus were no doubt already asleep. He decided to make himself useful and make his rounds in the recovery.

Lydia had gone to recovery herself, where the nurses had been on duty longer than her, and sent one of them to bed. Nancy was returning to the recovery tent, fresh from a break. Laura was already moving between the cots, methodically checking for signs of fever or bleeding. Without triage, and with the surgery closing down, the nurses' workload was reduced to just recovery. They wearily moved through the rows, each cot holding a wounded soldier, doing their rounds of analgesic, changing bandages, offering fluids... the mercifully routine work of helping the men try to heal.

Simon found her there working beside the other nurses. Her eyes met his, silently speaking volumes. He drew close to her, but resisted the intense desire to reach out to her. "Have you informed Nurse Mitchell that you fulfilled the nurses' request, Nurse Blackwell?"

"And what request would that be, Doctor?" Lydia replied, distracted as she assessed a bandage on a soldier's leg.

"A bushel of apples, I believe it was," he replied. "Or was it a small calf? Or a baby, perhaps?"

Nancy looked over at Lydia excitedly, grateful to be distracted from their ordeal. "Did you really bring us something delicious?"

Lydia smiled. "We were given lots of wonderful gifts by the French, in Nancy," she told the woman. "You have a great namesake. But it may all still be in the truck actually. We didn't have time to tell anyone to unload it."

Simon agreed. "I'm afraid it will have to wait until morning, now that we're in the blackout. Do you nurses need anything? Do any of the men need evaluation?"

"No, we've got this," Nancy said. "You should go get some sleep, Doctor. You'll need it."

Lydia looked over at Simon longingly from the bedside of a man, not asleep, but staring off into the peak of the tent over their heads. She bent over the wounded man.

"What can I do for you, soldier?" she asked softly.

"Je vais mourir," he whispered. "I am going to die."

"I do not think so," she reassured him gently, touching his face with the palm of her hand.

He looked at the ceiling of the tent. "Je vais mourir," he repeated. "Tonight. And I am afraid that God will not take me... après... after what I've done."

She knelt beside his cot, squeezing between the cots. "Why will God not take you?" she asked, stroking his hair as tenderly as a mother would her son.

"J'ai tiré sur un homme... I shot a man between the eyes," the soldier replied, "comme il m'a supplié, as he begged me... to let him live."

"God can forgive you of that," Lydia softly reassured him. "He knows you followed orders to find the enemy and to kill him. It is so difficult to follow orders sometimes. Tell God your sorrow and let him heal you."

The soldier continued to stare up overhead to the dark peak of the tent. "Tell God my sorrow..." he repeated, his voice hollow with spiritual guilt and pain.

She nodded, "Oui, tell Him all about it. Say the prayer. Focus on *forgive us our trespasses as we forgive those who trespass against us.* Forgive the commander who sent you into the battle with the order to kill. Forgive the Germans who pointed their rifles at you today, to kill you... God will forgive you, in His great love, for what happened today."

The young man turned his head then and stared at her, unblinking, with a look that penetrated her very soul. He said not a word but held her gaze, unwavering, for a very long time as she knelt there, smoothing his hair. Then he said, "I cannot think straight, mademoiselle l'infirmière. Would you say it avec moi... with me?"

Lydia nodded and took his hand in her own. "Our Father," she began quietly to pray in both French and English, "who art in heaven, hallowed be thy Name. Thy kingdom come, thy will be done..."

Standing in the pathway between rows of cots, Simon stood rooted in place watching and listening to this exchange. He saw the other soldiers, lying on cots on either side, incline their heads, listening as well, their lips moving as they recited the familiar words of the Lord's prayer. He watched Lydia touch the young man's face, stroke his hair as a mother would, drawing him out of the tortured isolation of memory. Simon now knew well the feel of that touch... the gentle, healing caress of his beautiful wife. In Simon's soul, he found himself also saying the words of the prayer along with them. It did not seem right to move away in the middle of the prayer. And when they had finished, he watched Lydia close the young man's eyes with her hand and heard her whisper, "sleep now," before she rose to her feet to go to the next prostrate patient.

A sudden sense of guilt washed over Simon, for wanting her attention. He was healthy and strong and their bond was undeniable. He quietly left the recovery, struggling to balance the giving and taking... the having and sharing. He secured the tent's inner flap before opening the outer flap, keeping the light inside. The light was all inside, in there, the light of his soul. He closed the outer flap carefully to protect that light and found his way through the darkness back to the little tent he shared with Marcus and Harold. Simon laid down on his cot, exhausted. He heard Marcus move.

"Finally decide to take my advice for a little nurse time?" Marcus asked Simon as he rolled over on his own cot.

"Shut up, Marcus," Simon whispered, trying to not disturb Harold. And he laid in the darkness for a long time, turning the pewter ring on the fourth finger of his left hand before sleep came at last.

Chapter 7
Holding the Line

Sometime in the night, well before dawn, Marcus awakened to a soft tapping on the wooden tent support. He was immediately awake, as they always seemed to be listening, even when they did not want to, especially when trying to sleep. Marcus stumbled to the door without pulling on his trousers, trying to let the other two doctors remain undisturbed. Slipping out from under the flap, he bumped into a woman just outside the tent. Quickly Marcus reached out and grabbed her, to keep her from falling back, over the tent rope, and realized in the dim starlight that it was Lydia's hand in his own.

"Nurse Blackwell? Lydia?" he whispered, knowing she had been on duty in recovery. "What is it?" He led her slightly away from the tent, trying to miss the tent peg, not seeing that she looked back over her shoulder through the blackout of night toward the place where her heart lay sleeping. "Is it one of the wounded?"

She struggled to control her voice. "It's... it's noth—" she attempted when she realized whom she had awakened.

Marcus was acutely aware he was in nothing but his boxers next to her. With his hand on her arm, he felt her tremble and heard the waver in her voice. He had never known this woman to waver.

Not ever. Never known her to weaken. She was the woman of the surgery, the woman of the renegade ambulance ride. A woman he had never had alone… for himself.

He wanted her.

"Lydia," he whispered, using her familiar name and desiring to rescue her. "Tell me—"

She pulled back. "I'm so sorry, Doctor Lovell, for disturbing you," she said, her voice breaking, tears staining her apology. "I'm sorry, Marcus…"

She tried to turn away, but he heard the pain in her voice and drew her back toward him, reluctant to release her in her distress or lose this opportunity to show her the man he could be for her.

"What is it? You can trust me," he tried again, coaxing her.

Then, they both heard movement as the tent flap opened and closed behind them.

"Lydia?"

She heard the voice for which she had been longing. "Oh, Simon," she started and wept openly.

Simon moved past Marcus and took the woman into his own arms. "What is it, my beloved?" he whispered, willing the familiarity of his body to comfort and console her.

She sobbed softly but pulled back from him in agitation. "He's gone… the young man… the soldier… he's gone."

Simon sighed, knowing immediately to whom she referred. "I'm so sorry. When did he die? Just now?"

"No, I mean, he's really gone, Simon," she agonized. "He slipped out in the night and left the camp. He went alone out somewhere in the dark and never returned. I was busy elsewhere… I didn't even see him leave… none of us did."

"Dear God," Simon breathed. "Come here, my love."

And she did. Simon held her in the darkness, pressing her head to his shoulder as she wept. The couple did not even notice as Marcus slowly withdrew back into the tent, where he took to his cot again and pondered what he had just heard. *Simon had just called Lydia his 'love'! There was no mistaking the word!*

Harold roused. "Everything okay?" he murmured sluggishly.

"Yeah," Marcus replied. "Go back to sleep."

Simon led Lydia to the mess tent, where everything was still. They sat on one of the benches at the long table and he held her against his shoulder until her sorrow eased and her tears subsided. He said nothing, just kissed her forehead and stroked her hair.

Finally, Lydia spoke in the darkness. "I didn't want him to die alone, Simon... and I'm afraid he did just that... walked right out into the night and died alone somewhere out there... his wounds were not even fatal, but he was so sure he was going to die tonight. The sentries say they didn't notice anything. I should have kept a better eye on him..."

Simon stretched out his long legs and felt her shift against him, wrapping one of her legs over his in an effort to get closer to him on the bench. "I don't think it is what you're thinking, my dearest one," he said.

Her voice was still grieved. "What do you think, Simon? Tell me, please..."

"I think," Simon said, his voice a little gruff from the emotion behind it. "I think you released him."

"To die?" she said, broken.

"No," he countered, one hand holding her against his shoulder and the other stroking her wet cheek. "No, I think you released that man to go meet God while they were still on speaking terms."

She wasn't sure what he meant and told him as much. "I don't understand."

He kissed her forehead softly. "I think you helped him make peace with God, Lydia. But his wounds weren't immediately fatal, you're right. He knew he was going to be sent back to the front, again, to face the same dilemmas: to shoot or not to shoot, to kill or be killed. I think he took the forgiveness offered and went out to find God while he could, free of the guilt and the shame... to cross over to God with a clean conscience... before anything else could go wrong."

Lydia raised her face to his in the darkness, unable to see him, but knowing so well what she would have seen if she could. She understood what Simon was trying to tell her... but the stabbing pain was still in her heart.

"I need you, Simon, now. Will you have me—"

He nodded. He removed his shirt and laid it on the ground between the long bench and the wall of the tent. He lowered her down onto it and took her slowly, in the darkness, inside the mess tent. He kissed the tears from her eyes... from her cheeks. She felt the cool earth at her back, seeping through his shirt. Simon poured pure love into her, creating an internal warmth far from war, pain, suffering, and death. And as they became one again in body, she gained strength from him; her soul quieted and soothed. He breathed heavily into her ear when they were complete.

She kept her arms around him and whispered, "This... this thing that we do now..." she struggled for the words. "It is protecting, and healing, and comforting..."

Simon kissed her deeply, still covering her on the ground. "I vowed to protect you. I'm here, Lydia, whenever you need protection, healing or comfort. I'll talk to Aubert tomorrow."

"Thank you, Simon," she whispered, and again, softly, a few more tears fell, but this time, they were not solely tears of sadness.

The wounded began to arrive shortly after 9 o'clock. The three doctors jumped from their cots at the sound of the trucks and ambulances rolling in and a quick alert from the bugle. They hastily pulled on their pants and boots for surgery. Marcus looked across to Simon as he threw on his clothes. "You missed your curfew last night, son!" he said, buttoning his shirt over his bare chest and identification tag. "How many times have I got to tell you be home by ten?"

"Leave it alone, Marc," Simon answered, remembering hearing Marcus outside the tent in the dark telling Lydia *'you can trust me,'* as she was crying.

"Just curious," Marcus replied evenly, looking closely at his friend for answers.

Harold looked over at both of them. "Am I missing something I should be aware of?" he questioned.

"No, sir," Marcus replied cheerfully, jumping up and rushing out toward the surgery.

"Simon?" Harold asked the remaining doctor.

"No, Harold," he said quietly, following in the wake of the crew all running to their stations.

In the surgery tent, the race was beginning. At the station, there was only one enemy, and it was time... not the Germans. Anesthetists snapped hoses onto tanks. Susannah was circulating. Orderlies were calling to each other. Laura, Lydia, and Charlotte were washing, masking, and setting up instruments at the three tables for the doctors.

"Nurse Blackwell," Marcus called over before anyone else could. "Assist me, please."

Simon looked up from the water spigot as he scrubbed in. This was irritating. He couldn't afford to let himself be irritated and distracted. Not on a day with casualties streaming through their doors. He needed to focus.

Susannah glanced over at Marcus, who was studying his first casualty. Then she shrugged. Hadn't she told the other nurses not too long ago that there was enough of the man to go around? She shouldn't mind him requesting her friend to assist.

Lydia wove her way through the corpsmen and wounded to where Marcus was already issuing orders for anesthesia.

"What have you got, Doctor?" she asked quietly, still thinking of the missing soldier.

He looked at the chest wound. "What do you think, Nurse Blackwell? I can see his heart."

She peered into the wound with the exposed heart pumping. "His lungs look pink," she returned. "The sternum is shattered, though. Can you sew together what's left? Can you see his aorta? Is it bleeding?"

"Damn, you're good," he said softly, under his breath. "No wonder Doctor Finney keeps you to himself."

She shot a look at Marcus. Their eyes met over their masks, across the fallen man on the table. "Let's try," she deflected the doctor as she saw the young soldier go limp under the anesthesia.

He nodded, "Let's do it." Marcus was very good with hearts, arteries, and bleeds. Together, they washed out the man's chest. Marcus peered into the cavity.

"Light!" Lydia called out, and the anesthetist pulled the overhead lamp closer for the surgeon to see. "No, flashlight!" she exclaimed.

A flashlight appeared in her hand, and she pointed it into the cavity in every direction under the soldier's loose rib cage, where fragments of sternum floated dangerously. Quickly, she began to receive the pieces of bone Marcus dropped into her hand.

"We need to keep that one there," he murmured. "Let's keep this one and this one and reconnect them together there... stabilize his ribs so he can breathe..."

She nodded, dabbing at bleeders with cloth sponges and watching the man's heart beating rhythmically, his lungs filling in and out in synchrony.

Marcus reached for suture, but Lydia stayed his hand.

"Wait, Doctor, look, there's fresh blood down in there." She pointed the light directly below to the aorta. "We have a bleed somewhere."

His eyes bored into the man's chest, searching as she directed her flashlight under the soldier's ribs. "Not the aorta," Marcus said.

"Blood's too dark," Lydia agreed.

"Something else..." Marcus was searching with his fingers and his eyes.

Then Lydia spotted the fresh ooze. "There," she said urgently, bending over to look and get it into the light held by her hand. "There, under the clavicle…"

"I see it," Marcus softly exclaimed, reaching in. "Clam—"

She pressed the clamp into his outstretched hand, and he swiftly blocked the flow of the vena cava, where there was a widening puncture wound. Quickly, Lydia soaked up the pooled blood with a sponge, threw it away and grabbed another.

"Sut—" he started as Lydia handed him a forceps already loaded with a needle and sutures.

"Damn, woman!" he breathed, never taking his eyes off the work he was doing. "You reading my mind or something?" She cut the sutures quickly, as quickly as he tied them, and then Marcus opened the clamp. Together, they watched the soldier's heartbeat, which had slowed.

With the restored blood flow, it steadily began picking up speed until the anesthetist said, "He's stabilizing."

Then Lydia handed Marcus the retention suture. "Perhaps you would like this now, Doctor Lovell?" she asked, her eyes twinkling over her mask at him.

He held out his hand. "I would, Nurse Blackwell," he stated. Then, taking the tip of the forceps, he tapped the pewter ring on her middle finger. "This a new trend in nursing attire?" he asked, curious.

"I think it rather suits the uniform," she said evenly. "I plan to keep it."

"There are other metals out there, you know… gold… silver… You might like one of them even more," he suggested as he started knitting together the remaining sternum they had salvaged to protect the precious organs beneath.

"Vastly overrated," she murmured.

He glanced up at her. "You just might be surprised. Never know unless you try it," he suggested.

"Suture, Doctor," Lydia replied, handing him the threaded needle.

Marcus took the sutures she offered and sewed the chest wound back together. He stepped back from the table as Lydia called for litter bearers to take the soldier to the recovery. Lydia moved away to the water spigot to wash her hands and was quickly joined by the surgeon, who soaped up next to her... entertaining the notion of washing her hands for her and feeling the soapy water slide over her skin.

"That was pretty impressive, Nurse," he said quietly in admiration. "We should get together more often."

"Sorry, Doctor," she said lightly. "My dance card is full."

Then he laughed out loud, causing the others in the surgery to turn at a sound never heard in this place. *So that was it then! Simon and Lydia had found each other on their little trip south! Well, good for them!*

Lydia spied an opportunity as Simon's table cleared, and he stepped away to make room for another patient. Quickly, she slid through the tables and told Laura, "I've got this one."

Laura nodded and moved over to Doctor Lovell's table, which was cleared and ready for the next casualty being heaved up into place.

Lydia was already standing and waiting when Simon returned from washing up.

"Everything okay?" he asked her quietly as they began to work on a man who had lost an ear and half of his scalp to a bomb blast.

"It is now," she said, looking over at him. "I'm right where I belong."

"Hope everyone else knows that soon enough!" he muttered under his breath so quietly that the anesthetist didn't catch it, but Lydia did.

There had been no time yet for Simon to approach Lieutenant Aubert due to the elevated flow of wounded. He was concerned that tomorrow would be the same, and the next day as well, if the bombardments continued like this. *Wouldn't these armies ever run out of soldiers?* he often asked himself. But it seemed they did not. He could leave a letter with the corporal. No, that wouldn't do. He needed to talk to the man directly.

Most of the surgical team was in the mess tent eating something hot. Simon took a tray and immediately saw there was cooked orange squash and some kind of meat with potatoes. "Fresh off the truck," Cook told him, plopping a spoonful of mashed potato down. "Thanks to you, cheese omelet in the morning."

"Thank the French," Simon returned. "It was a gift from them."

The cook lifted a ladle and waved it under his nose. "I'm out of flour," he said. "But the apples are stewed with the extra sugar we found."

"That so?" Simon said, interested. "Didn't know there was sugar."

"Yep," the cook replied. "Brown. Can do a lot with brown sugar."

"Well, I'm certainly relieved to hear that," Simon declared. He took his tray to the table where there was one space left between Susannah and one of the corpsmen. He saw Lydia near the end of the table, in focused conversation with some of the nurses. As he slid his legs over the bench into the only empty spot, the corpsman across from him finished and headed back to work, leaving the opposite bench open.

Marcus came through the chow line and into view across the table. "Mind if I sit here? No? Thanks!" He plopped himself down across from Simon and began eating with relish.

"You're in a good mood, Doctor," Susannah observed dryly. "Good day in surgery?"

Marcus lifted a fork full of potato and made a circle with it, waving it in her direction. "Any day we're done before the cook runs out of food is a good day in surgery, Nurse Boyton," he returned. "You off to recovery after this?"

"No," she replied gratefully. "For once, I get to go to bed."

His eyebrows rose in her direction. Her cheeks slightly reddened, and imperceptible to nearly everyone, she nodded his way.

Simon watched this subtle exchange unfold as he took a swig of hot, stale coffee. *How is it that I've never noticed this kind of thing before?* he wondered. He really had been oblivious to the social undercurrents in the camp.

Marcus waved his fork again toward the end of the table. "And there's a wounded man in recovery who owes his life to that one down there." He pointed to Lydia, who was intent on her own conversation. Her brown waves were still wet from the shower and her skin glowed.

Simon looked at his friend over the rim of his cup and set it down carefully. "How's that?" he asked.

"Didn't see it," Marcus said while chewing. "Didn't see the vena cava. Damnedest thing. She swooped a flashlight in there, and there it was. That woman is quick as lightning with clamps and sutures." Then he added, "I think that you've been teaching one or two... or maybe just one... of the nurses things you haven't told the rest of us about!"

Simon thought to kick his friend under the table, but restrained himself, knowing that he'd need to be able to stand in surgery all day tomorrow. "What's gotten into you, Marc?" he pressed.

Marcus laid down his fork, placing his elbows on the table, while enjoying a bite of the stewed apples. He glanced at Simon's left hand... Simon knew at once he was looking at the ring.

Simon continued to eat slowly, but his gut was knotting up inside.

"Damn good apples. By the way, thanks for getting those." Marcus continued, "I'm just saying that all the nurses should have the same advantage of learning new things. If they want to... you know... suture... and such. Each one can decide. Just saying. I told that to Aubert today when I took a break. Because we really want our nurses here, and we want to keep them happy. Because... if the nurses aren't happy, then the doctors aren't happy either." He looked over to Susannah and smiled cheerfully. Her cheeks turned pink. "And then the patients won't be happy. And the army wouldn't be happy with that."

Simon kept his voice even and calm. "That so? What did Lieutenant Aubert say to the idea that everyone should be equally happy, in a war zone?"

Marcus took another mouthful of food, chewed for a minute, and quickly glanced knowingly at Simon's left hand again as he picked up his coffee mug. He took a dramatically long drink. "He said, my friend," Marcus started, "that he didn't care what American nurses and doctors did, as long as none of the rest of them minded." He placed both hands on the table, looking at Simon's hand again and smiled broadly. "I told him that none of them minded at all."

Simon felt a wave of relief... and his stomach began to untangle. He looked down to the end of the table and saw that Lydia had glanced up his way. She smiled shyly and his heart picked up a beat.

"And I told him you would probably be paying him a visit, to back me up," Marcus said, looking directly at his friend. "That I wasn't the only doctor who thought the team was committed, no matter who decided to do, whatever."

Flushed with relief, Simon nodded, finishing his meal. He rose and slid out from the bench, but quickly leaned over the table to shake the man's hand before leaving the tent. Marc had figured it out and paved the way for him to go to Aubert. "Thanks, Marcus," he said, gripping his friend's hand tightly.

"No problem, Simon," Marcus nodded. Then he added, so that only Simon could hear him, "You lucky bastard!"

Simon looked straight back at his friend and chuckled quietly. "You have no idea..."

Simon left the mess tent, after catching Lydia's eye once more. He saw her finish her conversation and get up from the table, smiling in agreement to something one of the girls told her as she left the group. He walked over to the edge of the camp, behind the mess tent, where they had left the truck the day before. They hadn't even grabbed their haversacks as they jumped out yesterday, rushing to join the others in the surgery and then going right back at it again today. He needed to find their papers. Well... and he wanted her to find him, away from the others.

He waited for her behind the mess tent, knowing she was close behind. He grabbed her to him as soon as she rounded the tent, and she fell into his arms in a quick embrace. Then he said, "Let's find the truck."

It didn't take long to find as it had been pulled over nearer the mess tent where the foodstuffs had been unloaded for the cook. Simon searched the front floor of the truck and found their haversacks still tucked under the seat. "Well, at least these are still here. I woke up once during the night and realized our papers were still out here. Figured I wouldn't stumble around in the dark trying to find them. And, of course... other matters... took priority."

They went to the back of the truck and dropped their sacks. Simon looked in, noting that the two bolts of fabric remained inside, apparently deemed useless by the army. The basket of wine was nowhere in sight.

"Figures," Simon said.

Lydia looked over his shoulder into the truck. "What figures?" she asked.

"No wine," he replied.

"Figures," she echoed and laughed lightly, just glad to be in his presence. "We don't need it."

He lifted her up to sit on the open bed of the back of the truck and spread her legs so he could stand between them and face her. With an arm on either side of her, he could look straight into her eyes and have her full attention.

"How are you doing after last night?" he asked, concerned.

"Well, Lieutenant Aubert must already know that the man is gone. We keep lists of names of who comes and who leaves, and on which truck... and who dies. So, for now, he knows a name is marked as whereabouts unknown. Last night, what you said about that boy meeting God with a clear conscience, that took the burden away," Lydia said softly. "You knew the exact right thing to say... though I don't know how."

"I hope I'm always able to," he countered, thinking. "I also want to walk into heaven with a clear conscience when I approach that throne."

She took his face in her hands, as she loved to do. "And is your conscience clear, Simon? It should be."

He shook his head. "I'm afraid not. I almost decked Marcus last night, and again this morning in surgery, and then, again, in the mess. It was a close call all three times. I shouldn't let myself get that worked up."

Lydia looked puzzled. "Why did you almost hit him?" she wondered. "He's your best friend!"

Simon leaned over and kissed her lips. "You are my best friend now. And you are why I almost decked him. Has he ever been inappropriate... with y—"

Her blue eyes looked straight into his. "Never."

"I did say once that you can be an amazing liar."

Lydia was serious. "I've never let it get far enough to be inappropriate. I know he's a flirt, with all the nurses. And has been on occasion with me, as well. He is who he is, Simon. He's an excellent surgeon and I like him a lot. He just has trouble seeing where the line is. I don't think the man could settle down with one woman, even if he wanted to. The worst he's ever said to me is that I should try a little variety before settling down."

"Hm," Simon said thoughtfully. "Nothing wrong with 'black with one sugar', every day, year after year... or with vanilla ice cream being my all time favorite."

She traced his mouth, imagining the ice cream. "Yes, but that's because you tried chocolate once and made a choice. A fair choice. You've told me to tell you if I like or don't like something. You didn't have a chance to find out if you'd prefer something else... or someone else, so how do you know that I am what you like the most."

"Isn't it a little bit late for this kind of discussion?" he remarked dryly. "Most people discuss this kind of thing before the wedding day, don't they? Sort of already have this worked out in their minds?"

She pondered that question. "I suppose... but our marriage was a little spur-of-the-moment, shall we say?"

He nodded and stroked his beard. "The cathedral may have been spur-of-the-moment, but the decision was not... not in my mind, anyway."

"When did you decide you wanted me to be your wife, Simon?" she countered playfully, wanting to lighten the mood a little.

Simon swung himself up next to her on the truck bed. "About four months, two weeks and four days ago. Right after you walked into the casualty clearing station south of Verdun. I saw you get off the truck and come into the mess and thought to myself, she's the one... if I'm ever good enough." Then he looked around in the twilight as night began to fall. The camp was quieting down. No one was walking behind the mess tent. "Do you have duty tonight?" he asked her.

She shook her head. "I was on duty all last night, so..."

Simon reached behind him, pulled up one of the bolts of fabric left in the truck, and laid her back against it. He kissed her mouth slowly, lovingly. "This is why I don't need to look any farther than you, Lydia, when your your lips invite me in..." He opened the top buttons of her shirt and traced the curve of her breast, then opened the buttons of her trousers and kissed her stomach. "And I'm sure you are the only woman for me because when I do this, your body comes to me as if it already knows me, and we have only been husband and wife a few days."

"But you have not experienced the rest that follows with anyone but me, and what if someday, Marcus convinces you that you have missed out on something," she said half seriously.

Simon reached for the other bolt of cloth and began to unwrap its length, opening it out like a sheet over her, sliding down her trousers underneath it. "When a man like me is so blessed to find a woman like you to be beside me... why, in God's great name, would I ever look back wondering if there is more?" Then, he grew quiet. "I'm acutely aware that we have been together... often... this week, and I think I could want you morning, noon, and night. I'm concerned that I've enjoyed you too much for your body to handle it... I won't know unless you tell me, Lydia."

"I think my body wants you to enjoy it at least once more. Especially because we won't be able for the next five days, if my calculation of the moon is correct," she said quietly.

"The next five..." Simon groaned, then laughed. "You're worth waiting for." He moved to lay beside her and kissed the ring on her finger... she wrapped her fingers in his hair as he continued to gently awaken every inch of her body, waiting to couple with her until they were both satisfied that she would not need to refuse him at all.

Chapter 8

Fire and Brimstone

Lieutenant Aubert had been absent from the station for several days now, following a summons from Major d'Espèrey to report to headquarters. Upon the lieutenant's return, during a lull in the casualties, Simon seized the first opportunity to approach the man who was in charge of their destinies. It was to be a discussion about options... *Well, really,* Simon thought, *there are no options.* There was one clear path and one only. So, when he approached the camp commander, it was more to present an ultimatum, not a choice. He rapped on the tent's support beam and received the perfunctory "enter" in return.

Aubert leafed through files and memos with his aide by his side to help him quickly locate what was needed. Endless piles of patient records and transfer orders were in front of him, along with supply requests, medical requests, staff assignment changes, and military directives of every sort.

"Have a seat, Doctor Finney," the French lieutenant said as he drew on a cigarette and scanned a particular sheet of paper before him. Aubert rarely smoked in front of the doctors... Simon knew instantly that he must be concerned about something.

Several minutes passed in silence, save for the shuffling of papers. Simon cleared his throat. "Perhaps, Lieutenant, I should return later?"

Aubert waved away the comment. "No, just wait s'il vous plaît. We're going to be moving camp again. But say nothing until I am ready to announce to everyone. No, Doctor Lovell told me a week ago that you would be coming to discuss some concerns about doctors and nurses. Something about keeping everyone... happy." His voice was weary.

Another aide entered the command tent, handing him a communique received over the radio. Aubert scanned it quickly and, to the aide, added, "Send acknowledgement. Received. Understood. Keep it brief. Just those two words only."

"Yes, sir," the aide confirmed, leaving just as quickly as he had entered.

Aubert looked up from his desk to meet Simon's gaze. "So, what do those fragile people want, Doctor Finney? God knows we cannot have unhappy medical staff... or so Doctor Lovell insists."

Simon looked calmly across the man's desk and kept his voice and temperament casual, even indifferent. "I wanted to inform the lieutenant of a change in circumstance with two of the medical team—"

"Don't tell me someone has asked for transfer, for there will be no transfers," Aubert was resolute. "This station is moving again, as I told you. We have new orders from headquarters. Where we are going, there will be no time to train anyone new and every medical hand will be absolutely essential. You have my permission to tell them no transfers."

"Certainly, Lieutenant," Simon breathed a sigh of relief. "I wanted to inform you that Nurse Blackwell—"

"That woman's name just cannot stay out of my tent," Aubert interrupted. "No transfers, even for the nurses, even though they are volunteers... as you have been so quick to remind me! The nurses will be needed, and strength of this team cannot be compromised!" he finished emphatically.

"Very good, sir," Simon said, hastening to add, "Nurse Blackwell and I were married while in Nancy recently, and I just wanted to inform the lieutenant of the change in circumstance."

Aubert pushed back his chair, staring at Simon. "You what, Doctor Finney?" he pressed.

"We were married in Nancy, Lieutenant," Simon repeated smoothly. "Therefore, we just wanted to inform you, sir, that our commitment to the best welfare of the staff and patients is unchanged. We will, of course, continue to serve fully in our capacity to keep the team strong."

Aubert took a long inhale of the cigarette in his hand. Simon noted a slight tremor in the curls of rising smoke. There was silence in the tent. Simon waited... and waited... until the apparent internal debate within the company commander finally reached a conclusion.

"Well played, Doctor Finney," Aubert said at last. His fingers drummed on the desk.

Simon waited again.

Finally, Aubert dismissed him. "You may go, Doctor."

Simon rose, Aubert stopping him at the tent flap. "One thing, Doctor Finney," Aubert added.

"Sir?"

"Get your own tent. I won't have you Americans disrupting the station with impropriety. It's bad for morale."

"Yes, sir," Simon agreed, leaving the tent. He was unabashedly smiling. *My morale has never been better.*

Simon would have to wait to tell Lydia the good news, as the thunder of shelling nearby and the sound of bugles announced the beginning of casualties. People ran. The surgery erupted into a frenzy of activity. The flaps of the recovery were thrown open. From the elation of great news, Simon was plunged into the exhausting, repetitive grind that they had all come to know too well. Whatever had happened out there to the soldiers had been compounded by heavy rains over the previous five days. The men coming in were miserable with wracking coughs and foot injuries from standing in the muddy trenches with filthy water up to their ankles. The doctors had rarely seen so much gangrene, the men's feet soaked in muck. They asked the nurses to check the feet of the casualties regardless of the injury that brought them in. If the gangrene was too advanced to wait for a field hospital, amputation was required. One good piece of news was that the heroin did quiet coughing and seemed to help the wounded tolerate post-operative pain.

Lydia, Marlene, and Sally Winfield took the first triage shift and rapidly got soaked despite their ponchos. Gangrene complicated the process of nurses trying to establish the most likely cause of preventable death from external bullet and shrapnel wounds to gas gangrene working its way up inside of a man's leg, poisoning him just as quickly from the inside out. As the nurses followed the doctors' directions to remove boots before the patients came into the surgery, those with gas gangrene had to be evaluated and held. A hastily constructed amputation table had been erected outside of the surgery tent for that procedure to take place first, and then penetrating wounds were repaired inside of the tent. As Lydia and Marlene met halfway down the stream of patients, they found themselves side by side, pulling off soldier's boots in the rain.

Marlene sniffed. "This one's got it," she said quietly, but with certainty, removing the damp leather. She dropped the boots and pulled the man's sock off as several blackened toes also dropped to the ground. Carefully, she examined the sole and soggy heel of the man's foot. She looked up at Lydia. "Outside," she said, carefully placing a card with a large zero on it... the new triage number they employed for such cases. Marlene patted the soldier's shoulder softly. "Hang on, buddy," she said as he stared up into the grey sky overhead.

"Give me my boots to hold. Can't lose them, nurse. And can I have my toe for a souvenir?" the injured man asked.

She handed him his sock. "It's your toe," she said without judgment. Men kept pieces of shrapnel and carried a rabbit's foot just as often.

The surgeons, nurses, and orderlies took turns at the outside surgical table beneath the tent, now dripping with rainwater. They rotated often, lest any one of them should have to stand at that table for hours with the arduous task of patching together men who would never be able to stand without crutches, because all of their toes were in their pockets.

The team worked through the next several days until the wounded had all been treated, for now, and the surrounding hills grew quiet again. Mercifully, the sun emerged after two days to dry up the land once more. Lydia noted corpsmen burying tarps of body parts as far from the tents as possible to prevent the spread of infection. After this particular siege, the doctors and nurses had spent ample time in the makeshift shower, scrubbing themselves clean. Their morale was especially low. Worse, the mess tent had been closed briefly, she assumed it was to prevent the breeze from spreading any noxious bacteria to where the meals were served. People had been receiving a tray at the door of their tents all day and scooting off into private tents to eat. *A wise and necessary precaution against gangrene and respiratory infections*, she thought.

As the station fell into the quieter routine of transitory rest under the blessed sunshine, Lydia wanted only to find Simon and revive her somewhat flagging spirit. After leaving the shower and drying her long hair with a towel, grateful for the feeling of cleanliness, she was waylaid by Alice.

"Lydia, can you spare me a minute?" Alice asked anxiously, pulling her aside.

"Right this minute?" Lydia countered, glancing around, but not seeing Simon nearby. He might have gone to his tent to catch a few minutes of sleep. "Sure," she said. "What's the matter, Alice?"

"It's a personal thing... I'm really sorry to bother you with it, but I didn't know who else to ask," Alice apologized.

Lydia put her arm around the other nurse's waist. "It's okay, honey, what's up?"

"I have a lump," Alice whispered. "I want you to look at it."

Lydia was immediately concerned. "A lump? Where?"

"Can we go to our tent? I'll show you..." she said with urgency.

Lydia nodded, her fatigue leaving her with the concern she now felt for Alice, who rarely asked anything for herself and was usually the picture of health, beyond the stress of the job. They wove their way through the tents, arm in arm, skirting the recovery, and went to the tent they shared with Gretha and Laura. As they approached, they saw Gretha already stretched out on her cot and Laura putting a clean blanket on her own.

"What about them?" Lydia asked quickly. "Do you want them to know?"

"They will eventually, anyway, I suppose," Alice sighed. "But they can keep a secret, I trust them."

"Okay then," Lydia nodded as they ducked into the tent.

Upon their arrival, the two women looked up. Alice spoke first. "I'm glad you're my friends," she started. "I'm glad I can trust the two of you through thick and thin. I need to show Lydia a lump if you are okay with it..."

Gretha sat up. "Certainly."

Laura nodded.

Lydia waited. Alice went to Lydia's cot and pointed. "It's that one."

"One what?" Lydia asked, confused.

"That lump," Alice repeated, pointing again to Lydia's cot, where there was a lump underneath her army blanket.

"What the..." Lydia started as she slowly pulled the woolen blanket down. There, she saw the blue fabric from the bolt of cloth from the French villagers had rolled up, on her cot. She looked at the other women, who were smiling. Puzzled, Lydia picked up the fabric and it fell out into a long, soft dress. Lydia held it up against her body, astonished.

Gretha, Alice, and Laura then surrounded her. "Try it on!" Gretha exclaimed. "I think I can still sew pretty well. But we'll soon see."

"It was pretty easy to guess what size to make it," Laura added, "since we're all underfed, undernourished, and rather thin."

Lydia could not absorb what was happening. "What? Why?"

The girls laughed. "The word is out that that ring on your finger isn't just a souvenir from the town of Nancy," Laura said. "And we're as happy for you as we can possibly be. There's just been no time to get something together... until today, what with a war on and the rain earlier this week. Anyway, we'd all have to be blind not to see that your little trinket matches the one Doctor Finney is wearing now."

Lydia wiped her eyes. "You all are too much!" She exclaimed in wonder.

"Try it on," Gretha ordered her.

Lydia stripped off her army trousers and shirt. "I haven't any nice underthings to go with something like this," she said reluctantly. The other woman slipped the blue dress over her head. It had ruffled sleeves that fell to just above her elbows. The waist was crimped to fit her small contours. The bodice was fitted with darts that accentuated her shape, and the V-shaped neckline was almost appropriate enough to be worn inside a Red Cross dance hall. The ruffled hem fell just above her ankles. Lydia twirled around, watching the fabric move with her.

Laura surveyed her with satisfaction. "Nice job, Gretha," she complimented the other nurse as she buttoned up the back of the dress. "It's a really good fit. Now, here's the final touch!" She held out a white undergarment that looked suspiciously like it had been a pillowcase transformed into a pantaloon. Laura helped Lydia pull it on, tied the waist string, and looked at her again. "No slip or nice lacey brassiere. Oh well. In war, we must all make sacrifices."

Lydia looked down at the swirling blue fabric, the color of the early night sky. "It's so beautiful," she breathed. "And none of us have worn brassieres for months, just undershirts. I don't think I'd even remember how to put one on."

Alice lifted a strand of hair along Lydia's face. "Hmmm," she said. "Not much I can do about your hair with no bobby pins or flowers to style it."

Lydia looked up at the three of them. "It's okay, ladies. I haven't any place to wear such a lovely dress anyway."

"Ah, but you see—" Laura retorted. "You do. Hm, no glass slippers for Cinderella. Oh well, the dress is long enough that it almost hides your lovely army-issue boots."

As if on cue, there was a shadow at the door of the tent. Gretha pulled the flap aside and allowed the man waiting outside to enter. Harold Stockton ducked his head under the tent flaps, took one look at Lydia in the flowing blue dress, and smiled appreciatively.

"Doctor Stockton?" Lydia was, again, a bit confused.

He offered her his arm. "Madam Finney, I presume," he said smiling.

Lydia took his arm, her heart beating so loudly she was certain anyone could hear it, even without a stethoscope. "Where are we—"

"You'll see," he promised reassuringly. Harold led her out of the tent into the sunlight, where the breeze caught her dress and hair. Followed by the three co-conspirators, Harold led her around the recovery, where the duty nurses looked out through the screened sides and smiled. They passed the surgery, quiet and empty, and came into the clearing in front of the mess tent. The sides of the tent were now pulled back and sunlight shone on the faces of the entire rest of the medical team, the kitchen staff, many of the corpsmen, and several of the French soldiers. And there, flanked by Marcus... was Simon... waiting for her.

Simon watched Lydia approaching, holding the arm of their chief surgeon, the blue dress flowing, her long, wavy hair unbound and falling on and off her shoulders at the whim of the September breezes. His heart jumped into his throat. Lydia was intensely beautiful. He heard Marcus give a low whistle of approval.

"If you're not up for this, Simon," Marcus was smiling, "I can step in—."

Simon glanced over at his friend, but this time, there was no irritation at all. "She is everything I've ever wanted, Marc,"—*and she is already mine*, he added to himself, as he moved forward to greet his bride. There, in front of everyone, without any further need for discretion or subterfuge, he took Lydia into his arms and kissed her. The group assembled gave them an enthusiastic round of applause. Simon wrapped an arm around Lydia's waist and walked her to the open mess tent.

"Remember the wine?" he asked her; Lydia nodded.

On the long table in front of them, Cook had prepared the best meal he could manage, with what was available. The basket of wine was on the table. A layered white cake was waiting to be cut. The food was hot and steaming.

"You did all this, Simon? For me?" Lydia whispered, much too overwhelmed to speak any louder.

Simon shook his head. "Not me, my love. I'm as surprised as you are. It was Marcus. And it's been officially sanctioned, albeit reluctantly, by Lieutenant Aubert. The cook closed the mess tent just to have time to bake and set it up."

Lydia turned to see Marcus standing alone, just a little ways off, hands in his pockets, watching them. She walked over purposefully in her blue Cinderella dress. She threw her arms around his neck and hugged him. He in turn, wrapped his arms around her waist, thoroughly enjoying this innocent moment of closeness. "Thank you, Marcus Lucius Lovell..." she said softly, deliberately, "from the bottom of my heart."

He nodded, memorizing the feel of her body in his arms, knowing that after today, this would be the one and only time he would be able to do so. "Next time, we'll also get you lacey stockings and shoes... for the dance..." Marcus smiled at her, "even though I'm sure your card will still be full."

"You are so good at being bad," Lydia teased him as he reluctantly let her go to rejoin her waiting husband.

After they had eaten, after the wine was gone and the recovery nurses had been relieved from duty so that they, also, could join the well-wishers at the celebration, Simon took Lydia by the hand and pulled her up from the bench, to her feet.

"There's just one more thing," Simon told her. "Under direct orders from Aubert."

"Oh no!" Lydia laughed, her head a little dizzy with wine. "Should I be afraid?"

"That depends," he countered, leading her away from the mess tent, past the knowing smiles of the other doctors and nurses, past the surgery, past the shower, to a rather small tent tucked in the midst of the others, its flap open, but sides pulled down against the waning sun. Simon took her hand and led her inside, where two cots had been placed next to each other, and she noted her footlocker already on the ground next to his own.

She turned to him curiously. "I asked you if I should be afraid, and you said it depends... depends on what?"

"On the fact that I've noted that the moon is five days farther along its journey now..." he stated, "and we have our own tent, and that I have been patiently waiting... well," he conceded, "not very patiently, for five very long nights, despite—"

She turned her back to him and lifted her long brown hair, letting her neck feel the air. "You'll have to undo the buttons," she invited him. "I can't reach..."

Simon reveled in undoing the buttons one by one, coaxing the blue dress to fall from her shoulders until it gathered in a small pile around her feet. He softly kissed the scar on the back of her right shoulder. Turning her around to face him, he caught her hand, reaching for the tie to the homemade undergarment, and loosened it himself, letting it fall to her feet as well. He laid her back on one of the cots, then bent and retrieved both her new dress and undergarment, laying them carefully on top of her footlocker. He turned back to her and pulled off her boots and socks, one by one, until there was nothing left to remove. He stood over her for a moment, gazing down at her with longing. Then, finally, Simon said, "No more hiding for us, no more waiting, no more wondering when I will be able to hold you in my arms again."

Lydia relished the feel of the breeze caressing her body as it found its way through their new tent and over her skin. She welcomed the unwavering desire in Simon's eyes as he stood looking down at her, knowing she alone was the object of it. In anticipation, she watched him remove his own uniform until he lowered himself on top of her. Then she put a finger up and traced his lips. "Since you have already been waiting so patiently... would you do just one more thing for me, my dear husband?" she whispered.

He nodded, his brown eyes penetrating her soul. "Anything, you know that."

Her eyes danced. "Go very... very... slowly..."

And Simon nodded because, for now, they had all the time in the world.

A few days later, bugles announced that the time had come for the station to be taken down. They were moving again, farther up the front, to the countryside... this time north of Reims and closer to Somme, where the effort to push back the German army was taking place amid heavy fighting. They learned that several British casualty clearing stations were also setting up not too far from them. It wasn't long after their own station was set up in its new location, that visitors began to arrive.

The British were fully committed to the French effort to contain the German army on the continent. Earlier, in July, thousands and thousands of young British soldiers, who were covering the front line, got hung up on barbed wire fences. French and British alike had been cut down en masse by the German soldiers waiting behind the spiked barrier, which had been largely unaffected by a pre-battle bombardment of their own. Casualties were too many to comprehend. It was a couple of the British doctors from that incident that arrived at nightfall for a quick collaboration with the

French and American medical teams. Gathered around the mess table, they spoke of things to come.

One of the British doctors, David Winston, shook his head. "We didn't know the Yanks had doctors over here until recently," he admitted. "Glad to meet you, though."

Harold introduced himself. "Trained at Hopkins, orthopedics, before coming here and becoming a jack-of-all-trades, so to speak." He turned to Marcus.

"Lovell," Marcus said, shaking the man's hand. "Marcus. Vascular. Likewise now sort of a one-size-fits-all surgeon, I guess."

Simon reached over the table and shook Doctor Winston's hand as well. "Simon Finney," he introduced himself. "Neurology initially. Now, also trauma... and all the rest."

Doctor Winston looked at the nurses assembled. "And you have nurses? From the V.A.D., I presume? No, you can't be... you don't wear nurses' uniforms."

Lydia said, "Sorry, no. All of us are from the States. Red Cross. This is Laura Bertolli, Gertha Bernstein, Susannah Boyton, Laura Mitchell, Alice Miller, Marlene Sullivan, and Sally Winfield. The rest of us are already on duty."

He stood up to shake their hands. "Delighted, I'm sure, would be the response I'd use... in any other circumstance," the man said, nodding to each of the nurses in turn.

"And I am Lydia Finney," she replied.

"The Americans are sending over couple teams?" David said, eyebrows raised at recognizing the shared surname.

"Doctor Finney is my husband," Lydia confirmed, resting a hand on Simon's shoulder.

David Winston looked at the two of them. "Quite extraordinary," he exclaimed softly. "Forgive the impertinence, but doesn't that make things over here rather complicated?"

Simon laughed. "Getting married actually straightened things out quite a bit," he replied. "We met over here."

"God help you," David replied.

"He certainly does," Simon returned steadily, raising his hand to his shoulder, to gently clasp hers.

"Well then, gentlemen," Harold said, returning them to the matters at hand. "Bring us up to speed. What have the British been running into here? We've been working our way up the front from south of Verdun to Reims and now here to Somme doing front-line triage."

David leaned his elbows on the table and looked at the little group of medical staff. "Then you have saved the worst for last," he said, his voice carefully dispassionate. "We have had an estimated half a million British casualties alone, since early summer... just the King's men. That doesn't count the French, the Aussies or the other scattered Allies in the trenches."

"My god," Susannah breathed. "I am so sorry. In three months."

One of the other doctors interjected. "John Earl-Johns, here. Worse than that is that the Allies have gained less than four or five miles of French ground for that price."

"Sounds much like Verdun," Marcus commented. "The line is being held there as well, but at a high cost to the French. The trenches extend a very long way south."

Harold nodded in agreement and said, "Doctors, we're accustomed to treating infections, both respiratory and from wounds, gangrene, tuberculosis, pneumonia, shell shock, shrapnel, amputations. Sounds like we will expect the same here, but perhaps even more?"

David added, "Measles, venereal diseases, kidney failure from both trauma and inadequate intravenous capability to replenish fluids, dysentery. At the field hospitals, some of our surgeons are experimenting with grafting skin, especially for head and face wounds, repairing shattered jaws, improving blood transfusions and ways to store it so it can be transported without clotting so quickly, rehydration of the dehydrated."

"Do you have radiographic equipment?" Harold pressed.

"In the field hospital, yes, of course, but not at the front, in the CCS. But someone, maybe one of you Yanks even, started using magnets in surgery to pull out shrapnel pieces. Interesting little technique."

Lydia looked at Charlotte and they both nodded, mentally adding magnets to their medical supply order list, which was growing as they listened.

"And for wound infection?" Marcus asked. "Especially the deep tissue wounds?"

"Debridement and, of course, Dakin's," David Winston replied. "And clean water, as much as they can supply. I must also warn you the air comes in damp and cold at night off the coast. The bombardments are picking up again; no doubt the Allies are trying to take another mile before winter hits the region. And the aerial bombardments are almost continuous at times. We've been running the surgeries out here sometimes days on end before there's a break. They bring them in morning, afternoon, and night. I hope you have lots of tea."

"Does that make a good poultice, Doctor Winston?" Laura asked quickly, adding tea to their mental supply list as well.

"It probably would, Nurse," David said. "But personally, I prefer to drink it, hot."

The British medical team returned to their station, leaving the Americans more informed, but less encouraged. That night, they lingered after supper in the mess tent, knowing they should sleep, but not quite wanting to leave the calm of this evening with upcoming trauma looming all around them. Then, unexpectedly, Gretha tapped a spoon against a tin cup, drawing everyone's attention to her. She had a blue bundle in her hand.

"Not a dress for each of us, surely," Susannah laughed. "Though I wouldn't mind," she added, remembering how incredible Lydia looked in the gift that had been crafted for her.

Marcus looked up over his coffee mug at the size of the bundle. "If those are dresses for all of you ladies, then I would like a fashion show, for they must be fairly...abbreviated, shall we say?"

The entire company laughed, including Gretha, at first, but she continued to stand until they quieted down again. "When the fighting starts again, if it turns out like it sounds it will, then things might get a little confusing. I made these for the nurses so you doctors and the corpsmen can find us faster." She went around and handed each of the nurses two blue headscarves.

The women took a minute to tie a scarf around their hair until all eleven were capped in matching blue against the army green trousers and shirts they wore, just like the men. The doctors looked at them appreciatively. Harold Stockton nodded slowly and turned to Gretha, waiting, uncertain.

"That is the singular most sensible thing anyone has done around here for a good long time," he said appreciatively. "In the lines of soldiers, the rows of green, this will be a tremendous help for us to find you nurses."

Marcus picked up one of the spare scarves lying on the table in front of Sally, spread it out by the corners, and held it up in front of her comparatively. "I still think a fashion show is in order," he said. "Obviously, not as a head scarf."

Sally snatched the scarf away before pretending to smack the hand that held it. "It is fortunate for you," she scolded him, "that you will need that very capable hand tomorrow." The group laughed again.

Marcus stood up and bowed to the nurses. "I stand reprimanded."

Gretha started to speak again. "When I was a little girl, my father would tell a story while we sat outside the barn snapping green beans for canning. One time, he told a story about Hands and Feet."

The little group turned to her, attentive.

"One day, Hands looked at Feet and said, 'You are ugly and calloused, and we are glad we are not like you.' Eyes looked down at Feet and said, 'Hands are right. I am beautiful and blue and see very far off, but Feet are rather smelly and only see the ground.' Hands said, 'I am skillful and can grab things and create things.' Then Ears said, 'I am more important than all of you because I hear everyone's complaints, and I am above all of you.' Then, one sunny, hot day, Feet bumped into a great rock and swelled up badly. Toes started to bleed. So Feet told Brain, 'I'm not taking one more step,' and Body had to sit down under the hot sun.

Hands started to complain to Brain about shriveling up in the heat, but Brain couldn't do much of anything to make Feet move. Eyes said, 'It's too bright out here, the sun is burning me.' Arms complained that Skin was turning red and sore in the hot sun. Mouth said, 'I am dry as a bone, and there's no water.' Then Heart finally spoke up to Body and said, 'You all thought you were better than Feet until Feet couldn't walk anymore, and now what do you think? Feet carries such a heavy load walking all of us around all the time. We can do nothing without Feet.' Body apologized, telling Feet, 'We were wrong not appreciating all that you do.' And Feet said, 'Now I will take you wherever you want to go, even if it hurts, now that I know you value me.'"

The assembled group fell silent and absorbed her story, each in their own way.

Then Marlene said, "When we were kids, we heard a story about a poor housewife who was never satisfied. She told her poor husband he had to build her a bigger house. So, he went to the wise man in the village and asked what he should do. The wise man said, 'Go home and bring all of your chickens and cats and dogs into the house and see what happens.' The poor man did so. A week later, the wife was still complaining she needed a bigger house. The poor man went back to the wise man and asked, 'What should I do?'"

While she continued the story with the group, Simon quietly stood, taking Lydia's hand and led her to their tent, arm in arm. The blackout surrounded them. Simon stretched out on a cot, and in the darkness, Lydia reached down and pulled off his boots and socks. She sat on the cot, put his feet on her lap, and began to massage each of his toes, the balls of his feet, his arches, his heels. Feeling around in the darkness, she found the talcum and sprinkled it on her hands, rubbing it between his toes and on the soles of his feet before putting his socks and boots back on.

"You need to pay attention to your feet," Lydia admonished him quietly, "have to avoid those blisters." Then, she lay down alongside him, sharing the cot, curling her back against his chest and pulled his arm down over her. He quietly stroked her hair. After a short silence, she heard Simon softly speaking into the universe.

"God in heaven," he said. "Let those on their way to you die mercifully fast on the field. Send your angels to come and get them so they don't linger in pain. Help those who remain here awhile longer to get to us quickly so we can save some lives. Make my hands sure, my judgment sound. Put protection around my beloved wife, the gift you have given me even though I don't deserve her. Don't take your eyes off her since I don't think I'll be able to keep my eyes on her, as much as I would like, over the next couple of days. You know what all of us need and we leave it all in Your hands."

Simon finished his petition, and they lay in the darkness, still in uniform, ready to go at a moment's notice. A few hours into the night, they began to hear the planes somewhere overhead. Thunder began to roll on the hillsides just east of them. Even on the cot, they felt the ground shake. Lydia thought she could hear the whistle of the bombs falling through the air. She could still feel herself curled up on the hillside of dead bodies while dirt and debris rained down on the helmet she had clutched to her head in terror. She repeated Simon's prayer in her heart and sunk back against him. He held her tight against his body and gently stroked her hair in the night.

"So it begins," Lydia whispered, her voice trembled. As they listened to wave after wave of planes whine over the station and felt the earth rumble beneath them, she pulled his strong arm tightly around her.

"Fire and brimstone," Simon said softly. "Just stay close to me... I've got you." This night, they did not sleep.

Chapter 9
Earth Tremors

I t was only hours later, still well before dawn, when the first wave of ambulances tore into the station. The medical corps rolled out of their cots and jumped to work like a well-oiled machine. Within minutes, the three surgical tables held what would be the first of hundreds of wounded. Two additional tables had been crowded into the surgery, where medics who had been added to their staff tended to the less severely injured. The mess tent staff were up as well, keeping food at the ready, if a moment allowed, and coffee constantly brewing. The aerial bombardment in the east did not stop. The sun rose at dawn illuminating the horror below, lines of soldiers firing rifles and stabbing sharp bayonets into vulnerable spots, human bodies falling to the earth. But those inside the surgery did not see the sun rise.

At first, Lydia and Simon worked side by side. The usual chatter of the surgery had been reduced to brief directives of necessity. A nurse and a corpsman now circulated between the five tables. Simon glanced up briefly over his mask at Lydia as they closed scalps and chest wounds and packed stomachs gaping with revealed intestines. Suddenly, the entire tent would shake as bombs struck not far away. Overhead, lanterns would swing from their hooks changing the landscape as they cast swaying shadows. As one explosion fell exceptionally close by, the nurses struggled to stay upright. Linda, circulating, dropped an entire tray of instruments on the ground as she avoided falling into a table. Dismayed, she cried out in frustration only to hear Harold's voice, rising calmly over the din that ensued, saying, "Steady everyone, let's just keep it going." Linda dropped to her knees, retrieving the scattered surgical tools. She felt the ground shake under her palms. Then, clutching the dirty instruments to her chest, she rose back up and headed off to clean them, once again.

Lydia looked up at Simon, who was appraising a deep gash on a man's neck where a bullet had narrowly missed puncturing his vital carotid artery. He was still bleeding. "You need a break, Doctor," she told him.

"Do I?" he said absently in return, his voice weary from the hours that had passed.

Rumbling continued in the near distance, and they paused for literally a second as the instruments on the metal tray rattled in seismic rhythm.

"Yes," Lydia insisted, seeing his hands had slowed with his sutures, and he was delaying his decision about the wound in front of him.

His eyes were bloodshot looking up at her, his face creased with fatigue and sweat. He knew she was right... but this wounded man...

Lydia called over to the next table. "Doctor Lovell!"

Marcus looked up immediately at the sound of her voice calling his name. He was pulling sutures through the skin of a ragged leg wound.

"Nurse Finney?" he returned.

"Could you please—"

"On my way," Marcus said, immediately turning to Marlene assisting him and adding, "can you finish, Nurse Sullivan?"

"You know I can, Doctor!" Marlene declared and all but snatched the needle and snaking loop of suture thread from him... glad for the chance to use every skill the doctors had been teaching the nurses.

Quickly, Marcus washed his hands, leaving his bloody operating apron on, and crossed through to the table where Simon wavered. Marcus saw the artery exposed and throbbing in the wounded man's neck, the blood oozing. He turned to his friend. "Saving this one for me, Doctor Finney?" he joked lightly. "Guess you believed me when we told the Brits I was a vascular surgeon in another lifetime."

Simon lifted his weary eyes to his friend's eyes over the mask. "I won't be too long," he said, relieved, and watched his step carefully as he left the surgery under the swaying light overhead.

Lydia looked at Marcus gratefully as Simon departed. "He wouldn't quit... thank you." She shone a light into the stricken man's neck wound. "There's a bullet in there somewhere."

Marcus peered into the gash. "Can you get more li—"

Lydia directed the flashlight she held in her hand, placing the beam so he could see deeper inside the tattered tissue.

"One of the things I love most about you, Nurse Finney," Marcus said softly, "is you know what a man needs."

"Hmmpf," she scolded under her breath. "This man needs your vascular touch. That carotid is still intact."

He peered in. "It's going to be the devil getting that bullet out of the base of the skull with this shaking going on."

"The bombs are dropping in five-minute intervals," she advised him. "We've counted. We are on minute one."

Marcus shot her a curious look. "And then one for the drop and one to reach us underground?" he said quickly.

Lydia nodded, "Something like that. That's why I called you."

Marcus nodded. "I need you on this side of the table, right here."

She grabbed a handful of tools and scurried around the anesthetist as Marcus turned to him, "Don't let this guy wake up for five minutes under any circumstances. Count it off for me."

On the other side of the table, Lydia squeezed between Marcus and the anesthetist at the patient's head and neck.

Marcus said quietly, "I've got to make this gash just a little bigger to grab the bullet. I can just almost see it. You tie those bleeders off as fast as y—"

She held up the needle already threaded, with the waiting scissors in her left hand.

Shoulder to shoulder with the woman, Marcus took the scalpel in his right hand and opened the wound until they could both see the offending piece of coated lead where the bone had stopped it. The ground beneath them remained still. Marcus pushed a forceps carefully into the opening, past the patient's carotid and back to the base of his skull. He tugged on the bullet, pulled it back, then simultaneously dropped it on the ground and pressed his finger protectively to cover the vital artery. "Go!" he said under his breath.

Lydia's fingers flew, tying off bleeders as she would have stitched up a hole in a delicate hosiery stocking. Marcus shined the flashlight into the gaping wound. "Something is reflecting—" he warned.

"Sixty seconds left," the anesthetist announced worriedly.

"My left upper pants pocket, quickly!" Lydia hissed.

Marcus didn't waste one second. He reached his hand into the pocket of her trousers, and a cold metal object met his fingers. He pulled out a magnet and dropped it into her waiting left hand.

Lydia pushed it into the edge of the opening and watched as a small piece of shrapnel dislodged from out of its hiding place and stuck to the end of the magnet. "Would that be the something?" she whispered as Marcus took the suture from her and quickly sewed off the bleeders underneath. She dabbed at the incision with dry gauze, and they both saw no further oozing. Bullet gone. Wound rinsed. The ground started trembling just as the anesthetist told them, "Time's up."

The table swayed, but Marcus was already closing the neck wound, the man's vital artery intact.

Lydia and Marcus straightened and looked at each other.

"That was—" Marcus started.

"—amazing!" she exclaimed, her eyes sparkling with the emotional rush.

He looked at her eyes over her mask. "I love it when you finish my sentences, Nurse Finney," he said. "Let's wash up."

Marcus and Lydia continued to operate until it was time for Lydia to rotate out to triage. She removed her apron, washed up and stepped out into the daylight they had not seen today. What she saw horrified her.

There were wounded stretched out anywhere that the ground could offer up a two-foot clearance strip. Litter bearers were carting off the dead, one after the other. She saw the patients on the ground, all numbered. Some who could sit were holding their cards in their hands. One of the medics was moving along the rows of patients and tending the light wounds of the "twos" where they sat. Walking wounded were being helped into trucks by orderlies and French and British soldiers. Those trucks would pull out of the station as full trucks pulled into any vacancy, the casualties pulled out on litters or helped down by others waiting. Lydia immediately spied three blue scarves scattered amid the chaos and blessed Gretha for her incredible homespun wisdom.

Lydia was parched with thirst. She quickly made her way to the mess—a cup of cold coffee was placed immediately into her hand when she ducked under the edge of the tent wall—she slugged it down. "We also have tea, mademoiselle," the man told her.

"This is fine," she assured him, grabbing a biscuit and chunk of cheese to stay her hunger and keep her going. The surgery had erased her fatigue, and she knew she was running on an artificial high. Best to make use of the burst of energy because she knew she would crash when it wore off. Quickly, she swung by her tent and saw Simon was up again, no doubt back to the surgery. Her blue dress was still on top of her footlocker, a bright spot of sky blue in an otherwise olive green and brown space. Lydia smiled at the dress, turned the ring on her finger, and felt her energy regroup in a way that did not rely on caffeine or her endocrine system. She headed for the triage area, past the surgery, but stopping inside just long enough to see Simon already at work at one of the tables. As if he could sense her presence, he looked over at the door from the operating table and their eyes met... it was all they needed to keep the anxiety from eating away at them... to keep them going.

Lydia started her rounds of the waiting injured. She started rechecking the soldiers with the number two cards in case their condition was deteriorating. She offered many of them as much water from the canteen at her side as they could take in. Dehydration led to kidney failure and irregular heart rhythms which were more fatal than infection at the moment. She refilled the canteen at a water station and kept going.

She then saw a young man sitting outside of the tarp over the triage, leaning against a tree stump, his head lolling over to one side. A soldier stood over him. Lydia bent down over the man and lifted his face to look at his eyes. He focused them slowly. Lydia saw that he had no number card.

She looked up at the soldier. "Why is this man sitting in the sun like this? Where is his number?"

"Je ne sais pas," the soldier said. "I don't know. He is German."

"Of course he is a German!" she snapped back. "Get him out of this sun... dans l'ombre!"

The soldier reluctantly obeyed and helped her lift the man to move him under the tarp, offering some protection from the direct rays. Lydia opened her canteen and poured a small stream of water into the man's parched mouth. He drank it, coughing at first, then more smoothly before feverishly downing the water she offered. "Danke, danke, fräulein," the man whispered. "Danke."

Lydia did a brief once-over of the man and saw no overt bleeding on his filthy uniform. She lifted one finger and pointed at him, then held out her palm. "You wait," she said, hoping he would understand her sign language. She picked her way through the wounded across the camp to the recovery. Gretha was busy trying to feed a patient in front of her, and Lydia motioned for an orderly to follow her. "What's up, Lydia?" Gretha asked as Lydia approached her.

"Take over that care, please," Lydia directed the orderly who was following, then pulled the other nurse toward the edge of the tent. "Need you outside," she added. "Just for a minute."

Gretha followed her through the wounded to the man now under one of the tarps. "Can you talk to him?" Lydia asked. "I don't think he understands any English or French."

Gretha squatted down in front of the soldier. He was very young. "Ich bin eine Krankenschwester... a nurse..." Gretha said quietly. "My name is Gretha. Wie heißen Sie?"

The man looked up, "Henrich... fräulein."

"Henrich...? Hab keine angst," Gretha reassured him. "Don't be afraid."

"Henrich Miller, fräulein," he said warily.

"Hast du dich verletzt??" she asked him, feeling his arms, his legs.

"Mir geht es gut," the young soldier answered.

"Gut?" she countered, shaking her head in disbelief. "Ich bin eine Krankenschwester," she repeated. "You can tell me."

He looked at the two women hesitating, their blue head-scarves so civilian... and disarming.

Gretha put her hand on his thin shoulder. "Hier wird dir niemand etwas tun... no one will hurt you..."

He was still wary.

Gretha continued gently. "Hast du eine familie? I have a family... eine Kuh und ein paar Hühner... no, actually two cows and some chickens."

The thin face of the soldier relaxed, and he smiled a little.

"Hast du dich verletzt??" Gretha repeated again. "Show us."

He pulled up his shirt, and the area beneath his left rib cage was dark and swollen. The women looked quickly at each other in alarm.

"Ordonné, corpsman!" Lydia shouted. "Gretha, stay with him so he understands we aren't trying to kill the poor man. I'll get a table."

Lydia ran to the surgery. Scanning the room quickly, she saw the various stages of operations underway, all three surgeons up to their elbows in procedures. One of the medics was addressing a compound fracture. It wasn't bleeding. She ordered the table to be cleared and called for anesthesia. All three doctors interrupted what they were doing just long enough to try to find out what was going on as she set up the table. Litter bearers rushed in with Gretha in tow, right behind. They laid the soldier hastily on the table, and the man started to weakly fight them, crying out in German, "Nein! Halt! Nein!" He kicked over an instrument table that went clattering as it fell.

Gretha's voice rose over the din as the corpsmen caught his legs, and she tried to hold the man's arms down, "Hier wird dir niemand etwas tun! Hab keine angst! Hab keine angst!"

"Get him asleep!" Lydia demanded the hesitating anesthetist, who looked over at the chief surgeon questioningly. "His spleen is about to go..." she pleaded as he delayed.

Everyone looked at each other, considering the lifesaving work they were already engaged in, as the sound of the German words put a sudden and alarming hush over the surgery. Unbeknownst to Lydia, Harold had quietly, but quickly told Susannah to keep the patient stable at their table. Harold worked his way over to where Lydia was attempting to cut the young man's shirt and trousers open while he flailed weakly. Harold nodded to the anesthetist, who finally agreed to lower the ether mask over the smooth, young face. The soldier relaxed. Harold saw the concussion injury swelling below the rib cage and took the scalpel Lydia extended toward him.

"He's just a boy," she pleaded.

Doctor Stockton looked down on him. "Yes," he said. "He is." He cut the man's abdomen open while Lydia fell back to allow Alice Miller to take her place. And Lydia fled the tent, Simon's worried eyes watching her depart. There was no time to process what had just happened as Lydia headed to triage.

Night had come again. Fewer trucks rumbled into the station now, but more ambulances kept arriving. Trucks, loaded all the way full, to the cab, lumbered out of camp, carrying patients to field stations behind the front. Suddenly, everyone in the triage area stopped and looked up to the sky; there were no more planes. The ground beneath them was not trembling. Shades had been drawn around the lanterns. Muted flashlights were in the hands of many. No one could see the blue-scarved heads in the darkness, but the nurses continued triage. Two were now outside, just Lydia and Nancy, the usual third nurse having gone to the recovery where the need was greater.

As Lydia bent wearily over the litters, she saw, just ahead, that Nancy was kneeling between two French soldiers who were lying beside each other. There was a curious exchange happening between them.

"Non, mon ami," one man said, lifting his arm.

The other replied, "Non, non mon ami!" and waved the arm away.

The issue seemed to be that one man's card read the number one and the other had the number two. Having deciphered how the card system worked, the first kept trying to convince his friend to take the number one. Lydia watched as Nancy solved the problem by taking the card from the second man and giving him a number one as well. The two men clasped their hands together and continued to wait side by side, contented. Nancy moved off down the dark row as Lydia fought back the tears, knowing that if they started, like the shells, they might never stop falling.

Entering the recovery, exhaustion fell over her. Lydia had been on her feet for almost twenty-four hours and she was staggering. Alice saw her stumble and put out an arm to steady her.

"You've got to go to sleep, girl," she said.

Lydia pushed a stray lock of hair from her eyes. "How's the young German boy?"

"Stable," Alice responded. "So far."

Lydia stared off. "At first, I didn't think anesthesia was going to treat him."

Alice shook her head. "Where do you think they'll send him? Field hospital or prison camp?"

The other sighed. "Maybe both. But how do we know that in twenty years, he won't be the one man capable of forming some kind of peace treaty between two nations that can't figure out their differences? Where is he?" Lydia wondered.

"We put him down at the end of the row. Gretha said the other patients might get upset if he wakes up yelling in German. We're keeping him sedated until he can move out on the next truck. She's staying in recovery until he leaves."

Lydia nodded. "That's sweet of her. She's one of the best 'Feet' in the whole world."

Alice looked worried. "I sure hope, if any of our guys end up in one of their stations, that they're getting the same care. But I don't see how they could... we've got the best right here. The best in the world. I'm glad Doctor Stockton stepped in for him in the surgery. We haven't really talked about triaging any German soldiers that end up with us when we're overwhelmed like this."

Lydia placed her hand on her friend's. "You're right. We talked about triaging people... just people..." Lydia moved off drifting down the row, stopping to check on a few of the men sleeping restlessly.

Then, Sally Winfield pushed the flap of the tent aside, entering the recovery. She went directly down the aisle between the cots, stood before Lydia, and told her in her southern drawl, "Y'all are relieved!"

Lydia lifted tired eyes from a dressing she was in the middle of reinforcing on a patient's foot. "As soon as I finish this, I'll go," she promised.

Sally put both hands on her hips. "You'd better, girl. Get to bed."

After Lydia finished the man's dressing to her satisfaction, she made her way to the one marital tent in the station.

Picking up a towel, she then walked over to the shower in the darkness and stepped inside. She had blood and dirt all over her and urgently needed to wash. There, in the night, she scrubbed every inch of her body again and again. It took a long time to feel clean again. She rolled her shoulder around experimentally. It moved smoothly enough... Simon had seen to it. Would a German medic have sewn her up if they had taken her with Cédric that night on the battlefield? Or would they have just left her out under the sun somewhere to suffer? The boy from today looked to be not a day over fifteen years old. For the first time since her arrival to the continent, Lydia seriously wondered if any of them would make it home.

Wrapped in the clean towel, the woman left the shower and went back to her tent. She found her other set of trousers and a shirt and got ready to return to duty, automatically pulling on socks and boots while perched on her cot. Then, the fatigue took over. She toppled over sideways onto the cot and fell immediately into the sleep of the dead.

When Simon came to their tent later, he lifted Lydia's feet up onto the cot and covered her with a blanket. She didn't stir. He stretched out on the second cot and put his arms behind his head, staring into the dark. Not for the first time, he wished Harold had let Aubert send the nurses back away from the front when they had debated it. He could see the fatigue in everyone's eyes. The rattling bombardment made everything so much worse. Before, when the bombing stopped, they had all known the casualty lines had then been numbered. There was an end. But as the thunder and shaking of the earth went on, hour after hour, the length of the line at the station had grown into a writhing snake, wrapping itself around the surgery and squeezing the energy out of everyone, mentally. Simon wondered how long the team could survive this kind of onslaught without collapsing. He resisted the desire to reach out and touch Lydia in the darkness. God knew that she needed the sleep.

The German soldier weighed on his mind... well, not the boy himself, but their collective response to the youth in the surgery. It shouldn't have mattered to anyone. Simon himself would have changed tables immediately, except for the small fact that someone's liver was literally lying in his hands... still, it was probably better that Stockton had set a precedent. Simon knew that Harold had made the right call and put himself out there to take the case. But even so, why hadn't they been prepared for the probability that prisoners of war would be coming through, in this kind of fighting?

He'd never seen Lydia so agitated as when the German soldier was on the table while she waited to see who would help him. He had never seen her have to beg anyone to help. It unsettled him and made him feel ashamed. No, Simon decided in the darkness, this would never happen again. The doctors would meet with Aubert and the entire team and talk about this as soon as possible. As soon as the station emptied out of casualties enough to have all hands present. But as Simon lay there making this decision, he heard what he did not want to hear... the distant rumble of explosions resuming as dawn returned to the sky. Lydia stirred, hearing the same even in her sleep. She cried out softly. Then Simon did risk waking her. He moved over and lay down behind her on her cot, putting his arm over her protectively. She pushed back into his embrace, and he drifted into what would become a brief light sleep that would not restore his flagging body, but did strengthen his resolve.

No one watched the clock or counted the hours. Personnel moved between the tables carrying bodies, supplies, even tin cups of coffee and chunks of cheese which someone would down quickly, right at the tables, while continuing with whatever they were doing in the surgery. There was little banter between the team as the strain of continuously operating took its toll. Marcus stood over the patient in front of him, puzzling over how relatively few died in the surgery. He arrived at one conclusion. The triage nurses had another number in use... they were employing the number four. Foregone conclusions that some soldiers out there didn't have a chance. Forewarning that death was already imminent and would take time and resources away from some other guy who had a chance to make it, if he could get into their hands in the surgery. Forecasting when the lines of men on litters would be beyond capacity when the bombardments and fighting had no end in sight. Marcus hadn't thought about that aspect of things. Yes, in the surgery and recovery tents, they were doing everything possible to give a guy a chance to live. Outside the tents, the triage nurses were responsible for deciding who wouldn't get the chance. And all of the nurses moved in and out of the triage area. It was a heavy emotional burden to place on the nurses, deciding who had the best chance to live and it worried him now. *At what emotional cost?*

Marcus glanced up toward Sally Winfield, currently rotated in and working with him across their surgical table. "You're from the south, aren't you, Nurse Winfield?" he asked her.

She nodded, her blue eyes questioning over the mask. "Yes, Doctor…"

"Ahhh," Marcus said. "Clamp, please—"

"Why do you ask, Doctor Lovell? Do you like the south? Have you been there?" she wondered, relieved to be thinking of home.

"Once. I was at a bar… and the man sitting next to me had a beer in his hand, already half empty," Marcus nodded. "He told me, 'There once was a bartender in Dallas whose beer tap had turned rather callous. When the flow ceased to come, he said, don't switch to rum. In Texas, we just use our phal—'"

"Don't you dare say it!" Sally protested with an embarrassed laugh.

Marcus was glad when he saw her eyes light up a bit.

The anesthesiologist chimed in. "Well, after all, it is a medical term, Nurse."

She protested. "I don't care. There are decent women present in here."

Marcus looked at her. "More than decent, Nurse Winfield. Exceptionally, remarkably, decent women."

She blushed under his unwavering gaze. "We try," she admitted. "Even here…"

"How long are you in the surgery? Forceps—"

She looked up at some invisible clock while handing him the instrument. "Probably another hour or two till I rotate out. Why do you ask?"

Marcus took the offered tool. "I was just wondering if you'd ever been to Austin? Because 'I heard there once was a school marm in Austin who took off her shoes, and she lost them. Now under whose bed, it was oft heard she said, did I...'"

Harold, working at the next table, overheard, smiling under his mask. He thought of the storytelling evening recently, prompted by Nurse Bernstein, whose wisdom had led to far more than her contribution of the valuable blue headscarves. The station was sorely in need of a morale booster, and it had been right under his nose all the time. He chuckled to himself in the midst of his own exhaustion. Sometimes, the simplest things...

When the shelling finally stopped, the mess tent turned into a theater. The talent possessed by the people manning the station was surprising. One could sing. Another played the drums exceptionally well on Cook's pots and pans, using spoon handles as drumsticks. Some had a story to tell. Some had a poem, usually less ribald than the ones Marcus concocted in the wicked recesses of his mind. They laughed and clapped in appreciation for each member of the team who dared to get up and stand on the box platform acting as a stage. The side of the mess tent was open to the side of the recovery only ten feet away. Some of the wounded, and certainly the nurses moving through recovery, could overhear in the near distance. And at the end of the evening, Harold informed the talent that they had a week to practice their next act, as he intended that this show become an every-Friday-night affair, unless the war chose Saturday instead.

Everyone felt better when leaving for sleep that night... except for Cook, who checked his pots for unwanted dents. Simon and

Lydia had enjoyed the talent show enormously, the way laughter pushed the war from their minds. The couple walked back through the camp, to their tent, feeling momentarily relaxed. It was a welcome relief. Simon sat down on one of their cots expectantly. Lydia hesitated, standing close by, but not joining him.

"Simon," she started, seeing that familiar look in his eyes that he reserved just for her. "I feel so good at the moment. But I've been in the recovery all day."

He looked at her steadily, internally fighting a losing battle to take back command of his own body. "Of course, Lydia," he said, his disappointment evident. "I understand."

She took his face in her hands and kissed his head. "No, you don't," she countered.

He took her hands in his own and kissed them, trying to hide his feelings from her. "You may always say no to me, Lydia. Don't ever hesitate to tell me when you're tired and have been on your feet all day. That doesn't change a thing for me. After all, if I can wait five days out of every month, what's waiting one?"

She stroked his hair, leaned over and kissed his lips softly, letting her own lips part and linger over his, immensely enjoying teasing him and hearing the small groan she elicited from the man in response. "You don't understand," she repeated. "I don't want to say no to you... I was just going to say I need a shower. And I was wondering if perhaps, just maybe, you would care to join me?"

Simon jumped to his feet and reached for their towels, stopping abruptly as she put her hand on his arm. "What?" he said quickly, desperately hoping she had not changed her mind.

"Though, the shower is rather small," she said, eyes twinkling.

That night, they lay entwined together on one of their cots. There was a cooler turn to the night air. Simon was having trouble sleeping again while Lydia dreamt against his shoulder. He was still trying to absorb the reality that this woman was the wife he had never thought he would find. He'd assumed that, like Doc Albright, he would remain a single, country doctor, dedicated to tending to the people in his community... but this woman... he drifted off...

He awoke again, not to the coolness in the air, but to the memory, the feeling of washing her body with his hands, rinsing her with the lukewarm water of the tank, watching the small streams of water roll from the bucket down between the curves and peaks of her form. And in turn, she had washed him, the magic of her hands transforming the small, enclosed space of the shower into a universe without boundaries. How was it, he wondered, for the umpteenth time, that it could be the same biology with such wonderfully different results? Perhaps that was the mystery of marriage, the mystery of... becoming one.

All too soon, Simon heard the bombardment beginning another round of engagement in the battle for Somme. The enormous appetite of the war was not yet satisfied. Lydia's eyes opened in the dim light of dawn. She had heard it, too. She rolled over to straddle Simon, running her fingers through the curls on his chest with both of her hands. In response, the man reached up and fingered the waves of hair falling forward, off her shoulders. And as he pulled her down to him, they both were aware of an urgency, a need to meet and to remain joined together for as long as possible. There was a feeling of dread in the air.

Chapter 10

Schism

"Man, that was close," Marcus muttered under his breath as an explosion rocked the surgery tent.

"Think it was theirs or ours?" Susannah asked softly, as she helped the surgeon finish an amputation to a soldier's lower leg.

"Theirs, I think," he added, "but you know the saying, 'Yours, mine and ours—one big, unhappy family.'"

Susannah looked up at him. "There is one happy family at this station."

He glanced up. "You mean the Doctor and Mrs. Finney?" he returned. "Yes, they do seem rather happy together."

Susannah nodded as they moved to the sink to wash their hands. "I do mean them, of course, Doctor," she said, rolling the bar of soap between her hands and making as much of a lather as the military soap was capable. "I envy them... what they have."

Marcus reached for a towel. "Well, don't, Nurse Boyton," Marcus advised her. "Where there is much to gain, there is equally as much to lose."

She looked up after him as he turned to go back to the operating table. *Apparently, Lydia and Simon thought it was worth the risk,* she thought. It was time for her to rotate to recovery and she nodded to those remaining as she left the tent.

Marcus watched her go, her blonde hair tied up under the blue scarf. His brows furrowed for a moment, but he shook it off as quickly as the ground shook beneath them. Another casualty arrived at his table with a gash in his flank exposing a ragged kidney—*I like Suzie, but it's too much risk,* Marcus fell back into his spiraling thoughts. *To find something and then risk losing it all in a place like this! Why would anyone want to up the ante like that? And I can see that Suzie wants more... A real commitment? But... if Simon had not been here... if it had just been me and Lydia... would I have made that same leap of faith?* He honestly wasn't sure, and that awareness bothered him deeply.

"How's it going in here?" Susannah entered the recovery, making her way toward Lydia.

Lydia welcomed her with a smile. "No room at the inn," she said, "but that's nothing new now, is it!"

Susannah paused for a minute, appraising the two long rows of patients in front of them. Then, she looked back to her friend. "Hey, take a break," she offered.

Lydia stood, after ensuring that a soldier had gotten enough of the cook's best broth. "No, thanks. I think I'll stick around; there's a lot to do here."

Susannah bent over to check a man's chest bandage. "There's always a lot to do here," she murmured. The soldier looked up at her and reached for a blonde strand of hair that had escaped from under the blue scarf.

"Nurse?" his British accent identifying him, since his uniform had been reduced to a general drab army tee shirt and trousers, after his surgery.

Susannah was concerned. "Yes, soldier?"

"I don't know what you're doing here," the man said quietly.

Susannah touched his cheek gently. "I'm tending to your wound," she replied gently.

"You shouldn't be here," he said, a haunted look in his eyes, as the ground beneath them trembled. "They're coming for us. They aren't far over the hill."

Suzie placed a firm hand on his forehead. "You're shipping out on the next truckload to a field hospital, soldier. They are not going to get you."

He took her hand. "No, but they might get you."

Gently, Susannah placed the soldier's hand back onto his chest. "It'll be okay, soldier. You are ordered to focus on getting well."

The two women moved down the row, cot by cot, as some of the wounded were picked up by litter bearers to take them to the waiting trucks and others assisted those who could, to walk to the vehicles. Susannah took Lydia's arm. "Isn't it good to see them leave?" she asked wistfully. "More of them leave than get buried..."

"And some are still walking, sort of," Lydia replied. "Yes, it is good." She looked around the recovery and said, "This is the quietest place in the whole camp, you know?"

Susannah nodded. "And the simplest. No decisions of who's first, second, third. No poking instruments in people's body parts. Just feed them, change their bandages, wash them up, comfort them, listen to them..."

Lydia agreed. "But we lose some here, too, and it breaks my heart... when we've tried so hard... and it still isn't enough."

Susannah nodded. "You mentioned that once before, about doing everything right and people still die, and doing everything wrong and they still live. Do you still think there is some higher power determining all of this? After what we've seen?"

Lydia moved a bandage tray next to a young man whose head was bound up. "Yes, I do," she said. "The same God who brought me here, who led me to meet Si—Doctor Finney... He's still here, seeing all of this mess."

Susannah looked over from the next cot, where she was changing the bandage on what was left of a man's arm. "Do you ever think you made a mistake getting married here, Lydia? That maybe it was something driven by, you know, the passions of war, as they say? I mean, really... you went off to get supplies and came back married. Talk about sudden! How can anyone know in such a short period of time if someone is the right one, for forever?"

Lydia tied off the bandage she was working on, slid past Susannah in the aisle, and appraised the next man's wound before motioning for an orderly to take the man out to one of the transport trucks. "I'm not sure, Suzie," Lydia said softly. "When I'm with him... I'm complete. Just knowing he's nearby over there in the surgery, I'm complete. That's all I... what the...?"

They both turned at the roar of trucks skidding into the station. "Those are the British!" Lydia exclaimed.

The two women ran from the recovery at the arrival of the British CCS. A few of their team were wounded. Lydia searched through the faces for David Winston, who had come to see them weeks ago. Finding him in the confusion was going to be difficult.

She left Susannah to help some of the British medical staff as they limp into the recovery.

"Doctor Winston, what on earth happened?" Lydia exclaimed, pulling the man aside when she finally located him in the confusion.

He looked haggard. "Nurse... Finney, isn't it? The married one? Our post was overrun when the line shifted. We were ordered to pull back, had to leave all of our equipment. We came here, where we can at least lend a hand; it's all we've got left. The casualties will all be coming this way."

Lydia steered him toward the mess, her head swimming with this new information. "First, get something to eat. You look exhausted. I'll find Doctor Stockton." She left the man standing in the opening of the mess with others of their unit and ran for the surgery. Ducking her head into the tent, she noted Simon and Marcus and two medics at the operating tables. She put a mask over her mouth and wiggled through the staff to where Simon was deep into repairing a chest wound. Coming to his side, she told him quickly of Winston's arrival with his team.

"God knows we can use them," Simon exclaimed. "Stockton's done for... in his tent asleep... barely made it there. You'd better go straight to Aubert."

"Me?" Lydia exclaimed in surprise. Then, she nodded. "Of course... Lieutenant Aubert."

Simon could scarcely take the time to watch her leave as his patient's wound was critical.

Lydia hurried to the headquarters tent finding Lieutenant Aubert on the phone as she knocked, and an aide motioned her inside. Lydia had never been in the company commander's tent before. She was astonished by how military it appeared, with maps and file cabinets and well-ordered manuals lined up.

"Yes, what do you want?" Aubert said quickly. "Wait! Aren't you—the Blackwell nurse?"

"Lydia Finney," she corrected him quickly.

"Whatever." He called his aide back in the tent, but turned to her again, distracted. "Well? What is it, Nurse, and quickly. Germans are moving."

She nodded. "Yes, sir, I know. The British CCS just arrived. They're in the mess, Lieutenant."

Aubert turned to the aide. "Bring one of them here—someone in command—we need information."

Lydia hesitated, not sure of the protocol.

Aubert looked at her, "Well? Is there something else, Mrs. Finney? And don't ask for a honeymoon because you won't get it! You're lucky you're still here."

Lydia flushed with sudden anger and clenched her jaw to keep from misspeaking. *Lucky is not the term I would use for it today*!

The man saw it. "You are dismissed," and called for another aide.

She strode back to the recovery, fuming... not even noticing the ground rolling again beneath her feet. She did see the trucks, a convoy, full of wounded, leaving for a field hospital, and she was grateful of that. Reentering the recovery, Lydia could only think of how insufferable Aubert could be.

Linda registered her expression immediately, even as she was busy directing some of the British medical team who had come, offering extra hands. "You okay?" she asked quickly, in passing.

"Yes. Do you need me?" Lydia asked.

"Not with all of this extra help."

"I'll head to the surgery then," she told the other nurse. "There are wounded coming... lots of them."

"So, what else is new..." Linda looked at her carefully. "Try not to bite anyone's head off."

Lydia rewrapped her hair in her blue scarf. "I'll be sweet as a lamb."

With so many new faces in the station, she was grateful to be able to quickly find the blue scarves of the nurses, amidst the military brown, green, and grey of everyone else. The amputation table outside had a companion table next to it, with a medic, an anesthetist... occasionally a nurse. Lydia entered the surgery and took her time at the wash station, willing her anger to rinse away along with the dirt. Did Aubert think that she felt entitled to special treatment, now that she was married to Simon? Neither she nor Simon had missed a single beat in their service to the war. Could Aubert be so blind to what the medical staff had been doing under his leadership for these many months? Were the nurses so looked down upon by the man? She had to be missing something; she closed her eyes and replayed the scene in her mind. Then she remembered how Aubert's hand trembled when he was holding the field phone and then when trying to pick up the sheaf of papers on his desk. She wondered if he had been drinking... or worse, was he ill? Everyone in the station, from the lieutenant to the cooking staff, was exhausted and overwhelmed. And now a slew of new faces had arrived at the station needing to be organized and commanded under him...

Lydia looked for where she was needed and scanned for Simon. He was not there, but Doctor Stockton had returned after a much needed rest. She took her place at his side, and the corpsman moved off for a break. Alice Miller was circulating and nodded to her.

"Nurse Finney," Harold acknowledged her. "Glad you could join us. What's it like out there?"

"The British have come into the station. The German army forced them back. They evacuated without their equipment. The lieutenant is trying to figure out what to do with them."

"Hm, not hard to figure that out," Harold said quietly. "We've got a bowel here, Nurse."

Lydia nodded and set to the difficult task of looking for shrapnel in the open abdomen of the anesthetized soldier. She pulled out the magnet from her pocket and started lifting small pieces of metal splinters from the open cavity.

Harold raised his eyebrows. "Where did you nurses learn that trick?"

"The British, remember? When they first came to us, they talked about it—thought we might have even come up with the idea. Aubert got them for us."

"That so?" Harold mused while tying a loop of bowel together. "He's a smart man if he listens to all of you. Such a simple idea... a magnet..."

She looked at him. "I wish lead bullets were magnetic."

Harold shook his head. "No, you don't. I can find the bullets. But those sharp fragments of shrapnel worm their way in and cause all kinds of havoc later on, internal bleeding and the like. I wonder how many of these young men have to be reopened back at the field hospitals just because of fragments—"

For a long minute... Lydia could hear, nothing.

There was no sound in the... where on earth was she? Wincing in pain, she pushed a heavy metal table just enough to slide out from under it and realized she was on the ground. It was completely dark. She reached out a hand and felt soft bodies... forceps... trays... something sharp cut her hand. Vaguely, she thought it must be a scalpel. She smelled ether leaking out into the trapped air. The canvas of the tent weighed down on her. She started to crawl, feeling for the edge of the tent that had collapsed around them. Then, sound began to return to her awareness, slowly... then the moans and cries of others rose to a crescendo in her ears. A shaft of light hit her, blinding her for a minute. Hands lifted her to her feet, and someone asked, "Nurse, are you okay?" She struggled to stand up and nodded, bewildered.

Lydia looked at the disaster all around her. The rows of triaged wounded were no more. The mess tent lay hundreds of feet away in a pile of canvas. The recovery tent was blown away, and cots and bodies were strewn everywhere across the ground.

"Oh, my dear God! Dear Lord!" she breathed horrified. *Where was Simon?* A huge hole gaped in the ground in the center of the station. *The wounded... the nurses. Where was Simon? Where was Marcus?* Getting her bearings, Lydia tried to think.

Soldiers, who were able, started laying those they thought were still alive onto the ground in an area blasted free of debris. Those presumed dead were already being carried to the other side of the crater by others. She saw their cook standing, stunned, in the middle of the debris of the mess. He was holding a pot in his hand. Lydia saw soldiers and corpsmen peeling away the surgery tent walls, exposing the damaged contents to the light. The gaping hole in the ground was no more than three feet from the tent. Why one tent had collapsed, and the others were blown off, she could not fathom. Someone was helping Harold to his feet. He was alive, Lydia tried to slow her breathing. She looked for Alice Miller and found her lying in the middle of the surgical tables, helped her to get up realizing that, in some way, the thick walls and surgical tables had protected them from the concussion of the shell that had detonated with fury.

"Alice," she called her name several times. "Can you hear me? Can you move?" *Where was Marcus?*

Alice started to nod. "I think so," Alice finally said, clutching her friend's hand. "Anyone else?"

"Doctor Stockton's okay, I think." *But where was Simon?* Lydia scanned the faces of those getting to their feet and finding their bearings.

Lydia pulled an orderly to her. "Gather up as much bandage material as you can possibly find and pile it right over there," she directed him, helping him to focus. She pulled another toward her so his eyes met hers. "Gather up as many of the instruments as you can and pile them up right next to the bandages. We need two tables set up right out in the open. Anywhere you can find a clear space."

Lydia felt a hand on her shoulder, turning to see Marlene Sullivan—they hugged each other hard.

"I'll start checking the wounded over there," Marlene said.

"I'll get a couple of tables pulled together," Alice said, noticing that she was still holding a needle with suture hanging from it. She hadn't realized it was ridiculously still in her hand, as if ready for an invisible patient in front of her.

"I've got to find Simon," Lydia whispered, and they nodded. She picked her way through debris to where their tent used to be and saw that all of the medical staff tents were flattened. Marcus was just now crawling out from under the doctors' tent and Lydia helped him to his feet.

"What the hell..." he exclaimed, reaching up for her.

"Exactly," Lydia told him as she steadied him, and he pulled her into his arms, grateful she was still alive.

"Are you hurt, Lydia?" he asked her quickly, glancing over her body.

"No, I'm okay. It must have been an accidental drop, or a whole lot more would have hit us. Doctor Stockton is over... there... where we're trying to get the wounded collected. I think that's... yes, it's the British Doctor Earl-Johns... and looks like Doctor Winston, too. Thank God for that! I've got to go, Marc! I need to find Simon!"

Marcus shook his head to clear it. "He stopped by to wake me up. Said he was going over to the truck convoy to sign off on some casualties being transferred out, and then Aubert wanted to see him about the Brits."

"Okay, I'll head over to... where the trucks were... I think..."

"Lydia, are you sure you're..."

She waved him away, leaving Marcus to pull himself together and went in search of the trucks and ambulances had been lined up to depart. Several vehicles were turned over on their sides—she glanced in—empty. *Thank goodness.* Where the recovery had been was a tangled mess of canvas, cots, ropes, and moaning bodies. Lydia pulled cots off of the fallen, rolling some of the patients onto them so they at least were not lying directly in mud and grass... they didn't look dead. That was important. Gretha found her there. The two worked their way through the clutter, pulling Charlotte out of a tangle of debris. They found Linda staring off into space, not visibly wounded but not moving, just looking ahead. Gretha knelt down beside her, checking their companion, they needed to move her to a more sheltered location.

"Anybody see Suzie?" Charlotte asked. They scanned the crowd of people working through the disaster... searching for blue scarves. Far beyond the mess, they saw two who were assisting others. The work of reassembling the camp was already underway, with both French and British soldiers pitching in. It wasn't the first time either group had had to start over from scratch. The casualty clearing stations started over with every single move... just not with so much broken or so many wounded needing care at the same time. The nurses saw that tent poles were already being erected, in new locations.

Charlotte looked up at the sky. "My God," she breathed. "It's going to be night soon. What are we going to do?"

"What we always do," Lydia reassured her. "Treat the wounded."

She then went in search of Aubert and Simon. *Simon...where are you?*

Lydia found the remnants of Aubert's command tent, the file cabinet tossed aside like a wastebasket, the wooden desk splintered, and an aide hurriedly scooping up valuable military papers as they danced along the ground in the evening breeze. "Where is Lieutenant Aubert?" she asked him quickly.

"Je ne sais pas," he said. "I have lost sight of the lieutenant. Someone carried him away."

"Was he alive?" she asked quickly.

"Je ne sais pas, l'infirmière," the aide repeated, catching a few pages.

"Was he alone? Was, was Doctor Finney with him? Tell me quickly!" she demanded.

"Non, mademoiselle. He was carried off alone. Or maybe there was another. I do not know." The man was no help at all. Lydia looked in every direction. If she knew her husband at all, he would go where the wounded were—he would find where they were being treated—he would be looking for her, and he would know she would be where the wounded were being treated. *What in God's great name am I doing way over here?*

Lydia ran back to where the British doctors were rallying around an impromptu surgery being set up by lantern light, under a hastily erected tarp for some protection against the coming night. Lydia found Harold Stockton and took his arm.

"What is it, Nurse Finney?" he asked, his mind running in a thousand different directions.

"Lieutenant Aubert is wounded, I believe, or so his aide said... not sure if he's still alive," Lydia reported.

Harold Stockton looked up at Doctor Winston, "You'd better find your own station commander, Doctor. If he's alive, he's calling the shots now."

David nodded and went in search of the captain who ran their station. Harold looked at the woman still standing next to him. "Have you found Doctor Finney?" he looked worried.

She shook her head, unable to speak. It was growing dark.

"Find a flashlight and a corpsman and go look for him," Harold told her. "You there! Do you speak English?"

"Yes," came the reply. "I am Belgian, with the British. I am also a doctor."

"Then for heaven's sake, set up a table over here and get to work."

Lydia walked back into her nightmare. In the darkness, with her flashlight, a corpsman at her side, and the debris of the explosion all around them, she searched for Simon. They looked through the faces of the dead which were piled east of the blast crater. At least these bodies had been laid side by side respectfully, not tangled together in a mat of broken human remains. She recognized the faces of some that they had operated on just earlier today. Many others she did not know... they were faces in the darkness, faces that would no longer see the sun when it came up in the morning. With each body they examined, Lydia's breath would falter... until she saw for certain that it was not Simon. After an eternity of praying before each one that God would not let it be Simon, Lydia and the corpsman came to the end of the rows of the dead. Hope began to flicker in her again. If Simon was not among the dead, then he still must be among the living... somewhere...

They circled around the hole in the ground and started going through the wounded being tended by the team from the British station. They were efficiently moving patients into triage. A few lanterns shone in the hands of the medical teams that moved methodically through those waiting on the ground. Lydia saw lanterns clustered together over the makeshift surgical tables. The doctors were operating quickly, trying to contain the damage done. Anesthetists, reduced to dropping ether onto cloths to place over a patient's nose and mouth, were busy at the head of the tables, listening with stethoscopes to heartbeats and lung sounds, relying on what they could hear more than what they could see.

The anxiety and fear Lydia had been experiencing was turning into something she had never experienced before—despair. *Dear God, do not take him from me already*, she pleaded with the Almighty. *Not when we have just found each other here in this hell. Please, God in heaven, hear my prayer. Not that I am any more in need of my loved one than any other of those lying here... and am surely less deserving... but please don't take him from me so soon.*

The corpsman stayed with her as they found Susannah in the darkness of the triage. Susannah gave Lydia a quick hug. "Still haven't found him?" she pressed.

Lydia shook her head, her eyes hollow with the agony of uncertainty.

"I'll keep an eye out here," Suzie promised her. "If he's brought to triage, I'll send for you immediately."

Lydia rubbed her eyes. "I can't think; I can't focus."

"I know, honey," Susannah comforted her. "I know. You better go tell Doctor Stockton we're still looking."

The lights of the new surgery grew brighter as medics and corpsmen pulled together to construct more tables outside the tent. Lydia left the corpsman to continue searching in the darkness of the triage. She stumbled over toward the surgery, glad for its familiarity, glad for the simplicity of purpose... to save life...

Through the side of the hastily constructed tent, she saw Harold already at work and Marcus hovering over another table under the light of lanterns. She saw Alice moving in between them, handing out the instruments they had washed and made serviceable. She saw the water reservoir back up in place, the familiar wash station. And in the overflow outside that structure, operating in the night with just lamp light overhead, she saw the new doctors willing to jump in immediately to help the wounded. *Dear God, what would we have done without them today? How many more would have died?*

It was their dedication to purpose that drew Lydia back to her senses. She picked up her pace toward Harold and Marcus to let them know that she was still searching. As she wove her way through the waiting wounded, the litter bearers were busy in the dark, picking up casualties and carrying away others, like ants in a steady stream.

Lydia jumped out of the way of two men hurriedly carrying a soldier toward the temporary surgical tent. Stumbling backward, she found herself by the outside tables where surgeons were also hard at work under lantern light. Terrified, Lydia recognized Simon, being lifted onto one of the outer tables. A surgeon was bending over him, saw in hand. Lydia pushed past an orderly, knocking him off balance in her haste to intervene. "Stop!" she screamed, seeing Simon prostrate on the table. "Stop!"

The surgeon, someone unknown to her, paused, his hand raised above Simon's knee. Lydia sprinted to them, grabbing the man's arm. He shook her off sharply. "What are you doing, Nurse!" he demanded.

"Stop, please!" Lydia begged the doctor.

He pushed her to the ground. "You're hysterical. I'm trying to save this man's life!" he barked.

Lydia, summoning all of her remaining strength, screamed into the night, "Marcus!!!"

Inside the tent, Marcus heard the scream. He knew her voice. He heard the terror. He dropped everything, running toward the sound.

Jumping back up to her feet, Lydia threw herself over Simon's body, a medic attempted to pry her loose as she gripped the edge of the table. From the corner of her eye, she saw Marcus running toward them. "Marcus! Stop them!" she implored. "It's Simon!"

Marcus immediately assessed the situation, focused in on the bone saw and stayed the surgeon's hand, pushing the saw away from Simon.

"This is my patient!" the man barked at Marcus in confused disbelief. "For God's sake, let me save his life. The leg has to come off."

Marcus whipped around the table, grabbed the man, and in one swift move, placed the saw to his neck. "If you touch this man, I will cut your throat," Marcus pronounced coldly.

The other surgeon lifted both hands and took a step back. "Fine then, let him die,"

"This man is one of our surgeons," Marcus stated, "and my best friend."

Lydia looked up at Marcus, her face white with fear. It took her a second to register that Marcus was there, taking over... to release her grip on the table where she was bent protectively over Simon's still body. Marcus took hold of both of her hands.

"Let me have him, Lydia," he said quietly.

She nodded.

"Get me light over here," Marcus ordered the corpsman, who stood stunned for a second before jumping to action. "Get me a scalpel and clamps." He peered over Simon's leg, his pant leg cut open, the compound fracture exposed, his tibia a protruding jagged spear pointing up toward the night sky. "Get me another lantern, wash the whole leg... now... move!"

Lights emerged from somewhere; instruments arrived, from somewhere. Marcus scarcely looked up as he carefully made a long cut down the inside of Simon's right leg. The man beneath his hands stirred. "For God's sake, someone put him under!" he said, not stopping what he was doing, opening the leg, exposing muscle and bone.

Lydia gripped Simon's hand and whispered in his ear. "I'm here, Simon, I'm right here. Don't you let go."

Marcus and Lydia realized, at the same moment, that Susannah was the one holding out the instruments at their side. She had heard her friend scream and quickly ran to the new surgery area, scooping up tools and coming to their aid.

Marcus was speaking out loud, more to himself than to them. "The artery looks okay. There's some bleeding, yes, but the bone, let's see... corpsman, grab his foot and, when I say, give me some traction down there. Do not pull until I tell you, understood? Do not pull until I say!"

"Yes, sir," the corpsman replied, taking hold of Simon's foot, and waiting.

"Lydia," Marcus looked up. "Go wash up, quickly!"

She ran to the spigot, frantically scrubbed her dirty hands, fingers, and nails, and ran back to the table outside of the tent with them dripping wet.

Marcus looked straight at her. "Here's what I want you to do. The light isn't the greatest. Can you feel the pulsation there? That's the tibial artery, and there are the nerves running alongside. I need you to be the retractor, to get your fingers in there right under that muscle and bundle of arteries and nerves there and pull them back; protect them as I pull the bone back into alignment. If the bone rips that artery, he will bleed to death unless we cut his leg off. So squeeze those lovely, long fingers of yours right in there, there's not much room."

She nodded, letting him guide her fingers to where they needed to be. Marcus positioned his own fingers over the jagged tibial bone ends and said to Suzie, "Be ready with the clamps if this goes bad and we lose the luxury of choice."

Susannah nodded.

"Everyone ready?" Marcus said, "Now, slowly pull his foot, from the heel."

The corpsman began to pull on the man's leg with a steady draw down while Marcus guided the upper and lower bone pieces farther apart but back onto the same plane so that he could line them up...

"Keep going," Marcus breathed, angling up the irregular edges until they looked like pieces of a puzzle ready to snap back together. "Now, very slowly, release the pressure on his foot, just a little.

Let's see if this thing holds. Looks like it's lining up... Lydia, ease your fingers out of there, let the muscle slide back into place—No, wait, where's that artery... okay, okay, ease the muscle back... there you go, now let me take it from here... Suz, do we have a good pulse in his foot?"

"We do, Doctor," she whispered.

"We won't know if there is nerve damage until he wakes up. Get me full leg splints."

"We don't have any leg spl—" Susannah started.

Marcus turned to the corpsman at Simon's foot. "You, take one of those litters and break the damn thing in half. We need the poles."

"Wash it out, Suzie, and pack the incision with Dakins and gauze."

Between the four of them, they raised Simon's leg in unison, slid the folded canvas under it and the wooden poles alongside it.

"Find something I can tie this with," Marcus told the corpsman. "Rope, anything."

By the time the man returned, Marcus was calling for litter bearers. "This leg may not be moved for any reason. Once we get him on a litter, he stays on a litter. Do you understand me? This leg does not move unless I say it moves."

They nodded as Marcus helped them transfer Simon onto a litter to be carried over to the new recovery tent. The orderlies lifted the litter as one, carefully picking their way across the camp to where Simon would be cared for post-op.

Before turning to follow the orderlies who carried her husband, Lydia turned to Marcus, he was breathing slowly, deeply after holding his breath for what had felt like an eternity. Lydia went to him and he opened his arms. She leaned against his chest, softly whispering, "Thank you... thank you... thank you..."

Marcus held her there, at the foot of the table. He didn't need to warn her that it might not work, that Simon might never walk again, that infection might set in, that his leg might still need to be severed at the knee. He didn't need to warn her because she already knew. But he had at least given Simon a chance. Lydia finally looked up and kissed Marcus gently on the cheek before turning to catch up with her husband.

The Belgian surgeon who was operating at the next table said, "I wonder how many soldiers died while you were taking the time to do all that."

"We'll never know, will we?" Marcus replied quietly. "But I do know that one is still alive..." Then, he returned to the tent to take his place back at the table beside Harold. And Susannah went back to do triage in the darkness, pondering everything that just happened, her heart heavy with an empty longing.

Chapter 11
Waking Up

Inside the newly erected recovery, Lydia sat on a crate next to the cot where Simon lay supine, remaining on the litter as ordered. She had told the other nurses that she would take recovery duty for a few days so she could be near him and monitor the status of his wound. Marcus had determined it was safe to stop the frequent laudanum that had been keeping Simon from moving. When Simon began to stir, she rushed to his side to help him wake. Sitting next to him now, Lydia stroked his beard and kissed his lips, offering words, and her presence, for comfort. When his eyes opened, he was confused, looking up at the large tent peak overhead. Lydia motioned for Linda, who stopped what she was doing to come down the aisle of cots to join them.

"Ah, the patient wakes!" Linda said softly, noticing Doctor Finney's eyes attempting to open.

"Would you mind telling Doctor Lovell?" Lydia asked the other. "Or stay with Doctor Finney, and I'll go."

"I'll go find him," she assured her friend. "But he's been a little testy lately. If he's asleep in his tent, I'll just leave my calling card."

Lydia nodded and looked back at Simon, who was now staring at her. "Boy!" he complained. "Some nightmare!"

"No, my love," Lydia said very softly. "It wasn't a dream." She stroked his hair gently. "You have been sedated."

Simon tried to clear his mind. He attempted to reach out to her, but she laid a hand on his shoulder.

"You have to stay down," she told him, pushing against him gently. "You have a fractured leg."

He looked at her and then down at his leg, carefully positioned, between two poles with rope holding them in place. "I can't have a fractured leg," he informed her. "I've got surgery."

"Not today, my love," she countered, still brushing his cheek with the back of her fingers. "Dear God, you nearly scared the life right out of me."

Simon closed his eyes, trying to remember. "What happened?"

"A bomb detonated in camp, by the surgery, blew everything up. And you were injured in the explosion."

He searched his memory, but had no recollection of the day. "How many did we lose?"

Lydia sighed. "I don't know, honestly. Lieutenant Aubert was killed... and many others, I'm afraid."

Simon looked straight at her as his head cleared somewhat. "Marcus? Stockton? The nurses?"

"Our team is okay. Manageable injuries and concussions. The British are here, and they have taken charge of the station. Captain Adam Thornwall is their station commander. He says the fighting for Somme is probably soon over... it'll be too cold to fight soon, anyway. The battles are lessening in size and are not as often."

"Did anyone win?" he grunted, unsuccessfully trying to shift his position on the cot.

"It depends, is six miles of ground considered a win?"

"No one won," he concluded. "And no one lost, except the ones who died."

"Maybe so," she agreed.

"My leg, what was…" Simon started, then saw his friend enter the recovery and come directly down the aisle of cots to the one he occupied.

Marcus clasped his friend's hand. "Good to see you awake, Simon! Ready to go dancing?" he asked.

"Not with you! You have two left feet." It was a good sign to hear Simon ready to banter.

Marcus frowned at Lydia. "You nurses have been telling on me? To the patients?" he teased.

She smiled at him warmly. "This particular patient wants to know what his surgeon has done for him," she said.

"I'll itemize the bill," he countered. Marcus looked around for something to sit on, Lydia saw it, she stood and motioned to him. "Ah, the box step!" Marcus added. "I can do that one." He sat down on the box crate next to Simon, looking at him steadily.

Simon returned the look evenly. "That bad, huh?"

Marcus said, "Well, it depends on your point of view, really. You had an incredibly gifted surgeon open your leg, manipulate a hellish realignment of tibial bones, expertly navigate past your tibial arteries and nerves, and then leave you with the gift of an open wound. The tibia is, however, aligned. You must not move."

Simon closed his eyes. "I'm useless then."

"Oh, Simon," Lydia whispered…

"To the army," Simon said, explaining. "They'll ship me out."

Lydia shot a look of alarm over to Marcus, and he met her look evenly.

Marcus stroked his chin. "Well, that's actually something we need to discuss. At the moment, as your surgeon and your doctor, I have instructed the British army that you may not be moved. I would prefer your artery not be severed by a jolt from an army truck hitting a pothole in the road."

Lydia sighed, relief washing over her; Marcus noted it. "As your friend," Marcus continued. "I am ambivalent. After the bone heals, or at least begins to heal, you would benefit from the therapy at a field hospital, but I am not ready to have my friend escape the rigors of war just yet, and there is nothing that a field hospital can offer you immediately that we can't offer you right here, if we're careful about it."

Simon lay there, still, absorbing everything Marcus was saying and everything he was not saying out loud. *Will I ever walk again?*

"Just get me some crutches," Simon said out loud. "I can walk with crutches."

Marcus put his hand on his friend's shoulder. "Not now, you can't, Simon. No weight bearing whatsoever," Marcus said. "Spare the rod, spoil the child. The rods stay in place right where they are. First, I want to look at your wound."

Lydia left them, to retrieve clean bandages and antiseptic to change the dressing, and they watched her move out of earshot before they spoke.

"Marc—" Simon started.

"She's okay. She actually now knows your leg better than you do. Her hand was inside of it when we set it that night the camp was blown to pieces—"

"No, Marcus," Simon interrupted him. "That's not what I was going to say. You and I both know the risk of sepsis. You know how easily infection sets in, and people die in both places, whether here or at the field hospitals. It's a fifty-fifty."

Marcus looked at his friend. "We're going to try really hard not to let that happen, Simon, and your personal private duty nurse has expressed a very personal war on germs as far as your skin is concerned."

Simon reached up and grabbed his friend's arm. "Marc, promise me you'll take care of Lydia if I get septic and die," Simon demanded fiercely. "Swear to me you'll watch out for her! Swear it before Almighty God Himself that you will take care of her!"

Not even hesitating for one second, Marcus put his hand on his friend's hand. "I swear before God Himself that I will look out for Lydia if, and that's an unlikely if, anything happens to you," Marcus vowed quietly, before Lydia returned. And he had never made a vow that was more genuine in his entire life.

Lydia approached as Simon's hand fell back down to the cot in relief. She held a small bottle in her hand. "This is going to hurt," she warned, offering him the laudanum.

Simon shook his head. "Just do it, Marcus. I don't want my head to get clouded again."

Marcus knew what he was really saying... that Simon wanted him to be able to recognize any signs of infection-related delirium if it developed. Marcus also saw a rolled bundle under Lydia's arm. "What's that, Nurse Finney?" he asked curiously.

"I sheared a sheep... well, rather... someone in the countryside did. I want to put the wool under his leg, in the splint, as a cushion."

"Now why didn't I think of that?" Marcus wondered out loud.

"Well, it makes sense to pad his leg from the poles," Lydia returned.

Together, they carefully unwrapped Simon's lower leg. Marcus felt the top of his friend's foot and found a strong pulsation. Likewise, behind the ankle, his fingers felt what they had been hoping for, the softer rhythm of blood on the move. Marcus pulled the sponges from the incisional wound he'd created along the bone as Lydia poured antiseptic over it. They were gratified to hear Simon groan, as Marcus peered into the wound for bleeding and dead tissue.

"That's splendid!" Marcus exclaimed brightly. "You're in pain!"

Simon gritted his teeth. "You should try it for yourself sometime?" he said, with measured breathing.

"Nope!" Marcus exclaimed. "But it's good you can feel your leg. Now try to wiggle your toes."

The two watched, waiting. Then, barely, almost imperceptibly, Simon did move his toes.

"Well, this day just keeps getting better and better!" Marcus declared. "You've got movement."

Carefully, they repacked Simon's wound, filled the canvas with the wool, and rested the leg on its new cushion. Marcus situated the poles along his friend's leg from the sole of his foot to mid-thigh before pulling the canvas around and tying it with rope to hold it in place.

"All done," Marcus said. "Remember, no dancing, home by midnight, and for God's sake, use a little laudanum once in a while if you can't stand the pain."

Lydia momentarily resumed her place on the box, leaned over and kissed Simon's mouth, lingering just long enough for him to forget the pain and added softly, "Did that help?"

Simon looked up at her appreciatively. "A lot more than the laudanum... I am at your mercy, Nurse, for when the next dose is due."

For the first time in two days, Lydia laughed.

Marcus looked at his friend and his wife, a little envious. "Bill's in the mail," he declared before leaving the recovery.

Over the next two days, the station fell into a new routine as the battle for Somme slowed. Less intensive skirmishes to the northeast continued, but where the station was located, outside of Amiens, the pace had slowed and there was now fresh water from the Somme River. Mercifully, the station had a chance to stay put for a little while. The weather would be getting colder soon.

Casualties could still reach them and be cleared to go on to one of the hospitals around Paris. Without the mass damage from aerial bombardments, the men were now suffering more from lung diseases, malnutrition, and kidney disease. Accidental injuries, fractures, and falls increased, from slippery, rain-soaked ladders and ground cover. Marcus convinced Captain Thornwall, as the camp reorganized, that Simon should be moved to the private tent with Lydia, to minimize the risk of exposure to lung infection from the open recovery. Lydia asked that their tent be placed right near the surgery and the recovery so she could keep one ear open for his needs while she tended to other duties.

Lydia maintained her duty shifts and Marcus looked in on his patient daily. Camp stoves had been installed against the colder nights. Linda had been right; moving camp in the colder weather would be a challenge. There was wood enough, thankfully, to keep them going for awhile.

Simon was restless over the next couple of days, though he understood the nature of his wound. He didn't care for laying alone in the small tent, knowing that the surgery was running without him, knowing that the team was busy, with wounded still coming through. Even though he knew Marcus was absolutely correct in his prescription for bed confinement, Simon felt useless. He had to remind himself, again and again, that this was the only way to keep from getting shipped out. But even as he pondered that, the thought crossed his mind that shipping out might not be such a bad idea after all. Why not leave the war? Why not get shipped home? Why not recover in some hospital in Philadelphia and let them find a place to start their lives together in the States? Why not?

Simon tossed Marcus' baseball into the air repeatedly. His friend had assigned him the exercise of the ball toss to keep his arms moving... or just to stop him from fidgeting... either way, if he missed it and it rolled under the cot, he would have to wait until Lydia came to check on him to retrieve it. He was very careful not to drop it. He also regularly did leg lifts with his healthy limb, trying to keep it moving and functional. This evening, marked day six of his recovery. Six days of lying on a litter, on a cot, unable to do anything. In six days, God had created everything that is, and Simon had accomplished absolutely nothing in the same length of time. Lydia's mantra, *I need to make a difference,* crossed his mind repeatedly. He understood her better now. If he never did get to walk again, he wondered, why would God have even bothered to let him live?

When Lydia finally returned from duty, she brought a tray of food from the mess.

"There you are," Simon said, watching her lay the tray beside him.

She smiled at him. "I brought supper," she said brightly. "It's still hot."

"I'm not hungry," he told her flatly.

"Well, hungry or not, you have to eat," she admonished.

"For God's sake, Lydia, don't I at least have a say in whether or not I eat?" he snapped at her.

She stopped, fork in hand, and placed it back on the tray. "Of course you do, my love," Lydia said softly. "Of course you do. What can I do for you? What would help?"

He tossed the ball into the air over his head. "See, that's the thing," he told her as he watched the ball, careful to catch it on its descent. "It's always what you can do for me... not what I can do for you... or anyone else here... and I just lie here doing nothing."

Lydia sat next to him on their second cot, watching the ball go up and down rhythmically. She sat quietly beside him, not moving, just watching.

He didn't, couldn't, look at her. "I can't do six weeks of this, Lydia. I can't. I can't lay here for six weeks doing nothing. I can't help the wounded. I can't help the surgery. I can't be your husband. I can't do a damn thing, but try not to drop this damn ball."

Lydia's eyes widened. She was not unfamiliar with hearing wounded men express these exact sentiments... but it hit differently hearing them from Simon. She waited, knowing what was behind all of this... but allowing him the space to find it for himself.

"I wish God had just let me die," he declared. "If I'm not going to walk again, I'd rather He had just let me die."

There it is. "What makes you think you aren't going to walk again?" her voice was calm and quiet.

"Oh, I don't know," he started angrily, "Maybe because we're out in the French countryside where a single bomb, just one mind you, can put men flat on their backs for the rest of their lives... and we save them for what, Lydia? So they can go back to their families and lay in some bed, in some cottage, in some woods, so German soldiers can walk in and shoot their wives right in the middle of birthing a child? So some stupid people can throw apples and cheese in the back of some truck to take back to some doctor so he can patch up someone who won't ever be able to get out of bed and walk again?"

Lydia heard the rambling... the disconnection forming. She put one hand out and felt his forehead. His skin was hot. Very hot.

"I'm going to get Marcus," she told him, standing up.

Simon grabbed her wrist hard. "Okay, sure," Simon said roughly. "Go get Marcus. Go be with Marcus. I may not be able to walk, but I have eyes, for God's sake—"

Lydia pried his fingers from her wrist and fled their tent.

Marcus was in the mess tent with his own tray, enjoying a cup of hot coffee, while he talked to Harold and David Winston. The three turned as she ran into the mess, her agitation evident.

"Marc—Doctor Lovell, please come quickly!" Lydia pleaded. There was the sound of a loud clatter coming from the direction of their little tent.

Marcus and Harold both jumped up from the mess table at the sound, running straight over to the tent where Simon was trying, futilely, to get to his feet, though impeded by the heavy splints.

Harold immediately saw Simon was trying to cut away at the ropes with the knife from the tray that had been brought to him from the mess, the contents of that tray now lay strewn across the floor of the tent. He approached Simon warily. "Simon," he started calmly. "Let me help you get that off."

Simon looked at the other doctor, his eyes glazed.

"We'll take it off," Harold said quietly. "Let me help you."

"Alright then," Simon finally said, angrily staring the other man down.

Harold took the knife from him and bent as if to go for the rope, but instead swung his fist up, landing an uppercut squarely across Simon's jaw, knocking him out. Marcus was waiting behind him to catch him, and together, the two men lowered their injured friend back down to the litter on the cot.

"I hope you didn't break his jaw," Marcus observed dryly. "That was a good punch. Wouldn't want to have to wire him shut…"

"Medical school boxing team," Harold returned evenly.

Lydia stood behind them, mouth gaping in shock.

The two doctors lifted the litter while Lydia held the door of the tent open as they carried Simon into the surgery, only a few feet away. Someone called for an anesthetist. Charlotte had heard the ruckus from over in the recovery. She came on a run and, sizing up the situation, prepared for surgery. Lydia backed away, letting Charlotte take over the nursing care, but she didn't leave the surgery.

Before long, the two doctors had Simon's leg open and started debriding dead tissue along the muscle while Simon slept under the effect of the ether.

Harold looked at the bone alignment of the fractured tibia. "Nice job," he told Marcus. "There's already some bone regrowth starting there."

"Thanks," Marcus replied. "Nice to hear from the ortho."

"I couldn't have done it any better," Harold returned evenly. "Ah, well, a little dead tissue is to be expected. Wish we had an irrigation system."

Charlotte leaned over and looked at the tight space in Simon's leg. "What if we cut holes in one of the rubber tourniquets and laid it in there, letting the Dakin's drip in, between the muscle and the bone..."

The two doctors looked at each other.

"Or we could do that!" Marcus agreed, nodding his head. He watched Charlotte cut small holes every inch or so down a round rubber tourniquet, and they laid it inside along the muscle. They watched her push some antiseptic into the exposed end of the tourniquet, and it dripped nicely, the full length, into the wound.

The two doctors looked at Charlotte and she flushed. "Will it work?" she asked.

"Sure will," Harold said. "Remind me to put you in for a promotion, Nurse Stein."

She smiled under her face mask. "From volunteer, to..."

"We'll figure out the details later," Harold assured her.

They started packing the wound with wet, Dakin's-soaked bandages, knowing the infection could be halted with the drip. Marcus walked around an empty surgical table to the wash station and cleaned his hands. He turned to Lydia, still sitting there, quietly watching the efforts to save her husband's life.

Marcus crouched down beside her. He looked up into her face and rested a hand on her knee. "He's going to be okay, Lydia," he said quietly, reassuring her.

She looked down at him gratefully. "How many times are you going to save us, Marcus?" she asked him.

"As often as you need me to," he replied. "The two of you don't seem to be able to manage on your own, without me around."

"I don't know how to help him with this. He doesn't think he's good for very much right now," she reported sadly.

Marcus sighed, reached up, and casually brushed a hair back behind her ear. "It a common shortcoming among men that we define our worth by what we do... not by who we are, Lydia."

"Every one of you men is worthy, all the way along that entire continuum," she replied with conviction. "Especially you, Marc."

Marcus laughed lightly under his breath. "I think I may have a way to go. Even you have said I am... 'quite good at being quite bad', I think that's how you said it once."

"I could have been mistaken about that," she offered, a little tearful now, looking at his clear blue eyes, so different from Simon's deep brown ones.

"But maybe," he added, smiling, "I'm learning how to be, just a little, more worthy than I was before—if so, I have you to thank for that."

"Me?" she asked in surprise. "Helping you... be worthy?"

"Yes, you," Marcus continued so quietly, only she could hear. "I see how you are with my friend over there. And that makes me think that I want to be more like the kind of man he is... to be worthy of having a woman like you... who will look at me in the same way... someday."

"So there is hope for you, Doctor Lovell," Lydia smiled.

"Maybe so. Just please don't tell the other nurses," Marcus admonished her. "I don't want to break too many hearts all at once."

"Oh, Marcus!" she softly exclaimed, her eyes wet. Then she stood up and followed the two litter bearers who had come into the surgery to take Simon home.

When Simon woke, it was dark. His leg hurt, but not unbearably. His fever was gone and he felt better, physically at least. He slowly recalled some of what had transpired over the last day, or two... and as memory returned, he was not happy with the fragments coming into his mind. *It must be the middle of the night*, he thought. Lydia wasn't in the tent; the cot next to him was empty. Simon tried to get up to find her and cursed under his breath when he remembered the heavy splint was still on his right lower leg. He lay there in the darkness, praying to God that somehow, a way would be shown to him to make everything up to her. If a day ever came that Lydia was bedridden, he knew without a shadow of a doubt that he would care for her for the rest of her days... finding ways to still bring her joy... to love her, and ensure that she never had to question her value to him. She was doing the very same for him? Ah, but this was different. He was supposed to be the strong one, the protector.

The tent flap rustled in the dark. He knew instantly, of course, that it was Lydia returning from duty. He hadn't heard sounds from the surgery close by... she must have been in the recovery. There was a small red glow from the camp stove in the tent, offering them dim light and some warmth in the night.

"Lydia?" he called to her, softly.

She turned, "You're awake?" she questioned. "Are you in pain? Can I do something for you, Simon?" she asked.

"Why yes, actually, you can," he stated matter-of-factly.

Lydia was surprised, but pleased by the change in his voice, the calmness he projected. "What do you need, my love?" she asked, sitting on the extra cot she'd been using since his injury, pulling off her boots and rubbing her aching feet.

"First thing, do you know where that white stone is with the gold flecks that I got from the Meuse?"

She nodded. "It's in your footlocker. Just a minute." She opened his belongings, rummaging through, by feel, for the cool white stone... finding it at last, she placed it in his hand.

Simon looked at the stone, turning it over in his fingers, "I picked this up the day I made a vow to you that I would protect you. I can't protect you much right now, and it's eating at me, but I will be able, someday soon. I'm going to walk again and I will defend you, just as I promised."

Lydia reached out and touched his face with her hand. "I remember that day very well," she said softly. "You made me feel safer than I had ever felt before, even knowing we were coming back to... to this."

"As I recall, I was a little rough with you," Simon confessed. "But only because it mattered so much."

She nodded. "You didn't hurt me, Simon. You made me feel protected. Is there something else? You said that was 'first'?"

"Second, put your feet up here," Simon told her.

She swung herself around and angled her feet up onto his stomach. Simon began to massage them with both of his hands.

"That... feels heavenly..." she murmured.

The wood in the stove crackled slightly as a log shifted, exposing a new, red hotspot in the embers.

"Do you remember," Simon said quietly, "the red candle in the cathedral in Nancy? Near the lectern?"

She nodded, relaxing under his care. "Yes, in the little alcove in the wall. I remember."

One of his hands left her feet and began to travel up the inside of her trouser leg, where he massaged her calf muscle, feeling it relax. "Let's get a red, glass candle holder. For our living room mantle," he said.

"I'd like that," Lydia nodded in the darkness. "And we'll put the white stone right next to it."

Simon reached his other hand up, finding the buttons to her trousers, and unfastened them.

"What on earth are you doing, Simon!" she exclaimed.

"I know I've been a little out of it for a while," he admitted, "but I'm fairly certain that I just undid the buttons on your trousers."

"What on earth for?" she demanded. "You are injured. You must not move your leg, under any circumstance!"

"I may not be able to move a leg... but there's a lot more of me that can still move," he declared. "Look, you asked me what I needed... if you really want to know, then—"

"Oh, Simon," she said, wondering how far this was going to go. "How on earth would we explain to Doctor Lovell if something reinjures your leg?"

Simon relented. "Alright then, just humor me, at least give me the pleasure of looking at my wife while she changes clothes, if that isn't breaching medical orders."

"You have seen me change, hundreds of times," Lydia reminded him.

He nodded. "So I have. Then this shouldn't break any rules. Now, just take off your shirt..."

She did as asked. Slowly undressing in the night air, she pulled off her shirt and trousers and then stood, bathed in the dim red glow of the stove, where he could see her. He was motioning for more.

"Underwear, too. Now... turn around for me," Simon directed her, motioning with a finger as he lifted himself up on his elbows to better appreciate her. "Dear God, you are a beautiful woman," he breathed in deeply. "I'm the luckiest man alive. Come stand right over here, closer to me."

"I think you are doing this quite deliberately..." Lydia scolded, aware of a certain need inside of her that longed to be recognized.

"Doing what?" he asked innocently. "Come here... it's only my leg that's broken, other things are still working pretty well."

She stood right beside him, shivering at the touch of his fingers sliding down her stomach. "If you're thinking what I think you're thinking... you can't put any weight, of any kind whatsoever, on that leg," she warned.

"Can I use my hands?" he teased her, chuckling in the night.

"Yes, my love," Lydia said, gladly slipping back into their familiar terms of endearment. "You may use your hands, but..."

"Well, let me see what my hands can do," he said. "And, my dearest Lydia, I am so very sorry..."

She pulled a blanket over her bare shoulders and very carefully lowered herself down onto him, his apology had been interrupted by a deep sigh of anticipation... hers or his, she did not know. Everything was going to be alright... and he did not move his injured leg, not one little bit.

There was a folding chair in the cramped tent now, right beside the stove. Simon was sitting upright this morning, with his leg fully extended, splint and all, on a wooden crate. A surprise knock revealed Harold with some hot tea in hand. Apparently, it was the drink of choice at the station now, with so many British around. So, when Harold came into the tent with two mugs of hot tea, Simon was not surprised.

"How nice of you to call," Simon said sardonically.

Harold perched himself on one of their cots. "Nice little place you got here. The missus not home?"

Simon actually heard himself chuckle. "At the movies, with the girls, I imagine."

"Well," Harold offered, giving him a salute with the tin mugs, "it is Saturday, after all."

They drank their tea... at least it was hot. "Someone needs to get us some coffee," Simon observed. "So... is this just a social call?" he continued, mildly anxious when Harold was not forthcoming.

Harold looked over at his friend and fellow doctor, choosing his next words. "I think Captain Thornwall is getting a little edgy having you recuperate here," he admitted honestly.

Simon nodded his understanding. "Worn out my welcome? A bit of a burden on the army?"

"The Brits think a little differently than we do, my friend. I suspect he may come to call on you as well. You have another three weeks with the splint on. Then, the real work of therapy will begin."

"I'm not totally ignorant of medicine, Harold," Simon reminded him, "despite appearances. And Lydia still is committed to her work with the casualties, here at the station."

Harold nodded in agreement. "And Thornwall is aware of that as well. I think that's why he's stalled as long as he has, along with Marcus threatening to transfer if his medical opinion, regarding your care, is not regarded as sacrosanct."

They were both quiet until Simon started speaking again. "So, what's this Thornwall guy like?"

Harold sighed, "Oh, you know, career army, pretty much by the book. Probably wants to make a name for himself and rise up the ranks... for King and country and all that."

Simon drained his cup. "Well, I appreciate the heads up," he told Harold. "I have considered going stateside and setting up a little private practice with Lydia somewhere in the hills of West Virginia. Our own career advancement options here in Europe are a bit limited. But rumor has it that the military is finally getting it together back home regarding this war and the Allied forces. I feel like we still have a purpose here. If I could just buy some time, another three weeks, and get walking with these crutches... start exercising my leg again."

Harold looked down at the tea, swirling it in the bottom of his mug. "Tea leaves, supposed to tell your future, huh? Looks like gibberish to me. You know, I have someone back home...Tess. We're engaged. She's waiting for me to come back in one piece."

Simon nodded. He, of course, did know that, although Harold did not often speak of the woman.

"Maybe if Tess was over here, I wouldn't care if I could go home either. Maybe we'd finish out my tour and settle in some little village down around Spain, get some little villa, where the winters don't get too cold. But she isn't here, and I just want to get home to her in one piece myself. You know? Technically speaking, Thornwall can't order us to go or stay; we're not enlisted with the British crown... we're with the French army. He can, however, tell Washington he doesn't want us, and we'd be reassigned somewhere else... probably a desert in Africa or something."

Simon nodded again, waiting for him to get to the point.

"I'm just saying," Harold concluded, "that if Thornwall offers to send you and Nurse Finney out, and you decide to go, no one would blame you in the least for getting out of here. And if it works out that you stay, somehow, no one would be more glad than our little group here because when winter is over, all hell's going to break loose again... especially if the Americans come over en masse. You've been a good friend to me, Simon. And your wife is one helluva good nurse. We'd hate to see you go and hate to see you stay, if you know what I mean."

Simon put out his hand and Harold shook it with a firm grip. He looked up at the other doctor, "You really should come visit more often," Simon called out as Harold took his leave.

Simon assessed his situation, reviewing, in more depth, his conversation with Harold. Lydia was on duty in the surgery. Now that he was allowed to move, with crutches, to a sitting position, he had to find something else to do with himself.

When Captain Thornwall did come to the tent, Simon was sitting up and ready for him. Across his lap in the chair was a small writing board that was quite literally just a board. He had multiple yellow paper tablets in front of him there and several medical texts open on the cot. Hand-written notes were everywhere.

"Ah, Captain!" Simon said. "Forgive me for not rising, sir."

Captain Thornwall nodded. "Of course, at ease, Doctor Finney. You are looking surprisingly well."

"Thank you, sir," he returned. "I am told that I am a terrible patient, but actually healing rather nicely."

"May I inquire, Doctor, what is all of this?" the captain asked.

"Oh this?" Simon said, gesturing to the medical books and papers. "This, sir, is a medical paper that Doctor Winston and I are writing on British advances in military medicine during the war. Rumor has it that the Americans will be officially joining the campaign when winter is over, and American medicine is about one year behind the innovations that the British have acquired through hands-on experience. As I am temporarily unable to stand at length in the surgery, Doctor Winston and I believe that this is the optimal time to get these advances submitted to the journals so the Americans can prepare themselves."

Taken aback, the captain nodded. "Interesting. A professional article? Would you permit me to review your advisements, Doctor? From a military standpoint, there are extraordinary logistics involved in setting up casualty clearing stations."

Simon shook his head. "Of course, sir. I'm just a surgeon. I don't know that I could effectively communicate those issues for ranking American military, not at the level of your experience."

Captain Thornwall nodded. "Perhaps I could be of assistance in the manuscript," he offered. "I have been known to have some skill with the pen, myself."

"Much appreciated, Captain. And I'm sure Winston will agree. The War Department in Washington is removed by distance, and time, from the reality of this conflict," Simon reminded him. "I'm quite certain they could benefit. But when this is printed in the journals, sir, don't be surprised if the American majors and generals want to speak with you personally about the pragmatics of the CCS. There's nothing better than firsthand expertise. But we do need to get this finished within three weeks so I can just focus on operating again, as soon as I'm on my feet. There's some urgency to getting the manuscript off to the publisher."

Captain Thornwall rose. "Very good then, Doctor Finney. I will leave you to your assignment. Have someone run it over to me when you're ready for my part on the logistics. I shall begin a draft of some thoughts. Carry on, Doctor."

If I can't return to surgery, I'll go into psychiatry, Simon thought wryly, watching the captain leave the tent. He would not be getting sent away.

Chapter 12

When Hell Freezes Over

There was cold and then there was the kind of cold that made conversations freeze on the air, breaking into tiny shards before being heard. The close clustering of the tents in the station offered a small buffer from the winds of winter, while sandbags stacked along the bottom edges of the tents helped to trap some of the warmth, from the camp stoves, inside the surgery and the recovery. When the wounded came into the camp, the soldiers were grateful for the comforts of the station, for the brief reprieve from the bitter cold out in the trenches. Ice blocks, brought in from the river, were continually set to melt over banked fires as water had become even more of a precious commodity. Even in the cold, opposing armies found ways to lob missiles onto the battlefields, but mercifully fewer in number than during the fall campaigns. The station had received word from British Command that they were unlikely to move until the thaw. The cold was both a blessing and a curse.

Excitement rose, one icy day, when several teams of mules and wagons pulled into the station with much-needed supplies. Since they were frozen in place, the Allied army's postal service had finally caught up to their little group, for the first time in many months. The mess tent was crowded with soldiers and medical staff hoping to hear their name called out. Simon was also in the crowd, enjoying his newfound freedom, a freedom two wooden crutches afforded him, as he carefully navigated the snow laden ground with his good leg. It felt wonderful to be a part of the camp again. Cook had two large kettles simmering, one with tea and one with coffee. This day, both were requested as people received word from home and opened their letters and packages, hoping for good news.

Simon was in the mess primarily to avoid the confines of his small tent, so he did not really think his name would be called out by the private reading the envelopes. When "Doctor Simon Finney" was called, Marlene Sullivan brought the two letters to him where he was perched at the end of a table. She also had one of her own. Simon looked at the handwriting carefully. His letters had been long in the coming... the postal markings faded, but legible. One was from his sister and one from his brother, both in West Virginia. Each had been sent sometime during the summer. Simon decided to read them later as the news they contained would be history by now, but no doubt enjoyable. Marlene approached him a second time when the name "Lydia Blackwell" was called out. It was from her parents, the return address from Greensburg, Pennsylvania neatly written in a woman's fine pen on the outer corner of the missive. No doubt her mother's handwriting. Simon would take it to her when she got off duty from surgery.

Marlene took a seat near Simon, careful not to disturb his leg, and opened her letter on the spot. They both looked up when a cheer erupted over multiple, outdated, copies of the London

Times were passed out to the camp. "Do you mind, Doctor Finney?" Marlene asked.

Simon shook his head. "Not at all," he replied as he warmed his hands on the tin coffee mug he had precariously managed to carry to the table, while holding onto the crutches at the same time.

"*Dear Marlene,*" she began reading to him.

Simon raised his eyebrows. He had not expected her to read her letter out loud.

"*We hope this finds you well. It's September first and look how the fall is coming on us already. The apple trees are full and we'll have Tom come pick them for us this week. It's been a good year for the fruit as we had lots of rain. Dad is here and says he'll add onto the bottom, so not to tell you his news. But I can tell you I worry about you every day and hope you're in a nice hospital somewhere and seeing many interesting things. I pray every day and every night that you're safe from the war. Your brother got an excellent position with a medical team in Albany where they are working with new types of anesthesia that allow longer surgeries. His team is developing some way to take out more advanced tumors... your father can tell you more. Dan is the youngest doctor on the Albany team. Imagine that! What an achievement! We are very proud of you, too, even though news is not forthcoming. We received a letter from you in April that you had arrived in France, but you didn't say what you were doing exactly. No matter. We're proud of you regardless. Dad wants the pen.*"

Marlene paused, apparently feeling some kind of explanation was forthcoming. "My family are all medical, for generations," she told Simon. "My grandfather was a doctor in the Civil War, my dad and Uncle Samuel Sullivan are doctors in Syracuse, and so what else would my brother be, but a doctor... and me, a nurse? I mean, really! Was there any other option?"

It was a rhetorical question, but Simon answered her anyway with a question of his own. "Did you want to do anything other than nursing, Nurse Sullivan?"

She looked up at him evenly. "Yes," she admitted. "I wanted to be a doctor as well... but a woman doctor was unthinkable. So, I went into nursing, rather than follow my mother into a life of marriage and children."

Simon nodded. "You will have time to do both, if you choose to, when this war is over or you ship back to the States... whatever comes first."

Marlene sighed before she went on. "You don't understand, Doctor Finney," she said regretfully. "I don't want the war to be over... career-wise, anyway. I love it when you and the other doctors tell me to finish a surgery... close it up, clean it out, suture a wound closed. I love looking into the human body and seeing what it can be again, despite what damage might have been done... putting it back together."

"You could stay on in the American Army Nurse Corps, couldn't you?" he asked.

The woman shook her head. "I wish I could say that was an option. But if any of us enlist, we will be duty-bound to the army rules and regulations that don't in the slightest acknowledge the freedoms nurses have here in the stations. We would be bound to a rule book tighter than any sutures you could ever tie, rules that would hold us back to conventional nursing practices... which are good in and of themselves... but for me, are limiting, to say the least."

Simon listened carefully and nodded in understanding. "So basically, we have spoiled you in this hell hole experience?"

Marlene nodded, grateful he understood. "Something like that. Spoiled here, right along with the frozen water and two-minute wash-ups from a basin on top of a stove."

"And if you go back to New York, you won't be allowed to pick up a clamp or tie off a bleeder again?"

Marlene sighed. "If I go back and perhaps work in the operating theater, I will dutifully hand over a clamp, put a threaded needle into the hand waiting to receive it, say 'yes, sir' and 'no, sir' on command... and go home at the end of the day hoping to find some kind of fulfillment in doing what any other nurse does, in any routine surgery, in any city in the country."

Simon listened, hearing the frustration of lost opportunity in her voice.

"Not that I mind putting a clamp or a needle and suture into your hands... or Doctor Lovell's or Doctor Wilson's, mind you! Because I don't mind that," Marlene hastened to add, not wanting to offend him. "But I'm very glad, for instance, that we nurses don't have to stand up whenever a doctor enters the room, out here."

The doctor nodded. "A ludicrous gesture, of course," Simon told her. "I think I understand, Nurse Sullivan. Here, we might start a case, but you nurses do know how to finish it. You know as much as we do about most of these wounds. You could write books on post-operative recovery protocols and infectious disease management. We should stand, when you walk into the room."

Marlene looked down sadly at the unfinished letter. "Did you hear her pride in Dan's appointment to Albany? I'll never get that from my folks."

Simon leaned slightly onto the table, shifting his leg for comfort. "Nurse Sullivan," he said. "Even if you could tell them, I doubt your mother and father would ever be able to comprehend any aspect of this... this experience you've undertaken here. I'm sure, nonetheless, that they are proud of your character and your courage to come to a foreign country under dangerous circumstances. But if becoming a surgeon is really what you want, this I can guarantee you... the doctors at this camp will all write letters of endorsement for you for entry into medical school. There is not one of us who wouldn't. You take those letters and apply. Already, you could pass the entrance exam with flying colors because your aptitude for medicine is profound. Then, if you have any difficulty as a woman, after medical school, finding a surgical fellowship, you will always know where Ly—Nurse Finney and I are. I, for one, would be honored to sponsor you until you take your boards. My practice is, or at least was, rural surgery, not the most modern theater, but demanding of constant innovation and flexibility. If it's what you truly want," he concluded with conviction, "we'll make it happen. There will be another Doctor Sullivan in the family, I can assure you."

Marlene rose from the table, eyes beginning to hope again. "It is truly what I want!" she exclaimed softly. "Thank you, Doctor Finney. Thank you so much."

He watched her leave, a new spring in her step, despite her winter coat and heavy boots. The nurses were facing unforeseen challenges from many directions. Doc Albright had not held back any of his wealth of experience from Simon during all the years of mentorship he had provided. Medical school had been almost too easy for Simon. But even Simon, as a medical student, had had to learn to adjust to the "proper" way of doing procedures, to protocols better suited for the inside of the sterile hospital theater rather than his real-world experience with illnesses and injuries. He felt that he knew what Marlene Sullivan was up against as far as nursing expectations were concerned because even the doctors here were not "following the book", as they would have to if they were back home. In the war, it was permissible, at least for the surgeons, to toss protocols, when expedient. Circumstances drove their hands, not the army rules and regulations. He understood her frustrations and was grateful she had found new hope. As an afterthought, Simon wondered if any of the other nurses shared the same dilemma. He would talk to Lydia about it later and write a carefully drafted letter of endorsement for Nurse Sullivan without delay.

Simon didn't stay alone at the table for long. Marcus opened the flap to the tent, letting in a fresh movement of cold air and causing everyone inside to groan. Quickly pulling the flap shut behind him, Marcus bowed to the group as if receiving accolades. He searched the cluster of people and quickly approached Simon, when he spotted him.

"Got news for you!" he declared to his friend as he took a seat at the table.

Simon looked up. "Good, I hope?"

"Thornwall says that the British will be reforming their own, newly equipped, CCS when there is a thaw. We'll be getting a new

French commander and will be back under French control. Have to say I'm going to miss Winston. Great sense of humor, that one! Good surgeon!"

Simon acknowledged this news with a nod. "I'm sure the feeling is mutual."

Marcus nodded at the crutches carefully leaning against the bench. "Stockton and I assured Thornwall that you'd be up to speed by then and to not worry about our team being able to manage. You aren't completely up to speed yet, but the new French commander won't have to know that—I do such remarkable work, truly, I do," Marcus applauded himself. "Though that Belgian surgeon, who couldn't wait to amputate, probably still disagrees with my decision to leave it attached."

Simon looked at his friend appreciatively. "A decision for which I will forever be grateful." Every time his leg caused him pain, from the cold air or movement, he had an opportunity to thank God above that he still had a leg that ached and throbbed. He realized he had been only seconds from joining the other amputees on the next truck to Paris, then the States, leaving part of himself behind on French soil.

Marcus looked at Simon steadily. "It was a very selfish decision," he admitted. "I didn't want to share the glory of all of this with some new doctor, still wet behind the ears, who would have replaced you. And I wouldn't have been able to get your lovely wife's screaming out of my head, either."

"What?" Simon asked.

Marcus unbuttoned the top of his coat in the warmth of the tent. "Your wife called for me, over all of the confusion that night, with a voice that would have raised the dead. I knew it was her immediately… and there she was, holding onto the table, over top of you, telling that damned Belgian he'd have to saw her in half first." Marcus chuckled at the memory. "That woman doesn't take no for an answer."

"The way I heard it," Simon added dryly, "you threatened to severe his head from his body."

Innocently, Marcus looked up to the peak of the tent overhead. "Did I say that? Well, I might have. Ah, well, no harm done. But seriously, you need to start putting full weight on your leg, you know… without the crutches. You're favoring it, and it's time to loosen up that hamstring."

Simon nodded. He was favoring it. He knew that. He was also afraid of losing his balance and falling. "I want to start operating again."

Marcus looked at him. "Okay. Right now, only pain and balance are stopping you."

Simon looked at the crutches. "Pain is not a problem. And I've been working my muscles daily for weeks. I don't need to be sent off to rehab, so don't even suggest it."

Marcus studied his friend carefully. "Then figure it out, my friend. Get in the surgery… use a stool if you need to. Pick up the scalpel. The British Fifth is launching one more offensive across the Ancre River Valley, ahead of the snows, and we'll need every set of hands we've got. Maybe by Thanksgiving, we'll really have something to be thankful for and the British and Germans will take a break." He got up to leave, but then reached inside his coat for one more thing. A small letter. "I found this in the trash. Someone thought it wasn't deliverable, but I think it's for your wife."

Simon took the small note, it was addressed to *Ange de la Miséricorde*. Marcus was right; the letter could be meant for only one person.

Night had come. A few casualties arrived after dinner, nothing Harold couldn't handle in the surgery. Marcus went in search of Susannah and found her reading a tattered book by the dim light of the mess tent after most of the personnel had gone to their respective tents for the remainder of the evening. "Got a minute, Nurse Boyton?" he asked her. She looked up from turning a page, so he looked down over her shoulder at the title of the book. "Ah, reading a classic, I see. What is Heathcliff up to?"

Susannah looked at him in surprise. "You've read *Wuthering Heights*?" she was astonished.

"Of course," he stated. "A shining example of British literature. Bring it with you... I'll read you the good parts."

She allowed him to lead her through the freezing camp to the doctors' tent. Susannah raised her eyebrows when he opened the flap for them to step inside. A quick scan told her it was empty.

"Stockton's going to be in surgery for a while," he told her. The warmth of the stove reached her immediately. He'd stoked the fire before he had gone to retrieve her. Marcus opened her coat and slid his arms in around her waist, pulling her close to him. "While the kids are out, the house is all ours." Pulling her over to his cot, he took off her coat and pulled a blanket over both of them as he laid himself on top of her.

Susannah dropped the book carefully down on his footlocker, and Marcus took his time undoing her long blonde hair from the tight bun she'd twisted it into earlier in the day. He reveled in her hair, then teased her with his lips, and allowed her to feel his hunger for her. She hesitated in her response to him.

"What is it, Suzie?" he asked softly, plying her with caresses. "Is it Stockton? I promise you, he's not going to be back for a long time. He just started an abdomen. I made sure we won't be disturbed." He unbuttoned her shirt and watched her skin react to the cooler air passing between them. "I love watching your body wake up like this," he murmured.

"Marcus," she said softly. "I know you don't love me..."

"Of course, I love you!" he said quickly, pulling down her trousers and his own. "I love everything about you."

She put her arms around his neck, but made him look at her eyes. "I know you love, this—"

He kissed her insistently, fully, preventing her from speaking, showing her how very much he loved... this. And he persisted, pressing his advantage until he got the reaction he longed for. Then, he abruptly slowed. "I love the curve of your neck, and how your body fits into mine, and the taste of you here, and here, and here... I love every inch of you."

Susannah felt her body aching for him, knowing the man was deliberately holding her off, until finally she almost had to plead with him, "Oh, Marcus, please..."

"Ah, the magic word," he whispered. Then he unleashed himself upon her, enjoying the want he had created while stifling the eager sounds she made, his mouth covering her own until she gasped, clutching at him. "See?" he said, satisfied, nibbling on her neck. "That's how much I love you."

"You will always be my Heathcliff," she whispered, her body still trembling underneath him. He was very good at making her feel... very good.

He kissed her skin. "Is that so?" he murmured, idly wondering if they had enough time, before the surgery closed, to...

"I'm leaving in the morning, Marcus," she told him.

He froze.

"You're what?" he exclaimed, pulling himself off her.

She sat up, reaching for her shirt and trousers. "I'm leaving tomorrow. I'm going home," she told him.

He was genuinely confused. "But why? What for?" he demanded. "What about... what about us?" It was a stupid question, and he knew it. There were a hundred reasons she would want to go home, and he was the very least of them. There were a hundred more reasons he should want her to go, to leave the war, and leave him, behind.

Susannah pulled on clothing and heavy coat and retrieved her book from atop his footlocker. Standing over him, where he still perched, growing cold on the cot, she reached out one hand and fingered the dark curls behind his ear, at the nape of his neck. She leaned over and kissed the top of his head, and then she was gone.

By the light of their small stove, Lydia and Simon huddled under the blankets on one of their cots and talked late into the night. Lydia shared with him the neatly written letter from André Besimont, who had let her know he had survived the trip to the field hospital and was continuing to recuperate at his mother's home in a small town in southern France. She was deeply moved by the handwritten note and had carefully refolded it, tucking it away in her footlocker for safekeeping. Lydia lay with her head cradled against Simon's shoulder, enjoying the security of his arms around her.

He told her of his earlier conversation with Marlene Sullivan and his plan to get all the doctors to endorse her application to medical school. And they spoke of Marcus' news about the upcoming British campaign and of Simon's plan to be in the surgery with the very next arrival of casualties. Lydia shared with him the news of Susannah's planned departure in the morning.

Simon was truly surprised. "What on earth will we do without her?" he wondered.

"Do you mean what will Marcus Lovell do without her, or we, as in the entire station, do without her?" Lydia asked. "As far as the station is concerned, two French Red Cross nurses have volunteered, heaven only knows why, to join us. We'll be back up to an even dozen for the first time in a long time. It won't take them long to catch on since they've both come to the front from hospitals. As for Marcus..."

Simon looked up into the shadows playing overhead, from the firelight. He stroked her arm under their blanket. "Marcus will move on to someone new, I'm sure," Simon remarked. "Maybe you ought to warn the two new nurses what they're up against. He certainly couldn't have known about this when we talked earlier. I don't think Marc could hide that kind of information from me. I wonder if she's broken the news to him yet."

Lydia sighed. "She wasn't even going to tell him. Then she decided maybe she would tonight. I don't know where it ended up. I expect you'll be able to tell immediately when you see him in the morning."

"But why, Lydia? With no warning," Simon wondered. "You are such a tight knit group. I guess I just imagined you'd all pack up at once. Just all go home together some day. I sometimes forget you're all from different parts of the country, that you didn't just come over on the same transport. Is it getting to be too much for her? It's too much to ask of any of you... and now, with winter starting, it's harder yet."

Lydia faltered. "Susannah is pregnant, Simon," she softly confided. "And no, Marcus does not know. She does not want him to know, and you must promise not to say a word, even though he's your friend."

Simon's hand paused in mid-stroke. "Oh," he said.

Lydia looked up to meet his eyes. "She wants this baby."

"How far along is she?" he wondered, slowly caressing her hair as he pondered the implications of this revelation. The wood in the stove hissed as a wet log caught fire.

"She's just starting to show," Lydia told him.

"Oh, Lord..." he breathed. "She's four months? She's been working in this hell hole, with shells dropping around us, sometimes twenty-four hours a day, pregnant for four months? And Marcus hasn't noticed?"

Lydia nodded. "She's afraid he will, if she stays any longer... and this is no place to have a baby."

Simon put his hand up to her head and stroked her hair gently. "Marcus Lovell is an idiot."

"Yes," she agreed. "He is. A lovable idiot."

"He didn't even notice her body was changing... he's so damn self-centered!" Simon exclaimed under his breath. "What is the matter with him! How could he not tell? If it were you, if you became pregnant, I would know in an instant. I would probably know before you were even sure."

Lydia snuggled back down against his shoulder and lightly stroked his chest under the blanket. "That's true. I think we would figure it out at about the same exact time; we know each other so well. But they don't have the kind of love we have, Simon. And they aren't together every night like we are. I feel bad for Susannah. The baby is all she'll ever really have of Marc because she never won his heart. She never really knew where she stood with him."

"Do all the nurses know?"

"No, she only told me yesterday, after she met with Captain Thornwall and asked to be relieved. He couldn't refuse her, knowing we're volunteers."

Simon admitted, "This isn't going to be easy, not telling Marcus. Especially when I want to deck him for being such a fool. This is exactly why it was so incredibly important to me to get you to Nancy in September. I never wanted to put you in a position where you wondered about my commitment to you, my devotion to you... when we came together. I would never have left you in doubt of where you stood in my heart."

"And now... after these months of marriage... and with shells falling around us, and fractures, and winter coming..." Lydia asked. "Has anything changed?"

Simon nodded. "My commitment hasn't changed, but sure, I've changed. This injury changed me. You likely noticed, but men don't take feeling helpless very well." He smiled, but then continued. "I'm forever grateful for how you stood by me when hell froze over. I know I've put you through a lot and have thought a lot about the 'for better and for worse' part of my commitment...

and I know, with all my heart, I would do the very same for you. I can't live without you, Lydia. You are my heart... and, next to God, my soul."

Lydia reached up and pulled his face toward her to gently kiss his lips. "Someday, my love," she whispered, "I want to give you a child."

"When we get home, and I can carry you across a threshold, it'll be the first thing we do... make a baby." He held her tight against him. "Did you read the letter from your parents?"

She shook her head in the twilight of the tent. "It's an old postmark. Probably written in response to the letter I sent from Philadelphia before coming over here. I couldn't bear to tell them in person, so I mailed it to them just before I boarded the ship. I tried my best to explain why I needed to do this. I'm sure from the date that it's Mother's attempt to be understanding... and to translate Dad's anger into something protective. Whatever their reaction, it's been... let's see, ten, no, eleven months since I left for England? It was a long while ago... and probably nothing similar to how they feel now."

"Did you write to them at all after that one letter? Did you write them after you arrived in London?" he wondered. It was remarkable to him to think of her having two living parents, ones who had supported her intention to go for the Red Cross training. Ones who, though uninformed, must surely still be interested in the life of their child. "Or to your sister Peggy?"

"I sent a letter from London, yes, about the trip, about how big the Atlantic feels and how well we were received by the British Nurse Corp. I told them I'd be heading for a field hospital... somewhere; that was the last time I wrote," she said slowly. "Later, of course, I wanted to write them about you. I really do want to tell them about you. It's just, it's just been hard with the fighting and the wounded," she continued after a pause, while she sorted out her thoughts, hastening to reassure Simon. "I'm not sorry for a single second that we got married as we did. That second day in Nancy, I wish I could have called Mother and my sister, to tell them all about you, about us getting married, about the beautiful cathedral and the priest that blessed us right there. I wanted to write it all down and tell them it was the most important day of my life and that I wished that they could have shared it with us. But when we got back to find the station had moved and was in a mad shambles of wounded and all... I guess all that just got tucked away safe somewhere inside of me, and I just couldn't find a way to let it out onto paper."

Simon nodded. "Makes sense."

Lydia went on, her words rushing out. "And then I was worried sick about you for the past six weeks. And for a short time after you were wounded, I thought, I was afraid that... you might not—"

"That I wasn't going to make it," he finished for her. "And if I hadn't pulled through, then what would have been the point in telling them they had missed out on their daughter's marriage as well? I understand."

"Do you, Simon? Do you really?" she implored him. "You don't feel slighted that I haven't told them yet? You aren't hurt? Be truthful, please!"

"I don't feel slighted, my love," Simon told her. "I, of all people, understand why you tucked it away so you could carry on. And if the infection had gotten me, it would have been the very best thing you could have done, not to open that part of you, keeping the memory safe... to keep it sealed away. No, I don't feel slighted at all. In fact, maybe it's much better this way. Maybe together we should read the letter from your folks, and together, we could write them back... I would be honored to tell them about their lovely, loving daughter who gives herself so fully to her work, to the other nurses, to the wounded... the André Besimonts of the world. I can tell them that I have found the single pearl in this sea of war, worth all the hardships just to be able to hold it in my hand."

Lydia sighed. "Oh, Simon."

After a short period of silence, he continued. "I did tell my sister and brother, that is, if they got the letters."

"About the station or about us?"

Simon nodded. "About us. While you and the others kept the station running, with me flat on my back and good for nothing, I wrote to them about how we met and found the cathedral, about how the nun managed to convince a priest it was okay to bless our union, under the most unlikely circumstances, and the miracle of all of that. It was very comforting for me. I got to lay there reliving the day, and the night at the inn, over and over in my mind. So, I wrote it down in a letter."

Lydia's eyes widened. "Good heavens! I know you didn't write about the inn!"

"Came close," he laughed lightly. "No, it was enough to let the memory play, many times, in my mind."

She snuggled closer to him. "Which part of the inn? The first or the second part?" she teased him.

He laughed again, his fingers leaving her hair, to trace the shape of her mouth. "Well, all of it really... I had lots and lots of free time, so I got to just lay there and think back on the most minute details of the night. It's really rather remarkable how vividly the mind can conjure up the smallest details of a memory, when it matters so much." He felt her stir against him.

"I think my mind is conjuring right now," she whispered.

He moved her off of him and sat up on the cot. "Is that a fact?"

She nodded, watching him add a piece of wood to their fire. He dipped a finger into the pot of water they kept at the ready, on top of the stove, felt its warmth, and reached for a towel. "Then conjure up part two," he told her softly, "you know, it's long overdue for me to be the one giving the bed bath for a change. But, if I mess—"

"Don't worry," she assured him. "It isn't hard to figure it out."

Chapter 13
Crossing the Valley

During breakfast, in the mess, some of the team tried to figure out why the Ancre Valley was worth the fight. Paris was south and to the west of them, critical points at Somme and Verdun were south of them. North of them, was Ypres, where battles had already been fought. And farther north was Flanders and then the sea. The army was not fighting for the coastline which provided one hard northern boundary for the soldiers on foot. Lydia remembered being at Ypres; she remembered the Arctic, wet wind blowing in from the ocean when she and one other had arrived last February, from England. She recalled the screeching cries of the terns and gulls which seemed to warn the humans to turn back. None had gone back.

The Ancre Valley was in between France and Belgium, and the German First Army wanted it all. In the mess, speculation flew around the table about what they might expect from the British Fifth Army trying to advance. One thing was certain: there were casualties when the army, of either side, chose to advance.

Earlier that morning, several of the nurses had stood in the cold rain to wish Susannah well, as she boarded a truck, with a few wounded, headed west to a field hospital. There were many tears with the farewell, many good wishes, many long hugs. Lydia had made her promise to write once she got back home... although they both agreed that the baby would no doubt be a toddler before two letters could be successfully exchanged, what with the delayed mail delivery process of getting mail to "somewhere in eastern France." The women had agreed to meet up when they all returned home, a promise of reunion made, though unlikely to be kept, in times such as these. Lydia and Charlotte had stood for a long time, watching as the truck rolled out of the camp, taking with it Susannah's precious secret. Lydia had not made public Susannah's condition, as promised. She had told no one except for Simon about the woman's pregnancy. She had briefly looked around for any sign of Marcus in the morning light, but he had not appeared—at least, not within her view.

He was also notably missing at this breakfast gathering. Lydia and Charlotte filled their trays from the food line and looked for seats to join the others at the long table. She saw Simon engaged in conversation with Doctor Winston. The British were enjoying a last breakfast before heading out to reformulate their own CCS, in preparation for the next assault. The Brits and Americans had enjoyed this brief time together. It was hard to see them go. It had been hard to see Susannah go.

David Winston acknowledged both of the women, as others scooched aside, making room for them to join the group. Lydia noted that Simon did not have his crutches with him, not along the tent wall, nor beneath the bench. He had apparently walked without incident, through the rain and over slippery mud, to the mess. *Good.* He was regaining some confidence. Lydia glanced across to Simon; they hadn't gotten much sleep. He looked none the worse for wear, she thought. The man caught her gaze and his eyes twinkled as if he was enjoying much the same thought. She blushed and sipped from her cup of tea to hide behind it... a demure gesture that Simon found delightful.

"So, we likely won't be seeing any of you chaps anytime soon," Doctor Winston was saying, "but it has been a most memorable experience."

Harold nodded. "Feeling is mutual. We've learned a lot from your group. Good to know that you all are out there sharing the load. I do think that we should try to get together from time to time to exchange ideas, however. Old issues of the *Lancet* or the *JAMA* aren't quite the same thing as talking to someone who just practiced a procedure successfully in the field."

"Have you met your new commander?" Winston asked the Americans.

Simon shook his head. "Coming in tomorrow. No doubt you will pass him along the road."

Winston nodded, stirring his tea with a spoon. "Hope it works out. Always the luck of the draw. Either a good soldier and mediocre medical man or a good medical man with little experience running a mobile station. If you are fortunate enough to find both in the same man, then well done."

Charlotte smiled at the young doctor across the table. "We wouldn't have made it, without your team here. I hope you all make it back to your country when this is over. It would be nice to see England one day, your Big Ben and Buckingham Palace."

"And perhaps someday I will come to the States, although your country is so large, I wouldn't know where to begin," he agreed. "Where is your Doctor Lovell? I would like to give him my thanks before we pull out. With all of the mud and wet snow, I certainly hope our new station is already dug in and ready for our arrival. Dreadful, setting up camp with the ground half frozen. Oh, by the way, word has it that St. John's Hospital at Étaples is beyond capacity. Wounded will have to be trucked even farther than they have been. Be ready."

Harold nodded, "Understood. We're prepared to maintain a little extra space to hold the wounded, as needed. We'll repurpose some of the tents you folks have been using; even heavy snow can delay transport. It'll be important to hear what the new French commander wants as well."

Handshakes worked their way around the group as the British left the tent. The cold rain had begun to turn to snow. It would be easier for the trucks, and the new tanks they had heard about, to find traction across frozen ground than slippery mud. Harold watched as the trucks rolled out, finally turning to Simon.

"Where is Lovell, anyway? Not like him to miss a goodbye party. I'd better go hunt him down. I expect tomorrow we'll all be back here to get the lowdown from the new guy." With that, Harold got to his feet and buttoned his coat. He turned once more to the other surgeon, "So you're on your own two feet again? Good to see. You beat the odds, recovering out here, Simon."

"I had some help," Simon assured him. "Grace of God. It's a good feeling."

Simon and Lydia watched him go. "I hope Marcus is alright," she said softly as Harold went off in his search. "I didn't see him anywhere when Susannah got into the truck. It was hard to see her go, but I'm so glad she did, given the circumstances. I'm going to miss her so much." Lydia looked around at the nearly empty mess tent. "I don't know what to do with myself," she admitted.

He looked up and said, "Let's just go back to our tent. The surgery is empty, the recovery is empty. It does feel strange. The calm before the storm, I suppose." She nodded.

They pushed open the tent flap and watched as the snowflakes grew visibly discernible in the air. "Pretty, aren't they?" Lydia said, catching a few on the sleeve of her army jacket and studying their design. "I've always loved the snow. It was snowing when we arrived on the coast near Ypres. And now we've almost come full circle. I think I'd rather bundle up in the cold than be dreadfully hot in the summer..."

Simon felt her slip her arm around his as they walked across the camp between the tents. "Are you holding onto me? Or trying to hold me up?" he asked her, teasing.

"Both. Forgive a little extra caution. I'm glad you feel able to give up the crutches, though." She looked up, as a snowflake caught on her eyelashes. "Do you think the war will be over by Christmas, Simon? Do you think the powers that be will come to their senses if winter gives them a chance to slow down and think?"

He shook his head. "I don't think so. I think the factories will be using the lull to pump out more tanks and make more howitzers, rifles, bullets... I think it'll take another round of seasons before someone gives up, or gives in. So far, no one seems inclined to do either."

"I'm a little nervous about the new commander, Simon," Lydia confessed. "About us."

"Don't be," he reassured her. "Captain Thornwall briefly took command out of necessity, but remember, Major d'Esperey is still over this station, and you ladies have already won him over. He already knows about us, as well. I don't think we have anything to be concerned about. When do the French Red Cross nurses arrive?"

"I don't know. Maybe they will come in with him."

They slipped inside their tent and out of their wet coats, pulling heavy dry sweaters over their clothing. Simon stretched out on a cot and briefly closed his eyes. "I'm going to take ten. What a luxury!"

Lydia nodded, but his eyes were already closing, enjoying the absence of being needed, of expectations... there would be no casualties, for the moment. She sat beside him on their second cot, visually tracing the line of his profile and the steady rise and fall of his chest... down to his abdomen and further to his two feet... his two feet.

How many times in the past six weeks had she sat and watched him as he battled to keep his two feet? And today, he had walked alone. She thought back to the conversation of last evening. Marcus well deserved the moniker Simon had given him... but he had also saved Simon's leg... he had saved her husband from being crippled. And because of Marcus, she and Simon had not been shipped out; she was still able to be at the station where she loved to serve. And Marcus had told her that he was trying to be a better man, a more worthy man. Lydia couldn't help but wonder what would have happened if Susannah had told him that she was pregnant. Would it have made a difference to him? Would Marc have married her? Lydia would not break her promise to the nurse, her dear friend, but perhaps in the future, she might persuade

Susannah to tell Marcus, herself. Give him a chance to do the right thing.

She put a log in the stove, debating if she should take a nap herself. Then she decided it was time. She pulled out the letter, addressed in her mother's fine script. *"Dear Lydia, Dad and I received your letter from Philadelphia and of course it gave us quite a shock. I think we both thought you'd settle down back home with Derrick after you took the nursing training, perhaps working at one of our hospitals. So, you must forgive us, dear, but this is quite difficult to understand, and Derrick must be devastated. Now you're headed off to England and we will have no idea when we'll be hearing from you again. At least England is relatively safe and has good hospitals. I comfort myself with these things and that they speak the same language, and you can ask for help if you need it.*

"You've always been a determined young woman once you've set your mind to something. I wonder where this idea of getting on a ship and crossing the ocean came to you? Did it come from the Red Cross? I hope it wasn't because of something your father or I said. Your father loves both his little girls and only wants the best for you. We'd hoped you and Derrick would start a family like your sister did and we'd have more grandchildren on the way soon. Your sister is worried sick about you going overseas. She has the children and Tommy to distract her, but you two are so close, she can't imagine you being thousands of miles away. I can't bear the thought of anything happening to you in the Red Cross. The people in Philadelphia will tell us nothing except to give this address to write you. They did assure us they take good care of their nurses. So awful to have such a great valley of time and space between a mother and her daughter.

"I know you'll do what you think is best and right. Your father can't write because he is too distressed for your wellbeing. Say your prayers every night. We all love you here and pray for your safe and quick return. Your loving mother."

Lydia put the letter down and wiped her tears away with the sleeve of her sweater. She hadn't realized she was crying. Now she was glad that she'd mailed the second letter from England advising them of her safe crossing and arrival there. Perhaps they would be content, believing she had remained on the island.

Simon was softly snoring on his cot. Lydia covered him with a blanket, picked up her coat, and slipped out of the tent to see how the other nurses were passing the time this quiet afternoon.

So odd that no one had to be on duty and a strange emptiness with the British medical team gone. A few folks were playing cards or checkers in the mess tent, others were reading. Out of sheer habit, she wandered over to the recovery. The cots were lined up neatly in two rows, waiting for the inevitable. At the far end, the supply shelves were stocked to the brim. Lydia wandered into the area and smiled at the neatly assembled piles of dressings, stacks of bedpans, urinals, wash basins, neatly folded towels and cloths and blankets for the wounded. She loved the orderliness of the shelves when they were full and waiting. She enjoyed the feeling of reassurance that the supply room afforded. She almost tripped over something that had dropped to the floor in the dim tent and bent to retrieve it and to put it back in its place.

Marcus was on the ground, almost passed into oblivion, with a bottle of whiskey in one hand.

"Oh, good grief!" Lydia softly exclaimed under her breath. "So this is where you've been hiding. Here in the cold no less…"

She crouched down beside him and gently shook him. "Marcus, what on earth are you doing here? You can't stay on the ground like this. You'll freeze to death."

His eyes opened, unable to focus. Too much drink. The bottle was nearly gone. Bleary-eyed, he looked up at her. "Ah, miss nightingale…" he managed. "You came to sing me… a song…"

"No, you foolish man, it's Lydia. What have you done to yourself? Come on, let me help you get up. The ground is freezing cold."

He waved the nearly empty bottle of whiskey in the air, found his mouth and swallowed the remaining contents.

Lydia reached out and wrested it from his cold fingers. "That's quite enough of that, mister! Hand it over, if you please… although, I guess it is a little late to tell you not to finish it off." She held the bottle up against the light, assessing its emptiness.

His voice was slurred. "I'm… lousy surg… surg… lousy man…"

"You are not a lousy surgeon, you are an excellent surgeon," she countered, trying to sit him up. "But the man part is negotiable at the moment."

"She's gone," he mumbled, his head lolling against his chest.

Lydia sighed. "I know."

"Becuzza me—"

He was too heavy for her to lift. She had to get him up on one of the cots. "Come on," Lydia said, "put your arm around my shoulder. Let's get you off the ground and warmed up… and some coffee in you…"

He slung an arm around her shoulder, haphazardly trying to focus. "My fault... she's gone," he said, the whiskey thick on his breath.

"I know," Lydia murmured, trying to get a grip on his trousers to help him stand up between the supply shelves. "On three now..."

He was dead weight. He fell back down with his arm still around her, pulling her down to the ground right along with him.

Lydia tried to wriggle out from under the man, knowing now she needed an extra set of hands and wishing she could have spared him the embarrassment of someone else seeing him in this predicament. But Marcus had fallen on top of her, his face above her own. "Is 'cuzza you," he slurred. "s'always been you..."

He opened his eyes wider and briefly looked at hers. "You wan' me a little bit, don' you... Lydia... wan' me?"

"I want you on that cot over there, drinking coffee," she said, pushing up against him with all her strength, "because you don't know what you're saying and won't remember a word of it to-morrow, anyway."

To her dismay, Marcus began to cry. "How 'bout jus' a little bit?" he said, planting a poorly aimed kiss on the corner of her mouth, pushing his hand in between her legs. "I' be really good... for you... promise... Lyd..."

Lydia reached up both of her hands and pinched his cheeks hard. "Marcus Lucius Lovell, you stop that!" she scolded him fiercely, her eyes boring into his own through the haze of the alcohol. "Now get off me! And let me get someone to help you, or else I swear I will gladly let you freeze to death right here in the recovery!"

A tall, lanky form filled the entry to the supply room, cutting off what little light was in there. "Need some assistance, Nurse Finney?" he said, his voice thin as polished steel.

"Thank you, God!" Lydia breathed. "Help me get this poor drunken man onto a cot, please, Doctor Stockton."

With almost no effort, Harold pulled Marcus off of her by the nape of his coat. Lydia crawled out from under him and pulled one of Marc's arms over her shoulder. Together, the two half-dragged Marcus to a cot, where he fell awkwardly down onto his side. Lydia turned and got several blankets from the supply shelf to cover the man up while Harold stood over him with thunder and lightning in his eyes.

"Are you okay, Nurse Finney?" he asked very controlled, very quietly.

She nodded, tucking her shirt back into her trousers and putting herself back together. "I'm fine, Doctor Stockton. I was afraid something like this was going to happen. You know, Susannah left us this morning."

Harold nodded. "I was aware. But this drunken fool—"

"She didn't tell him she was leaving until sometime during the night. He didn't take it very well."

"Apparently not," Harold agreed.

"Got to get something hot in him. Laying there, he's probably got hypothermia already," Lydia said, exasperated.

Harold pulled up a crate. "You get coffee. I'll stay here. When he comes to his senses a bit, he and I are going to have a little man-to-man talk."

She nodded, pulling her coat around her as she walked back between the two rows of cots to the tent door and crossed over into the mess.

Lydia picked up a tin mug for the coffee, then, on second thought, filled a pitcher taking the whole thing with her. She ran into Charlotte outside, enjoying the snowflakes.

"Am I missing a party?" she asked, wondering at the steaming drink in the other's arms.

"Not one you want to go to. Doctor Lovell found out Suzie's gone," Lydia said quietly. "He's somewhat intoxicated. Found him in the supply closet..."

Her friend sniffed her. "Perhaps a lot intoxicated? And was perhaps trying to share an entire still with you...?" Charlotte added. "Want some help?"

"No thanks, Doctor Stockton is over there and..."

The other woman rolled her eyes heavenward. "God help Doctor Lovell when he wakes up to that one!" Charlotte finished. They both knew very well that Doctor Stockton held deep convictions about alcohol use among the medical staff, who needed to be ready for duty at a moment's notice.

Back inside the recovery again, Lydia offered the hot liquid to the doctors.

"Um, Doctor Stockton," Lydia started. "We all knew this would be hard for him to take..."

Harold looked up at her as he received the cup and pitcher. "Don't worry, Nurse Finney. He'll get all the mercy he deserves. He's got to be ready for surgery, so I can't be excessively hard on him," he added somewhat regretfully, Lydia thought.

Lydia nodded and, turning, left the prostrate man quite literally at the mercy of the other doctor.

Upon entering their tent, Simon stirred as Lydia slid out of her coat and put a fresh piece of wood in their stove. He lifted the edge of the blanket for her to join him, and this time, she was glad to slide under the cover with him where it was warm and inviting.

Simon's nose wrinkled. "I have always found you intoxicating," he admitted. "But did you run into a whiskey barrel out there? I could get drunk off of you."

"In a manner of speaking," she replied. "Marcus is totally soused. He was on the floor of the recovery... back in supply."

Simon looked at her face. "What did he do, pour half a bottle on you too? Smells like pretty strong stuff."

"Doctor Stockton helped me get him onto a cot. He's over there now working to sober him up."

Simon chuckled dryly. "Wouldn't want to be in Marc's shoes. How long was I asleep?"

Lydia closed her eyes and rested herself against him. "Not long enough..." she whispered, "to make up for being up last night... that was the best bed bath in history..." She reached up and kissed Simon fully on his mouth, finding the smoothness of his lips between beard and mustache, and then nestled her head again under his chin against his shoulder. "Let's both nap a little longer," she murmured. And as they lay there, before sleep overcame her, she thought back to what Marcus had said in his stupor. *"It's always been you." It must have been the whiskey talking*, Lydia concluded, and allowed herself the luxury of sleep.

Casualties arrived before the new station commander did. With the previous rains no longer a deterrent to battle plans, the offensive to take the Ancre Valley was fully underway. British, Scottish Highlander, Canadian, and occasionally French wounded were rushed to the station as fast as the rescue vehicles could navigate the frozen mud and icy slush. Due to the cold, the triage tent was now manned with staff solely assigned to keep the stoves burning and the wounded men warm. Along with the physically injured, the nurses found themselves triaging men with the rash and pounding headache of measles, those with throats inflamed and swollen from mumps, and countless numbers with incessant coughing from bronchitis. Other soldiers came in blinded by mustard gas, their newer gas masks ineffective against the chemical which entered through the skin, to poison them. Many, losing their sight, were anxious for help to write one last letter to loved ones while they could still sign their name in their own shaking hand. For some, the last image they would see was the shattered, ice-coated shards of trees and buildings in the valley they had fought to retain.

On the first day of casualties, Doctor Lovell had appeared no worse for the wear, despite repeatedly asking a nurse to check him for rash, as he expressed a fear that he might be coming down with measles, due to his pounding headache. Lydia had observed the man carefully for any symptoms affecting the steadiness of his hand with the scalpel, but had seen nothing that would have prevented him from performing his duties. She was acutely aware that Doctor Stockton had also cast an eye on his fellow doctor, from time to time. For the most part, Marcus seemed to be maddeningly normal, teasing the nurses and often uttering irreverent jokes in the middle of pulling shrapnel and pieces of barbed wire from his patients.

The surgery was now running for long hours, every day, without pause. Lydia was concerned about Simon standing for hours on end and noticed when he pulled over a stool, to operate from a seated position. She cast him an inquisitive look, over her mask, half disbelieving him when he assured her that he was 'doing fine'. For the first time in over six weeks of bed rest and healing, he was doing what he did best... his hands were wonderfully steady and his mood cheerful. In fact, he seemed happier than she had seen him in a long time. He was, he would later assure her, in his element again, back in control and feeling useful.

Inclement weather hindered the trucks from transporting stable patients to the field hospitals. By the end of the first day of the Ancre assault, a second recovery tent was needed to accommodate men waiting for their turn to be transported. The same weather did not, however, prevent the new station commander from arriving in the middle of the siege, along with the two new French nurses. When word came to Lydia that the nurses had arrived, she called Linda to cover for her at the table with Simon and went to greet the new arrivals.

She found the new station commander had been met by an army corporal assigned to his service and abruptly whisked away to the command tent, behind all the medical facilities, centered in the station. Lydia quickly approached the two women disembarking the truck with their footlockers.

"Welcome to the station," Lydia assured them as they looked around nervously at the tents flapping slightly in the cold, wet wind. "I am Lydia Finney, Red Cross. Corpsmen, take these foot-lockers to one of the nurses' tents, please. Come with me, ladies." She led them to the mess tent and quickly secured the flap against the wind as the women stepped inside. She gestured to the long table and said, "Help yourselves to coffee or tea, as you like, and let me introduce you to the camp after you've warmed up. When did you last eat?"

"This morning, mademoiselle," one of the women said grate-fully, pouring herself hot coffee and one for her companion.

"It's just Lydia, please, "Lydia assured her. "Only with the doc-tors are we formal. Between the nurses, we are family. If there is any food laid out, you are welcome to it. Cook tries to keep something hot available to us while the surgery is running."

"Forgive me," the woman apologized, "I did not know you were a nurse."

Lydia understood the error, dressed as she was, in army olive green with her hair pulled back in its blue scarf. "Indeed, how could you? We don't look like what you might be accustomed to."

"You do not wear the uniform of the nurse?" the other asked.

"We do not. There is no time or energy to keep anything that is white, white out here. If we can find an army shirt and trouser that is clean, it's enough. These scarves, however, are our own personal uniform of sorts. They set us apart for the doctors when they're trying to find one of us quickly. And you are...?"

"I am Monique Despirite, and this is Adrielle Marchendeaux," the one identifying herself as Monique introduced them both. "We are from hospitals in Bordeaux."

"You've come a very long way," Lydia observed. "And in poor weather, I'm afraid."

"Almost, we were sent to St. Johns at Étaples," the other nurse, Adrielle, told her. "There is much sickness there in the nursing staff. They have a lot of measles and need assistance, but our orders are to come here, so we are here."

"You are very welcome, we have need of you too," Lydia assured them. "We have three surgeons here, many corpsmen, and a few medics—some of them are also new. The nurses are all engaged at the moment, as casualties started coming in yesterday from a campaign to the northeast near Beaumont-Hamel. The British are advancing there."

"In the winter?"

Lydia nodded, "In the cold. The rains finally let up, so the British are attempting to move the Germans eastward before winter fully sets in."

"Where is Beaumont-Hamel?" Monique asked.

Lydia calculated. "What is left of it is about six miles from us, to the northeast."

"Mon Dieu," Adrielle breathed, looking quickly over at her companion. "We are near the front."

Lydia looked at her, concerned. "Didn't you know?" she asked them. "The mobile stations serve as close to the front as we can get, without being directly attacked. It is how they get the wounded to us so quickly. Did no one tell you?"

Adrielle looked frightened. "They said there would be little fighting now as winter is come and so..."

Monique shook her head. "We were told the front had been pushed back close to Belgium and so, no, we would have little chance of any fighting."

Lydia sighed. "I am sorry to hear that you were told that. They were correct that winter is coming and we will have less fighting. Yes, that part is true. But this is a mobile station, and we move to be closest to where we are needed. For now, we are needed here. I am afraid that news travels very slowly back to the Red Cross, and so perhaps they were not aware of our situation. I send updates once every month to the American Red Cross in Philadelphia, where we all shipped out from. For the French Red Cross, we go through our station commander."

"Is this not very dangerous, mademoiselle, Lydia?" Adrielle said quietly.

Lydia nodded. "It is dangerous. I don't want to mislead you. I have been here since May, along with eleven other nurses. One of ours was sent out early last summer with pneumonia and did not return. None of us have been killed. None of our doctors have been killed, and they have been here since January. We have a small group of soldiers here guarding our station and moving us where we need to go, and they do try to protect us."

"The Germans, they do not come to here?" Adrielle pressed.

"Sometimes, yes, we get wounded and some prisoners passing through. We have not been overrun. There is a British casualty clearing station north of us also serving near the front as we do. They were overrun once and joined us here for a time. But they have gone back to their own station now. We are not out here alone. The entire British Fifth Army is just to the north of us, and the Sixth to the south. Before you decide if you go back or stay, I would like you to meet the other nurses. I would like you to see what we do here."

Monique nodded. "We have been trained in first aid, and to do dressings, and to care for the physical needs of the soldiers. These things we have done at hospital."

Lydia hesitated a moment before answering the unspoken question that hung in the air: *Is that enough?*

When she spoke, she tried to convey the deepest confidence in these women that she could muster. "Those things are needed here as well. We came here from the States with the same training you received. We have learned many more things while here. If you choose to, you will learn to assist in the surgery tent, to help the surgeons open and close the patient, to set broken bones and put on splints... to tell which patient must come first and second, and which does not have a chance to survive. Our doctors are very good teachers and will teach you whatever you wish to learn." She saw that the women were taking in her message. "However, we will not ask you to do anything that you do not want to do or do not feel you can do. The ten nurses here are all excellent women. We will ask only that you do your best and that you tell one of us if you cannot do something being asked of you. You may stay, with our welcome, and learn or you may go back and be assigned to a hospital again, if you wish. But please," Lydia urged them, "do not decide until you meet the nurses."

Monique and Adrielle looked at one another. "Show us," Monique said with more curiosity than fear.

"Very good," Lydia replied. She stood up, buttoned her coat, put her cup in with the dirty dishes for washing, and led the two new nurses from the mess.

They saw the ambulances arriving, the litter bearers taking the wounded into the triage tent. Lydia led them past the surgery and triage to the recovery, where there would be the most sense of calm. Once inside, the newcomers quickly took in the two rows of cots, inches from one another, three-fourths full of wounded men. Some with bandages covering blinded eyes from the mustard gas, others missing arms, legs, or both, with bandages well-wrapped over stumps. Other patients were staring into space, not responding to the sounds around them.

Mary and Gretha moved among the men carrying their trays of antiseptics, gauzes, bandages, and pain relief, quickly and efficiently directing the orderlies with personal care and hygiene orders. Lydia led the new nurses through the maze of well-ordered confusion as a new patient arrived from the surgery and was deposited carefully onto an empty, waiting cot. Mary took a quick head-to-toe glance over the man, listening to his heart and lungs, before writing the name from his identification medallion into a ledger, next to a quick diagnosis. "Open chest wound... measles."

"This is Mary Atkins, one of our best," Lydia introduced her as the other smiled at the new women, without slowing in her tasks. "Meet Monique and Adrielle."

Mary nodded and said, "Good to meet you. A little busy right now. Glad you came."

Monique looked puzzled at Lydia. "Nurse Mary, she listens with the stethoscope, no?"

Lydia nodded. "Yes, we all do."

"But this is not what nurses do...?" Adrielle added with some misgiving.

"It is what we do here," Lydia explained. "It is necessary to be both eyes and ears for our doctors."

The three continued to where Gretha was changing a dressing on a bloody stump of a man missing his foot.

Lydia knelt, lifting the man's limb for Gretha so she could wind the clean bandage more quickly around the stump. Gretha unrolled the clean bandage swiftly and talked while she wrapped. "Hello, ladies," she nodded, "can't shake your hands right now, you understand."

"Of course," Monique assured her. "You do that so quickly! I am amazed."

"It's easy when you've done thousands," Gretha smiled disarmingly. Then, to Lydia, added, "Oops, maybe I shouldn't have said that?"

Lydia patted her arm as she lowered the man's leg back down and carefully covered him with the blanket. "No, Gretha, you were right. It comes more easily the more we do it. But we all started out with the first one."

Continuing, Lydia showed them where the supplies were kept and introduced them to some of the orderlies, knowing they would never remember all of the names. Then, she led them out of the recovery to where triage was being conducted. She quickly introduced them to Laura Mitchell and Nancy Miller, their blue-scarved heads bent over dozens of wounded newly arriving as they directed the litter bearers in to position the wounded and assigned them appropriate number cards. Laura and Nancy waved quickly from where they were working, but did not stop to talk. Medics assisted them in containing superficial lacerations, intermittently relieving tourniquets and applying pressure bandages.

"Is it always like this?" Monique asked Lydia.

"Only when the wounded are arriving in significant numbers. When it's only a few, we triage them right in the recovery. What is important now is to get them warm and hydrated. The cold is a blessing in keeping bleeding down. It's a curse for... many other reasons."

They left the triage tent, and she took them to one of the nurses' tents, finding where their footlockers had been stowed. It was a little cold inside the tent, the stove being banked against a future time someone would come in off duty to rest. "We have three tents for the nurses, so they have obviously put you two together here. Our tents are always close to the recovery and the surgery in case we're needed quickly. You are welcome to warm up the stove and rest today. I know that this has been a long and difficult trip."

The two women looked around at the sparse tent. Four cots, one stove, four footlockers, pairs of socks drying on the ends of two of the cots. It was difficult for them to imagine that some women had been living in here for almost seven months. Adrielle observed simply, "I think this makes sense if you must often pack up, to move?"

Lydia nodded. "Always keep your canteens full. We use snow or ice on top of the stove, to thaw into water. The latrines are on the edge of the camp. Important things stay in your footlocker. We do not unpack. Perhaps, though, with winter coming, we will unpack a little, if we stay here very long." She did not tell them of the utter destruction of the tents when the bomb had recently fallen on their little station. It had not made sense, after that, for any of the staff to redisplay the few scattered, decorative personal items they had been lucky enough to recover. The war too quickly took things away.

"You did not take us to the surgery," Monique observed carefully.

Lydia shook her head. "No, not today. This is not the time. And I must return there, I've been away long enough. Rest… and if you choose to, go back to the recovery to Mary and Gretha… you could be of help there. We do work in shifts when we are able to. Your hands would be appreciated helping to feed and wash the men and reinforce their bandages."

"When are you able to take shifts?" Adrielle wondered.

"When the wounded stop coming in," Lydia replied and took her leave. She was anxious to see how they were getting along in the surgery.

Slipping back into the surgery tent, Lydia washed up and grabbed a clean apron. Sally was circulating. Lydia passed between people running about, doing their jobs, slipped between the tables, saw what Harold and Marlene were working on at the table they shared, saw Simon and Laura working intensely to repair a torn tendon in a man's exposed leg. Then she saw Marcus approaching a prostrate form being lifted onto the table in front of him and knew where she was needed. The soldier had an open gash in his flank… he had fallen on a coil of barbed wire, a section of which was still lodged in his skin. As the man began to warm up, his wounds started bleeding, profusely. Lydia moved into position next to Marcus. He reached for an instrument, from the corpsman across the table, and promptly sent it clattering to the ground, dropping it.

"Lots of bleeders," she noted to the surgeon. "Mind if I help?"

Marcus was sweating. "Sure," he said, "if you've got the time."

"I have the time," she said softly. She quickly began tying off any bleeding arteries while the corpsman cut the sharp wire into sections, making it easier to remove from the soldier's skin and internal organs where it had lodged. The three of them worked silently, cutting the wire, pulling it away, staunching the blood, suturing vessels closed. Lydia rinsed the wound as the last of the barbed wire came free. She peered into the cavity where a loop of bowel was exposed.

"I can't see," Marcus said quietly.

Lydia pulled the light over closer.

"No, I can't see, Lydia... anything," he murmured.

"Corpsman," Lydia said quietly to the man right across the table, "Get Doctor Lovell out of here before he passes out. Get some liquids and food in him."

Quickly, the corpsman dropped his instrument on the tray, grabbed Marcus, and supported him as they quietly left the surgery.

Lydia stood pondering the open belly wound in front of her. "Um, gentlemen," she said calmly to no one in particular. "Either of you doctors have a spare minute?"

Harold and Simon looked over to her, from their tables, having scarcely appreciated that Marcus had left the surgery. It was a foregone assumption that each of them needed to go out for a quick breather from time to time.

"Give me a sec, Nurse Finney," Simon said, "almost done here."

But before either of the other two doctors could move, another voice said, "I do." A man who had been quietly circulating in the surgery and reloading the stored anesthesia supplies came to her side. "What is it?"

Lydia looked up into piercing blue eyes, a shock of black hair, and an air of calm. "Are you a new medic? We have contained all the bleeders, and the razor wire has been removed, but I think a section of the large bowel has been torn. Looks like the colon is spilling out stool right here..."

As Simon and Harold Stockton looked over, now quite curious and listening, the stranger peered into the soldier's belly with alacrity. "You would be correct. You are a nurse, I assume?" he asked her, reaching already for the forceps she was holding in one hand while she irrigated the wound with antiseptic solution with the other hand.

"I am... Lydia Finney," she said softly. "And you are..."

"Your new station commander. Doctor Henri Fortraine," he replied.

"Welcome aboard, Doctor Fortraine," she replied without hesitation, handing him a needle and suture before he asked for it, while adjusting the overhead light so he could see into the wound.

He smiled at her under his mask. "Indeed."

Chapter 14
The Frozen Trek

"The best way for me to get to know how a system is working is to observe it, in action," Doctor Fortraine stated to the assembled medical staff in the mess tent. "To that end, I have been observing how this team operates and functions over the past few days. Your care of the wounded is efficient and commendable. I see little room for improvement. However, I will be meeting with Doctor Stockton to discuss matters so that I am fully up to speed. When we have a meeting such as this one, all ideas are welcomed. Otherwise, you will take your concerns to Doctor Stockton, who will convey them to me in the appropriate chain of command."

The medical team listened, nodding. They had been accustomed to Doctor Stockton being their intermediary with Lieutenant Aubert as well. The new commander looked around the little group. "The floor is, shall we say, open?" he offered.

Simon decided to speak up. "One of the things that makes this station unique is how our team works to improve our clinical skills as a group. We valued spending time and sharing best practices with our British colleagues recently... it was a benefit to everyone. If there is a way that can be continued, as the war allows, we'd like to be able to periodically share advancements, face-to-face, with the other stations."

Doctor Fortraine nodded. "I will speak with their commander—"

"Captain Adam Thornwall," Simon offered.

He nodded, making a mental note. "Is there something else?" Fortraine questioned. He looked around at the group.

"We've heard, Doctor, that St. John's has exceeded capacity in Étaples, all five hundred plus beds," Marlene reported. "Do you know if the British were correct about that?"

"I have also heard this to be true," Fortraine replied. "The operations of the hospital are not technically under any military supervision, but the implications are something I wish to speak with Doctor Stockton about. I appreciate that any changes to hospital bed capacity has an impact on all of the stations. Hopefully, some of the fighting will diminish through December, but word has it, from command, that the Allied efforts to push back the Germans, even in winter, will continue. We can expect lower numbers of casualties, but there will still be a steady flow.

"The area of the Somme remains of strategic importance, and the lines will be at least held, if not advanced, before the spring offensive. New mobile tanks are being employed on the battlefield. They are less hampered by weather and terrain than men on foot and obstacles such as the barbed wire fences do not hinder them as they do human bodies. Therefore, we can expect that tanks may make breaches in German lines that were previously impassable. We will not be relocating south."

Harold nodded. "So, business as usual," he acknowledged. "However, we also hear that some Germans are surrendering to

Allied troops. We need to be prepared for this as well. It will not be the first time we've treated wounded German soldiers, but there must be clear protocols for our sentries and the medical staff, should larger groups wander into this station, under a white flag."

Their new commander nodded. "You shall have them. You will also find that our soldier compliment has been enlarged. Additionally, everyone must have a typhoid shot. And while we are a bit more stationary, the army will make efforts to move mail with improved efficiency. Especially as the holiday approaches."

With this last remark, the flap to the mess opened, and a private entered quickly to speak in Fortraine's ear.

"You will excuse me," he said to them all and left the table abruptly.

The group remaining behind looked at one another after the man left.

Marcus spoke up, appearing refreshed and back to his usual self, after some rest and fluids. "Well, I like him!" he declared to the group.

Harold chuckled. "I'm sure he'll be glad to hear that he has your endorsement, Doctor."

"No, seriously!" Marcus explained. "He's even willing to pick up a scalpel. We've gotten a station commander and another surgeon if we need it."

Laura sighed. "Did you hear what he said about mail? It would be nice to get more mail. Now is the time to write home and ask for fudge, while it can get here without melting."

Gretha glanced over at the mess line. "Do you think the cook will have something special for Thanksgiving? Do the French celebrate Thanksgiving? If not, they should."

Marlene reminded them all, "He found something good in July for Bastille Day. I'll bet he finds something for Thanksgiving... even if they don't celebrate, less fighting is worth being thankful for."

Harold added, "Sounds like the Thanksgiving menu should be a topic for my next strategic planning meeting with Fortraine. In other news, for the past week, we haven't had more than twenty to thirty casualties a day, and not all of them needed the surgery, so that's something to be thankful for at any rate. I imagine our British counterparts haven't fared so well north of us."

"These measles cases are rampant," Laura said. "I can't imagine why here and why now, but so many cases are coming through. What will we do if everyone here comes down with it? We won't be able to function at all."

Simon spoke up. "The fact that so few of us have contracted it suggests that most of us had it already, years ago. We're probably able to fight it off." He turned to the new nurses sitting at the table, listening in, quietly. "How are you nurses adjusting to life here at the station? This must be a bit hard to get used to."

Monique answered him. "For myself, Doctor Finney, I'm finding the change a surprise. I did not expect... the expectations of here to be so... not like at the hospital at all."

"Is any of it a good surprise?" Simon asked her, genuinely interested.

"So far, Nurse Finney put us first in recovery. So many dressings. So many sick men, coughs, and such. And poor ones unable to see, frightened. Is it very sad. There is much learning here."

"And you, Nurse Marchendeaux? Also a surprise?" Simon pressed.

"Oui, monsieur," Adrielle replied quietly. "I enjoy recovery, yes. I feel good to help there. I miss hot, running water. Very different from Bordeaux."

Marcus chimed in with his usual casual demeanor. "If you nurses want to learn about the surgery and more, just ask any of us. We're all happy to make you comfortable with the rest of the operations of the station."

"Merci, but for now, Doctor," Adrielle replied, "the recovery is best for me. Nurse Finney says I stay with soldiers and give help to them."

Lydia smiled at the newest nurse. "You have a particular way about you that is very calming and soothing to the men. I see them relax quickly under your care... especially those who have seen too much of this war; you have a gift of helping them to have courage."

Adrielle reddened at the well-earned praise. Privately, Lydia thought it unlikely the woman would ever want to step up to the rigors of the surgery or the triage, but she was certainly needed where she was, and her presence freed up the rest of them to make the difficult choices elsewhere. Monique, however, was more confident, more apt to take risks. She would no doubt do well in the surgery, and Lydia was already discussing it with Marlene, who she felt would be a good tutor for the new nurse.

It quickly became apparent that Fortraine would not be returning to the mess tent. Harold decided they had given the man enough time to settle whatever affairs he was addressing, so he told them all that they may as well go back to their duties. He called out to Simon for a moment of his time, no doubt to discuss the new camp commander. As the two men left the mess tent, Marcus approached Lydia.

"Nurse Finney," he began. "A moment of your time?"

Lydia nodded to Marcus as she finished her conversation with the two new nurses. "I will meet you both in the recovery." She watched as Monique and Adrielle buttoned their coats and headed out to their duties, then turned to Marcus, who gestured to the table. Curious, Lydia sat back down as Marc straddled the bench beside her. He looked down at his hands, sheepishly.

"Um, Lydia," he started, faltering. "I just want to... I want to apologize for..."

She put a hand on his arm gently. "It's okay, Marcus," she said softly. "I understand."

"I don't think that you do," he corrected her. "I do remember some of what... happened in the supply area."

"If this is because Doctor Stockton told you to come talk to me, it isn't necessary, Marcus," Lydia said softly enough for only their own ears to hear. "You have been a wonderful friend to Simon, and also to me. I owe you more than you could possibly know, and I totally understand how hard it was for you when Suzie left. I do understand."

Marc looked at her with troubled eyes. "Thank you for that, Lydia, truly," he said. "But what I want you to know is... meeting you has... raised the bar, so to speak. For me. You've become... the goal... no, don't misunderstand. I don't mean you are my goal.

What I mean is... I want to be a man... I want to be the kind of man—"

"Doc!" one of the soldiers burst in, cutting short their conversation. "Doc, you gotta come quick. One of the guys fell on a tent peg. Got it stuck in his leg."

Marcus nodded and quickly stood. He glanced at Lydia, still seated, obviously wanting to say more to her.

"Go," she told him. "It's all good."

He nodded, following the soldier, his face still telegraphing a deep concern. Lydia rose to go meet the nurses in the recovery, wondering what this was all about.

The surgery was currently not in use. The few trucks that arrived had brought in men with frostbite and trench foot and fracture injuries, but they were not in need of the doctors, beyond diagnostics of their various ailments. The recovery, however, remained busy and Lydia caught up with Adrielle and Nancy. Soon after, Monique joined them as well.

"Mind if I tag along?" she asked Lydia.

"Not at all, but you certainly deserve some time off, if you want it," Lydia exclaimed.

Monique shook her head. "No, I wish to see."

"Very well," Lydia said.

The four women observed the activity in the recovery and relieved the nurses on duty, who welcomed the chance to return to their tents after grabbing a bite to eat. Susannah had left her copy of *Wuthering Heights* in the camp for the nurses to share. Darkness came so early these days that in the comfort of the warm, stove light, they had taken to reading chapters to each other in the privacy of their tents... it was a wonderful distraction into a world of fiction.

All day, none of them had heard any planes overhead and no bombs had shaken the earth. Perhaps those new tanks the commander had mentioned were replacing aerial offensives. Lydia taught the two new nurses the record-keeping system they were using, the carefully kept ledgers of names of men who came under their care. Then the women set about their shift work. Nancy turned her attention to the soldiers with trench foot, whose feet were swelling, causing them excruciating pain and administered laudanum, freely, to those moaning or asking for help. One of the soldiers pulled Adrielle aside almost immediately and asked her, in French, to help him write a letter home. Lydia looked around at the orderlies moving about, helping attend to the daily physical needs of toileting and bathing.

Monique looked around as well. "It is, as you say, well-oiled machine," she observed.

Lydia nodded. "That is our goal."

"The doctors come here too each day?"

She nodded again. "Yes, and as we need them. They know us and know we will call them if something looks suspicious, si quelque chose semble suspect..."

"Why do you speak French... avec moi?" Monique said. "We must learn English."

"French is a beautiful language," Lydia smiled at the woman. "We like to practice our French as well."

"And you marry here, yes?" Monique wondered aloud.

Lydia laughed. "This is where Doctor Finney and I met. And we do not know how long this war will continue. We did not want to wait until the Allies decide to send everyone home."

"At hospital, nurses may not marry," Monique stated, puzzled. "This is a new thing to me."

The two women turned a man on his cot and put clean blankets beneath him. "It is a new thing to everyone," Lydia admitted.

"It does not take your mind from your duties?" the other pressed her.

"One time it did," Lydia said evenly, thinking back to the day of the bombing when her entire being was focused only on finding Simon in the ruins and getting help for him, regardless of the countless wounded all around them. Only one thing had mattered at that moment, and she would do it again, the same way, if disaster ever befell the station again. "But most of the time, duty comes first, to the wounded, to these men."

Monique carefully positioned a pillow beneath the stump of a man's leg needing elevation. "And you Americans do this for us, for France? You do not have family at home for you?"

Lydia paused as they moved to the next prostrate soldier. "Most of us have families at home, yes. But we do this because we believe we are called to do this."

"I am called also," Monique replied quietly. "I feel this."

Lydia looked at her clear eyes and saw the focus and determination in them. "I know that you do. And Adrielle also."

Monique gently lifted the head of a man in front of them to help him drink. "Adrielle, as well. But she is unsure if to stay or to go."

"I know," Lydia nodded. "But look at her there, how good she is with that man in pain and confused. She must find her own way. Whatever she decides is good for her will be acceptable."

"Soon, you put me in the surgery, please?" Monique added. "Je suis prêt."

"Very well. Marlene Sullivan is a wonderful surgical nurse. You will work with her," Lydia assured her. "I've already talked to her about it. The surgery requires a different kind of skill. Equally important as this, but different."

"You like the surgery?" Monique asked. "More than others?"

"I like it all," Lydia assured her. "Except when the men die."

Monique nodded her head, understanding. "That is why I come."

Lydia looked around. "If you all are okay here for a minute, I am going to go to freshen up."

"This freshen?"

"To the latrine!" Lydia laughed.

Monique rolled her eyes and laughed as well.

Lydia left the tent, bundled in her coat, carefully securing the flap from the wind and cold of the night. She hated going to the latrine at night, in the cold. The only redeeming feature of the latrine in winter was the diminished odor, with everything frozen. She met Charlotte outside, coming from the mess. The woman handed her a chunk of cheese and bread.

"Want some?" Charlotte said.

"Sure, why not?" Lydia replied, accepting the offered food and sticking it in the pocket of her coat for later. "Where are you off to?"

"Got to use the necessary," Charlotte replied. "I hope it's for the last time tonight. It's getting colder."

They fell into step. "Do you think the new girls will last?" Charlotte asked. "We sure miss Susannah, but I don't know if it's right to ask these girls to stay much longer. They're still like frightened deer."

Lydia nodded. "Adrielle is, that's for sure, but I think Monique is going to be fine. She already wants to take a stab at the surgery, and I talked to Marlene about taking her under her wing."

"Not going to pair her up with Doctor Lovell, are you?" Charlotte pressed. "Don't throw her to the wolf yet, please! She'll run for sure."

Lydia chuckled. "I think he's learned his lesson," she said. "Doctor Stockton just might have had a conversation with him about his adventures with women and urged him to reconsider his choices."

Charlotte shook her head as they walked. "I don't know. In the meeting this morning, he was still offering to be very... helpful... shall we say? With the new nurses?"

The women reached the latrine. There were sentries around the station at intervals. In the starlight, Lydia could see where one was perched on duty, restlessly stamping his booted feet, against the icy ground. "Those poor fellows. There's frostbite waiting to happen!"

"Wait until you pull your pants down inside, then tell me about the cold!" Charlotte laughed.

The latrine was a two-holer with sandbags around the base, keeping the cold air from blowing up inside while people were most vulnerable to the elements. It was relatively warmer than the outside. Charlotte shivered, pulling her trousers down. "Yikes, I might freeze right to this plank of wood."

"Just don't get any splinters down there," Lydia teased her friend. "Or You Know Who will offer to take them out. And that will ruin any conceivable New Year's resolution he might be considering."

They tended to their business and dressed quickly, each breath visible in the dim light.

"This," Lydia said, "is what the new girls were talking about, missing running hot water! Oh, for a sink and soap, right here!"

"And real tissue paper that doesn't rub half your skin off," Charlotte added longingly.

"Ready?" Lydia said, pushing the door open, ready for the cold wind in her face.

They stepped out into the brisk night. Immediately, hands covered their mouths and voices spoke softly in their ears.

"Sei ruhig!" a deep voice commanded.

Charlotte nodded and swallowed the scream trying to leave her throat, assuming there could be only one interpretation of that message. She was unable to see Lydia clearly in the darkness, but quickly became aware there were several figures clustered about them. Where were the sentries?

Lydia felt the barrel of a gun poking against her back. The two women had no choice, but to let themselves be half dragged and half pushed toward the dark night outside of the camp boundaries, across the rough, frozen ground. The soldiers did not release their grips on the two women for a long time, and it soon became apparent that two of the sentries were also being dragged along, by those carrying rifles. Lydia pulled at the hand on her mouth just enough to speak, hoping she was saying it correctly, and asked, "Was willst du?"

"Krankenschwester," the man breathed in her ear.

Lydia had heard Gretha use that word with the German soldier they had helped in camp.

"Yes, oui, krankenschwester," she said, her heart pounding in her throat. Nurses. They wanted nurses.

He did not reply again, but pushed them onward into the countryside. It seemed they walked for several miles before they stopped briefly on the edge of a small uprising where they were slightly sheltered from the wind. There, one of the soldiers pushed the two women together. Charlotte grabbed Lydia's cold hand in a vise-like grip in her fear. They could just barely make out the faces and figures of the German soldiers around them.

To her horror, a German soldier put his rifle up to a sentry's head.

"No!" Lydia cried out. "No! No!"

"Oh, please!" Charlotte begged. "Don't hurt him! Please! S'il vous plaît!"

The soldier who appeared to be in charge of the group looked at the women closely. He motioned with his hand, pointing to them, then to himself, then out into the dark countryside east ahead of them.

Lydia and Charlotte both nodded. "Okay, okay. Just don't hurt him."

Then, the same soldier pulled Charlotte over in front of him and pressed his pistol to the side of her head, looking intently at the two French soldiers. They both quickly put their hands up in surrender. Lydia felt pure terror wash over her.

"Ne leur fais pas de mal," one sentry said quietly, calmly, keeping his hands elevated and visible. "L'infirmières."

The German soldiers spoke to each other quickly and appeared to be having some debate amongst themselves for several long minutes. Then, their leader lowered his pistol and pointed again over to the east, out into the night.

"I don't know any German," Lydia whispered to Charlotte.

"Me either," she whispered back, grabbing her friend's hand again tightly after the soldier released her.

"Fangen Sie an zu laufen," the German told the four of them, now assured that there was an understanding, of was expected of them, that surpassed any language barrier.

Without protest, they started walking, stumbling at times over hillocks of frozen grasses and protruding rocks, burrowing themselves into their heavy coats to keep warm. The exertion of walking was enough for now, but they knew that the cold sweat would be painful when they stopped. Lydia looked up into the night, trying to locate the Dipper and the North Star to help her with direction. It seemed they were heading due east. She knew the front was only six miles away. Surely, they had covered at least three or four miles already.

"What do you think they want?" Charlotte whispered once.

"Sei ruhig!" The guttural command was immediate; better to save her breath for walking.

As they trudged along, Charlotte and Lydia thought about their earlier longing for hot water and soft tissue... both useless and irrelevant at the moment. To each of them came the thought that there were wounded somewhere who needed help. These Germans clearly knew they had entered a Red Cross station. They knew the women were not soldiers. The sentries, though, were in grave danger, although it was a good sign they had not been killed outright. Lydia thought back to her experience with Simon at the checkpoint and wondered how she would communicate that she needed the sentries to assist them in helping any wounded men they might find. It was their only hope of keeping them alive. An hour seemed to have passed and still they walked. To the east, a bright star had risen over the horizon, and the women were glad to see it. It was a jewel in the velvet black of night and gave them something on which to focus other than the German soldiers pressing forward around them.

Finally, when she thought she could walk no further, Lydia said out loud, "Please, s'il vous plaît..."

One of the soldiers turned and looked at her. He said something long and complicated that she couldn't comprehend, but his motions indicated, perhaps, that they were nearing the end of their journey. Rows of barbed wire came into view, glinting in the light of the stars overhead. Expertly, the soldier navigated his way through the loops of sharp wire. There were tanks looming in the darkness, the first tanks the women had ever seen. They were staggered by their size and the great tracks upon which they ran. Some soldiers were posted by the tanks and looked at them curiously as they passed, speaking only in German to the escorts around the four. Finally, in the darkness, they stopped. The women were exhausted.

A soldier pointed to a ladder, the handles extending just above the ground. One of the Germans swung around and started climbing down. Charlotte hesitated but, following a harsh command, took hold of the ladder herself and began to descend, Lydia right behind her, followed by the two Frenchmen. They were in the trenches. Numb with cold and confusion, the four followed single file along a narrow wooden board where heavily armed German soldiers stood on post, glancing curiously at the new arrivals. The wooden walkway was slippery, and, more than once, the women had to reach out to grab something for support to keep from falling… usually it was a, not-unfriendly, hand that steadied them as they passed. There were a few wires running along the trench and an occasional lightbulb. Some of the men were smoking cigarettes. Others appeared to be resting, perched in small alcoves cut out of the ground, below the surface. On and on, down the slippery walkway they continued, passing several turns until the four were hopelessly disoriented.

At long last, they came to what appeared to be a wide room cut out of the ground and lined with wooden beams. There was light inside. Lydia and Charlotte bent to enter and immediately saw what they had feared the most. There were dozens of wounded men lying on wooden boards perched precariously on log posts in the ground. It was an underground aid station of sorts. Charlotte looked around them for any indication of medical personnel in action. The wounded men just lay quietly or moaned in the dim light.

"Oh my," the women said in unison.

Lydia bent over the first man lying there, his right arm a bloody and torn mess of flesh. She looked at the second and saw the man's leg askew, no doubt fractured, but at least with no bone protruding. Charlotte leaned over a third and saw the bleed from his abdomen coagulating in the cold on the uniform. She gently probed the man's stomach, and he moaned, but here was no new gush of blood when she did so.

Lydia motioned to one of their captors, making the gesture of washing hands. An order was barked, and someone emerged with a bucket of water. The two women rubbed their cold hands briskly, letting it run on the ground. Lydia said to the other three, "Let's pair up. I am hoping they will think you are orderlies, so act like orderlies and do exactly what we tell you."

The men nodded.

Charlotte stood in front of the soldier who had marched them there and patted her chest. "Charlotte, I'm Charlotte." Then she patted the German's chest and raised her eyebrows, questioning.

"Frederick," he said.

She nodded, "Frederick. Good."

Lydia nodded and patted her own chest. "Lydia." She pointed to their two companions, who dutifully offered, "Paul" and "Philippe."

"Glad we got that out of the way," Lydia breathed.

Charlotte was already formulating a plan, "This man, here, with the abdominal wound... he has to come first, if they have suture." She made a sewing motion with her hands to the one in charge. He opened his hands to show they were empty. There was a conversation in German behind them, and turning, Lydia saw a soldier come through the door carrying some kind of first aid knapsack. It was better than gold. Eagerly, the women opened it and examined the contents. Lydia removed a rolled gauze and held it up to the man named Frederick. "More like this," she said, holding up the singular roll before him.

He shook his head, but pretended to tear his shirt.

"Yes," Lydia nodded. "Like that."

He issued a clipped order, and one of the soldiers scurried out in search of torn fabric they could use as bandages. The two women started to pull away the sodden mass of clothes over the stricken man's abdomen.

Lydia looked to one of the newly appointed orderlies, "Paul, pull that lantern down here for me." He did so, and she peered into the wound, gently using tweezers which she had found in the first aid pack, to explore the damage, while trying to not disturb the clot in the wound.

She looked up at Charlotte. "I don't feel a bullet or anything. Can we roll him and see if it came out the back?"

With Paul's help, they gently rolled the man to his side. There, a large, gaping wound was clearly visible. Charlotte and Lydia's eyes met over the man. The German leader, Frederick, saw and understood the significance of the look. Immediately, he issued an order, and two soldiers appeared and carried the fallen man outside, not to return. The soldiers brought in another to take his place.

The women worked as quickly as they could. They bandaged open wounds, pulling together torn skin to minimize bleeding before carefully wrapping the limbs to hold staunching cloth pads in place. With the help of Paul and Philippe, they realigned broken bones under the skin and applied homemade splints from pieces of wood brought to them. They applied iodine to scalp wounds before wrapping heads with cloth bandages. The German wounded were appreciative, thanking the women for their care as they left the little alcove, murmuring, "Danke, danke," as they left. Some men had no obvious injuries, but were clearly unwell, most undernourished and thin with flank pain. These, they encouraged to drink water, hoping there was some in the trenches they could access. Lydia fashioned a stethoscope of sorts from a small piece of pipe to help them hear heart beats or lungs filling with fluid from pneumonia.

The four worked for several hours until Charlotte whispered, "Lydia, I'm exhausted. I'm about ready to drop right here, after that long walk... and now this. Will they shoot us if we stop?"

"They know we have to sleep, too. They aren't without understanding. They were just desperate for help for their wounded. Whatever happened to their medics?" Lydia whispered back.

"Killed, no doubt," Charlotte replied.

"No doubt," Lydia agreed under her breath. "Paul, help me with this man's ankle. It's probably shattered, but maybe we can get it lined up a little to ease the pain."

Paul helped her apply gentle traction on the ankle, and she applied splints and wrapped it. "Why are you doing this, Nurse Lydia?" he asked her very quietly.

"Because these men are in pain and suffering."

"These men would kill you if they had a chance to do it," he observed quietly.

"They already had the chance to kill us, and they didn't," she replied softly.

Paul shook his head, hollow-eyed. "My life is worthless. I'm already making my last confession to God."

Lydia looked him in the eyes. "As long as I need you, then they need you, too. Just keep working right by us and don't do anything stupid to hurry up their decisions. And as far as God is concerned, He heard. Just in case."

There was a brief lull in injured men arriving. Charlotte fell down onto one of the empty boards and curled up in a ball on her side, almost instantly asleep. When a soldier arrived at the alcove, Lydia was still awake, beginning to become aware of how badly her feet and legs hurt.

"You," a voice said in English. "You come with me."

Lydia turned, looking at Charlotte asleep and reluctant to leave Paul and Philippe.

"Come now," the order was issued. She followed, as she was told.

Back into the bewildering line of trenches they went. Lydia had a chance to look up to the sky and saw a suggestion of light beginning to the east. *Oh god,* she breathed, *is the night over already?*

Finally, the soldier stopped at a door and motioned her inside.

Lydia stumbled in wearily over the threshold and saw she was in some kind of command post. A German captain sat at a small desk in the center of the little underground room where there was a telephone, some papers written in German posted on a wall board, a few maps. He appeared little more than twenty years old, perhaps as old as she, and his uniform was impeccably clean and neat, given the circumstances.

He spoke in French, then in English. "Parlez-vous français, madame?" he began. "Or do you speak English?"

"I prefer English," she said.

He looked surprised. "You are an American?"

Lydia nodded, her own weariness threatening to overtake her now that the pressure of the patient care had paused, at least temporarily. "I am an American, yes."

He nodded, blue eyes sharp. "Where are you from in America?" he questioned her.

"Pennsylvania," she answered.

"I have heard of this place," he said. "It is where much history happened, yes?"

"Yes," she replied carefully. She waited.

"The German army has need of your services... unless, of course, you prefer that we overrun your entire Red Cross station and simply take it for our own use."

Lydia still waited, not certain how to respond. She remembered the rout of the British CCS from a German assault. She would protect the others at the station at all costs, this she knew. Simon... the other nurses... for the first time since leaving the latrine, the faces of everyone she loved flashed through her mind. She didn't realize the awareness could be seen on her face.

The German captain saw it, though, and nodded. "I see you are considering your options. Since the Americans are not officially part of this conflict, you are not a prisoner of war. You will be our... guest... for as long as I have need of you." He stood and walked around the little desk from which his center of control radiated.

Lydia knew she had no recourse. "We've already cared for many of the wounded men during the night."

"I am aware of that," he said evenly. "There are many more."

"If we are to care for these men, then we must have supplies," she said, meeting his gaze almost eye to eye. "They need water and food. And my people need those things too. And sleep."

The man circled her as she desperately hoped to remain on her feet, with fatigue now soaking into her bones worse than the cold. He lifted a leather crop from his side. "This is not a complicated matter at all," he added. The man put the crop under her chin, lifting her head slightly. "Such a pity if beauty is ever wasted," he said quietly. "What are you willing to do for your people?" he asked her, keeping his voice expressionless.

Lydia looked straight into his eyes. "Whatever it takes," she said immediately, surprising herself by the strength of her conviction. "As long as it ensures their safety."

He nodded. "A simple thing, really," he said. "Just one small thing then. Remove your head scarf."

Lydia raised her cold hands and pulled the blue scarf from her head, letting her hair tumble down to her shoulders.

The commander raised his crop and, with it, lifted her long brown hair off her neck, the cool air of the damp office touching her skin.

"Do you see how such a little thing makes such a difference?" he said calmly. "That wasn't hard now, was it? You see—you may go." He called for a soldier just outside of the command office to take her back to the aid station as the sun rose into the sky for a new day.

And Lydia thought he was right. It had been a small command. Not too bad. Not if it saved the others.

Simon was beside himself. Lydia had not returned from her shift in the recovery that night. Charlotte was also missing from the camp. Two soldiers failed to be located with the changing of the sentry guard. The last anyone knew was from the new nurse,

Monique, who told Doctor Stockton that Lydia said she was going to the latrine around nine o'clock, the evening prior. There had been no reports of gunfire, nothing that had set off the alarms in the camp. The camp soldiers had searched the perimeter of the camp and seen no signs of heavy truck lines on the ground. The four members of the station were simply gone. Henri Fortraine was now facing the first major challenge to his command since his arrival.

Harold stood seething, arms crossed, in Fortraine's tent.

Fortraine met him squarely, facing off with the doctor in the tent. "I've sent word to Major d'Espèrey. Like you, I must wait for orders."

Harold glared at the man, risking insubordination, his anger rising from the realization that, indeed, there was nothing that could be done. Their tiny casualty clearing station was not manned by the French to take on the German First Army camped across the front six miles away. The British army was not about to pursue four missing personnel, risking major campaign strategies, in the face of countless tens of thousands of soldiers already dead, wounded, or missing in the ongoing conflict for the Somme region. What were four more to the insatiable machine of war?

Harold knew he had to help his friend waiting for his return. It had taken threats of bodily harm to keep Simon from marching into Fortraine's tent himself. And even as Harold stood fuming, he berated himself for not having sent the nurses away from the front before... before the shelling had decimated their station... or even after the British CCS had been overrun and the awareness of the close proximity of the German army was thrust upon them. He, Harold, had allowed the nurses to remain. He could have sent

Simon and Lydia home under medical discharge. And he had not. He could have insisted the nurses had guards with them at all times in the camp... but of course, two of their own soldiers were also missing, presumed taken as well.

Fortraine appreciated Harold's internal war. "I will apprise you the moment I hear from Major d'Espèrey," the commander told him. "You may convey that to Doctor Finney as well."

"Yes, sir," Harold said perfunctorily, turning on his heels to go have the conversation he was dreading. The doctor left the tent and strode back across the camp to the mess where he had left Simon, Marcus, Marlene, and Gretha Bernstein.

Harold pushed the flap open and shook off the cold as he entered the tent. Eight eyes bore into him. He could not sit, he himself also at risk of losing control and knowing that he must maintain calm for their sakes, as well as his own.

"Fortraine sent a telegraph message to Major d'Espèrey and is waiting for orders," he told them.

Marcus stood up. "That's it?" he demanded angrily.

"Now, just what did you expect the man to do, Doctor Lovell, send our tiny detachment of fourteen soldiers out to the Western Front themselves on a rescue mission?"

Marcus slammed his fist on the table; they all jumped. "We can't just sit here and do nothing!" he exploded.

Looking at Marcus, Simon said, "No," the quiet in his voice belying the undercurrent of raw emotions. "Fortraine is right. We don't have an army to send. That doesn't mean I can't go myself." Simon stood up.

Harold moved over to stand near him. "And you know you can't do that either, Simon. You can't take on the German army by yourself, and you getting shot or killed, searching the countryside, doesn't save Lydia, or Charlotte, or those two sentries either, now does it?"

Simon heard Harold, but had already stopped listening. *Lydia...where on earth have they taken you? Dear God, put a band of angels around her... around the four missing... if any of them so much as touches her... what? What are you going to do Simon? Nothing! That's what you can do... nothing!*

"Do not make Fortraine put a guard on you, Doctor," Harold said very quietly. "Because he will put you in a makeshift brig if he has to, under lock and key for the duration, and that will be worse for you sitting in there with nothing to do, but feel powerless."

Marlene looked over at the men, frightened. She was remembering the story of the nurse, Edith Clavell, who was shot by the Germans in a prisoner-of-war camp. There was no option. There was nothing any of them could do. That feeling was terrifying enough. The war had come into their own team, more destructive, in its own way, than the recent explosion had been. She looked fearfully at Simon, who stared at the ground.

Gretha got up and walked around the table to where Simon stood, rigid, in place... his soul in torment. She reached out a hand and put it on his shoulder, startling him.

"Doctor Finney," she started, waiting to see if he would look at her and actually see her.

He focused, barely. "What is it, Nurse Bernstein," he said flatly.

"I have an idea," Gretha said.

They all turned to this quiet, unassuming nurse. Any idea was welcome. "Abril," she told them.

Simon's eyes bore into her. "Abril what?" he demanded.

"Abril," she repeated. "Give Abril one of Lydia's shirts and let her smell it. She will find Lydia. She's a splendid animal... and they know things. The Germans will not shoot a dog. Take something to tie around Abril's neck so the others will know we we're trying to find them."

Simon looked at Harold and Marcus. It was an idea... and the only one to be found.

Together, the five went to Simon and Lydia's tent. He retrieved her heavy sweater from her cot. Then he fumbled in his footlocker. "I need something... something..." He reached up, removing his identification medallion from around his neck and clasped it in his hand. "I don't need this without, her."

They took the sweater and found the dog in the care of the corpsman who had adopted her. They led Abril to the latrine area at the edge of the camp, and Simon buried the chain in the thick fur around the dog's neck, fastening it securely. He knelt down next to the animal and pushed her nose into the heavy sweater that Lydia had slept in the night before. Then he took the dog's face in his hands and looked her in the eyes. "Go find her, girl," he whispered.

She looked back at him as if she understood. Sniffing the frozen ground around the latrine, at the edge of the camp, the dog started running in a beeline, heading straight east across the uneven wintry countryside beneath the stars and sliver of moon. The five of them watched her never veer, continuing east until she was completely out of sight over the horizon.

Simon stood shocked, staring, as Marcus said, "She's heading straight toward the trenches... they're about six miles away."

"Dear God, don't let them shoot her," Marlene whispered.

"Can't believe it," Harold murmured. He took Gretha in his arms and hugged the nurse. "Blue scarves and sheep herding dogs. God brought you to us for many reasons, Nurse Bernstein."

Swallowing the acidic fear in his throat, Marcus put his hand on his friend's shoulder. *God, if You're real... what they do to women... to prisoners... if You're real... do... something. Please.*

Simon stared off into the distance, overcome with despair and with very little hope to counter it. *Dear God, get the medallion to her*, he prayed. *Find a way to bring her home again. Find a way when all other ways fail. Infinite God...*

Chapter 15
Beyond Freezing

Days had passed. Charlotte pushed her hair back under the blue scarf, tying it back. She thought of Gretha, hand sewing the scarves for the nurses, and blessed God for the woman. While she was at it, she blessed God for the doctors, each by name, the cook, the orderlies, the corpsmen, and everyone else she could think of. She looked over at her friend working with Philippe on a man who had come in, with a tear from a bullet through his upper arm. She saw Lydia carefully extract the bullet with the tweezers and patch the hole with some medicated gauze that the trench commander had located. The soldier in her hands looked at the bullet she had extracted and thanked Lydia many times as he experimentally moved his arm.

"No, no," Lydia shook her head at this. She wrapped a sling around the arm. "You keep this still, see?"

The young man looked up at her and nodded in understanding, pulling his coat around his shoulder. Lydia buttoned the top buttons as a mother would her young son and sent him off. Their perpetual guard, Frederick, watched her do this small gesture and just shook his head.

"Who is next, Philippe?" Lydia asked wearily. The four of them had been tending to the wounded for most of the day, as they had the days before.

The sentry said, "I believe this man has been hit in the head."

Lydia moved over to the man, looking carefully into his eyes. There was nothing she could do for a concussion other than have the man rest and hope he would recover. He looked at her vacantly. That was when she realized the man could not see her. She waved her hand in front of his eyes. He did not blink. The nurse turned to Frederick and motioned for him to come over. "You look," she said, knowing he couldn't understand her. "He can't see anything." She waved her hand in front of the man's vacant eyes again, showing the German the sad situation in front of them.

Frederick shook his head and had the man led off by the hand.

Lydia sadly watched him go. He was so young.

While he was gone, Charlotte said softly, "Where did they take you the other night, Lydia?"

Lydia's voice was measured, even, as Phillippe glanced over. "The commander just had a question. That's all."

"Just a question?" Charlotte asked again.

"Yes," Lydia said. She did not tell Charlotte what the man had asked her to do for him. It kept them all alive. It didn't matter.

Charlotte was examining a man's toes after pulling off his boot. Lydia glanced over. She heard Charlotte saying to Paul, "It's not gangrene. But it is trench foot, and his feet are going to swell terribly." Charlotte picked up the man's boot and showed him with her hands, putting the boot to the outside of his foot so he could see the difference in size. "Too small..." Charlotte looked at Frederick who had returned and held up the boot for him to see as well. "Too small." He nodded and spoke to one of the soldiers assisting them, ostensibly sending him off to find the man a bigger boot.

Charlotte sighed. Malnutrition was hurting these men more than the weather or gunfire, she could tell. They were so painfully thin. Just as the four of them were now feeling painfully thin. The little bit of cheese and bread she had given Lydia previously had been divided four ways, days before. Charlotte's stomach gnawed at her. She knew that in time, it would stop. For a treacherous moment, her mind wondered what Cook was preparing in the mess tent today. Had they really wondered about the possibility of a Thanksgiving dinner?

A soldier appeared at the door. The one who knew a single line of English. "Come with me," he motioned to Lydia, as he had twice before. She followed him along the narrow trench, and now, some of the soldiers at their posts nodded to her as she passed. She had helped treat some of their injuries. He led her back to the commander's office, shutting the door as he retreated, and she stood inside again before the desk where the German commander examined a single piece of paper.

The commander finally looked up at her from the written sheet before him. "Did you get the supplies that you demanded?" he said calmly, undoubtedly already knowing the answer as his order to obtain them would not have been questioned.

"Yes," she replied, watching him carefully. "Thank you."

"My men tell me that you still treat everyone who comes through without complaint," he said.

"Wounded men are wounded men," Lydia replied evenly. "It makes no difference where they are from."

The man pushed his chair back and rose to his feet, coming out from behind his desk, and she watched him warily.

"So what do you want from me today?" he asked her, calmly pulling out the crop from his belt. "You must be hungry."

"Nothing," she replied.

He poked her in her stomach with the leather device. "Would you like some food for your friends?" he asked. "Or would they prefer catching the plump rats that run through these tunnels in abundance?"

Lydia swallowed hard, her mouth dry. She knew Charlotte and the sentries were hungry.

"If we are to care for your men, then you must care for my team," she countered, "as I've told you before several times."

He stood in front of her, his clear blue eyes searching her face. "Ah, but that was not our deal, now was it, Nurse Lydia... you said you would do whatever it takes if it meant your people would be taken care of. And so far, I've asked so little of you."

She nodded. "Yes, I did. And I have not seen anything come for them except some bread."

"You can change that," he suggested. He walked over to a chair upon which a small box was perched and tapped the top of it with the crop he held in his hands. "Open it."

Slowly, she walked over and pulled the lid apart. Inside the box was a loaf of bread, a circle of cheese, and two dried apples, large, but wrinkled with age.

Lydia's voice caught in her throat, but she fought to make it clear. "They will be grateful for this."

"There is a bigger price for this food," he said to her, circling around the chair to stand in front of her.

She waited, standing in place, not moving.

"It is very simple, really," he told her smoothly, almost apologetically. "All I ask of you is another small thing, a very little thing really, almost trivial, and then you take the box with you to your team."

Still, she did not move, waiting while her heart pounded.

"Open your shirt," he ordered her.

Lydia hesitated only long enough to pray, *Simon, please forgive me...*

"Take it off... the undershirt as well..." he said calmly.

She did as he told her and stood silently in front of the man. He leaned back against his desk and studied her for some time, lifting the leather crop and running it slowly over the curves of her skin. She did not take her eyes from his face. The tip of the crop lingered where her skin was the most sensitive.

"Do you see how very easy this is? Not difficult at all," he said quietly. "Such a little thing to do... to feed your people..."

"Give me your hand," he said. She held it out and he moved it for her to his desired location and closed his eyes with a sigh. Then, he abruptly lowered the crop, walked back around his desk, and sat down, watching her. "You may go."

Pulling her clothing back on, quickly, Lydia buttoned her shirt and tucked it back into her trousers, walked to the chair with the box, and picked up the food. She turned and walked out of his office, where the soldier was waiting to escort her back down the trench to the aid station.

It was going to be almost too easy, the commander said to himself as he watched her retreat.

Back in the makeshift aid station, Lydia shared the food with the others and urged them to eat it all before the rats got into it.

"However did you convince him?" Charlotte exclaimed, cutting the wrinkled apples in half for each of them.

"He wants us to take care of his soldiers. If we die of starvation, that will never happen. You saw how quickly he got supplies for these wounded men. He wants them cared for." Lydia shrugged. "What did I miss?"

Paul made a checklist. "A busted eardrum, more bullet wounds, a fracture from someone slipping and falling in the mud... and a couple of people with a rash."

Lydia groaned. "Measles here, too?" she wondered.

Charlotte bit into her fourth of a loaf of bread. "Probably. Fever, rash, white spots on tonsils... this bread isn't too stale, actually. You aren't eating, Lydia. You have to eat too."

The other nurse nodded. "I know, I will."

Frederick stood in the doorway at his post. Lydia turned to him and, tearing her bread in half, gave some to him. Charlotte broke off a chunk of her cheese for him as well. He put up his hand to stop them, but they left the offering on his lap until he bit into it.

"Why did you do that?" Paul hissed at them. "You are feeding the enemy."

Charlotte shushed him. "We are the enemy here. This man is as hungry as we are!" she declared. "They all are. They're getting almost nothing to eat. I'll bet they do eat the rats. Fortunately, we aren't reduced to that yet."

Philippe shook his head. "I'll die of starvation before I eat a rat," he declared.

The other three looked at him. "Let's hope it doesn't come to that," he added quickly.

They had not realized that darkness had already fallen for the day, Lydia had insisted that Frederick take them to a latrine area, refusing to use the corner of the room where they were treating the wounded. He had finally agreed. Now, the route was familiar, to the alcove that allowed virtually no privacy, but did offer a glimpse of the sky. Lydia looked up and saw the Dipper overhead. It was comforting. It was over the end of the trench, so she knew the section they were in was running north and south. She tried to see Simon's dragon, but there was not enough night sky visible. That's when they heard a commotion overhead, out on the ground above the trenches. Men's voices were calling, and Lydia and Charlotte looked over at each other, wondering if the trench was under attack. They soon realized that the calls were not unfriendly, they were cajoling. Soon, the women heard a dog barking and realized some animal had strayed into the trench area, and the men were enjoying the creature, calling to it as they would one of their pets at home.

Frederick tried to hurry them up to finish their business and get them back into the underground room. Overhead, at the edge of the trench, they heard the snuffling of the animal, following along the ground. It made a small whining sound. The two women followed Frederick, and Paul and Philippe brought up the rear along the narrow boardwalk as the German soldiers looked up in wonder at the bright eyes peering over the edge down into the trench. Suddenly, there was a large bound and plop as the dog jumped into the trench, landing squarely in front of Frederick. The man fell back, causing Charlotte to fall into Lydia and Lydia into Paul and then Philippe, like dominos.

"Shoo," Frederick exclaimed. "Shoo!"

The soldiers lining the trench were laughing now, their spirits lifted by the sight of the energetic dog. The dog had one person in her sights, however. She wove her way through the legs of the people in the trench and sat right next to Lydia expectantly.

Lydia knelt down in the dim light of the trench at night. She looked up at Charlotte. "This cannot be..."

"Abril?" Charlotte said incredulously. "Is that Abril?"

Lydia stroked the dog's head and looked at its face. "I think it is, but I can't imagine how."

Frederick ordered them to move, and Abril moved right along with them into the aid chamber, staying right at Lydia's feet. Once inside, Charlotte and Lydia knelt next to the animal and rubbed the fur around her neck and under her ears. "This has to be our dog," Charlotte breathed. "How on earth did she find us all this way? She must have been searching the trenches."

"I can't imagine," Lydia said. "It's the dog that keeps the buzzards off the wounded at the station when the men are laying outside of the tents waiting for surgery," she reminded Paul and Philippe, who looked on amazed.

Lydia buried her face into the familiar neck of the animal. That's when she felt the chain around Abril's neck. "What is this, girl?" she murmured softly. She undid the catch and the medallion fell into her hand. Immediately, she saw the name on the disc: Simon J Finney. Lydia buried her face into the dog's fur and wept silently. He knew what had happened. He guessed where she was. He had found a way to tell her his heart was with her no matter what happened, no matter where she was. The dog sat patiently, quietly, while Lydia clung to her, and Charlotte held onto them both. They dared for a fleeting second to believe they might survive this. Frederick watched from the door, and this time, he did not order the dog to leave.

The next order for Lydia to visit the commander's office came all too soon. After the string of wounded had come through the aid station, the voice came again at the door. "Come with me," he said.

Lydia followed and Abril moved to go with her. She turned then. "Abril, stay!" she ordered the animal.

Abril looked up at her questioningly, but obeyed. Lydia fingered the medallion in her pocket as she followed the soldier through the trench. She was greeted by many of the men along the wall, who now called her by her name, Fräulein Lydia. Frederick watched her leave, his brow furrowed.

As usual, the commander was sitting in his position of authority at his desk. The top of the desk was bare. He left her standing in front of him for a long time. Lydia took a quick glance around the room and saw yet another box on the chair next to the wall. She looked back at the commander and said nothing.

"Have you been enjoying your food?" he asked her politely.

"It nourishes the body," she replied. "It strengthens us to help many, many wounded German soldiers each day."

"That is good," he stated. "Such a small thing that helps so many people. It is most remarkable, isn't it? You help your team, and your team helps my men. This is a very good thing. Do you see what a good thing this is, Nurse Lydia?"

Lydia fingered the chain and identification disc in her pocket, knowing that somewhere Simon was praying for her, waiting for her, longing for her safe return. Knowing that no matter what happened next, Simon would still love her.

The man finally rose to his feet. He closed the door to the underground office, the guard just outside.

"There is another box of food for your people waiting over there for you."

"I see it," she said, trying to keep her voice from quavering.

He nodded. "If you do just one small thing for me, it is yours, as always," he reminded her, taking the crop from his belt again.

Lydia waited, feeling the cool metal of Simon's medallion, not giving the commander the satisfaction of a reply. She would not beg. And after he gave the order for what he wanted her to do, she did not beg, not even once... until she finally was permitted to leave his office, the box of food in her arms, and tears in her eyes. She was limping with pain.

The next day, Abril refused to leave Lydia's side. She stayed with her in the aid station, she walked beside her to the open-air latrine area. Frederick tolerated the dog, realizing it was pointless to even try to separate the two of them. Lydia asked the soldier to take her to the latrine several times over the day, and he took her a little farther down a side trench where she had a bit more privacy. As before, each evening, she shared her food with him. Now, he waited while she addressed her physical needs but was surprised to suddenly hear her vomiting into the alcove. The dog whined softly. The soldier turned to look over his shoulder and saw bloody, angry welts of a crop crisscrossing the woman's buttocks as she gingerly pulled up her trousers. The soldier's stomach twisted, also rebelling against its own contents.

Frederick looked away again and waited until the woman's stomach quieted and she had situated her clothing. He led her slowly back to the aid station, where the dog immediately sat beside her. Several times, she was called back again to the commander's office. Each time the guard watched her go down the trench, Frederick grew more troubled in his spirit. The woman didn't complain each time she returned white faced and limping, and she still shared her food and still she tended the wounded.

A night came when the commander's aide came to the underground aid station with the order for the nurse to come with him, and Frederick sent the man away with a few guttural words that the four occupants of the room could not understand. It was dark and cold that night, with a light snow falling into the trenches. It promised to be a very, very cold night. After they had been sleeping for a few hours, Lydia felt herself being shaken awake.

"Come with me," she heard a man say, and she groaned.

Charlotte immediately woke up. "What is it?" she whispered.

It was the soldier, Frederick, waking them. "You come," he said, his voice urgent. The four of them quickly got to their feet and pulled their coats tightly around them. He led them into the trenches in the dark, and around them, other soldiers nodded at the four, urging them to hurry. Reaching one of the ladders, Frederick climbed quickly up into the night. Charlotte followed immediately after him and waited above ground as Paul lifted Abril up the ladder into Frederick's waiting hands. A small group of German soldiers were also waiting above on the snowy ground. After Lydia painfully climbed the rungs, she felt strong arms lift her out of the trench, with Philippe right behind.

"Come, come," Frederick whispered. Other German soldiers whispered, "Go!" and "Run!" The group of some fifteen Germans and the four medical staff took off running along the frozen ground. Abril sensed the urgency and took off doing what she did best, herding them along the straight path west away from the trench, allowing the German soldiers to lead the dog through the barbed wire, then taking the lead again for all of them, the full six miles back to the station. Abril never wavered in the night. She needed no North Star to guide her... certain of her path, she circled, guided, and drove the group forward.

When the women could run no further, they were forced to walk and catch their breaths, which froze in clouds on the night air. Abril whined anxiously, urging them on, pushing at Lydia's aching body, propelling her forward. There had been enough Germans who were sympathetic, but not yet ready to surrender, who had covered their absence. No one seemed to be chasing them. After hours of walking in the subfreezing weather, there was the faintest light of a single candle on the horizon. They knew it was the camp in blackout.

Frederick stopped them all as they drew closer to the camp. "Krankenschwester, we surrender to you," he told Lydia in English. "We are your prisoners. Do as you see fit to us."

Lydia turned to Paul and Philippe. "Run ahead, if you can, and alert the guards that we are coming and they must not shoot. These men mustn't be harmed in any way. They surrendered in good faith."

"Oui, l'infirmière," Philippe assured her. "It will be as you say." They ran ahead, calling out in French, into the crisp frozen air, as they drew close to the station tents and heard the alarm raised by the sentries on duty, who were glad to hear familiar French voices approaching in the darkness.

Lydia turned to Frederick and the other soldiers and said for herself, and for Charlotte, "Thank you. Danke."

Frederick looked at Lydia in the starlight. "I am sorry," he said simply and dropped his eyes in shame.

She put her hand on his arm. "It is over now," she assured him. "You will not be mistreated."

Charlotte wrapped her arm in Lydia's, and she and a limping Lydia made their way as quickly as possible through the remaining quarter mile back into the camp, following Abril.

Simon heard the clamor of French voices calling to the sentries. He jumped from the cot where he had been talking with God about the situation with no small amount of fervency. He knew, he just knew, she was back. Running from his tent, around the surgery, the commander's tent, and the soldiers' tents, he sped toward the sentries' calls. He heard Abril barking, now that she was back within the familiar confines of the camp, as she herded the group to safety, at long last. Simon saw all of the German soldiers, and then found Lydia, stumbling forward, half frozen in the night. At the commotion, Harold and Marcus had also run from their tent and when Marcus saw Charlotte, he scooped her up in his arms and twirled her in the air. Some of the other nurses threw on coats and ran to join them. Harold stood in the melee and blessed God above, smiling broadly and wondering at the fifteen Germans, with hands held over their heads in surrender, being marched through the tents under close guard. Fortraine emerged from his tent, looking on in amazement at the reunion. Simon went directly to Lydia and wrapped her in his arms as she buried her face in his neck.

"I'm home," she said to him. "I am so cold."

He led her immediately to their tent, and once inside, she took his medallion from her pocket and slipped the chain back over his head. Quickly, he threw wood into the stove, and it sparked, caught, and crackled, filling the tent with warmth. Simon helped her get her heavy coat and boots off, rubbing some warmth back into her hands and her feet. He took the warm water from the stove and gently washed her face and hands.

"Simon," she whispered. "I know that you love me."

He looked at her worriedly, tenderly. "I do," he reminded her. "All my heart and soul."

"There is something I have to tell you—"

"No, my beloved, you don't." He reached for her dirty shirt to unbutton it, but she stopped him and held it closed. His eyebrows raised slightly in surprise when she balked at his gesture.

"No, you don't," he repeated. He took her hand down. Lydia didn't move as he unbuttoned her shirt and gently washed her neck and chest and arms just as he had not too long ago, patting her dry before she chilled. Then he moved around behind her as she continued to stand motionless. He dropped her trousers, exposing crisscrossed raised red stripes of congealed blood, and he suffocated the rage that erupted within him. *Oh my God...* Simon gently washed her back and bottom, slipping a dry shirt and warm sweater over her. "I'll be right back," he told her, thinking to go to the recovery and getting ointment for her.

"No, don't leave me, Simon," she begged him. "The commander, he wouldn't give the others, us... any food, unless..."

"You don't have to tell me, my love," Simon assured her. "Nothing has changed between us." He washed her legs and gingerly pulled up a warm pair of boxers over her, forgoing the heavy trousers.

"Can I lay against you?" she asked, trembling.

"Of course," he reassured her. He lay on the cot, and she rested on her side against him as he covered them both with warm blankets until she finally felt warm and the shivering lessened. Simon put his arms around her, locking his fingers together, tears running from his eyes.

"I have to tell you something," Lydia said again, the warmth finally invading her bones and bringing a sense of safety and security.

He listened, dreading what might come. "Okay."

"People can be really evil," she said finally. He waited, listening, his soul in agony from her pain.

"But there were men in the trenches who also were very kind and grateful for what we did for them. The commander though, he was evil of a kind I've never known. I've never known anyone who enjoyed being evil." She paused a long time, and Simon almost wondered if she had fallen asleep, but she went on. "But in the middle of the evil, I felt you praying for me, Simon. I held your medallion that Abril brought in my hand, and I felt you praying for me. I had trouble finding God in the trench though. He didn't stop the man from being evil, but maybe He kept me from becoming evil in the middle of it. I felt you with me though because of the medal."

Simon felt his eyes well up. He didn't know what to say.

"And maybe God heard me after all," she said. "I asked God to keep the commander from wanting… I asked Him to make the man want other things… instead of…" She faltered, "Our oneness is still ours. I just wanted you to know that. It's important to me that you know that."

Simon caressed her cheek softly, kissed the top of her head, whispered how very deeply he loved her, until he felt her fall asleep in his arms, tears running down his cheeks, without a sound.

It was only a few hours until morning. They awoke in the same position as they had fallen asleep. Lydia woke first and was watching Simon's deep, steady breathing. She could hear the slow, rhythmic beating of his heart, in his chest, against her ear. She didn't want to move, but she was hungry, which surprised her. When he stirred, she was fingering the medallion lying on his chest.

"How about breakfast?" she asked him.

He looked at her, surprised. "Are you up for it?"

Lydia nodded. "Yes, but I also need to see one of the Germans. And I need to… to use the latrine…"

"I will go with you," Simon said quickly.

She stood up gingerly. "Okay, ouch. Today, maybe some salve."

They pulled on their heavy clothes, and as soon as they opened the tent flap, Abril, who was waiting just outside the entry, jumped up.

"Looks like you have a new best friend," Simon observed, wrapping his arm around Lydia as the dog followed them.

They visited the latrine before walking over to the mess tent, a new coating of snow crunching under their boots. When they entered, the smell of the hot food was almost too much. Lydia accepted the eggs and sausage and coffee from the cook, and she sat gingerly, at the end of a bench. Cook's creations had never tasted as good to her as they did that morning. *It would make a splendid Thanksgiving meal*, she concluded as she shared a bite of sausage with the dog at her feet.

"Where are the German soldiers being held?" she then asked Simon quietly.

"I'll show you," he told her. "But I'm going with you."

Helping her to stand, they left the mess, and again, Abril fell into step at Lydia's side. Crossing through the recovery and triage tents, they came to one tent surrounded by French soldiers. There was little need for the armament. The Germans were submissive and grateful to be warm and fed.

Lydia nodded to the French soldiers and said, "I need to speak with them." She pushed her way through the tent flap. The fifteen under guard all looked up at her anxiously. Frederick dropped his eyes in sorrow. Lydia went to him and knelt beside the cot where he sat. She took one of his rough hands in her own. Abril sat patiently beside her on the ground.

"Have you eaten?" she asked, gesturing to her mouth.

He nodded. Looking up briefly at Simon, hovering over her. "Kommandant?" he asked, pointing.

Lydia shook her head. She pointed to the ring on her hand and then to Simon's matching one. "No," she whispered. "My husband."

Realization dawned in Frederick's eyes, tears began to collect, and he dropped his head. He said something in German, his voice breaking several times.

One of the other German soldiers spoke up. "He says, Krankenschwester," the man offered. "That he cannot bear the shame of what happened to you."

Lydia looked into Frederick's face while speaking through their intermediary. "Tell Frederick," she said, "that I am forever grateful he brought me back to my husband. That all of you brought us back."

The German flowed between the assembled men.

Wincing, Lydia tried to stand, and Frederick saw it, quickly reaching out a hand to help her. Simon was faster. Back on her feet, Lydia looked at them all. "We aren't bad people," she told the one translating. "I hope you're treated well where they are taking you."

Their interpreter nodded. "The Germans are not bad people," he said in return. "Only some. I hope you know."

"I do," she assured him.

She turned to leave, and Simon met Frederick's eyes. The two men were so close in age, divided by the geopolitical forces of the war. But regardless of whatever had happened in the trenches, of which Simon only knew a small part, this German soldier had risked his life to bring Lydia back. Simon glanced at Lydia, departing the tent with the dog at her heels. Reaching out his hand, he shook Frederick's hand firmly. Understanding passed between the two, beyond any translation. Then, Simon turned, following Lydia out into the cold air to take her to Fortraine's tent, where their own commander was waiting to be briefed.

They stepped into Henri Fortraine's command tent after being announced by his aide. Fortraine motioned to the folding chair in front of his desk, and Lydia perched gingerly on the edge of the seat with Simon standing beside her. He said, "I regret your unfortunate experience, Nurse Finney. I've already spoken with the others, but now I also need you to tell me what happened."

Lydia nodded. "Nurse Charlotte and I were at the latrine, and when we came out, we were grabbed by German soldiers."

"Where were our sentries?" Fortraine asked her.

"They were being held at rifle point. The Germans said they would shoot Charlotte unless the sentries did what they were told, and so they did. It was very sudden."

Fortraine nodded. "Go on."

"They made it clear that they were looking for medical personnel, nurses, and led us over the fields to the front lines through the barbed wire and the tanks until we reached the trenches."

"Can you describe the tanks to me?" he asked.

She said, "I've never seen anything like them. They were oval-shaped and sat on top of great flat metal ribbons instead of on wheels like the ambulances. They had very large guns sticking out from them, and there were many soldiers gathered around the machines."

"So, you passed these tanks. And then?"

"Then we were taken down ladders into the trenches where men were lined up in little dugouts along the dirt walls, and there were some lights hanging from a wire lining the edge. We were led down these wooden walkways a long way past other turns and underground rooms and then to a room dug into the ground where there were many wounded men lying on planks. I think they thought our sentries were, maybe also medical people, so we maintained the ruse in the hope of keeping them with us and alive."

"You helped the Germans who were wounded?" Doctor Fortraine asked her, jotting notes on a yellow tablet in front of him.

"Yes," Lydia said. "Their wounded were just like the ones we see here. There were many with bullet wounds and fractures. Some were blind, and some had rashes and coughs. Others appeared to have concussions. Some were nearly dead, and we could do nothing to help them. One of the Germans found some basic medical supplies. We did what we could to help the wounded like we do in our own triage."

Fortraine asked then, "The others said they did not talk with the kommandant. Did you have any contact with the German commander?"

She tensed. "Many times, I was taken down through the trenches to what seemed to be a command center of sorts. There was one German leader, maybe he was a kommandant, at a desk, with his aides there. I think there was a telephone, though, and chairs."

"What did the German commander want from you?" Fortraine pressed her.

Her voice catching, Lydia faltered. "I don't know why he asked for me in particular. He asked me what we needed, and I told him food, bandages, gauze, iodine, and things to make splints."

"Did he ask you anything about our station complement, the number of soldiers or wounded we have, plans regarding any movement of our station or that of the British stations near ours? Did he ask about our weaponry? Where we send German prisoners?"

Lydia thought back, felt puzzled, perhaps overwhelmed by the long string of questions Fortraine had asked her. "Why no, he did not ask anything about the station or any German prisoners at all. He didn't ask if we were staying or moving. He only said that if we did not help their wounded, that the German army would attack this station... I think like they did with the British—kill all of our people and take all of the supplies they need."

"So, you decided to help their wounded rather than risk them attacking this station, Nurse Finney?" he asked.

She nodded.

Simon glanced up at Fortraine, anxiously wondering where this was heading as neither he nor Lydia had shared with anyone about her injuries in the trenches.

Fortraine continued relentlessly. "The other nurse, Charlotte, told me that they refused to allow the four of you to eat for quite some time. And yet, somehow, Nurse Finney, you were able to convince the commander to let you have food."

"Yes," she whispered, descending down into the icy trench of, remembering. Simon saw the look of pain in her eyes with growing concern. He and Marcus, both, had seen that same look before, after she had returned from rescuing André Besimont months ago.

"What information did you have to give him in order to get food?" Fortraine pressed her, all too familiar with military information revealed under physical duress and hunger, during war. Had she told the Germans about the British CCS, the army to their north, the plan of holding Beaumont-Hamel? The delay of the offensive until a thaw?

"He didn't ask for any information in order to allow us to have food," Lydia whispered, her voice so low that Fortraine had to lean over the desk to hear her. "He said he needed such a small thing from me," she repeated in a small voice as she returned to the cold underground of the commander's office in the trench.

Fortraine pressed her, "What small thing from you?"

"He said, 'It's just a trivial thing, of no consequence at all, really...'" she said in a frightened voice. "'Just take off your shirt for me, and you can have the box of food on the chair. Do you see now how simple that was? Such a little thing I ask of you and, there, you can have the box... just as I promised...'"

Doctor Fortraine stopped abruptly, having become suddenly aware of the signs of trauma and shock that masked her face.

Simon dropped to one knee beside her, careful not to touch her as she followed the memory through the trenches. "You made sure Charlotte would be safe," Simon assured her quietly. "You took care of Charlotte... and Paul and Philippe. You got them food to keep them alive."

She could no longer see Simon, but she could hear the almost apologetically calm voice of the commander as time collapsed in on itself, and he was coming again around the desk with the leather crop in his hand. "He made me come back, over and over..."

"I ask such little things of you..." she again heard him say, "and they are so hungry. I will strike you once... you will scarcely feel it, really, and afterward, your friends will not have to eat the rats... it is such a simple thing you will do for them..."

She felt the hard wooden edge of the desk against her pelvis. The whistle of the crop took her by surprise, and she gasped when it struck her skin.

"That was of no consequence at all, was it?" the commander said quietly with authority. "The crop is irrelevant... listen again to how it whistles through the air... did you feel it this time? Was there perhaps a little pain? So unnecessary... but see now. You may stand up. You need not hear it again."

She stood, involuntarily wincing in pain, intensely relieved by his assurance. Then her heart sank as she saw him undoing his trousers. He took her hand and placed the leather crop in it. "All you must do is strike me once the same way, and you may go for tonight."

She shook her head. "I can't do that," she whispered, dropping the hateful crop by her feet.

"Such a pity when I ask so little of you," the man told her, shaking his head as he retrieved the leather crop from the ground beside the desk. His voice had grown cold. "You do realize that you have brought this upon yourself?"

She gripped the medallion in her hand as she felt the cold wooden desk again pressed against her cheek. She felt fire searing her skin. "I give you permission to change your mind, Nurse... just take the crop from me and strike me once, and this will be over for you. No? Then you force me to apply it harder than it needs to be... why do you make me hurt you...?"

Simon saw her body flinching with each remembered lash. Simon ignored the white-faced aide behind the desk while also raising his hand to stop Fortraine from speaking. Quickly, Simon pulled the chain and medallion from around his neck and placed it in her hand, careful to loop it so that it would not fall to the ground. He watched her reflexively clutch the medallion tightly in her fist, the cool chain wrapped in her fingers, knowing it was the anchor that would pull her back to the present.

"Such a pity... now you are bleeding," she heard the commander observe. "Such a shame. You will regret that you forced me to hurt you. I will allow you to get dressed. Next time, it will not be so simple, if you do not obey me," she echoed his words. "You may take the food to your friends. I keep my promises... all of them. You will obey me."

Simon spoke softly, making certain he could conceal his rage before he directed her. "Charlotte is waiting for you to come back," Simon reminded her. "Go back through the trenches. Take the food to Charlotte."

She nodded, seeing the slippery wooden board in front of her, clutching the box of food as she followed the guard, feeling the pain as she walked. "It hurts..."

"Give Charlotte something to eat," Simon urged her. "Give the others the food."

He waited, now guiding her through the rest of the memory, the parts he already knew. "Now listen for Frederick. He wants you to come with him."

Lydia nodded, feeling Frederick waking her in the darkness.

"It's time to go now, it's time to leave with Frederick," Simon reminded her quietly, keeping his voice calm and even. "Go with Frederick. Abril wants all of you to follow Frederick through the trench."

They followed the soldier along the winding, slippery trench to a ladder.

"Climb up the ladder, get out of the trench... and follow Abril in the dark."

She felt the dog gathering them together and driving them in the right direction. They were running hard, breath coming in tight gasps of cold, icy air. "I can't go on..." she whispered, "it hurts too much... it's too cold... and so far..."

"Yes, you can," Simon told her. "Just follow Abril, she knows the way. I am looking for you, I am watching for you. I can almost see you coming now. Just a little farther. I'm running toward you now. Can you see me?"

She nodded. She could see Simon coming for her.

Simon positioned himself between her and the offending sight of the bare wooden desk in front of her in Henri Fortraine's tent.

"Run right into my arms," he said quietly. "I've got you."

He enveloped her in his embrace, and she collapsed against his chest with shudders, releasing all of the terror of the recent past.

"Abril, come," Simon called, knowing the dog was waiting outside Fortraine's tent flap. Immediately, the dog bounded inside and pressed herself up against Lydia's trembling legs, watchful and protective.

Lydia felt Simon protecting her and the dog supporting her. She had escaped the Kommandant in the trenches. She was safe.

"He never even said his name," she whispered.

Doctor Fortraine silently slipped out of the tent, past them, followed by his astonished aide, and left the couple alone in the tent. It had been imperative for him to know if she had revealed anything that could give the enemy an advantage. But he hated himself for having had to do that.

Returning to the surgery was a blessing. It kept her mind from going backwards, to the trenches. Marcus watched Lydia closing. Simon was taking an hour to sleep after being on his feet for far too long during this current influx of wounded, from the last skirmish.

"Retractor, Nurse," Marcus said softly, prompting Lydia to find the right instrument. He had pulled Simon aside repeatedly and Simon had only said to give Lydia time; she needed time. *Time from what? What had happened? Why won't Charlotte tell me anything?* He was deeply concerned. They finished the surgery and as he sutured the patient's incision, she didn't leave the table to wash, instead, waiting for him.

"Come on," Marc finally said, with the last snip of the scissor. "Let's wash up."

Leading her to the sink, Marc started the hot water and handed her the soap. Slowly she washed off the blood, watching it disappear down the drain of the little scrub sink. Marcus saw her shudder and pressed his shoulder against hers.

"I'm right here, Lydia," he said softly. "You're safe now."

She looked up at him and the tears filling her eyes pierced Marc's soul.

"Need a break?" he asked her kindly as another patient came in born on a litter by two soldiers.

"No," she whispered. "Simon is asleep. Can I... just keep working with you, Marc?"

He smiled at her gently. "Of course!" he said, trying to keep his voice light and confident. "No one I'd rather have at my table. The one who just came in doesn't look too bad. We'll do it together. Then afterward, if we're all done here, I can challenge you to coffee-chugging. See who can down black with one sugar the fastest! Or gin rummy."

That brought a small smile to her face; he was glad, taking her elbow protectively back through the tables to their own where they finished their last procedure without incident and were glad no others were brought through the door. After the surgical tent shut down, Marc looked at her as they bundled their coats around them to head out.

"Need to wash up?"

"Yes," she said, then, "no. I mean… maybe later. Or not. I don't know."

"Lydia," Marcus said kindly, walking her back to her own tent to see if Simon was awake. "If you need anything, I'm here."

"Thank you, Marcus," Lydia whispered. "I don't know what I need." She ducked into their tent and saw Simon, on a cot, under a blanket.

Sadly, Marcus shook his head as he walked the distance to the doctors' tent, just ten feet away. He didn't know what to do to help because he didn't know what had happened.

Chapter 16
Resolutions

1917

A month had passed and, along with it, Christmas and the New Year while the station remained situated outside Amiens, along the Somme River. True to expectations, the skirmishes, between the Allies and the Germans, had diminished. Fearful cold had brought with it an influx of Germans surrendering from deprivation, hunger, and hopelessness. Both of the French nurses were still with the team, neither having abandoned the Red Cross nor the mission of the station, yet. True to his promise, Henri Fortraine worked with Captain Thornwall to arrange a holiday get-together, just after New Year's Day, at the British casualty station. Both medical teams were excited to share some time and ideas. The French station team eagerly loaded themselves into the back of a truck for the ride north. Abril stood outside, her front paws perched on the edge of the truck, her nose reaching over the edge of the truck bed. She whined.

"Stay, Abril," Lydia ordered the dog, as she climbed in with the others, but Abril persisted, not wanting her to leave without protection.

Simon climbed up into the back of the truck, following Lydia. "Oh, let her come," he said and called the dog, who immediately bounded up and in between the staff. "She won't be happy seeing you ride off without her."

Marcus jumped up into the truck and wormed his way in between Gretha and Charlotte. "Damn, it's a cold one," he said, rubbing his hands together. "Everyone cuddle up... just for the sake of staying warm, of course." The women rolled their eyes but obliged him with little smiles, pressing against one another as it was indeed very cold outside, and with all of them squashed into the back of one truck, there was no room to spread out even if they had wanted to. Only Abril was comfortable, her thick fur coat was her built-in blanket. She plopped herself down on Lydia's feet, looking quite content.

The truck started off down the frozen dirt road, and Marcus started to sing, "One hundred bottles of beer on the wall..." as everyone else groaned.

When they arrived at last at the British CCS, they were promptly ushered into the mess tent of the camp. A fire was burning hotly in a stove, and there was a Christmas tree of sorts set up in the tent, it was decorated with popcorn and pine cones and a, precariously perched, paper star on the topmost, vertical branch. It looked cheerful and festive in the eyes of the newcomers.

"Stockton, Lovell, Finney!" David Winston exclaimed, greeting them and extending his hand to shake each of theirs in turn. "And we are delighted to welcome the nurses. Did you leave no one in your camp to cover your absence?"

Harold extended a hand to Doctor Earl-Johns as well and clapped him on the shoulder. "We left directions for the wounded to just come here," he assured the team.

"Splendid," Doctor Earl-Johns exclaimed, leading them to where their cooks were preparing something that smelled delicious. He noticed the dog entering the tent.

"Are the Americans training dogs for the surgery now?" he asked curiously.

"That's Abril," Lydia laughed, "and yes, she is part of the team... refused to be left behind."

"Well, do come in, come in," David Winston said, ushering the small group past the many familiar faces of the Brits who had worked alongside the Americans earlier in the fall. "How has the war been treating you? Have any of the wounded had to make the trip down your way, or did all of them stop here and give you a vacation?"

"We've had our share, you can be sure," Harold assured the man. "This little holiday event gave us something to look forward to, I must say. When our commander informed us it had been arranged, everyone's spirits rose noticeably."

"Well, do we have a surprise for you!" Winston continued as the teams removed their heavy coats and allowed themselves the pleasure of the warmth of the tent.

"Santa Claus and a few elves?" Marcus asked curiously.

"Better than that," Doctor Earl-Johns said.

Charlotte exclaimed, "What could be better than Santa Claus and a few elves!"

"We just received a truckload of supplies from England and wait until you see what the cook has made up for all of us. And some kindhearted soul back home sent, yes, it's true, a huge box of incredibly warm mittens and socks, no doubt hand knitted by a local church ladies' fellowship who had nothing better to do than think of us over here, in the dead of winter.

"But that's not the best part," Doctor Earl-Johns added, waiting for their curiosity to peak and enjoying the suspense he was building. He moved close to Marlene Sullivan and bowed to her. "May I have the pleasure, mademoiselle?" he asked.

From somewhere in the tent, the magical sounds of a wind-up Victrola rose into the warm air. The music of a Beethoven waltz filled the room as the two long mess tables were hastily pulled back, allowing for an open space. The lovely melody needed no introduction. It took mere seconds for the assembly to join together, men with women, women with women... coming together to enjoy the rare luxury of music. By the time Captain Adam Thornwall arrived at the mess tent, it was clear that the symphony was now in command of the dreamy-eyed couples, clutching one another while their bodies moved to the music. It was as though the veil of heaven had been lifted slightly, allowing the pure beauty of chord and harmony to leak out, spilling down onto the Earth, with all of its struggles.

Simon took Lydia into his arms. "Is your dance card full? I'm actually not a very good dancer," he murmured in her ear as he put his arm around her. "But I'll try not to embarrass you, too much."

She wrapped her arms around his neck, pressing her body against his as the notes of the waltz moved them with nonverbal directions. "You may step on my toes! This is the most beautiful thing I have ever heard," she murmured. "How I have missed music!"

One shellac record after another was added to the turntable, with someone dutifully turning the crank as needed. With each new piece, people changed partners, seeming anxious to share the experience with as many as possible, for remembrance. Marlene found herself dancing with Marcus to the strains of Mozart. Lydia twirled with Harold to the melody of a Bach rondo. Gretha, Linda, Nancy, Monique, Laura... all of the nurses, were in great demand with the men of the British camp and had ample chances to dance with them all. But it seemed as though Laura and Doctor Winston spent the most time dancing together.

When the smell of the food came to its own crescendo of sorts, the cook rapped on a pot to get everyone's attention. The music changed to Christmas carols—lively, sad, endearing... powerful reminders of better times and safer places. The tables were drawn back together, and everyone lined up to follow one another through the holiday fare, carrying their trays to an open spot at the table where they mingled. They ate, talked, and periodically stopped to listen to a familiar chorus or hum along.

"You know," Thornwall shared with Harold as he motioned around them, to the tent full of people, "we should have done this long before now. Why did we wait so long?"

"The war got in the way, my friend," Harold replied.

"Are you getting on sufficiently?" Thornwall asked the other.

Harold responded slowly, "Had some bad times and some worse times. Overall, though, we pulled through."

"You have an excellent team," Thornwall remarked, "resilient."

Harold corrected him, "We both do."

"I sometimes wish we had more nurses," Thornwall sighed. "They are good for the morale of patients and staff alike. Our complement is just up to six now."

"And they are a persistent source of concern," Harold added.

Curious, Thornwall replied, "I don't remember that to be so."

Harold looked around him at the happy faces lining the tables. "Not here, not now at this moment, but when the times are tough, I often struggle with the notion of exposing them to such risk."

"These women are tough," Adam said slowly. "Hardened in many respects."

Harold nodded, "Yes, but at what cost? How will they go back to their lives in the States, being wives perhaps, mothers perhaps, with all of this in their minds?"

The captain picked up his cup of hot tea and took a sip. "The same way the men will," he said. "One day at a time... and some memories will never fade. Others they will never talk about. And now, let's you and me pass out socks and mittens compliments of some British wives and mothers. And find some kind of treat for your dog."

"Not to worry," Harold assured him, having noticed the many hands that had already slipped Abril something savory from a tray. "The animal has been far too spoiled already, I can assure you."

The ride back to the French station was quite different from the ride over. The entire team, once again sardined into the back of the truck, was content... filled with warm food, wearing warm mittens, and carrying with them, warm memories. When they arrived at the camp, they quickly moved off to stoke their stoves and warm their tents against the bitter cold. They were collectively grateful for the absence of wounded, as everyone had the night off duty.

In their tent, Lydia and Simon found the fire banked with only glimmers of red embers waiting. They invited Abril to join them; she immediately nosed the flap to be let out again, where she took up her position, just outside, snuggled between the inner flap and the outer tent wall, her sharp nose catching all of the scents on the cold night air, her thick fur sufficiently insulating her against the winter night.

As the fire began to crackle and the air inside became more comfortable, Simon and Lydia were able to pull off their coats. Lydia looked at the mittens she had worn home, soft green with bright red stripes of yarn woven through. She was reluctant to remove them.

"Still cold?" Simon asked her, seeing her hesitate.

"No, it's not that," she murmured. "I was just wondering what grandmother sat and knitted these somewhere in England. Did she wonder who would receive them? Did she pray over them, that God would protect the person that would wear them? I know I would have."

Simon hung up his coat to dry. "You can wear them to bed if you like!" he declared. "The socks as well."

She laughed at the idea. "Now wouldn't that look silly?"

He stood after dropping a log into the stove and looked at her. "Only if that was all you were wearing," he said carefully, mischievously. He had been treading very gently with her since her ordeal at the hands of the German commander. She had never resisted or pulled away from him, as she had the night she returned, when he tried to remove her filthy clothes to wash her, not knowing of her severe wounds.

"Well, we've been sleeping with socks on, and everything else we own, every night. It's been so cold," she turned down the cots before taking a seat.

Simon nodded. "That it has. Spring will be here before we know it, then summer... and then we'll wish for relief from the heat." He sat down on the cot near where she was perched with the mittens in her hands, thinking of the love that went into their making.

"Simon," she said. "I've made a New Year's resolution."

"What's that?" he asked curiously, gently.

"I'm going to write my mother and father and tell them all about you."

Simon studied her face, the serious look in her eyes. "Okay, if you think it's time."

She nodded, pulling the scarf off of her hair and letting her waves fall down around her shoulders.

Simon wanted to run his fingers through her hair. "Do you want my help?" he asked. "I'm willing to write something to them, as I told you before. Let them know how I feel about you."

"How do you feel about me?" she asked, laying the mittens aside.

Simon was genuinely puzzled. "What do you mean, my love? You are the love of my life. You are everything to me, the one that gives me a reason to wake up every morning in this hell hole."

"I know you love me," she said quietly. "I don't doubt that for a minute. I mean, how do you feel about—about the kind of person I am?"

He sat across from her on the second cot, their knees touching, and he took her hands in his. "Out with it, Lydia. You can tell me... something is still eating away at you."

"Simon," she said. "I told the German commander I would do whatever it took to get food for Charlotte, Paul, and Philippe."

Simon nodded. "I know," he acknowledged her statement.

"I didn't know if anyone would ever find us again or if we'd be taken off to a prisoner of war camp... or get shot. I didn't know if I would ever be able to see you again, not until Abril showed up."

He listened quietly.

"I said I would do whatever it took, Simon."

Simon nodded, his rage captured just below the surface with the thought of what had been demanded of her against her will. "It took a lot of courage to tell him that."

"But I meant it," she confessed in distress.

He swallowed hard. "You wouldn't make such a statement lightly."

"Why did I tell him that right off the bat?" she asked him angrily. "Why didn't I tell him no from the beginning? That's what is eating away at me. It's almost...it's almost like I willingly threw us... no, threw you away... for bread and cheese and a few wrinkled pieces of fruit in a box. As if you didn't matter. I stood right there in front of the man and said I would do whatever it took. That's exactly what I told him."

Sitting silently, Simon did not let go of her hands.

Then he said carefully, "In that moment, Lydia, it was the very best thing you could have said."

"How can you even say that!" she exclaimed angrily, knowing the anger was misdirected. "Aren't you furious with me? I know I am!"

He looked at her, his brown eyes full of compassion. "And what would have happened, if you had said no?"

Lydia looked at him, puzzled. "But I didn't. I did what he told me to do... almost—"

"Let's think about it," he urged her. "You were the only one there in the room, the only one that heard his voice, his tone, his intention. What would he have done next, if you had kept saying no? Would he have allowed you just walk back down the trench and catch the rats?"

She shivered, looking startled. She saw the crop in the man's hand. She remembered the guards stationed outside of the underground office. "He would have... he would have found a way to force me to do whatever he wanted."

"There are many ways to force someone to do something they don't want to do. How do you think he would have forced you? A man like that, who doesn't care at all about whether or not anyone is hungry, but only cares about taking control over another human being? Especially a woman," Simon said, relying on sheer willpower to keep his voice even, analytical, and practical.

"Well, I suppose he would have..." she faltered, exhaled, gathered her thoughts. "I suppose he would have called in the soldiers by the door..." Then she thought further back, to the bitter march away from the latrine when she had watched Frederick put the pistol to Charlotte's temple, trained to shoot her dead in front of them if they did not follow orders and start walking into the night. So... the four had started walking. And a dreadful thought finally dawned on her. Lydia looked up at Simon. "Or he would have done it to Charlotte... wouldn't he..."

Simon nodded. "Or he would have done it to Charlotte. And do you know what Charlotte would have told him?"

Lydia looked straight at Simon. "I would never have put her in that position!" she declared emphatically. "Charlotte is my dear friend. I would never have allowed Charlotte to fall into that man's hands."

"Nor would I have wanted you to," Simon held her hands tightly, not letting her look anywhere, but at him, "because there is nothing, no German commander, no hunger, no suffering, nothing on this Earth, that could change us. We have been bound in heaven before God, my precious Lydia. There is no evil on Earth that has the power to ever change something that God Himself has bound in heaven."

Simon allowed the words to sink into her soul, to find where the connection had needed mending. The truth of his words permeated every part of her being with the full and immediate release of guilt and remorse. "Nothing can break us..." he stated quietly.

"Except me," she said sadly. "I have kept us apart."

He looked into her eyes, patiently reassuring her. "That changes nothing."

For the first time in a month, Lydia reached for him with a sudden urgency. She pulled off her shirt and reached for his, but he was already ahead of her, quickly dropping their clothing down to the floor beside the cot. Lydia drew his body to her, wrapping her legs around him before memory could change her mind, and

Simon immediately found her. Simon lost himself in her, covering her with his soft caresses after their long abstinence. He reached one hand beneath her hips, pulling them up to meet him. And deep inside of her body, she pulled him in as far as she could toward the sacred place that only he had ever entered, had ever stroked, had ever loved... blocking out all other images that could threaten their oneness.

"My precious Lydia," he whispered urgently, "I will not be able to hold back for long..."

She nodded. "Then don't. Let everything go..." she whispered as she went there with him.

As they lay spent with the warmth of their bodies trapped beneath their blankets, Simon was sure that somewhere the angels of heaven were singing with joy that at least in one tiny corner of the world, torn by war, one conflict had finally found resolution... if not a little healing.

At the mess table, Simon and Lydia had a yellow-lined tablet in front of them, along with cups of the cook's best brew. "So, what do you want me to tell them... your mother and father?"

Lydia tapped her pencil against her chin thoughtfully. "I was just thinking about that. How about just starting with where you're from, where you went to school?"

He laughed. "This isn't a job interview, Lydia. We're talking about mother who birthed you. The one who wants the world for her daughter." Simon had read the letter her mother had sent last year. This was not like Marlene Sullivan's mother lauding a son's appointment in Albany. No, this was a mother who had expressed her fear for her daughter, and with good reason, as he knew all too well. Through his words, he wanted to be seen as Lydia's protector. This worried woman back in Pennsylvania needed to know that someone was watching out for her daughter. There was no list of job requirements to meet this situation. "And how about you?" he countered. "What are you going to tell them after not writing since England?"

"I shall share with them my deepest apology for worrying them. And then I will blame the postal service." She looked over at Simon, and drank some coffee, adding, "I forgot the sugar."

Simon stood back up and grabbed her tin mug. "Sugar, we can do," he assured her.

Lydia watched him retreat and picked up her pen.

Dear Mother and Father,

January 1917

Where do I begin? First, I must tell you I carry the burden of guilt for your worry over me. I hope my leaving has not taken its toll on either of you. That was not my intent. Let me assure you that I know I was born to do this work.

When I am taking care of the sick and injured, I feel confident that I am doing what God has called me to do. I was never meant to continue working at the bank or to be a professor's wife. I knew that the very day I got off the train in Philadelphia and sat in my first class learning how to do a bed bath with the Red Cross instructors. I've caused you much distress by leaving without notice, but how could I bear the look in your eyes when you learned of my intention?

I needed to be strong the moment I arrived over here. So I wrote you of my decision in a letter. Your own letter in reply only arrived just before Thanksgiving, so you know that it takes quite a bit of time for any news to change hands. I did receive one letter from Derrick before he and Linda moved out west and am glad that he found someone with whom he could share his life.

I was shipped to a place I could never have imagined existed. I'm in a country at the center of the war with the most dedicated nurses and doctors I could ever hope to meet. We have been in France. It doesn't matter where, as all of France is engaged in this struggle for freedom, and they will not let me tell you any details anyway. One of the doctors in our company, his name is Simon, quickly became very dear to me. After working together for many months, we found we were linked not just in the care of the wounded, but also in spirit and in our hearts.

I am excited to share with you that Simon and I married, here in France. You must forgive me, Father, but it was a Catholic priest who married us, and that also was God-driven. Whenever we get home, there will be much to share with you about that. For now, let me assure you both that Simon is such a worthy man. I want more than anything for you to meet him and come to love him as part of our family. For myself, I have found in him a place for my heart to call home. He is the one I turn to when I am confused, or sorrowful, or need to share the beauty of a sunrise or sunset that is beyond words. He is the one whose children I want to bear and raise if we are so blessed. Someday, when this war is over, we will come home and sit in your kitchen and make new memories involving all of us. I'm amazed that I will turn twenty-two this year. Sometimes, I feel as though I am already fifty. Simon makes me feel as though I'm still a schoolgirl with the whole of life yet ahead of me to explore. In the absence of any creature comforts in the war, I find that with him, I want for nothing at all..."

Lydia laid down her pencil, imagining her mother reading this letter to her father at their kitchen table or beside their fireplace in the parlor. She thought it was a letter acceptable to share with her sister as well. There was more she was forbidden to say than she was allowed to share in this apology... this explanation... this entreaty for understanding.

Simon noted when she set down her pencil and was rereading what she had written. He did not ask to see it, working out his own thoughts and getting them down, before they slipped away. Surgery was still easier than relationships, but he realized he had gained some experience in these things over the past year. How to even address these two from Greensburg? Not as mother or father, not mister or misses—Simon skipped that part.

I asked Lydia to allow me to add on to her letter to you, knowing that it may be difficult for you to accept that she had graciously accepted my offer of marriage last summer, causing me to be the happiest man living under God's heaven. For through your daughter, I have become like Boaz in the Bible when he found his Ruth and was amazed that she would find him worthy to receive her love.

In the midst of this war where we serve, I want only to be her protector, her defender, the man she can trust for all of her days. Here, we don't know what tomorrow brings. The end of the war? Or the ongoing efforts of men to conquer and defeat other men, for ideological reasons?

I desired to honor your daughter in every respect. Therefore, when the opportunity came unexpectedly for us to say vows properly in a church before a priest, I took it gladly, for only that blessing would allow me to take her under my protection and my care in the manner of a husband. I can't begin to describe to you the respect she has rightly received from the entire medical team here and also from the soldiers serving with us.

Her courage and commitment are well known to all. The patients and the other nurses rely on her leadership, compassion and skill to see them through many difficult days. She will not be the same daughter as the one who left you a year ago, when she returns. But she will be a daughter you will love even more for the depth of her wisdom. I understand fully your wish for her safety and wellbeing. I will give my life to ensure both, if that should ever be asked of me. If it is not, then I will look forward to the day when we can meet and I can tell you a little more about myself and to learn about you all. I hope to resume my practice in West Virginia upon our return from the war. And I recognize that Lydia will also need to be intimately involved in her family life in Greensburg. I will ensure that she is able to do both. It is only with great difficulty that I imagine living a day without her. I wouldn't wish you to be without her longer than necessary, either.

Simon also set down his pencil. Then they exchanged what they had written, read the words appreciatively and folded up both, slipping them into an envelope addressed to home. It was enough.

In the mess, the team was arriving for a briefing before their upcoming move. The spring thaw had come as expected, offering dry ground over which the machinery of war could easily move; the war had resumed, with its insatiable appetite. The Ancre Valley advances of the Allied army, in the Argonne region, had held through the bitter winter months. Staff at the one major hospital, St. John's, were recovering from the devastating February outbreak of measles.

Now, Doctor Fortraine, following a private briefing with Harold, who had urged him to include the entire team for this news, called the team together. It was not just about the upcoming move, but also to cover the major changes in the world scene. Henri Fortraine stood while the others sat, listening.

"So here is the situation," Fortraine stated. "On April 6, America officially declared war on Germany. We expect mobilization of American troops in the upcoming months, perhaps by summertime, when troop transport ships should arrive on the continent. Once the troops have established themselves here, you Americans may be asked if you will stay with our station or go support one of the American Army battalions and come under their direction. For now, fighting is already getting underway at Arras, about 40 miles northeast of us, and we are too far away to be of service to the soldiers at the current front. We need to mobilize immediately."

The medical team nodded, always willing to move where needed.

"There is fighting across Europe," Fortraine continued, "and even naval battles at sea. There is political unrest in Russia. Where it will end, no one can foresee, but the Americans joining the war will likely change the nature of the conflict. If the war is not ended quickly by this additional army presence, then the fighting may intensify even more in the coming months. Each of you nurses, as always, is free to decide what will be best for you as our situation changes. For the immediate issue, this station must move out by this afternoon, so pack it up."

As they dispersed, to secure the surgery and their personal items, the nurses looked at each other in unspoken agreement. None was willing to break up their team, and all hoped they would not be asked to do so. For Lydia, there was no question; where Simon was ordered to go, she would go as well. The nurses and doctors returned to their tents to ensure their footlockers were organized and nothing would be left behind. At least they were moving during the warmer spring and not in the dead of winter. Within the next few hours, the army corps had disassembled the tents and stacked them onto trucks and wagons, filled with all of their supplies. They were ready to move out, heading northeast.

In the trucks, while traveling the forty miles across northern France, the group had an uninterrupted opportunity to debate the news contained in Doctor Fortraine's update. The Americans joining the war would, they all agreed, be monumental with many implications for their own work in the field. So much war had already been fought over the past several years. They wondered if the entry of the States was because Europe was losing? Or because the Allies were at a bitter stalemate? From watching the last year of merely incremental gains in the Argonne, they suspected it was more likely the latter. When would the countries run out of young men to send into battle? Doctor Fortraine had not shared any insights regarding what lay ahead. But whether or not to join with the American troops once they finally arrived in Europe... that was the foremost question on everyone's mind.

Marcus looked around at the nurses carefully. "You do know," he said as the truck and wagon convoy bounced and slogged its way forward, "that for all the talk over the past year about you nurses being either sent away or leaving by choice, none of us wants any of you to leave us."

Charlotte laughed at him. "We've become indispensable to you now, Doctor Lovell?"

"No... I mean, yes!" Marcus replied, the truck lurching through the ruts in the road. "You've all been indispensable from the first day you arrived. You heard what Winston said at the New Year's party! They're still just up to six nurses and wishing for more support. We've had the luxury of having almost a dozen of you for a year now... that is to say, we've been more aware of our need for you women... I mean, we've been more clinically astute about what is best for our patients, that is—"

Marlene laughed and tapped his knee reassuringly. "It's okay, Doctor Lovell, we knew what you meant from the start of all of that. I believe you are attempting to compliment us."

Marcus nodded. "Well, just so that I made myself completely clear on that," he said quickly.

Harold agreed. "I was one of the most vocally hesitant to allow you nurses to continue on with us as the fighting got worse. But I must admit, from the information Captain Thornwall and Doctor Fortraine have had to share with me, our station has triaged and treated more than most others at the front, and I know that it is, in no small part, because of you. Our mortality rate is lower and our successes are more easily counted because you women are running the show."

Lydia put up a hand. "I will grant you that we run the triage and recovery, Doctor Stockton. For the most part, we've taken that off you doctors. I think we have proven we're worth the hassle, in that respect... but let me be sure I understand you... no one in charge is actively considering sending us away anymore?"

Harold gave her a small smile. "No one is actively planning to send you nurses out anymore. For better or worse, the decision is now completely yours. You've more than earned the right to choose."

Marlene jumped in, "Speaking only for myself, I'm not breaking up our station to go with the American Army. My American Army is right here."

Gretha nodded. "No one in Washington or Philadelphia decides where I go!" she exclaimed. "My next stop will be home whenever that next stop comes. Not to an American Army camp somewhere."

Laura added, "Although, after the war, it might be nice to stay with the Red Cross in England for a little while and keep working with soldiers after the fighting is over. We've been here. We might be able to help the casualties in the hospitals to heal because we have an idea of what it's been like for them when they were wounded. Doctor Winston told me that the Brits are always looking for experienced nurses and would recognize our years of service, even as volunteers. He said some of the volunteer nurses at the field hospitals had even been given stripes on their uniforms for their years of service."

Nancy looked at the others. "I don't need any stripes," she told the others. "Every boy who made it safely out of our camp is a stripe on our sleeves."

"Doctor Winston was just saying that the Brits recognize the sacrifices of the volunteers," Laura added. "He thought our service deserved some recognition."

Though she was also absolutely certain that not one of the nurses wanted to leave their station, Lydia addressed the women.

"Regardless, no one has to commit to a decision, now. It should be made individually and there is plenty of time before it has to be decided, from the sound of it. We are all coming up on our year of being at the station and it's been a really long year. Everyone needs to feel free to go home at any time or, later on, join the army formally, if the American Army offers the chance to do it. You are not getting paid for this. None of you are sending any money home to family or loved ones. None of you will have any pay waiting in a bank somewhere after this. We'll be sending each other home with nothing more than memories and the satisfaction that we did our best." The image of Susannah going home, with a baby, flashed through her mind as she spoke.

The trucks ground to a stop, pulling over to the edge of the road. The horses drawing the wagons needed water and rest. Everyone was glad to get out of the truck to stretch their legs. Abril briefly left Lydia, taking off over the new grass of spring emerging across the countryside. It was a beautiful day in April. The sun was warm, the air was clean. A few spring flowers dared to poke out from the dirt along the side of the road. Lydia and Simon walked slowly, watching Abril bounding after some small creature in the grass.

"What about her?" Simon asked.

Lydia looked at the dog. "Abril? You mean Abril? Is there any question; she goes home with us whenever you get discharged?"

He laughed. "I assumed as much. Just asking. We've got the wife, the dog... all we need is the white picket fence."

"And two or three little toddlers running around," Lydia continued. "I wonder how Susannah has made out, Simon. I've written to her… but of course, we've been moving. I've heard nothing yet."

"Give her time," he assured Lydia, putting an arm around her waist. "She's got a lot to sort out."

Lydia looked over to where Marcus was stretched out on the ground near some of the nurses, relaxed and laughing with them.

"He still has no idea…" she murmured, "that he is a father."

Simon shook his head. "None at all," he assured her. "But his tone with the nurses seems to be more controlled, I think. Whatever Harold told him seems to have stuck. For sure, he hasn't touched the whiskey, not even once."

Lydia watched the dog playing on the hillside. She wondered just what Doctor Stockton had said to Marcus that next day after Susannah had left them. She wondered if he even remembered anything when the whiskey had worn off. Simon was correct about one thing. He had been holding himself in check, so far, with the other the nurses.

The group reboarded when beckoned, and Abril came leaping back through the field with a single call from Simon. She jumped into the back of the truck, settling in at Lydia's feet, as was her custom now. Their little convoy took to the road again. As they crossed over the next rise, there was no further talk of the army, nor of leaving, nor of home. For many, many miles, their wagons and trucks passed shells of bombed out buildings… single stone walls still standing, against all odds… trees reduced to stumps of jagged spears which poked up into the sky… holes in the ground from the impact of the shelling, some filled with muddy water, others empty reminders, like open tombs waiting to receive the dead.

They passed broken-down wagons with shattered, useless wheels. The newer tanks, already taken out of service, lay half-buried in craters or sideways in the dirt. Remnants of barbed wire fences still stretched across the ground. Mile after mile, they passed through the devastation, fully aware of the lives lost—the price paid so that their own trucks could roll over the countryside in relative safety. Also visible, in every direction, was the earth attempting to renew itself. Spring ivy gained a foothold, climbing the deadly metal spikes of wire. Small yellow flowers bloomed next to the abandoned war machines. Birds could be seen perched on the lone walls, where a home, a shop, a church, had once thrived. Everywhere, life triumphed over the death wrought by human invention.

Inside the truck, the nurses and the doctors found comfort in each other. They could visualize men running forward with bayonets or rifles in their arms or the litter bearers carrying the wounded off the line to bring them out to the casualty clearing stations. They knew the cost the ambulance drivers paid to steer their way through the battlefields, trying to get to the stricken soldiers on the ground. The doctors and nurses knew. They also knew that where they were headed now, the need for their services would be great... and they were all ready to serve.

Mercifully, there was a light, warm breeze flowing over the wounded under the newly erected tarps. Lydia and Monique moved through the rows of triage, examining wounds, assigning numbers to the men, and calling litter bearers to move some of the casualties to the front of the line, for priority care. All of the surgery tables were running at capacity. The wounded German were separated by armed French soldiers, not to prevent care—and not that the risk of violence was prevalent, as they had all been disarmed—but more to define the two groups clearly for the sentries on patrol.

Lydia could see that Monique was becoming increasingly adept at recognizing which wounded soldiers were most in need of care. The French nurse often called Lydia over to confirm her findings and strengthen her judgment skills. She was a blessing to French soldiers, who could speak fluently with her, unhindered by translation obstacles. Lydia observed the woman gratefully. She had become a valued member of the team.

Lydia stood and let the breeze refresh her. The sun was just warm enough to be comforting, rather than imposing. She noticed one of the German soldiers motioning for assistance to the women moving down the rows. Lydia called over to Monique, affirming that she had seen and was heading over. Picking her way carefully through the wounded, she made her way to the man's side. His left leg was mangled. She could see the severity of the damage even as she approached. Undoubtedly, it would not be able to be saved; she felt sorry for the young man. Abril moved cautiously beside her, careful not to step on any of the wounded. As Lydia drew near to the man on the ground, she stiffened in sudden panic. Abril whined slightly and ran off.

The German commander was lying on the litter at her feet.

He looked up at her, and his face suddenly relaxed with recognition despite his physical pain. "Ah, it is the nurse of the trench," he said. "At last, we meet again, Nurse Lydia, don't we?"

She nodded, her throat tight, choking her words. She fought a deep desire to turn and leave him unattended.

"You want to help me, don't you," he stated, observing the struggle in her face. "Yet, you hate me."

She stood over him. "I don't hate you," she said in a measured tone.

"Is that so? Give me some water," he said, pointing to the canteen over her shoulder. "I am parched laying here."

She lifted the canteen, hesitated, then slowly unscrewed the cap. Then, she knelt beside him as he attempted to rise up on his elbows to drink. She lifted his head and put the canteen to his lips, and he took a long sip, water droplets escaping the corners of his mouth to run down his chin where a blond beard was forming, and then he lay back down.

"Water," he said. "Such a simple thing. That was not very difficult now, was it, Nurse?"

She stared at him, incredulous. "Have you learned nothing of compassion..." she said softly, but loud enough for him to hear. "Don't you realize you will lose your leg? That you are a prisoner of war?"

He looked up at her with his piercing blue eyes. "You were so easy to control. I will always have the satisfaction of knowing that you did exactly what I told you to do."

"I did only what I had to do," she stated, "not what you told me to do."

"You just gave me water because I told you to," he corrected her. "You are not in control here, Nurse. I am. And when we were together, I could have made you beg for mercy, but it was I who chose not to."

She shook her head. "I did beg for mercy, but not to you," she told the commander. "I begged God to forgive your soul, to take the horrible evil from you and give you another chance."

The man spat, and it landed on her breast where he had aimed it. He reached up one hand and grabbed her shirt where the spittle clung, pulling her down toward him. "Even now," he told her, "I could make you scream if I wanted to…"

"If you don't have the power to make me hate," she told him, grabbing his hand, "then you have no power over me at all." She heard him ripping the fabric of her shirt in the iron grip of his fingers; other wounded were now looking on in troubled astonishment.

Suddenly, there was a blur of fur, and a shadow fell over the both of them. Abril lunged, sinking her teeth deep into the muscles of the man's outstretched arm. The commander screamed in pain, jerking Lydia down toward him. At the exact same moment, Lydia felt arms around her as Simon pulled her back up to her feet and away from the man, now howling in the dog's vice-like grip. Armed French soldiers came running toward the scream, rifles loaded and pointed. Lydia watched Simon smash his fist into the German commander's face. The German lay unconscious, on the litter.

"Abril, come," Simon ordered the growling dog, who obediently released the commander's arm from her teeth. Simon shook the pain from his fist. He saw the bitten muscle of the soldier's arm bleeding profusely. As Lydia tried to pull her torn shirt back together, Simon whipped off his own shirt and wrapped her in it. He had her in his arms, and Abril sat watchfully at their feet, still softly growling from time to time. "Good dog," Simon said, reaching down to rub her head between her ears. The dog growled at the unconscious man.

"How did you know?" Lydia asked him, relief washing over her, yet aware of a slight tremble, likely adrenaline.

"Abril came and got me in the surgery," Simon explained. "Marched right in... to Stockton's horror... wouldn't let go of my pant leg." The doctor looked down at the man. "So, is that the one?"

She nodded. "That's the man."

"Well! Someone else is going to have to saw that man's leg off. It would give me far too much satisfaction, and I would have a great deal of trouble repenting to God for it," Simon admitted, leading her away to their tent for a new shirt and directing one of the corpsmen to wrap the commander's bleeding arm.

Inside their tent, Simon attempted to help her remove the ripped shirt, but she stayed him. She slipped out of it herself and held it in her hands for a moment before letting it fall, leaving both of them standing half-naked and unashamed. She pressed her body against his bare chest as he held her. Then, Lydia took the shirt he'd pulled off himself only moments before and clothed herself in it, tucking it into her trousers. "You have always been my covering," she told him. "Always."

He nodded, bending to get a new shirt for himself from his footlocker. "Always."

"No more demons," she told Simon. "I didn't know if I would hate him if I ever saw him again."

"And you don't," he offered, eyeing her quizzically before looking at the slightly swollen, bloodied knuckles of his right hand.

"No," she admitted, amazed and relieved even as she heard the words come out. "I don't hate him."

"Well then," Simon said, kissing her face after he took it in his hands, "you will have to pray for me, Lydia, because I most assuredly do."

Chapter 17

Clearing the Air

Simon returned quickly to the surgery and to the waiting casualty, there at a table.

Harold looked up from his own patient, glanced around at the ground, and said, "Did you leave the dog outside?"

Simon nodded, his face tense and resolute. "I did."

Marcus glanced over. "Heard a bit of a ruckus a few minutes ago. Anything you'd like to share with the rest of the family?"

Simon shook his head. "Not at the moment." He took a quick look at the prostrate man in front of him and said to Marlene, "Nurse Sullivan, would you pull the bullet out of this shoulder and just pack the wound? It won't even need to be sutured. I'll take the next one."

"Yes, Doctor," Marlene said, moving into position while Simon went to the next table where a man was being carried in with a gaping chest wound.

A corpsman poked his head through the door and called over to Simon. "Uh, Doctor, what about this one out here? He's still bleeding all over the place... and not just from that arm."

Simon didn't look up from the chest wound in front of him, but called out in response. "I'm busy and I don't care... he'll have to wait."

Marcus and Nancy shot looks over at Simon's unusual remark.

The corpsman hesitated. "If you say so, Doc."

Harold turned to Gretha beside him, "Finish up here, please, Nurse Bernstein." Harold walked around the table, toward the opening of the surgery, and washed his hands. He assessed the man outside on the litter, at the feet of the puzzled corpsman. Kneeling down beside the soldier, Stockton immediately realized the German had lost a significant amount of blood from the mangled leg. The amputation would have to be very high, almost to the groin. Harold saw the fresh, blood-soaked dressing on the man's arm as well and recognized the deep purple swelling of the man's jaw, undoubtedly a new injury. He glanced over the rows of waiting wounded on both sides, Allies and Germans alike, filling the ground under the tarps. He said quietly to the corpsman, "This man has no chance of survival whatsoever. Take him over to wait it out with the rest of those we can't help."

Relieved to have clear instructions, the corpsman turned to the litter bearers and told them to take the German commander out to the tarp where the critically wounded were being left to end their time on Earth, assisted with laudanum if needed. Harold watched the German be moved off and scanned for anything amiss in the rest of the collection of humanity, both prostrate and those tending the wounded. The nurses were busy down the rows. He saw Lydia among them, moving between the injured French men with the dog near her side. Nothing he saw looked out of the ordinary beyond a difficult day of war. Harold shook his head and returned to the surgery. *Neglecting the wounded, assaulting one, even a German, can't be tolerated.* The explanation for Simon's unusual behavior would have to wait until there was a lull in casualties.

It was nearly midnight when the surgery shut down and the energy of the station shifted focus to the recovery. The three surgeons were exhausted despite taking breaks as needed. While they scrubbed their hands at the surgical wash station, Harold said quietly to Simon, "A word with you, Doctor Finney."

"Yeah," Marcus responded. "What was that all about, Simon—"

Harold looked at Marcus. "Another time, Doctor Lovell. You can hit the shower if you want to."

Simon looked at both of them over the running water from the reservoir. "No, Harold. I'll tell both of you right now what that was all about," he said, his voice tight with rage.

"Have anything to do with your fist turning purple?" Harold said then, motioning to his hand.

Marcus whistled. "Wouldn't have wanted to be on the receiving end of that one."

Harold looked sternly at his fellow surgeon. "It's completely unethical, it's downright morally wrong to hit an injured man, no matter which side he's on. That would cost you your license, in front of a medical board, Simon, in France or in the States."

Simon picked up a towel to gingerly dry his injured hand. "They can have my license, if they find out," he said defiantly.

Harold looked around them. There was no other medical staff in earshot.

"Okay. Explanation. Now!" He demanded.

Simon looked at the two other doctors. "That was the German commander who held Lydia and Charlotte and our two sentries hostage in the trenches last winter. That was the German commander who forced my wife... to do unspeakable things in order to keep the four of them from having to fry up trench rats to ease their hunger. That was the German commander who put his hands on my wife and ripped her shirt open right here in our own camp just to satisfy some sick perversion of his own, even as she was trying to comfort the wounded.

"Hell yes, I punched him, and he's lucky I stopped at one. And hell yes, I'd let him bleed to death, and gladly. Report me to the board when we get home, Harold. Hell, report me to the French army. Go wake up Fortraine right now and tell him. Let him revoke my privileges and dishonorably discharge me. I don't give a damn what you do. That man laying over... well, wherever he is... will never touch my wife again because if he so much as lays his eyes on her again, I will most certainly kill him."

Harold and Marcus looked at Simon, dumbfounded. They had never seen him this angry in the entire year and a half of serving together. Realizing the implications of what Simon had just told them rendered them both, momentarily, speechless.

"The German died about two hours ago of irreparable, massive blood loss from an artillery shell," Harold told Simon. "That is what I wrote in the ledger regarding the prisoners of war for the French Command."

Simon looked at his friends, relief flooding over him. "Then he'll rot in hell, unless he did some heavy-duty repenting under that tarp while he waited."

"Fortraine already knows," Harold continued. "And one of the wounded told a guard, who told Fortraine, that our dog attacked a wounded man, and Fortraine ordered that she be shot."

Simon ran the fingers of his good hand through his hair in distraction. "I can't believe this!" he groaned. "That dog saved Lydia's life... and not only hers, the other three as well."

Harold nodded. "I know that. Abril is in your tent with Nurse Finney. I told Fortraine I'd explain later. So, what I need from you is what else should I tell Fortraine in order to explain all of this?"

Simon breathed a prayer of thanksgiving that the dog was safe and Lydia even more safe. "Fortraine already knows what that man did to Lydia. He made her tell him the very next day, after the four of them had returned to the station. He made her tell him almost the entire story of what that man did to her... almost. And I have scarcely had one good night of sleep since, thinking about that German commander, knowing he was still out there somewhere and wishing I could get my hands on him myself. Then he shows up here, of all places, right here. That's why Abril came and got me in the surgery. It took every ounce of willpower I had to stop with one punch when that man grabbed Lydia. That isn't malpractice. That's justice."

Marcus looked at Simon with a newfound admiration. "Truthfully, Simon, I didn't know you had it in you!"

Harold gave Marcus a look that halted his accolades before addressing Simon again. "Just try to keep the dog out of the surgery from here on out, will you?"

Then Marcus said, "I know you haven't told us the half of it, Simon, but is Ly—is Nurse Finney alright? I mean, is she suffering any long-term effects from..."

Simon put his hand on his friend's shoulder. "You want to know the truth, Marcus? She's been doing better than I have. She already forgave the bastard, and all I've been thinking of is how to make him pay."

Harold looked them both, but his message was meant for Simon alone. "I think sometimes it's a great mercy when God takes that choice out of our hands. Vengeance is supposed to be His, Simon. I doubt the German crossed over to the other side looking forward to what was waiting for him there."

"I'm glad the decision is out of my hands," Simon admitted. "Now, if that's enough of an explanation, Harold, I'm hitting the shower and going to check on—oh. Does she know about—?"

Harold shook his head. "Not from me. I will leave that to your discretion. And Simon, when there is a lull in the fighting, I need to teach you how to throw a punch without breaking your hand."

Simon paused. "Fair enough, Harold. I missed that in med school."

"Some extracurriculars come in handy."

Marcus nodded enthusiastically. "You can say that again..."

Simon hurried to the shower and hastily soaped up, dumping buckets of water over his body and quickly drying off. After Harold's update, he was anxious to get to Lydia. As he pushed open their tent flap, Abril came bounding out to take her place, just outside of the tent door. "Good dog," he whispered, rubbing her ears.

Lydia was already under the blanket holding a folded-up, outdated, London Times—even old news was better than the other options which she'd already read a dozen times before. She set the paper down, noting that Simon looked surprisingly at peace, considering the challenging day they had had.

"Simon!" she exclaimed. "Did you hear that Doctor Fortraine was going to have Abril shot!"

"I know," he nodded. "Stockton told me. It's all cleared up now." He sat down by her on the cot. "How are you holding up?" he asked in concern, reaching out to touch her hair.

"Oh, dear god, your hand!" she exclaimed softly. "Simon!"

He gingerly stretched out his fingers. "They all still work," he assured her. "Are you okay?"

Lydia took his hand and softly kissed the purpling, abraded knuckles. "Yes. I'm so sorry."

"Don't be," he told her. "I'm not." He took her hands in his. "The German died a few hours ago, Lydia."

She absorbed that information. "Did anyone even try..."

"Harold took a look at him, didn't even know who he was, but decided he was too far gone already. Wounds far too extensive. And I'm glad."

She nodded. "Me too. So we both can put it completely behind us."

He nodded in agreement. "Yes, we can." *I hope...*

She sat up and laid the paper, linking them to the regular world, aside. "You need to let me help you out of your clothes," she told him.

"Well, I already did that successfully in the shower and got some back on again too, busted hand and all..."

"Perhaps, but now I'm here, so let me help," Lydia helped him undo his shirt and trousers. He laid back in just his boxers, stretching out on the cot, grateful for the woman beside him, the resolution of the emotional turmoil he had been carrying, the warmer weather, the fire in the tent. The moon was almost overhead now, casting a sliver of silver through a crack in the tent siding which allowed in just a bit of fresh air. Lydia looked down on this man whom she loved so deeply. His eyes were already closing as he drifted off, from fatigue.

Simon started lightly snoring. Lydia quietly slipped out of her clothes to lay down on their spare cot, close to him, and softly reached out to touch the medallion nested in the hair on his chest. The cool round surface gleamed in the moonlight and she felt the indentation of his stamped name... Simon J Finney... that small metal circle had kept her from losing all hope. *It is such a little thing... It is such a little thing, really...* Lydia heard the hated echo repeat itself unbidden, trying to connect itself to something she loved. The German commander's declaration that he was still in control of her had troubled her. The awareness that his words could still echo in her head... she forbade her body to make any sound while her eyes overflowed. *No,* she told herself fiercely, try-ing to sever the link, *there was nothing small about the medal at all!* That precious medallion was a huge thing! Because it represented such a great love.

Simon stirred slightly. His voice came softly in the moonlight. "I think you forgot my boxers, if you wouldn't mind..."

Without speaking, she rose up, pulling his boxers down over his feet. Then she caressed him, her tears dropping on his abdomen like falling stars.

Simon sank the fingers of his good hand into her hair as she ministered to him, knowing it would take time for her to heal from the memories. He felt the wetness of her cheeks against his skin and wished it was in his power to speed the healing along. Then he said, "Lydia, my love, don't cry. Come up here."

She moved up over him where he lay, his good hand still cradling her head, drawing her face to his. But before their mouths touched, she heard him say regretfully, "I want to comfort you... but some things may be a little more complicated with just one hand—"

She stopped him with her lips against his; she still had two willing hands, and she was happy to use them any way he wanted.

In the morning, there was snow again in the April air. Abril bounded ahead of Lydia to the latrine, enjoying the colder weather, and then followed her to the surgery. Lydia had already determined she would work in the surgery beside Simon with his throbbing hand. Abril plopped herself down outside of the surgery tent where she could people-watch, her tongue lolling in the fresh, crisp air... and she was sure to get a few scraps of something good, sitting where all of the people were coming and going.

Marcus nodded to Lydia as she washed up. The wounded were coming in from Arras, where there had been an intense bombardment. "How are you this morning, Nurse Finney?" he asked somewhat anxiously, wishing he knew the entire story hidden inside of her.

"Quite alright... thank you, Doctor Lovell," she reassured him. "And you?"

"Ready to serve," he assured her. "Are you... really alright? Is there anything I can do to help you with all of the... recent events?"

She reached up, pulling her hair up into a bun, while wrapping it in her blue scarf. "Did Doctor Finney say something to you?"

"Will he get in trouble if I say, yes?" Marcus countered, noticing the stray curl by her ear.

"No," she said slowly. "But I wonder if he spoke to anyone else?"

Marcus nodded. "Doctor Stockton and I were the only ones... he didn't go into much detail though... and I guess, Fortraine was brought up to speed at some point."

Lydia reached for a surgical apron. "Yes, he knows all about it."

"You know I would have gone after you myself—we all wanted to," Marcus added quickly, "but that dog beat us to it."

She looked up at Marcus's face, the intensity in his eyes. "I know you would have helped us in any way you could, Doctor Lovell. I'm glad you didn't have to. You're so irreverent, you'd have gotten yourself shot!"

"I can be very reverent when I need to be, Nurse Finney. I swore to take care of—" he stopped abruptly.

"To take care of what?" she asked him curiously.

"Simon made me swear a long time ago, when he was sick, before God, to take care of you if anything ever happened to him. And I did swear it, Lydia," Marcus told her by the wash sink. "I meant every word."

Lydia's eyes welled with tears. "Did you really, Marcus?" she asked, slipping into the familiar.

"I did, I still do... I mean... I will if it's ever needed," he said, wanting to wipe her eyes himself. "I'm not a very religious guy, as you might have already figured out. But I don't mess with the swear-before-God promises. No, that's serious stuff. If you ever need to talk, to just let it all out, you can count on me."

She saw the earnest expression on his face. "Yes," she said softly. "A vow is serious stuff. Well, thank you for that reassurance. If it was that important to Simon to ask you to take care of me, then it is that important to me as well. I'm alright. Truly."

At just that moment, Simon came through the tent opening and they moved aside to let him wash. He gingerly ran his hand under the cool water, finding it to be surprisingly soothing.

"I don't know, man," Marcus observed, shaking his head. "Looks pretty bad, that. How are you going to operate with one hand?"

Simon smiled and glanced over at Lydia. "Can't put an undue burden on the rest of you, can I now? I was offered the assistance of two very capable hands all day today, Doctor Lovell."

Lydia blushed almost to scarlet, thinking of him only a few hours ago, and reached for a mask to cover her face.

Marcus's eyes laughed at that. She was still a blushing bride after all these months. He liked that about her. "Just let me know if you need these hands today," Marcus said, waving his own ten fingers in the air. "Here to help. All ten, in working order!"

The three of them moved to surgical tables as the wounded began arriving, being brought in on litters and placed in front of them. The anesthetists immediately got busy, putting the soldiers to sleep.

Marlene stood at a table waiting for Doctor Stockton, who hadn't made his morning appearance yet. A patient with a gash across his thigh from barbed wire was placed before her. Simon stood between her table and his own, where Lydia was prepping a man's abdomen for the surgery to follow. He looked at the torn thigh and looked at her.

"You've got this," he assured her. "Clean up the tear, cut away the loose fragments of skin to get a clean line and wash it out well, and suture that one shut loosely... every inch and a half, so we can irrigate it if we need to later."

"Yes, Doctor," she replied. She was happily in her element.

He turned back to his own table, where Lydia had the abdominal wound retracted and washed out, waiting. She shone her flashlight into all aspects of the wound for him to see deeper inside. "Gut wound, right at the ileum," he said.

"I see it." She pointed with the tip of a clamp. "Suture or resection?"

"Suture," he returned. "Let's try to keep him connected."

She picked up the needle and suture. "Do you know it was a British man who invented that little light?" she asked him. "Misell. David Misell. Not even twenty years ago."

Simon was appreciative. "You mean when you nurses were asking for equipment, you wanted the very latest, most modern inventions? Amazing." He smoothly clipped her sutures with his left hand. "Let's rins—"

She was already rinsing out the wound again to take another look for more tears.

"Geez," Simon breathed. "If you two ladies no longer have need of me, I'll just go read on my cot!"

"Now, Doctor Finney," Marlene corrected him. "You're the only surgeon in here running two tables at once. Give yourself a little credit."

It wasn't long before the tables were cleared and they looked up as more casualties were brought in, followed by Harold. He had come from a private update with Doctor Fortraine about the battle for Arras. Apparently, the French defense minister had recently resigned. New attack formation strategies had been formed, with such little ground having been gained at Verdun and Somme, during the previous year. Harold was told that Canadian forces were attempting to draw the Germans slightly to the north, at a place called Vimy Ridge, so that the French army could advance along the front to their south. The twenty-four miles of front line were being heavily bombarded by millions of shells, in advance of the foot soldiers. All of the casualty clearing stations were already positioned, in anticipation of the arriving onslaught of wounded. The French were determined to break through the line of German trenches. And it was snowing again.

Harold washed up and joined Marlene at the surgical table and they got to work. He valued working with the nurse and appreciated her quick aptitude for the surgery. The doctor had happily written her a letter of recommendation for medical school, upon Simon's request, last fall. Harold knew she would get in, if the social mores of the medical community would welcome a woman, back in the States. No doubt, she deserved the chance. Her hands were quick and her eyes were sharp. He knew they were treating twice as many patients as other stations, because their nurses were trained to actively assist. And why not? Medics were trained to assist. *Why on earth*, Harold often wondered, *would a good nurse be left doing only dressings, putting a few drops of ether on a mask, and carrying away bedpans?*

Taking a moment, he called for the attention of the team under the tent. Everyone grew quiet, listening, even while they continued their work.

"I've just come from Fortraine's tent," Harold said loud enough so everyone could hear him clearly. "The battle for Arras is intensifying. The Allies want to break through the trench line."

The others looked up. They had been expecting this and had already heard the echoes of the shelling.

Harold continued, "It is unlikely that the British Expeditionary Force and the French will lose ground… although they may not gain much. Sounds like there is minimal chance of us being overrun. There are multiple casualty stations positioned in the area, all prepared to absorb the flow of the wounded, so we aren't alone in this. This battle is likely to go on for several days. Take care of yourselves. Take breaks and get rest. Cook will be keeping the mess open around the clock, since it will be needed. The nurses and medics, who can be in surgery, do the same thing. Relieve each other in shifts, as we're likely to be working through the night for several days. We'll need all the hands we have. If the Allies can break through the German defenses, this could start a new chapter in the war. If not, many more lives will be lost."

Marcus said, "Sounds like Verdun and Somme all over again. Nothing new. We've got this."

Harold nodded. "Perhaps so."

Simon spoke up, "When this one is over, can Fortraine send someone to go check in on Winston and the others, to the north? It would be good to know how they're faring."

Marcus agreed. "And it's our turn to play host if they can come to visit… only, they'll have to bring that Victrola down. I, for one, am ready to fill some of the nurses' dance cards." That broke the tension as the team remembered the wonderful January event at the British CCS. If they hosted, it would be hard to plan a better party.

As they worked through the next few days, it was difficult to imagine that the Allies were winning, given the intense flow of casualties coming through. They followed Harold's orders, relieving each other, and resting, as needed… and holding onto the idea of hosting a reception for the British team… a thought that never failed to lift their spirits.

Lydia hated to wake Simon, but it was time. He groaned.

"Didn't we just fall asleep ten minutes ago?" he mumbled.

She nodded, pulling her boots back on. "Fifteen. Yes. And it's time to go back."

He sat up, stroked his beard, and yawned. "At least I don't have to take the time to shave."

She reached over to touch his bearded cheeks. "I like your beard," she said as she tucked her shirt into her trousers. "I don't ever want you to shave it off. It tickles when you rub it between my breasts."

His eyes flew open. "And… anywhere else?"

She looked down at him and caressed his chin. "Oh my, yes!" she said softly, teasing. "Most certainly a 'somewhere else.'"

He laughed and pulled on his own boots. "Well, I'm certainly awake now!" he exclaimed.

She kissed him lightly on the top of his head. "That was the idea," she smiled. "I'll see you in a few minutes in the surgery.

Come, Abril." The dog fell into step at her side as she left the tent, stopping at the mess for coffee.

Charlotte and Monique were deep in conversation at the long table, while they hastily ate some supper.

"How are you two doing?" Lydia asked, sitting down beside them for a quick moment.

"This is a long one," Charlotte groaned. "Don't think it's ever going to end. What day is it, anyway? Does anyone even know?"

"April 15," Monique replied. "Almost a week they fight. Now we are glad we came in winter. If we had come in the middle of this, I think we would have both turned around the first day."

Lydia sat briefly with the other two nurses, just long enough to drink her coffee and eat some baguette. "I know I certainly would have!" Lydia agreed. "Let's see, when we came... yes, it was spring and the start of an offensive, but we were down south of Verdun then."

"And we were in Bordeaux," Monique said, thinking back. "At hospital learning to change beds."

Charlotte leaned over the table. "Is it true what I heard?" she asked Lydia, a somber expression on her face.

"About?" Lydia pressed her.

"About the German commander? I heard he was right here, in our own station, and died," Charlotte said softly.

Lydia nodded. "Yes, that is true. He died two days ago, here."

"Why didn't you tell me, Lydia?" Charlotte demanded. "I would have wanted to know... at least, I think I would have wanted to know."

"We've been so focused on the wounded... there wasn't time. Why, we've hardly even had a chance to see each other, except in passing. Does it change anything for you knowing this, Charlotte?" Lydia asked her curiously.

Charlotte slowly shook her head. "No, I guess, not really. I mean, I never met the man. I wouldn't have known it was him even if I had seen him. So, probably no. But I heard you saw him here, Lydia, and that he remembered you. I heard that Doctor Finney decked him."

Lydia nodded. "Yes, I saw him and recognized him. He remembered me. And yes, Doctor Finney hit him."

"Why?" Monique asked the others. "Why did the doctor hit this man?"

Lydia looked at Charlotte before answering. "The commander was still being a cruel man, Monique, even here. He was someone who enjoyed using his power against others. He thought he could take one more shot at me."

"But isn't that just the way Germans are? Isn't that why they started this war? For power?" Monique asked. "This is why we try to kill them, no?"

Charlotte shook her head, denying the other woman's underlying assumptions. "When we were with them, we saw so many young men in the trenches, all Germans, of course, and they were no different from our own wounded. They were hungry and cold and hurting. I think they probably just wanted to go home to their families, as soon as they possibly could."

"Except for the ones in charge," Lydia added. "Having power, when men get power, it can change them."

"I wonder," Monique said. "Doctor Fortraine has power, and he does not seem to be... the word you say, cruel, is same in French, oui? Doctor Finney had power over the wounded, no?"

Lydia nodded her head. "Yes, the same word. Not everyone with power is cruel. When Doctor Finney hit him, he was defending me... il me défendait. He hit the German commander because he had to make him stop."

"Ah. Cruel to you, and maybe not just here, no?" Monique said astutely. "Maybe also before he was cruel to you? This is why Doctor Finney hit him."

Charlotte grew pale wondering if Lydia would be ready to talk. "Lydia?"

Lydia looked at her friend. "Why are we even talking about this at all?" she asked them both. "War brings out the evil in people sometimes. But we can offer the world something good in spite of it. That is all that matters."

Charlotte stared at her, her eyes penetrating Lydia's barriers. "He hurt you a lot didn't he," she stated, sadness overwhelming her soul. "Because of us. Because of me. God in heaven, Lydia, I never wanted you to be hurt for me. I knew something had happened... when he kept calling for you. We all thought he was doing something..."

Lydia came around the table and hugged Charlotte. "You are a sister to me, Charlotte. The man is dead, and he didn't die well, either. No regrets." Lydia lifted her friend's chin to look her in the face. "No regrets," she repeated emphatically. Monique watched them, wondering what had happened that had deepened their bond so.

Charlotte nodded. "Okay, Lydia. No regrets."

There was no break in the volume of wounded. The team had fallen into a routine of four hours on duty, two hours of sleep. Quick showers and hastily eaten meals kept them going. Doctor Fortraine himself now came to the surgery each day for several hours to relieve one of the surgeons. Simon's hand had healed. Another week passed of the grueling pace, but one night, after sunset, no ambulances appeared. Somehow, the opposing armies had either run out of soldiers or had briefly grown weary of using up the ones they had. Either way, the eye in the middle of the storm was welcome. Some people used the lull just to sleep continuously. Others tried to engage and distract themselves with something normal and mindless, like cards or checkers. The April snow had lifted, and the air had warmed again. Trucks pulled out of the station loaded with wounded, for the hospitals. A collective sigh of relief could be perceived throughout the station.

Pulling into camp, was a supply truck from the quartermaster corps. Its team had used the lull, for safe passage through the torn-up countryside. With them, they brought the mail; there had been none since Christmas. In the twilight, everyone in the station, who could, joined a little crowd in the mess for the excitement of mail distribution. As names were called out, there were many letters, small parcels, carefully wrapped in brown paper, outdated newspapers, and a few medical journals, all placed into eager hands. A letter from the Red Cross, for all of the nurses, was addressed to Lydia. The backlog of mail delivery meant that it took some time to ensure everything packed into the truck was officially delivered. Those who stood waiting, only to end up disappointed, tried their best to share in the good fortune of the others. The supply truck had also brought a priest, a rare visit by the clergy, to minister to the wounded.

Simon and Lydia took their precious mail back to their tent to open. Simon had a letter from his sister in West Virginia, dated the previous November, and a small parcel wrapped in brown paper. Lydia had one from her own sister, also postmarked in November. And there was a small envelope from Susannah.

"Finally!" Lydia breathed. She put a log on the fire to brighten the tent. "It's from Susannah, Simon! Look!" she exclaimed, as the warm light spread around them, and she stretched out onto one of the cots to read.

He nodded, absorbed in his own mail.

Dear Lydia, she read as she leaned on her elbows over the letter.

I am so sure this will take forever to reach you, but hope that when it arrives, you are still alive and able to read it. My family has not disowned me despite my condition when I finally got home. Let me tell you, pregnant on the ship, crossing the ocean was not fun at all. I spent most of my time on the ship just trying to keep water down. My pregnancy went well, and I can tell you that feeling the baby moving inside of me was a joyful experience. I hope you and Doctor Finney will have the chance to know that same joy. Of course, it would have been so much better if Marcus would have been able to share it with me. But I have accepted that he could not.

I gave birth a little earlier than expected, February 22nd, to a precious little girl with a head full of dark curls just like her father. She was only five pounds. I named her Marcie Nichole, sort of after Marcus, I suppose. But I am calling her Nikki because she is such a sweet little thing. My family adores her and that is fortunate for me. They can blame my having a baby on the 'terrible effect of the war on their own little girl' so they can excuse her accidental birth and treasure her.

I have gotten a job working at one of the hospitals near my parents and my mother watches Nikki while I work. It is really rather boring, but it provides me a small income. You would hate it. We must stand up when the doctor comes in the room. I detest wearing white dress uniforms.

One day I tried wearing my blue scarf, but got in trouble for it. And we are not allowed to have an opinion about how a patient is doing. We have to call one of the doctors in for that. I sometimes wonder if they forget we each have a brain.

And no one at all talks about the war. No one even asks about it. I guess that's okay since I don't really know how to describe what we've seen and been through. Maybe it's better that way.

Maybe someday I will find a different job and a little cottage for Nikki and me. But for now, I'm content to let my mother and father adore her right along with me, in their house. They were so glad I wasn't killed in France that I think they would keep me here forever if I asked them.

I worry about you and all of the girls. I hope that Marcus is behaving himself as well as can be expected. I do miss him and his sense of humor. I hope Nikki inherits that at least. If you want to write back to me, I would welcome a letter. Just send it to my parents' address.

Yours fondly,
Susannah.

Lydia read through the letter three times before putting it down.

Simon was watching her lying there reading. He had a small parcel in his hands. When she finished her news from Susannah, he held out the box, still wrapped in paper and twine. "This is for you. It was supposed to be for Christmas, but... well, you know. I asked my sister to have it sent a long time ago."

Lydia rolled onto her back. "But we agreed no gifts, my love. I have no money."

"I wanted this for you," he said simply. "I thought it would be a good thing for you to have."

She sat up curious. "It had better not be a gold ring, my love. I don't want another."

He shook his head. "It's not a gold ring."

She examined the securely tied parcel. "We need something to cut this twine."

Simon took a piece of kindling and put the tip in the fire until it caught the flame. He held it like a candle to the twine until a section blackened and snapped before throwing the tinder and twine alike into the stove.

Lydia carefully tore away the brown paper. The plain brown cardboard box was slightly larger than her hand. She glanced up at Simon, wondering. "You have been keeping secrets from me! What have you done..." She opened the top. There, nestled inside a protective lining of crumpled newspapers, was a small wooden box which she carefully withdrew. A small brass knob on the side revealed its purpose. She turned the winding key and the Swiss movement released the sweet notes of Brahms's Lullaby into the night. Lydia had no words... she could only hold it in her hands.

Simon knelt beside her. "I have never made love to you, to music."

She nodded a little breathless. "Right now? Do you mean...?"

He nodded. "Yes, I'd love to." He undressed her as the refrain repeated. He lifted her hair and kissed the back of her neck, causing chills to run down her spine. Simon knew he could not have prevented the injuries the war had inflicted upon her. He could, however, play a key role in her healing and recovery from those insults. So now, he kissed the scar from the bullet wound on her back, tracing its path along her shoulder. He lowered her against the cot, rolled her onto her stomach, and wound the mechanism of the music box again. With his fingers, Simon traced the long, white, shiny scars stretched across the roundness of her bottom, following with tender caresses from his lips. Only then did he roll her over onto her back so he could look down on her. *If I could have just taken it for you, I would have!* he thought to himself for the hundredth time.

"Don't you think you should take off your clothes now and join me?" she asked softly, her body aching for him. "I want to feel you against me..."

Simon wound the Brahms one more time. "You will," he assured her, "but not just yet. Didn't you just say this morning as you walked away from me that you liked the tickle of my beard against you...?"

"I did say that," she whispered as she felt him positioning her legs where he wanted them.

"I could think of little else as you stood beside me all day long..." he teased.

She allowed him to enjoy her to the lullaby, rising as the notes rose, her entire body feeling healthy and whole. The intensity of the response he, and his beard, elicited from her, sent her spinning off into the heart of the music, just as he promised...

When he felt her body begin to quiet, he stood, finally removing his own clothing, and winding the box once more. Simon lowered himself onto her, letting the melody carry them both away, into the movement. And long after the disc of the music box ceased to turn, the notes still enveloped them, the symphony finding its climax in and around them, and they remained entwined. Tomorrow, the war would return. Tonight, the music had replaced reality as they lay holding onto each other, savoring the moment.

After a quick lunch, Marcus made his rounds through the recovery tent, checking in with the nurses, conferring with them about the stability of those waiting for transport to the hospitals. Charlotte was on duty as Marcus made his way through the rows of men. He saw her halfway down a row, standing between two of the wounded, looking down at one... not moving. Then, she leaned over to listen with her stethoscope and used her hand to close the eyes that would no longer see anything of this war, again. She called softly for the corpsman assisting her and gave him quiet instructions.

The doctor moved over to her. "I'm sorry, Nurse Stein," he said simply.

"He didn't have much of a chance," she said softly. "His wounds were severe."

"Who was he?"

She answered, "Daniel Mitterande. He had a bad chest wound. He wouldn't have survived the trip anyway. He was the fourth one this afternoon, here in the recovery."

Marcus put his arm around her waist. "I'm sorry," he said again. "I think we sometimes—I sometimes—forget how often you have to shut someone's eyes like this."

"It's hard on the other men as well, when they're awake," she said, glancing at those resting on either side of the young man as the litter bearers came in to take his body away. "I wonder sometimes if they can still look down on us... see us carrying off their bodies. I'm always careful to remember their spirits might still be hovering somewhere close by until they are sure they're leaving Earth for good."

Marcus nodded. Sometimes, even when a soldier died on the surgery table, the doctors wondered the same thing. Could the spirits of the dead see them trying to save the body? Did any of them want them to stop... wish that the doctors and nurses would stop trying to bring them back into a body torn to pieces?

The priest who had come in on the mail truck entered the tent just before the litter bearers carried the man away. He saw and came quickly to Charlotte's side while pulling his satin stole around his neck.

"It's too late, Father," Charlotte whispered.

The priest shook his head. "It's never too late, Nurse." He took out a small vial of oil, anointed the man's forehead with the sign of the cross, and prayed over him anyway. Then he stood up and said, "Are there any others who should have the Rite?"

"Everyone here should have the Rite," she told him. "But many are medicated right now, Father. If you give them an hour or two, they will awaken and welcome your ministry, I'm sure."

The priest looked at the nurse. "And you? Would you like prayer?"

"Yes," she whispered. "But not now when I am on duty. Perhaps afterward, if you are still here."

He nodded. "I will be here for a day or two," he said to her. "I am Father James. Whenever you are ready, I will be happy to pray with you, Nurse—"

"Charlotte," she replied. "Just Charlotte."

"Nurse Charlotte," he finished. Then he turned to Marcus. "Would you walk with me, Doctor—?"

"Lovell. Marcus Lovell," Marcus said, falling into step with the man as he watched him restore the vial of oil to a velvet-lined wooden box he carried. The priest carefully removed the stole from around his neck, kissed the cross woven into its fabric, and carefully folded it up in his hand.

They walked out of the recovery, toward the mess tent.

"Do priests drink coffee?" Marcus asked. "Or tea, maybe?"

The man laughed quietly. "Both, and in great quantities when we can get it!"

They poured some for each of them and Marcus led him to the long mess table, swinging his legs over the bench. "What can I do for you, Father James?"

The priest sighed. "I was just wondering what I can do for the nurses and doctors at this station? How can I help? It is obvious that you all face tremendous challenges every day. So much death and destruction all around you. What can I do to ease the weariness of the souls of your team?"

Marcus replied, "I'm probably not the one you want to be asking, Father. If you sit next to me too long, your white collar, might just turn a dark shade of grey."

Father James raised his eyebrows. "Is that so, Doctor Lovell?"

"I'm afraid my sins will rub right off on you," Marcus assured him. "You'd have to do a penitence yourself!"

The priest smiled slightly. "Dealing with sin is rather up our alley, as they say."

Marcus laughed. "I suppose that's so. Just like dealing with bullet and shrapnel wounds is our turf."

They both drank from the tin mugs, each appreciating the other's contribution to those around them.

"Don't you ever get tired of hearing peoples' confessions, Father James? I mean, how many times can you hear all of the rotten things inside of people and still get up every morning glad to be a priest? Who takes care of you, when you need some relief, anyway?" Marcus countered.

The priest rolled his eyes heavenward. "We turn it all over to the higher Priest. He takes it from there... and from us. If we held on to everything we hear, we would probably throw the collar away and take up gardening."

"Gardening is good, too," Marcus said. "I wouldn't mind turning in my scalpel sometimes for a hoe and wheelbarrow... a few onion shoots, some parsley, mint."

"Perhaps you would make a very good monk!" Father James chuckled. "Tending an herb garden."

Marcus shook his head. "No, I'm afraid not. I have been guilty of too much sin with the ladies, to be a monk."

"They are marvelous creatures, are they not?" Father James agreed. "Marvelously fashioned."

Marcus looked over at the man in surprise. "Did I just hear a priest say that women are marvelous?" he asked, astonished. "I thought you guys weren't supposed to even look at a woman."

Father James' eyes twinkled. "When the Lord God made Eve, she was incredibly beautiful. Adam himself was most impressed. He said, 'Well now, this is bone of my bones.' He was most pleased with what God gave him."

"But that was different. First of all, Adam didn't have to face what we face here," Marcus objected. "And second, wasn't she made especially for him? That first man and woman deal? But there is no kind of Garden of Eden here. And holding a woman in your arms here is sometimes the only thing that makes sense. The only thing that is soft and warm and real when everything else is dying and in pieces and mutilated."

The priest answered him evenly. "I cannot imagine how you could not want to find some kind of warm, real comfort in the middle of all of this destruction."

Marcus set down his cup a little hard, some coffee splashing out onto the table. He ignored it. "Yes, but my looking for comfort drove someone away, one of the nurses that I think I did care about... maybe more than... casually. Maybe if I'd had more time, I would have wanted more than just physical comfort. Or maybe not. I don't really know. Anyway, she left and went home because I couldn't figure it out in time."

The priest said, "That's very difficult... letting go of the person who gives you comfort, who makes you feel alive when people are dying all around you almost every day... like what happened, only minutes ago, over in that tent with Nurse Charlotte."

Marcus nodded. "Charlotte is one of the best. She was even taken prisoner by the Germans for a time. It was a miracle they made it back in one piece. Two of the nurses were taken, that nurse, Charlotte and... and Lydia."

"These nurses were taken by the Germans, you say?" the priest clarified. "Out of the station?"

Marcus nodded. "And from what little I've been told, what happened to Lydia was... well, at least she made it back. I'm not a real religious kind of man, Father James, you understand, but even I asked God to bring Lydia back in one piece... though I doubt he heard me."

Father James looked at him directly. "Why on earth would you think that an all-knowing God wouldn't hear that kind of a prayer, Doctor Lovell?"

Marcus sighed and gripped his hands around the tin coffee cup. "Because she's the woman I really want to love, Father. So, it wa a sinful prayer. I think she's the kind of woman I always wanted to be with forever."

"Perhaps she will one day accept your devotion to her?" Father James offered.

Marcus laughed a bit sadly. "I doubt that, Father. She is married to my best friend here... one of the other doctors."

"Oh... I see."

"So now you know why your collar is no doubt turning all kinds of shades of dirt right now. Because I know that it's wrong. I think I loved Lydia, in a way, long before she even married my friend, Simon. I think I will always love her, somehow."

"But you did not, shall we say... take comfort with her before she married your friend?" the priest asked.

Marcus shook his head. "No, but I think I heard it said some-where that if you think about it, you've done it. And, yes, Father, I have certainly thought about her that way, many times."

"And you have 'done it,' as you say, with others?" the priest pressed him.

"Yes, several. And I would never put Lydia in the position of having to tell me, no." Marcus sighed heavily. "Are you going to try to tell me there is some kind of forgiveness for all of the above, Father James?"

The priest nodded slowly. "Yes, my son, there is. Would you like me to say a prayer with you, to God, about this?"

Marcus looked around them. "Sure, why not? Can't hurt, can it?" he said, feeling suddenly relieved to have actually admitted all of this out loud to another human. "But isn't there supposed to be some kind of wall or screen or something in between us, for something like this?"

Father James laughed. "God would see right through it, anyway, my son. I can pray with you without it."

"You know, Father James," Marcus observed, "forget garden-ing. You're pretty good at this. I think you should stick with it."

Chapter 18
A Different Battlefield

The letter, from the Red Cross in Philadelphia, had spelled out upcoming changes to the role of the nurses in the war. Lydia had read the directive with concern. Thousands of nurses had been recruited from the States. The Army Nurse Corps was preparing to send them with the American soldiers to Europe, to join the conflict. Lydia carefully reviewed the entire update. Then, she found what she was looking for, "No volunteer may be asked to serve at the front against her wishes." The nurse took a deep breath. They were safe. There was no directive for them to step down from the CCS, join the Army Nurse Corps, or abandon their French alliances.

She wondered about the nurses who would be coming over as an official component of the American contribution to defeat Germany. How were they being trained? What would they be expecting? And she still worried about what would happen to their American doctors, currently serving under the French. Included in the typed letter, were updates on pneumonia, meningitis, tuberculosis. There was an encouragement for everyone to be inoculated against typhoid. There was an admonition for all nurses to engage in conduct befitting the highest moral standards, under all circumstances.

She paused... there was a final page with a single paragraph at the top. *It will be expedient for one of the supervisory staff to visit with the volunteer units to assess the current needs and situation, prior to the arrival of new nurses at the front. We will be contacting the nurses in forward units by messenger once plans have been solidified.* The Red Cross was coming here? That could be... a good thing, perhaps? Or would the activities of the nurses be met with full disapproval of those stateside, who knew little of the pragmatics of the war on the Western Front? Lydia would have to meet with the nurses, and they would need to discuss this in some detail. Maybe they could hide much of what they did each day from the supervisor who would come. That person did not need to know the entire story. Not everything.

As the Arras offensive continued, Lydia was back to rotating through recovery and triage, now that Simon's hand was healed. She worked off and on with Charlotte, but had become a bit worried about her. Charlotte seemed preoccupied since their short conversation with Monique. Lydia hadn't even considered telling Charlotte about the German commander being at the station. What would have been the point? Lydia realized she must have given off some tell-tale sign, from memory, for Monique to have picked up so quickly on her reaction a few days ago in the mess tent.

One thing was true about the war, more was often left unsaid than was spoken. Secrets were easily generated. Some things were never shared. Many things were nearly taken to the grave by the soldiers left in their care, who whispered a confession with their dying breath. The overwhelmed medical staff treating them had their own private thoughts, which they shared with no one. Keeping secrets became a necessary part of life, whether they were working in the recovery, surgery, or triage.

While Lydia moved through the recovery tent recording admission names, diagnoses, and dispositions on the ever-lengthening list of wounded, she also considered what she would add to the note in her pocket, a letter she had started for Susannah. It was going to be easy to write back, as there was no need to write to her friend about censored subjects. Susannah already knew everything. Lydia wanted to ask her if she had considered letting Marcus know about little Marcie Nichole, but was still unsure how to broach the subject.

"You look preoccupied," Laura remarked, passing her with a stack of clean blankets in her arms.

Lydia nodded. "I am."

Laura inclined her head over to where the priest was still ministering to the casualties. He had remained in the camp longer than the two or three days he'd first anticipated.

"See the priest over there? Father James. He's willing to talk to you if you need him. I think he's talked to almost everybody."

Lydia looked up from her clipboard in surprise. "Really? You mean the patients?"

Laura shook her head. "No, everyone... anyone. Rumor has it, even the doctors."

"Wow," Lydia exclaimed under her breath. Another secret. "He must have heard a lot." She wondered if Simon... surely Simon would have told her if he'd talked to the priest! Or maybe that was something no one was supposed to know?

"Nice guy," Laura assured her. "Easy to talk to. If you get a minute, you should try him out. I did." She moved off to the supply area with her bundle.

Lydia hung the clipboard on a hook on the central tent pole. She turned to the men lying beside her. One was becoming restless, so she went to him.

"Are you in pain, soldier?" she asked him kindly.

"No, l'infirmière," he replied. "But I have to get back to my unit, and I can't seem to get up."

She put a hand on his shoulder to gently restrain him. "You are injured. You can't go now. What's your name?"

"David Schofield," he replied.

"Where are you from, David?" she asked him. "Are you British, perhaps?"

He nodded. "Yes, and you are not French, are you?"

She shook her head. "No, I am an American."

"We hear the Americans are coming soon," he said. "It is a rumor in the units out on the battlefield. It gives some of the soldiers hope that maybe this war will finally be over."

"We've heard they're coming too. It would be wonderful for this war to end soon," she said. "Will you let me check your wound?"

He nodded. "Sure, where is it? Where did I take the bullet?"

She took his hand. "In your legs, David. A shell exploded."

"Wow!" he exclaimed softly. "I can't believe I'm not in pain. Shouldn't I be in a lot of pain, Nurse?"

She stroked his head gently. "Not this time, soldier. Your legs are gone, so there is no pain to feel."

He stared up at her, in disbelief. "What are you talking about? I feel my legs, even my toes. They can't be gone."

She held his gaze, saying nothing, as he reached a hand down and realized there was nothing below his knees. The young man suddenly began thrashing wildly with his arms, trying to get up off the cot. "Give me back my legs!" he shouted in agony. Everyone, who was not sedated, in the tent was roused by the sudden noise.

Lydia held him with her arms to keep him from falling off the cot. Laura looked over in concern and went for the laudanum that would calm him. Father James left the man to whom he was ministering to cross the tent and offer his assistance.

The soldier, David, was now sobbing heavily as the realization sank in that he had indeed lost his lower legs.

Lydia held him close and let him cry, offering no platitudes or assurances and he clung to her as if the whole world would spin off its axis if he let go. She stroked his hair, his head against her shoulder, until the sobs subsided... she waited.

"Nurse," he finally said in a broken voice. "Help me die."

"You think death is better than this..." she said simply.

"Yes," he nodded, still clutching at her and the escape he thought she could arrange. "Please—"

"I don't have anything to give you to help you die," she said. "But I can help you live, if you decide to."

He looked up at her, his eyes filled with agony.

"My girl back home," he said. "I'm not a man for her anymore. I can't help my mum. I can't do anything if I can't walk, if I don't have any legs."

Lydia just held him in her arms. "Your legs make you a man?"

"Hell yes!" he exclaimed, the anger that she had expected, now erupting, as unstoppable as a tsunami. "Well, not completely! But hell yes!"

"But not completely," she offered.

"Sure, but what good are my hands, my brain," he pulled back, pounding on his chest with a fist, "or this! What good is this, without my legs?"

She took the hand he had balled up in a fist and placed it against her own chest, above her heart. "What good is this, David? When you can't see my legs? What good am I when this is all you see?"

He stared at her. He saw the curls of brown hair escaping her scarf. He saw the compassion in her eyes. He grabbed her by both arms, his grip tight and compelling. Finally, he said, "I don't know if I can do this."

"You won't be able to by yourself," Lydia agreed. "You will need God helping you every minute of every day. You will need your mum. And your girl at home, you will need her to remind you, often, that you are a soldier who has faced the evils of war and survived it. That you are a man who did not run away in terror on the battlefield. That you are a man of strength, of courage, not cowardice."

David still had not released her, but his breathing was beginning to calm. The frantic look in his eyes was beginning to fade. Only then did he really notice the priest behind Lydia.

"Did someone send him here to give me the last rites?" David asked.

Lydia shook her head. "No, David. He's here to help you get started on this new part of your journey, not finish the last. If you will let him."

The young soldier looked up at the priest. "I'm Presbyterian."

"I'm Father James," the priest extended his hand to the man on the cot. "I'm very glad to meet you."

David let his hands fall away from Lydia's arms. She gave him a reassuring nod, then stood and continued moving down the row of men, bending to check some, lifting blankets to look at the wounds of others. The young soldier watched her tending to the wounded. "If losing my legs makes it so my mum and my girl don't have to, then, then I guess it's all worth it... I can try."

Father James knelt down on the floor by the man's cot. "Let's talk," he began quietly.

Lydia took her two-hour break, dropping down on the cot in her tent, unable to sleep. She wanted to sleep, to shut off her brain, but she simply couldn't. Then she thought of the music box. The little brown box was resting on top of her footlocker, beside the cot. She picked it up gently. *If Simon had had his leg amputated, I would have loved him just the same.* She was grateful Marcus had saved Simon's leg, but she was absolutely sure she would have kept on loving Simon even if Marcus had not been there to spare him that outcome. Simon was so much more than his leg. Lydia wound the little key. The music of the lullaby softly filled the tent. It took her back to several days ago when Simon had traced her scars and covered them with his caresses... accepting her damaged skin; loving her anyway. The music box was a different matter than the touch of his hands, his mouth. The music touched her soul where words had inflicted more damage than a bullet, or a crop, ever could. Words of hatred, of control. Simon had known she needed help dispelling the words that had penetrated her core.

She lay there listening to the gentle refrain created by Brahms and wondered what had happened in his life that had caused those particular notes to find their way to each other, in this particular pattern... those same notes reaching out to her now. She wound the music box several times, letting it play over and over, feeling the music as it soothed the deepest recesses of her being. Simon knew her so well... he loved her so well.

She decided that maybe she would find Father James later on. Perhaps she would find out if he really was as easy to talk to as Laura had suggested. But now, it was already time for her to go to triage, where Gretha would be waiting to be relieved for her own two-hour break. This siege felt like it would never end.

By the time the casualties stopped coming through triage, it was late. Lydia was exhausted. Abril had stayed with her in the outer tent where the overflow of casualties had been lined up, to wait. Some had died while they waited, having arrived at the station already one step away from death. There were not enough surgical hands to save them, even though Doctor Fortraine himself had manned a table inside the tent to help the other surgeons, who worked tirelessly. Lydia remembered their own rule; they didn't count the numbers... not the number saved, nor the number lost. But she knew they had lost many because Father James had also followed her to the triage and was very busy administering the sacrament of last rites to the fallen, before their bodies were carried away, to shorten the line.

At last, the brief nightly lull had come. The onslaught subsiding, there was a chance to rest. Lydia and Abril headed straight for the mess tent. She was starving. She hoped they could both find something decent, at this hour of the night.

As she ducked under the flaps, she noticed that Father James was already there, drinking something hot. He was sitting alone, his face looked haggard and drawn. This must have been an extremely difficult day for the man whose two days had turned to four, then six... now seven.

"May I join you?" Lydia asked him, waiting with a tray in hand. "Or do you need this time for prayer and reflection?"

He looked up at her, some of the weariness disappearing. "No, I'm alright, thank you. I was told you are Lydia Finney." He thought immediately of Marcus Lovell's confession of love for this woman, glad he could finally meet with her.

"I am," she said. "When I'm awake enough to remember it."

He nodded. "Please, join me, yes."

"Thank you," she said, placing her tray down and offering him bread and cheese to share. She also had a bowl of something that looked like a vegetable soup with chunks of beef in it. It smelled delicious, actually.

He took some of the offering and broke off pieces of the bread, making her think of Communion and how many times he must have done the same thing in a sacristy somewhere, with his parishioners.

"How did you end up here, Father James?" she wondered. "If you don't mind my asking. Shouldn't you be back somewhere baptizing babies and performing marriage ceremonies?"

He smiled. "That would be nice, wouldn't it? To baptize a baby or do a marriage ceremony. Instead of the last rites, but I could ask the same thing of you, Nurse Finney. Shouldn't you be back somewhere delivering babies or putting iodine on a child's scraped-up knee?"

She laughed. "I deserved that. Yes, that would be nice, too. Although, I did get to deliver a baby here. Once."

His eyebrows went up. "Here, in the war? At this station?"

Nodding, she took a spoonful of soup and tasted it gingerly. "Not at the station, but yes, here in the war, outside of Nancy. My husband, Doctor Finney, and I were there. We had just gotten married at the cathedral in Nancy... that's another story that is really amazing. But we found ourselves in a little village, and a woman who had been shot was in labor. She delivered the tiniest little premature baby. I wonder if he survived his abrupt entry into this world. The odds were stacked against him."

"That's an incredible story," he said.

"One of many," she assured him.

"I'm sure."

"I hear," she said, taking a sip of coffee, "that many in our little group have found their way to you... to tell their stories. I suspect you could write books by now."

He nodded tiredly. "Yes, several. Between the soldiers who are dying, the ones trying to live, and all of you... everyone has a story to tell..." He waited, extending the opportunity.

She ate her soup.

"You were very compassionate with that soldier whose legs were amputated," he observed. "You have a gift that makes others reach out to you. They feel safe and comforted."

"Aren't you awfully tired tonight, Father James, to go searching for one more story?" she wondered. "Or don't priests get any breaks in their day? Maybe breaks don't come with the collar? No need to encourage me to tell you my little tales of woe tonight."

He drank from his tin cup. "I assume that you are as tired as I am. And carrying around heavy burdens only adds to the general weariness that comes with serving, as we do, all day and all night."

"My burden, Father," she said softly, "isn't being unable to forgive. I can do that. I can forgive. But it is difficult for me to forget, to get things out of my head once they have gotten stuck in there. Words have hurt me more than anything that has been done to me."

"You are referring to when you were taken prisoner in the German trench line?"

She looked at him in honest surprise.

"The fact that you were taken, is rather common knowledge among your fellow workers here. It was brought to my attention."

Lydia winced. "I'm sorry that you have had to add that to your book of tales, Father. I forgave the one German, and he is actually dead now, from his own battlefield wounds."

"I see," he nodded. "Yes, our memories for words are long. We make vows, commitments, and we must remember them for a lifetime. We are bound to secrecy by others and carry their words with us to our graves. I think that sometimes nurses carry many things they never reveal, while giving such intimate service to others."

Lydia pushed her tray away and lowered the bowl of soup, beef chunks still remaining, for Abril, at her feet.

Father James saw it. "The dog loves you and rarely leaves your side."

"She found us in the trenches. She led us back to the station in the middle of the night when we were half frozen with fear and the cold of winter. Abril led us right back to the camp."

Father James looked at the dog with a new appreciation. "They are impressive creatures, aren't they? Very loyal."

Lydia rubbed the dog behind her ears, and Abril looked up at her.

"The German soldier that I forgave hurt me, Father," Lydia said. "With his leather crop. A lot."

The priest fell silent.

"He said it was necessary because he couldn't let the four of us taken prisoner eat, without getting something in return. We still... tended to their wounded, though. Many of their wounded. Charlotte and I did the very best we could for the injured German soldiers."

"As our Lord would have done Himself," Father James said. "The highest Christian charity is to love thy enemy."

Lydia paused. "I am not a saint, Father. I did not love my enemy. I hated the German commander."

The priest nodded. "After what he did, I'm sure that was a normal reaction."

"I didn't hate him because of what he did. I understood him using the crop, the anger he projected through it onto me. I hated him because of what he said... the way he used his words to turn everything upside down so that being hit by him was an act of charity on his part and not being hit was somehow a wrongdoing on my part. Somehow... he took simple words and turned them into something that wormed their way inside of me and still come out at the most unexpected times, even now. I can't get his words out of my mind sometimes."

Father James nodded with understanding. Psychological warfare was not unknown to him after all of his years of hearing confessions and counseling others.

"The last time he made me come to him, he was so apologetic when he beat me. He used his words to make me feel guilty about it, like it was my fault that he had to be cruel. And for a moment... I believed him. I never told anyone, not even Simon, the things he said to me in the trench..."

Abril whined softly, sensing her distress, putting a paw on her leg in comfort or, perhaps, protection.

"The man saw my ring. He knew I was married. He told me that the next time he called me down, that he would rape me. He said if I gave it to him right at that moment, that he would show mercy and be, I guess... more or less gentle, for my sake... but that if I said no, then the next time, if I made him wait, he might not be able to show his mercy, of not letting it hurt too much. The longer I made him wait, the more it would hurt. So... I did... I did start begging him to just get it over with, thinking terrible thoughts of everything he could possibly do that would make it hurt even more. And his words got into my head... and I can't seem to get him out of there."

After a long moment of silence, Father James said, "So you told him to go ahead and hurt you?"

"After a couple of times of saying no and getting more and more afraid... yes. I did. Then, well, then it turned out there was no next time for him to rape me," Lydia said. Abril rested her head on Lydia's leg, looking up at her anxiously. "We escaped with some of the German soldiers who we had helped and with the help of Abril. I didn't have to face that. When I saw the commander again, he was one of the wounded here in the camp. He grabbed me and told me that he still had the power to make me beg... and that's when Abril clamped her teeth into his arm, and he had to let go of me, and Simon knocked him unconscious. Then the man died hours later. I wasn't there. Physically, he's gone. But he was right. He still has power over me. The terrible thoughts still come."

Father James nodded, his eyes full of concern.

"Sometimes now, with Simon, I feel guilty when he makes me feel good. I'm afraid that I will want him to hurt me so I don't feel guilty. It gets... confusing." Her voice dwindled off to a whisper.

Father James said to her, "Lydia, can you look at me, please?"

She struggled. But finally, she raised her eyes and looked at him.

The priest continued, recognizing that she was open to hearing more. "There was a prophet in the Old Testament. It was on the eve of a battle. The prophet slept. His assistant said, 'How can you sleep at a time like this when the enemy is encamped all around us and we are sorely outnumbered?' The prophet prayed to the Lord and said, 'Oh Lord, show this man what he cannot see.' And the assistant looked out again and saw a huge army of the Lord God, of angels and chariots surrounding the camp, far outnumbering the enemy coming against them. The protection of God was all around them. He just couldn't see it. Inside of your mind, God will put an army of protection against any force of evil that comes against you. The battle has already been won. The enemy is outnumbered. The victory already belongs to God and to the ones who want to serve him."

Lydia let the priest take her hand. "Your desire to protect the sanctity of your marriage to Simon, that desire is a holy thing. God prevented you from being violated in that way, physically. Now you must see how He is safeguarding your mind, your thoughts, even now. The enemy must run in defeat. You may ask anything of your husband and he will honor you. There is no guilt between a husband and his wife. When you have been made one, what you want is what he wants, and what he wants is what you want. It is the miracle of oneness."

Lydia felt as though the floor was dropping out from beneath her. Had she not at some point asked Simon about this "oneness" they had found that defied explanation? The oneness was miraculous in its own way for healing... and pleasure and fulfillment. Had she not said those very same things and yet somehow let them be forgotten? The concept reawakened in her now as if it had simply been sleeping.

Father James came around the table and stood over her. He placed his stole around his neck and took out his oil of anointing. She felt him trace the sign of the cross on her forehead with his thumb. When he prayed over her, he prayed in Latin, resting his hand on her head where the offensive thoughts had collected themselves. She didn't understand the words, but she felt the spirit of peace all around her. The enemy, her shame that she had begged the commander to rape her, was driven away by an angel of God wielding a heavenly sword to protect her.

It was almost May now, and the fighting still continued for Arras. Spring had come. The sun was warm. Grasses waved with the winds on the hillsides. And the wounded arrived in a steady flow. It seemed as though both armies were growing tired, as the lulls at night had became noticeably longer; sleep now came in longer intervals as well. Sometimes, the camp spent the entire night sleeping—except for in the recovery, where the nurses kept to their tighter shift schedule. In their tents, the off duty nurses made the most of the luxury of a night off. Their tent sides were partway opened, inviting the cleansing, fresh air to move through.

Charlotte could not smell the fresh, damp earth with sprigs of new grass. *Odd*, she thought. She was restless. Charlotte laid down on her cot and took off her trousers and shirt. She was too hot to sleep and thought to herself that she should have skipped supper at the mess; it wasn't agreeing with her. She was troubled by the recent death of the German commander in the station. It weighed heavily on her that he had been in their station and she hadn't known. As she lay on the cot, tossing, the truth came to her that she wouldn't have known him if she had seen him... and that maybe she had. Maybe she had relieved his pain with laudanum. Maybe she had tended his wounds, not knowing who he was. Maybe she had offered him words of comfort and tried to soothe him, not knowing what he had done to her friend. It was eating away at her.

The nurse dozed, off and on, until midnight. Then, she was awakened by a searing pain in her abdomen. She tried to sit up on her cot, but couldn't.

"Gretha," Charlotte called out in the darkness. "Get Doctor Lovell."

The other nurse stirred. She came to the cot and put her hand on Charlotte's forehead. "You're burning up," Gretha said, alarmed.

"And get Lydia, please," Charlotte whispered, sinking back down on the cot in pain.

Lydia woke immediately to the soft sound of Gretha's voice at the tent flap. She quickly dressed, without waking Simon, and followed Gretha to the nurses' tent before she ran to fetch Marcus.

Beads of sweat covered Charlotte. Lydia felt the rapid pulse in Charlotte's wrist. "Where does it hurt?" Charlotte pointed to her abdomen as Marcus came through the tent flap with Gretha on his heels.

Lydia looked up. "She's got a high fever... abdominal pain, Doctor Lovell."

He bent over the nurse and gently probed her belly. "Probably appendix," he said. "Gretha, get a litter in here, would you? And let's get her to the surgery." He looked down at Charlotte on her cot. "I would have been happy to make a house call without you going to all this trouble, Nurse Stein."

She groaned in pain. "I didn't doubt you'd come," she said. "Lydia, come with me."

Marcus smiled down at her. "You don't trust me, Nurse? I promise, my hands will only touch your appendix."

Lydia assured her quickly, "I'll make certain he behaves while you're asleep."

They quickly moved Charlotte to the surgery, Lydia dripping ether onto a face mask. "Ready, honey?" she asked Charlotte as Gretha pulled down the woman's boxers and washed her abdomen with antiseptic solution. Marcus picked up a scalpel.

Charlotte reached up stop Lydia from lowering the mask over her face. "Lydia, I just want to tell you how sorry I am... it should have been me. The commander... he should have taken me—"

Lydia cut her off. "No regrets, honey, remember? Let's get you to sleep so Doctor Lovell can fix you up."

Charlotte shook her head. "Wait. I have to tell you. I knew he was doing terrible things to you, I should have gone instead of you. I need you to know that I would have gone."

Lydia stroked Charlotte's sweat-soaked hair. "I don't doubt you for one second, honey. And I felt just exactly the same way about you. No regrets now. Let's get you to sleep." She lowered the ether mask over the other nurse's mouth and nose, watching her drop off, her body relaxing, then nodded to Marcus, who was ready.

Quickly, he cut the incision low in her abdomen and found the ruptured appendix. "It's already draining," he alerted Lydia and Gretha. "Won't take long to get it out, but we'll have to clean her out well, so the infection doesn't spread all through her. We'll leave it open and pack it." He worked quickly. "I wish she had said something sooner. This was building up for a while."

When he was satisfied that his brief operation was a success, Marcus looked over at Gretha and at Lydia sitting near the sedated woman's head. "You nurses need to learn how to complain."

Gretha looked over her friend on the table, then back to the doctor. "It's not in the job description!" she said softly.

He nodded sadly, looking especially at Lydia. "Well, it should be."

Charlotte was resting well in the recovery. Lydia stayed with her briefly, until she knew that the fever had broken and that she was able to sleep on her own, and not from any remnant of the anesthesia. Then, she went back to her tent... Simon stirred on her arrival. She slipped out of her clothes and lay back down beside him under the blanket. She felt his arm reflexively move around her as he slept. Lydia was glad that Charlotte had gotten that off her chest. Yet again, she felt the relief that came with knowing Charlotte had been kept safe from physical harm, but she now recognized that even Charlotte had suffered guilt, emotional harm. And Lydia thought of Frederick, their German rescuer, who had wept, saying that he could not bear the shame. War did terrible things to people.

It brought out the very worst in those who needed little excuse to do their very worst... and it brought out the best in those who were merciful, noble and courageous. *War is an awful thing*, she proclaimed, in thought, to the heavens above. It did, however, eliminate any neutral zone for morality. She wondered if humans would ever be able to reach a point where true mercy and compassion were the norm.

When morning came, she had only dozed. After breakfast, she went to the surgery where she was stopped, just outside of the entry, by an aide.

"Nurse," the man said, "Doctor Fortraine wants to see you now. Please, come with me."

Lydia fought back the unbidden response which rose up inside of her. This was that unseen battlefield where angels must surround the camp of her mind. Fortraine was not the German commander. Being summoned by Fortraine was not the same as being summoned by the German commander. Lydia prayed for angels with flaming swords to protect her mind, now, as she answered the conveyed order to appear at Fortraine's tent. Abril stood up beside her and Lydia did not tell her to stay. "Come, Abril," she called clearly and the dog immediately fell into step at her side.

Lydia followed the aide to the command tent, entered when directed, and stood before the man's desk, where he sat looking at a communique. Unbidden, her heart began pounding against the inside of her chest. An intense feeling of dread washed over her; she felt dizzy. *Angels with swords*, she thought, *angels with swords*. She had not been in the command tent since his interrogation of her, right after their return from the trenches. She felt Abril sit, pressing against her legs. Simon was not beside her this time, but Abril was.

"Please, sit down, Nurse Finney," Fortraine invited her. He saw the color draining from her face. He came out from behind the desk. "I apologize for causing you to feel uncomfortable," he said. "I realize the circumstances under which you were last here might still be... an issue."

"I'm fine," she said quietly, keeping her voice even. "What can I do for you, Doctor Fortraine?"

"Do you need anything? Can I get you some water or something?" he asked quickly as her face had paled.

"No, thank you," she said.

"Do the nurses need anything?" he asked her.

Abril growled softly, protectively, and Doctor Fortraine backed away, returning behind his desk to put a sturdy obstacle between himself and the animal that had recently demonstrated fully, her loyalty to this woman.

"No, Doctor, the nurses do not need anything other than sleep and for this battle to wear itself out. Although, you should know that Doctor Lovell operated on Nurse Stein a couple of hours ago for a ruptured appendix. Charlotte is now in the recovery," she told him.

Doctor Fortraine let his surprise show. "I see! Well, let us hope she recovers smoothly." He lifted up a piece of paper, a telegram.

"I have received this word from the States," he told her. "A representative from the office of the director of the Red Cross division of mobile unit volunteer nurses will be arriving any day now, depending on the trains and their ability to get a truck to us, out here on the front. Is there anything you need from me to help you get ready for that arrival?"

Lydia, at last, breathed a sigh of relief. That's what this was all about. The color returned to her cheeks. Fortraine was glad to see it.

"No, Doctor," Lydia told the man. "I was aware that they were preparing many thousands of nurses to come over with the American troops. The last notice I received from them confirmed, again, the status of the volunteer nurses, though, to stay at the front... at their own will."

Fortraine laid the telegram back on his desk. "What is the will of our nurses, Nurse Finney?" he asked.

"We all want to stay with our station, Doctor," she told the man. "Every nurse has expressed that wish. Although, I do have one concern."

"And that is?"

"When the representative arrives, she will undoubtedly see that we do many things here that were not taught in the Red Cross classes. I really don't know how she will react to that... she may feel that we've overstepped our bounds."

Fortraine nodded, understanding. "Let me take care of that, Nurse Finney. That's something I can address. You just keep the nurses doing what they are doing." He paused, thoughtful.

"Is that all, Doctor? I am scheduled to be in surgery," she told him. "They will be looking for me." *Simon will be looking for me,* she thought to herself.

He nodded. "One more thing before you go. I want you to know that I did not want to hurt you when you were last here. When I asked you to tell me what had happened during your terrible experience with the Germans. I regret causing you any pain, but it was necessary, as commander of this station."

Angels with swords, Lydia said to herself as she heard the words echo from the past. *The enemy is already defeated by angels with swords.*

"You needn't be concerned, Doctor Fortraine," Lydia said. "It's in the past."

He stood up, as did she. "Very good then," he said.

"Come, Abril," she called softly and, turning, left his tent. He watched the two of them go. There must be something he could do to help the nurses. He would talk to Stockton and see if, together, they might come up with an idea.

Lydia left Abril at the entrance of the surgery and ducked inside. She washed her hands and found a clean apron and mask. Looking around quickly, she saw a medic working with Harold and went to relieve him. Simon glanced up, asking a question with his eyes. She tried to reassure him with a glance.

"Ah, Nurse Finney," Harold said. "Just in time to retract that bowel, if you would." She did, noticing the surgeon was removing a spleen. "I heard that you and Doctor Lovell didn't get much sleep. How is Nurse Stein?" he asked.

Lydia shook her head. "I don't know this morning. She's in good hands, though, you can be sure."

He laughed lightly. "Well said. We've had to take care of our own more than once, haven't we?"

"Indeed, we have."

"Damnedest thing… an appendix! Can you get that bleed under there…"

"Yes," she said, reaching in with a clamp. "Is Nurse Sullivan doing as well as I think she is?"

He didn't take his eyes off what they were doing, but said, "You mean learning surgical techniques? Yes, she's very good. Very good."

"About that," Lydia said, "someone from the Red Cross will be here any day now, to observe and report. I'll be talking with all of the nurses. The recovery will be fine. Triage will probably be a concern. Surgery could be a problem."

"How so?" Harold asked, lifting out the damaged spleen for disposal, while she washed out the cavity they had created.

"The observer may conclude that we're not doing things the proper way."

Harold peered into the wound, then up at her. "What should you be doing exactly?"

"I would say, the same thing we've been doing for the entire year, plus more. All of it. But how to convince someone from Philadelphia who has never been here?" Lydia wondered.

"Want some advice?" Stockton asked her.

"Gladly!" she exclaimed, thinking of Susannah's complaint that nurses weren't allowed to use their brains, where she worked, back in the States.

"Let your work speak for itself. This battle isn't yours; it's theirs. Let the bureaucrats fight it out. By the time they get finished arguing about it, the war will be over."

Lydia looked up at him, amazed. "That's really good advice, Doctor!"

He laughed at her softly. "Don't compliment me, Nurse Finney. That was guidance from Father James... I'm just repurposing it."

And Lydia laughed, too. Angels with swords must be working overtime for all of them... including Harold Stockton.

As the truck door swung open, Lydia was there to greet the newest visitor to the station. Extending her hand, she introduced herself. "I am Lydia Blackwell-Finney. Welcome to the station. I hope your trip wasn't unpleasant."

"Ah, Nurse Finney! A pleasure," the woman answered kindly, and with a firm handshake in return. "I am Nurse Mary Baxter from the Red Cross office, overseeing the forward mobile stations. This is my first trip to France."

"A pleasure to meet you, ma'am. I'm sure you're aware there is major military activity just east of here and, therefore, we will have little time to talk. The Allies have been sending us casualties for three weeks now."

The woman shook her head. "I am an observer, Nurse Finney. Don't worry about talking. I'll be following you as you go about your duties and helping to determine how we can better assist our nurses in the field."

Lydia looked at the woman's neat blue skirt and jacket with its clean stripes on the sleeve, her white shirt, and her navy tie, wrapped neatly around her neck. Her white head scarf moved in the breeze on her shoulders. Lydia thought she looked rather like a nun. "Perhaps you would like to change to an army uniform?" Lydia offered.

"This is my uniform," Mary Baxter assured her, looking at Lydia's boots, gray-green trousers and shirt, and curious blue scarf. "It will suffice."

"Very well. I'm in triage at the moment if you'd care to follow me," Lydia said. She saw Abril come bounding over to her, curious about the new arrival at her side and sniffing at her shoes.

"You have a dog?" Mary asked, surprised.

"Yes, she helps keep the buzzards and wild dogs off the dead and dying, over there, under the tarp."

Mary nodded. "Oh, I see."

"Would you like to freshen up first?" Lydia offered.

"Yes, please," Mary replied. "It was a long way to come."

"I'm sure it was. This way." Lydia led her through the camp to the latrine, pointing out the central mess, the large surgery and recovery tents, the medical staff tents sprinkled in between, and then the military soldiers and administrative tents surrounding the medical core. As they walked, they frequently moved aside to allow litter bearers and soldiers to come through. The nurses, however, were all occupied. Lydia showed her the latrine and took advantage of the opportunity to use it herself while they were there. She stepped back out of the tent and washed her hands under the spigot from the water reservoir on a plank outside, shaking them dry in the air.

Mary followed shortly after, adjusting her skirt. "It's not a very good hotel, is it?" she laughed.

"No, indeed... it is not."

They walked back around to the field of suspended tarps where the casualties waited. A blue-headed figure bent between the men. "That's Sally Winfield," Lydia said, "there with the blue scarf. She's one of our nurses."

"What are those numbers in her hands?" Mary asked as they approached and started their own round through the soldiers. She held her skirt close to her as the breeze picked it up, understanding a little better why these nurses opted for trousers.

Lydia explained while she knelt down to look at a man newly arrived with a blood-soaked leg dressing. She pulled the heavy scissors from her pack and started cutting away the trouser pants on his uniform. Quickly finding the source of the blood, she pulled out a roll of heavy bandage and a tourniquet. She cut off the blood-soaked wrap and saw where the artery was leaking blood steadily, applied the tourniquet just tightly enough to stay the flow, and checked the man's foot for a pulse. It was still there, but thready. "Corpsman!" she called out, and one came immediately, as she changed the fallen man's number, from a two, to a one. "Get him in next and release this tourniquet if you see his foot change color at all—and don't lose the tourniquet." She looked up at Mary. "They're like gold."

"Yes, Nurse Finney," he said and called for litter bearers to take the man to the surgery tent.

They moved to the next man in line. He lay very still. Too still. Lydia pulled her stethoscope and listened carefully for any sign of a heartbeat. She looked around the busy triage and spied the man she was seeking. "Father James!" she called and motioned to the man on the ground. He nodded and came quickly through the men.

"You said once that it's never too late, Father, remember?" Lydia asked him, her eyes sad.

He knelt on the ground next to the young soul departing the Earth. "That's right, Nurse Lydia, never too late." He began anointing the young man, praying over him. Lydia put her hand on his shoulder briefly in appreciation, paying no attention to the slight imprint of blood she left behind. At the end of the row was a water reservoir. She'd wash when they got there and anyway, there would be much more blood on her hands between here and there.

The women saw a wounded soldier trying to rise, and Lydia ran over, Mary at her heels. Lydia knelt down.

"What is it, soldier?" she asked softly.

"Those big black things... Je pense qu'ils essaient de me manger!" he exclaimed angrily, watching them soar overhead.

"Abril! Come!" she called. The dog came bounding over the fallen to her side in just seconds.

She rubbed the dog's ears. "Abril, stay with him a while." She turned to the man to reassure him. "Abril, elle ne les laissera pas te faire du mal." She knew the blood was attracting the buzzards, but Abril would not let them hurt him. She looked at the man's blood-soaked abdomen and lifted his shirt. "Let me check you while I'm here," she said to him. "Mary, please help me."

Mary knelt on the ground, her bare knees in the dirt and bloody grass. Together, the women reinforced the man's belly with a heavy bandage and wrapped it around his waist to secure it. It would deter the large black birds. Lydia patted the man on the arm. "It's not as bad as it looks, soldier. The doctors will be getting to you shortly."

"Merci, l'infirmière," the man whispered, reaching out for Abril, who had plopped herself down next to him for protection.

"What did he call you?" Mary asked as she brushed off her knees and, with nothing else to use, wiped her hands on her skirt.

"L'infirmière... it's French for nurse," Lydia said. "Most of the men are French, but a few are British, Belgian, Canadian... Scot..."

"You speak French, Nurse Finney?" Mary asked her.

"Oui, mademoiselle... I do now." Lydia smiled at her. "But not terribly well. It is a necessity."

Mary looked down the rows of wounded. "How many surgeons are there in the camp, for all of these wounded?"

"Three, plus medics who help. And the station commander is also a surgeon. He helps when it is overcrowded."

Mary looked around. "Seems fairly crowded to me."

Lydia paused over a man writhing in pain. His fractured leg lay crooked, askew. Lydia felt the long bone with her fingers, feeling at the point of injury for any jagged edges beneath the skin and finding none. "Mary, can you grab his foot and pull on it for me?"

Mary looked at her with a puzzled expression. "I don't think I know how to do that."

Lydia nodded, calling for Sally Winfield as she worked her way back up the row. "Sally? Do you have a second?

The other nurse came over. "Oooo. Ouch," she said quietly. She took the man's foot and said to Lydia, "Ready?"

Lydia put a hand on either side of the break to stabilize it. "Ready."

Sally pulled down on the leg gently as Lydia felt the bone re-align. She reached into her sack, pulled out a bottle of laudanum, and gave the man a few drops of it. "This will help, soldier."

Sally waved for the litter bearers. "Get a splint, please, and this man can move over to the transport to wait for a ride out once we have it wrapped."

While they waited for the splint to arrive, Lydia introduced Mary to Sally. "You came on a busy day," Sally told the woman. "It's been pretty steady while they fight for Arras, beyond those hills."

Mary looked at the women. "The military keeps you informed of the actions going on around you?"

"They do," Sally said. "So that we can be prepared." They looked at the hills, where there was the sound of distant rumbling.

"Are those trucks, cannons?" Mary asked.

"A combination of that, plus some shelling from those planes overhead. Although most of the shelling was first thing this morning before the ground troops started to move forward," Lydia explained.

"It doesn't seem very far away," Mary observed.

"About five or six miles," Sally said. "We stay close, to be ready to receive the wounded."

A litter bearer arrived with a splint, and the two nurses wrapped the soldier's entire leg, immobilizing it for the ride ahead.

"Where did you ladies learn how to splint fractures?" Mary asked them.

Sally looked at Lydia. "I don't really remember... we've been doing it forever. I suppose the doctors showed us way back at the beginning. If they are complex fractures, we wait for the doctors, since surgery might be needed immediately. If it is a simple fracture, we stabilize it and move the soldier to the field hospital."

Mary's eyebrows furrowed, puzzled.

"Nurse," a corpsman called. All three turned in unison. "There's a soldier over there who says he thinks his legs are on fire. Can you take a look at him?"

They went together. The young man on the ground was ashen with pain. "My legs are burning," the man groaned.

The nurses felt his legs for wounds. Lydia and Sally nodded at each other and rolled the man in one smooth movement onto his side. They found the injury in his lower back, a piece of shrapnel close to his spine, protruding from the skin just above his buttocks.

Lydia knew immediately what needed to happen, "Sally, run ahead and tell the surgeons and send some litter bearers. I'll stay here." She looked down at the soldier. "Can you stay still, right where you are, on your side? I will give you something for the pain. There is some shrapnel near your nerves, and it is confusing them. You must not move... you need to convince your body that it is not really burning."

The young man nodded, frightened. "Am I going to be paralyzed?"

"I don't know," she answered him, truthfully. "The surgeons will take out the shrapnel so it can't harm you any further. They will look inside along your spine for any other little pieces of metal. Then, you'll know if you can wiggle your toes and move your legs. Nurse Winfield went ahead to tell the doctors that you are on your way."

The litter bearers arrived. "Now, you hold onto the pole here on the side of the litter, soldier. Keep yourself as straight as you can," she told him. "Try not to move much, and we'll get you inside the surgery."

"Will you come with me?" he asked Lydia.

She shook her head and touched his cheek softly. "I cannot right now. But I will see you in the recovery after the surgery is over. I'll come and find you."

She stood next to Mary as they watched him be carried away toward the surgery tent.

"What are his chances?" Mary asked her.

"Of living? As good as most. Of walking again... I don't know," Lydia said. She shaded her eyes with her hand. A new truckload of casualties and several ambulances were rolling into the camp. "Let's go see what they have brought to us."

By the end of the shift, hours later, Mary was spent and filthy. Lydia finished her rotation and took the woman to the showers. "Here's a bucket, and the soap is inside. I will bring you some clean clothes."

"My footlocker was on the truck that brought me." Mary confirmed.

Lydia put her hands on her hips and surveyed the disheveled woman from the Red Cross. "You need pants, and clothes that can be burned... and of course, a shower and some food."

Mary looked down at her uniform, covered with everything imaginable and much more that she could never have imagined. "Okay," she conceded. "You're right." She stepped into the tiny tent and took the bucket in her hands, noting the water in the tank perched outside the walls, its spigot pushed inside through a small hole. She found the bar of soap and removed her clothing. With no cloth to use, she rubbed the soap in her hands and spread it over her skin before pouring some of the water in the bucket over her body to rinse. It was lukewarm, and she shivered. She realized these nurses had been doing this for over a year. "I don't know how they do it," she admitted aloud, to herself, as she washed, then waited, growing chilly in her nakedness, until Lydia returned with something for her to wear.

The next morning, Mary followed Lydia to the surgery. Lydia had been dreading this since receiving notice that an observer was on her way to the station. The doctors coming in were all well aware of Nurse Baxter's presence and purpose, but as Harold Stockton had told them, "It's going to be business as usual, ladies and gentlemen."

The tables started running with the first light of day. It was warm enough for the tent flaps to be opened a little, so both light and air moved through. Mary noticed that, at least here, there was a workable sink for hand washing, she was grateful for that. She was wearing the army green-browns and boots that Lydia provided and accepted the surgical apron and mask. She followed Lydia through the maze of anesthetists taking their positions at the head of the tables, the nurses joined the doctors as they arrived from their tents or the mess, corpsmen were bringing out newly cleansed instruments, and Nancy began to circulate.

Lydia turned to Mary. "Shall I introduce you?" she asked.

Mary shook her head. "No, I won't remember them all, and I'll be embarrassed to keep asking them to repeat themselves. I'll just watch."

"Okay," Lydia said as she took position, waiting for Simon to come from breakfast. A patient was brought in and laid in front of her on the operating table. Lydia and one of the corpsmen started cutting off the man's clothing. He had been caught in an explosion, and his abdomen was open with a jagged tear, a section of bowel visible from the open wound. They cut his pants off and washed him thoroughly with antiseptic solution as Simon came into the tent and scrubbed in. Lydia saw him enter and told the anesthetist, "Go ahead and put him out. Doctor Finney is here."

He nodded, and as the man drifted off into the ether sleep, Lydia picked up a scalpel and began trimming the edges of the jagged wound as Simon had shown her numerous times before. She saw some larger bleeding blood vessels as the wound was irrigated with the Dakin's solution and reached for a suture already threaded on a needle. Simon joined her across the table and looked into the man's abdomen. "Good morning, ladies," he said to both of them.

"Doctor," Mary acknowledged him.

"This is Mary Baxter from Philadelphia, Doctor Finney," Lydia introduced them as she started tying off the bleeding vessels as Simon watched. "There is something behind the small bowel, pushing it forward, Doctor," she reported.

"Any exit wounds?"

She shook her head, "No exit wounds. His right lung has very little air in it. Something is inside."

"Hm, let's see what's back there." He took the scalpel she offered him and widened the jagged wound, giving him room to see as she lowered the light overhead, closer to the table.

"I'm going to pull aside his liver and pancreas, Nurse... your hand is smaller than mine. Can you get back there and feel what's going on?"

Lydia slid her hand under his, as he held back the vital organs. Something irregularly shaped and rough met her fingertips. She pulled on it gently. "Oh," she said. "That explains it."

He looked at her over his mask. Lydia continued, "It's a clump of grass and dirt... and... a body part... from someone else," Lydia said quietly, and she pulled a clod of grass and a piece of a severed limb from the man's abdomen. "They must have been standing right next to each other when the shell exploded." She tugged the debris free and dropped it onto the tray by the table, then quickly reached for the irrigation solution and her flashlight, to look back under the right lung for signs of puncture. "Diaphragm looks intact," she muttered, more to herself than to Simon, who was looking intently for tears. She turned to Mary then, but the woman was gone. She had left the surgery. "Nancy?" Lydia called out, and the nurse came quickly to her side. "I think we might have lost Nurse Baxter."

Nancy looked over to the door of the surgery. "I'll try to send someone to check on her," she nodded and called to another as she continued moving between the tables with supplies and surgical tools, being summoned by all of the tables simultaneously. Nurse Baxter did not return to the surgery. She didn't need to. The woman knew everything she needed to know about the nurses at the station... although she had no idea how she was going to put it into a report.

Morning came quickly. In the mess tent, a small group had assembled for breakfast. Fortraine, Harold, Mary, and Lydia gathered, at the end of the table, while the others were busy at the surgery with the newest casualties. Mary picked at the hot cereal and bread. The three others eyed her anxiously. It was Lydia who decided to break the awkward silence.

"Have you any recommendations for us?" Lydia asked the woman, who had planned to leave the camp, after eating.

The Red Cross observer took a deep breath and let it out slowly. "A few. There should be hand washing stations throughout the triage area and a second one in the recovery. There should be hot water for the shower and hot water at the surgery sink, not tepid. Repositories for bandage waste should be placed at more accessible locations throughout the camp and frequently emptied... and not by the nurses, to reduce the spread of infection. And you need more dogs to keep the wounded from being preyed upon by those birds!"

Doctor Fortraine was taking notes. *More dogs!!* he wrote with exclamation points. "All of these are good suggestions, Nurse Baxter."

Lydia took a deep breath. "And as far as the nurses are concerned?" she started.

Mary laid aside the spoon, which had been pushing around the cereal in front of her. She folded her hands in front of her thoughtfully, tapping her fingertips together, while the doctors looked at each other, wondering. "I cannot condone what I have seen in the brief time that I have been here. The nurses are not following Red Cross training protocols, scarcely at all. From what I have seen, it is as if almost all protocols have been cast aside."

Doctor Fortraine responded to that. "I am sure you are correct, madame," he said. "We ask a great deal of our nurses due to the extenuating circumstances we face daily."

Mary regarded him steadily. "Nurses are not, shall I say… assistant doctors. They are patient caregivers, assistants to doctors."

"Is that not one and the same, madame?" Fortraine asked her. "The patients, the wounded soldiers that come to us, they are the focus of all of our work, whether doctor or nurse or corpsman."

"Certainly so," Mary agreed. "I said almost… all of the protocols… not all. The one overriding protocol is to do what is best for the patient to recover, to heal, to survive. And that is being carried out by the nurses in exemplary fashion, from what I have seen."

Lydia breathed a sigh of relief. "Thank you for noticing that," she said gratefully.

Mary looked at her fellow nurse. "The problem I have, Nurse Finney," Mary continued, "is that I cannot prepare other nurses to do this kind of work. There is no way to teach the women we have recruited and who are coming over from the States how to do the triage as you do, to prioritize wounded from those less likely to die to those with a good chance to live. I cannot write a list of protocols for a nurse to enter the surgery and be prepared to assist a surgeon in amputating a limb or reassembling someone disemboweled. There is no protocol I can put into a manual to cover these types of eventualities which you see every day when the shells start falling."

Lydia waited. "I'm not sure what you are suggesting then—"

Mary raised a hand to stop her. "I am suggesting that what the nurses do at the casualty clearing stations must stay at the stations. This kind of nursing practice may not be extended to the field hospitals or to the general practice of nursing in the States."

"Would you not agree," Harold Stockton interjected, "that the work these nurses do only further defines the role of the nurse in the medical care of the wounded, wherever they are?"

Mary nodded. "You said it correctly. It further defines a nurse's role in medical care, not nursing care. As such, while the practice of nursing may someday allow for that kind of nursing judgment and discernment, it is still years away. We are not there. Nurses engaged in the practice of medicine may indeed be necessary in some situations, such as this one where there are only three—forgive me, Doctor Fortraine—four doctors on site, for many hundreds... if not thousands of patients coming through this station. But at this time, in the general hospitals in the States, and probably other countries as well, there are ample numbers of doctors to practice medicine. Nurses must define nursing practice and keep it within the limits of, acceptable, patient-driven practice. They must teach principles of health, control infection, and administer comfort with medicines and dressings, allowing the doctors to practice medicine."

Lydia felt sad, hearing in the woman's words the obstacles Susannah Boyton was facing in the States and knowing that all of the nurses in the station, not just Marlene, would be facing a similar dilemma when the war ended and the CCSs were disbanded. "Where does that leave us, then, in terms of your report to the directors in Philadelphia?"

Mary took a moment to reply. "I think, Nurse, that all of you must prepare yourselves to reenter the world of nursing upon your return home... and I do hope that you all make it home. I will recommend that nurses in the CCS, at the front, practice nursing to the fullest humanitarian extent demanded by the unusual and exclusive dictates of war, under the direct supervision of the physician staff at the stations—mind you, I said demanded by the dictates of war... not in times of peace. I will further recommend that the practice of nurses serving in the CCS remain on a strictly voluntary basis due to the extenuating circumstances of patient care demands, near the front. I will also implement guidance on how to assist the nurses leaving the front with reacclimating, shall we say, to the traditional role of the nurse, upon returning to a field hospital or the hospitals for long-term recovery, both on the continent and back in the States. And perhaps, if we all live long enough, I will recommend that as nursing practice continues to define itself, the collective wisdom of those who have given so much of themselves to the survival of the wounded men, here, will be taken into consideration in that new definition."

Nurse Baxter stood, ready to take her leave. "And for goodness sake, get these nurses a real breakfast," she told Doctor Fortraine. "They certainly deserve that, at the very least."

Lydia walked her to the edge of the camp where she would board one of the trucks, with the wounded who were leaving for the hospital at Étaples.

"You have been more than fair to us," Lydia admitted to the woman as they walked through the station.

Mary took her hand. "I am surprised, frankly, that all of you are still alive and that only one has gone home after a year of service. I cannot commend your spirit of commitment highly enough, to do it justice. You will receive no pay, no recognition, no tangible reward for this work. No one will understand what you have done here other than yourselves… and in some way, Lydia, I envy you." She climbed into the truck, holding her skirt closed and keeping her head garb from blowing away. "Look me up when you get home," she called from the window. "I will take you out for a good breakfast!"

Chapter 19
Sidelined

It was mid-May, when the battle for the region around Arras ended. There was an incremental fallback of the German troops, but their trench lines were not taken, as the Allied forces had hoped. In the face of staggering loss of life, on both sides, the German defenses endured, through the mud and rains... and eventual sunshine. The casualty clearing stations breathed a sigh of relief as a brief respite from the war fell over them. As quickly as the calm was confirmed sustainable, Doctor Fortraine announced that half of the medical team could go on a brief furlough for rest and a chance to rejuvenate their flagging spirits. For those leaving, it would be their first reprieve from the war since their arrival.

With very little convincing, six of the nurses, along with Harold and Marcus, had filled overnight packs and made ready to leave the station. Father James also joined them, along with most of the remaining wounded who were now ready for transport. Simon and Doctor Fortraine arranged to carry on station responsibilities for the few scattered wounded that might come through. The two French nurses who had more recently arrived at the station deferred to those who had been serving the longest, but still watched enviously as the group departed.

The priest stood on the grassy area of the triage, waiting near the vehicles which had lined up along the edge of the camp. He stood with Simon and Lydia for a last-minute exchange. Gratefully, Simon shook the man's hand in farewell.

"We really didn't expect you to stay as long as you have, but I think your being here made all of the difference in the world, during this last long siege," Simon assured the priest. "Made it bearable for the wounded soldiers and staff alike. You ushered a lot of souls on their way. I hope we didn't completely wear you out."

"We can't thank you enough, Father," Lydia gave the priest a quick hug., "for reaching out, not just to the casualties, but also to our team. I hope you find some rest, and support for yourself, where you're going. We won't forget your words of wisdom. At least, I know I won't. Keep the angels around you, too, wherever you end up."

He smiled at them both and patted Abril's head as she watched the bustle of human activity. "It's been the longest I've stayed in any of the casualty clearing stations, if you want to know the truth," he reflected. "Coming right at the start of that battle, it just didn't seem right to leave in the middle of it. Your little medical group has also strengthened me, knowing that others are doing everything in their power to save these young lives. And God has blessed you both, to have found each other here. I will pray for you. I may not pass this way again. Hopefully, I won't have to, if the Americans make a real difference this summer, in helping to bring this war to an end."

"You are welcome to come back and visit anytime, as long as you can find us out here, Father," Simon said. "I know you'll be needed anywhere you go, in the churches or hospitals, but I hope not the military for too much longer. The world is going to need a long time for healing, even if everybody lays down their weapons sooner—"

"—rather than later? And, God willing, for the last time?" Father James finished the thought for him. "We can only hope. How could the world survive another war like this? And even when the war ends, there will always be the sick to care for, no matter what happens next, politically. I'll never lose hope; it may be a fallen world, yet there are bright spots that can always be found, like here."

The horses nearby snorted and pawed at the ground. Drivers started moving the wagons out. The three heard a shout from one of the trucks, its engine coughing as it came to life. "Come on, Father James!" Marcus called over to him from the back of the truck. "You're holding up the convoy, and Paris is waiting for us!"

The priest turned with a slight wave and smile. "I believe I'm being summoned by Doctor Lovell."

Simon wrapped his arm around Lydia's waist as they watched the priest be hoisted up into the truck by their friends, happily heading off. The trucks lurched over the roadway, heading for the train station that would take them to Paris. As the sound of the trucks faded, the entire station suddenly felt very empty to those remaining behind.

Fortraine was sequestered at his post, carrying on with administrative duties, until, if needed, Simon called for him in the surgery. Monique and Adrielle were caring for the few wounded left in the recovery who were still unable to travel, needing another day of healing. Gretha waved at their departing companions and turned to find some leisurely activity to fill her time. The other two nurses, Marlene and Alice, were already resting in their tents. Simon and Lydia looked at one another.

"Now what?" she asked him curiously. "We have nothing to do! What a strange feeling."

"I could hardly wait for them to leave!" Simon exclaimed, relieved.

Lydia lightly scolded him. "Is that any way to talk about our devoted friends and co-workers?"

"It certainly is! I remember how anxious I was to leave when you and I took our little holiday last year!" he returned. "I'm sure they are just as glad to be on their way. I just hope Marcus doesn't come back married to anyone."

"Anyone in particular?" Lydia wondered, suspecting, but not sure who he would name.

"Nurse Stein might favor him with a second glance," Simon suggested. "She seems to have taken somewhat of a shine to him."

Lydia put her arm through his as they walked back through the station. "Yes, but she hasn't forgotten Susannah, either. She doesn't know about the baby, of course, but she remembers him showering his attention on Suzie. And if she knew little Marcie Nichole was in the picture, she might not allow herself to feel any special way about him at all."

"That would influence her decision, I'd imagine," Simon replied. "I certainly don't think I would ever be able to date one of your good friends if I were in Marcus' shoes, though. Of course, he might be put off from dating altogether if he knew about the baby. I've often wondered how it might change him."

"You would never have been in his shoes. You've never given your affections so casually," Lydia added. "For which I am most grateful... So, what would you like to do now, Doctor Finney? Sleep, read... play checkers, perhaps?" The quiet and calm of the station was a balm to their souls, after the last grueling month.

He paused thoughtfully. "We have some new equipment that Fortraine ordered after Miss Baxter left. It might have been something she suggested. The supply shipment came in with the last convoy. I wonder if you'd mind checking it out with me. Fortraine said he thought it would make the lives of the nurses easier."

"My, my... how a visitor from out of town can change things!" Lydia exclaimed. "I can think of many things now that would make things easier for the nurses. But a week ago, when Doctor Fortraine called me to his tent to ask me that same question, not one blessed thing came to my mind. I told him we didn't need anything at all."

Simon pressed his arm against hers. "Well, then, let's see how clever our leader has become, even without any suggestions from you." He led her through the tents, past the quiet surgery, the nearly empty recovery tent, and the staff sleeping quarters. Abril, sensing the absence of any pressing human demands, went bounding off over the grassy field, searching for her own diversion.

"Um, Simon, the supply area is back over there, in recovery," Lydia had to remind him as he led her through the camp.

"I was told that this is too big to fit in the supply area," Simon assured her.

"It isn't... is it hot, running water?" she exclaimed. "Mary Baxter told him we should have hot, running water for the surgery and for—"

He nodded, finishing her thought, "And for the shower." He took her hand and led her to the shower tent. There, they saw several things: a large, metal holding tank for water had been erected outside of the tent; a banked fire smoldered in a brick-lined pit beneath it, keeping it warm.

It looked, to Lydia, as if the tent itself had been replaced with a slightly larger one. "God bless the woman for suggesting this! I must surely write her a thank you note!" Lydia breathed. "And maybe actually two can shower at once now, instead of waiting in line, when we're all dirty after a long, tiring day?"

"Maybe," Simon said, his eyes twinkling as he pulled open the flap to the tent. It was dimmer inside, but they could see that, indeed, the tent was larger now.

Lydia's eyes widened. "Will you look at that!" she declared in astonishment as he escorted her inside.

"Madame Finney, have I told you recently that I'm in love with you?" he murmured. "Welcome to the best hotel in France."

Before her was a metal tub, its edge just under the spigot to the water tank. The tub was filled with warm water, coils of hot steam rising up into the air as if beckoning her to come in. Lydia had no words.

"I'm at your service, madame" Simon said softly, turning to tie the tent flap securely closed before pulling the scarf from her head. In no time at all, she was undressed and anticipating complete re-laxation. Then, Simon took her hand as though she were a princess entering a coach, and motioned to the waiting water.

Lydia hadn't been in a bath since her arrival in France. She lifted one leg over the metal rim of the tub, letting the sole of her foot find leverage on the slippery metal floor. Feeling the support of his guiding hands at her waist, she drew her other leg in and sank down into the water. She leaned back, closing her eyes against the slanted headrest. Then, holding her breath, she submerged herself under the water. She was grinning when she finally came up, hair dripping. "You knew about this the entire time, didn't you?" she accused Simon, splashing him with the hot water from the tub.

"Maybe," he laughed. "You can hold it against me... it was worth it to see your face."

"I couldn't possibly hold it against you. You are very much forgiven," Lydia murmured, luxuriating in the soothing water. Simon knelt beside it on the ground. She felt Simon's hand moving through the warm water and down her neck, drawing back her wet hair that was floating like seaweed over her chest. "Oh my," she started, "I do hope you have something in mind..."

He chuckled softly. "Yes, I do," he assured her, making ripples in the water, letting his fingers follow the curves and folds of her body, inviting the warm bath to invigorate her senses. Then, Simon undressed and climbed into the large metal tub, between her legs. She shifted her position, allowing him to lower her down onto his lap, her legs wrapping around him. "I don't tell you nearly enough how beautiful you are," he reflected, scooping steaming water over her shoulders with his hands and kissing her neck.

Lydia reached past his head and found the bar of soap on the wooden plank bench. "May as well do this right," she said matter-of-factly. "Think of all those bed baths when you were injured... all those lonely, bucket showers in cold water at the end of a day..."

He nodded, taking the soap from her and lathering his hands with it as well. "I enjoyed your bed baths! But then there were all the icy sponge baths from the pan on the stove during that long, cold winter when all you wanted was to get it over with as fast as possible..."

"And now, my darling husband, you can just lay back and let me take my time finding every nook and cranny..." she advised, pushing him back against the headrest, her hands soaping the muscles and broad band of hair across his chest.

"This is a two-way street, you do realize," he assured her.

"I certainly hope so," she encouraged him, leaning forward to take his face in her hands and kissing him. "I love you, Simon."

They lingered over the simple act of washing each other, deliberately taking their time, gently teasing each other until Simon pulled her closer to him and murmured, "This part I didn't plan... but my god, you... wet and slippery... is more than I can resist..."

She positioned herself over him, wrapped her arms around his shoulders, and pulled his head to her chest. "I think it's even better unplanned..."

They opened the drain at the bottom of the tub, emptying it after rinsing everything, and refilled it with fresh hot water one more time, reluctant to leave the experience of their private spa. Lydia rested back against Simon's chest, her feet balanced on the far rim of the tub while he continued to stroke her under the water with his hands. Her long hair floated over and around them.

"This is exceptionally nice," she murmured, tracing the lines of his arm. "Simon, do you think we will ever have a fight, a real fight?"

Simon laughed. "What a time to bring that up! Have you been thinking of anything you want to fight about?" he asked her, wondering.

She shook her head, "No, but after all this time, you'd think something would have come up."

Simon circled her navel with his finger. "It's not like I'm going to get angry about burnt toast or something equally as foolish. You don't snore, and you don't criticize me... so what else do people get angry about?" he asked, pondering the question. Then, he told her, "I certainly was angry when the Germans took you. I do get angry at what you have to see... I worry at what you'll have to remember years from now."

She pulled his hand to her lips and kissing it. "What I'll remember years from now is that you were always here for me, in the middle of it all."

"Hm. Well, it appears that we have nothing to fight about... I can't seem to stop touching you," Simon said softly in her ear. "So... if you want me to, you'll have to tell me..." he murmured, hesitating.

"Don't stop," she whispered. "Can we just spend the night here? I feel like I'm returning to the proverbial womb."

He laughed, using his hand to drip water over her and watching how it made rivulets across her chest like streams finding their way down to the sea. "I suspect the word will get out pretty fast that this tub arrived. Others will want to try it out."

"They won't like it half as much as we do," she said, relaxed and content.

"Probably not," Simon admitted, tracing her lips with his wet fingers.

"Simon," she started. "I'm glad we didn't go to Paris. This... this is better than Paris."

They lay together until the water started to cool again. Lydia kissed each of his wrinkled fingertips. Finally, she stood, and the water cascaded from her long hair down her back and buttocks, before him. As she lifted one leg out over the tub, he stopped her and turned her around to face him.

She looked down and admonished him gently. "We mustn't be greedy, my love. We aren't filling it three times!"

"I just wanted to know," he said, rubbing his face against her, "if it's different with my beard wet."

She bent over and kissed the crop of hair on his chin. "It's always different," she replied softly, her hand on his cheek, "every single time." Resisting his hand attempt to pull her back into the water, she reached for their towels and began drying her face and arms.

Simon got up and stood by her, releasing the water to drain out of the tub, into a trough. He took a towel and dried her back and bottom, then turned her around to hold her one more time against him, before they dressed. "Lydia," he faltered. "Am I... do you think the day will come that I'm not enough..."

"Goodness gracious, Simon," she said, wrapping her arms around his neck and looking into his brown eyes. "How can you even ask that? I'd love you even if we were never be able to be together like this again."

"We've been married now almost nine months," Simon reminded her, holding her against him, "and, yet, sometimes I ask myself if it's still real. So much has happened in just nine months."

She looked up at him and smiled. "If I ever am blessed to be pregnant with your baby, you can tell me again how much can happen in nine months." She placed both of her hands against his chest. "We are solidly bound, my dear husband. Each time we're together doesn't have to be a moment of great discovery...although this particular surprise of yours is certainly high up on the list! But as wonderful as it is when we touch, it's still just a reflection... a mirror. It's an act of renewal of the promises we made in the church in Nancy. Why do you ask?"

He said, "Just something Father James said to me..."

Lydia pulled on her trousers and tucked in her shirt. "What did he say?" she asked him, confirming her suspicions that Simon had indeed talked to the priest.

"It's just that sometimes I want you so much that I was concerned that it sometimes wasn't the right thing to do, that I needed to practice self-control. So, I asked him about it. He said that in war, in this kind of circumstance, it's alright to seek you out, any time, for comfort—to 'take refuge,' I think he said, in the God-given gift of marriage. But that it should always be more than just an escape or a diversion. That the honoring has to be there. I should equally seek you out in times when I'm not inundated with the war, when the pressures of the injured and dying aren't weighing heavily on me. So that's why I wanted to... to show you today that I love you even when the shells aren't falling... that I want you because I want, you, not just because I need you sometimes."

Lydia waited until he finished his explanation and they were ready to leave their tiny escape from reality. "I know you've struggled with relationships in the past, Simon," she finally offered, "but we are truly alright... and Father James was right. Don't you think that sometimes I just want you... and sometimes I need you, and sometimes I just want to comfort you or renew our promises to each other? He told me that anything we ask for between us is okay because, in this marriage, we want the same things for each other."

"You talked to him, too, while he was here?" Simon asked in surprise.

"I did..." Lydia smiled and kissed him one more time before leaving the tent. "He got to me, too."

The truck bounced, jostling the little company, as the convoy headed for the train station outside of Arras. Many of the wounded in the trucks and wagons would be continuing on to St. John's Hospital in Étaples, along the coast to the north, but the nurses and doctors from the station would board a train for Paris. As they drew closer, the anticipation of exploring the grand city began to build, but as the convoy pulled into the train station, the six nurses and two doctors looked somberly around them at the milling crowds... the war crashing back in around them.

Countless wounded were sitting, lying on the ground, walking, leaning on crutches, sitting in carts. Corpsmen, Red Cross personnel, and litter bearers were everywhere, helping the wounded to board the trains or carrying others forward to wait in line for passage. These wounded had come in from all of the surrounding casualty clearing stations along the front, not just their own. The sheer number of injured from the battle for Arras was staggering. It was a sobering reminder of the fuller extent of medical interventions, attempting to preserve life, across the front. Some of these soldiers were too ill to travel far. Others would be able to stand the longer trip to rehab hospitals that were waiting to receive them, far away from the front. A few might actually be heading home, their injuries ending their military service completely... hoping that a family member or friend would be waiting for them at their final destination. The train station was a mélange of journeys.

There were others, not wounded, milling about as well: passengers, not unlike themselves, waiting to board... soldiers finishing their tours and heading home... civilians with suitcases and others with small children, whose hands were clutched firmly, to keep them safe. A few stray dogs, hoping for a friendly pat or sniffing for a morsel of food, ran between those waiting. Huge piles of supplies, artillery shells, sacks of foodstuffs, tires, barrels of gasoline, and bags of coal were stacked awaiting pickup by army trucks and wagons making their way to the front. The army was attempting to refill the larder before the next round of fighting began. It was organized bedlam as railroad personnel jumped on and off the train cars, calling out orders to others and inviting some of the waiting to climb aboard while the giant steam engines hissed from time to time, waiting.

Harold looked at the others. "Find a place to perch while I take care of tickets. Don't get separated. I don't want to have to chase you all down. Father James, I bid you farewell, with our gratitude."

The priest shook hands all the way around the group. "May God continue to bless you with safety and give you wisdom and comfort when you are in need. I'm heading now for a train to St. John's Hospital."

The medical team watched him go as Marcus said, "If priests were all like him, I might even go into a church!"

"They have churches in Paris. Huge cathedrals like Notre Dame," Charlotte told him. "Want to try one out?"

Marcus shook his head. "I did say 'if'," he reminded her. "Just talking to this one priest was enough, for now."

Harold made his way through the crowd of soldiers toward the ticket booth, trying not to pay too much attention to who might need medical care. He was off duty, he reminded himself, over and over, as he saw those with red-stained bandages sitting, waiting. Counting the Red Cross personnel with the identifying armbands who were working their way through the crowd, he finally felt easier in his spirit. Once though, Harold could not help himself, stopping one of the workers briefly, pointing out a soldier whose bloody stump above the knee looked too bright a red, for Harold's comfort. The worker nodded and went to check on the man who was perched in a rolling cart, while waiting to board.

At the station ticket booth, there was a counter, a window, and line of people. Harold knew he'd found the right place. Above the window was a sign that read: *Billets*. He waited in line behind a soldier until he heard the anticipated "Suivant..."

"Eight, please," Harold said, holding up eight fingers and trying to speak loudly enough to be heard through the small, open circle in the glass enclosure. "For Paris."

"Aller-retour ou aller simple?" the agent asked impatiently, the question thrust back through the small opening like a ship in a bottle.

"Round trip, um... retour," Harold fumbled with the language. "Do we have to change trains?"

The station agent behind the counter looked at Harold's military garb. "Non, c'est le train pour Paris. Un train direct. Voiture quatre, juste devant la voiture de l'hôpital. Car four—"

"The what?" Harold questioned, checking his hearing.

"Car four, right before the hospital car, monsieur... where the doctors go."

Harold nodded. *Car four... right in front of the hospital car... of course. Just can't get away from the war, can we?* he thought to himself. "Thank you, uh, merci," he said aloud to the man, through the hole in the glass. "Have a nice day."

The man behind the counter rolled his eyes as he surveyed the line behind Harold. "De rien."

Harold wove his way back through the crowds and reconnected with his companions. "Car four," he told them, studying the train, to count the cars following the British engine labeled ROD 1328, with its attached tender.

"Do we count the coal car?" Charlotte wondered out loud.

"If you get into the hospital car, you've gone too far."

"The what?" she countered.

"That's what I said," Harold remarked. "There is apparently an entire car serving as a mobile surgery along with transportation for wounded. This entire train is meant for troop and supply transport... and extra passengers, if there is room."

Laura looked over at him, considering this information. "A mobile hospital on a train is not a bad idea, actually. Take the operating tent on the rails. Think how quickly they could get to another village if fighting breaks out suddenly. And they don't have to take the time to set everything back up again each time they stop."

Harold clarified. "Can you imagine trying to resect a bowel while a train car sways around a curve in a track? I wouldn't want a scalpel in my hand at that moment."

"Nor I," Laura replied. "It's still a good idea, though. Why not have train surgeries?"

Charlotte nodded. "And just look at all these wounded fellows. There must be thousands here. What if one of them needs something on the way to Paris? We've all wondered at times, if we've sent boys from our station before they were ready to leave the recovery and what might happen to them. I think it's reassuring that the trains are prepared. It says ROD on the engine; that's British for Railway Operating Division. Sounds like something the British would think up."

Marcus attempted to propel them through the bystanders. "British or French, wounded or not, they certainly don't need us. For now, this train is the fastest means we have of getting to the city. Let's get on board, boys and girls... before we lose our seats and have to ride in a box car with a bunch of sheep."

The eight of them moved with the current of humanity toward Car 4. They came to the steps where a train conductor was calling, "*Monter à bord du train!*" He asked to see tickets and motioned people up the steep wrought iron steps to the waiting cars. One by one, they boarded, turning left toward seats, which were rapidly filling with people, also anxious to get on their way. To their right, the window on the door of the hospital car had a shade that was raised up, and taking a quick glance inside, Harold saw a most remarkable sight.

There were two examination tables set up. Electric lamps were suspended overhead. Stands with basins and water containers were fastened to the walls of the train car to prevent shifting. Along the rear two-thirds of the car, he could make out three tiers of berths mounted, one on top of the other, many already occupied by wounded soldiers. He saw a nurse with a long, floor-length white apron over her skirt and a white headband and veil. She was helping the men settle in their various berths. She had a red cross on the front of her pinafore. The entire scene looked organized and completely under control. Harold rapidly turned left to find the others saving him a seat in the crowded passenger car.

"You looking for a new job?" Marcus asked Harold curiously as the other man finally settled into his seat.

Harold shook his head. "Just never saw one of those before," he admitted. "Pretty impressive setup."

"Don't get any ideas," Marcus reminded him. "Our orders are for rest and recreation, from this point on."

Harold stopped one of the conductors moving down the aisle between the seats. "This train... how many wounded can it hold?"

The man looked up as if counting. "This is a smaller train... three or four hundred... I do not know for sure. Sometimes more cars are added."

Harold nodded. "Thank you."

Laura looked out the window at the crowds in the station. "This is what happens to them when they leave us... their journey just keeps on going..." She saw how men were in wheeled chairs, unable to walk on their own, but pushing themselves along with effort. Others were being propelled forward in hay-padded push carts, depending on someone else to get them close enough to the train for others with strong arms to pick them up and carry them up the wrought iron steps. Only weeks, or perhaps months before, Laura knew that these same young men would have bounded up those steps on two strong legs and swung themselves into the seats without a single thought of the effort that it took... How one shell or one bullet or bayonet could change a life forever.

Marcus reached across the seat and patted her knee reassuringly. "Now, Nurse Bertolli, you have to keep your eyes on the goal. We're going to have fine French wine and wonderful cuisine, hear music on the street corners, and sleep in real beds. You're supposed to forget about the war when you're on vacation."

"We're not escaping the war, Doctor Lovell, just the active fighting," she replied, still looking out at the sea of faces. "It's keeping step right along with us."

This time, even Harold nodded in agreement. "Paris has seen its own share of the war... in the beginning, it was the Western Front. It won't be all wining and dining. When we do get there, you ladies must at least pair up. Don't want any of you getting waylaid by a bunch of drunken soldiers somewhere. And make sure you're back in time for the return train. I can't lose any of you or Fortraine will have my head."

The train suddenly lurched ahead. A whistle blew and people on the platform moved back as conductors pulled up their wooden stepstools and inch by inch, the train started moving. The wheels screeched as they began to turn and gain traction against the iron rails. Smoke slowly began to spread out from the stacks of the engine in rhythmic belches, then faster and faster as they picked up speed. Finally, those on board saw that they were free of the station and the nearby countryside began to blur beyond the tracks. They were on their way.

Reaching for the seat in front of him to steady himself, Harold rose to his feet. "I'm going back to the hospital car. I want to talk to the doctors and find out what this has been like for them."

"I'm going with you," Laura said. "I like the idea of a hospital train."

Holding onto the back of the seats for balance, as the car swayed, they waited, letting the conductor pass by, then walked back through the doors, and across the noisy, windy coupling, to the car behind them.

Marcus shook his head and said to the remaining nurses seated nearby, "Those two just don't understand the concept of R&R... rest... relaxation. Or revelry and rejuvenation... take your pick. Personally, I prefer the latter."

Charlotte laughed and rested her head back onto the seat comfortably. "Oh, don't mind those two, Doctor Lovell," she returned cheerfully. "They'll be fine. They'll relax once we get there."

Nancy chimed in, sounding a bit worried. "I sure hope our own station doesn't get slammed with casualties while we're away. It's a big risk for all of us to be gone at once. Remember how Doctor Finney and Lydia had to follow our trail when we moved the camp while they were gone? What if the station has to pick up and move out while we're away?"

Marcus was quick to reassure her. "Fortraine was confident it was a good time for us to go, or he wouldn't have sent all eight of us at once—now you're doing it, too, Nurse Mitchell... you've got to let it go, even if it's just for a few days."

"I will eventually," Nancy promised. "It's just hard to change gears so fast. All those wounded guys at the station back there... they have to figure out how to get on with their lives. I wonder how long some of them had been waiting for a ride. Maybe they could have even used our seats."

Nodding, Marcus added, "Maybe, but we have to get on with our lives too. We need rest if we're going to be able to keep taking care of them. So, just fit as much as you can into three days of bliss, ladies. Make some good memories to hold you over. I know I sure will. Nurse Winfield, I'll bet you southern girls don't know much about French wine or opera, but I hear the opera house in Paris is incredible."

Sally shook her head. "That's not for me. I'm going to find a nice street corner along the Seine where a cafe serves coffee and croissants, and a violin player is pulling music from a tattered old instrument, and some nice gentleman asks me to dance right on the street."

Charlotte patted the doctor's arm. "Don't worry, Doctor Lovell, I'll go to the opera with you. It's a good idea. I've never been to an opera house."

Marcus settled back in his seat as the countryside slid past. Having spoken his piece and secured the assurance of some companionship from at least one of the nurses, he was content now to just sit back and enjoy the ride.

Paris in spring was everything they hoped it would be. Streets were crowded with taxis, bicyclists, pedestrians, fruit and vegetable vendors, newsboys trying to sell papers promising the very latest headlines. The trees along the river and canals were in bloom, leaves waving in the warm breeze. Windows in the shops were open, some giving off inviting aromas. The little group of nurses and doctors disembarked the train, mindful of the many soldiers in wheelchairs and on crutches also looking for a clear path through the crowded station. They separated from the sea of human need and took off to find Hôtel Florida, a YMCA-managed facility, run by an International Hospitality League known for providing respite for Allied troops. In the multi-story flat iron building, the women found simple but adequate rooms to share, and they quickly changed into the only skirts they owned—the ones they had worn when arriving at the casualty clearing station, over a year ago. Feeling energized and feminine, they took to the streets of Paris, seeking out the wonders of a city, which had been the front, less than three years ago. They emerged from the building to meet up again with the two doctors waiting outside of the hotel. Marcus whistled in appreciation at their sudden transformation, looking at them from head to shoes.

"All of you have legs!" Marcus exclaimed.

"Is that a new medical condition, Doctor Lovell?" Charlotte teased.

He looked at her approvingly. "No, mademoiselle, it is strictly male appreciation."

"So, you don't think we look as good when we're back at the station in our army trousers, is that it?" Linda challenged him. "Now, with skirts, you appreciate our gender."

Harold put up a hand, warning Marcus not to answer. "Dangerous question, Doctor. Don't take the bait."

Flowing hair, flowing skirts and beaming smiles surrounded the doctors. Marcus took one of the nurses on each of his arms and headed onto the street, hailing two taxis willing to take them around the city. "Champ-de-Mars," Marcus told the driver, who nodded, not surprised. Most visitors staying at the hotel asked to be taken to the Eiffel Tower or the Arc de Triomphe first, when visiting the city. The team chose the Tower.

Stepping out of the cabs, they stared up in awe at the extreme height of the Eiffel Tower, which seemed to reach the clouds. All eight of them climbed the wrought iron steps to the observation deck, taking in the uncomparable view of Paris. They could see the Arc de Triomphe, only two kilometers away, and spires of great churches and cathedrals. Leaning on the balcony, with the light breeze blowing, Marcus looked out over the green grass below. Charlotte walked over to stand beside him.

"Penny for your thoughts, Doctor Lovell?" she asked him curiously.

"I'm thinking how great it is to be in this old city, in spring, with eight beautiful women," Marcus looked back to her. "Ya know, your red hair is very pretty, Nurse Stein. I never really noticed, but in the sunshine... you nurses always have to keep it hidden under those scarves."

She blushed. "Why thank you, Doctor," she said. "It's nice for you to notice. Nice to feel feminine for a change."

"We don't help you feel feminine in the station very much, do we?" he asked regretfully.

"It's more, the circumstances of war," she corrected him. "You have nothing to do with that."

"I envy Doctor Finney," he had returned to looking out over the crowded buildings, the straight lines of the streets fanning out below them. "He's allowed to make Nurse Finney feel feminine whenever he wants to. The rest of us don't have that opportunity."

"Why ever not? You don't have to be married to have that," she observed, leaning on the rail next to him while the city went about its day, in the warm sun.

"According to Doctor Stockton, it works better that way," Marcus informed her.

Charlotte was quiet. "He probably declared that when Susannah left, didn't he?"

Marcus nodded. "We had a talk... well, he talked and I listened."

"Do you miss her?" Charlotte asked curiously, watching the couples walking below them or sitting together on blankets laid out on the green grass below. Some of them looked like they might be on holiday as well. There were many people on bicycles, weaving their way between taxis, coming and going. She watched the clusters of pigeons circling, dropping down nearby for handouts. It was a long way down to the ground.

"Susannah? Sure, I miss her," Marcus told Charlotte. "I know she left because of me. I couldn't make a commitment. Her leaving probably hurt all of you nurses and made it harder on you, until replacements came... even though none of you complained. None of you blamed me... at least, not out loud."

"She left. It happened so suddenly. I don't think anyone is to blame, really." Charlotte seemed convinced of her appraisal of the situation.

Marcus didn't look at her. "I blame myself. Susannah is a wonderful woman. It was bad timing."

Charlotte put a hand on his arm lightly. "Susannah will be fine in the States, Doctor Lovell. She was ready to leave the war, and we all wished her well. Anyway, it really didn't matter that she left that way. We're all going to go home sooner or later, hopefully. She just left a little earlier."

He shook his head. "I don't know about that. I think it was more than her just feeling her time was up. I don't really understand why any of you stayed in the first place, but I think she loved what she was doing over here. Susannah leaving is the one thing I'm grateful that I got to talk to Father James about. Glad he was there to listen."

Charlotte looked over at him, surprised. "You, talked to Father James?" she asked, with obvious incredulity.

He couldn't help but laugh. "Yes, I did. You don't have to sound so shocked, Nurse Stein. I'm not a total heathen."

"I'm not shocked," she corrected him. "I'm... impressed... and... while we're talking about personal things, do we have to be so formal—Doctor and Nurse—while we're here in Paris? Don't you think we can just be Charlotte and Marcus while we're off duty, miles away from the front? After all, you saw my insides when you did my appendix."

He met her gaze, admiring her copper hair blowing in the breeze... and appreciating their candor. "I certainly did, under Nurse Finney's watchful eye. Yes, I think we can. At least when we're alone." Then he added, somewhat casually in response to her directness, "Would you like us to be... alone, Charlotte?"

She nodded and smiled over at him without hesitation. "Yes, Marcus, I would."

"Then let's make it happen. You did promise me the opera, I believe," he reminded her.

"I did," she said. "Was looking forward to it, actually."

The two took their leave of the rest of the group and made their way through the crowd, back down the metal lattice steps, to the street, where they hailed a cab. They were transported through the busy streets to the Palais Garnier, where they joined a group touring the famed Napoleonic structure. They peered up at the carved friezes, busts of musicians, and gilded sculptures from mythology adorning the gables, gleaming in gold and the bright green copper-covered roof dome, lit by the afternoon sun.

"These sculptors weren't hesitant to put the human body right out there, for all to see..." Charlotte said, looking up at many nude and seminude figures. She shaded her eyes from the slanted rays of the sun reflecting brightly off the metals as they walked around the building façade. "The statues are incredibly intricate, I must say..."

"Trust Greek mythology to be shameless with the human form," Marcus agreed. "Let's go inside."

The sculpted figures, holding lyres, torches, and harps, stood guard from their elevated stone perches as the two passed beneath them. Inside, even Marcus had to let out a soft exclamation of awe as they approached the central, grand marble staircase, flanked by brightly lit candelabras. The looked up, taking in the intricate paintings on the vaulted ceiling before walking up the marble staircase and into the auditorium, where row after row of empty seats waited for an audience.

The lighting was subdued, with no shows or practices, at the moment... the thousands of lights in the famous chandelier, suspended from the lofty ceiling, were currently extinguished. The heavy velvet stage curtain was drawn, closing off the backstage. It was calm and quiet. The two of them slipped into one end of the back row, overwhelmed by the grandeur around them. They imagined what this great stage would be like when it came to life with a full orchestra playing and dancers gliding delicately, on point, through the space.

Charlotte's voice was just a whisper. "This is the most beautiful building I have ever seen," she murmured. "I'm glad you suggested the opera house, Marcus."

Nodding in agreement, he said, "It's certainly one of a kind." They sat quietly, not speaking for several long minutes, simply soaking in the grand atmosphere of the building. Then, Marcus stretched his arm out on the back of her seat as they contemplated what was ahead of them.

Finally, he spoke. "When I asked if you'd like to be alone... how, alone, were you thinking, Charlotte?"

She answered him almost matter-of-factly. "I assume there has been a bit of a hole left, after you found yourself without... companionship. I think alone means a place where two people can find companionship, out of sight of others, who don't need to know about it."

Marcus concluded their definitions, and expectations, matched. He allowed himself the pleasure of stroking her long copper-colored hair, then ran his fingers along her neck, behind her ear, feeling her shiver against his arm. Charlotte countered by casually allowing one hand to drop down to rest on his lap. He immediately responded to her touch... to the unspoken invitation she was extending. Leaning over the seat, he pulled her toward him with his arm around her and kissed her until, finally, she paused.

"There are supposed to be many rooms in this building where people can... socialize alone..." Charlotte suggested, her heart pounding.

Marcus felt her breathing quicken. His long unmet needs were longing for the kind of attention she was intimating. "Let's go find one of them," he suggested.

They left the massive auditorium through one of the side portals. In the corridor, they found a small, curved, carpeted staircase leading to one of the many tiered boxes, overlooking the stage. Running up the stairs, the two slipped into one of the private enclaves. Charlotte dropped down onto the carpeted floor of the small, gilded balcony, kicking off her shoes. Marcus urgently lowered himself to her and lifted her skirt, to her hips. Charlotte reached for him, wrapping her arms around his neck, continuing where they had left off. Until that moment, Marcus hadn't fully realized how badly his body missed having Susannah regularly. He reached down and opened his trousers as Charlotte slid down her undergarment. As he attempted to enter her, he was surprised at the sudden resistance he encountered. He paused, whispering, "Charlotte, are you a—"

Charlotte didn't answer, wrapping her legs around him, pulling him in past any barrier, pressing her mouth to his. The deed was done. She wanted this, right now, in this place, even though she knew little about what to expect. But Marcus realized his sudden predicament. With considerable effort, he controlled his urgency. He began to help her awaken the womanhood within her that she did not even know existed. He stopped long enough to whisper, "Try to relax... just allow your hips to move in rhythm with mine as I move you... let your body feel the sensations it will create... there will come a moment when you feel like you're going to lose control... don't be afraid of it, just give in to it, let it take over. I will guide you... it will be intense, but in the best way."

Charlotte obeyed him, following his instructions and letting him guide her to the mysteries of womanhood as his lips roamed over her face and throat and his hands moved over her body, introducing her to the sensations he was creating. Then, she felt something strange taking possession of her, something that she had never experienced before.

"I think someth—" she whispered, but he stopped her from speaking with his lips.

"Let it build... it will feel very good..." he murmured gently.

Charlotte uttered a gasp as her world exploded in his arms.

"I've got to keep moving a little longer," Marcus warned her. Then, finally, he groaned with the effort of releasing all of the months of pent-up desire, everything being held back since the night before Susannah left, into this woman. He remained on top of her, breathing heavily, intense relief washing over him... along with feelings of guilt that it had felt so good. They didn't move for some time.

"I guess I should have told you—" Charlotte began.

He kissed her forehead. "It wasn't necessary. I'm glad you trusted me enough..."

"I had no idea..." she was spent.

"And now you do," Marcus answered her matter-of-factly.

She pulled up her undergarment, as he closed his trousers. With his fingers, he straightened her tousled hair and helped her to stand as she found her shoes. He kissed her forehead again, softly. "You really are a lovely woman, Charlotte. You may be a little uncomfortable, for a day or two, after your first time though," he cautioned her.

Charlotte nodded, grateful that he had taken her arm in his as they left the little alcove. The two returned down the curved stairs behind the box seats, down the long, quiet hall, and then outside, by way of the marble staircase. On the street, the reliefs of Eros, Apollo, Pegasus, and the composers were unchanged, but Charlotte was changed. She didn't know if it was for the better, or worse, but knew that she was now different than she had been, before. And Marcus wondered where Susannah had gone, when she had returned home.

Back at the Hôtel Florida, during their last evening in Paris, the nurses were comparing notes about how they had spent their days. Laura and Linda chattered on about the people of Paris, the welcome sight of children running in the streets, mothers with babies in prams, and greying, older men unable to serve in the army, who sat playing checkers and smoking pipes, while talking politics at outdoor tables in the parks. Nancy described how she went to several little shops, including bakeries where apologetic bakers told her regretfully that the offerings were limited, due to a shortage of flour. Some of the nurses had visited a few music venues where unfamiliar melodies were being practiced by cellists and violinists, complimented by haunting silver flutes, offering harmonic tones. Alice had found a dust-filled bookstore and spent hours poring over volumes of gold leaf pages. She had also made it to the Cathédrale Notre-Dame. All of them had seen signs of the war, some buildings still remnants of their former selves—not yet replaced from prior bombardments, when Paris had been under attack. They each saw the city from a different point of view. When asked, Charlotte held her peace, other than to describe the magnificent architecture of the opera house.

Nancy looked over at her curiously as she lay stretched out on her bed. "You spent the whole day with Doctor Lovell, and he behaved himself?" she asked incredulously.

"He showed impeccably good manners," Charlotte replied simply.

"That's amazing," Alice agreed with Nancy. "I figured he would pounce on one of us while we were away from the station."

"Yes," Laura chimed in. "Of course, there was no question about Doctor Stockton being a gentleman, but Doctor Lovell, that's a whole other matter. I wonder if Susannah were here if he and Suzie would have run off and gotten married like Lydia and Doctor Finney did. After all, we all knew they were a couple for quite some time. I wonder if she's written him since she got home."

Charlotte shook her head slowly. "I don't think he ever wanted to marry Suzie," she concluded. "Everything they did was on the sly."

"Well, I tried to stay out of it," Alice told them. "Didn't he date you, Laura?"

"We dated," she admitted. "But I knew where that was going to go. I mean, he was nice enough when I was with him, but I could tell it wasn't going to go anywhere. He's a man who just likes to keep his options open. I wasn't going to get locked into something like that. Especially not when we have to work side by side every day like we do."

"People change," Charlotte offered. "Maybe he didn't know what he wanted?"

Laura shook her head and sighed. "Well, he certainly did know I wanted... in certain respects. I'll give him that."

Nancy looked carefully at Charlotte again. "You sure nothing happened between you two, Charlotte? You can tell us if it did. He's been a flirt with all of us... probably Monique and Arielle, by now, too."

"Nothing happened," Charlotte kept her response light. "Now, you all ought to get some sleep. We have to go back tomorrow, and heaven only knows what we'll run into when we get there." She rolled over and feigned sleep. Charlotte determined then and there that she wasn't going to let Marcus Lovell treat her like just one of his many women. No, he would realize that things could be different with her. She would see to it.

As the group reboarded the steam train for their return trip, most of its passenger cars were still empty. This train was heading back east to deliver supplies and, in return, collect the newly wounded soldiers. The train was longer this time, with a hospital car, a kitchen car, and sleeping quarters for both the medical and support crew. Cars with stacked rows of empty berths were stark reminders of what was to come. Box cars, filled with much-needed food and fuel, followed after. This time as they boarded, Marcus avoided idle conversation with the nurses by taking advantage of the opportunity to tour the medical facilities on board. He went back to the hospital car. Talking to one of the surgeons, he asked about the pros and cons of the arrangement. The surgeon perched himself on an empty lower berth.

"The best part is knowing that even if we must operate, a hospital is waiting when we pull into the city," the surgeon told him. "Most of the time, we do minor operations, although we have everything that we need for more extensive procedures, right here on board."

Marcus shook his head. "I don't know, seems like it would be easy to slip up on a moving train."

The other surgeon laughed. "You would be surprised how fast you get used to the movement of the cars."

One of the nurses came into the car with an armload of long fracture splints. "Here," Marcus said, taking the pile from her. "Let me help you with that. Where did you want them?"

"Down a couple of more cars, monsieur," she said lightly. "We are replenishing supplies."

Marcus followed her through the cars, through the doors she slid open, and across the open space, between the cars, over the loud banging of the iron couplings. Finally, after going through several empty cars, they arrived at their destination. Marcus crouched to stack the splints where she directed, just as the train took a sharp bend. He lost his balance, falling to the floor, the wooden splints clattering around them as he landed with his back up against the edge of a patient berth.

The nurse chuckled. "You have now been initiated into train service, Doctor. An official member of the staff!" She knelt down on the floor of the car and started gathering up the scattered wooden rods. He found his knees.

"I'll get those," Marcus protested apologetically. "I was the clumsy one."

"We all do that until we get used to the sway of the cars," she reassured him. "But at least you do not wear a dress when you tumble to the floor."

Marcus smiled at her. "No, that much is certain. Why do you do this work, Nurse?" he continued curiously as she stacked the wood in his arms again. "Especially here on the train?"

"Because it is my country. Because I like to help the soldiers. Because I like the way they look at me when I come into the car and they reach out to me for comfort... reassurance," she answered cheerfully. "All of these things. And because, on the train, time goes very fast. We don't stop long, we don't stay long. Now, let me help you stand. Spread your feet for better balance."

Arms loaded, Marcus got back to his feet, trying to move with the sway of the car, keeping his feet slightly apart. He followed her to the end of the aisle and lowered the remaining splints into a waiting bin, secured to the wall.

"Oh, my goodness, did you strike your back on the berth?" the nurse exclaimed, looking at his side.

He straightened up and winced. "Maybe."

"Let me see. You have a spot on your shirt," she motioned to a nearby berth. "Sit down, here."

He did, and she pulled his shirt out of his trousers. He heard her say "ouch" as she clucked her tongue. He tried to bend to get a look, but couldn't see the injury. As she took his shirt off, he felt the pain when he pulled his arm from the sleeve.

"You must have hit the corner where it is very sharp. It is bleeding ever so slightly. But no stitches. Sit down here, while I get a bandage for this," she told him.

Marcus said, "Now, I am one of those, reaching out a hand to you. What's your name?"

Her eyes sparked as she looked down at him. "Beatrice," she replied. She turned away with a swish of her long skirt and apron and effortlessly navigated the swaying train, rummaging through the supply shelves to get what was needed, to tend him. Coming back, she cleaned the abrasion, along his lower rib cage. "I am afraid you will be a little black and blue before long. Let us hope you don't need to stand and operate for a day or two."

"Most likely not," he said, feeling as she gently washed his injury. "Why do they make you cover all of your hair with the headdress? Why must you wear the long dress of a nun? Are you from a convent, then?"

Laughing out loud, she said, "No, no, nothing like that! This is to demonstrate to others our modesty and our chaste behavior."

He enjoyed her humor and her laugh and appreciated that she had not teased him for falling and making a fool of himself. "And do all of you practice this chaste behavior?" he wondered as she reached around him, wrapping a long gauze around his waist to hold the dressing in place.

"This is what we must project, but is not always what is practiced," she clarified mischievously, adding, "Lower your trousers slightly so I can tuck this in and keep your waistband from chafing."

Marcus obliged her. She wound the gauze around him and, satisfied with her handiwork, helped him pull his shirt back up over his arms. "Just what color is your hair, Nurse Beatrice?" he wondered curiously.

Pulling off the headpiece and veil, her jet-black hair spilled out around her face. Then she pulled the headpiece back on and pushed her bangs underneath, concealing her hair under the veil once more.

Marcus reached up. "You missed one," he murmured, tucking in a lock of black hair behind her ear and pulling the white band over top. "Now you are very chaste again. Your eyes are very blue," he observed.

Then, reaching down, she lifted the long skirt she wore, revealing small ankles and white legs. "And the long skirt is to tell soldiers we are unavailable. But as you can see, my legs have been given much attention."

Marcus could not resist her invitation to touch her legs, for the hair had been removed, and they were smooth as a baby's skin beneath his fingers. He had not seen a woman who had maintained her legs in this manner since long before the war. Beatrice stopped his hand just above her knee, pressing it there for a moment while she whispered coyly, "Some of us remove the hair all the way up... everything! It is a shame no one can enjoy it... time goes so fast on the train, and we don't stop long or stay long..."

Marcus swallowed hard. "Yes," he said, becoming immediately frustrated. "It most certainly is a shame..."

"Do you think you can make your way back to your car?" she asked him, somewhat wistfully, Marcus thought.

He rose carefully, holding on to the upper berth for stability. "I believe I can."

Lowering her long skirt, she said, "Just let me know if you need to be taken care of before we arrive." Cheerfully, smiling at him, she turned to the door of the train car, leaving Marcus to find his own way back to his fellow travelers and to figure out if there was any conceivable way to make the trip last a little longer.

Marcus took his seat with the others, sitting back gently, not wanting anyone to notice his discomfort. "What did I miss?" he asked them all.

Laura said, "I was telling them I found the Seine and my croissants and even a fiddler. It was positively delightful."

Nancy told them, "We saw a newspaper boy, and he said that though it may not be in the papers, some of the French soldiers are staging a mutiny on the front! That they refuse to advance out of the trenches under fire where they risk getting shot before they even have a chance to stand up."

Harold commented, "Sounds pretty smart to me. I never could understand the concept of 'going over the top' as some of our wounded have described to us. Jumping up out of a trench under a hail of bullets sounds a bit like suicide. I think I'd want to keep my head down, too."

"The newsboy said he heard the soldiers weren't running away. They just weren't running toward the Germans. He said there is a new French chief of staff, as well. I tried to get a paper, but he had already sold out."

"Did you know," Linda chimed in, "that they're rationing a loaf of bread now, things have gotten so short for them? We eat better at the station than some of the French do, even in the city."

"Poor things," Nancy sighed. "Their country is just overwhelmed. We heard whispers everywhere that when the Americans come, things will turn out okay. I sure hope they can hold on with the Allies helping them."

Linda leaned back with satisfaction. "We saw a movie," she told the others. "Doctor Stockton and I. It was wonderful to see a movie. Even if it was all in French and I didn't understand ninety-five percent of it. How about you, Charlotte? What did you and Doctor Lovell see after the Eiffel Tower?"

"The opera house. The Garnier," Charlotte sighed. "I've never seen such a magnificent building in my life, not even in Washington, D.C. I will never forget it. But the hot shower at the Hôtel Florida was a true gift. Just being able to stand in hot running water was heavenly. And the French do know how to make a breakfast worth eating, even with the rationing."

Marcus listened to all of their information and said, "Sounds like you all followed the advice I gave you when we set out on this little journey. I said make some memories to take back with you to the station. Sounds like everyone did." He leaned back and shut his eyes, avoiding Charlotte's glance.

Left to their own thoughts, they relaxed and eventually dozed with little else to do. The train rolled along, occasionally letting a whistle blast out into the air, no doubt to warn some animal or cart crossing the tracks of the approaching engine. But after a time, the train slowed for no apparent reason and sat quietly, chugging in place. A conductor came down the aisle and Harold stopped him.

"Is everything alright?" Harold asked the man.

"Oui, monsieur," the man reassured them all. "But a train filled with wounded is coming the other direction, and we must go off on a siding."

"Does that take a while?" Harold asked.

The conductor nodded. "The train is far, but there is no other siding. So, we must pull off here and wait. You may wish to go to the dining car and get some supper, as it will take some time before we go again."

The eight looked at one another. Of course, a train full of wounded was priority. They wouldn't want it any other way. Harold watched the engine steer off onto a long siding and pull the entire length of cars after it until the rail was clear. As the train curved onto the side track, the engineer and the signalman on the end could see each other, signaling to shut down the engine. The locomotive slowed to a soft, intermittent hiss of steam. Harold looked at the others. "I'm up for some supper. Let's find the dining car," he suggested.

They all rose, with the other passengers, and headed down to the open doors at the end of the car, across the couplings, and through the surgery... then the cars of empty patient berths... the crew quarters with privacy curtains pulled around their berths. Finally they located a kitchen car, with a dining car beyond. It seemed as though the conductor had shared his advice with the entire train. Tables were full of travelers. In the dining car, a server told them they could safely take something to eat outside and sit on the grass beside the tracks if they chose. The train would likely be parked for several hours while they waited, and there would be no rush or risk of being left behind. Most of the passengers and the train medical staff took the conductor's advice. It was a warm, sunny late afternoon, and there weren't enough seats at tables in the dining car anyway, to accommodate their numbers.

Marcus looked around the crowd, scarcely able to believe his good fortune. He saw the group of "chaste and modest" nurses on duty, as they entered the same dining car. He broke off from following his own companions outside, saying that he forgot something back in his travel pack and would join them a little later. Charlotte looked at him quizzically, then followed the others, choosing the grassy knoll. They took their trays of food and disembarked the train to find clear green spaces outside to enjoy their meals.

By the time Marcus rejoined them, they were relaxing in the sunshine. They could see the other train when it whistled and came into view around the curve along the main track. It was a huge train filled, they surmised, with hundreds and hundreds of casualties coming in off the front. The Paris-bound train slowly lumbered past them as they watched from the siding. Some of the soldiers near windows waved to the onlookers in the grass. Marcus ate heartily from the plate he had carried out as he joined the others.

"What on earth did you forget, Doctor Lovell?" Charlotte asked, looking up at him. "It took you forever!"

He dropped down carefully onto the grassy slope, holding his plate and cup in an effort not to spill anything. "This train cuisine is actually quite good, isn't it?" he said. "A custard of some sort, the fish is seasoned well, and rice, instead of the army's multi-purpose potato. They may be rationing, but I'd say the cook on this train does a great job of making the most of what he has to work with. Tastes delicious!"

Harold watched the other train lumber past. "Will you look at that... every single window has the face of a soldier in it. I can't imagine where all of these wounded are coming from. Far more than we will ever see at the station. I don't think I'll ever complain again about the volume of wounded we have to manage. There are so many more than I realized, until now."

Nancy looked over thoughtfully. "Yet many of them wouldn't even be on that train if we hadn't gotten to them first... they'd be on a hill somewhere under a small white cross."

"We do make a difference..." Laura added softly.

They lost track while trying to count the number of cars. At long last, they saw the signalman on the final car give their train personnel the all-clear to switch the tracks back over from the siding again. They didn't need the conductor to warn them it was time to reboard. Steam began rising in the smokestacks in rhythmic bursts. The passengers gathered up all plates, cups, and flatware before taking their place in lines to reboard. As the engine came to life, the following cars jerked forward, in obedience. The train slowly maneuvered, from the siding, back onto the main track, heading east once again, toward the front. It incrementally picked up speed until the countryside blurred, and only trees and hills on the far horizon remained clear.

The mood of the eight was now uniformly subdued. Paris had been lovely. It had been good to take off the uniform for a short time, but now it was time focus on their return to the station. Charlotte sat by one of the windows of their divided group of seats. She could see Marcus ahead of her, two rows up. His head rested back, and he appeared to be sleeping. She looked out the window at the countryside slipping by. There was the occasional cluster of farmhouses, a group of cows near a small barn. She saw horses drawing curved plows to rake the ground, preparing it for seed, with farmers, who were surely hoping for a better harvest this year... something always left to the whims of Mother Nature, who never made promises.

The woman thought about Marcus. He would never make promises, either. This she had known from the start when she had prompted him to be with her. Susannah had never gotten him to make a promise to her, even though she'd been with him most of the time she had lived at the station. Of course, even Charlotte realized that Marcus had been with many women, not just Susannah... anyone he could cajole into a brief interlude. But now, as the train sped along, Charlotte relived the moment in the private alcove at the opera.

It hadn't been quite what she thought it would be. He had helped her feel many new things... but he hadn't held her and whispered sweet nothings in her ear after he left her body. He hadn't kissed her and told her he thought she was beautiful or special. Just '*now you know*', she recalled. Charlotte realized she would have to be content with the memory that her first time with a man was in a grand opera house, in a grand city. She hoped it would be enough. At least it wasn't at the hands of a German soldier, against her will.

It was early morning, when the train finally pulled back into the station at Arras. The air was beginning to cool. Trucks were waiting to pick up supplies from the train, and one truck had been arranged to convey the team back to the station. From a box car, a herd of pigs was being encouraged down a wooden ramp and into a hastily erected pen. While waiting for someone to help them board, casualties watched the pigs squeal and push into each other in the small enclosure... if the soldiers didn't make this train, there might not be another to take them away from the front, tonight. As the medical team disembarked the train car, they saw significantly less wounded, than when they left three days ago. Harold was glad to see that the temporary lull in the fighting had held. He glanced around, counting heads to make sure their own group had all made it off the train, and in so doing, spotted some more familiar faces.

"Winston!" Harold exclaimed and reached out a hand to greet the British Doctor. "Very good to see you."

David Winston was jovial. "Lovell! And you all as well... Nurse Charlotte... Laura..." He seemed very happy to see Laura.

Laura shook the hand he offered to her. "Good to see you, Doctor Winston," she said, smiling at him. "We've just come from some time off in Paris."

David shook his head. "Certainly wish I had known that earlier!" he exclaimed. "We're heading there now, five of us, doctors and medics. If I'd known you all were going, we might have arranged this better and gone to see the sights together!" His eyes were fixed on Laura and she felt deep regret that the timing had prevented their two teams from seeing the city together.

"That would have been lovely," Laura admitted modestly, in return.

Marcus chimed in. "Three days doesn't do it justice, Winston," he declared. "But it was a nice diversion."

Wincing, Charlotte heard him say that. She held her peace.

"You'd better board," Harold advised the British group. "Looks like they're calling everyone already."

David gave them a small salute. "Hope we run into each other again soon, when there's more time," he said, and the five British medical personnel headed off for the train.

Marcus watched them go, idly wondering if the British team had ever discovered the nurses on the train, with legs smooth as silk, or if that was a pleasure that he alone had discovered. His own group climbed aboard the truck; their driver was anxious to get back to the station before the dark of night made driving difficult, over the rutted road. They were not pressed together as they had been before, when there had also been wounded in the truck. Now, in place of the wounded, there were bags and bags of foodstuffs, bandages, and medical supplies stacked in the back. They each found a place to perch among the stacks for the ride back. Marcus was glad for that... there was no pressure to sit next to anyone in particular. He slid between stacks of lumpy potatoes and leaned back, trying to ignore the discomfort in his lower rib from the hard potatoes pushing into the abrasion there. Realizing that was too uncomfortable to tolerate, he got up and found a spot beside a pile of new army blankets. Charlotte saw the opportunity of a narrow space beside him and sat down next to him. It was dim now, in the fading sunlight.

"Do you mind, Doctor Lovell?" Charlotte asked.

"Of course not, Nurse Stein," he replied, patting the floor of the truck beside him.

She pushed her way between the piles and was not unhappy that they were pressed together in the small space. Her heart began to beat a little faster, feeling him next to her; she was confused by it. *Just let your hips move with mine...* that's what he had instructed her. Charlotte felt the truck kick into gear, pulling out of the station, horn beeping lightly at the animals and people in the road as it found its way out to the open countryside.

Marcus held his haversack on his lap in front of him and focused on his bruised side. Sometimes physical discomfort was a good diversion... it was now... as she sat pressed up to him.

"Are you glad you were able to see Paris, Doctor Lovell?" Charlotte asked finally, keeping her tone and voice casual.

He nodded in the dim light. "A very nice city to visit. Wouldn't want to live there, though," he replied.

"Really? Why not?" she countered curiously.

"Some cities lose their mystery if you get too familiar with them. If you only go once in a while, then there is always more to discover. Go too often, and it becomes routine," he explained.

She couldn't see his face anymore in the darkness. "But sometimes routine is a comforting thing," she suggested. "When you just need to unwind and feel relaxed, routine is a really nice thing to have."

"I suppose," he admitted. Marcus pulled the top blanket from the pile next to him. He kept it folded and stuffed it between them, along his shoulder. "You might as well rest a bit," he invited Charlotte to make use of the makeshift pillow, for whatever little comfort it would afford her.

She leaned against the rough, woolen army blanket. The barrier between them had not been broken after all. If leaning her head against his shoulder, was all she was going to get for now, she decided she would take it and closed her eyes.

By the time the truck pulled into camp, the night was well upon them. There was no welcoming committee to match the previous send-off. They climbed out of the truck and made their way to their tents, wishing each other a good night's sleep. Marcus and Harold headed for their own tent, but Marcus paused, "I'm gonna find Simon and let him know what he missed out on, if he's still up."

"I'll quickly report in with Fortraine's aide… let him know we're all back, in one piece," Harold said. "I'm beat."

Marcus took a quick look and found Simon and Lydia's tent dark and quiet; he briefly wondered how the couple was doing… he'd meet up with Smon in the morning. Making his way to the doctors' tent, he laid down on his cot, pulling up a blanket. He was too tired right now to figure out what he was doing with his life anyway… for tonight, he was going to focus only on sleep.

Chapter 20
The Explosion

Early the next morning, as the medical team gathered for their first breakfast together in days, they heard the command to break up camp. It was already time to uproot again. They were to move out immediately, to the north, across the Belgian border. The British had been planning an advance to take back the important Messines Ridge, overlooking strategic Ypres. The attack plan was complete. Now, the medical stations needed to move.

"Finish your meals quickly," Harold ordered, unnecessarily, "or they'll pull the mess tent down around us. Good to see you, Simon."

"It's back to work, everybody! That didn't take long," Marlene observed, standing up from the bench and brushing crumbs off of her hands. "By the way, we missed all of you."

Marcus wolfed down the last of his eggs and potatoes, adding between bites, "I see you all kept the home fires burning! Well done, Simon! The war gave us almost two full weeks off, at least. That's something."

"Ypres," Lydia said to the others, as they finished the last of their coffee and filled their canteens for the trip, "was where this all started for me, after England." Marcus looked up quickly and filed away this little tidbit.

Simon took a moment to put his arm around Lydia's shoulders and hugged her. "Maybe it will also be where the war ends. Wouldn't that be a great coincidence?" he added, kissing her cheek. The entire group quickly went their separate ways, assembling their belongings as the soldiers collapsed the poles to load up the tents.

In short order, the camp was packed up, wagons loaded, trucks full, people aboard, and they started the trip to the northeast. They passed Vimy, where the Canadian battle for the ridge had been fought only two months prior, during the grueling Arras offensive, which was still fresh in all of their minds. They continued, crossing over the French border into Belgium, just northeast of Armentières, where they would camp outside of the village.

This entire region along France and Belgium had seen more than its fair share of this war. The fighting around Armentières had been fierce back in 1914. One year later, in nearby Ypres, the deadly chlorine gas had been deployed, leaving the soldiers with a healthy fear of the canister bombs. Small, clustered groups of crosses dotted the countryside. The communities that had been decimated, had not been rebuilt... and the land was trying to heal, but still visibly grieving the injuries of war.

Rumor had it that the battle would begin within the week. They would have just enough precious time to set up supplies and prepare the surgery and the recovery. And then they would wait. The waiting was always hard, no matter how many times they moved and set up the station again. And all of France was waiting for the Americans to arrive. Scraps of information reached the CCS that an American unit was forming to the south, as soldiers arrived off the coast of France and made their way to the front. The American Army was waiting for orders to engage. The medical team knew better than to speculate about when the waiting would end.

As they drove along, Lydia noticed that, despite the recent R&R, the spirits of the nurses were subdued. They were not revived as she had hoped they would be. She immediately took note that Marcus and Charlotte were not paired up within their little group. Lydia was almost relieved, concerned that a bad encounter might cost the station another nurse, and her, another friend. She hadn't had the opportunity to finish her letter to Susannah... or to write a thank you note to Mary Baxter, for that matter. Now, the mail would be delayed by the move... no more mail and parcel deliveries for a while. She decided to talk with each of the nurses individually, to see how she could help them with this new change. The trucks bounced down the road, mile after mile, matching the speed of the mule-drawn wagons. Sitting next to Simon with Abril at her feet, Lydia felt herself start to doze off as they rumbled on. Simon shifted himself to put an arm around her, inviting her to nestle her head into his shoulder, so she could sleep.

Marcus watched the couple's small, simple maneuver and closed his eyes. *Lydia and Simon made relationships look so easy.* Gingerly, Marcus laid back against the side of the truck and tried to get comfortable. His mind drifted back to the nurse on the train. Relationships with nurses in the station were so complicated, but on the train, with Beatrice, it had been very straightforward... easy. He thought back to how Beatrice had caught his eye in the dining car and had ever so slightly nodded her head, guiding him back up through the train. He let himself relive how he had made his way through the passengers waiting to be served their supper, following the black-haired beauty, with silky legs, through the empty patient cars with anticipation. When Beatrice had entered the crew quarters car, she had ducked behind the curtain of a low berth and motioned for him to quickly slide in next to her. Marcus let their encounter replay in his mind as the truck droned on.

In the low light of the enclosed berth, Beatrice had pulled off her white headband and veil, and her black hair had tumbled out. The French nurse had whispered, "Others may be in their berths. I do not think so, but I do not know for sure, and people may walk through the aisle right beside us. This makes it more fun, non?" she had whispered to him mischievously. "I'm very glad you followed me. Now, do not stop your hand at my knee…" She had raised her skirt, revealing her long, smooth, bare legs, encouraging him to feel the softness of her skin. Her eyes had danced with delight, watching his reaction to her.

"Do you like me then?" she had teased him, whispering in his ear, running her fingers between his lips.

He really did like how she had felt under his fingers. "Yes, I certainly do like you," he had whispered back, his anticipation growing. "It's like I'm touching pure silk." The woman clearly knew what she was doing.

She had leaned over to kiss him, letting her black curls fall around him. "Ah, but keep going… it is also pure silk where it matters most, Monsieur Doctor." Then, she had encouraged him to further his inquisitive exploration. After a time, Beatrice kissed him lightly and whispered, "Now it is good we are delayed, oui?"

She had made it impossible for Marcus not to fulfill a rather intense desire for her. Beatrice had laid back again, enjoying how Marcus committed the feel of her to his memory.

Marcus had then leaned over to kiss her lips again and looked into her perceptive blue eyes. "But what about you?" he had whispered in her ear, lingering, concerned that she might not be enjoying his presence, as much as he was hers.

"Oh, monsieur," she had breathed, her eyes twinkling. "I have already danced several times, but I do not make a sound, so you do not hear me. Now, when you get back to your home, you will ask your lover to remove her hair, and you will enjoy it all over again. Perhaps you will even think of your Beatrice."

"But I'm asking my Beatrice to enjoy again, right now, so that I'm absolutely sure she does... sound or no sound," Marcus whispered because he did not believe in things being one-sided. This time, she had let him know, without any lingering doubt.

As the truck bounced along, Marcus thought how simple and easy it had been to be with Beatrice on the train. He regretfully knew he would never see her again, so he considered his options. He assumed Charlotte would be with him again if he needed her, now that she had tasted the forbidden fruit. He looked around at the women in the truck, and his eyes landed on Monique. French Monique, who might offer the same mysteries—or perhaps new ones—as Beatrice. Monique was bold, too, perhaps adventurous. She might be a woman who knew what a man wanted. And she didn't know about Susannah. Her eyes were shut. She was probably asleep. He looked at the very full curves under her shirt. He determined he was going to find out what mysteries she might offer a lonely man such as himself.

Many of the team slept or dozed lightly, still thinking about the city of Paris and what they had seen. The encounter with the wounded at the station, both coming and going, had made an impression on them. Seeing former soldiers on crutches in the streets of the city or being pushed in wheeled chairs had kept the war foremost in their minds. The wounded were all around them. A generation of young men dead and injured... with no end yet in sight. Some of the team wondered how it was that they were allowed to escape the injuries that the soldiers had endured. The medical team stayed near the front, but somehow, they had suffered only one shell landing on top of their camp... the one that had wounded Doctor Finney and claimed the lives of Lieutenant Aubert and several others. The shell that killed many of the wounded they had just tried to save. They had been fortunate, so far, to have only been under fire once, while this country had endured so much.

When the little convoy finally stopped, everyone roused, and the team climbed out of the truck to take in their new surroundings. There was little left of the countryside, but shrubs and holes in the ground from prior bombardments.

"Hope nobody walks in their sleep," Monique observed.

"If you do and you need an escort, let me know," Marcus said, also surveying the hazardous terrain with skepticism, thinking of the horses.

Harold called out, "Everyone knows the drill. Let's get ourselves set up and ready to go. Don't know how much time we've got."

"It'll be hard for the casualties to get in here, with these craters," Charlotte observed cautiously, imagining ambulances trying to navigate the terrain.

"The army thought of that," Harold told them all. "They'll be covering many of them with wood plank bridges."

Nancy shook her head. "Then let's hope it doesn't rain," she added, thinking of litter bearers crossing slippery wood planks with their precious cargo.

Lydia watched Abril exploring her new domain, sniffing out the new smells, alert to each new sound. She turned to Simon with a resigned expression on her face, knowing what was ahead of them all. "I'm going to set up the shelves in supply. See you in a bit."

Simon headed toward where the surgery was being erected. He hoped Fortraine hadn't misjudged this location for the station. They were certainly right out in the open and the environmental hazards were abundant. The armies of the Allies were certainly working hard to be able to claim this particular parcel of destroyed earth. The German army seemed to be just as resolute in their desire to take it again. He watched soldiers efficiently raising the tent poles. Their four surgical tables were assembled side by side, three feet apart. He advised soldiers bearing crates of instruments where to lay them, but by and large, it was an unnecessary gesture. There were a few new people in the station, but most had been with them for the duration and already knew where things should go. Simon saw Harold approaching him from the direction of Fortraine's new command post.

"Got a minute?" Harold asked, as he approached.

Simon answered, "Lots of them, for a little while, at least. What's up?"

"Fortraine told me a little about what he thinks could be coming at us, and soon," Harold started.

Simon quickly noted the worry in his voice. "You sound more than just a little concerned."

"That's an understatement," Harold admitted. "Fortraine relayed that intelligence is suggesting that the coming battle will include very heavy land and air bombardment—large explosives; might change the kind of wounded coming in. It's also, likely, just a prelude to an even bigger battle, also close by. Which means—"

Simon nodded. "Which means we're in it for the long haul, again... so soon after Arras. It also means a greater likelihood we won't be able to save people with concussion injuries."

"My thoughts exactly. And I'm thinking two things," Harold continued. "First, closed concussion, high impact injuries might be better served with a watch and wait, and rapid transport, so we don't fill the recovery with soldiers solely under observation. And second, the role of triage seems heightened. We won't have the ability to perform cranial burr holes for everyone coming in with brain bleeds... or take out ruptured spleens and collapsed lungs." Harold paused. "Which means the nurses, who are making all of those decisions, may need additional support and medical input. But we don't have additional hands for support and input, unless one of us takes a hand at triage. Can we afford to run two surgeons in the surgery so one of us can be out in triage or making rounds in the recovery?"

Simon leaned back against one of the surgical tables with his hands in his pockets. "Well... you heard Mary Baxter. What's learned here in the clearing stations stays in the clearing stations, but can still be learned. Let's teach the nurses about concussion injuries and maybe some of the corpsmen who have an aptitude for working with the wounded."

Harold leaned against another of the tables. "What are you thinking? A crash course in concussions and brain injuries in the next two days?"

Simon nodded. "yeah... but not just brain... soft tissue and organ damage too... the wounded that can turn on a dime. If they don't have a collapsed lung on arrival, they aren't likely to lose one after twenty-four hours post-trauma. If they do, then we can remove a lobe. And then we have to decide if we'll take spleens out here or let the wounded take their chances trying to make it to the field hospitals. But the delayed brain bleeds—different story. Twenty-four or even forty-eight hours post-trauma, they may crunch. It'll make a big difference in how we triage. And we'd have to try to get them to the hospital within forty-eight hours."

Shaking his head, Harold added, "I don't know, Simon. You should have seen that train station with the thousands of wounded waiting for transport. The trains were carrying many hundreds, with every berth and bunk full, and were apparently running constantly during daylight hours, but the casualties were just waiting at the station largely unattended... even ones still bleeding from their wounds. Closed head injuries, those with collapsed lungs, they'll be sitting in that mix without any obvious wounds—"

"And will get the least attention without any obvious signs of injury," Simon finished. "We'd effectively be sending them on from here just to die on the train... or en route to a hospital, in some truck."

The two doctors fell silent.

"You know what I think we need to do?" Simon said. "We need to go ask the nurses for suggestions."

The doctors gathered up Marcus from the doctors' tent and called the nurses together at the newly erected mess. Twelve faces turned to them with curious expressions. Harold explained the situation and what they were anticipating regarding both seen and invisible injuries and turned the discussion over to the twelve for suggestions.

Marlene said, "I can help with the surgery, take some of the load off you doctors."

Harold nodded at her. "I expected you'd say that... was already counting on it, actually."

"We need a way," Lydia interjected, "to start the clock running when a concussion patient comes in. And a separate quiet triage tent to gather them together without all of those with open wounds, with one of us staying with them and watching for subtle changes. Their arrival times can be added to the clipboard so we can watch them for the first two days, and if there are no obvious signs of decompensation, we can send them out on the first available truck after that waiting period. We can monitor their heart rates, breathing, their pupils, and alertness without having to stop for dressing changes on the post-surgical patients."

Charlotte said, "If heavy explosions are going to be used, there are going to be many of those young men arriving deaf, ruptured ear drums... they'll have trouble communicating how they feel. We need to make up some picture and word cards quickly, so they can just point and let us know if they're having headaches and pain... in English and in French."

Nancy added, "We also need a way to elevate the head of the cots for the ones with a collapsed lung having trouble breathing. Maybe some kind of wooden blocks under the head of the cots so they aren't flat on their backs... tilt them up a little."

Then Alice spoke up. "Every one of these boys is going to need their bellies and lower backs checked for bruising and swelling. As long as one of you doctors can come out of surgery when someone looks suspicious, this could work for us to just keep a close eye on them."

"But fractures are going to go up, too," Gretha chimed in. "If they're flying up into the air with explosions, they are going to come down hard. Extra splints and wraps should be on hand."

As the ideas kept coming, Simon finally put up his hand and stopped the nurses. "Better write it all down, and we'll put all of these ideas into practice, immediately. They're all good. Do you nurses all wear watches?"

The nurses looked at each other. One showed her trench watch with its protective lid fastened to one of her wrists. Lydia had a pocket watch, but she rarely took it out of her footlocker, afraid to risk its fragile crystal face breaking, so she just shook her head.

Laura looked at the watch on her own wrist. "I got a military watch from Doctor Winston at the British station," she, shyly, confirmed aloud. "At the New Year's party. He said a nurse should have it. I don't know where he got it from, though."

Simon added, "The British give every single soldier a military-grade wristwatch so they can better coordinate timing while following battle instructions. You nurses must all have one so that you can let us know if a change in a patient is happening over thirty minutes or an hour... and for monitoring heart rhythms. Harold, we've got to talk to Fortraine about the urgency of getting these nurses military-grade wristwatches as quickly as possible... even if we have to find Winston's outfit to get them!"

Harold nodded. "I'll get on that, and the wood blocks for the cots, and another tent for observation, and paper supplies for word cards... and everything else you nurses put on a list. And we're going to teach all of you about concussion injuries and organ collapses to help you better recognize the signs of complications. This afternoon, right after lunch, we start. The more you understand what's happening internally, the better you'll be able to see subtle changes. Doctor Lovell, have you anything to add to this discussion?"

Marcus looked compassionately at the nurses. "I just want to remind everyone that there will also be more Germans wounded with this kind of assault. Just be ready. Also, it's more than reasonable for us to rotate out of the surgery through the triage so we can support you in making these decisions. And concussion injury casualties will die for no obvious reason while they're in our care. Doesn't mean anyone missed anything or did anything wrong. It's just going to happen. No blame involved."

Harold nodded slowly. "That's exactly right. Some will not make it and no one is to blame, except the war. We've always done the best we can as a unit, as a station. Now is not the time to start second-guessing ourselves. We just keep going. And just in case no one has been informed yet, the suggestions Nurse Baxter left for water for hand washing in the triage rows, triage trash bins for dressings, and—"

"and hot water," Monique breathed with a look of content-ment on her face.

Harold continued, "and hot water have all been put into place. They are building the pits now for the fires."

Marcus looked at Monique. "Hot water?" he asked when she sighed in pleasure, raising his eyebrows curiously.

She smiled. "You did not see the new shower when you got back from Paris?" she returned with a little smile in his direction.

He shook his head. "I wasn't aware we had a new shower," he said. Marcus looked at the woman's faraway look of satisfaction while imagining her in the shower. He determined that he would ask her more, before the day was out. If the expression on her face was any indication, it would be well worth the effort.

As soon as the meeting was over, the group dispersed to their fi-nal preparation tasks. Marcus was restless. He took note of Char-lotte hovering in the mess tent and left, avoiding her. Following the others, he noticed where the nurses' tents had been positioned. He berated himself for his curiosity, but after letting himself wake up again with Charlotte and Beatrice, he felt like he had to make up for lost time. He saw Monique head for the recovery tent and decided to follow her in.

She saw him enter after her. "Can I help you, Doctor?" she asked.

He picked up the empty clipboard waiting on the central pole. "Everyone's suggestions were superb," he told her. "Our nurses are incredibly gifted, smart women. We're lucky to have you all."

Monique took the board from him and looked at the sheet. "Hm," she said. "Here, we will add a column for time in and then, on the other end, time out. This will work. I am fortunate Adrielle and I got to come here."

Marcus looked at one of the cots as he stalled for her attention. He lifted the head of one. "I think perhaps three inches on blocks will help them breathe better," he said. "It was a good suggestion. All of the nurses had great input; it's why we save as many soldiers as we do."

She smiled at the compliment. "Did you enjoy Paris, Doctor?" she asked curiously. "I did not hear if you enjoyed your visit to our capital."

Marcus sat on one of the cots. "I did," he said. "It's a magnificent city. There were far too many things to see and do in just three days. We only got a glimpse of everything such an old city has to offer."

"I understand," she admitted. "It would take many months to see everything. I have been there many times, since I was a little girl. I am always glad to go back and see new things." She hung the clipboard back onto its nail on the post and started making up the blankets on the cots. Marcus immediately got up to assist her in smoothing out the rough army browns and folding them to be ready for use.

"Mon Dieu!" she exclaimed softly. "A doctor who makes a bed!"

He smiled. "The army saw fit to teach us how to make a bed and fold things neatly enough to pass inspection, along with how to shoot accurately with a rifle," he reminded her. "Oh, but... you did not have to take basic training. Well, we did and had to pass close inspection of our quarters. The army likes things neat and clean."

Monique moved down the row, preparing the cots, with his help. "You do not need to help me, Doctor Lovell," she protested, but smiling at him.

"My pleasure," he returned. "Too much of the routine work of this station falls on you nurses... I'm very glad that Doctor Fortraine was able to improve things around here, for you."

She looked up as she carefully joined the corners of a blanket together in a neat fold. "Oh, do you mean the shower?" she asked, brightening up. "Yes, that was a very nice thing for Nurse Baxter to recognize as a need... and for Doctor Fortraine to so quickly make it happen. I think he also visited it... as must you, Doctor..."

"A real shower was long overdue," Marcus started.

Monique remained focused on the task at hand. "Yes, but not just a shower! You will see! There is hot water from the tank and also a soaking tub."

Marcus' eyebrows raised. "Really!" he exclaimed. "A tub, here? In the station? With hot water? Can't remember the last time I took a bath..."

Her eyes twinkled. "Yes, really," she returned. "You must try it out. Your toes, they will wrinkle. While you played in Paris, we played in a hot water bath!"

Marcus shook his head regretfully. "And we missed it... the bath, I mean..." He handed her a pillow for the next cot.

"Do not worry, Doctor, there will be time for you to play, after the next battle... or perhaps even before it begins, if you get in line. Since word got out, the line has been long, of people waiting to enjoy."

Marcus laughed, sensing an opportunity. "Then people will have to shorten the line by doubling up!" he said, tucking in the linens as they continued down the row.

She looked at him curiously, leaning close to him as she folded a spare blanket for a cot. "What is the doubling up mean?" she asked.

He winked at her. "Two go in at the same time... to make the line shorter."

Monique considered this. "Two at once makes the line shorter, but the time longer... two at once makes the bath much longer, n'est-ce pas?"

Marcus paused. "Yes, I suppose it would make the bath, much longer... if the two were able to relax and enjoy themselves."

Monique looked around the quiet recovery tent, satisfied with their work. "Two have made this task much shorter!" she told him gratefully. "You have time to go see for yourself the new, hot shower."

"Care to join me?" he teased her lightly, hoping she would say yes.

But Monique just smiled at him, touching his shoulder. "Not now, Doctor. For now, I go to do my nails and enjoy my book. Later... I think, yes?"

He nodded hopefully. "And what are you reading?" he wondered.

"*Wuthering Heights*. I found it in a box of things in recovery. It is English and many pages, so I read so slowly. Many words I do not understand." She sighed, looking at his dark, wavy curls, then smiled.

Marcus nodded. "Well, if you need help, let me know. I know this book and will gladly read it to you. You'll enjoy the story better if it flows smoothly."

"Perhaps we will do this," she nodded. They left the recovery tent to go their separate ways, but Marcus, as he wished her a good evening, now was more hopeful than ever that their paths would cross again, and soon... she seemed to indicate they might.

Two days had passed quickly. The camp had just started to rouse with the morning light, when it happened. Cook had breakfast well started. The camp flag had been raised. The medical team, along with soldiers waking up, were dressing and pulling on their boots or already starting their morning routines. When the first explosion came, the ground beneath them rolled like a ship on the high sea, facing a tremendous wave in the midst of a tempest. Anything not fastened down quickly clattered to the ground. A few of the small tents collapsed around the people still inside. The thunder of the explosion shook through their bones and caused them to clap their hands over their ears in pain. Some who were standing, lost their footing, many falling to the ground. The horses and mules tied to the lines screamed and pulled against their tethers in terror.

As the doctors and nurses stumbled from the tents into the open air, they joined the soldiers who were staring toward the Messines Ridge, just to the east of their camp, where an enormous cloud of dirt particles and debris had risen, towering into the air. This was followed in rapid succession by another, and yet still another, in a series of earth-rending explosions, shaking the ground beneath their feet. More clouds rose, followed by thunderous booms, delayed by just seconds—long enough for the sound to travel the few short miles from where they stood watching the new battlefront forming.

"Dear God," Lydia breathed, clinging to Simon for balance as they looked at the horizon where the sky and earth had merged as one. "What have they done?"

He shook his head, "That's not cannon fire or shelling…"

Harold stood, stricken with concern. "It's worse than I could have imagined… those explosions were from underground."

Overhead, they saw planes approaching in formation, from the west. Under the cover of the clouds of dirt and smoke, the shells fell invisibly from the sky. Onlookers reflexively clung to, whoever was beside them, for support, as the planes dropped their payloads into the melee on the ridge. Simultaneously, land-based missiles arced across the countryside, heading toward the east.

Nancy said, to no one in particular, "How can any wounded make it out of that…"

"They are only miles away," Simon reminded them all. "We can expect wounded within twenty minutes."

Harold nodded. "Do whatever you have to do, and quickly people. Once we start, we're likely to be busy for quite a while."

Soon, trucks and ambulances were skidding into the triage, unloading Allied and German wounded, alike. Most of the German soldiers were triaged for immediate surgery as most of them had missing limbs and bones poking out through their skin. They had been the target of the underground explosives planted by the Allies to decimate the German army in their maze of trenches. Allied soldiers at the front lines, near the blasts, arrived as expected, ears bleeding and shocking, blood-red eyes from ruptured capillaries. Some were blinded. The team swung into well-practiced motion. As the triage nurses directed blast casualties into the dedicated quiet tent, for observation, they carefully recorded the time of arrival and started the ticking clock against major internal bleeds.

Simon remained out in the open-air triage for several hours with Monique, Alice, and Laura as they practiced their assessment skills: looking into the eyes of the wounded, listening to lungs for consistent breathing, checking abdomens for signs of bruising forming deep within. When he was satisfied that they were proficient in their new role of directing the wounded to wait for surgery, either under a tarp or in the observation tent, he left the triage and rejoined the surgery. He saw the steadily growing line of Allied and German casualties, intermingled, too many to even separate, with soldiers patrolling the entire triage... and Abril circling the perimeter, ever vigilant over her charges. Inside the surgery, Simon scrubbed in and donned an apron. Marlene was at work doing minor surgeries under Harold's watchful eye. Nearly a fourth of the casualties were German. Simon saw Gretha at her favorite post, circulating; giving reassurance and explanations in English and German, as needed, to calm the frantic and confused.

Lydia, Adrielle, and Nancy moved through the recovery and observation tents, receiving the post-op wounded with their fresh bandages, as well as those who sat and stared, unseeing, unhearing—stunned into an involuntary silence by the circumstances. They carried their word cards—pointing, gesturing, watching for understanding or small responses—grateful when a wounded man could be reached and his needs communicated. They had not done any cards in German, Lydia noted regretfully, but picture cards of faces displaying various expressions of fear or pain were helpful. Still, the need for words in German would have to be rectified. Adrielle came to Lydia's side in observation and said softly, "The recovery is backing up, now that surgery is in full swing."

Lydia nodded, shining her flashlight into a soldier's eyes. "Go on, help them out. I'm okay here, just send a corpsman, or who-ever else looks available, for an extra set of hands, here."

Adrielle slipped out to help in the recovery, and soon after, one of the corpsmen came into the observation tent to support as needed. Lydia kept the sides of the tent largely drawn from the daylight. The dim lighting made it easier on the men with eye injuries and created a sense of quiet and calm. She moved down the rows of men, checking for tremors, loss of movement on one side of the body, sudden abdominal pain, and changes in the size of their pupils. It felt otherworldly, looking into the many pairs of bright red eyes with black pupils, as tiny arteries had ruptured under the pressure of the bombs and explosions. It was eerie to look at their faces, and she strove to look past the damage, to the men underneath.

One of the wounded pulled at her hand as she passed by. He was British. "Nurse," he said quietly, "my head hurts pretty bad."

She bent over him and checked him for changes. "Which side?" she said softly. "Show me."

He pointed to his head over his right ear. "Here," he said. "Is there something for pain? Is there whiskey?"

"You can have something soon," she reassured him. "Right now, I need you to stay awake to tell me how you feel and if the headache changes. Squeeze my fingers. Show me how strong you are…"

He obeyed. She felt the weakness starting in his left arm and turned to the corpsman. "Go tell the doctors one of the head injuries is coming over and get some litter bearers to take him."

The corpsman nodded.

The soldier rallied briefly. "Am I going to make it, Nurse?" he asked Lydia.

"We're going to get you to the operating tent very soon," she reassured him. "The surgeons will take the pressure off of your brain, and that will help."

He reached out and took her hand again. "You didn't answer the question. It's okay. I already know the answer. Will you reach in my pocket and take the picture out for me, Nurse?"

She retrieved what he was seeking and tried to put it in his hand, his unnatural bright red eyes watching from a face, pale with pain.

"No," he slightly shook his head. "On the paper around it is her name and address. Please… keep it, Nurse, and if I don't make it, tell her she was the last thing I was thinking of up till the very end."

Lydia felt her eyes fill. "I'll keep it safe," she assured him, reading the tag hanging on the chain around his neck. "Byron Hereford. I'll take care of the picture, Byron. I'll make sure she knows… if you can't tell her yourself, that is."

He nodded with relief. "It took us over a year to dig all the tunnels under the trenches for the explosives. When the TNT went off, I thought the world had ended. Everything was moving all around me. It got so dark, so black… it was like night came, and I couldn't tell which way was up, or down. Turns out I was down. How about that, huh? I can't see very well right now, Nurse…

things are getting a little fuzzy. My head is splitting. I sure hope I don't go blind... I don't want to go blind..."

The litter bearers arrived to take Byron directly to the surgery, where one of the doctors was waiting. Lydia touched Byron's cheek and watched him be carried off through the tent opening. She already knew she would be writing the letter, for him, to the girl he had carried to war in his pocket. Her heart broke, and she tucked the tiny pieces deep inside, where such things must go, when the need all around is so great. And then she turned to the next wounded man being brought in, already filling Byron's place on the cot in the dim tent. Carefully, Lydia noted the time on the clipboard next to the name on his tag—Heinrich Stauffer—she checked him carefully and continued to make her rounds.

By the time night fell, Lydia was exhausted. She had rotated from observation to recovery and out to triage, in four-hour intervals. Now, she stumbled over to her tent for some sleep. She didn't see Abril in the darkness, but was certain the dog was shepherding the wounded under the tarps. Lydia sat on the edge of her cot briefly and took the picture of the dark-haired young girl in the tiny black and white square tin type from her pocket. She peered at the words on the inside of the brown paper wrap, lettered neatly in ink. The name and address were clearly printed so there could be no mistake.

Mary Stevenson. Mary, who Byron was not going to come back home to. She looked like she was barely out of school. What it must have cost them to have procured an actual likeness of her. How carefully he must have tended to the little square, wrapped as it was in a brown piece of paper. How often had he taken it out while he waited for the call to charge forth into battle? How difficult it would be for her to receive the letter that now had to be written and sent to England. *By the time Mary receives my note, weeks will have already passed*, Lydia thought sadly. She wondered if somehow the young girl could sense in her spirit even now that Byron was gone. People sometimes reported that strange sense of loss, even over a distance. Lydia placed the tiny picture into her locker for safekeeping and fell onto the cot. A few tears slid from her eyes before exhaustion took her.

In the darkness, she had to fight again with her demons. They came to her with penetrating red eyes, staring at her in the night, mocking her helplessness. They chased her down the trenches, where a single light bulb made the shadows of the menace grow ever larger, narrowing the distance between them. She saw the ladder up ahead in the trench... if she could only reach that ladder...but the rats ran around and over her boots, causing her to stumble. She slipped off the wood plank beneath her feet and fell into the muddy trench, where cold brown ooze sucked her feet up to the ankles so she couldn't move, as the bright red eyes with black pupils bore down on her. Lydia tried to scream for help, but no sound came from her mouth, only garbled nonsense as the shadows caught up and reached for her in the mud.

She had screamed and not realized it. Tears ran from her eyes as she batted at the blood-red eyes overtaking her. Then, Lydia felt strong arms around her and heard the words, "You're safe, Lydia. It's okay now." She burrowed into the arms, sobbing into his chest in very real terror.

He held her tightly against him. "You're safe with me..." he murmured to her again, stroking her hair for comfort, pulling her closer.

But she felt her shirt rip open, cold air striking her bare breasts as he mocked her. "Beg me to hurt you," he hissed in her ears. "This is meant to hurt." She felt his hands thrusting inside her trousers, fingers groping, grasping, tearing at her. The hardness of his crop pressed into her. She tried to push him away and realized he was much, much too strong for her. "It's such a little thing you have to do," he taunted her. She felt his hands around her throat until she couldn't breathe, pushing her down where piles of amputated arms and legs reached up, pulling at her clothes and hair. Then there was a scuffle and a pulling away, and the dismembered hands actually let her go. She fell back onto the plank in the trench, and the rats ran over her, fleeing. The red-eyed demon hesitated, angry and brooding over her, mocking her nakedness. The ladder was up ahead, and Abril was barking and whining, pulling her forward, her furry body pressed against her legs. She climbed and climbed the never-ending ladder until her legs ached toward the black sky overhead, never reaching the top.

Lydia heard Simon's voice. "Just look ahead until you can see me," she heard him say from far off. "I'm waiting, I'm watching for you. You can make it. Follow Abril and come back to me, my beloved. I'm waiting right here."

"I'm afraid!" she whimpered, her voice broken. "I can't make it."

"Yes, you can," he told her firmly. "Open your eyes, you'll see me. I'm watching for you, my love."

Abril whined and licked her hand. The dog put a paw up on her arm, and Lydia felt it. At last, she realized her eyes were indeed closed and that she had to open them. There was a lantern lit in the tent. Simon was sitting cross-legged nearby on the floor, anxious but calmly watching, waiting, giving her space, keeping his distance. Lydia tried to focus, the night terror still hovering too near the edge of her awareness, confusing what was real from what was not. Abril was alert, beside the cot, watching... and nuzzling her with her soft nose.

Slowly, Lydia sat up. She saw that she was fully clothed. Nothing was out of place. There was no one in the tent except for Simon and Abril, who now, satisfied that the crisis was over, plopped down comfortably on the ground. Lydia looked over at Simon, who was still sitting, waiting. She saw his familiar brown eyes, full of concern, and held fast to them. Brown eyes... not piercingly red... brown, familiar eyes. She clutched at her closed shirt, hiding behind it.

"Simon..." Lydia whispered, trying to find what was real. "What day is it? What time is it?"

"It's Thursday..." he told her, "... around ten... at night."

"Would you come closer?" she asked, trembling violently.

He nodded, scooting himself over to just beside the cot. Lydia reached out a hand and traced the lines of his face and eyebrows, feeling the soft beard covering his chin and how his mustache stopped short of his mouth, leaving a border of smooth skin around his lips—lips that her fingers had traced many, many times before. It should have felt safe. It should have felt right and good. It didn't. He looked up at her sitting on the cot.

"See me now?" he asked slowly, noticing that her trembling was easing and her eyes were clearing.

"I see you," she whispered. "Simon, I'm afraid to sleep…", *with you.*

"I know. The trench again?" he replied softly. "Can I sit up there with you yet?"

She nodded. "Yes, please," she said, but she wasn't actually sure.

Simon got up from the ground, stepped over the reclining dog, and carefully sat down beside her on the cot.

Lydia took his hand and traced the fingers she knew so well. She lifted his hand to her cheek and pressed it there, finally kissing his palm. He waited quietly, his soul wrenched in his chest, thinking—for the thousandth time—that he should have taken her back to the States, long ago.

"Simon," she said finally, feeling guilty and ashamed of her internal conflict. "Remember when we talked about Father James?"

"Yes," he answered, "of course."

"About sometimes it's because of want, sometimes it's because of promises, sometimes it's for comfort?"

"I remember."

"Is it wrong to do it when we're… I mean, when I'm, afraid?"

Simon looked puzzled. "Help me understand," he implored.

She swallowed. "I know being with you isn't supposed to be a bandage against pain. I know it's not supposed to be about using a good thing to drive away a bad thing… but remember the music box and how it took us somewhere else? And how usually, we can get above any ugliness around us, to where the light is shining, the air is pure, and everything makes sense again? It's awful, but right now, I'm afraid that I can't make it there again, with you…

to where the light is shining, because there's something telling me that our being together is... ugly... and it's inside me, and if I don't try to fix it, right now, while I'm afraid... then I'll be too afraid to ever try, and the lies, inside, will win."

"Just tell me what you need to do," he reassured her. "I want you to know that you are stronger than this."

Lydia looked down at the dog watching them. "Abril, door," she said softly. Abril quickly got up, stretched, pushed her way through the tent flap, and fell to the ground out in front of their tent door, without ceremony.

Simon stood up and followed her, then tied the tent flap closed. Then he turned to Lydia. "Okay," he said. "Just tell me... whatever it is..."

"Don't you need to be in surgery?" she asked him.

Simon shook his head. "Nope. Marcus took it for me. We now have whatever time we need."

Lydia stood. "This isn't going to make sense. I need my body to belong to me, and you, without letting the ugliness lie to me about us. I need to be in control so that if I have to stop to chase, something, away, I can stop. I need to get rid of... the shame. Can you do this for me?"

He sat down on the cot after following her cue. She undressed until she was vulnerable. She sat down next to him and said quietly, "I hope this is the last time I'll need to ask this of you. I hope the nightmares end. I need the light to shine on every inch of us, so there is nothing saying it's unclean or shameful anymore."

He nodded. "Remember that I love you, every inch."

"I'm counting on that," she said.

Lydia moved to the foot of the cot as he laid back. She reached out her fingers and traced his toes, the arch of his foot, the line of scar running up his lower leg from the terrible explosion that nearly cost him his life. She remembered fighting to save him and to bring him back to her, when he was in his own despair. She renewed her covenant with his feet and his legs, his knees and his thighs.

Simon let her chase away her demons in her own time, in her own way. She moved up and renewed the wonder of his face and his neck, his shoulders and his chest. And, always, she looked back into his brown eyes, seeking in them the solid bond of his love for her, while casting out any lies lurking within her. Simon braced himself for the possibility that she might have to stop there, watching for any sign that she was slipping back into the terror of the night. Once, he involuntarily reached up for her, hovering over him, and immediately realized it was too soon when she pulled back. He willed himself to lay still under her hands. After a bit, she started reacquainting herself with his manhood, silently wrestling with any demon claiming the right to make her afraid of the power rising in Simon's body to love her, trying to turn it into something that should be despised. Simon sensed her struggle and urgently prayed to God above that she wouldn't be swept back into the nightmare that had violated her, yet again.

Finally, Simon heard Lydia let out a long breath that he felt against his skin like a caressing whisper. The light was shining all around her again. There were no mocking red-eyed demons, left anywhere, to steal her away from the one she loved. She had made it into the pure air again. She sat back on the cot beside Simon and nodded, feeling peace.

"I love you. What we do is a beautiful thing," she was free once more. "Simon... please make love to me."

Immediately, Simon did so. He laid her down, moved over her, and took her, keenly aware of the power in his body as he did so, holding her gaze with his, keeping her connected with him, even at the same time that he was causing her to lose herself to him. And when he was absolutely certain that she would not need to turn back, Simon took her right along with him up into the light.

Chapter 21
Second Time Around

Lydia slept for hours. It was dawn when she woke, still wrapped in Simon's arms. The day's early light crept into the quiet tent. For a moment, she wondered if she was dreaming. Was the war still on? Were they still in France? Oh wait, they were in Belgium now, weren't they? What had happened through the night with the others, with the wounded? Where should they be? She felt Simon's body, lean and hard against her back, felt his arms holding her, his hand cupped around her breast even in his sleep. He breathed softly into her ear, sensed her awakening, and stirred against her. He kissed her neck, and she turned her head to look into his eyes.

"What on earth are we doing? The sun will be coming up!" she whispered, feeling guilty. "I should be in the recovery! You should be getting ready for surgery!"

Simon kept his hand where it was and gave a gentle squeeze. He kissed her neck again and her shoulder.

"We'll be in both places soon enough," Simon assured her. "But before we get up, I need to know... did you sleep as soundly as it seemed?"

She rolled over onto her back, causing his hand to shift, dropping lower, protectively, over her softest curls, where he let his hand linger. She allowed him to rest there, feeling a sense of safety. "I really did. Did you?"

His eyes twinkled. "I had no trouble at all."

"Last night seems like a long time ago," she started. "It feels a little unreal, a little supernatural, sort of…"

"Hmmm, supernatural lovemaking," Simon observed. "That's a new one, but… I like it. Yes, that describes it pretty well. It was a very good thing, Lydia." He leaned over her and kissed her.

She nodded after he lifted his lips from her own. "It really was a good thing, my love. I'm not feeling ashamed now. Parts of last night are still a little confusing, but I think I'd rather let that just go… because I feel whole right now, and I don't want anything to change that."

His hand shifted a little farther down. "We could have breakfast in bed…" he offered.

She laughed softly. "You would still be hungry."

He leaned over her chest and teased her, "I could fill up on you…"

Lydia only laughed, reaching for her shirt and trousers. She was glad that she felt free to laugh with him.

Reluctantly, Simon watched her get dressed, pull her hair into a bun on the back of her head, and tie the scarf around her hair. "I enjoy watching you get dressed as much as I enjoy watching you get undressed," he observed.

"Is that so?" she teased. "Well, I shall get dressed more than undressed, and we'll test your theory."

He shook his head. "I stand corrected. It isn't the same thing at all… Well, I can see you've made up your mind. It's going to be biscuits and hash, then." He got up quickly to dress: pants, shirt, boots. As he ran a comb through his hair, he cocked his head to one side, listening. "I don't hear any planes yet."

"Might be a good sign," Lydia added, waiting for him to join her as they headed to the latrine and then to the mess tent. "But the sun is just coming up, so they still have time to make a run at the ridge."

"Harold says the explosions are over," Simon told her as they headed into the mess. "He was told the battle for the ridge today will be back to foot soldiers and artillery… no more underground detonations."

Lydia reached over and squeezed his hand. "Thank God for that! Bullets are bad enough."

Many of the team were already in line, ready with trays, for breakfast Cook had prepared. Marcus was ahead of them as well. He collected his breakfast and tin cup of coffee and found a seat at the table. Lydia watched Cook fill her plate, thanked him, and went over to join Marcus where he sat. She saw immediately that he had a bruise on his face, and in dismay, she leaned over to touch it very gently.

"What on earth happened here?" she exclaimed, concerned.

He looked up and gave her a little smile as Simon joined them with his own breakfast tray. "I walked into a tent pole in my sleep last night," he told her. "Just too tired to see where I was going."

Simon looked over at him with an appraising eye. "Series of unfortunate events, buddy. That looks like it hurts."

"A bit," Marcus admitted dryly. "You look like you got some rest."

"A bit," Simon answered. "Thanks to you, my friend."

Lydia looked over at him. "Why thanks to Doctor Lovell?"

Marcus took a bite of hash. "I owed him one, so I went over to the surgery for your husband last evening," he explained to her.

"Oh, thank you, Doctor," Lydia told him gratefully, starting in on her breakfast. "But I'm sure you must be exhausted."

Marcus shook his head. "Least I could do for a friend. Wasn't that big a deal," he told them both. "Anyway, Stockton and I wrapped it up in an hour or so after the armies figured out that they'd wreaked enough havoc for one day. Lots of havoc going around yesterday."

"That's certainly true," Lydia said quietly, thinking of fighting her way through her own personal battle. But there was no shame, she noted gratefully, in the reflection, now. She was at peace. "I think I'd like to join you in the surgery today, gentlemen," she added. "I'm going to see if Nurse Mitchell will switch out with me." Peace or no peace, she wasn't entirely sure she was ready to look back into the rows of red eyes, in the observation tent. Perhaps those sleeping under the anesthesia would be better. She looked up to the top of the tent as the sound of planes and the distant boom of artillery fire reached the camp. Everyone in the mess tent looked up.

"And so it begins again," Marcus said, finishing off his coffee. "I'm very glad that you were able to rest, Nurse Finney. See you soon." He got up, returned his tray to the mess line, and walked out of the tent.

"He's too tired if he's walking into tent poles, Simon," Lydia observed, shaking her head. "That was nice of him to let you rest with me last night, but he'd better get some sleep today."

"I've never walked into a tent pole," Simon stated. "Some people just lose their way, and it smacks them right in the face." He recalled seeing how Marcus had bounced off the tent pole last night after Simon had pulled him away from Lydia. Marc was still a work in progress. Simon understood that Marcus had heard her scream and wanted to help. But he should have known better than to approach her in the middle of a night terror. Since he had had the sense to send Abril for Simon, he should have had the sense to just wait for Simon to get there instead of trying to hold onto Lydia—for her own safety—even with the best of intentions.

"Well, it looks like it hurt," Lydia said, unaware of what Simon was keeping to himself. She followed him out of the mess tent over to the surgery. There, she found Nurse Mitchell, who was more than willing to trade duties for the morning. Lydia scrubbed her hands to get ready for the wounded, still marveling at the hot water of the holding tank. They knew that some of the casualties coming into the station first thing this morning would have been lying in the field for the entire night before, not being found till the light of day.

Old wounds were harder to treat than fresh ones. It always meant more cutting and clearing away of the things that ate away at people during the darkness. It was frightening how quickly wounds could fester and gangrene could set in, on the battlefield. Especially now that summer provided a warm, fertile field for bacteria and flies, eager to lay their eggs at every opportunity.

In the surgery, everyone took to their duties. There were two nurses on duty in the observation tent, carefully monitoring the men without visible wounds—men who could be bleeding internally and required immediate care if any symptoms changed. The recovery readied themselves to ship some of stable wounded to field hospitals, just waiting for trucks to arrive that could convey them. The triage area filled rapidly with the wounded who had been gathered from the field of battle at the first light of day. Many of these casualties had lost a great deal of blood during the night. Some too weak for even the simplest surgery were wrapped, splinted, and waiting for the first available truck to get them to a field hospital where there would be blood transfusions and intravenous fluids available.

As the day's fighting intensified, the newly wounded started coming in by ambulance, now with bullet and burn wounds or shrapnel from artillery lobbed over the ridge by the Germans to the east. Most of the casualties coming in were British troops. All of the fighting to secure the ridge was to gain the northern line of the trenches to protect Ypres, so the Allies could circle the German army from the north and try to drive them back through Belgium. Doctor Fortraine relieved Marcus for the first half of the day while he slept after breakfast. The nurses held to their shifts, taking time to rest, knowing more would be needed throughout the upcoming night, in the recovery.

Lydia was grateful to be in the surgery with Simon. She was glad for the quick efficiency of the scalpel, the clean removal of the debris of war, the blessed sleep of the ether protecting the wounded from pain, and the hope of healing they provided. There was an unending, but purpose-driven, rhythm to the surgery, like the eddies of a stream, always in motion, but at least heading somewhere. On occasion, the doctors followed suit with Simon, who had continued to, periodically, operate from a stool beside the table, even long after his leg had healed. It was good to be relieved of standing hour upon hour, and the others realized it helped them endure long periods of time on their feet.

When Simon took a break, Lydia joined Marcus, who was starting up at his table. He received her assistance gladly... the shy and a bit hesitant Adrielle being less of a help to him, during difficult operations. When Lydia had offered to give Adrielle a break, the younger nurse seemed grateful. Lydia slid into place with washed hands and a clean apron. She peered at the bruise still marking Marcus' face.

"You look a bit more rested, Doctor Lovell, but I'm worried about your bruise," Lydia observed as he appraised the open abdomen of the wounded man in front of him. "Were you able to sleep at all?"

Marcus smiled at her behind the face mask covering his mouth. "I did, thanks to Fortraine this morning. Didn't expect that from him... my head is fine, don't be concerned."

"I think Doctor Fortraine must have also been concerned, if he saw you were too tired to see where you were going," she concluded. "I think he's keeping track of who is working late into the night."

Marcus took the scalpel she handed him and began cleaning out the wound. "And that was me... and Stockton, of course. But we were done by midnight. How about you, Nurse Finney? Are you sleeping okay in our new little home away from home here in the bosom of Belgium?"

She glanced up at him. "Sometimes it isn't so easy," she admitted.

"Ah. Longing for the creature comforts of hearth and home, I expect... clamps, back under the bowel there, please," he offered.

She placed the clamps, avoiding the large aorta pulsating in the man's open body. "That always amazes me," she said, marveling as she looked down.

"What's that?" he countered. "How people can sleep at a time like this? Or..."

"No," she shook her head. "The aorta... the lifeline for the heart, for the body. How remarkable that so much rests on that single vessel... there's a bleeder..."

"Got it," he nodded. "You were really paying attention in your classes, weren't you, Nurse... retract the bowel there..."

She reached her hand in and pulled the bowel away so he could see. "And look how narrowly the shrapnel missed it... lodged right at the juncture. Wait! Is that the renal artery? Did I get it right, Marc?"

"It is. Good for you," Marcus said approvingly. "We need to try to get out that piece of debris right where the renal arteries are branching, without causing damage. It's awfully close. Could sever the renal, and he'll bleed to death or lose a kidney if I have to clamp off the artery."

She shined a light deep inside the opening where the shrapnel gleamed. "I know that you are really good at this, but... how are you going to suture that if it bleeds so close to the artery?"

"We'll use the new cautery we just received and hope we don't fry anything important," Marcus said casually.

Lydia looked over at him worriedly.

"You did say once my hands are pretty steady, didn't you?" he teased her, his eyes twinkling at her skepticism.

"At some point, I'm sure I did," she admitted. "When you weren't so worn out."

Marcus held out his hand, and it was absolutely still. "Is that good enough?" he asked, waiting for her approval.

She nodded, "It is for me," and she called Gretha to bring their newly acquired cautery probe and the burner they used to heat it.

Marcus eyed her over his mask. "You unwedge the shrapnel, I'll use the cautery right after you," he said. In one smooth motion, she tugged the shrapnel free, and he touched the bleed in several spots with the tool that hissed slightly, releasing the smell of burned tissue. Lydia shined the light back into the wound while Marcus peered closely at the outcome.

"What do you think, Doctor?" she whispered. "Did it work?"

He nodded, not taking his eyes from the wounded man's cavity. "Everything is still pulsating, including the collaterals. Nothing is bleeding. I think it's going to be okay. You have a quick, steady hand yourself, Nurse Lydia."

Lydia returned the cautery to the holding unit and breathed a sigh of relief. She enjoyed doing surgery with the skilled man beside her.

He looked into her eyes, and Lydia saw that he was amused. "You didn't trust me, did you, Nurse Finney!" he said softly. "That's okay, sometimes I don't even trust myself."

"I do trust you, Doctor Lovell, more than you realize," she returned evenly, holding his gaze. She had trusted him with Simon fully.

Marcus was taken aback. He hadn't expected her to say that, especially at that moment, and he didn't know what she was referring to. This morning at breakfast, she hadn't seemed to recall anything at all about the night before when he'd gone into her tent during her nightmare. Now, he didn't know if she was referring to that or something else and had just been reluctant to say so in front of Simon earlier.

He finished up in the wounded man's abdomen and turned to Lydia, "Well, that's a good thing... that you trust me. I haven't always come through for you in the way I've wanted to. It's hard on me, to see you afraid."

She rinsed the wound out carefully with the Dakin's solution and reflected on this. "You've seen me afraid on more than one occasion, that's certainly true. I don't want... I don't want to be a burden, on anyone."

Marcus remembered each time clearly. He remembered her flashbacks and her terrified cry for him when Simon was lying on the table, about to be amputated, her frantic plea for him to help her when the infection took hold in Simon's wound. She had specifically called for his help, for him above all of the others. How could he not have run to her side when he heard her scream in the darkness last night, their tents less than ten feet apart? How could he have waited for the dog to do its job?

They followed the wounded man to the door of the surgery as the litter bearers carried him off to the recovery. The two stopped at the sink and started to wash the blood from their hands.

"You're safe with me," he now told Lydia, quietly, as they stood at the sink where no one could overhear. "I only want you to know that I care about you. No burden. Never let anyone make you think otherwise."

She looked up at him oddly over the running water. "I do know that, Marcus. And I care about you, too. Next to Simon, you are very important to me. I only wish that—"

She was interrupted by traffic at the door: new wounded being carried in, the switching out of staff as they rotated in and out, and Simon returning from his break. Lydia looked at Simon, as he came close to the sink, with unrestricted love in her eyes, which Marcus also saw, making him feel the familiar surge of both appreciation and jealousy. Simon met her gaze, equally focused, and the other doctor suddenly felt the gnawing emptiness he sometimes experienced when he was around them. Simon leaned over the sink and plunged his hands into the warm running water.

"What did I miss?" he asked cheerfully, soaping up. "Boy, does that hot water feel great!"

"You wouldn't believe it! Doctor Lovell used the cautery and saved a renal artery from bleeding where it branched off the aorta," Lydia said in a rush. "He was so quick. It was amazing." She dried her hands on a towel.

Simon looked over at Marcus with respect. "Wow! It really worked? Could you pinpoint with it? Is the tip fine enough? Did it hold the heat long enough? What do you think about using the cautery when we..."

Lydia was momentarily invisible. The two surgeon friends made their way back to their tables, talking quickly about the advantages of having this new device in the surgery. Marcus never got to hear what Lydia was going to wish for. The genie was back in the proverbial bottle, once again. Lydia returned to the table to work with Simon, as was her usual preference, but Marcus wished she had stayed with him a little longer, so they could have finished their conversation and his question could have been answered. It was going to drive him to distraction, unless he found an outlet somewhere. That was the moment he realized Charlotte had rotated into the surgery and taken the position of his nurse assistant for the next wounded man being brought to the table.

"Nurse Stein!" Marcus said softly, noticing the stragglers of copper-colored hair framing her head scarf. "Good to see you. It's been an intense couple of days since we've been back, hasn't it?"

She blushed slightly. "It has been intense," she said, moving into position at his side. The patient before them had a significant amount of burnt tissue on one of his arms and half of his chest. It was going to take time to clean the man and debride the crackled flesh, giving him the best chance to heal. And Marcus felt Charlotte's nearness. He settled himself in for the operation ahead and decided just to appreciate her willingness to work closely beside him, knowing already she had chosen to be there for the duration of his shift in the surgery. *May as well make the best of it*, Marcus thought to himself. Lydia's wish, whatever it had been, began to recede to the back of his mind where it would wait for later satisfaction. "So, Nurse Stein," he said lightly. "How have you been since the ground started heaving all around us?"

Charlotte looked at him over her mask as they set to work clearing away any skin that was no longer viable. "I just did what you told us to do, Doctor," she replied. "Thought back on some nice experiences made during our R&R and enjoyed them all over again."

"That so?" he said. "That's good advice. Are you sure I was the one who gave it?"

She nodded, "You did. Some of the nurses are still going on about what they got to see and do. It's been a good thing for them to have something to share other than how many dressings they've changed in a shift."

"And how about you?" Marcus asked carefully. "Have you had good things to share?"

She shook her head. "I prefer to keep things more to myself, actually," she said evenly. "Seems like it kind of spoils things otherwise."

He nodded. "Hm, I'd like to hear about it sometime. Maybe later this evening if the powers that be decide to let up on us a little? Let's not go too deep around the axilla here... I don't want to cut down too close to the artery and risk losing blood flow to his arm..."

"Maybe later," she agreed as she helped position the wounded man's upper arm. She felt her heart speeding up in her chest with his nearness, and it was confusing. "We could do that."

They set themselves to the task in front of them, but the wounded kept on coming. The clipboards of names hanging on the pole of the recovery tent kept adding pages. The sun moved across its zenith. And the stream of the surgery just kept flowing... so later never came.

On day three of the battle for the ridge, they were all getting tired. Gretha had dropped a tray of instruments; Stockton had missed a gauze in a wounded man's belly and had to reopen him to find it. Numerous patients had died on the tables in the surgery almost before the surgery had even gotten underway. And the anesthetists were complaining they were running low on ether.

Harold sent a message to Fortraine that something had to be done about the ether situation. They could not operate on men lying there awake, looking back at them. Fortraine himself came to the door of the surgery to find out what was needed. Harold Stockton motioned him inside, close enough to talk.

"Can you send someone for supplies?" Harold asked the station commander. "Maybe one of the other stations has ether to spare. If not, let's find these men some whiskey, or else we'll have to knock them out with a club."

Fortraine raised a hand to stop him. "I got the message," he said calmly. "I'll see what I can do, Doctor." He left the surgery and headed to the recovery to talk to the nurses there about their situation as well. In the recovery, he found Lydia rounding with Alice and Laura as they tended to a long line of men on cots. "It's getting crowded in here. What do you need?" he asked them. "As long as we're making a list, I thought I'd better ask."

"We're running out of space," Lydia told him, looking at the rows of casualties stretched out around them. "And we haven't been able to ship out the wounded yet. We didn't get a truck of supplies yesterday. We're running out of the usual: bandages, Dakin's, blankets, gauze," Lydia rattled off her mental checklist. "And flashlight batteries are sorely needed. We're using them up rapidly checking the soldiers with head trauma."

Fortraine nodded. "I'll send someone to the field hospital near Amiens, right away, to see what we can find."

"And Doctor Fortraine," Lydia added. "What about the watches for the nurses? Can we get at least one for each tent to tie to the clipboard in the observation tent, one that we could all share?"

Fortraine nodded. "You deserve better than that," he said. "I asked for eleven, one for each of you. They just have not arrived yet."

"We're using Nurse Bertolli's right now in the observation tent. It's the only one we have. But the flashlight batteries are critical," Lydia added. "And more cots for the wounded. We're running out of room to lay them down."

"The Dakin's is more critical," Alice added.

"So are the bandages," Laura chimed in.

"I understand, nurses," he said again. "It's all critical. I hear you. Here, take my watch for now and use it for this tent. That will at least give you two of them." He looked around at the crowded space where easily over seventy-five men were packed in, side to side. "By the way, when exactly did the last group of wounded go out to the field hospitals?"

Lydia mentally calculated. "Not since the battle started. None have gone out today yet, either. Where are the trucks? It's really unusual not to have them coming in and out daily!"

"I don't know where they are," Fortraine replied. "But I intend to find out before the day is out." Fortraine immediately withdrew, to his tent, where his aide was already working on the supply issues. So far, his efforts to find out where the trucks were had been in vain.

"Private Seymore," Fortraine said.

"Sir?" the man looked up from the box holding the short wave and field phone on his desk.

"Where are the trucks?"

The young soldier shook his head worriedly. "I don't know, sir. I'm trying to raise someone on the lines. I have no idea what's happened. Maybe after the explosions, something broke our connection."

Fortraine leaned on his desk. "We had contact yesterday, Private. A message should have been sent out yesterday when the trucks didn't get here. Trucks and wagons bring supplies, and trucks and wagons take the wounded out. This is not a complicated process. Find a soldier and a corpsman who can go hunt supplies down. Tell them to take horses. We can't spare our petrol or trucks in case we have to move the camp. If there are no supplies at the train station, tell them to go to the British CCS over by Ypres and see what they can spare. How on earth are we supposed to run a casualty clearing station with all these casualties not being cleared out and no supplies? It's unacceptable.

"If we're out of trucks, then find some mules and wagons, and let's get the wounded who are able to travel out on them. And get some men to put up another recovery tent right beside the first, in case it starts raining. The one we have is full. And find some more cots. Men can't be laying all over the ground post-op."

He sat down and considered his options. The battle for the ridge would likely continue for another couple of days. They had fewer German wounded showing up in the station today for their care, but if he had to prioritize, the Germans would be dropped down the list for any available resources. Having no supplies was a real crisis. He got up again and walked quickly back through the station to the mess tent, where he found the cook.

"How are we situated for supplies in here?" Fortraine asked the man, fearing the answer.

"Got enough for a day of fresh now that it's summer and things don't last long," Cook responded in frustration. "Then some canned rations. Enough maybe for the personnel, but not to feed all the wounded. Hadn't planned on them still being here, and with so many mouths to feed, we've run out of supplies faster than expected."

Fortraine's eyes furrowed. "That's not good enough," he told the cook. "We must feed these people."

The cook nodded. "Yes, sir, but with all the wounded and nothing coming in since we arrived here, what else can I do? If I don't cook up the fresh stuff today, it will spoil. Then I've got nothing."

Fortraine shook his head. "Why did I not know that you've had no supplies delivered?"

"It's the army, sir, and I'm just a private," Cook replied, shrugging his shoulders. "I don't ask the army to explain things to me."

"Don't let anything go to waste," Fortraine instructed him. "Dish out smaller portions all the way around. Stretch out what we have. Something has interrupted the arrival of supplies, and we haven't been informed yet what the problem is."

The cook looked dismayed. "They don't eat the best as it is, sir," he admitted. "Giving them even less isn't going to make anyone feel very good."

"We've had to tighten our belts before," Fortraine told the man. "We can do it again. There isn't anything left in this wasted countryside to appropriate for the army. Hell, there isn't a single village left standing. Do what you have to, and send anyone with complaints to me."

"Yes, sir," Cook replied dismally. He could not work magic. He didn't look forward to lunch when the staff would be coming in to revive themselves. He turned to the privates helping him and told them to cook up the perishables that were left before they spoiled. Then, he thought of his menu. Gravy with a bite of meat was better than no meat at all.

When the personnel started coming through, everyone noticed the servings were being shorted. No one complained out loud, but there were eyebrows raised as the food was spooned onto the trays and kettles of thinned hot cereal were carried to the recovery for the staff to distribute to the wounded. Charlotte came into the mess in response to their meager provisions and asked for the cook.

"I can't feed these wounded men a thin gruel for long," she reported. "Is this a temporary thing?"

Cook leaned over the serving counter and apologized. "I'm sorry, Nurse Stein. It's all I can do to put a little something in everyone's stomach. You know that no trucks have come in, don't you?"

She looked puzzled. "I didn't really pay attention. We've been so busy with the wounded. Is that so, then?" she asked the man. "Does Doctor Fortraine know?"

The man nodded miserably. "Yep. He knows. I'll do what I can, Nurse, but there's a whole other tent full of wounded to feed, too, and I'm trying my best to stretch it out so everyone gets at least a little."

Charlotte nodded. "I'm sure you are," she reassured the man and went to find Lydia.

The two women gathered together in the recovery with Marlene and Alice to assess the situation. "What can we do?" Alice asked in real concern. "The men are weak enough as it is. How are we going to nourish them? The number of dying is increasing, even as we're talking!"

Lydia was in problem-solving mode, "We've got to keep the post-op patients hydrated, at least with water, if we don't have soup or broth to give them. It's the ones who are already too weak, upon arrival, who aren't pulling through, ones we've been just watching."

"Water is not going to nourish them, that's for sure," Marlene observed. "I can't imagine what happened to the supply trucks! They must have fallen under fire somehow. Or heavens! Maybe they got captured."

"With this countryside, they could have driven into craters and been stranded," Charlotte said unhappily. "The cook said he's run out of options other than to make do with less."

"We have to keep the doctors fed, so they don't pass out standing at the tables all day," Alice added. "This recovery tent is at capacity and there are some soldiers putting up another one, right now. None of the wounded are going out; if we run out of cots, we'll have to lay them on blankets on the ground."

Charlene added, "Remember in Paris, the bakers said they were already being rationed to sell one loaf of bread per family each day. Maybe the shortage is all the way back to the cities... maybe there's really nothing available to come all the way out here, to us!"

"How's our Dakin's?" Lydia asked. "We can always tear up sheets for bandages, but keeping wounds clean is another matter. If we can't count on more antiseptic, we'd better save the Dakin's for the surgery. If we can get the wounded cleaned out in there, then we'll just have to keep the wounds covered and use soap and water in the recovery. That much we do have, at least. Let's not change any of the post-op dressings for at least twelve hours unless they are heavily soaked. Except if there is gangrene, then we have no choice. And maybe by tomorrow, things will be different."

"Time to go on a diet, ladies," Marlene attempted to lighten the mood. "We'll all look great in our bathing suits in no time!"

Charlotte looked at Alice's tiny frame. "Some of us don't have much to spare!" she exclaimed.

Alice looked down at her own profile. "I've always been tiny," she said. "It's hard to find nice clothes."

Lydia critically appraised the three of them. "I don't think any of you have an ounce of fat on you. The powers that be had better figure this out quickly, or I'm stealing an ambulance and going to hunt for some supplies myself, even if I get in trouble again for doing it!"

By the next morning, they were all feeling the lack of both calories and nutrients. Lydia had worked the recovery, all night, with five other nurses—extra hands being required for the many patients who needed constant monitoring in the, now, three tents. At the end of her shift, she saw Simon before he left to start his next shift.

She tumbled down onto a cot. "I'm hungry," she whispered tiredly, lifting her feet up for a rest.

He looked down at her while he tucked his shirt in. "Hungry hungry? Or just hungry?"

She picked up a sock hanging to dry on the nearby footlocker and threw it at him. "Just hungry."

"Darn," he said, retrieving the damp sock to hang again. "I can't give you that. I can give you something else though—"

She closed her eyes wearily, her stomach grumbling. "No, you can't give me that either. It's that time..."

He groaned. "Five days without even that? I may not survive. If there's anything left in the mess, I'll bring it back to you." He looked at her, lovingly, on the cot with her arm over her closed eyes, blocking the daylight.

She shook her head. "Don't bother. Eat it yourself... you'll need it... and I have to sleep a couple hours and get back to recovery. The men are lying on blankets on the ground... we ran out of cots. We lost nine of the wounded just during the night, Simon. Nine. We don't have what we need to keep them going here. The trucks can't come soon enough. How on earth do we write to their families and tell them their loved ones died in the war by starvation because we couldn't feed them?"

"I don't know," he told her softly. "I don't know what Fortraine is going to do, but he says he's working on it."

"Good," she said, her voice dropping off as fatigue commanded that she sleep.

Simon stood a moment, noting that her breathing slowed. He heard the artillery beginning to fire in the early morning air and cursed under his breath. *It just doesn't stop,* he thought. *And we're already up to our eyeballs.* Simon hoped she would sleep without nightmares.

He went to the door of the tent and called for Abril. The dog soon came bounding into sight, and Simon motioned inside the tent toward Lydia. "Stay," he commanded the dog, who instinctively went inside to take up her post near the sleeping woman. *At least she has that,* Simon thought as he headed to the mess to see if he could find a cup of coffee. He would come back and check on her in a couple of hours.

In the mess tent, the undercurrent of frustration had finally surfaced. Many were holding mugs of watered-down coffee. Others preferred tea to the less-than-satisfying alternative. There was a white cup of watery cooked cereal, hot, but very thin. Simon drank his instead of trying to spoon it up. He felt bad for the cook's crew, who were trying to make the best of a truly terrible situation. As he sat at the table, Marcus soon joined him. He had a smile on his face despite the circumstances.

"Ah, the savory smells of breakfast in Belgium," Marcus exclaimed. "I think I'll look for dandelion greens during a lull in the wounded today, my friend. And will be sure to share—the drums are already beating out there—you'd think they'd have taken the damn ridge by now. They've blown it to pieces, dropped bombs on it, bombarded it with artillery, fired on it. How could anything possibly be left!"

Simon sipped his brown water. "The Germans have a huge reserve army, not too far away, to the east. The British may hold what's left of the ridge today, but there will be more Germans coming tomorrow."

"I don't think there will be anything left for them to claim victory over. Just our latrines and some dirt—" Marcus said, looking around at the corpsmen and soldiers coming through the mess and those sitting, disgruntled, on the benches. He didn't see Lydia about.

"She's asleep," Simon answered Marc's unspoken question. "Peacefully... I hope. The nurses doubled up their numbers last night, with so many wounded in the tents. She said they lost nine patients during the night."

"Damn!" Marcus exclaimed. "We can't keep them here like this!"

"I know we can't."

Marcus finished his cereal in two swallows. "Is she... are the nightmares... any better?" he asked carefully.

Simon knew Marcus was genuinely concerned, but he was reluctant to answer. "I'm not sure," he admitted. "I thought so for a while, and then being here with the explosions and more German wounded just made it worse again. I hate to see her going through it again. It tears me up inside." He drummed his fingers slowly on the table as he felt the tension rising.

"The guy is dead," Marcus said slowly. "But he sure did a number on her. Nurse Stein was there, too, but she doesn't seem to have the same kind of problems."

Simon shook his head. "No, she doesn't," he admitted. "It wasn't the same for her."

"I, uh... I know I overstepped my bounds a night ago," Marcus admitted. "I just really wanted to help, Simon. Really."

Simon nodded slowly. "I know, buddy, but yes, you did."

"I don't think she remembers it, though," Marcus said hopefully, then added quickly, "but of course you do, and I am sorry about that."

Simon finished the coffee, placing his mug on the table. "Marcus, you're my best friend, and you've saved my life more than once. I'll never forget that. I don't know what it is that possesses you sometimes, though. You, of all people, should know better than to try to hold onto someone in the middle of a hallucination, or a nightmare, or flashback... whatever it was she was having. You just get sucked inside the trauma, and that makes it worse because you can't be any help at all when you become part of it. Did you, like... sleep through that class, in medical school?"

Marcus looked down at the table where he had clasped his hands around his coffee. "I can't stand to see her suffer either, Simon," he admitted honestly. "I saw what she went through when you were hit in the bombing. And when you were hallucinating with infection. She was scared to death you were going to die, both times. Then, having to go through what I can only imagine... whatever happened in the trench... when I heard her scream a night ago, I seriously didn't give it any thought other than to try to snap her out of it, so she wouldn't be terrified."

Simon didn't look at Marcus. "I get that. I know you wanted to help. Sometimes, though... I have to wonder if you want more of a relationship with Lydia, Marcus. Do you?" Then he raised his eyes and looking at the other man who was too slow to answer.

There was dead silence between them.

Marcus shifted uncomfortably on the bench in front of Simon, holding his coffee mug a little too tightly. "Listen, Simon," he started, "I would never do anything to..."

"I'm not saying you would," Simon told him quietly. "I think our friendship is strong enough that you wouldn't do anything, intentionally, against me. And I don't think she'd allow it, anyway.

But sometimes, hidden desires and extreme circumstances make people do things they wouldn't do otherwise."

Marcus flushed. "Now look, Simon, if you're referring to the incident with Lydia and Stockton, I was really drunk because Susannah left. It was only the alcohol talking. I've been very careful to never cross that boundary again."

Simon felt anger rising inside him. He didn't know anything about the incident other than that Lydia had smelled of the whiskey the night she came into their tent and told him she'd found Marcus drunk in the supply room. Simon held his breath, considering how the whiskey could have gotten on her, and he didn't care for the suggestions coming into his mind... but then he exhaled again and tried to relax. He was too hungry. He was way too tired. He was stretched beyond capacity with the wounded all around them... and no end in sight. And Marcus was his best friend. Simon rubbed his hand over his eyes and looked up at the man still squirming on the other side of the table.

Simon reached out over the table to shake Marcus's hand. "I'm beyond fed up with the war and death... and drinking thin cereal to survive, while we go try to put human beings back together. I'm sorry, Marcus. I'm overreacting," Simon told him truthfully. "I apologize."

Marcus reached over in relief and took the peace offering. "Me, too," he said. "But if we don't get something to eat around here soon, I may have to take a scalpel to the resident milk goat the cook has behind his tent."

Simon stood up. "Let's get to the surgery. I hear the ambulances coming. I've never had roasted goat. What's it taste like?"

Marcus stood up and joined him, intensely relieved the other conversation was over. "I don't have any idea, but it's got to be better than gruel."

Fortraine had decided against sending a truck out for supplies. When the soldiers had checked, they indeed had very little petrol left in the station, and if they couldn't move the camp when the battle line shifted, they would be stuck behind enemy lines. Two of the soldiers had been dispatched by horseback and given written orders to conscript two trucks and load them with whatever they could get their hands on and get back to the station as quickly as humanly possible. It was faster than if they had to pull a wagon. Fortraine knew the hunger in their own bellies would give them extra speed. He had given them orders to wire command with their location and critically urgent needs.

Their own field phone line remained useless. Fortraine now wondered if the French army had simply lost them, in the last move into Belgium, where the British forces were more prevalent. It was possible. And if so, he would move the station without orders just as soon as this bloody mess on the ridge was over and get back into French territory.

The station couldn't move, loaded with wounded stretched out on cots and blankets, though. As a commander and as a doctor, Fortraine appreciated the strain this situation was putting on everyone. They would not be able to function much longer without food and supplies. He decided to head to the surgery, to relieve Stockton. The men would be more tired with fewer calories... they would need to be relieved more frequently. At least he could give them that.

His first patient was at a table with the French nurse, Monique. The man on the table had multiple bullet wounds to the groin and stomach. Fortraine probed the incision for fragments, pulling them out one by one. He reached a clamp deeper into the wound to fish out a fairly intact bullet he could just barely visualize. As he pushed the clamp in, probing for a hold, the wounded soldier lying in front of him jumped. Fortraine jerked his hand back in surprise.

"Get this man under!" he shouted at the anesthetist, making the nurses turn and causing Marcus and Simon to both quickly look over at his table in concern.

"I'm sorry, sir," the anesthetist said regretfully. "We don't have enough ether left to put them out fully. It's the best we can do. A light sedation."

Fortraine froze, clamp in hand, hesitating to push inside further. "Of course," he told the anxious man at the head of the table. "You're right. My apologies. Is the laudanum equally as low?" He looked up at Monique, questioning.

Her eyes were troubled. "We're rationing it out for the most severely injured, Doctor," she said.

"Well then, I'll have to be as gentle and fast as I can, won't I?" Fortraine said. He increased the speed at which he was working, trying to be precise while conserving the limited resources available and saving the wounded man from any further pain. "Wash it out well."

"We are just using hot water, Doctor," Monique told him. "It's all that is left, but I will be complete."

Fortraine rattled off something in a long stream of French that only Monique was able to follow clearly. Her cheeks turned red at the forceful diatribe that he was expressing with more skill than his scalpel, and she did not offer to translate the one-sided discourse to the rest of them. He strode over to the sink, washed his hands in plain water, and returned to the table for the next casualty being brought in to him, not heeding the questioning looks of the other medical staff. *Unacceptable!* he thought to himself. Marcus and Simon just looked at each other, in mutual concern.

That night, no one slept well. All three tents were now full. The night was warm, so wounded were laying on cots outside, under a tarp, while those inside were reduced to laying on blankets on the ground. The nurses were left to stand and kneel, stand and kneel until their leg and back muscles protested. Seven nurses were on duty for over two hundred wounded in various states of: dying, recovering from surgery, or shellshock, waiting for something they could not even verbalize. The corpsmen and some of the soldiers were helping to minister to their needs, including the use of the urinals, washing and changing soiled bedding, and putting cups of very thin cereal and water to the lips of those awake enough to drink it. Fortraine hovered around the tents in the lantern light, watching the nurses care for their patients... essentially getting in their way... Lydia finally pulled the man aside.

"Doctor Fortraine," she began. "I realize how worried you are about this situation. But sir, frankly, we need you elsewhere, more than here in the recovery all night. Just let us do what we know how to do. Please, sir."

Fortraine looked at Lydia intently and saw no disrespect in her face, heard none in her tone of voice. Finally, he nodded. "Very well, Nurse, but I expect you to keep me informed of your situation, frequently."

She nodded, relieved. "I will, Doctor. Please try to get some sleep," she told him and gratefully watched him leave the area. He was the last person the nurses and soldiers needed hovering over them, watching their every move. Lydia left the tent to pass through the outdoor cots. Abril stood up as she approached and followed her through the cots as the nurse tended the wounded, talking briefly to some who were awake. There was a half-moon that night, a better substitute for the precious kerosene which was needed inside the tents, in the blackout.

"How are you holding up, soldier?" she asked a man who was staring up into the night. She wished she could see his face better.

He let her hold his remaining hand. "I think the guy next to me died. I haven't heard him take a breath for a long time. Maybe you could check him? I heard him for a while, kind of gurgling."

"Thank you, soldier," Lydia told him, giving his hand a little squeeze of reassurance. "Are you in pain?"

"Not so much, Nurse," he admitted. "Not like some of the guys over there who sound pretty miserable."

Lydia nodded in the moonlight. "We'll do what we can for them. We're trying to get all of you moved out to the field hospitals just as soon as possible." She bent down over the man on the nearby cot and listened with her stethoscope to his chest, putting her hand on his lips to feel for any sign of life. She knew he was gone, just as soldier next to him had thought. Lydia walked back through the cots and found a corpsman who could fetch the litter bearers. They were lining up the dead on the other side of the tents and just covering them up with tarps, unable to dig graves in the night.

Marlene saw the man being carried off and approached Lydia in the dark. "That's the fifth one tonight already. Nine last night. Geez, these men are hungry. They're getting weaker by the minute. My stomach stopped growling, at least."

Lydia put her hand on Marlene's arm. "Probably a bad sign, Marlene," she said, "when we aren't feeling hungry anymore."

"I think the army forgot all about us in the last move, Lydia. I think we fell off the map when we left France and crossed the border," Marlene observed. "I think we're alone out here."

Lydia absorbed this. "That may be true. If so, British intelligence should know we're over here. They have stations nearby. The ambulance drivers surely know to head here, and wherever the other units are."

"Yes, but the ambulance drivers don't know we've run out of supplies. They fly in, drop off, and just shoot right back out again."

"Maybe tomorrow, in triage, we'll tell each of the drivers to spread the word, when they see commanders out in the field. Maybe it'll find its way to someone in charge."

"Tomorrow is day four with nothing but water and the cook's 'white water', as some of the men call it. If more wounded come in tomorrow, we won't even have a tarp to put them under. There are already three hundred and seventy-two names on the clipboard... of course, that includes the ones who've died—Are you as tired as I am?"

Lydia nodded. "Yes. But we aren't holding scalpels, so it's okay if our hands shake from hunger."

Charlotte stepped out of the enclosed recovery tent for a brief moment of fresh air and saw the two shadows talking. She walked over to join them. "How are you girls holding up?" she asked, pulling off her scarf and letting the night air blow through her hair to revive her. "I was falling asleep in there, had to get some air to wake myself up. Oh, my, look at how many men are lying out here. They're a pretty quiet bunch. I don't like that. I hope they're just sleeping."

"We just lost another one," Marlene said. "They just carried him away."

"Geez... I hate this," Charlotte breathed.

Marlene said, "Listen, stay out here awhile, and I'll go inside. I don't mind being inside for change."

"Okay, thanks," Charlotte replied and Marlene slipped inside the tent, carefully keeping the dim lantern light inside. She put an arm around Lydia. "I'm hungry, and it makes me think of the trench."

"I know," Lydia said softly. "I was worried about you."

"I was worried about you," Charlotte countered. "This is not good for either of us or the two sentries."

"Not for any of us." Lydia folded her arms over her chest. "This also isn't a very good welcome back... after being away Paris. To go from having the options of the city to having nothing. I saw you all after you returned, and it seemed like everyone was so subdued, so quiet. I guess the idea of coming back to all of this weighed everyone down... even though we didn't really know that this was coming."

"No, we didn't know what was coming," Charlotte agreed. "But remember when you and Simon got back from getting married? You had to track us down, since we'd already moved the station closer to the front while you were away. It was pretty much the same thing when we came back. Only we got back just in time to get on board the caravan."

Lydia nodded. "Simon thought Doctor Lovell might take advantage of the situation being in Paris and come back married to you!"

Charlotte laughed lightly. "Married to me?" she exclaimed. "Why ever would he think that Doctor Lovell would want to marry me?"

"Just because he thought the two of you were getting a little more involved, and with Susannah being gone, he thought Doctor Lovell might be looking for another relationship. He was just speculating on Doctor Lovell's next move. He's a good guy, Charlotte. And a great surgeon."

Charlotte cleared her throat. "Well, we were... together... once in Paris," she finally admitted out loud. "But I haven't told any of the others."

"Already, Charlotte?" Lydia whispered. "Are you okay?"

Charlotte nodded. "Sure, why wouldn't I be?"

"Was it your first time?"

"Uh-huh. He was nice enough about it when he realized," Charlotte admitted, thinking back briefly to the opera house.

Lydia slipped her arm around the woman's waist. "It's not supposed to be that way, Charlotte, casual. We waited because it's supposed to mean something... represent something, wonderful."

Charlotte's voice was a little wistful. "You mean like what you have with Doctor Finney."

Lydia nodded. "Yes, like that. It can't mean nearly enough without the promises that should be going right along with it. Don't you know that's why Suzie left, Charlotte? I don't want to lose you the same way. Don't let what happened with Doctor Lovell turn into something that doesn't mean anything at all. You deserve more than that."

"I don't know what I deserve," Charlotte told her finally. "After what you and I went through, I thought, what if we ever got captured again, and the next time, I was the one taken? I thought it would be better to choose a man that I, at least know pretty well, to be the first one I'd be with, that way... rather than have some German soldier just take advantage of me in a trench somewhere. I was afraid that maybe that's the way it would happen and my first time with a man would be horrible. Doctor Lovell wasn't horrible... quite the opposite. He didn't want to hurt me... in fact, he made a point of making me feel good, too. Things I never felt before."

Lydia stood next to her friend in silence. She wanted to offer support and encouragement, but she truthfully didn't know if Marcus could offer Charlotte anything more, emotionally, than he had already.

"Are you... could you be pregnant?" Lydia said, half afraid to broach the subject.

Charlotte shook her head. "I don't think so. I'll know soon."

Lydia gave her friend a small squeeze of reassurance. "Let's hope you aren't. But with us having nothing to eat this week, don't be surprised if you skip a month or are late. We won't panic.

Let's make our rounds through the men. I'm glad you told me about what happened in Paris... and why. Please, don't keep it to yourself, if anything happens. It's too heavy a load to carry. And, who knows, maybe Doctor Lovell will sort things out in his own head."

The two nurses split up and resumed their duties. Overhead, the stars were hanging bright in the sky. It wasn't raining, the air wasn't too cool, there were no sounds of war. It would have been a lovely night except for their hunger, the dying, and the war.

When day seven dawned a few days later, Lydia did not even bother to go to the mess tent for the weak coffee that she knew would be in a pot; someone else could have it. She felt a little dizzy, realized she was probably dehydrated, and filled her canteen with water. It was odd how the water had gained a flavor in the absence of food. It felt good to have something in her stomach, even if it was just cold water. But after drinking it, she felt a little nauseated. She was so tired. Simon would probably be getting up soon to start in the surgery. It was a good thing she was to be in triage this morning because Lydia didn't feel capable of assisting the doctors today. She was too weak. How were they all supposed to keep going?

Abril followed at her heels, whining slightly. Lydia looked down at the dog. "It's okay, Abril, go hunt, find yourself something to eat," she told the animal, who left her and went bounding out over the grass, avoiding the craters and working her way up a nearby hill. Lydia fondly watched her go. The dog hadn't seemed to feel the wasting effect of the lack of food. Lydia guessed she was able to fend for herself better than the humans in her care could. Lydia saw another pair of litter bearers coming through, between the tents, with yet another body. She rounded the surgery tent and saw the field of bodies covered with tarps lying on the grass. There were many dozens lined up in a solemn row... now just mounds of human beings, the remains of what used to be vibrant, hope-filled men. She thought of the letter she had promised to write to Mary, the girlfriend of the fallen soldier, back in England, but without a means of delivering it, it would have to wait. The little picture was still safe in her footlocker.

The first ambulance pulled in as the sun broke over the eastern hills, shining its rays onto the dew soaked ground, making the manmade craters shimmer. The ambulance had two wounded soldiers in it, and Lydia approached them as they arrived.

"Nurse?" the driver said with an British accent, jumping out of the ambulance and opening the back of the vehicle. "We found these fellas this morning. They're in pretty rough shape. Say, you don't look so good yourself!"

"We haven't had any supplies for over a week," she told the man regretfully. "The wounded are starving here. We ran out of pretty much everything several days ago."

"Damn! Begging your pardon, miss," he said. "Look, I've got a sandwich and some rations in my vehicle here... take them."

Lydia shook her head, though her empty stomach objected. "Thanks, but we need enough for three hundred wounded and our small staff. Unless God would multiply it like the loaves and the fishes, it wouldn't go far enough. I'll wait, right along with the others."

"Whatever you say, Nurse," the man replied, shaking his head. "But you gotta know there's more coming after me on the road back there."

Lydia nodded. "We thought there might be. We'll do the best we can."

The driver turned back to his vehicle after his helper deposited the wounded on the ground, but called out from the window, "The good news is this battle for the ridge is winding down. Might get a break soon."

"Thank God for that!" Lydia exclaimed tiredly. "It'll be welcome."

Only after the ambulance left did she remember that she and Marlene had decided to tell the drivers to contact headquarters or a command post somewhere and tell them about their station and the situation. *Oh well,* Lydia thought, *what could one driver do anyway out in the middle of nowhere in Belgium?* She bent over and assessed the two wounded men who had waited in the field all night to be rescued. She lifted the bloody pant leg of one of them and saw maggots crawling through an open gash in his flesh. *Bad, but not awful.* She gave him a small word of encouragement and turned to the other man. He was barely alive but could open his eyes and saw her, when she took his hand.

"There's the sun," the soldier said, squinting his eyes in the early morning light as it streamed over the hill. "You're the prettiest thing I've ever seen..." he whispered, looking up at her.

Lydia took his hand and touched his brow. They looked at the sun together, shining in the early blue of the morning sky. And his eyes fixed on the shining orb as the last thing he saw on the earth. Lydia gently closed the eyes that were hopefully now seeing something much more glorious than a sunrise, before motioning for the corpsmen to come and carry his body over to the growing row of the dead.

She saw Sally crossing over the grass to join her in triage. Marlene was not too far behind... Lydia saw the woman stumble as she covered the distance.

"Marlene, go rest," Lydia called to her. "You need to sleep."

The other woman smiled wanly at her. "So do you. We need food. All of us."

Then Lydia saw motion over in the field. Abril came running back with something in her mouth. It was a rabbit she had caught somewhere over in the grasses. The dog dropped the creature at her feet and looked up. Lydia knelt down and gave the dog a squeeze. "Good girl!" she exclaimed excitedly, for the first time in many days. "Go get another one!"

Abril took off with a bound over the grass, and Lydia actually laughed. "Wait till Cook sees this!" she said to Marlene.

Sally smiled at the good-sized furry mound. "It's a start. Let's hope she finds a hundred more! We'll give the dog a medal of honor! She deserves it!"

"In more ways than one!" Lydia said and took the rabbit over to the mess tent, where she found the cook and presented Abril's prize. *You would have thought it was gold,* Lydia thought, seeing the expression on the cook's face as he reached for his sharpest knife and immediately headed out back of the mess to skin the creature before putting it in a pot to cook down even the bones.

"If that dog can keep them coming, I'll keep them cooking," the cook called over his shoulder at her happily. "Bring anything she finds straight to me." In his mind, he already envisioned rabbits, groundhogs, maybe even a grouse or pheasant or two...

Lydia took a moment before returning to triage to make sure that Simon was up and on his feet. She found him sitting on their cot, looking down at his hands, and she immediately put her arms reassuringly around his shoulders. *They feel thinner,* she thought, feeling his bones beneath.

"God help us, Lydia," he said softly to himself as much as her. "My hands are shaking."

She took his hands in her own and looked at him. "I'd rather have you with shaking hands operate on our boys than any other doctor whose hands are still. It's going to be okay—You'll never guess what happened!"

He looked up hopefully at her with his pinched cheeks and tired eyes. "What's that? Something good, I hope."

"Abril just brought in a rabbit she found in the field that I gave to Cook, and she went right back out to hunt for more!"

Simon just shook his head and laughed softly. "Who knew? If God knows every sparrow that falls, then He must be aware we're going down. That dog sure is a gift, straight from Him."

"There's a guy out there who just came in. Needs his leg wound debrided pretty badly," she told him. "I'm out in triage this morning. Even one of the ambulance drivers this morning said we weren't looking real good today."

"Maybe he'll spread the word," Simon said and sighed, stretching and standing up. "Okay, tell the surgery I'm on my way." He combed his hair, and she touched his bearded cheek.

Lydia gave him her canteen to take a long drink. "You need a haircut. Keep your fluids up," she reminded him and kissed him lightly on the mouth. "And remind me later to tell you about Charlotte and Marcus."

"Oh, no, good or bad?" he groaned.

"I'm not sure yet. But it'll give you something to think about other than your stomach grumbling," she teased.

He reached for her and pulled her to him in an embrace. "I hope someone feeds me before I'm too weak to have you." His hands drifted down to press her hips tight against him. He felt his body stir, and so did she. "And I love your haircuts... so does Marc. It's a bright spot, here!"

"Well, now you can think about that!" she said, reaching up and kissing him again, and she turned and headed off to receive the wounded as he watched her go. *Seeing her retreating shape isn't breakfast, but it is quite satisfying,* he thought as he headed to the surgery to clean out the wounded man's leg of its carnage.

The wounded streamed in over the course of the morning. With every incoming ambulance, Marlene, Lydia, and Sally planted the idea with the drivers that the station was in trouble and badly needed supplies. Word-of-mouth was sometimes an effective means of communication when all other sources had failed. Abril returned all day with ground prey she had sniffed out and captured. Each trophy she brought to the feet of Lydia, where she received endless praise, before bounding back out over the grassy field of craters. For her, it was a game. For Cook, it was a lifeline against despair, every creature simmering in the white cereal soup, adding some protein to each small cup he served up. He ground up the bones and mixed them right in. One of the soldiers went out and dug up wild garlic, the tiny bulbs offering a hint of flavor. At any other time, it would have been an unpalatable mixture, but to those in the station, it was widely appreciated. The newly wounded had to wait for the broth, as those most hungry had greater need.

By noon, Lydia couldn't stay on her feet. She refilled her canteen, and she and Marlene headed off to sleep after having been up throughout the night in the recovery. The two instantly collapsed into restless dreams upon reaching their cots. In the surgery, Simon tried to keep focused on each wounded man placed in front of him. He saw Marcus and Harold hesitating, both men moving slowly in their efforts to complete a surgery. They were making mistakes. He looked up as Harold cursed out loud.

"Damn it! Damn it! Nurse, grab that bowel and pinch it off. Damn it, I slipped!" Harold exclaimed in agitation to Nancy, who was assisting him.

"I've got it, Doctor," Nancy reassured him. "He's not going to miss a couple inches of bowel. Let's just take that piece out and put him back together."

"Need a hand, Doctor Stockton?" Marcus called over from his table. He could see Harold swaying.

"Yes," Harold replied, rubbing his eyes with his forearm. "I can't see straight."

Marcus immediately left his table, telling Gretha to clean the wound out and finish packing it for him. He rinsed his hands and went to relieve Harold. "Oh, that's not bad," he told the other surgeon. "Just needs a couple stitches, and we'll get it right back together. Go take a break. I hear there is rabbit, or gopher, or some kind of stew coming out of the mess tent, compliments of Nurse Finney's dog. Go grab a cup while you can."

Harold shook his head. "Let it go to the wounded."

Marcus looked at Stockton with serious intent. "If you don't get something in you, we'll lose you, too. Simon and I are the best, but we need help. Go to the mess tent and get a cup of whatever the cook's got."

Harold wavered. Marcus had never given him an order before, but in the fog of hunger, he realized Marcus was right. Harold washed his hands, took off his soiled apron, and left the tent for the mess. Marcus peered into the wound at the damaged loop of bowel.

"Okay, Nurse, let's do this before my eyes go blurry, too," Marcus told Nancy. She looked across the table and smiled over her face mask.

"Thank you, Doctor Lovell," she said, "for helping him get out of here. It was a really kind thing to do."

"Oh, it was nothing, Nurse," Marcus said, taking the scalpel from her and beginning to resect the damaged section of intestine. "We have a reputation for surgical excellence here that must be maintained."

There was a sudden commotion as one of the medics fell to the ground in between the anesthesia tanks and their steam sterilizer. Laura, who was circulating, bent over the man. "He's okay, he just passed out," she told the others after finding a strong pulse in the man's wrist. "Take him outside for a bit of air and get him to the mess, too," she told the corpsmen who came to help. She looked at Simon. "We're all going to drop like flies pretty soon. Do you want the stool?"

"That's not a bad idea, Nurse Bertolli," he said tiredly. "I'll use up less energy sitting than standing. Can you find Nurse Sullivan to give us a hand?"

"She was up all night with Lydia, Doctor," Laura told him. "She just went off duty for a couple of hours of sleep."

Simon nodded tiredly. "Of course, I'm sorry, I forgot. Let it go. If anyone else in here feels like they're going to go down, just try not to fall over the tables. At the very least, move away to the edge of the tent."

"We'll drag you out feet first," Marcus warned them all. "Just make sure you tell us which direction you want to be dragged. Blink an eye or something so we don't accidentally put you in the wrong place."

They kept going, tending to the wounded as best they could, taking frequent breaks, drinking water, collapsing in their tents for short naps. Fortraine wandered through the camp, feeling forlorn, but hiding it under an expression of anger and sternness that belied his worry for the people under his care. He heard about the dog bringing in game and now remembered Mary Baxter telling him that they needed more like Abril. He realized too late that he should have heeded the suggestion she'd made for more dogs, back when she had visited. But more than ever, he appreciated the spirit of the team to which he'd been appointed and the fortitude of the wounded who fought the war and now fought to live.

He wondered where the two men were, the ones he'd sent off on horseback to the train station, hoping they would be successful and return soon, with supplies. Fortraine checked in on the three crowded recovery tents and also on the wounded out under the tarps. He saw the nurses still at work. They had been reduced to tearing up bedding into strips that they were rolling into bandages while washing the used bandages and hanging them to dry in the warm sun to reuse, letting the sun's rays bleach them. *These nurses are so goddamn good, and I can't even get each of them a watch,* he thought to himself. It was unacceptable.

At supper time, as the surgery wound down and the ambulances stopped coming in as frequently... the artillery fire to the east had stopped. Either the battle was slowing, or the ambulance drivers, knowing their predicament, were taking wounded to other stations. Either way, the number of wounded dropped off to a pace that more closely matched the weary feet trying care for them. Anyone not required was lying down, trying to recoup some strength. Cook continued to make the most of what Abril brought, tirelessly, to his tent. Marcus finally went to his own cot and fell into it, exhausted. He was too tired to think. Even his usually steady hands were shaking now, and he knew he was on his last leg for the day.

Simon left the surgery and gratefully accepted the small cup of whatever it was the cook's staff gave him. He swallowed it in one gulp, hoping to bypass the taste, but found it wasn't unacceptable after all. Then he went to find Lydia. She was still asleep. He sat on the spare cot and gently pulled the wavy brown hair off her face, traced the outline of her ear, and kissed her forehead. He didn't want to wake her, so he lay on the spare cot in their tent. To divert his mind, he thought back to the news that they'd never had time to discuss, concerning Marcus and Charlotte. He hoped to heaven Marcus hadn't made a foolish mistake again. He thought of Susannah raising little Marcie Nichole, back in the States.

He then wondered what their children might look like, that he and Lydia might have someday... and what their house back in West Virginia would look like. His brother and sister would welcome Lydia, and any children they would be blessed to bring into the world. It would be so good to take Lydia back to see her parents and her sister's family. Simon imagined waking up beside Lydia, setting their children around the table for breakfast, and watching them dig into a stack of pancakes, covered in buttery syrup... and bacon... then Simon forced himself to stop thinking about food. His hunger was driving him to distraction.

Just as Simon was drifting off into a troubled sleep, he and Lydia were startled awake at the same exact moment by a loud shout coming from the edge of the station by the recovery. They looked at each other in alarm and jumped up off their cots, heading together for the door of the tent, running out into the evening light and right into Marcus, wondering if another bomb had dropped nearby while they were sleeping. The station personnel were starting to gather outside of the recovery tents, and many started to cheer.

Something had dropped in, but it was not a bomb. Not at all. It was a mule-driven wagon steered by Father James. The wagon, covered with a mounded tarp over its ample contents, creaked over the final rise and into the camp. Father James was waving at them as the sun was going down behind the eastern hills. Marcus, Simon, and Lydia joined the others running over to meet the priest.

He pulled in the team of mules, shouting aloud, "Whoa up!" He then called out to those who had gathered, "Did someone here order dinner?" and climbed down from the wooden seat of the wagon. He loosened the rope of one corner of the tarp. As others pulled back the canvas, they saw the wagon loaded with bags of flour, sacks of potatoes, bread, cheese, fruit, vegetables, several squealing hogs, a crate of chickens, and papers of wrapped dried jerky and bacon. They miraculously found the strength needed to unload the wagon, taking the much-needed food to the cook who waited at the door of the mess tent with tears in his eyes. "Give me an hour," the cook shouted over the commotion. "Or a half an hour!"

Marcus and Simon shook the priest's hand heartily. Father James looked at them closely. "You all look terrible," he said. "I got word through a soldier in Ypres who'd been taken there instead of here. He said they had heard you were in a bad way out here. Lost in the wilderness like the Israelites, so to speak. I came as fast as I could gather things together. I don't have anything medical. Could only get food."

"Only?" Simon declared in relief. "It's just what we needed. We are overrun with wounded, and they are dying of hunger, literally, Father James. You are a miracle from God Himself."

The priest took Lydia's hands in his own when he saw her. "I'm no miracle," he told them. "But I'm glad I was in the right place at the right time. It's the Lord who multiplies the resources. This wagon came from the people of the churches in Ypres who don't have that much themselves but said they had this to share."

"You'll have to thank the congregations for us," Marcus told the priest with genuine gratitude. "You need to stay! It's going to be dark, don't go back tonight."

Father James nodded. "If you have an extra cot, I'll spend a day or two and see what I can do for the wounded. If you don't have a cot, just give me a blanket on the ground."

Simon smiled, his arm around Lydia, who also nodded. "We have a spare cot for you, Father. It'll be in the doctors' tent if you don't mind sharing it with Doctor Lovell... and Doctor Stockton, who should be here somewhere... Ah, there he comes, finally. He's with Fortraine. They must've also heard the commotion."

The station commander was striding through the tents, with Harold close behind, toward the wagon being emptied. He dispensed with formalities and grasped the priest's hand. When he saw what was being unloaded from the wagon, his relief was apparent on his typically expressionless face.

"What a surprise! You've returned sooner than expected, Father James," Fortraine said. "This is very good."

Harold leaned around and reached out his hand to the priest as well. "How did you find us, Father? Even the army doesn't seem to know where we are. And somehow you figured it out?"

"God knows where you are," Father James replied, smiling as if he and the Divine had shared some heavenly secret. A message came through many people before it found me. But here I am. Perhaps I can be of assistance to the cook in the mess tent? I believe I shall go help stir whatever he's pulling together for you. Everyone eats tonight."

Chapter 22
A Lull Between Storms

The quickest meal, for Cook, was breakfast for supper. It was easy to scramble eggs, fry bacon and potatoes, and whip up some hot biscuits. In half an hour, to the minute, he had a serving line readied in the mess tent and was gratified to see everyone waiting patiently to eat. The mood was lighter, and people were feeling revived, both mentally and physically.

The first wave of recipients, had filled their bellies and then moved to one of the three tents with wounded soldiers and they all set to work, spooning nutrition into parched mouths and dipping biscuits in the warm liquid, making them easier to swallow. As soon as he could, Father James joined them out in the twilight, under the open-air tarps and then inside the enclosed tents. The need was so acute and even though the cook had made the meal in short order, it had not been fast enough for many of the wounded who had already slipped into death, while they lay waiting. Even as some were being fed, others were being carried away to the field behind the station. Father James saw the suffering in the faces. He was overwhelmed and glad he had been able to come.

As the night nurses and corpsmen took their shifts in the recovery tents, Father James continued moving between the cots, kneeling over men lying on blankets on the floor, giving last rites, and praying over the multitude of wounded. The hundreds of injured welcomed his ministry. The nurses periodically stopped to put an appreciative hand on the priest's shoulder as he knelt at the side of a cot, praying over one of the men. As he went, he heard snippets of stories about the huge explosions that, unknown to this station, had been heard all the way in London... the subsequent battle... the perception of being left to die, by the army, in their hunger. He puzzled over the situation, unable to fathom how the station could have been left to fend for itself in the war-torn countryside.

Finally, he succumbed to his own fatigue. He found the doctors' tent and saw the empty cot waiting, next to Doctor Lovell and Doctor Stockton, who were already asleep, resting for their morning shifts. The priest prayed for the two men, then for the camp as a whole, then for some individuals he knew by name, then for the generosity of the people who had provided, from the little that they had. Then, despite a small feeling of guilt over having a cot while some of the wounded were on the ground, he fell asleep for the remainder of the night.

When Lydia finally returned to her tent, Simon was already there, lying on the cot in his boxers, relaxing as only those with full stomachs could. The tension and apprehension of the week were easing, and he was grateful beyond measure for the ministry of the priest who, yet again, had kept them on his spiritual to-do list. Lydia smiled at the sight of him. She pulled off her shirt and trousers and then heard a soft whine at the door of the tent. Dimming the lantern, she pulled open the flap. Abril came in immediately and dropped down on the ground next to the footlocker. Lydia looked concerned.

"What is it, girl?" she said softly. "It's not like you to want to be inside. Did you eat something that didn't agree with you? Maybe when you were catching rabbits?" She knelt down beside the dog. Abril looked up at her, then lay down.

"Simon?" Lydia looked up at him, worried.

Simon rose from the cot and knelt beside them. The years of being asked to care for many of the farm animals in West Virginia, even doing surgery on some, came back to him. He ran a practiced hand over the dog, feeling for some sign of disease or injury. Then, he sat back. "Ah—"

Lydia felt her anxiety climb. "What, Simon? Is she going to be alright? I can't lose her!"

Simon kissed Lydia's forehead. "You are going to be a grand-mother."

"What?" Lydia asked, astonished. "Out here in the wilderness? I haven't seen a single other dog about!"

"She must have found one at some point, maybe back in the other camp. It'll be soon... I think..." Simon said, standing up and going back to the cot. "Don't worry, Lydia, she knows how to do this."

Lydia remained kneeling at the dog's side and rubbed Abril's head fondly. "When Mary Baxter said we needed more dogs, I don't think she had this in mind. But now Private Rudell, the one who found her, perhaps he'll feel much better if he gets a puppy. He didn't want to give her up to me."

Simon laughed, motioning for Lydia to join him on their cot. "He didn't give her up. She chose you."

Lydia patted the dog's head one more time. "Yes, she did choose me. And I'm glad. I never had a dog when I was little. I'm surprised by how close I feel to Abril now."

"I want to feel how close you can get to me now!" Simon urged her. "I think I've revived!"

Lydia stood up and snuggled in beside him. "It was so incredibly good to be able to feed all those men out there. Father James is a treasure. Those men weren't even complaining, only appreciative."

Simon turned on his side next to her. "You're my treasure," he declared. "It'll take a while for everyone's strength to get back up to par. Having the padre in camp again is a good feeling, for everyone's morale."

Lydia smiled and kissed him lightly. "I'm certain the cook is already hatching up ideas for the morning meal. He probably hasn't even gone to sleep yet tonight, contemplating how he can surprise us all. It really troubled him that he wasn't able to feed the camp. You could see it in his eyes."

Simon kissed her. "What do you see in my eyes, Lydia?" he asked, longing for her.

She gazed at him and shook her head. "Nope... still in the no man's land for another day or two, my love."

He pressed himself next to her and let his hand wander down over her. "Just because I can't doesn't mean you can't!" he declared, his voice growing persuasive.

She lifted his hand and placed it back firmly on her belly. "I can wait for you!" she declared. "Till we can do it together."

He leaned over her, kissed her throat, and moved down to her breast. Nuzzling her, he said, "We'll be fattening this up, too..."

"That's not fair," she whispered. "Not fair at all…" She felt his hand move back down over her skin.

"You can lodge a formal complaint later," Simon murmured, but he continued to coax her, arousing himself through her pleasure. And with the needs of one hunger met, the other hunger grew even stronger. Or maybe it was the feeling of relief from the priest's arrival, or the realization of the dog about to give birth, or from his belief that Marcus had desires for Lydia that could surpass what Simon thought were appropriate boundaries… whatever it was, Simon decided in that instant that he needed her as his own again. He rolled over her and pressed his mouth against hers, stilling any words of caution. He thrust himself into her, telling the universe this woman was his and his alone. He felt her arms around him and her legs wrap over him. Her body trembled beneath his as it drew him into her soul, where he filled her with his love, his commitment, and his claim to her.

They lay coupled together for a long time. Simon kissed her eyes, her face, her neck, murmuring his love for her with every move. She kept her arms around his neck, pulling him back down to her mouth, still eagerly seeking him out. Finally, he slid down, laying his head on her breasts, where she gently stroked his hair and traced the line of his ear with her fingers. She remembered what she had told Charlotte. The recent starvation had probably altered all of their cycles… Of one thing, Lydia was certain, this was Simon laying on her breasts, the Simon who loved her fully. No matter what else might happen to them in this war, it would be okay as long as Simon was there.

Another day passed of delicate surgery, the doctors making do with minimal sedation and being as careful as possible to avoid inflicting further pain. Lydia moved back into the surgery for the day, along with Marlene, who was excelling in the repair the lightly wounded. Charlotte was at the table with Marcus. Lydia watched for any nonverbal language passing between the two, for Charlotte's sake. She could see that Marcus remained intent on his patient, without his usual banter, which she'd come to expect when his stomach was full. Perhaps he was more subdued due to the lack of ether and concern that the soldiers were semi-conscious while their bodies were being reconstructed. Lydia herself was careful to keep talking to the soldier lying in front of Simon, reassuring him that he was going to be alright, that they were fixing his wounds, and that soon he would be better. She didn't know how much he could hear, but assumed that he was at least taking in some of her reassurance as his body stirred from time to time. The anesthetists were dolling out the ether in drops.

Harold was steady again... full belly, calm hands... there had been actual coffee. The atmosphere of the station was measurably calmer. The wounded, however, continued to die from the week of want. They were so famished that their systems had been rendered unable to stave off death. Father James remained at the station, seeing how many young bodies were accumulating in the field out on the edge of the station, staying in the recovery tents where he was being called upon frequently to minister. All of the camp watched the skies. There were no aerial attacks this morning. Some random thuds of artillery fire reached them, but none of the bitter barrage the ridge had been experiencing over the past week.

They could only hope that maybe the fighting really was winding down to the east of them.

Lydia checked on Abril frequently throughout the day. The dog hadn't moved from her spot by the footlocker in the tent, but lay panting softly, waiting. She also stopped in the mess, to thank the cooking staff, who were creating something with pork and potatoes. Then she checked in on the recovery, where the rows of men continued to grow, but much more slowly. With the concussion soldiers out of danger, all of the recovery tents were now a mix of post-surgical and men simply waiting for transport. The nurses were on alert for fever and infection. With only water for the washing of wounds, the risk of infection was climbing with every day that passed. A great many had developed fevers. The nurses now had to start returning casualties to the surgery, for the surgeons to clean out existing wounds matted with infected tissue. Lydia took note of the clipboard and the tally of numbers. The nurses needed more help from the non-medical staff for feeding and trying to keep dressings clean. Lydia wondered, along with the rest, where the trucks could be.

Within days, two events caused quite a stir in the station: the birth of Abril's pups and the arrival of Fortaine's soldiers, with their horses roped to two trucks which they had filled with medical supplies. Other vehicles, from the army, followed close behind them to finally take the wounded out of the CCS. By afternoon, a great many of the casualties had been loaded and were finally on their way to the trains and field hospitals. One of the recovery tents and the outdoor tarp were taken down as they were no longer needed. The army intended another run of the vehicles that evening, as the longer days of summer light permitted them to continue to travel. The collective group of those manning the station breathed a sigh of relief. They now had the critically needed medical supplies and some additional rations that had been dropped off at the mess tent. Doctor Fortraine was assured by this activity that the French Command was now fully aware of their location, and he confirmed with one of the drivers that communications were being restored. Additionally, written orders were received that the station was to move as soon as the wounded were fully evacuated. A new battle line was forming north, closer to Ypres. They would be needed there.

In the middle of this burst of activity, various staff stopped in to welcome the new puppies, and each of the new members of the station were claimed quickly, after weaning. Abril tolerated the visitors as long as a distance was respected. Lydia marveled at the tiny creatures, odd blends of spots and streaks of color, with closed eyes, but ready to nurse. There were five curled up inside of the dog's legs, and Abril seemed content to call the space next to the footlocker home for now. When Simon came from the surgery to see them, he stood with his arms crossed, looking down at the tiny creatures. He told Lydia the only problem would be watching where they stepped at night, in the small tent. The nurses all stopped by between shifts, appropriating two of the puppies for themselves.

Twenty-four hours later, the station was half emptied of its casualties, the dead had been buried, and Father James had departed again, with their deepest gratitude. The particularly long trial had finally come to an end.

That evening, Marcus took advantage of the calm to discover the benefits of the new shower tent, before it was taken down for their move. Even in the Paris hotel, he hadn't soaked in a tub. So now, with the surgery quiet for the evening, he decided he would finally check out the new accommodations. He filled the tub and let himself sink into the water, relishing the time to relax and unwind. It was the first time, in a long time, that he had let his mind, wander. He was just himself, immersed in a bath, and he laid back and thought about where his life was going. For the first time in a year, he wondered what he was going to do after the war was over... or after his enlistment was complete... or when the Americans were established... whichever happened first. He decided that he wasn't going to join up with the American Army. His enlistment would be up by December, along with Simon's, as they had come at the same time, a year and a half ago. *My god,* Marcus thought in alarm. *It's been a year and a half over here! A year and a half, but a lifetime...*

He could travel once the war was over. He could see Europe, without having to worry about battle fronts. He could even spend more time in Paris... but he would be alone. That prospect was not ideal. He could go home and try to find Susannah... if she would even consider rekindling a relationship with him. He could return to the hospital in Richmond, where he had practiced before enlisting and take up a staff position again. Some of the nurses he had known there might still remember him and welcome his return. It would be a big change from this... to have time to go to parties, enjoy leisure time, work a regular schedule, give some lectures to new medical students. Yes, he could join a faculty in Richmond.

Or maybe he could go into practice with Simon. *Where is he from again? West Virginia,* Marcus reminded himself. Sounded very back woods. Maybe he would just visit. *But then I would rarely see...*

No, Marcus stopped himself. That wouldn't do. He couldn't let himself think about Lydia like that. Marcus closed his eyes and leaned back in the warm bath. It was physically very relaxing, but he felt very much, alone.

He felt the air move when the flap of the tent opened and closed again. Surprised, Marcus turned suddenly to the door and saw a woman slipping inside. She was wrapped in a towel, which she dropped beside the tub as she approached.

"You invited me," Monique reminded him. "To share the bath?"

He nodded up at her, taking in her full, round, and desirous curves. "So I did!" Marcus exclaimed softly. "You are simply... stunning."

"This stunning is a good thing?" she smiled, eyebrows raised at the unfamiliar term.

Marcus smiled and extended his hand to help her slide her foot into the warm water beside him. "It's very good indeed," he said. "But it might make the bath much, much longer."

She laughed softly. "I think it will," she agreed and slid into the water, where he welcomed her gladly for the first, of many "baths" to come.

In the morning, the trucks returned to retrieve even more wounded. The station was now down to one tent of just fifty casualties still awaiting transport out. Some newly wounded did come in by ambulance, mostly falls and injuries, but there were no serious battle wounds as the fighting for the ridge had ceased. The Allies had taken the high ground, for now. Mercifully, there was ample ether for the wounded undergoing surgery. Those soldiers with only minor conditions would be returning to their units instead of going to hospitals. A few had symptoms of influenza and were shipped out that afternoon.

Doctor Fortraine was back in communication with command via the short-wave radio; they would stay in place until the morning... the evening was theirs. With the Germans pushed back, they were permitted some lights at night. Some of the soldiers lit a small fire between the tents where there was space for people to gather on blankets and watch the flames crackle and spark.

Harold stretched out on the ground and watched shadows flicker on the faces around the fire. They had made it through this very difficult half of June. There would be more difficult days to come, but they had made it through, against all odds. Everyone was aware of the simple graves marked by small crosses, over the nearby hill to the east. When the station moved, the graves would remain, a lasting testimony to the deprivation and suffering that had happened here during the last couple of weeks.

Lydia and Simon lay back on a blanket and watched the fire. It was a cool, but comfortable night. The smell of the burning wood was soothing, reminding them all of happier times. They saw the stars appearing overhead in the night sky and watched the moon begin its transit over the war-torn earth.

"It's been a long time since we've seen the Dipper together, not since down by Verdun," Simon said softly as Lydia lay back against him on the blanket and brushed away a buzzing insect.

She nodded. "I remember that night very well," she said. "And you pointed out the dragon, which I didn't see."

He chuckled. "I did say you needed a good imagination for that one."

"So much has happened since then..." she started. "It's hard to wrap my mind around it."

"I know," he agreed. "Hell and back again. But also a touch of heaven in between to keep us going. Only you could have brought me a touch of heaven in a place like this. You keep me sane, my beloved."

"When we get back home, let's make a point of spending some nights out under the stars so we can remember how we found each other," Lydia said.

"I'm not about to forget." he quietly insisted. He reached down, touching the ring she wore on her right hand. "Every minute we've had together is forever in my memory." She squeezed his hand, the presence of the others around them holding her back from showing more affection. It was all fixed in her memory as well.

Lydia looked over at some of the others gathered around the fire. She saw Charlotte across the way, sitting with her arms wrapped around her knees. She noticed Marcus lying back on a blanket with his hands under his head, just relaxing. He caught her glance and gave her a quick smile. He seemed content. Gretha and one of the corpsmen were poking long sticks into the fire and watching the tips glow in response to being lit and laughing over some small joke they shared. Alice, Sally, and some of the soldiers were lying back, watching the stars as well. Even the cook had joined them at the fire this evening... for once, not panicked about what would be available for tomorrow's meals. Lydia saw movement at the edge of the shadow around the fire, as Doctor Fortraine came into view.

Fortraine came into the circle, looking at the fire briefly. "How is everyone doing?" he asked.

Harold spoke for all of them. "Just relaxing. Welcome to join us if you like."

Fortraine shook his head. "Just checking on the camp before I retire."

"Everyone is doing well now. Taking a breather," Simon assured their commander that the crisis was past them.

"Glad to hear it." Fortraine cleared his throat. "It's quite an honor to serve with all of you," he said gruffly, and then he walked away toward his tent, leaving them all in shocked silence.

"Well! I'll second that!" Harold exclaimed. "I guess that's a good enough way to say good night for me!" He rose to his feet and headed off for his tent as well. As if on cue, one by one, the others began to take their leave for some sleep, before the morning move.

Simon stood up and looked down at Lydia. "I'll be along in a minute," he told her, heading down to the edge of the camp, toward the latrine, before they retired to their tent.

Before they knew it, Marcus and Lydia were the last ones around the campfire. Marcus got up and moved to sit down beside Lydia, on the ground. He liked how the fire light danced in her eyes.

"You look rested," she told him, relieved. "I'm very glad to see it."

"Been one hell of a couple weeks, hasn't it?" he stated. "I'm glad it's over! Wish more of the soldiers had made it through..."

She nodded. "As long as we have supplies coming, the next siege won't be nearly as bad. We lost too many because of no supplies."

"Are you okay?" he asked, looking directly at her. "Are you sleeping better? Have things inside settled down a little now, especially at night?"

"I think so," Lydia told him a little hesitantly. "Sometimes I still get nightmares, but they pass. The strangest things seem to set them off."

Marcus almost took her hand, but refrained. "I'm really sorry, Lydia. I told you I really care about you, and I meant it. I'm sorry you had to suffer. You deserve so much better than all of this."

Lydia saw the genuine concern on his face. "We've all suffered, Marcus, no one deserves any of this," she reminded him. "And we pull through it by relying on each other, like you and Simon. None of us does it alone."

"Lydia," Marcus started, "I want you to promise me that if you ever need something or need help, you will remember you can call me."

Nodding, she said, "I know that, Marcus. Really, I do know that. I just hope you find someone to settle down with... someone to love."

"But I mean even back in the States when we go home. No matter where I am or who I'm with, if you need me, I'll come. I think... I think knowing you has been the closest I've ever been to knowing what loving someone must feel like," his voice faltered with its honesty.

She put her hand on his arm to stay him. "Marcus—"

But he continued. "No, really, hear me out... please. I know you and Simon love each other in a way I can only imagine. And I'm not trying to intrude on that. I'm trying to learn from it. I told you once before that knowing you makes me want to be a better man, one that can be worthy of a love like you have. That's still the same... though I fall short, a lot."

"I remember you telling me that," she admitted. "It was a lovely compliment. I wish Suzie could have been here to hear you say it."

"I just hope that if anything ever did happen to Simon, that you would... that you'd consider me... not that anything is going to happen, of course," he stumbled. "But I wouldn't want you to ever have to be alone. I'd be there for you. And I just need you to know that. When I was drunk that one night after Susannah left, I was stupid with you, and I'm really sorry because that must have given you the wrong idea. I mean, yes, I think you're a beautiful, desirable woman, I do, but it's not just about that with you, and I want you to know that."

Lydia slowly got to her feet, and he joined her. "Marcus, you know I love Simon."

He nodded, "I know, I know. I'm not trying to change that," he said again to reassure her. "I'm trying to understand that kind of love."

She continued. "But in addition to loving Simon, there's Suzie. It would hurt her... perhaps... if we ever... and you... connected that way."

He looked surprised. "You've heard from Susannah? Did you get a letter?" Marcus exclaimed. "It sounds like you have. Is she okay? Do you know where she is? Has she said anything about me?"

Lydia nodded. "Months ago. But she's asked me to leave her relationship with you up to her to figure out in her own time, Marcus. It was really hard for her to leave you. I haven't said anything to you because she wasn't sure she was ready for me to tell you."

Marcus nodded. "I'm just glad you've heard from her and she's okay. If you write to her, would you tell her I asked about her, please?" he begged her. "I want her to know that I think about her and want her to be okay. I didn't want her to leave. I wasn't ready to make any permanent commitment then, but I didn't want her to leave. I talked to Father James about it and told him I felt guilty about it.

"I don't know why she left without any warning. Maybe I could have figured it out if she'd said something, told me she was think-ing. Maybe I could have gotten my head together in time. There was no reason for her to go so suddenly. We were good together, we were fine, we hadn't been fighting or arguing or anything of the sort. And I wasn't with anyone, but her. Honestly, Lydia, I wasn't. Suzie was the only woman I was with that entire time. There wasn't a reason for her to leave so abruptly... unless she left for another reason—" He stopped cold. "Unless she left because she had to? Lydia, did she have to leave for another reason? Did she have to leave?"

Lydia couldn't look him in the eye. He was in too much pain. "It's not for me to say why she left, Marcus," she said sadly.

"Oh my god!" he exclaimed. "I should have known!" He dropped back down on the ground and put his head in his hands as the realization hit him. "I should have known... how could I have been so blind?"

Lydia knelt down beside him and put her hand on his shoulder, feeling it shaking. She realized Marcus had quietly started crying... it was heartbreaking. She looked up to see Simon through the darkness, approaching the fire. He looked concerned and quickened his pace. Lydia stood up and went to him.

"What's going on?" he asked, concerned.

She took his hand and held it. "He just realized why Susannah left. Simon, please, talk to him..."

Simon ran his fingers through his hair. "I'll listen, but I don't have any words of wisdom for him. How could he not tell Suzie was pregnant?"

"I'll wait for you at the tent. He just needs his best friend right now," she pleaded and was grateful when he nodded.

Lydia turned away as Simon sat down next to Marcus by the fire. It would be burned down to embers before either of the men got up to leave.

The next day, they all ate before the mess tent came down. Lydia saw Marcus had circles under his eyes from a lack of sleep. She herself had fallen asleep waiting for Simon's return from the fireside talk, and she was anxious to hear how it had gone. From the look on Marcus' face, it must not have been great. The man's guilt was palpable.

Simon brought her a mug of coffee, but she moved it aside. "No, thanks, my love," she said. "We're getting ready to roll out. Look at him. He looks utterly drained."

He sat down next to her and pulled her mug over next to his own, to drink them both. "Should be. Long and very painful talk."

"I'm sorry I couldn't stay awake for you," she apologized. "I boxed up the puppies. Found some old newspaper to pad it with."

"I saw," he nodded. "They'll be fine. But Marcus... I don't know. He's feeling guilty... not that she was pregnant, but that he wasn't there."

She nodded. "I'll bet."

"He's figured out that little Marcie Nichole is about four months old already and growing up without a father. That's a lot to process. He's missing out on all of it," Simon told her, quickly eating his meal before the tent would be collapsed around them. "You didn't eat much, my love. This really got you down?"

She picked at a biscuit. "That, and seeing all the little grave markers out there on the hillside. I didn't notice them as much when all the tents were up. But now those crosses look so lonely out against the hillside. It's sobering to think how we tried to save all of them... there are eighty-seven, Simon, I counted them... and other bodies went out on trucks... and most of them died because they didn't have anything to eat."

Simon swallowed a mouthful, then corrected her, "They died because they were caught in this awful war. And you are still here with me; you need to eat. None of us are back to ourselves yet. Not taking care of yourself doesn't honor those dead boys out there."

Lydia looked down at her untouched hash. "I know you're right. I just don't feel up to it. I'll be alright." She pushed her plate over toward Simon, and he dove into the hash, finishing it up before they gathered their utensils and took them to be washed.

They left the tent and found a spot on the dry ground to wait near the trucks while the last tent, the mess, was dismantled. The rest of the nurses, Harold and Marcus were there as well, no doubt thinking of what was to come. Another battle ahead. But this time, the army knew where they were. This time, they would be able to do their work fully supplied. Doctor Fortraine had assured them all that he was in regular communication with Army Command, and their location was well known. The disaster of the last couple of weeks wouldn't be repeated. The station moved out as soon as the last of the tent poles and crates were loaded. The trucks and wagons pulled away, in a line, leaving nothing but the graves of the dead and the cratered earth behind them... but the memories of the medical team were all on board.

As the trucks dodged craters and rolled over rutted roads, they were all lost in their own thoughts. This time, it was Simon who dozed off against Lydia's shoulder, after having been up much of the night discussing Marcus' personal challenges. This next offensive would be the third time that Ypres would come under siege from the Allied and German bombardments. The convoy was drawing nearer to the coast, and the smell of the salty ocean lingered on the air, when the wind blew in from the north.

Some seagulls flew over the fields with raucous calls to the crows clustered in the grasses below them. Abril and the little box with the puppies were at Lydia's feet in the truck. Lydia looked down at them from time to time. They were so tiny... so vulnerable... just like little Marcie Nichole, who at least had a devoted mother and doting grandparents to care for her. She felt bad for Marcus. The sins of the father were catching up to him... but not being passed on to the child, who would make it without him, if need be. Lydia wondered again what Marcus was going to do. She hadn't told him where Suzie was. He hadn't asked for her address. She would have to write Suzie first and get permission before divulging that information, and it would take months for a reply.

She also had a letter still to write to the woman, Mary, the love of that British soldier, Byron, who was buried on the grassy slope they had just left behind. At least she would be able to tell her where his body was laid respectfully, along with many other heroes of the war. Perhaps one day, Mary would come here to place flowers on the grave... or perhaps she would choose to move on, as Susannah might have already done.

Lydia's thoughts rambled on as the trucks and the mule-driven wagons creaked along. They stopped once to rest the animals and let people stretch. Boarding again, they finished the trip, still in Belgium territory near Ypres, with Dunkirk and the sea to the north. The camp was set up quickly, and the medical team moved quietly around the tents, getting ready for the next round of casualties that would come to their station. Now, again, it was time to wait.

Lydia decided to write her letter. She took out the photo of Mary, carefully addressing an envelope she had gotten from Doctor Fortraine's aide. She wrote with compassion, knowing that as soon as the woman saw the photo in the envelope, there would be no further explanation required. But later, after tears had been shed, Mary might read, and reread, the words that only a woman could send to another woman, in similar circumstances. She wrote from the heart and gently sealed the letter shut.

She then pulled out another sheet, to write to Susannah. It was necessary to let her know that Marcus had, at last, figured it out. She had no idea how Suzie would respond. Lydia hoped that the mailbags would catch up to them in this new camp and that there might already be a letter from her friend, giving her some guidance about how Susannah was doing now... whether she had found someone new to love. Lydia also wanted to write to her mother and father, but how to begin to describe what had been happening? There were simply no words...

She took the blank sheets of paper to the mess tent while Simon met with Fortraine and the other doctors, planning out their next round of battle response. Some of the nurses were in the mess as well, also writing letters, playing cards, and sipping on hot coffee. Lydia joined Marlene, Charlotte, Nancy, and Gretha gathered together at the long table.

"How're you all holding up?" she asked them as she laid her paper and pen down beside her.

"We are playing cards and thinking up names for our puppy," they said while holding cards in their hands... but without very much secrecy from one another.

"Who's winning?" Lydia asked curiously.

"We aren't keeping score!" Marlene laughed. "Seems we all forgot how to do it, so, we're just laying out cards."

"What about the puppy names?" Lydia asked as she slid her legs over the bench.

"Has to be a French name," Charlotte replied, "for Abril's sake. Simone... Marie... Lorraine..."

"Sounds like you're naming a baby girl! What if the puppy is a boy? You haven't figured that out yet." Gretha laughed. "We're taking our puppy right into our tent, Lydia. It's going to be Nurse One Dog. The other girls are taking Nurse Two Dog into their own tent. They'll be much adored."

Lydia straightened her paper and pencil and leaned on the table, watching them lay down cards, in turn. "They've been a bright spot, in the most dreadful time."

The others nodded in complete agreement. "Do you know what's with Doctor Lovell?" Marlene asked her then. "He's pasty as all get out, this morning."

Nancy agreed. "He looks like he's got a bad case of the flu or something. I wonder if he's got a fever. Should we check on him?"

Lydia shook her head. "I don't think it's physical," she said carefully. "Simon talked to him last night. He just has a lot on his mind, from what I understand. Things have been hard on all of us lately. Simon tried to help him sort some things out. Wouldn't it be wonderful to get some mail out here? I want to hear from home and send some letters out. It's been so long since we've had a mailbag delivered!"

Marlene nodded. "It's been forever. I sent everything off and am still waiting to hear if I'll be accepted to medical school. The doctors were all gracious enough to write recommendations for me. That was such a shot in the arm! Sure hope their opinions count for something, back in the States."

"I hope you do get in if that's what you really want, Marlene," Charlotte said gently. "But what are you going to do if they say, no?"

"Oh, I don't know," the other answered lightly, belying her want. "Open a bakery. Sell croissants. Bake pies... eat pies..."

Nancy laughed. "Sounds thrilling. But you know what I think? If you don't get into medical school for some absurd reason, then become a midwife! It's as close to surgery as you'll get without being a surgeon. Bring babies into the world. You'd be on your own a lot, sometimes in life-or-death situations... a lot like here!"

Marlene paused, holding her cards in her hand without laying one down. She looked over at Nancy seriously. "You know what, Nancy? That is actually a really good suggestion. I hadn't thought of that, but it's true. I could be a good midwife. I really am going to consider that for my backup plan. Did you do maternity ever?"

"Just in my own family. Helped deliver the babies for some cousins of mine. But it's too much screaming for me. Those women in labor looked like they were dying... but glad the suggestion helped," Nancy said. "For myself, I'm going to take a break from nursing. Maybe I'll run a school for orphaned kids or something... or go work for the Red Cross. See if Mary Baxter can find me a position somewhere in Philadelphia. I could still travel a little. Still help the cause."

"I'm sure she would," Lydia told her. "She knows how skilled you all are, and she'd have been truly amazed at how we all pulled together through the last several weeks. She would probably welcome any of you... not for war, God willing, but maybe for relief in floods and earthquakes and natural disasters like that. There are always plenty of those. How about you, Gretha? What will you do after the war?"

Gretha smiled peacefully. "My grandparents' farm is waiting for me. I'm going to take care of the cows, the sheep, and the goats.

I'll sit at night and listen to the corn growing in the fields. I have no desire to see any more bullet wounds or broken bodies. I just want to go home to the farm. And any of you who want to visit, can come and sit at the pond, catch fish, sit by a fire at night, and listen to the owls calling out from the barn. They have a big old farmhouse with five bedrooms in it. It's very quiet there in the country. It's very soothing."

"Where is that again?" Nancy asked her.

"Ohio," Gretha said. "I'll make sure you all have the address."

Lydia asked them all, "Do you think we'll keep in touch, really? After we go home? I mean, I want to, but will we really do it or just say we will, like people promise after school is finished?"

"Sure we will," Charlotte replied. "Why ever not? You hear from Susannah, don't you? We'll write each other, and visit, when we get home. It'll be good to have a reunion from time to time and talk about our war stories."

Lydia nodded. "I do hear from Suzie. I hope to again. I really do want to see all of you when we go home, though. I don't want us to lose touch after everything we've been through together."

Marlene laid down a card on the table. "Suz was the smart one, to leave before the last disaster here. I sure hope she's okay. How'd she sound in the last letter, Lydia? Is she happy?"

"She said she missed everyone here and was bored to tears at the hospital, changing bedpans and saying 'yes, sir' and 'no, sir' to the doctors," Lydia told them. "She said nurses aren't allowed to think or have an opinion about anything. They have to stand up when a doctor enters the room."

They all laughed.

"If I ever make it to being a doctor, no nurse is going to say 'yes, ma'am' or 'no, ma'am' to me… or stand up when I enter!" Marlene declared.

"What's that in your hand, Lydia?" Nancy asked, looking at the small, wrapped square.

Lydia opened it and showed them. "Her name is Mary. Her boyfriend's name was Byron. I had to tell her about his death; I promised him before he died that I'd send it back to her with his love."

"Ouch," Charlotte said. "That's tough. We've had to write too many of those letters. I've got a couple waiting for the mail to go out, myself. It's important for those boys dying in our care, I know. Never easy, though."

They all grew quiet. It truly did not ever get easier.

"Well, ladies," Marlene said, rising from the table. "It's been lovely to play cards with all of you. I'm going to go lay down for a bit and enjoy the freedom to simply do nothing."

"Well said," Charlotte agreed. "I think I'll go sit in the tub, if it's available, and enjoy getting wrinkled from head to toe. What a luxury that tub has been!"

Gretha added, "Lydia, do you mind if I go visit the puppies?"

"Not at all," the other replied. "I'm just going to sit here and write letters awhile."

The four women moved off, leaving Lydia alone with her thoughts and pencil. Finally, she started to write:

Dear Mother,

It's been a long time, I know. We haven't been able to send out or get any mail for many months, so I apologize for the long delay and hope you and Father are well. Just because I haven't written doesn't mean I don't think of you constantly and pray for you. Maybe there will be a letter from you in the next mailbag, if we ever get one. I did write you about Simon. Hope you got that letter.

I hope your joints aren't giving you grief. It should be warm there, too, now, and I bet the heat feels good.

Simon and I are good. I mean, we're good for each other. Nothing much is good about being here lately, but he is very, very good to me. I'm so looking forward to you meeting him. He's a remarkable man. He knows when I need my spirits lifted. And he's very gentle with me. I'm sure I try his patience sometimes when I get down and frustrated with everything going on here. But if I do, he doesn't make mention of it. Just keeps on loving me.

The priest was here twice, Father James. He seems to come to the station right when we need him most. I guess that's God bringing him around. What a kind man, spending hours with the wounded men, but not forgetting us as well.

Did I tell you I have a dog here? Yes, me! Her name is Abril, which comes from the word for shelter, in French. She adopted me, and Simon says we're bringing her home with us, whenever we make it home. She just had five puppies, who are the focus of everyone's affections here. What a treat to see their tiny little bodies against her. I'm glad she had them now while it's warm out, so they'll be strong before winter hits us. It gets pretty cold in the camp in winter, but we don't need to worry about that now.

I wonder how Sis is doing and the children. I think about them all the time. I hope someday Simon and I have children. I'd love to see them all play together. It feels sometimes like that will never happen the way things go around here. Everything is so demanding. Life feels so short when there are people dying all around, but maybe we'll make it home. God willing, we will, and we'll have a good chance to talk and be together. I'd love it if you'd make your meatloaf and your soft, baking powder biscuits. They're the best ever. Makes me hungry just thinking about it! Tell Father that I love him very much. I hope you've forgiven me from my last letter of explanation... if you got it. I love you both.

    Lydia

Lydia signed and sealed up the letter and addressed it. Then, she put the two together and tucked them into her shirt pocket to take to Doctor Fortraine's aide, for the mailbag. Rising up from the bench, she decided to take the short walk around the station. Abril joined her as she left the mess, her tail wagging happily out in the summer air. She bounced around, sniffing the ground and checking out the various tents as they made their way around the camp. *She has more energy than I do,* Lydia thought. Together, they dropped off the letters. There was one more she wanted to write, and that would be to Susannah, but not just now.

The smell of the ocean reached them, on the breeze, and Lydia was glad for it. She recalled sailing across the channel from England to the Belgian coast, landing at Calais, just over a year ago. What a lifetime ago that seemed now. She was not the girl from Pennsylvania who'd left Philadelphia to make a difference, not by a long shot. She was a nurse and a wife and much wiser to the sorrows of the world. At the edge of the camp, she peered out over the horizon. There was a little cluster of crosses marking the ground, far off in the distance, to the east. The war had already been here, she realized with a pang of emotion. It would come again. Suddenly, she felt sadness beyond measure. Kneeling down at a patch of small yellow flowers growing close to the ground, she plucked a couple of them, marveling at the softness of the petals and their perfect design. Nature seemed, effortlessly, to get it right... while humans seemed to go to great trouble, just to get it wrong.

She wondered if there was anything she could do for Marcus... and why he treated relationships so casually. Did he not have a good role model for intimacy as she had had? But then, Simon never had a model for close relationships either, with both of his parents lost at an early age, and he seemed to have overcome that limitation quite well. She thought to herself that he would no doubt be an even more conscientious father, not wanting to miss out on the experience for a single minute... not wanting the past to repeat itself.

Then, Lydia noticed something metallic glinting in the flowers. A shell casing lay beneath the greens, then another, and another. There must have been a battle right on this very ground. Suddenly, she leaned over and vomited into the grass. Everything beautiful was tainted by the war. Abril came bounding over to her as she knelt on the ground. Grief washed over her. Grief for Mary and Byron and the eighty-six other young men they had left behind at their last station, grief for the eighty-seven more that would probably die at this new one, grief over Marcie Nichole not knowing the arms of a loving father, for Susannah carrying on alone, doing the best she could... for Marcus, missing out on it all...

Lydia couldn't stop the tears from flowing. Everything from the past several months seemed to have come to a head. She leaned her head on the dog sitting still beside her and wept as if her heart was broken. That was where Simon found her. He sat down on the grass beside her and gathered her into his arms. They didn't speak, and he didn't hush her. He saw the shell casings in her hand and the plucked yellow flowers and surmised the source of her distress easily enough.

After a moment, she wiped her eyes on her shirt sleeve and took a deep breath. They sat together in silence, watching seagulls fly high overhead, taking in a buzzard soaring effortlessly in circles, the clouds moving on the breeze from the sea, watching the grasses, growing over the battlefield, wave slightly, as the air commanded. He kissed her forehead as he often did when he wanted to comfort her. Finally, he spoke in a matter-of-fact tone.

"I do push-ups," he told her.

"I know," she said softly. She saw him do it regularly.

"No, I mean to let it out. To try to push back against the war and all the things we see. I try to just push it back into the ground, push myself up away from it in return. Sometimes the more, the better."

"Does it work?" she asked him, still sniffling slightly.

"Most of the time. Harold taught Marcus and me some boxing moves a time ago. But I'm afraid I'd hurt someone if I started throwing punches, even in a sparring match, so the push-ups work better. Unless my arms get so sore that I can't operate." He reached up and squeezed her upper arm. "Nope, don't think you could do it. Not enough muscle."

She felt her own arm. "There's enough there to hold onto you."

He hugged her. "That's enough, then. I've been thinking, Lydia. We should go home as soon as my time is up. I'm not signing on with the American Army. We aren't staying here in Europe."

She nodded. "I was hoping you'd say that," she admitted, taking a moment before continuing. "I just wrote my mother again, and I don't even know if she got my last letter. What if they haven't forgiven me yet for coming over here?"

"They're going to be so glad to see you that they will forget everything else. Just like Susannah's family did. I'm sure of that," Simon told her. "Even my brother and sister said they hope I make it back in one piece, and we aren't nearly as close as your family is. I think all was forgiven before you were even halfway across the Atlantic." He looked up and saw the sun dipping over to the west. "We need to go back inside the camp before it gets dark and the sentries shoot us."

She stood up and dropped the shell casings back to the ground where wind and rain would plant them back into the earth again. But the yellow flowers she took with her. Simon stood as well, wrapping his arm around her waist, and they walked back to the tents, with Abril bouncing along at their heels.

"Let's grab some supper before we go in," Simon suggested as they neared the small collection of tents.

Lydia shook her head and turned toward their little tent. "You go ahead. I'm tired, and my eyes are probably all red and puffy. I don't want people to ask about it. Bring me something that you can put in your pocket and I'll eat it later. Please, my love."

He looked at her with concern and kissed her forehead again. "I think you're beautiful, puffy eyes or not," he said softly. "See you in a little bit."

She slipped into their tent, where Abril settled in next to her puppies, to nurse. There, Lydia stretched out on the cot and pulled off her boots. She laid down gratefully, wound the music box Simon had given her, and closed her eyes, listening to the soft refrain of the waltz, playing several times until the mechanism wound itself down and stopped. It soothed her to hear the sweet notes fill the tent, and she wound it once again. Then, she decided to get back up and take a quick shower before going to sleep. She grabbed a towel, left her boots at the foot of the cot, and padded over through the grass to see if the shower was unoccupied. It was, as everyone else eating in the mess tent. Unlike Charlotte earlier, Lydia didn't want the big tub tonight. She just wanted to feel clean from the war, and turning on hot water was a welcome respite, washing away the cares of the day. She dried off, feeling refreshed, and made her way back to the tent. Simon was coming back from the mess at the same time and met her at the door. He saw her hair wet and dripping.

"Didn't want company?" he teased her, sounding more than a little disappointed.

"I'm happy to go back with you," she assured him. "It's still open."

"It's okay," he said, grabbing a towel for himself. "Give me ten minutes. I'll be right back, I promise."

She reached up and kissed him softly on the lips. "I'll be here." She undressed and slipped into their cot. Before she knew it, her eyes were drifting shut. When Simon returned after showering in record time, he saw she was already dozing. Simon took off his clothes and slipped under the light blanket next to her, hopefully. She stirred and snuggled against him, but didn't open her eyes. Sighing deeply, he wrapped an arm around her and, after a time, fell asleep himself.

Chapter 23
Round Three

July had come. There were minor skirmishes, but no major campaign yet, by either the Allied or German armies. Tensions were rising as the station wondered what might be coming and when. Doctor Fortraine decided to send the medical team to the British CCS for a chance to relieve the anxiety of waiting with some socialization between the two teams. The British station was just north of them between Ypres and Passchendaele. They were well positioned to receive wounded when the fighting began again. The last time the two teams had gotten together, it had been winter, and they had enjoyed dancing to the music of the Victrola. This time, in the warm night of summer, the British team had another surprise for their guests, a large white sheet had been stretched between two poles, and they had found a movie projector that could be run by a small generator. On blankets, outside of the tents, they laid out and laughed, watching Douglas Fairbanks on the screen in a movie called *Double Trouble*. The diversion was well received by both sides and worth fending off a few hungry mosquitos as they watched.

Tonight, there was no speculation about what would be coming in the next week or so. It was understood that the get-together was to preserve sanity and not prepare for war, so the conversation was kept to light, friendly banter. It was also apparent to both teams that David Winston and Laura Bertolli had become more than casual friends and didn't want to hide the fact anymore. His gift of the watch had now taken on an added significance as the group of friends noticed the two interacting comfortably during the course of the evening. Lydia was glad to see that Laura and David had made a connection. She had always thought highly of Doctor Winston ever since their first encounter. Simon, watching Lydia, was relieved to see her relaxed and enjoying herself, laughing at the romantic comedy on the make-shift movie screen. Her distress in the grassy field back at the station seemed to have passed. They were all going to spend the night with the British and head back the following day. Tonight, for once, there was no rush to leave their friends and return to war.

The Third Battle of Ypres began near the end of July. The German army had intermittently clashed with British, French, and Belgian troops in skirmishes earlier in the month, and a strategic artillery bombardment had begun in earnest in preparation for an offensive move by the Allies. The medical teams in both the French and British stations knew that an intense period of battle was coming. The triage station had had more than enough time to prepare. They efficiently moved the small numbers of incidentally injured soldiers and those with influenza symptoms in and out of the station, confident that their connection with the army was strong and their supply chain intact. They were as ready as they could be.

Then, as July was coming to a close, the sky grew overcast and the air grew thick with moisture, smelling of the sea. Rain started falling in sheets. Before they knew it, the ground was soaked and muddy. Ditches were rapidly dug in, to drain water away from the surgery and recovery tents. They now had to make ready to receive triage casualties under the cover of tents and on hastily erected cots to keep the men out of the rain. Sanitation depended on the ability of the soldiers to keep ahead of any standing pools of water turning brown and sticky. The artillery bombardment continued day after day to the east, pounding into the wet earth. The medical team could only imagine what the foot soldiers were going through in the torrents of rain, with the ground too soggy and muddy for them to run or flee enemy attacks. It was rapidly turning into a miserable state of affairs. Cases of pneumonia were on the rise, and the station hastily erected a separate tent for those men with lung infections who needed transport to field hospitals.

In the surgery tent, they found out quickly where every hole existed for water to leak through onto the operating tables. Harold swore, as water dripped down into his patient's open wound.

"Corpsman," he called, and one of the soldiers came running "Get a tarp erected inside of this tent over us somehow. We have to have some protection from the rain for these patients." So, while the surgeons operated, the station crew put up poles inside of the surgery and stretched a tarp overhead to catch any rain that found its way inside. Though it limited their head space and made it difficult to keep light positioned where it needed to shine, it kept everyone dry.

Simon, taking a break from the surgery, ran through the rain to the latrine and then back to his own tent. He ducked inside and saw leaks coming through there as well. Taking out their ponchos, he erected one as a shelter over Abril and the puppies by their footlockers, covering what little possessions they owned, and he stretched the other out over the cots to give them a little bit of a dry spot in case they got a chance to sleep. Then, he set out for the mess tent, where hot tea and coffee were in high demand. The cook had a hot potato soup on hand just to provide something comforting and warm for the team. It was not a particularly cool day in July, but the heavy rain required some comfort. Another inside tarp was erected over the cooking equipment and serving line, keeping the staff, and food, reasonably dry. Simon found Lydia in the mess, wiping water off the table with a sleeve, and sat down beside her, giving her a quick kiss on the cheek.

"How are you holding up?" he continued. "I think we're going to have to build an ark soon."

"Is everything working in the surgery?" she asked. "I'll be over this afternoon when I'm done in the recovery. I'm okay, but lots of these soldiers are coughing and feverish. Influenza or pneumonia, I don't know which."

"It's better over there with the inside tarp up," Simon told her. "At least we aren't washing out wounds with rain water!" he added, sighing. "Are you drinking tea? That's not like you! There's coffee on. Want me to get you some?"

She shook her head. "No, for some reason, the tea tastes good in the rain, and you should eat quick before your food gets diluted."

"Did you get your breakfast this morning after your shift last night?" he wondered anxiously.

She nodded. "More than enough. This weather is enough to turn anyone off from a meal... except you, of course. I do believe you could eat in the middle of a tornado!" she declared. "Could you eat when you sailed over here from the States? I'll bet you didn't even get seasick."

He nodded. "I ate just fine on the ship. Didn't bother me at all. Some poor guys wretched the entire trip. Felt bad for them. Marcus did okay. I didn't mind the waves."

"Yuck!" Lydia exclaimed. "Makes me nauseous just thinking about it!"

He laughed and stroked her soft cheek affectionately. "I'll remember to take a bucket along when we sail home!" He leaned over then and kissed her lips quickly as he downed his meal. "I miss you when you work through the night. Hurry over to surgery."

She nodded. "I'll be there soon. I want to check on Abril and put on some dry socks, and then I'll be over."

He stood up and kissed her once more on top of her head before running back out through the rain over to the surgery, where it was humid, but mercifully dry under the tarp inside the tent. Soon, he was back at work on the next casualty. It wasn't too long before Lydia came in as well and scrubbed her hands before donning her mask and apron. She made her way through the busy tables to where Marcus was just starting a case and needed an assistant.

"Ah, Nurse Finney," Marcus said. "Welcome to the surgery. The only good thing about the rain and thunder is we can't tell artillery from the weather. For all I know, the battle is over out there and it's just the rain that won't give up."

She took her place beside him. "I'm afraid the triage is still growing, Doctor Lovell. I think the artillery is firing, even in the rain. They must still be fighting out there. Look at this poor man, mud up to his knees. Oh, my. What if he's wounded under all that mud?"

Marcus looked at the prostrate man in front of them. "He needs a good wash, doesn't he? How are the nurses situated in the recovery for getting these fellows cleaned up? Bullet wound, left groin..."

"And his upper arm... right here... I'll get his sleeve off," Lydia replied. "We're trying to rinse the guys off in triage before they even get in here. Some of the corpsmen are helping us bring warm water out under the triage tarp so we can de-mud them first, but there's a lot of work to go around. Just getting their boots off is a challenge. Stuck to their legs. The ditches are a huge help, though. The soldiers are keeping them free of debris to let the rain run off."

"I need you on this groin, Nurse Finney. Can you open this wound more so I can see where the artery is? I need a little l—"

Lydia shined a flashlight down into the groin, so Marcus could see the femoral artery pulsing. "Better?"

"Better," he said softly. "Just what I needed."

Then, Lydia called urgently over to Alice circulating through the tables. "Alice, I need you here now!" she said in distress. Alice came over immediately, and Lydia thrust the flashlight into her outstretched hand. Lydia turned and fled the surgery tent through the tables and out into the rain beside the tent, where she vomited her lunch. She held her stomach and felt the rain pelting her, feeling the dizziness and nausea pass. She had been in the influenza tent all morning and now couldn't feel her forehead in the rain to see if she was feverish or not. Simon saw her run out of the tent with concern. He couldn't leave his patient, and there was no one free inside the surgery tent who could go. Moments later, he saw with relief that she was already returning through the tent opening, looking a little wan. She scrubbed her hands again and returned to her spot beside Marcus, retrieving the flashlight from Alice, who looked at her questioningly.

"You okay, Lydia?" Alice asked, concerned. "You look a little pale."

Lydia nodded. "Between the rain and all those boys with fevers in that recovery tent coughing all night, I'm trying to avoid getting sick!" she stated. "I refuse to be sent out to a field hospital with influenza. If I get a fever, just put me to bed in my tent to sweat it out!"

Alice gave her a quick nod. "Same goes for me. Tell the cook to make me chicken soup… if there's any chicken around… and I'm doing the same. You aren't the only one looking pale. Linda and Marlene are under the weather, too! They're both lying down in their tent right now, trying to fight it off. Gretha sent word they won't be coming over for their surgery shifts. We'll have to keep it going ourselves, with them out sick."

Lydia sighed, worried, as she handed Marcus instruments. "Oh, dear. We can't run short on staff with all these casualties coming in like this. Maybe we should be wearing masks over in the influenza tent like we do here, just in case. We did that last fall, and it seemed to help us fight off the pneumonia. Let's do it again. And we can set up a separate tent just for influenza cases amongst ourselves, if we need to quarantine, so it doesn't spread."

Simon, listening in, thought, *Except for you! You won't be apart from me if you get sick!* Lydia had tended him through his long recovery from his infected leg wound. He would care for her in their own tent. Now, he was anxious to listen to her lungs and check her for himself. He wanted to evaluate the other two nurses as well before Marcus got the idea to do it. He considered how last autumn the medical team had largely escaped the various illnesses brought in to them at the station. This year, they might not be as fortunate. If a major outbreak happened in the camp, Doctor Fortraine would have to find a way to divert the wounded from the station until it ran its course and everyone was back on his or her feet. He decided to talk to Harold and Fortraine about how that could be accomplished at the first lull in the fighting. They did not need an epidemic of influenza.

A brief lull came by early evening. With the heavy rain, the mutual armies seemed to have given up the day's quest for superiority. The artillery stopped for the night, but the rain did not. The surgery emptied out and the triage closed down, all the care shifting over to the recovery. Simon went to the tent where the sick and feverish patients lay. He wore a mask from the surgery in an effort to keep any bacteria or virus from being coughed into his face. In the tent, he examined several of the casualties, determining what their primary symptoms were and if they were adequately hydrated. Swollen glands, fevers, generalized weakness and fatigue, and headaches seemed to be the majority of the complaints for these men. Some were coughing severely. He encouraged the nurses and corpsmen to wear masks and wash their hands as often as they could. Then, Simon went to find the two sick nurses, Marlene and Linda, both prostrate in their own tent, and on examining them, found they were describing similar symptoms with swollen glands, headaches, and fevers. He didn't need to encourage the other nurses to check on them frequently, he knew that they would be well cared for. He went to find Lydia, his anxiety growing that he would see her in the same condition.

Lydia was lying down in their tent, resting quietly. The rain wasn't dripping in too badly at the moment, and she had moved the poncho aside and closed her eyes, exhausted. Simon sat by her and reached out to feel the glands on her neck, and she stirred under his touch.

"How are you feeling?" he asked her, concerned. "I've already checked the other two nurses. They've got almost exactly the same symptoms as the soldiers. Same bacteria, for sure. And look at you... washed out and exhausted. You don't feel hot, though."

"I'm so sorry to hear the girls are ill. I'm just tired," she said, and even her voice was weary. "Thank you for checking on them and also for making the little tent for Abril. I'm so glad the wounded have already stopped coming for tonight so we could shut down. How long do you think this rain will keep pouring down, Simon? I really miss the sun."

"You're welcome for Abril's tent. And I wanted to check on the other nurses before Marcus got the idea!" he exclaimed softly. "Figured I'd better do the poking and prodding of swollen glands instead of him touching them all over and weakening his newest and most noble resolve to be somewhat chaste. Maybe for this week anyhow. Now it's your turn for a check-up, my lovely one."

Simon began poking and prodding Lydia, pressing along her throat on the sides of her neck, the back of her neck along her spine, and then her armpits. He took his stethoscope and opened her shirt to listen to her chest.

"Simon," she admonished him. "I'm just tired, I'm not dying!"

He raised a hand to hush her as he listened to her chest. "Take some deep breaths for me, please."

She obliged him so that he could take the earpieces out of his ears and listen to her. "Were you this thorough with the other nurses? If I just sleep a bit, I'll be fine, and we'll go get some supper," she insisted. "Or you could just go ahead, and I'll meet you there in a little bit..."

"I'm not done checking you yet," he said gently and opened her trousers to check her abdomen and the glands in her groin. He said, "Hm..." as he pressed all over her belly, and then he got up and tied the flap to their tent shut against any intrusion. Simon came back to the cot and said, "Lydia, I need to slide your trousers down."

She sighed. "Simon, I love you with all of my heart, truly I do, but I'm just worn out. Not that I won't enjoy your touch, but if you want to be together right this minute, you'll have to do all the work!"

"I'll do all the work... you might feel some pressure," he assured her. He slid her undergarment down and bent up her knees on the cot.

"Simon, what on earth are you d—" she started as she felt him put his fingers inside of her and press his hand into her belly above her pelvis.

He leaned over her as he examined her, his expression indecipherable. "It's been a while since I had maternity experience, but you don't have influenza. You are very pregnant, my love," he told her softly.

Lydia's eyes grew round as saucers. "Simon... that can't be."

"Really?" he said, standing back up over her, his eyes a mixture of love, caution, and anxiety all at once. "I'm quite sure that I know what I'm feeling, my beloved. Your uterus is nicely rounded and growing. Your ovaries are alright. I thought your breasts seemed more full to me."

Lydia touched her breasts. "They've been a little firmer, but I thought I was just regaining the weight I'd lost when there wasn't enough food. And I thought I was off my cycle for the same reason. Are you absolutely sure, Simon? Absolutely?"

Simon laid both of his hands protectively over her pelvis for a moment and then leaned over, tenderly kissing her where his hands had been. Then he kissed both of her breasts before helping her dress again. Finally, he took her in his arms. He kissed her for a long time. "I'm absolutely sure. I love you. We'll go home in November as soon as I'm released from service. That's four months. Can you handle this? Here? For four months? We'll be able to get home long before it's no longer safe to travel. We'll get you back to your family, and then your mother and sister can be with you for the birth."

Lydia rested against him, still trying to absorb the realization that she was carrying Simon's child. She pressed one hand against her abdomen. "It's not influenza...? I'm sorry. I'm still stuck on you saying that I'm pregnant..." she whispered. "With your baby...?"

"Gosh, I hope it's mine!—" he teased her, his eyes now twinkling as they filled with joy.

She lightly slapped his upper arm. "Of course, it's yours!" she scolded right back. "I'm happy, but I'm scared, all at the same time, my love. I can't even think yet about four months... or of going home. I'm gonna need a minute to think... to let this sort of settle in somewhere in my head..."

He nodded. "Same." They lay together on the cot, holding each other quietly, thinking of the numerous implications before them.

"Simon, what if something goes wrong here at the station in the first few months? What if I can't carry a baby all the way, under these circumstances? I don't know what to do!" Lydia exclaimed, her eyes suddenly tearing.

He held her tightly against his chest in reassurance. "We're young and healthy... mostly healthy, anyway. You'll eat right and get extra sleep, and your body will do the rest... just like Abril. And wasn't Susannah was here for about four months while pregnant... and she kept right on with her duties even in the thick of things. And now, little Marcie Nichole is doing just fine. Your body knows how to do this. There's no reason to think anything will go wrong. In fact, the baby is safer inside of you than anywhere else on Earth."

Her voice was almost imperceptible. "The baby... inside of me... I'm having your baby..." she repeated. "Oh, Simon. I loved you before this. I loved you completely. But this, this changes things. I didn't think about getting pregnant."

Simon just held her and kissed her forehead. "Do you want to tell any of the others?" he asked.

"Not just yet," she declared firmly. "I'm still trying to get used to this myself... and what if I lose the baby? A lot of women lose the first one. No, I don't want to say anything yet. And what would Fortraine say? Would he send me away? Let's keep it to ourselves for right now, please?"

He nodded, understanding her concern. "Fine with me," he told her. "Tell the other nurses when you're ready. But it'll be hard for me not to want to protect and watch over you a little more... keep you from overdoing it. People might begin to notice that I'm hovering a bit. And it'll be hard not to tell Marcus; he knows me so well!"

"People already see you hovering over me," she corrected. "But your eyes, they're positively beaming. People might reasonably wonder what you've found in the middle of war and rain... and mud and casualties to make you look so happy. You... you don't seem scared a bit... you seem, excited."

He looked down at her, snuggled against his chest. "Yes, I'm happy. I want children with you. Always have, from the minute we said our vows. I figured we'd wait until we got back this winter... and it's all my fault, really."

Lydia gently corrected him, "I think it's both our faults! It did take the two of us."

He explained, "No, really, I mean the timing of this. I'm the one that put you in this predicament because I took a chance six weeks ago, and I knew it was a risk."

Lydia looked puzzled. "Six weeks ago... I don't even remember six weeks ago..."

"You warned me it was no man's land for another day or two, and I chose to ignore it. It was when Father James was here," Simon reminded her, thinking back on that night. "I wanted you so badly that night after we'd finally eaten that I couldn't stand it. It was a risk. But this baby was conceived in love either way. A rather intense love... I do remember that night fairly well."

She nodded, now recalling the night herself, when their relief at Father James's arrival with food and the security of his presence in the station touched all of them so deeply. She remembered then, the urgent need to come together. Yes, that would be about the right timing. "Let's forget about fault altogether. How do we tell our baby it was conceived in Belgium, in the middle of a war?" she teased him.

"We don't, not until they're fully grown and would get a chuckle out of the story that I couldn't keep my hands off of you. We'll just always tell our children they were conceived in love," Simon told her matter-of-factly. "Now, what about supper? I'm famished, but I know this is a lot to take in. Do you feel like eating?"

"You and your insatiable appetite!" she exclaimed. "Well, if I'm eating for two, I should do a better job of it." She sat up on the cot as he released her from his arms and pulled her boots back on, preparing for the mud puddles she'd soon be navigating. She embraced Simon one more time before leaving the tent. "I love you..." she was deep in thought, "It's no bigger than a walnut... Simon, you're a father."

He laughed. "Wow! Do I like the sound of that!"

They ran out of the tent, through the rain and across to the mess, dodging the raindrops. Upon entering the mess, they shook off as much of the water as possible, before they got in line. The majority of the team was already eating. Simon and Lydia joined Harold and Marcus and several of the nurses at the long table.

Harold looked up immediately. "You checked the sick nurses, Doctor Finney?" he asked Simon quickly. "What do you think? Is it influenza after all?"

"My guess," Simon confirmed, getting situated on the bench and picking up his fork. "Fever, headache, fatigue, enlarged glands.

No major chest congestion, no rashes. Just what many of the soldiers are saying over in the recovery. Nurse Bernstein seems to be a very proficient caretaker for them. The nurses and corpsmen in the recovery are now masking and washing to see if we can contain the spread, among ourselves."

"How are you feeling, Nurse Finney?" Marcus asked her in genuine concern. "You ran out of the surgery rather abruptly earlier."

She smiled at him. "Not to worry, Doctor Lovell. I've been thoroughly checked out! I passed inspection."

Marcus looked intently at her before taking another bite of food. "That's good. You looked a little pale earlier, but your color is better now. Didn't want you falling under someone's feet in the surgery."

"I think I just needed to eat something and get a little rest," she assured all of them, feeling Simon's hand squeezing her leg, beneath the table. "I feel much better now."

Harold nodded. "We can perhaps be grateful for the rain. It might slow things down tomorrow and we can get by with fewer hands. The army is no doubt having trouble advancing the troops in this steady downpour. It may reduce the casualty numbers, if they're stuck, literally, behind the lines."

"That's exactly what the wounded are telling us," Nancy chimed in, between mashed potatoes and meatloaf. "They've said the horses and mules are breaking their own legs trying to pull through the deep mud. Have to be shot. It's a terrible thought. A different kind of casualty in this terrible situation. One of the men said that soldiers were being shot, where they stood, their feet stuck in the mud, unable to run for cover. I can't imagine how awful..."

Lydia imagined the scenarios. "And think of the poor men under their ponchos, their feet soaked through. Nothing hot to eat. They must be more miserable than ever. They won't be able to get supply wagons through to the front, and we all know, too well, what that feels like! Thank goodness we can keep them mostly dry here and at least feed them hot food when they come in."

Harold agreed. "Well, keep me apprised of how many of our staff fall ill. I need to make sure Doctor Fortraine is aware of our capabilities—and limitations, as the case may be—if our own numbers climb. And take care of yourselves while you're at it. Try not to breathe in any sickness if possible. Get as much rest tonight as the rain permits."

They finished their meals and returned to their respective tents, aware of the risk of contagion, to everyone. Once inside again, Lydia and Simon slipped out of their wet clothing and into the cot, covered with a poncho against leaks from any sudden downpour. Lydia curled up against him as he rested his hand on her belly again, and they picked up where they'd left off earlier.

His voice was low against her ear as his hand caressed her pelvis. "I have to admit that I wanted to tell everyone at the table, Lydia! A baby... the miracle of life happening right here. I want to be a really good father, Lydia, to our child. Since I didn't have a father most of my life, I'll be winging it sometimes. But I think if I just keep holding onto this feeling that I have now, I'll be fine."

She rolled onto her back so she could see his face. "You're going to be a wonderful father, Simon," Lydia reassured him. "I don't doubt it for a minute. I'll have my mother and sister to help me, but you'll have me helping you, and we'll give this baby a good life."

Simon raised himself up, leaned over, and kissed her. "You have more faith in me than I have, sometimes. But I promise you, I'll do my best... Do you realize what else this means?"

She reached up and touched his face, tracing his brow and bearded cheek tenderly. "What's that, my love?"

He leaned on one elbow and ran his hand down her thigh. "It means for about eight more months, you won't have to warn me about a five-day no man's land. We can have each other, completely, every day of every month, from here on out. Think about that!"

Lydia traced his lips with her finger. "I'm thinking about it right this minute... in case you couldn't tell..."

It rained all night and continued to rain for the rest of the week. There seemed to be no end in sight to the sheets of water pelting them. The medical staff was noticeably affected by the constant rain, heavy grey clouds, wet wind, and the casualties which came, not in unmanageable numbers, but in a constant flow. Thankfully, the French army was able to get their trucks through, over swollen streams and waterlogged roads, with makeshift plank bridges to routinely get their wounded out to the hospitals. True to its promises, the army also kept supplies coming into the station, which eased the stress of their difficult circumstances.

Many of the station personnel had fallen ill with fevers, headaches, and cough. The nursing staff had dropped down to only eight on duty. Nancy and Adrielle had joined the other two nurses in what they now called, the nurses' sick tent. The remaining nurses took turns directing corpsmen to cover for many of their tasks. The eight women continued to rotate in their four-hour shifts, with the help of any asymptomatic soldiers or corpsmen.

Although Lydia hadn't changed outwardly yet, inwardly, a maternal mindset had taken hold. She now considered everything she did, with the baby in mind. She thought of Susannah often, knowing that her friend had worked through adversity, even through a shelling that had devastated one of their stations. Suzie hadn't stopped any of her activities while she was pregnant, so Lydia tried to do the same. She did avoid checking in on Marlene, Linda, Nancy, and Adrielle for fear of getting influenza. How had Susannah kept up her spirits without having anyone to talk to about her pregnancy? Lydia was so grateful she had Simon to share this with. He needed to tell Marcus soon. Suzie had told no one... and now Lydia felt a new depth of sadness, that she'd had to go through it alone.

When Simon had declared that they would leave in four months, that decision had changed everything, too. There was now an end point to her service, to tending the wounded, and to being part of this enormous undertaking. As she moved between the wounded in the recovery between midnight and four o'clock, watching them sleep, she thought about the new direction their lives were going to take... and she considered the others at the camp. What would it be like to leave Marlene, Nancy, Gretha, and the others, behind? What would it be like to leave Marcus behind? And Charlotte... with whom she had shared so much... she would be leaving Charlotte to face the war, without her. How does one leave people behind, who mean so much? What would happen to them after she and Simon were gone? The thoughts made her feel tremendous guilt about leaving... she had not wanted to go, until they could all go together. The baby was changing... everything. Could she be happy feeling safe at home with her family and Simon, all the while knowing that her friends and co-workers were still living in danger, daily? Lydia gently touched her abdomen again. She would have to deal with this... for the sake of the baby.

At four o'clock, when Lydia was relieved by Sally, she returned through the downpour to her tent. As she shook out her poncho, she saw that Simon was sleeping, as she had hoped he would be... a new day was starting for him in just four hours. She had four hours to rest, and she was weary to the bone. She quietly undressed and lay on the spare cot to avoid waking Simon. Pulling up the blanket, she rested her hands again on her belly and tried to imagine herself as a new mother. She should give birth around March or early April. A spring baby. And she would see her sister and parents again... meet Simon's brother and sister... they would get a little house somewhere... she fell asleep thinking of having her own little kitchen.

Simon kissed her awake at eight o'clock, to start another day. Lydia felt as though she had just closed her eyes.

"You didn't wake me when you got in during the night! Did you get some sleep?" Simon asked her anxiously. "It's only been four hours, and it worries me."

She nodded. "I slept. Not enough, though. I can't wait for the burst of energy people talk about, near the end of pregnancy. I could use a dose of it now..."

Simon stood over her, his brows furrowed with concern. "Maybe we should tell the others. Maybe they should know, and they could make some allowances for you."

Lydia pulled herself up to sit on the side of the cot and get dressed. "Now, Simon, you know I cannot do that. They're as tired as I am. Suzie didn't tell a soul, and she didn't skip a single shift, the whole time she was here. I can do this."

He bent over and lifted her chin so he could kiss her. "Susannah was not my worry... you are," he reminded her. "And I'm just saying the others would understand if you need a little extra rest."

She looked up at him. "Yes, they would. And I would feel guilty asking for any special consideration."

"Hm," was all he said as he stood there, looking down at her.

"I'm going down to the latrine. You go for breakfast, and I'll be there as soon as I wash up. I'll be quick," she told him. "I promise."

Simon hesitated. "Okay," he finally gave in. "I need to be in the surgery, so I'll go, but I'll be waiting for you."

She nodded, pulling on her boots and reaching for a poncho for the walk through the rain. "Coming, Abril?" she asked. The dog looked up, carefully stepped over her puppies, and followed Lydia out of the tent and into the downpour. Lydia groaned, aware that the sun was up there, somewhere behind the heavy clouds, lighting the sky just enough to see that it was, still raining. Would it ever shine through again?

Simon walked over to the mess. The rain had been with them for so long, that it now seemed pointless to dodge the drops... he'd shake off inside and just get wet again, in a little bit, on his way to the surgery. He sat down with the doctors eating their breakfast. "Everyone okay today?" Simon asked the others.

"Waterlogged, but yes," Marcus answered. "I think a hole opened up directly over my cot during the night. Dripped the whole time I was trying to sleep. Lousy European weather. I wonder if the entire summer is going to be like this!" He wiped a raindrop from his arm with visible irritation.

"Last July, we roasted, as I recall," Harold calmly observed as he enjoyed a biscuit with his coffee. "The wounded were sweltering under the sun and dehydrated. This is better for them."

"And I suppose you're going to tell me to be grateful we haven't run out of water, and the laundry guys can just hang everything out in the rain to do the wash?" Marcus objected. "There is only so much room for optimism in this kind of weather."

"And your point is, what? You aren't grateful?" Harold replied. "You'd rather it be ninety degrees, under a blazing sun?"

Marcus considered this and said, "I want seventy-eight with a light, warm wind... blue sky. That's all."

Harold grunted. "Put in a requisition."

Simon dove into his breakfast. "Cook outdid himself this morning!" he chimed in cheerfully.

"You're certainly in a good mood!" Marcus exclaimed. "You know something we don't know?"

Simon paused. "Probably a lot of things. But just think. In four months, our enlistment is over. I'm taking Lydia home. She's going to be able to see her folks again, her sister. I'll get us a nice little house somewhere and reopen my practice in West Virginia..."

Marcus nodded approvingly. "You sound like Harold here, who can't wait to get home and get married to his sweetheart. What's her name again?"

"Tess," Harold reminded him. "Short for Teressa. And I certainly hope she's still waiting for me! No mail for all these months. I hope she hasn't given up on me and married the man who runs the local meat market."

"Probably get five letters, all from her, in the next mailbag," Marcus reassured him. "All waiting for us at a train station somewhere. Four months isn't that far away. Then another month to get back across the ocean. Another train ride, and voila. You're home. You'll beat your last letter home from the Western Front, and you and Tess can read it together."

"That's quite a thought," Harold observed. "Sitting at home reading a letter, from myself, from way over here. Have to think carefully what I want to say to myself if that's the case. Some parting thoughts of learned wisdom from two years working over here... we should all do that..."

Simon finished the food on his plate and drank his coffee. "I'm going to consider that idea, too! Hm, Lydia's not here yet. I think I'll just run back over and make sure she's on her way." As he stood, he saw her duck into the tent, dripping wet. She left the poncho at the entry and smiled at him before gathering up some breakfast for herself. Coming over, she sat down and joined them.

"I stopped at the recovery. Three of the men died during the night," she told the doctors. "High fevers, coughing. These are young, healthy men dying of this influenza. I'm worried about our nurses, but Nurse Bernstein says they all slept through the night and took broth this morning. She thought Nurse Sullivan looked a little better, but of course, she was the first to become ill. Sure hope she's past the worst of it now."

"Do you want them sent to the field hospital with the men? They can be on the next transport," Harold assured her.

"They wouldn't go," she reminded him. "And if it's running its course now, they'll start to recover soon. As long as they aren't any worse, let's keep giving them a chance to just get better."

Harold nodded at her. "It's your call. They can be on the next truck if you change your mind, at any time."

"I'll keep that in mind. At least it's still just the four of them. No one else seems symptomatic," Lydia added. "It would help if the sun would come out and start drying things up!"

Marcus smiled at her. "Exactly what I was saying, before you came in!" he exclaimed. "We need the sun. You see, Doctor Stockton, great minds do think alike."

Harold stood. "Just take your great mind over to the surgery in time for the afternoon shift, Doctor Lovell. See you two over there shortly?"

"Yes," Simon assured him. "Give us just a minute and we'll be there. I'm sorry to hear about those men, Lydia. I know that never gets easier on the nurses."

She nodded, picking at her food. "Must've happened after I left at four. I knew some of them were barely breathing, but I'd hoped they'd hang on until the trucks came today to get them out. Sally said it was peaceful. They just gave up to it. One was a surgery patient. The others were from the influenza group."

Simon rubbed the beard on his chin. "If it isn't one thing, it's the other... a constant reminder that life is so short, Lydia. I want that chance to make a home and family so much."

"So did they," she added softly.

Week three of the rain, proved that the earth was not a sponge capable of absorbing an infinite amount of water. Puddles became ponds, and rivulets became rivers. Every crater, from previous shelling, was filled to the brim, and occasional pairs of waterfowl could be seen paddling about. Tent pegs lost their traction in the saturated ground and were hastily resecured before the heavy, wet tents fell to the ground. The soldiers regularly elevated the sagging tent fabric, using the ends of long rifles, to force accumulating water to flood down the sides, dousing unwary passersby, if they walked too near the tents. The latrines overflowed, causing men to have to ditch the sewage away from the encampment, toward lower ground. The day finally came when the vehicles could no longer get through to take out the sick and wounded, until more planks could be obtained to cover the deep muddy ruts.

Seagulls regularly flew over the station in great clusters. Often floating on crater ponds and pecking into the wet earth for small creatures that had been forced up to the surface. Even the number of ambulances had dropped off considerably, unable to travel over the boggy countryside, from the battlefield to the clearance stations. Although the sound of artillery persisted, the number of newly wounded rose much more slowly now. Only airborne missiles were able to travel across the countryside.

The medical team valiantly continued to slog their way from tent to tent, caring for new arrivals and feeding the men who were now stuck at the station, for lack of transport. They looked to the sky, acutely mindful of running out of supplies without the support of the army, and automatically began cutting back to conserve the resources available to them. And there as another serious complication—burying the dead outside of the station was now impossible, with muddy graves filling back in as quickly as they were being dug. As Lydia made her rounds in the tents with Laura, Alice, and Sally, caring for those triaged and those in recovery, she curiously noted that the number of men with fevers seemed to be down.

Lydia bent over a cot to change a bandage for one of the wounded, just as he jumped, cursing when a large raindrop fell onto his face.

"I'm sorry, Nurse," he exclaimed. "I didn't mean to use such foul language, but the rain just smacked me right in the eye."

Lydia nodded. "I know, soldier, it's alright. I feel the same way... even if I don't say it. Where are you from?"

"Merry old England where it rains, yes, but not like this!" he declared. "We're no stranger to passing showers, that's for certain. But this has been going on for weeks. What I wouldn't give for a nice dry, cheery fireplace. And a mug of brew."

She laughed lightly. "If I find either of those, I'll take you there myself and join you," she told him emphatically. "This is pretty discouraging, and when the sun finally comes out, it'll be hot and humid, waiting for all the water to dry up; we'll be busy swatting mosquitos. There now, that wound looks pretty good. You're healing well, even in the middle of all this."

"I hate to bother you, Mum," he said. "But I'm getting a bit hungry. Think the cook will find something for us?"

"Absolutely he will," she assured him. "Soon."

She stood and straightened her back; it felt good to stretch it out after bending. Maybe Simon would rub it tonight when she got to lie down for a bit, before returning to duty at midnight. Being pregnant, she found he was more than willing to massage the small of her back if she mentioned it to him. She walked down the aisle, between the cots and passed Laura giving out heroin to the men coughing. The substance worked well to calm the coughs and help the men sleep.

"How's our supply of laudanum and heroin?" she asked Laura.

"We're okay now that the number of arrivals have slowed," Laura told her. "I wish we had clean, dry blankets, though. The shelf is empty, but it can't be helped since we can't get them washed and dried out. At least it isn't winter, and the men aren't cold."

Lydia looked down the rows where many of the men were under ponchos. "Where did all these ponchos come from, anyway?"

"I think Doctor Fortraine got them in for us last week," Laura replied. "It was good foresight. They're better than blankets in a lot of ways. How are the puppies?"

"Safe in their crate!" Lydia exclaimed. "Stop in and see them." She went on past Laura down the row and stopped to check a man whose cheeks were flushed. Laying her hand on his forehead, she felt he was getting hot. "How are you holding up, Brent?" she asked, checking his identification tag for his name.

"I'm okay, Nurse," he said. "Just a little sore in my leg."

She bent over his leg and started unwrapping the wound to look at it. "How did you get hit, Brent?"

"I wasn't hit, Nurse. We were ordered over a trench, and I slipped off the ladder, climbing up the far side to get back out. In the rain, my muddy boots just didn't hold. Went down sideways on my leg," he recalled. "I sure saw stars then. Can't exactly say I was hurt in action just climbing a ladder."

She corrected him. "I know those ladders! They're awfully hard to climb up, even with dry feet. I can only imagine trying to do it dripping wet and in the mud along the trench bottom."

"How do you know, miss? You been there or something?" he asked curiously.

"Yes," she admitted, "I've been there. Lots of hazards down in the trenches. Trying to climb down and then climb back up the other wall during an advance would be dangerous."

He looked up at her, wondering. "You don't mind my asking, why were you there? No nurse ought to be there."

She carefully focused on the man's fractured leg where the doctors had reset his bone. "It wasn't by choice, that much is for certain," she told him. "The Germans took us. It's a long story."

He reached out a hand and stayed her arm. "Sorry, miss. You shouldn't a had to be there like that."

Lydia patted his hand on her arm. "It's okay, Brent, I'm not there anymore. But I do want one of the doctors to take another look at your leg. It's a little puffy, and you're a bit feverish. They might need to clean it out a little. I'll ask one of them to come and look at it."

"You nurses been real good to us boys, miss," Brent told her. "Thank you."

Lydia stood up and carefully placed his hand back down on the cot. "You're welcome, Brent," she said simply.

Lydia turned to find one of the other nurses; she saw Sally and crossed over. "That one looks infected," she reported, pointing over to Brent. "I'm going to see if Doctor Lovell will stop in and check his ankle. And then I'm going to pick up a pot of soup for these boys."

"Okay," Sally said, trying to spread a little cheer. "Watch your step out there. If you see Noah and the ark, tell him to save me a seat... just not next to the hyenas."

Lydia laughed. "How about next to the sheep? Woolly blanket built right in." She went to the tent door, pulling a poncho over her head, knowing full well that it wasn't going to do much to help her in the driving rain.

Lydia knew Marcus would be getting up soon, to cover the afternoon in the surgery, and called to him through the opening to his tent.

"Are you up, Doctor Lovell?" she raised her voice over the sound of the rain.

He heard her, quickly meeting her at the entry. "What's up, Nurse Finney? Care to come in for a hot toddy? Tell me you need me for something, please!"

"I need you to check on one of the wounded. His leg looks nasty and he's getting feverish," she told him while still standing in the rain at the doorway. "Sally knows which one. I'm going to get some soup for the men."

"Just for you, I will," he assured her as she turned, and he closed the tent flap again against the weather.

Lydia slogged her way to the mess, where she greeted the cooking team. "I'm glad to see all of you surviving. We're all choosing seats on the ark. What do you want to be seated next to?"

The cook held his ladle in his hand and looked up at the ceiling, considering the question. "Better put me in the section holding the hay. The animals might be mad at me for cooking up so many of their future relations here. Might want to get even," he offered.

"I'll bet they'd understand how you had to keep us going!" Lydia laughed. "I've come for a pot of soup for some hungry guys over in recovery."

"We'll bring it over," the cook told her, looking around to see who might be available.

"I'm already soaked through, I can take it," she offered.

"We're all soaked through!" the cook declared. "But if you want, you can take one of the smaller pots over and tell the wounded guys more is coming. I know we have a few more mouths to feed today, with no trucks."

"A few," she agreed. She pulled her hood back over her head and accepted the warm pot of soup, grasping the handles with mitts. The warmth of the metal was soothing against the poncho, and she considered how it would cheer the wounded, as she made her way back outside. A soldier ran past her, splashing up muddy water.

"Want some help with that, miss?" he called out as he dodged the rain.

"No thanks," she said. "Just get where you're going."

"There's an ambulance stuck out there in the mud. We're going to try to push it out and get it through," he called back over his shoulder.

"Good luck!" Lydia exclaimed, concerned that there were wounded so close, yet unable to complete their journey. She'd warn Marcus. As she rounded the recovery, Lydia didn't notice a dislodged tent spike still tethered to the rope, but loose and jutting out at an odd angle, by the entry to the tent. Her boot caught on the spike, and she fell forward into the rain-soaked ground, landing on top of the pot of soup she was holding. The wind was knocked out of her briefly as she hit the ground, and she felt a ragged gasp as it finally flooded back into her waiting lungs. She groaned. There was a pain in her right hip. The rain pelted the poncho over her, drenching her hair as the hood fell away. She pushed up against the soggy ground to try to stand, and the pain in her groin stopped her. Immediately, she thought of the baby.

"Sally," she called out through the rain, toward the tent. "Laura! Can anyone hear me?"

After what felt like a lifetime, Laura ran out into the rain and knelt beside her. "What happened?"

"Tent peg," Lydia said. "Knocked the wind out of me, but my hip hurts."

"Let me get some hands," Laura said and ran quickly back inside.

Then Marcus was beside her, bending over her in the rain. "Lydia, what on earth..."

"Long story," Lydia said. "Just help me up, would you? I can't put weight on my hip."

Marcus looked worried and nodded. He bent over, picked her up, and carried her inside the recovery to an empty cot, where he laid her down, gently. He and Laura pulled off her wet poncho. "Which hip?" Marcus asked her.

"The right one," she said, frightened. "When I move. But the baby... oh, Marcus, did I hurt the baby...? Laura, see if Simon isn't in the middle of a surgery?"

Marcus and Laura looked to each other, in shock. Marcus was the first to speak, "Wait, Nurse Bertolli, I'll go. Lydia, let me quickly check your hip."

She nodded, her eyes wide with worry, as Laura helped ease down her trousers. She felt Marcus expertly move his hands over her hip, feeling for displacement, gently probing as Laura helped her bend her knee and move the joint.

"Ouch," she breathed in one position. "That's where it hurts."

Marcus nodded as Laura straightened her leg and hip again. "It's not displaced," Marcus said, "might not be broken. Most likely, it's just a wrenched ligament from the way you went down."

She put her hand on his arm with a pleading look. There were tears in her eyes. "Marcus, I landed on the soup pot, though. Right on my stomach. What if I hurt the baby?"

Marcus touched her face gently. "It's going to be okay, Lydia," he reassured her softly. "You'll rest, and we'll watch for any signs of bleeding. But the baby is still largely behind your pelvis, I suspect, and it's very much protected there. It's going to be okay. I promise. I'll go get Simon, and if he's in surgery, I'll take over for him so he can come check you. Just rest here, and then they can get you to your tent. I'll send Doctor Finney... Nurse Bertolli."

Lydia watched him leave, and Laura took her hand. "Why didn't you tell us?" Laura demanded. "Never mind, I understand. Lydia, let us help. You don't need to keep up this pace!"

"That's exactly why I didn't say anything!" Lydia protested weakly. "I don't want special treatment."

"My god!" Laura exclaimed softly. "You're having a baby! Doesn't that deserve some special treatment? If you don't want it for you, fine! But let us help the baby!"

Wiping away a solitary tear, Lydia said, "I just want to keep going."

"How far along are you?" Laura wondered. "Does anyone else know?"

"We haven't told anyone. I'm just finishing my second month. It's still very early," she admitted. "And I thought it might not take even in these circumstances, so I didn't say anything."

"No wonder you looked so pale! Morning sickness?" Laura asked.

Lydia nodded. "Some, but I thought I was getting sick like Marlene and Alice."

"Okay," Laura said resolutely. "But we're going to help you get through this. And you're going to let us!"

Lydia nodded. It was the right thing to do, for the sake of the baby.

Marcus hurried through the rain to the surgery, his mind whirling with the realization that Lydia was with child. He pushed aside his personal feelings in his concern for her welfare, but he was angry with Simon. Hadn't Simon seen what happened when Susannah got pregnant? Hadn't he learned from Marcus' experience and guilt? He had poured out his own remorse over getting Susannah pregnant, and Simon had gone and done the exact same thing! How could he have put Lydia in the same predicament? He pushed into the surgery, determined just to concentrate on Lydia's wellbeing, for now. Quickly, he washed his hands, donned a mask and surgical apron, and made his way through the tables to where Simon was working.

"What's up?" Simon asked quickly. "You look upset."

Marcus moved up to the table. "What are you working on here? You're needed in the recovery."

Simon hesitated, scalpel in hand. "It's shrapnel in the thigh. What is it—"

"Lydia," Marcus said.

Simon immediately handed over the scalpel and turned from the table. He washed his hands rapidly and ran through the rain, not even grabbing a poncho. When he got to the recovery and saw her lying on the cot, his anxiety spiked. Laura was beside her as he bent over Lydia and took her hand. "What happened?" he asked quickly.

"She fell outside and wrenched her groin. Doctor Lovell says her hip is okay, but she can't walk without pain," Laura rushed to inform him.

"Simon, can you help me get to our tent?" Lydia pleaded.

"Of course," he told her. "Are you able to stand at all?"

"I'll try," she said. The other two helped her sit and swing her legs over the cot, but when she went to stand, she grimaced when she put weight on her leg.

"We'll do it the other way," he assured her, picking her up as she wrapped her arms around his neck and held onto him. Laura pulled open the tent flap.

They carefully covered the short distance from the recovery to the medical staff tents. Simon lowered Lydia down onto one of their cots and reached for a damp towel, it was the best he could do. "Now, will you listen to me?" he demanded.

"I'll listen," she surrendered.

"Just take it a little easier. I married a woman and promised to take care of her. If you keep trying to do everything on your own, you won't need me anymore!" he declared with mock severity.

"I need you. I landed on the soup pot and it knocked the wind out of me," Lydia told Simon. "What if I hurt the baby?"

He slid down her trousers and examined her for himself, feeling her hip and groin, and then he slid her undergarment down and checked her inside. "No bleeding," he breathed with relief. "I agree with Marcus that you strained a ligament, and it's just going to be sore for a while." Simon sat back on the second cot and looked at her. "What am I going to do with you?"

She felt the fear and anxiety begin to fade. "A crutch would be helpful so I can hobble around for a day."

He nodded. "That I can do," he assured her as he helped to dress her again. "Can you stay put while I finish my shift in the surgery? Or do I have to tell Abril to force you to stay down?"

"I promise to lay here and rest, for both of us," Lydia said firmly. "I told them, Simon. I told Laura and Marc. It slipped out; I was so afraid."

Simon shook his head approvingly. "Well, I'm glad you did!" he declared. "It's better that some of the others know. Then you won't have to carry it alone, and I can have someone to talk to about it as well."

"Do you think it'll be complicated for Marc?" she said, worried.

"Cat's out of the bag. He's been a really good friend. Makes it easier on me." Simon bent over her and kissed her before he left. "Stay put."

He trudged back over to the surgery, where he scrubbed his hands and returned to his table so Harold could take the afternoon off, as scheduled.

"Everything okay?" Stockton asked as he took his position at the table and waited for a patient to be carried in. Marcus looked over as well, intending to overhear.

"Everything's fine," Simon assured him. "Nurse Finney slipped and fell, but she just has a sprain. She'll be okay."

"Damned rain," Harold grumbled. "It's a wonder we aren't all falling all over the place, in the muck underfoot. Well, I'm finished up here, gentlemen. I would take a shower, but I doubt it will be necessary by the time I get to my cot. See all of you good people later."

Simon nodded at Stockton as he left the tent. He looked over and saw Marcus glance his way and smiled his thanks through the mask. Marcus just shrugged his shoulders as if to say, "Of course, any time," and the two continued to work until the casualties stopped coming, for the night.

The next morning, the station woke to a pronounced silence. Simon rubbed his eyes as he rallied and tried to figure out what was wrong. Lydia was asleep on his chest. He reached down, pulled the tousled hair away from her eyes, and looked at her profile. *God*, he thought, *how I love this woman*. He stroked her shoulder and watched her start to stir. He loved that about her. He enjoyed watching her come to wakefulness and realize where she was and that she was on his chest. She always smiled when she opened her eyes and saw him looking down at her. This time was no exception. But then she looked puzzled.

"Something's wrong!" she exclaimed softly.

He laughed. "No, something's right. It stopped raining."

She looked up. "Oh my goodness! You're right! The sun is coming up. Help me get up, Simon. Did you find a crutch for me last night? I want to feel the sunshine."

He slid out of the cot and pulled on his trousers and boots. Bare chested, he went to the tent flap and stepped outside, looking around. He wasn't the only one. Others emerged from their tents and smiled. It was humid and warm out. Simon looked through the tents and over to the surrounding hillside. Already, the rising sun was forcing the moisture out of the ground and tendrils of mist were beginning to rise. A foggy layer of cloud was forming on the surface of the earth, its gentle movement being stirred by the fresh breeze, from the southeast for a change. It was mystical and almost magical to watch. Simon went back into the tent and helped Lydia finish dressing. He handed her a crutch, and she experimented with standing. It helped take the weight off her strained groin.

"That's much better!" she said, pleased. "I can function again! What's it like out there?"

"Wonderful," Simon told her. "You'll see."

They made their way down to the latrine together and watched the sun work its powerful conjuring of the elements, all around them. It was pale yellow, through the vapors rising around them and looked otherworldly. As they walked, the tents behind them almost disappeared into the mist. Abril playfully bounded in and out of the morning fog, chasing at wisps as they moved around her. Her fur glistened with dew... even she seemed to enjoy the absence of rain. They finished their morning ritual and headed for the mess tent, for breakfast, where everyone present was in an exceedingly good mood.

Marcus greeted them as they sat down at the table. "Now we know why the Druids worshipped the sun," he told them. "Who wouldn't, after weeks of rain! It's a much welcomed sight!"

"And it's going to be hot and humid today," Simon ventured. "We'll be soaking in the rays before we know it and wishing it would cool off. But you got the breeze you ordered, Marcus, and it's at least in the seventies."

Marcus was enjoying his breakfast. "Happy to oblige. How are you feeling, Nurse Finney?"

"A little sore in the groin, but otherwise, everything seems to be fine," she told him with relief in her voice. "Thank you for helping me out yesterday. I'm very grateful, Doctor Lovell."

"Not to worry," he replied casually. "All part of the day's work." He looked across the table at her with new eyes. She was pregnant. He hadn't known Susannah was pregnant. And now, as he saw the glow in Lydia's face, he wondered for the thousandth time how he had missed it in Susannah. It was as if he was being given a second chance to experience Suzie's pregnancy through the woman sitting across from him now. "You should take it easy today," he advised her, putting his private thoughts into words.

"Did you talk to Doctor Finney this morning or something?" she demanded. "I'm hearing the same thing from him."

They were interrupted by one of Fortraine's aides. The soldier entered the mess and immediately crossed over to where Simon was sitting by Lydia. "Doctor Finney," the aide said. "Doctor Fortraine wants to see you immediately. Please come, sir."

Simon nodded. He downed his coffee, placing the cup on the table, and stood... a curious expression on his face. "I'll be right back," he told Lydia and Marcus and left the mess, following after the aide. Entering the command tent, he approached Fortraine quickly. "You called for me, sir?"

"Yes, Doctor Finney. You are to leave immediately for the British CCS. They have several doctors out with influenza and are critically short of surgical hands. Pack your bag."

"How long will I be gone, sir!?" Simon asked, dreading the answer.

"Till the men are back on their feet, I would imagine. They can't very well operate with one remaining surgeon." Fortraine looked up from his desk at Simon. "It's an order. Is there a problem with this, Doctor?"

"No, of course not, sir," Simon replied. "May I take Nurse Finney with me, sir?"

Fortraine considered the question for a moment. "No, I think not. I can replace you in the surgery myself, Doctor, but I cannot replace a nurse, and we are still down four nurses ourselves. We'll all have to make sacrifices."

"Of course," Simon replied, his heart sinking. He did not want to be away from Lydia for even a day.

"We are told there will be trucks coming for the wounded today. You'll go out with the first, and they will drop you off at the British CCS, north of Ypres—"

"One last thing, sir, if I may? Why me?" Simon asked.

"They asked for you by name," Fortraine replied. "That is all."

"Yes sir," Simon answered and left the tent, wondering. He went back to the mess tent, dreading having to tell Lydia that he would be leaving the station. When he reentered, he sat back down at the table, where she was laughing at something Marcus was saying. Simon's expression caused Marcus to stop mid-sentence.

"What was that all about?" Marcus asked him quickly. "You look like you got sucker punched."

Simon cleared his throat before grabbing the fork he had left stranded on his tin plate of half-eaten food. "I have been informed I'm to go to the British CCS today. Their surgeons have influenza, and they are down to one surgeon. I'm to leave when the next truck comes in for the wounded, this morning."

"Good god," Marcus exclaimed, shocked.

Lydia said nothing, but looked over at Simon. The blood had drained from her face. "How... long do you have to be there?" she whispered.

"Until they are back on their feet, apparently," Simon answered them, hoping to hide the anxiety churning inside of him. He resumed eating his breakfast.

Lydia reached out and grabbed his hand. "Simon..."

He reached out and gave her a quick squeeze. "It'll be okay, Lydia," he said quietly. "It'll be okay. It's orders that have to be followed."

Her eyes were huge. What if she lost the baby while he was away? What if she started to bleed? What if he got into an accident on the way or came under fire in the other camp? What if he got injured and she had no way of knowing? A thousand what-ifs clamored in her mind, and she felt the panic begin to rise.

Marcus saw and quickly intervened. "At least we'll know where you are," he reminded them, "and you'll be with Winston and Earl-Johns and the crew we know really well. We were just there not long ago, and they are all friends. I know they'll watch out for you, Simon. Just don't get used to movie night or dancing to the Victrola without us!"

"I doubt there will be much dancing," Simon stared at his food. "Unless it's in the sunshine—if they're enjoying it as much as we are. Let's finish our breakfast, Lydia. I have to pack a few things and I want to see you in our tent before I go—"

"I'm done," she whispered, leaving the hash on her plate.

Simon ate her remaining hash and picked up their utensils. "Come on then," he told her. Turning to Marcus, he added, "I need to see you, too, before I go."

"I'll be around," Marcus assured him as he watched the two of them leave the mess, Lydia hopping with the crutch and Simon with his arm around her waist. *Why Simon? Why not him?*

Simon and Lydia returned to their tent. He tied the tent flap shut and sat her on the cot. Quickly and gently, he opened her shirt, pulled off her trousers and boots, and laid her back to pull off her undergarments. She lay naked before him, and he looked down at her. He bent over her and kissed her mouth and her neck and her breasts, then moved down and tenderly stroked her belly, kissing her just above her pelvis. Undressing quickly, Simon lowered himself over her. "I'm sorry if I hurt your hip," he murmured, "but I have to have you."

Lydia reached up for him urgently. She had to have him just as much. Ignoring the pain in her groin when she moved her leg, she gave herself to him. Simon took her slowly, making every movement meaningful. He covered her with his body, felt her want, and covered her in kisses. When they had come together, he lay on top of her, breathing hard. "Never, ever, ever forget how much I love you, Lydia," he whispered as he kissed her eyes and lips.

"Never, ever, ever forget how much I love you, Simon," she repeated, her arms around his neck, pulling his mouth back down to hers, wishing he could stay inside her forever.

But of course, he couldn't. Reluctantly, Simon pulled himself off of her and dressed. He helped her as well, then threw extra clothes into his haversack, not knowing the duration of his stay. He reached into the footlocker, found the white stone with the gold flecks in it, and put it in his pocket. "I have to go find Marcus for a minute," he told her. "I'll be back. Wait here."

He left their little tent and went to find Marcus, who was getting ready in his tent before heading to the surgery. Walking into the tent that Marcus shared with Stockton, Simon sat on Stockton's cot and looked at the man trying to shave in an old, dim piece of silvered glass. He stopped and looked at Simon. He was still appalled at the turn of events.

"Take care of her," Simon demanded of Marcus. "I'm counting on you."

Marcus wiped soap off his chin with his towel. "I will," he promised again, sincerely. "You know that. I made you a vow a long time ago."

"I mean it, Marcus," Simon said again. "Treat her the way she deserves. The highest gentleness, the highest respect. Just as much as you would if I was right here."

Marcus nodded. "I will, Simon. I will not let you down."

Simon stood and looked Marcus directly in the eyes. "Just as if I was right here," he repeated with emphasis, knowing Marcus would read between the lines and respect the boundaries that had to be enforced. Knowing his friend had learned from all their past experiences together and had gained insight. Hoping that Marcus realized Simon was entrusting him with his deepest treasures. "And... the baby, Marc, the baby..."

"Simon, I understand. I will," Marcus answered, meeting his direct gaze, unwavering. Marcus reached out his hand and shook Simon's tightly. "Be careful. Don't take any unnecessary chances."

Simon shook his head. "You know I won't!" he said quietly and left the tent to see if the trucks had arrived.

With the break in the weather, the shelling had resumed, over to the east. He heard the thuds. The sun was shining brightly... all of the early morning fog had lifted and the countryside was visible... overhead, clouds, white and moving rapidly, were scuttled in the wind. Buzzards circled, against the blue. The rays of the sun were blinding, after the weeks of gloom, and he shielded his eyes with his hand as he looked over the horizon toward the road, now beginning to dry out. Off in the distance, he saw the small convoy take shape on the dirt road, moving slowly, but making its way to the CCS...and to him. His heart was heavy. But he turned resolutely and went back to Lydia. Inside their tent, he took her onto his lap and held her against him as if she were a young child. They didn't speak. He stroked her hair, her head on his shoulder. He touched her belly, where the child was growing. He caressed her breasts beneath her shirt and kissed her forehead while she reached up and touched his beard, felt his lips, and laid her hand against his chest. They heard the trucks come in, together.

"I'm going to the recovery," she said. "To see the men off."

He nodded. "I'll walk you over." He helped her to her feet and slung his haversack over his shoulder. They walked to the recovery, where there was a flurry of activity, loading the men onto the trucks. Lydia took the clipboard, recording entries for each of the men leaving the station, as the nurses always did. At the bottom of the list, she added Simon's name. Under destination, she wrote *British CCS-Ypres*. Then she hung the clipboard back up on the center pole, and Simon put both hands on her arms, pulled her close, and kissed her forehead one last time.

He turned and left the tent, got in the front seat of one of the trucks, and didn't look back. But the white stone with the gold flecks was in his hand as the little convoy moved back out over the rutted dirt road to their destinations. And Lydia stayed in the recovery all day, hobbling around on the single crutch, giving laudanum to the wounded and heroin to those coughing... writing names and taking dictation so some of the men could send letters to loved ones, letting them know that hey were still alive or about to die. Nothing would be right again, until Simon returned. Nothing.

Chapter 24
Sacrifice

Lydia could not get used to sleeping alone. Of course, she had before, after she had worked the night shift elsewhere and Simon was still in the surgery, but he had always been just a hundred feet away, then. They hadn't been apart since she'd been taken by the Germans. Now, she considered what that must have been like for Simon. Everything in the station was familiar... and everything in the station, was changed, because he wasn't there. She avoided the surgery due to the discomfort of standing for hours, on her leg. And she avoided the bending and stooping of the triage. But the recovery was just what she needed, keeping her mind busy with the emotional and physical needs of the wounded and sick coming through. Marcus had been right about the relief of knowing Simon was with David Winston. It did give her some comfort to know where he was and who he was with.

Marcus checked on Lydia several times, each day, making certain she was up for breakfast and eating, and that she was safely settled down with Abril in the evenings after supper, before retiring to his own tent. He knew that he would hear her if she called out in her sleep... it had already happened once before. If she had a nightmare, he would know it. And now, with the hot, early August weather, the tent sides were pulled up to let air move through, so he was acutely aware that she was only ten or fifteen feet away as they slept. Each day, he was glad to see her out with her dog, who, followed by a trail of five puppies jumping around after their mother, was a delight for the entire station to watch. Even Marcus had to admit that he enjoyed watching the puppies frolic playfully. They were such an odd mixture of colors, each one so different. Marcus was keeping an eye on Lydia as much as Abril was keeping an eye on her puppies.

One day, while sitting with Lydia at the long table in the mess, Marcus noted that she was just picking at her dinner. "You know, you're going to offend our deeply committed cook, if you don't eat," he admonished lightly.

She looked up from her plate, pushing some peas and potatoes back and forth with her fork. "I surely wouldn't want to offend anyone," she managed a couple of forkfuls before drifting off into thought again.

"You can't lose any weight on my watch, or Simon will have my head when he gets back," Marcus warned her. "You must look robust, healthy... pink-cheeked, upon his return."

She met his penetrating look. "I was sitting here thinking about what it was like for him when I was taken from the station, last winter."

"He was as miserable as you are now," Marcus assured her quickly, enjoying his own food very much. "But he still ate. Really now, how's your ligament? Are you ready to put some weight on your leg? I know you're avoiding the surgery, and I realize that the recovery needs you, too, but what do you think?" He avoided the more important issue, due to listening ears.

"I'll try if you think it's had time to heal, Marcus," she said, looking distracted. *I have to eat for the baby... I have to...*

"He's okay, Lydia," Marcus said softly so the others couldn't hear them talking. "He'll be back before you know it. And I'm sure they're more than grateful to have his help. They've no doubt had the same steady stream of wounded that we have, especially now that the ground is drier and there's forward progress. You need to take care of the baby... eat."

Her gaze finally met his. "What if we have to move out?... and we don't even know if he got there in one piece!... And I'm worried that if they have to move their station suddenly, we won't even know about it."

"Well, Fortraine can probably find that out," Marcus assured her. "We can ask him, if it would make you feel better. But I assume that he would have already heard if Simon had not shown up, as expected. They would have been sending communications asking where he was, with how badly they needed a doctor. They'd have been looking for answers or asking for another one of us to come."

She nodded, resting her head on her hands. "Of course, you're right," she realized. "Thank you... that does make me feel better... I'm glad you're here. Okay, I'll walk tomorrow without the crutch and see how I do in the recovery. At least there's no more risk of me falling over muddy tent pegs... I'd still be on the ground there, if you hadn't come and picked me up."

Marcus shook his head. "Not likely, but not to worry... we've got to look out for each other in this camp," he said, but in his heart, he was glad he'd been able to come to her rescue. He did have a noble side. "And you might try soaking in the hot tub. The water would probably relax the muscles that have gotten tighter in your hip. It might help loosen them up."

Lydia took his advice. She walked gingerly, without relying on the crutch, to her tent, gathered up a towel and soap and headed over to the shower. The water was hot in the reservoir and she filled the tub. Carefully, she stepped over the side of the tub and lowered herself down into the water. Marcus was right. It felt good on her hip, and she realized she hadn't soaked in the tub for a long time, with the rain and steady stream of wounded.

She allowed herself the luxury of relaxation, wishing Simon was there, but willing her muscles to unwind even without him. She wondered what he was doing this evening. Was he thinking about her... or too busy with the wounded to even have time to think? She said a quick prayer for him before she washed herself and rinsed off. Lydia pulled the drain from the tub and let the water begin to drain around her, feeling the weight of her body return as the water disappeared. along with its uplifting buoyancy. In the last little bit of water, she saw what she had feared the most, a trickle of red in the shallow, being carried along down into the drain. She was bleeding.

Lydia felt her abdomen. She was not in any pain. There was no cramping in her belly. She stood up carefully, dried off, and got dressed while she pondered what to do. Surely, in the early months of pregnancy, it wasn't uncommon to have a bit of bleeding. Surely, it could be normal, given the stress and circumstances. As she slowly and gingerly made her way back toward her tent, her panic began to take hold. How could she tell Simon, when he returned, that she had lost the baby? How could she face the sorrow in his gentle brown eyes? He wouldn't forgive himself for not being here, even though he had to follow orders, and they both knew it. She felt lost and desperately alone.

At the entry to the doctors' tent, Lydia hesitated. Harold Stockton might be in there resting, too. Deciding that she had to know, she called softly through the netting on the door flap. "Doctor Lovell?"

He heard her, jumped up from his cot, and came immediately to the flap of the tent and saw her hair was wet. "What is it, Lydia?" he asked her in the evening twilight. "Did you get your bath?"

"Marcus..." she faltered with tears in her eyes. "I saw blood."

He stared at her, already accessing the clinical diagnostics in deep memory. "Oh. Well then, let's get you lying down and get your feet up."

She turned and walked the ten feet back to her own tent and obediently went straight to the cot. Marcus followed behind her and pulled off her boots. "You need to be on bed rest," he told her. "Probably stress."

She nodded. "Am I losing the baby?" she asked in a trembling voice, her eyes wet. "Marcus, I can't lose the baby. It would destroy Simon."

He shook his head, his eyes compassionate. "I don't... I won't know unless I examine your cervix. But are you okay with having me do that?"

Lydia considered her options. She didn't want anyone else, like Doctor Stockton or Doctor Fortraine, to examine her. She didn't want either of them to know yet that she was pregnant. And there weren't any midwives in the camp. Better Marcus than one of them. Finally, while he waited, she nodded. "I need to know. You can tell from feel?"

"I can tell if your cervix is softening, starting to dilate," Marcus explained. "That would tell us if you are going into premature labor."

"Then I'm okay with that," she said anxiously. "I have to know..."

Marcus helped her take down her trousers and undergarment. He kept his eyes and emotions focused solely on the medical aspect of examining her, and he was acutely aware of her vulnerability on the cot. Even in his most remote fantasies about this woman, he had never, not even once, envisioned touching her for the purpose of pregnancy. He took her canteen and washed off his hands with her soap before he examined her. "It won't hurt, but I need you to..." he started.

"I know," she whispered, raising up her knees, allowing him entry.

Marcus leaned over her and, as gently as he could, felt inside of her with his fingers while he pressed her belly softly. He felt the bulb of her cervix with his fingertips and found miraculously that it was firm and round and fully closed. As he touched her uterus, he measured its height above her pelvis and felt the firm round fundus under his hand. He looked into her frightened eyes. "Lydia," he said softly. "Everything feels absolutely normal. Everything is closed tight inside. There is no indication at all that you're dilating. Your baby is lifting out of the pelvis as it grows, and it's likely this was just a random stretching that made you bleed a little."

Marcus withdrew his fingers from inside of her and helped her pull up her underthings before covering her with a blanket. "You have to stay on bed rest for a couple days. I'll bring you your meals and a bedpan. If you don't have any more bleeding, then I think everything will be fine." *It's the miracle of life growing in there... Lydia and Simon's own baby...*

Lydia grabbed his hand in her relief and held it. "Thank you, Marcus," she whispered. "Thank you so much." She wiped the tears from her cheek with her other hand.

He leaned over, moving her wet curls from her face, kissing her forehead much like Simon would have done if he had been there. Marcus also wiped the tears from her eyes with his fingers. "Don't cry. It's going to be okay. Call me if you need me," he said in a voice husky with emotion. He left the tent reluctantly, wishing he could remain and give her comfort. But as he laid down on his own cot, he kept one ear open, listening for her should she call for him. He was satisfied with himself for doing his part. He had protected her dignity. He had treated her with gentleness and respect. He had kept his promise to Simon. Now, he would have to find a way to sleep without thoughts of her coming into his awareness. That would take effort... and he wanted to do what was right by Simon and her, both.

The next morning, Marcus took Lydia a plate of food. She was still sleeping when he went into the tent. He sat down beside her on the spare cot and gently touched her hair. She stirred, and her eyes opened as he held out the plate to her. "Time to nourish the wee one and its beautiful mommy," he admonished her. "How do you feel?"

"I slept well, thanks to you for easing my worry," she said, looking over to where he sat. "I was so frightened when I saw the blood in the water. I can't thank you enough, Marcus, for being a good friend to us." She stroked her belly tenderly.

"Well, it's not altogether unselfish," he admitted, smiling wryly. "That husband of yours promised a sound thrashing if anything happens to you while he is gone. And I'm already curious... boy or girl?"

"You mean you couldn't tell?" She laughed lightly. "How many days do I have to keep my feet up, Doctor?"

"Three, and I will inform Nurse Bertolli. Officially, you'll have some influenza-ish symptoms, unless you want everyone to know."

"Influenza will be fine," she frowned. "Is that coffee?"

He held out the tin cup. "No, tea with one sugar. I've noticed you were off the coffee for the past several weeks."

She accepted the cup gratefully. "Ever since I got pregnant, I haven't been able to drink coffee. Strangest thing."

He laughed outright. "At least you aren't craving chocolate ice cream or bonbons! That would be impossible to satisfy. You know, Lydia, I really wish I had known Suzie was pregnant. I would have enjoyed sharing it with her, even finding her a piece of chocolate if she had wanted it. It's really an amazing thing feeling your uterus growing in there."

"I have a letter going to her, Marcus," Lydia told him. "And I've asked her to let me give you her address. I want you to know your little daughter. You know Marcie is for Marcus, don't you?"

Marcus reached out and squeezed her hand. "I want that, too," he admitted and realized, surprisingly, that he really did. "But you can tell her I also want to see her, too. That's true, just as much as the little one."

Lydia smiled up at him serenely. "I already told her that, in the last letter. You're a changed man... you're caring... and gentle... and sensitive."

He stood. "Well, let's just say that I'm still a work in progress. But I'm closer than I was, that's for sure. And now I'd better get off to the surgery after I find Nurse Bertolli... and before Fortraine sends out the bloodhounds to look for me. Send Abril if you need me."

Lydia dropped her hand down beside the cot where Abril was nursing. She stroked the dog's head affectionately. "I will."

She made herself eat everything on the plate that Marcus had brought her. Then she snuggled back down on the cot, the blanket lightly over her undergarments, and she listened to the warm breeze whistling through the tent screens which were open to the air. She heard the sounds of the station as it moved through its daily routine, the occasional clatter of instruments from the surgery, the occasional cries of the wounded coming from the recovery. She heard the heavy sounds of the trucks arriving and then departing soon after, taking the wounded from the recovery. The artillery thudding on the eastern hills occasionally reached her ears. There was the sound of metal on metal and voices coming from the mess tent. And, sometimes, she heard the nurses calling urgently to each other when the ambulances arrived in the triage area.

Life was going on around her, and without her, much as it would after she and Simon went home in November. She realized the machinery of war was just, relentless. It ground on and on, regardless of who was serving or where. As she listened, feeling like an invisible bystander to the station activity, she realized she was finally at peace about going home and leaving it all behind. Everything that mattered now hinged on the baby being whole and healthy and Simon returning safely, so they could get on with their lives. With that, she drifted off to sleep and didn't wake until Marcus returned with her supper.

In the British CCS, Simon joined Winston in their doctors' tent and threw his haversack down on the cot. Winston looked haggard.

"How long since you slept, David?" Simon asked in concern.

"Quite a while," the man replied. "We're pretty close, here, and it's picked up a lot since the rain stopped and the army pushed forward again. The Germans are putting up a good resistance. I'm pretty well spent... and more than glad you could come."

"Not a problem," Simon assured him, although he didn't really feel that way. "Glad to help. Where's the surgery? I can start right now."

Winston nodded. "Appreciated. Nurse Sarah Timons will take you under her wing and get you set up. She's expecting you in the surgery. When we got word from Fortraine that you were on your way, she undertook laying out the welcome mat. I believe she met you when you were here for the movies. Really appreciate you coming, Finney. I've had it."

Simon stroked his beard. "I may not be able to pick Nurse Timons out. If you can save me the embarrassment, point her out to me, then come back here and hit the sack, and don't get up till morning."

"You don't need to offer twice on that one," David assured him. "I'm asleep on my feet. There was a late ambulance that pulled in during the night. Picking out shrapnel after midnight two nights running isn't very restorative—for me, anyway. By the way, is Nurse Bertolli okay?"

"She's fine. Escaped flu symptoms herself," Simon reported to Winston.

The two men went to the surgery tent, and Simon washed up. "Everyone," David announced, "Doctor Finney is here from the French station. Please give him whatever he needs. I'm planning to retire for some much-needed sleep."

Nurse Timons, Simon assumed, came immediately to his side. She was tall and slender, and her auburn hair was uncovered, not like the nurses at his own camp who wore their blue scarves. "Doctor Finney!" she exclaimed with a small, tense smile. She was clearly overworked. "How lovely to see you back at our camp. Your wife could not come?"

Simon shook his head while taking the surgical apron she offered him. "No, I'm afraid not," he said in reply. "Our nurses are down with influenza. Four of the twelve are in bed. It's been difficult for them to keep up with the wounded, so she couldn't be spared."

"Well, we're certainly glad you've come to help," Nurse Timons replied while leading him to a table where the orderlies were settling a patient on a litter. "When we needed help, I suggested you to our captain. You made quite an impression on our little station when you were here with us before."

Simon looked at the prostrate man in front of him. "I appreciate your kind comments, Nurse, but I think our surgeons are all the best of the best, actually."

"Shall I put him under, sir?" the anesthetist asked, waiting for his go-ahead, to Simon's surprise. The man should have already been out.

"Yes, please," Simon said as he took in the scope of the man's chest wound and Nurse Timons took her position next to him at the table.

"What would you like, Doctor?" she asked him as she stood by her instrument tray expectantly, making Simon feel somewhat as though he was the star of the show instead of just one of the medical team.

"Scalpel, please, Nurse. Let's open this up a little more and clean him out before we hunt around for bullets," Simon said, surprised by the obvious differences here... Lydia always anticipated everything he needed in the surgery, before he had to ask for it. Simon forced himself to concentrate on what he was doing. He needed to appreciate that the British did things a little differently and try to put everything else out of his mind during the task at hand. He had already spent enough time agonizing, in the truck on the ride over, deep in his feelings about leaving Lydia behind.

The hours in the surgery progressed with one casualty coming in after another. Between patients, he was asked to go to their triage area and assess priorities for several of the wounded waiting for care. There were corpsmen moving between the soldiers and tending to urgent needs, mindful of those bleeding or fading from life. There was a medic intermittently moving amongst them as well, giving directions to the others providing care. Simon assumed the nurses at the station were primarily in the recovery, tending to the post-op patients. He advised the medic on priorities and returned to the surgery to wash again and take the next patient they brought in.

Nurse Timons did not take a break. Simon admired her fortitude, as she worked all day with him, without faltering. "What kind of nursing background do you hold, Nurse?" Simon asked, curiously. "I can certainly see, that you have an excellent command of everything surgical."

"Thank you for noticing, Doctor," she replied. "I worked surgery for many years, before the war, in London. It is what I enjoy the most. I am a career military nurse now."

"What made you join the war effort, if I may ask? Clamp, please," Simon always wondered why the nurses had chosen to come here.

"My brother is serving and I wanted to help," she said simply. "That is all."

Simon nodded. They finished up with the patient in front of them. "I need a five-minute break, Nurse. Where is your facility?"

"I'll show you," she said. "I could use it myself."

They washed their hands and removed their aprons. As they left the surgery, she pointed to the right, to where the latrine had been set up. She went inside, but turned to face him before closing the door. "Come on in, it's a two-seater," she offered, "with a little divider in between."

He waved her on. "It's okay, Nurse Timons, I'll wait my turn."

She laughed as though he had said something ridiculous, but went ahead of him. Soon the door opened gain, "All yours. You don't have to stand on ceremony here. When things are moving so fast, we just take care of things as quickly as possible."

"Do things slow down here, at night?" he asked as he passed her, holding the door to the latrine.

"Usually, then we unwind a bit. You'll see," she reassured him.

By the end of the day, the wounded arrivals did indeed drop off. There would likely be no more ambulances for the night. Simon was glad to leave the surgery tent for some fresh air. It was warm, but not too humid, and he smelled the sea air and heard the gulls calling overhead. They were just a bit closer to Dunkirk and the sea, here. Nurse Timons led him to the mess tent, where a hot meal was waiting along with a large mug of lager. Simon was surprised. The rules were different here for alcohol and medical staff. Then Sarah Timons leaned over and said softly to him, "Now you'll see how we unwind..."

One of the soldiers had risen to his feet and walked to the front of the mess tent. He held a small violin in his hands and tuned it briefly in front of them all, then he started to play a soft, haunting melody that Simon didn't recognize—not that his knowledge of music had much depth. The song made him think of ancient castles with moats... and of knights riding across drawbridges... with the plumes of their helmets blowing in the winds that crossed the moors. He felt a longing rising in him, elicited by the music.

After the violin player was done, someone else stood up and recited a long poem, a little bawdy and very entertaining, and they were quickly all laughing. As the talent show continued, Simon felt Nurse Timons slide a little closer to him on the bench where they were sitting. Careful to wait until the performers were changing places, he politely excused himself, explaining his long trip and day in the surgery and the need for sleep. Simon left the tent, their laughter lingering in his ears, but he needed to be alone.

Once inside the doctors' tent, he collapsed onto the cot, arms raised, resting his head on his hands as he gazed up at the tent's fabric above him. He thought only of Lydia. He thought about them coming together just before he'd left the station early this morning. It bothered him tremendously that he didn't have any way to get word to her that he was alright or to find out how she was faring. And he pondered Nurse Timons' request for him. Apparently, she held some sway around this station to request his presence. He really didn't recall meeting her at any of the few previous visits they'd had. He didn't remember her being at their station when the teams worked together briefly, either. Simon pulled the white stone with the gold flecks from his pocket and thought of Lydia on the banks of the Meuse. He needed to sleep and, fortunately, was tired enough to let it happen. Tomorrow would be another long day.

Three days had passed with Marcus tending to Lydia's well-being. She confirmed that there had been no further bleeding, and he almost dared to hope she'd ask him to check her rising fundus, but she didn't. The miracle of life in this setting was profound. When he let her get back to her duties, he still advised caution. "Take it easy. No lifting, minimal bending. Give meds or something. Check hearts and lungs. You can change dressings."

She stood up by her cot and put her hands on her stomach protectively. "Yes, Doctor," she said. "I'll be a good patient, I promise."

He put his hand on her arm and looked at her closely. "And no bleeding or cramping? None whatsoever?" he pressed her.

Lydia shook her head. "None whatsoever, Marc," she assured him.

He still looked concerned, still hovered over her protectively. "If you feel bad at all, come back right away and lay down and send for me."

"I will, I promise," she said with enough conviction to convince him that she meant it, so he walked her out of the tent and over to the mess, for some food.

Harold was glad to see her at the breakfast. "Nurse Finney!" he exclaimed. "Did you overcome the influenza already?"

"It must have been some other bug," she told him. "I'm feeling better already, and Doctor Lovell has released me to get back to doing what I want."

"Like joining us in the surgery? Nurse Sullivan also says she's ready to come back, thank goodness!" Harold told her. "And the other sick nurses all appear to be on the mend, as well. I checked on them this morning. This thing is running its course, apparently, before taking all of us down like the British team experienced. I expect our number of casualties might rise, as ambulances divert to us from the British station, due to their drop in staff. Doctor Fortraine is going to take Simon's place... to join us if we need him."

"Has Doctor Fortraine heard from the British station?" Lydia asked Harold. "Do you know if he's heard anything?"

Harold looked at her reassuringly. "Doctor Finney is fine, Nurse Finney. I'm sure of it. Try to stay focused."

She nodded. "I'm focused," she replied firmly. Inside, though, she was far from it. Her mind was all over the place, from the baby to checking for cramping to Simon and his wellbeing.

The trucks were efficiently and routinely moving patients out to the field hospitals, so fewer staff was now required in the recovery, so Lydia decided to take a shift in the surgery after all and, after washing up, joined Marcus, to his delight. It would make it so much easier for him to keep a close eye on her and notice if she was in any distress. He enjoyed hovering over her as if her wellbeing was his sole responsibility. *So! This must be like what it feels like to be in a committed relationship!* he thought to himself as Lydia joined him. It was a good feeling, and he wanted it to last... practice, for Suzie, if she ever gave him another chance.

They started operating almost immediately, the first ambulance pulling in ahead of a string of vehicles, all bearing wounded. Lydia found she was able to stand on her feet without any discomfort at all; she was relieved. She loved being back in the surgery. If she couldn't operate with Simon, she was glad to be working next to Marcus.

As they worked, the sounds of artillery intensified off to the east of them. This battle, in the valley east of Ypres, had been underway for over a month. There didn't appear to be an end in sight, but the battle line hadn't shifted enough for the station to need to move, suggesting that little ground was being gained. Lydia was relieved that they hadn't had to move. She didn't want Simon to have to hunt for them... for her.

She saw Marcus checking on her frequently and knew he was monitoring her closely. Simon must really have put the fear of a thrashing into the man, before he left. Lydia remembered Marcus telling her a long time ago that Simon had once made him vow to watch over her. He certainly was fulfilling that vow, but there was really no need. She was glad to be back on her feet... and to feel like she was, at last, making a difference again.

The days passed slowly. Lydia's sleep grew more restless the longer Simon was away. The puppies were weaned and already settling into their new homes, being properly adored by new owners who had been waiting, anxiously. Lydia and Abril looked at each other in the quiet of the tent, missing the yipping and frenetic energy of the tiny dogs. During the day, a few of the puppies ran with Abril outside around the triage area, learning how to herd or chase buzzards, returning at night to their respective tents. At night, when it was quiet, Lydia frequently reached down to rub the dog behind her ears... easing her own loneliness.

One night, her sleep troubled, Lydia dreamt that Simon had been caught up in battle and she was unable to run to him... one of the maddening dreams where one's feet refuse to follow the command to move, no matter how much effort is spent to will them forward. She called out softly for him and immediately felt Abril nuzzling her hand, with her nose. She said another prayer for Simon and tried to go back to sleep, without success.

At the British CCS, Simon had been equally restless. He hadn't slept well and didn't feel great either. His throat was sore and his glands were swollen. Surely, he may have picked up the influenza which was moving through the camp with alacrity. That would be the damnedest thing, to travel all the way here, just to get sick himself and be of no use to anybody. He went to breakfast and forced himself to drink fluids and eat something. That's when he knew he wasn't well. Simon never lost his appetite.

He went to the surgery, where Nurse Timons was waiting for him. She saw immediately that he didn't look himself, even through his beard.

"Are you ill, Doctor?" she asked. "Your color is off."

"Sore throat, Nurse," Simon confirmed. "Don't know where it's heading. Maybe nothing."

She looked at him worriedly. "I hope you're right."

They started caring for the wounded, and she kept a close eye on him as he worked on the casualties laid in front of him on the table. David Winston was working beside him and overheard the exchange.

"Pace yourself, Doctor Finney," he advised the other surgeon. "If you need to sleep, do so. No heroics. We'll carry on one way or the other."

Simon nodded, rubbing his forehead. The only good thing about getting sick here is that he wouldn't be passing it on to Lydia, in her condition. For that, he would be grateful. He could protect her, even from afar. He focused and took the tea offered to him periodically by Nurse Timons, who might have slipped some honey into it, unless his taste buds were mistaken. Must be a British remedy being used in the camp. By late afternoon, Simon was washed out. His head was beginning to throb, and he left the surgery for the latrine, glad for the fresh air. He sat in it for a minute with his head in his hands. When he stood and left the facility to make his way back, the warm August wind actually gave him a chill... he knew, then, that he was going down a bad path and would have to convalesce.

Making his way back to the surgery, he poked his head in the door and motioned for Nurse Timons. "I'm done for today," he reported, regretfully.

She immediately felt his forehead. "You're burning up," she said quietly. "Let's get you to the sick tent." She took his arm, unnecessarily, Simon thought, guiding him to the tent set aside for those of the staff afflicted with illness. Grateful to be laying down, Simon took to one of the cots, covering up with one of the blankets despite the eighty-plus-degree August sun beating down on the tent. He knew that he had to stay hydrated, but all he wanted to do for the moment was close his eyes and make the headache fade away. He said a prayer for Lydia and the baby and dropped off into a troubled, restless sleep, aware that Nurse Timons was putting cool cloths on him from time to time and making him drink.

Doctor Fortraine stared at the communique from the British CCS, as it lay on his desk, staring back at him, demanding action. He finally stood, accepting that there was no point in delaying the news. He had to go find Nurse Finney. It was a brief communique and quite to the point. The doctor put it in his pocket and made his way over to the surgery, where he knew that the nurse was on duty. Entering, he saw her scrubbed in. Catching her eye, he motioned with a hand for her to come outside with him.

Lydia looked up anxiously at Marcus as she left the table, her eyes immediately filling with fear. She moved around the tables to the sink to quickly wash her hands before stepping outside. Marcus tried to angle his head toward the opening of the tent to see what was happening and was frustrated when the two moved out of view. He heard Lydia cry out and, summoning a medic to step in for him, rushed out, between the tables. Lydia was slumped to her knees on the grass outside of the tent.

"What happened!" Marcus demanded of Fortraine while he knelt down beside Lydia and immediately wrapped an arm around her.

The doctor showed him the communique: *...notify you that Doctor Finney succumbed to influenza.* "I'm sorry," Fortraine said simply. ""

"What the hell does that mean?" Marcus demanded, staring up at Fortraine. "What the hell does 'succumbed to influenza' even mean? Is that British for he's sick... or dead... or what? Get someone back on the radio or send a telegram... or send someone on horseback, for God's sake... and find out what the British meant by that.

"Lydia, listen to me, this doesn't mean anything," he told her firmly, taking her face in his hands and making her acknowledge him. "Means nothing at all. The Brits have a different way of speaking, that's all. Simon probably just caught the bug that's been getting them over there. Don't let your imagination get ahead of this."

She looked up at him, absolutely stricken with grief and fear, and his heart was wrenched. She leaned against him, wordless, her hand pressed against her belly, unable to even question the unspeakable communique. She let him help her to stand, but her knees buckled, refusing their burden.

"Can you finish my case?" Marcus asked Fortraine, who simply nodded and went to wash his hands, replacing Marcus at the table.

Marcus picked up Lydia in his arms and carried her to her tent, calling for the dog to come, knowing she would help Lydia cope. Abril came at a run and fell immediately into step beside him, sensing Lydia's distress. In the tent, Marcus sat and held her against him, the offending message still in his hand. He was concerned that she was not crying, not speaking, not moving. And he was anxious about the baby inside of her, knowing how her recent stress had affected her. This shock could be enough to cause her to lose the baby.

"Lydia," he finally said. "Talk to me."

She looked up at him, wordless with the shock of Simon, possibly, being gone forever. There were no words...

He took her face in both hands and made her lock eyes with him, again. "Lydia, we have to wait for Fortraine to confirm what this thing means. I think if anything had happened to Simon, you would have known. You'd have felt it... spiritually, somehow... the way you two are connected."

She stared at him as Abril nudged her knee, as if in agreement.

Marcus put his arms around her and held her tightly against him, trying to block out her fear. "Simon is going to be okay," he said over and over. "We need to wait. It will be alright. Fortraine is French, remember? He couldn't read the nuance in a communication like that, not if he wanted to." Finally, with nothing else to do, he just sat with her, offering small reassurances as they came to him, doubtful she was even listening, but needing to say something, for himself as much as for her.

Her eyes closed and he continued stroking her hair. Then he saw her hands move down, protectively covering her belly, and he knew that she was still in there, still aware, still concerned about the new life inside of her, and his own anxiety lessened.

"Think of the baby," Marcus told her softly. "We'll get through this, Lydia, for the sake of the baby. Talk to me."

Her voice was a whisper, and he had to lean over to catch the barely discernible sounds. "I dreamt I couldn't go to him... that he'd been caught in the battle, and I couldn't make my feet move, no matter how hard I tried to get to him..."

"It was just a dream," Marcus reassured her. "You probably sensed he was getting sick. The two of you are so closely intertwined you probably sensed it. Simon loves you so much, he'll fight off any enemy that tries to take him down... even a virus or bacteria... you can be sure of it."

Then she did open her eyes and looked at Marcus, his blue eyes intent on hers. "Do you really believe that, Marc?"

"Without any doubt. He loves you and this baby enough to fight for you with everything inside of him. And he's healthy. If anyone can fight off influenza, it will be Simon," Marcus said emphatically. "He won't let it take him. I'm sure this was just a misguided notice that he's sick."

Lydia hadn't thought about how hard Simon would fight for her. It was a comforting thought and the only one that sank in.

For the sake of their baby, Simon would fight. Marcus was right. She did not cry, but leaning against Marcus, she tried to borrow his strength and forced herself to, breathe. It felt as though she had had the breath knocked out of her, similar to when she had fallen in the rain. Now, she felt the air moving in her chest and willed it to reach the baby. She had to be strong for their baby. It was more important now, than ever, that she not lose this part of Simon growing inside of her, this human link to the man she loved with all of her being.

"Marcus," she finally said as she leaned against him. "I've needed to thank you over and over for helping Simon and me. And yet, here you are doing it again. I cannot do this alone... please give me strength."

He nodded, pressing her head against his shoulder. "All that I have is yours. I'm here. We'll wait for more information. We'll do it together."

It was a couple of days, before Fortraine received an answer to his inquiry. The other half of the communique had not come through. When he read the full message, handed to him by his aide, he couldn't see how it would be very helpful to Nurse Finney. Nevertheless, he walked with purpose and found her working in the triage, where she was asking every ambulance driver about the British CCS and if it had changed location.

He spotted the blue scarves of the nurses and saw them busy assessing those newly arrived. When she saw him approaching from a short distance, she froze. Fortraine kept his face neutral, another dreaded communique in his fingers.

"Nurse Finney," he called to her. "May I have a word?"

She nodded, fear stuck in her throat. Automatically, her hand moved down protectively over her abdomen. Lydia could see the paper in his hand, fluttering lightly in the hot breeze.

Fortraine cleared his throat. "It appears the earlier communique we received was incomplete. This is the full missive."

Lydia took the paper. *Doctor Finney succumbed to influenza and the decision was made to transfer him to the field hospital outside of Calais.* Simon was still alive! At least at the time of his transport to the field hospital. Where was the field hospital outside of Calais? How could she get there? "I need to leave," she told Doctor Fortraine. "I need a truck or something... I need to go find him."

He nodded. "I thought you would say that. However, I do not have anyone to take you with the volume of wounded coming in."

She placed her hands on her hips, looking over her shoulder. "Well, couldn't I just ride with the wounded? Surely some of them are going to the field hospital in Calais? Or I can walk... or, something." She was grasping at straws.

"And what if, by now, he has been moved elsewhere, Nurse Finney? The field hospitals do not keep patients for long. They are also triage stations, and Doctor Finney could have been moved by now to St. John's Hospital... or transported even to Paris, to the American Hospital, there. You would be trying to find rides all over the French countryside, without currency, without resources... during a war."

Lydia looked around her at the open fields of the countryside as if she were trapped. "Well, what can I do then!" she demanded angrily. "Are there no other options? There must be something..."

He looked at her, not without compassion, but his voice was firm. "I will send messages to command, for them to locate Doctor Finney. He is still in the employ of the French army, which keeps track of its troops, as you well know from the careful lists that we, ourselves, keep here. Let me find out if he is still near Calais or if they have also triaged him and moved him on elsewhere, maybe to St. John's. The moment I receive word from Major d'Espèrey, you will be the first to know."

Lydia removed her scarf, using it to wipe the sweat from her face... and to hide her tears. She turned from him, running from the triage area. Charlotte, who was working triage with her, saw her friend fleeing from Doctor Fortraine and surmised that the news had not been good. Charlotte shook her head slowly, unsure of exactly how bad it was, but knowing that she had to continue her work, with the new arrivals... and stepping up her pace to keep up with the flow.

Lydia ran to the tent that she and Simon shared and threw herself down on her cot, sobbing. *How could this have happened? How could this be?* She remembered, all too well, that the army had completely lost their CCS in Belgium, just a couple of months ago. Would they be any more careful about one of their doctors? She felt the hysteria growing inside of her, perhaps triggered by her shifting hormones or perhaps solely by circumstance, but it was frightening. She was losing control.

Marcus ran into the tent, hearing her distress through the thin canvas of the tent walls. He picked her up in his arms and held her tight, unsure what news she had received, but realizing it could not be good. She beat on his chest with her arms in anger and fear, but he did not let her go, glad she was not holding the power of the emotions inside. Finally, she collapsed against him as the hysteria passed and the dim realization started to enter her mind that it was not good for the baby... Simon's baby... she had to get a hold of herself. She felt Marcus rubbing her back and hair, soothing her, comforting her, offering her his strength and support. She threw her arms around his neck and softly cried into his shoulder, and he simply held her, until the tears were spent. And finally, they stopped. She drew in a long, tremulous breath.

"Tell me," Marcus said quietly.

"Doctor Fortraine said that the British sent Simon out to a field hospital near Calais. He was alive, but too ill to stay at the CCS. He said casualties are not kept long at the field hospitals, and Simon could have been triaged anywhere from there... St. John's, Paris... anywhere. And we have no idea if he is still alive at some other hospital. I need to leave. I need to get out of here, Marcus. I have to go..."

Marcus held his peace. Obviously, she could not go. The Red Cross volunteer nurses received no pay; she had no money... she was pregnant, she could not travel alone, and he could not go with her. The army would not allow it with the battle at Ypres raging on, incessantly, month after month. He held her against his chest, feeling her body quiet and the trembling cease.

"What we are going to do," he started, "is take care of the baby, first... take care of you. When Simon shows up, he needs to find you both whole and healthy and safe. That's first." He saw her hand move down to her stomach and knew that he had reached her. "Then, second, we'll hound Fortraine daily for communications from the army until they find Simon. And third, the minute this battle is over, I'll make Fortraine give me a truck or a mule and wagon, and I'll drive you myself to wherever they find Simon. We'll get you there." Marcus looked down and saw her wet eyes looking up at him gratefully.

"Would you do that?" she asked.

"Of course," he declared. There was no question, though he'd need to learn how to drive a mule.

She reached up and pulled his face down, then kissed him on the corner of his mouth. "Thank you, thank you, thank you."

Marcus kissed her forehead. "That's what friends are for," he reminded her of the old cliché as he felt his body stir in response to her. He willed himself to be calm; she needed him as a friend. He could not allow old patterns to betray that. He needed to be in charge of himself now, more than ever. Gentleness and dignity. Just as if Simon were here. That's what he had agreed to. Gentleness and dignity. He sat her on the cot and knelt down beside her. "Can you go back on duty? It would keep your mind busy, and I don't want to leave you, but I'm due in the surgery."

She looked down at his face and appreciated him more than ever. "I'll wash my face, get a quick cup of tea. And then, yes, will you tell Charlotte? She's in the triage. I'll be there in just a little bit."

Marcus stood up. "I'll tell her. But join me in the surgery if you need to, Lydia." And he left her.

He strode out of the tent and across the grass to the triage, where he easily picked Charlotte out, by her blue scarf, moving among the men. She stood after placing a number card on one of the wounded. "What happened?" she asked him in concern, pushing back her sweat-soaked bangs from her forehead.

Marcus said, "They've lost Doctor Finney, apparently. Moved him from the CCS to a field hospital, and then, God only knows where. Fortraine is trying to get the army to locate him."

"How is she?" Charlotte asked, assuming he had been with Lydia—she pushed away a little pang of jealousy.

"She's washing her face, getting some tea, and will be back out to help you shortly, Nurse Stein... or she'll take over for someone in surgery. Get her mind off of things. Not good to dwell on the unknown, all the what-ifs... I'm going to the surgery now, if you need me." Marcus turned and made his way through the row of waiting men, knowing his work was cut out for him, for some hours to come.

By the time night fell, Marcus was plain exhausted. He was worried that Lydia might not have eaten. She had apparently stayed in triage the rest of her shift. After the surgery and triage had shut down for the night, he went to the mess. Lydia wasn't there, but he was starving and needed to eat something, so he grabbed a tray of food and found a place at the table, near Monique, who was also eating.

"What a day!" Monique said. "You must be very tired, all those patients and no break."

He nodded. "I am. To the bone."

"Your bone?" she questioned, raising her lovely arched eyebrows.

Marcus nodded wearily. "It's an old expression. Means tired all the way through the whole body."

"Ah," she smiled. "To the bone. I understand. Perhaps you need to rest and relax? Perhaps a hot bath to soothe the bone would help?"

He looked at her and remembered how very pleasing she had been, many times, in the hot bathwater... it seemed a lifetime ago, when they'd come together. "It probably would," he admitted truthfully. "But no doubt I would drown from exhaustion. Just fall asleep in the water and go right under!"

She laughed lightly and patted his thigh. "I would make sure the water does not drown you," she teased him suggestively. "I would keep you up..."

He looked at her with admiration in his eyes, but said, "Yes, I know you certainly would! But then I would never want to get up for the surgery in the morning! Doctor Fortraine would be most unhappy with me."

She laughed out loud. "I will take care of Doctor Fortraine!" she exclaimed softly with a knowing smile. "He will not be so unhappy."

Marcus stopped short. He hadn't considered that Fortraine might have found his own comfort with any of the nurses. Had she already been with Fortraine? It was a novel concept. Well, why wouldn't they? They were both French. The absurd idea came to his mind that he didn't know any French words to utter in just such a circumstance, but of course the two of them were fluent.

"There are always more baths," he teased her back as he finished his food and gathered up his tray.

"You leave so soon?" she said curiously as he stood.

"To the bone, remember?" he smiled down at her. But the truth of the matter was right in front of him. It no longer appealed to him to have the casual dalliance in the tub. The awareness of this was as much of a shock to him, as it might have been to Monique. When had he ever turned down such an offer? He stepped out of the mess and saw that the sun was setting, in the August evening sky. There were early stars starting to shine. He really was exhausted from the emotions of the day. He made his way to the private medical tents. In the dim light, he saw Lydia on her cot where she'd fallen asleep, her tent flap still open. Abril was on the ground by her side, as usual.

"Good girl," Marcus said softly to the dog, whose eyes glittered in the dim light as she looked up at him and stretched. Marcus quietly pulled Lydia's tent flap closed and went to his own tent. Harold hadn't come in yet. Likely in the shower himself, unwinding. Marcus stripped down to his boxers in the hot, humid air and collapsed down onto his cot. It was the right decision to sleep.

It was the middle of the night, and pitch black except for the starlight, when Marcus woke. He was momentarily confused about where he was, having been dreaming heavily, and he didn't know what had startled him. He looked out through the screen by his cot and saw two glittering eyes pressed against the tent, staring at him, and he jumped in alarm. Abril softly woofed against the screen. Immediately, Marcus rose and went to her, following the dog into the night. The warm night wind met his chest. It felt good after being in the hot tent. Abril led him to the edge of the camp where Lydia was standing, staring out to the north where the Dipper hung low over the countryside, where the well-worn dirt road stretched out in the darkness to... to everywhere else, but here.

Abril reached her first and sat down at her feet. Marcus didn't want to startle her and called softly as he approached. "Lydia, what on earth are you doing out here all by yourself?" he demanded quietly, not wanting to attract the attention of the sentries. "You're lucky the soldiers didn't shoot you!"

"He's out there somewhere, Marcus," she said. "And he's alone."

Marcus put his arm around her. "My god, woman, you aren't even dressed! Come back into the station," he urged her. "You can't help him this way, Lydia." He couldn't see her face in the darkness, but he was reasonably sure what he would have seen, if there had been light. "Come back to bed. You need to rest, and you shouldn't be out here alone in your underthings with the soldiers around."

"I couldn't sleep. I kept dreaming that he was in pain, hurting, alone... I couldn't sleep," she faltered.

"Come on," he insisted, walking her back, his arm around her waist, guiding her through the tents in the dark, careful not to step on anything harmful, even in boots. She went along with him, Abril leading the way. He pulled back the tent flap for her, and she went in and felt her way back to the cot.

"Will you please stay put?" he asked her in frustration. "If you don't, I won't get any sleep at all."

She reached for his hand in the darkness and squeezed it. "I am so afraid for him..." she whispered.

Marcus sat down beside her on the spare cot. "Don't you realize, Lydia, that Simon will try just as hard to get back to you as you're trying to get to him? As soon as that man is strong enough to travel, he's going to make a beeline back here to look for you."

"If he gets strong enough," she corrected him. "If they are able to pull him through... wherever he is. He must have been awfully sick for them to move him out. We kept our people here and pulled them through. They sent him out. That means he was really, really sick."

Marcus said, "The way he feels about you is better medicine than anything they've got. You have to sleep and take care of yourself. Do you need me to stay with you for a minute while you fall asleep? Would it help?"

"Is it asking too much?" she wondered.

"Nope." He moved out of the way so she could lie down on her cot in the darkness, but he felt her hand still holding his.

"Please, Marcus..." she whispered. "I'm so afraid."

He hesitated, knowing what it would cost him. Then he lay down beside Lydia and put his arm around her. She put her head on his bare chest, and in no time, he heard her breathing deepen and slow, as she drifted off to sleep, laying against him with perfect trust in him. He lay there holding her, aware she was half-clothed, aware he was only in his boxers. His body was wide awake, and he pondered this. It was a different kind of wakefulness than he had ever experienced. It wasn't a competition. It wasn't a lust. It was a response to someone he... cared deeply about. Had she not been married to his best friend, he would have wanted to take her for the sole reason of giving her comfort and making her feel connected and loved... to extend to her a tenderness for her distress. Using his body for that purpose was a revelation he'd never known or felt. And likewise, not taking her for the same reason was a sacrifice he realized he was willing to make. So, after he was sure she was asleep, he slipped out of the cot, easing her back gently and leaving her tent so no one would get the wrong idea about his presence there. That, too, was its own revelation. Marcus returned to his own cot and quietly went to sleep. He was not frustrated; instead, he was satisfied with his choices.

A week passed, yet again, the station still waiting for news about their missing surgeon. Marcus peppered Doctor Fortraine daily with questions and urgency. Fortraine was frequently in the surgery now, making up for the other doctor's absence. He. often, had to remind Marcus that while he was up to his wrists in someone's intestines, he wasn't over in his command tent to receive communications . Marcus also noticed Monique in frequent attendance at the commander's table, he smiled at this. Lydia was in the surgery, assisting him at the moment, and he looked carefully at her. She seemed rested, and he was relieved that her sleep had improved and she hadn't taken any more middle-of-the-night strolls. They were all just... waiting for word.

Simon moved in and out of delirium from the pneumonia that had settled into his lungs, which had been compromised by the influenza that swept the British CCS. He was vaguely aware that he'd been lifted onto a train and settled into a narrow berth on an adapted passenger car, along with a crowd of other sick and wounded passengers. He could recall the feel of the car swaying and clacking along the track as it carried him farther and farther away from everyone he cared about. As the fever and wracking coughs seized him, he drifted in and out of awareness... the whistle of the train reorienting him to his situation. At times, images of Lydia would come to him in his dream state. He wondered if she was real or a hallucination. There was a caring hand checking on him, leaning over the berth, a face draped in a white headdress… or maybe an angelic being checking to see if he was ready to meet God. He pushed the angel away. *Not yet, Lord*, he told it. *Not just yet. I want to see the baby first.*

On arrival at a station, somewhere, Simon found himself being loaded, half-aware, onto an army truck along with the other soldiers and bounced over cobblestone streets to a large imposing stone and brick structure of many floors and wings extending out on either side of the central hospital. There, he was carried in on a litter, down long white hallways of tiled floors with many doors that passed by in a maze of confusion. He was rolled onto a bed in a ward filled with men in rows of metal beds with thin mattresses. There was the constant sound of coughing there day and night as others with lung infections struggled to catch their breath. Simon just wanted to sleep and knew he had to keep breathing and moving. He would only get weaker laying in the bed, hour after hour, but he had no strength left to get up, and in his mental state, he had trouble remembering why he should.

Simon did not realize that he had been taken to the American Hospital in Paris. Thousands of wounded were being treated by American doctors, from across the sea, who were rotating here, to improve the care of soldiers on the continent. Volunteers, American financial aid, and medical school students all came together to serve and prepare for the arrival of American troops who would soon join the Allied forces. It was here that Simon lay in a ward and found himself subject to nurses and therapists who came regularly to pound on his chest and try to clear his airways and help him breathe. He knew a doctor came briefly and put a stethoscope to his chest, listening to the wheeze and rattling of mucus in his airways. When his eyes drifted open, he could see white-gowned nurses moving around the large ward of men. He heard them speaking in English, and in a more lucid moment, he wondered how he'd been sent back to the States without Lydia. *How could he have left her behind? How could he get back over the ocean, to her, again? Didn't they see his ring? Didn't they realize he had a wife? What was wrong with these people?*

He tried to put his legs over the edge of the bed to get up and realized he didn't even have clothing, just a hospital gown. No matter! He had to find his way back to France.

Gentle hands pushed him back down. "Now, Simon Finney, you can't get up yet. You're too ill," the nurse scolded him gently as she read the identification tag around his neck. "You have pneumonia. You need to rest."

He tried to resist her hands pushing on his shoulders and started coughing. "Have to get back," he wheezed. "Have to get back..."

"Not today," she said firmly. "Your fever is too high, and you must rest. Drink this broth for me."

He felt her put the cup to his mouth and tried to take a sip of the salty broth, but immediately started coughing again. Taking the cup from her, he forced himself to try again, knowing he had to hydrate somehow. After a few swallows made it down, he sank back against the mattress, sweating with the exertion of just trying to sit up and take the drink. The nurse placed the cup next to him on a very small table. His muscles were trembling from the effort.

"Try to finish this if you can," she told him. "Take your time."

He grabbed her hand to detain her a moment longer. "My wife..." he wheezed.

"She is not here," the nurse replied. "You are in the hospital. Where is your home? Is she at your home?"

Simon shook his head. "Belgium..." he wheezed, coughing hard. "The army..."

The nurse put his hand back down on the sheet and tucked him back in. "You have a Belgian wife? That is very good to know. We will let the Belgium authorities know later when you can tell us where her village is." She moved away, leaving Simon frustrated and frightened for Lydia's sake. He was too weak to call her back and try to explain.

Later, he roused from what felt like a medicated sleep, vaguely aware that a man was washing his sweat-covered body in the bed. He wished he could be left alone. The pain along his rib cage was sharp, and coughing sent waves of it through his chest.

Once, Simon awoke, just long enough to look at the other men in the other beds. White beds, white walls, white angels with wings. There was something he was supposed to be remembering... something important... but it took too much effort to try to remember it. Oh, well. Maybe it wasn't that important after all.

Maybe nothing was.

Simon thought once, that he saw lights rolling overhead in a neat row, then white-covered heads leaning over him. Something went over his mouth, and he didn't think it was ether, but it was impossible to say in his confusion. Then, much later, he realized the tight band around his chest was still there. He drifted in and out of voices talking and the wracking coughing fits. Lydia drifted through his awareness, and he called for her... his voice too weak to be heard. She walked away, always just out of his reach... she was holding a baby. He wondered who had thrown a baby away for her to pick it up and carry it around like that. No one should give up a baby like that.

During the nights, Simon weakly tossed and turned in the bed. He instinctively knew that he had to change positions to try to drain the fluid out of his lungs. So, he tried to turn from side to side every few hours and get his lungs to open up. With every turn, a spasm of coughing erupted, and he worked hard to get the mucus out of his lungs. Finally, an orderly came over to his bed and put a spoonful of liquid in his mouth. Simon didn't know what it was, but it quieted the cough and his mind drifted off to a place of confusing images. He drowsed, seeing pictures of Lydia flash through his awareness: on the cot making love to him...standing in the surgery by him and looking down at the horse lying on the table... no, that could not be right... there were no horses in the surgery... then he saw his sister and brother, but they were looking for a cot to sleep on in the casualty clearing station. *Why were they in Belgium*, he wondered? *How did they find the station there?* Then, Marcus drifted through Simon's subconscious awareness... Marcus holding hands and walking with Lydia... Marcus holding hands and walking with Susannah... the baseball hitting him in the back when Marcus threw it at him, hitting him over and over and over on the back with the damn baseball.

Simon tried to stop the baseball from smacking him!

"Whoa there, buddy," a man said firmly, catching Simon's swinging arm. "Just trying to help you here, soldier. We have to pound on your back and loosen up all the fluid in there. It's part of your treatment. Doctor's orders."

"I'm a doctor!" Simon snapped back with a moment of clarity. "Stop it!"

"Really now?" the man answered, humoring him. "Well, I'm an orderly, and your doctor has ordered you to have chest therapy, and that's exactly what we are going to do."

"You imbecile," Simon spit out. "I am a surgeon from a French casualty clearing station, and I want to talk to this doctor you're talking about immediately!"

The orderly stopped and looked at Simon carefully. "You really are a doctor?" he asked incredulously.

"Yes, I really am a doctor. I am an American doctor serving with the French army," Simon said in return, already growing tired from the exertion. "And I want to see the doctor in charge of me right away."

"I'll tell the nurse you asked," the orderly agreed. "But on one condition. We are finishing your treatment first."

"Very well," Simon said weakly now, his strength already waning from the exchange. He turned on his side with help from the man and allowed him to pound on his rib cage until the orderly was satisfied that he had done his full duty. Simon coughed up some foul-tasting mucus and decided the treatment prescribed was, after all, effective and that he should go along with it, just as he would tell one of his own patients.

Later in the day, another nurse came and checked on him. "We are going to take you for a radiograph," she told him. "Are you strong enough to be in a wheeled chair, do you think?"

"I'll try," he told her, a little doubtful, but willing.

With the help of an orderly, she took Simon by the arms, swung him out of the bed and into a wheeled chair. Simon almost passed out from the change in position, the ward and its occupants swirling around him in a blur of confusion. He fought to clear his head and see straight. The nurse bent over him and looked into his face. "Are you alright?" she asked, a hand on his shoulder, checking a dressing on his chest.

"Yes," he said, his vision clearing. "Just a little dizzy... it's passing."

"Not surprising," she told him. "You've been in bed for many weeks. This is good that you're able to get up."

Weeks? Simon's confused mind tried to make sense of time. He'd been back in the States for weeks? How many weeks? That couldn't be possible. That means he had been away from Lydia for over a month. It was impossible to conceive that much time had passed.

"Orderly," he said as the man started rolling him out of the ward down a long, tiled hallway. "Where am I? What day is it?"

"It's September 20th," the man told him. "And you're in the American Hospital, of course."

"No, where, what town? What state?" Simon asked urgently.

"Not the States, sir," the man said. "Paris. You're in the American Hospital in Paris. Didn't you know?"

Simon almost laughed for the first time since he'd taken sick. His mind started to clear. He was still in France. He was just in Paris. He could get back to Lydia and the station after all. He would make it happen. "I have to get word to my unit where I am," Simon told the man firmly. "It's critically important they know where I am."

"Later," the orderly assured him. "Right now, I have an order to get you to radiography."

Simon didn't try to tell, yet another person, that he was also a doctor. He decided to just go along with being a patient, for the moment. With help, he stood in front of the machine that flooded his body with invisible rays. He didn't need the roentgen examination to know that his lungs would improve and that he had made it past the worst.

He was now fully aware that he had been through a surgery for his lung; the bandage was still there... he also knew his body and could tell. He wanted to refuse whatever medicine they were giving him at night, though. It just confused his mind, and he needed to concentrate and think. As the orderly wheeled him back to the ward and helped him get back into the bed, he realized how big the place was. There must be a hundred soldiers in the one ward alone. It was massive, with high ceilings and many windows. He laid back down, exhausted and weak from the exertion of having been moved around.

September 20th. That's impossible, Simon thought. *September 20th*. He'd been away more than a few weeks. The frightening thought came into his awareness that the station might not even know where he was; Lydia might not know where he was. *Oh, Lord*, he breathed. *She might not even know if I'm alive, after all this time*. Simon considered that carefully. And the baby... how would she have handled the stress of him going missing? *Was she still carrying the baby? What if the stress of this caused her to lose the baby?* And him not there to be with her and help her? He remembered his parting words with Marcus, who had promised to take care of Lydia. *Wait! What if the unit has been bombed again? What if they were not alive! What if they had come under attack, and I'm the only one left behind? Oh, God in heaven! What if they are all gone? What if Marcus had not been able to keep his commitment to maintain the boundaries with Lydia? What if, in her fear and confusion, she had turned to Marcus for comfort, and the man had given in to his own impulses, the ones for which he often lacked self-control? What if the medical station had been overrun again, and Marcus wasn't able to protect Lydia from the Germans? What if...* Simon forced himself to stop and refocus.

In a real panic, Simon lay on the bed, staring up at the white ceiling and imagining the scenarios. *If Marcus did have Lydia, if she did turn to him for comfort, it would be understandable,* he decided. If they thought he was dead, missing... well, in the middle of war and pain and confusion, he would have to understand if they had been together. He would have to prepare himself for that possibility. And if they thought he died, well, *Lydia shouldn't be alone with the baby coming, anyway. She would need support. But if the camp was bombed, overrun... if they were all dead...*

His sudden terror was interrupted by the arrival of a man in a white coat wearing a stethoscope. Simon could only assume he was a doctor. He thought vaguely he had seen him before, in a lucid moment. The man was middle-aged, a younger man behind him, no doubt a medical student, trailing after. The two of them approached Simon's bed.

The doctor spoke first. "I heard you wanted to see your doctor, soldier? Well, here I am, Doctor Mark Hayes, and this is my student from Hopkins. Your film shows some improvement in your lungs, I am pleased to inform you. You are beginning to heal from your surgery."

Simon nodded. "How much of my lung did you take out? I'm having trouble sorting things out in my mind."

"It's the pain medication causing confusion," Doctor Hayes told him. "Your right lower lobe collapsed. But as you had three lobes in that lung, you will be fine with the two that are left. They will expand and fill your chest. You just need time to recover from not only the pneumonia, but the surgery as well. No bending or lifting. Rest is what I prescribe."

Simon corrected him. "I believe I'm over the worst of it, and I'm ready to go back to my unit. I have to find my unit. Immediately."

Doctor Hayes shook his head. "That's not possible yet. You're far too weak. You can't tolerate the travel, and you aren't fit to return to duty, although your desire to is very commendable."

"You don't understand, Doctor Hayes," Simon informed him. "My wife is at the unit, and she is pregnant. I must get back as quickly as possible. She likely doesn't even know if I'm alive or dead because I helping another unit when I fell ill. I don't even know where she is... the unit is..."

"Hm," Doctor Hayes said. "You have a pregnant wife serving in an army unit in the middle of the war?" The doctor looked knowingly at his medical student as if to say that Simon was not yet in his right mind with such an impossible story. There were no pregnant women in the military, and certainly very few soldiers were permitted to marry. To Simon's great irritation, the medical student nodded back as if in complete agreement.

Simon was seized with a bout of coughing. Then he cleared his throat, angrily trying again. "Doctor Hayes, my name is Doctor Simon Finney. I am a surgeon, and my wife is a volunteer nurse with the Red Cross. We serve together in a French army mobile casualty clearing station only five or six miles from the front lines, last known to be in Belgium outside of Ypres. And yes, she is pregnant. I was temporarily reassigned to the British CCS north of Ypres because their surgeons were down with influenza. While there, I also contracted it and now find myself waking up here.

"If I do not get word to her that I'm still alive, I'm very much concerned that she'll lose our baby with the anxiety my absence has caused her. I don't even know if the battle outside of Ypres has ended yet or if the mobile unit has had to move out. We've already moved many times to stay near the front lines and take care of the wounded. It's imperative I get word to the French army of my whereabouts so they can get word to the station... wherever it is at the moment. My god, if the station is even still standing!"

The medical student stared at Simon. "You're serious, aren't you! You're serving at the front?" he asked him. "As a surgeon on the front lines?"

Simon looked at the young man beside his bed. "Yes, I am... I do," he stated wearily. "My two years are up in November, and I'm finally going to get my wife home and away from this beastly war. I have to know the medical unit is still standing! I have to know if... if my wife is alright... if the camp is in one piece."

Doctor Hayes took Simon's hand and shook it. "I admire you, Doctor Finney," he admitted. "Being on the front lines for almost two years. I'm not sure I could handle that myself. I want to ask you about it later when you can talk without coughing. But for now, you really are too weak to even walk on your own, let alone make the trip back to your CCS. I'll send someone over from the American army to talk to you and get more information, and we'll try to send a wire or somehow get word through the French army concerning your whereabouts. If they can be found. After all, if they're still in Belgium... a whole other country... or in battle...

I make you no promises that the army can find anything out quickly."

Simon laid back against the thin pillow in relief. "Thank you," he said. "It means a lot. I need to get back to the station as quickly as possible, though, and I mean to do so. They've been down a surgeon the entire time I've been here, and the army has not chosen to surrender the front to the Germans yet... nor has it beaten them back over the trenches. I'm needed there in more ways than one. They have to still be out there... they have to be..."

"May I inquire, Doctor Finney, about your leg?" Doctor Hayes asked.

Simon looked down at the shape of his leg underneath the white sheet. "Oh, the scar? Compound tibial fracture from a shell exploding in the camp. One of the other surgeons, my friend, reconstructed my tibia rather than amputating the leg, and it took a while for the infection that followed to clear... but it healed up. Hence the scar."

"And your friend, the other surgeon, did that just at a CCS? You didn't go to a hospital for that kind of surgery?"

Simon laughed wryly at the thought. "I couldn't leave my wife. She's one hell of a nurse... she got me through. And Marcus, the surgeon, my best friend, wouldn't let them move me an inch, without his approval."

"I can certainly see that the treatment worked. Let's hope mine is just as effective." Doctor Hayes said in amazement. "Your team must be remarkable."

"You have no idea..." Simon exclaimed softly. "Nor could anyone possibly imagine, who hasn't been there."

The other two nodded, but Simon knew they couldn't conceivably understand. After they left his bedside, Simon realized that this was exactly how it was going to be when he and Lydia returned to the States, to set up his practice again, making a home for themselves and their child. No one was going to be able to understand what they had been through unless they had seen it for themselves. The two of them would get the same stares, the same quizzical expressions, the same marginal comprehension. Thank God they would have each other to understand what it was like on the front lines, in a medical station. Thank God for Lydia. *Thank you, God, for Lydia. Help her to somehow know I'm still here. Somehow, find a way. But if they're all dead, please, just take me too, right now.*

Chapter 25
Redemption

They were well into September, and still, there was no word. Lydia was barely eating... she felt weak and listless. Daily, she waited for Doctor Fortraine to come with news. He repeatedly assured her that he had communicated with Major d'Espèrey and that the army was working on it—working on finding Simon. But the major also wanted Lydia to remember that tens of thousands were in the same predicament of not knowing where loved ones were. She was only one of thousands. He felt no news was good news. Lydia wasn't so sure.

Her head told her that the longer she went without any word, the more likely it was that Simon was dead. The army did not recognize her marriage to Simon. Someone would read his identification tag and work through Washington to contact his brother or sister back in the States in West Virginia, as next of kin. No one would reach out to her, especially not out in another country altogether. She realized anew how incredibly important the letters were that the nurses wrote for the dying at their station. Those last words provided desperate families some way to face the finality of loss. Her quiet despair grew with every passing day. She wasn't sleeping. She knew she was losing weight.

Marcus was worried beyond measure. He shared everyones's concerns that the longer Simon was missing, the less likely it was that he would be found. He watched Lydia carefully in the surgery, in the mess tent, seeing that she was only picking at her food and looking pale. She never laughed and rarely smiled. Marcus was aware that Doctor Fortraine had asked her if she wanted the Red Cross to send her home. She had refused. She didn't want to leave the last place she had been with Simon. But, given her condition, this probably was the last place she should be. Finally, Marcus decided to broach the subject with her himself.

In the evening, Lydia had wandered to the edge of the station toward the road again, walking with Abril and looking out over the horizon for any sign of vehicles coming... just as she checked every truck or wagon that pulled into the camp, daily. The horizon was again empty as the sun went down, and she obediently returned to the camp and went to her tent. She had promised Marcus she would put her feet up after being in surgery for almost ten hours earlier. They had operated continuously and the wounded had been many. She knew she needed to rest. So, she dragged herself to the tent, pulled off her trousers and shirt, and washed the late summer sweat off of her arms and face. The cool water in the basin was soothing. It would be hard to sleep tonight with no breeze, just hot, muggy air. Lydia sat down on the cot and opened her footlocker, taking out a light undershirt to sleep in. There, she saw the music box. Simon's Christmas present seemed to beckon to her. Gently, she picked it up and started to turn the winder. The first few notes began to slowly play... and she simply broke down.

The light rap on the tent entry frame made her carefully lay the box aside on the footlocker. Marcus poked his head in the door and she nodded. He came in and sat down next to her on the cot, immediately taking note of the small music box, his eyebrows raised in curiosity. "From Simon?" he asked unnecessarily... *of course it was from Simon.*

She nodded and showed it to him. A few notes slipped out as the little box exchanged hands. "I can't bear to hear it now, though," she said sadly.

"Lydia, there's something I want to talk to you about," Marcus started, looking at her and then at his hands in his lap.

She waited, too listless to speak.

"I want you to let me take you home when November comes. You know Simon and I enlisted at the same time. My time is up then, too. If there is no word about Simon by then, please let me take you home to your family."

Lydia looked down at her belly and stroked it gently. She nodded. "I suppose that would be best. I can't stay here when the baby comes. Suzie left when she was four months along. I'll be almost five. I'm starting to show."

"Not if you don't eat enough to help the baby grow," Marcus admonished her. "I see you at the mess, and I know you aren't getting enough food in for the two of you. It worries me."

She looked up at him, seeing genuine concern in his eyes. "I'm sorry," she said simply. "I know—I'll do better."

He took one of her hands in his own. "Listen to me, Lydia. I want... I want you to consider letting me help you raise Simon's child—if it ever comes to that. I mean, it may not. But just in case...

I would be honored to give you and the baby a home, and I would love both of you and care for you."

Lydia's eyes welled up. "Oh, Marcus, I know you made that vow to Simon a long time ago, and he made you promise to take care of me if anything happened to him. But you have Suzie and little Marcie Nichole to think about, too, and I wouldn't ever want to complicate the chance for you to be a father to your own daughter."

He nodded and took her hand. "I thought about that, too," he admitted. "But I also realize Susannah may have moved on in her life. She's a beautiful woman, too, and it's likely that another man has invited himself into her life by now and offered to help raise little Marcie. I'm prepared for the fact that she may have set up a home for them, and I wouldn't want to upset their lives by intruding into it with unfair expectations of my own... But with you, I do love you, Lydia. Not like Simon, I'm sure, but in my own way, I really do. If... if we ever find that the worst... then marry me and let me provide a home for you and the baby."

Lydia didn't know how to respond. To do so, to agree, would almost be admitting that Simon was not coming back. She cared for Marcus—next to Simon, probably more than anyone else she'd ever known. And she wondered at what point does one have to face reality? At what point does someone in her situation have to decide to move on? How would anyone know if it was time? She couldn't answer any of those questions at the moment. This was so far beyond anything she had had to experience in her life. There was nothing to prepare her for it. All she knew was that she was alone, her hope fading.

Marcus leaned over and took her in his arms. He very gently put his mouth on hers and kissed her softly and tenderly, offering her the reassurance that he meant what he had just told her, that his feelings were genuine. Lydia felt that honesty in his touch. She was surprised by how gentle he was with her, and the gratitude welled up in her for all of his friendship and faithfulness over the past year, all of the times he had saved Simon and given her the precious time she had shared with her husband, all of the times he had helped her in her own distress and asked nothing back of her, ever. So, now, she put her arms around his neck in return. Marcus eased her down on the cot, kissing her lips again, and her eyes, and her forehead, not with passion, but with tenderness, surprising even himself. He leaned over her, stroked her hair, and looked at her. He laid one of his hands down on her belly over her undergarment. "I promise I will love you both and care for you if it comes to that... and if you will have me," he told her once again. And tenderly kissing her lips once more, Marcus got up and left the tent to go to his own cot.

Lydia laid back, listening as the camp grew quiet in the night. She felt Marcus nearby, on his cot, not far away if she needed him. And she thought about his offer. *If Simon is dead, I will go home with Marcus in November as Simon and I planned. I will take the baby to safety and keep that part of Simon alive and well and happy,* she said to herself. This Marcus was a different man than the one who had groped her in his drunken stupor. He was a different man than the one who used the mess tent at night as his personal retreat to entertain, more than a few of, the other nurses. This Marcus was a man growing in his soul. *Oh God,* she prayed. *I have to know if Simon is alive. I have to know if Simon is coming back. The not knowing is killing me slowly. I can't go on like this... please hear me...*

She lay thinking for a long time. Abril lay quietly beside her cot. A peacefulness had stolen over her that everything would work out one way or the other. She was blessed that if Simon were gone, his best friend would not be. Lydia thought about her wedding to Simon in the cathedral. She revisited the inn in Nancy where they had discovered the wonders of coming together as husband and wife... she remembered the feel of his arms around her and his beard against her body as he pleasured himself and her, discovering the depths of love in its various manifestations. She remembered him striking the German commander and protecting her. She felt his love again when he ministered to her wounds. She felt his sturdy presence whenever she felt afraid or troubled. She thought of his arms around her when they danced or sat by the fire. There was only one Simon for her... there would never be another Simon for her. There was an offer of a Marcus, yet it would not replace Simon, to whom she had surrendered her entire being, heart, body, and soul. In the darkness, she reached out across the invisible distance to wherever he, or his body, lay.

"I love you, Simon," she whispered aloud into the realm of the Spirit.

And at that very moment, the music box resting untouched on the footlocker released a few more notes that had been trapped by the semi-wound spring inside. Lydia froze, listening to the few notes weave their way through the hot night air to reach her ears. Just a few notes. That was all... before the silence of night returned and settled in around her. For a split second, Lydia thought she'd imagined hearing the music box play, but Abril nuzzled her hand

and woofed as she sometimes did when she knew Simon was needed. Lydia had not imagined it. Word would come soon. Simon, or God, had heard her need for confirmation and had answered. The waiting was over. Either he was returning, or he was in heaven, blessing her decision to go home with Marc. She fell into a very deep, peaceful sleep.

In the morning, Lydia woke just as dawn was breaking. She got up from the cot, sweating with the early heat of the day, and went to the shower to quickly wash herself. She had an appetite this morning and intended to eat and take better care of herself. She returned to her tent, quickly finished dressing, and tied her hair in her scarf. When she came out, Marcus was emerging from his own tent. She hooked her arm through his and fell into step with him, looking earnestly up at his very curious eyes as he wondered at her transformation.

"Yes, Marc," she told him, continuing the conversation of the night before. "If it comes to that, I would be honored to be your wife. But I have to tell you, I hope to God that Simon is alive and still coming back, and I hope we hear soon. And if that is the case, you and I will find a way to stay in each other's lives, always, for you are very important to me as well, and I would not want to lose you."

Marcus felt the change in her and was relieved. If Lydia and he ended up together, he would endeavor to be the best husband he could be for her. If Simon returned, Marcus would be the best friend he could be and an uncle to their baby. And maybe, if the stars aligned, Susannah would give him a second chance after all. Either way, the course of his life had taken a new direction, and he knew it was permanent. Once before, he had told Lydia that she was making him a better man, and she hadn't understood what he had meant by that, but the truth of it was emerging now. They went into the mess tent, and he was glad to see her eat breakfast as he brought her a cup of tea.

The afternoon artillery bombardment was particularly heavy. All day, they heard the thuds of missiles hitting the earth, to the east. Ambulances flew into the station one after the other. Lydia worked beside Marcus the entire day in the hot, stifling surgery, but she listened when he reminded her to take a break or hydrate and even when he made her use the stool, which Simon had used at times, to rest her own legs and back. Marcus saw her smile at him again, over the face mask, and he was glad. She was at peace... and it felt good knowing he had been a small part of that.

As Marcus was reconstructing the pieces of a broken skull, he caught her looking at him and asked, "Nurse Finney, why do you think good guys wear white hats?"

She laughed then. "I don't know, Doctor Lovell. Why do good guys wear white hats?"

"I don't know either," he declared. "I was just curious. But I'm going to buy one when I get home, and I'll let you know if it changes anything in my head or not."

She looked up from the patient's open head. "You've earned a white hat just by putting this man's head back together."

"Like pieces of a puzzle!" he declared. "He must've gotten hit by the butt end of a rifle or something to have this much damage."

Lydia peered down in the wound. "Do you think his brain is damaged?"

"Don't see how it couldn't be, blunt force trauma and all," Marcus replied. "But at least the skull fragments overlapped instead of pushing inside. That'll help."

"Which part of the brain is that, Doctor Lovell?" she wondered, shining her flashlight where it was needed.

"Frontal and temporal lobes," Marcus replied, happy to see her inquisitive nature reemerging. "Judgment and emotional processing."

Lydia frowned. "Hm, I think mine has been frozen for a while."

"That's more than understandable, Nurse Finney, given the circumstances. It's good to see you smile."

Lydia hesitated, but decided to tell him. "The music box went off on its own in the middle of the night."

"Really?" he said, looking at her, his blue eyes curious. "What do you think that means?"

She furrowed her brow. "I'm not really sure. I think it just means that there is an answer on the way... one way or the other. And that has given me a measure of peace... not sure if that makes any sense?"

Marcus nodded. He decided at that moment that he was going to have to work on that spiritual side of things, too. She seemed to have a pretty strong faith and he'd never really thought too much about it, himself. "It's not my area of expertise, but I'm willing to keep an open mind."

"I can already see you in that white hat, Doctor Lovell," she said softly as she focused on helping him suture the skin back over the man's repaired skull.

That evening, a truck came rolling into the station while the staff was gathering for supper in the mess tent. When Lydia heard the sound of a single truck engine, she ran out to meet it, hope springing up inside of her. A single truck was never just for wounded... and not at this time of night. She eagerly scanned the front windows, searching for a familiar face. Was her prayer being answered so soon? A man jumped down from the truck.

"French station?" he asked tiredly.

"Oui," she answered, hope quickly fading.

"Mail," he said, walking around to the back of the truck and pulling out two large sacks of bound letters, magazines, and small parcels. It was the culmination of months of correspondences.

"Come and eat," Lydia invited him, trying to hide her disappointment. "You must be hungry."

"I will, thanks, miss. You a nurse or something?" he asked curiously.

"Yes," she nodded. She felt rather than saw Marcus come out of the tent behind her. He saw instantly that she had been hoping for more than mail, and her shoulders now slumped. He put an arm around her lightly.

"It's okay. Maybe the next one," he said softly and moved forward, offering to carry one of the heavy sacks of mail. They all returned to the mess tent, and when the others saw what they were carrying, a round of applause and cheers went up. There wasn't a single person in the station who hadn't been anxiously waiting for some word from home. While the soldier delivering the mail made his way through the serving line, one of the cooking staff opened the first sack and started calling out names. Nearly everyone there had their name called out, including some who weren't present:

nurses in the recovery, soldiers on sentry duty, Fortraine... and Simon.

Marcus went forward and took the letters held out for Simon and brought them back for Lydia, who sat quietly on the bench, watching. She also had been given letters from her parents and her sister, Peggy. These lay before her on the table. She couldn't bring herself to tear into them, as others were eagerly doing all around her. Lydia took the letters for Simon—two were from his sister, Rebecca.

"Recognize the names?" he asked her as he slid his legs back over the bench and under the table.

She nodded. "His sister. West Virginia. You got a letter, too."

He held it up. "From my dad. No doubt telling me to behave myself and to get my act together over here."

She smiled at him, and he noticed that her smile was more reserved again. "I'll tell him he has a wonderful son, a man he can be proud of."

"Well, if you ever get the chance, he probably won't believe you," Marcus told her. "I gave him a lot of trouble during my younger years. You probably won't believe this, Lydia, but I was a bit rebellious in my youth. Stayed out all night. Still got good grades, but never listened to his fatherly advice. I did not, uh, learn from his corrective actions."

She patted his arm. "He'd believe me now," she assured him. "I'm going to take these back to my tent and maybe read them there. I haven't heard from my folks since last year. I don't know that they've even forgiven me for coming over here. I may be in for a good scolding myself."

Marcus nodded as she rose from the table. "You okay?"

"I'm okay," she replied quietly, smiling gently at him.

"Check on you in a bit," he told her, and she nodded and left the mess tent. Moments later, he felt a rustle beside him, and Charlotte slid into the space Lydia had occupied just moments before.

"How's she doing?" Charlotte asked him. "I saw her run out of here like her life depended on it, when that truck pulled in."

Marcus nodded, his letter remained unopened in his hand. "I think you're right, Nurse Stein. Her life really does depend on it. Surely, it'll be Doctor Finney coming back on one of these trucks."

"She watches every one that comes in for the wounded every day. It's heartbreaking," Charlotte said. "I think she'll have to face facts soon. I doubt he's coming back... I can't imagine what she's going through."

Marcus studied the nurse beside him for a moment. "You've both been through too much," he said regretfully. "You and Nurse Finney. This war has been especially hard on you two women. I'm really sorry. Neither of you deserve to go through all of this."

Charlotte looked around at the busy tent of people opening their packages and envelopes, absorbed in the news from home, both good and bad. "None of these people deserve what we've been through."

Marcus pressed her. "But none of them were taken by the Germans like you and Lydia, Charlotte. That's what I was referring to. You two went through more than any of us have had to. I can't figure out why whatever powers-that-be allowed that to happen to you girls."

Charlotte looked at him, amazed. She wasn't used to hearing Marcus talk like this, and she couldn't understand the change in him. "You mean in the trench? Well, it was hard, for sure. When we weren't allowed to eat and had men with rifles standing over us all the time. But the whole camp had to go through not having food, not that long ago... it wasn't that different. Of course, Lydia had it worse than I did. It took a long time before she ever told me how the German commander whipped her to get us a few lousy pieces of bread and some cheese. Better than eating rats, I guess but I still feel so guilty that she went through that willingly for us."

Marcus felt a sudden hard lump in his throat, threatening to choke him, and tried to swallow. He couldn't speak. Simon had never let on a word of what Lydia had gone through in the trenches. Only that it had been difficult. After what felt like forever, he knew he needed to respond. He forced himself to say something. "Well, like I said, I can't understand why that was allowed to happen to either of you. I'm really sorry you had to suffer in that trench, Charlotte. I wish to God it hadn't happened."

Charlotte looked at him steadily. "It's okay, Marcus. Really. It's in the past. Lydia said she forgave the German. I don't think I could have forgiven someone who'd tortured me like that."

"Is it over? I mean, for you?" he pressed her in concern. "Can you put something like that behind you?"

She nodded. "Yes. Now, I think I'll go read my mail, if you'll excuse me. I hope it's only good news in yours!"

"You too," he said as she left the tent for the night. Marcus sat alone. A new wave of emotion flooded over him. Now he realized, some, of the burden Simon had been carrying all this time. Now he understood fully why Simon had almost destroyed his fist when he'd flattened the German commander and drawn Harold's severe reprimand in the surgery that day the German had died. Now it all made total sense to him.

Marcus would have done the same thing, knowing now what Simon had known then. It seemed unreasonable, but Marcus felt enraged, and it was difficult to agree with Charlotte that it was all in the past. He realized his jaw and fist were clenched, just considering the German laying stripes on Lydia, and he had to force himself to relax. Simon had kept Lydia's secret... he had helped her heal. Her occasional nightmares now carried a different meaning for Marcus, as well as Simon's admonition regarding how to help her through the night terrors. Marcus was furious at the dead commander and, at the same time, glad he now knew the truth.

Marcus put the letter from his father in his shirt pocket and got up from the table. He said good night to those around him and stepped outside. He'd promised to check on her before he retired, and now, he went to her tent. The flap was open, and she was lying on her cot, the unopened letters on the spare cot beside her.

He softly called her name, but she didn't stir. He went in anyway and saw she'd already gotten ready for sleep. It had been a long, emotional day... and a long surgery day. He sat beside her on the spare cot and looked down at this woman with her secrets. The thought of her enduring whippings stabbed right through him. It was another hot, humid night, and there were beads of perspiration, dampening the loose, wavy strands of her hair... her undershirt clung to the moisture on her skin, outlining her body. He realized how hard it must have been for her to see the empty truck. Simon had been helping her carry her pain. If Simon did not return, Marcus was determined to pick up that burden.

He gently pulled the strands of hair away from her forehead. She stirred and saw him beside her, and the sadness on her face struck him hard. "May I?" he asked.

She nodded. Marcus took off his shirt, laid down beside her, and kissed her softly. He took her in his arms and held her. "I'm sorry," he told her softly. "I'm sorry he wasn't on the truck for you."

Lydia couldn't find any words to say that she hadn't already said a thousand times. She reached up and touched the stubble on his chin gently. "I don't think he's coming back, Marc. I think that was my answer," she said simply. So, she just took comfort in his arms and eventually fell asleep again, knowing already that he wouldn't be there when she awoke but that he was there now. It was enough.

October came and fighting still raged to the east of Ypres. It was obvious to everyone at the station that the battle was at a stalemate and men were dying unnecessarily as there would be no favorable outcome, for either army. Yet, the wounded still came daily, and the station attempted to meet their needs.

Lydia stopped running out to meet the trucks as each one arrived. She spent more and more time in the surgery, where she focused her mind on the instruments in her hand and the rhythm of patients being carried in... and back out, shortly thereafter. It was much, much harder to see one of the wounded die on the operating table. With each man's death, she felt her own heart shattering, as if Simon was dying, over and over again, in front of her.

Now, the American soldiers were flooding into France by the tens of thousands. Finding one American man amid the shuffling and organizing of troops, command posts, and battalions out in the field was a daunting task for any army. Doctor Fortraine could only offer that Simon had fallen seriously ill at the wrong time in the war.

Laura, knowing of the pregnancy, often checked in on Lydia. She expressed her concern, but kept the secret, which was known only to Marcus and herself. When Lydia failed to eat well, Laura would try to entice her with something special she asked the cook to conjure up—a baked apple, a sugared biscuit. Anything to spark her appetite. Lydia knew what the other nurse was up to and always took the offering gratefully, tucking it into a pocket for a later time, which sometimes, actually did happen, but sometimes not.

After surgery, Laura confided that she would be leaving the station at the end of the week. Lydia was surprised. They sat out on a patch of open grass in the afternoon sun, watching birds soar far overhead in the blue sky, and talked.

"Where are you going?" Lydia asked her. "Where's home?"

Laura looked over at the other nurse shyly. "I'm not going home," she finally admitted.

"You aren't—" Lydia started with a little excitement. "Let me guess! You're going to the British CCS, aren't you!"

The other woman nodded. "I'm going with David Winston."

Lydia leaned over and hugged her friend hard. "I am so very happy for you, Laura! That's wonderful news. Why didn't you say something before?"

Laura looked down at the ground. "I didn't want to hurt you, what with Doctor Finney missing and all. I thought my finding David would make you more sad, so I didn't say anything."

"Oh, Laura, I couldn't possibly be sad for such good news. You and Doctor Winston make such a lovely couple. Even when we went for movie night, everyone could tell that he adores you." Lydia realized with a pang of sorrow that she really was happy for Laura... just sad that Simon wasn't with her to share the news. She'd have to tell Marcus. "Do you think you'll marry over here?"

Laura nodded. "He asked me, and I said yes. I saw how you... how you and Doctor Finney made it look so easy. Oh, Lydia, I am so sorry. I shouldn't have said anything." She stopped abruptly when she saw her friend's eyes well up with tears.

Lydia took the woman's hand, giving it a genuine squeeze. "I am happy for you, really, I am, Laura. If you and David can be half as happy as I was with Simon, you will be so fortunate. And I think David Winston is a fine man. I'm glad you found each other... and that you told me. Truly."

"Thanks, Lydia," Laura said. "I have to write my family. Will you keep in touch after you leave with Doctor Lovell in November? I want to know how you and the baby are doing."

Lydia noticed immediately that Laura did not include Simon in that. She let it go, realizing the woman didn't mean any harm, and was just assuming, as so many were, that Simon wouldn't be coming back. "Of course, we'll stay in touch. I'll look forward to having a pen pal from England!"

Laura stood and brushed off her trousers. "Well, I've got the first of the night shifts. I hope you get some good sleep. Make sure you eat this fresh slice of cheese bread. Cook made it just for you!"

"Promise," Lydia said and watched her friend leave for the recovery. She called for Abril, who bounded over the hills back to her side.

They walked over to her tent, and Lydia got her towel for the shower. She had to wait outside for one of the soldiers to finish up, but it was warm and evening was closing in, and she didn't mind waiting. When he left, she slipped inside, letting the water run over her. She washed slowly and felt the growing bulge of her belly... just a nice roundness taking shape as the baby was developing. She guessed she had been eating enough for two, no matter what anyone else thought. She stroked her belly gently. "I wanted so much for your father to see you growing..." she whispered aloud to the life inside of her. In the shower, it didn't matter if she wept. Her tears fell right alongside the drops, and no one saw them run out into the ditch behind the tent, except for her. She had to face facts. Simon would have recovered from influenza long ago. There was no other explanation for him not coming back other than the one she still refused to accept.

She dried off and walked back to her tent barefoot. Inside, Abril was waiting, and she looked up at Lydia expectantly, waiting for a head rub. Lydia rubbed the dog's ears for a time as she thought about, perhaps, reaching out to Simon's brother and sister in West Virginia. Their addresses were on the unopened letters from the last mail sack. At least they could meet Simon's child one day. That would probably be important to everyone, and Marcus would take her without question.

Finally, she laid down in the deepening darkness and dropped off to sleep. Suddenly, she was back in the trenches again, running along the duckwalk, slippery with mud and blood. This time, though, she was pregnant. She had to protect her baby at all costs... she had to keep the baby hidden from the commander in his office. *You only have to do one small thing for me,* he said to her, *just one.* A heavy feeling of dread flooded over her, and she felt herself grow cold with fear, waiting. *Remove your clothing*, he told her with a quiet evil in his voice... *show me your baby.* She watched in horror as he came near her and ran his leather crop over her bulging abdomen. She tried to scream for help and couldn't. She forced her feet to move and, leaving her clothing behind, she fled to the trenches, running and running... as rain began falling in torrents, rapidly filling the trench... she fell into the mud, and the arms reaching for her from the mud now were from Simon... he was dead and in pieces in the mud... one arm reached up for her and she screamed in absolute terror...

Marcus came running in the dark, in his boxers. He stopped abruptly, realizing she was having a night terror and not being physically assaulted. He remembered what Simon had told him... *What, did you, like, sleep through that class or something?* Marcus was careful not to touch her. He dropped down near her like he had seen Simon do on at least one occasion and spoke softly to her. "Lydia, come back out of the trench to me," Marcus told her. "I'm here."

"He wants the baby," she whimpered, still in the dream.

"He's dead now. He's dead," Marcus told her softly. "He can't get the baby now. The baby is safe."

"Simon is dead," she cried. "In the mud..."

"You can leave the mud now, Lydia, come out of the trench," Marcus urged her. "You'll be safe up here. I'll take care of you."

"I can't get out..." she whispered.

"Yes, you can," he told her. "Can you take my hand? I will pull you out."

She paused, quieting, her breathing slowing. And, cautiously, Marcus reached out and let their fingers touch. He saw that she didn't pull back, so he took her hand in his own and very gently began to pull it as if he were lifting her out. "I'm pulling you up out of there, Lydia, it's Marcus. I've got you, you're safe..."

Then he felt her hand grab him with a grip that astonished him. It was as if she were actually letting him pull her out of a deep hole. He stood and pulled her up off the cot until she was standing. "You're out," he told her. "You're safe now. I'm right here. Open your eyes and try to see me."

They stood, holding hands with each other in the darkness. Finally, the dream snapped shut and sealed itself away again, somewhere in her subconscious. Lydia eyes opened. She realized where she was and fell forward against his chest, but Marcus caught her and lowered her down to the cot. She reached immediately for her stomach and touched her belly.

"The baby..."

"The baby is fine," he calmed her. "The baby is safe. You're safe."

"Oh my God..." she groaned in despair. "Will it never stop..."

Marcus stroked her hair. "It will, Lydia. It'll stop. It takes time, but it will stop." He saw movement at the door of her tent and saw Harold standing there, somewhat bewildered.

"Is everything okay?" Stockton asked him, rubbing his eyes.

"She had a nightmare," Marcus reassured him. "She's okay now."

"Oh, well then, good night again," Harold said, half asleep, and stumbled back to his own cot in their tent next door.

Marcus stayed, stroking her hair while her body calmed.

"I hate this," she whispered.

"I know," Marcus said, now much more acutely aware of why she kept being troubled by the dreams. This time, he didn't ask if he had permission to stay with her for a bit. He simply slid down next to her, pulling her into his arms, reassuring her, his physical presence holding back her fear.

Then suddenly, Lydia rolled onto her back next to him. "Marcus, feel this," she whispered, lowering her undergarment and putting his hand on her belly. "Sometimes, I think I feel it moving... see if you can feel it..."

He felt the round mound of the baby taking shape, and a sense of wonder washed over him. Not that he hadn't seen pregnant women before—naturally, he had in his medical training—but not like this, as the first awareness of life was emerging, in someone he cared about. He said softly, "That is a beautiful thing. You are beautiful, Lydia." Marcus wondered why he had not felt the mound growing in Susannah and then realized with a deep sense of guilt that he hadn't been paying any attention to Susannah and her needs... only his own. He would not make that mistake twice. So, now, he shared the wonder with Lydia on Simon's behalf and said as much to her. "If Simon was here, he would be in awe of your belly."

"How I wanted to share this with him," she whispered in return. "Thank you for taking the time, Marcus."

He leaned over her and kissed her softly on her lips, caressing her baby mound. "That's for Simon," he said tenderly.

She kissed him back, her hand on his rough cheek. "And that's for you," she said softly in return, to Marcus' amazement.

He laid next to her with his hand on her belly until she fell asleep again and he was convinced she was not in any distress from her subconscious mind. Then, he withdrew his hand gently out from under hers and slid off the cot. He left the tent, closing the flap behind him, and went back to his own, still marveling at the wonder of pregnancy and of the human mind's ability to absorb trauma, finding ways to make sense out of an experience that defies explanation... and marveling at her kiss.

The following day, Marcus found time to talk to Doctor Fortraine about getting replacements for Simon and himself and Lydia. Doctor Fortraine accepted the request for discharge, assuring him that the paperwork would be ready, Simon's posthumously, if needed, for an honorable discharge. Realizing how slowly the army moved at times, he would put in the requisition for two more doctors and another two nurses, that day. With any luck at all, replacements might arrive before the end of October for a smooth transition into November.

Marcus told Lydia what he had done... the realization, that she had only a month or so left at the station, hit her hard. Leaving would be hard. She had already carefully placed Simon's letters and leftover personal items in her own footlocker. She would write to his sister and brother in West Virginia about the baby... remembering that Simon had told them about her and wanting them to realize how much she loved him. The day progressed as all of the others had, lately, and soon enough, it was time for dinner in the mess and everyone began to turn in for the evening.

In the middle of the night, she woke, needing the latrine. Abril padded alongside her, silently enjoying the warm night excursion. A sentry saw her and nodded with familiarity. She was still anxious about going out at night, but less so as the months had passed. Returning to her tent, she washed and settled herself down. So much for having screens. Without a breeze, it was still and hot in the tent. Then, she felt something. The baby was turning. Lydia gasped and jumped up. She ran the few steps to the doctors' tent.

"Marc, Marc? Marc!" she whispered loudly in her excitement.

"What, what? What!" he echoed, teasing her as he woke immediately to her voice and came to the tent flap.

"What?" Harold mumbled, starting to awaken from his cot. "Is it wounded?"

"Go back to sleep, Harold," Marcus called over softly. "I've got it."

Lydia grabbed his hand, pulled him the few feet into her own tent, and dropped down on the cot, dragging him right along with her. She dropped her boxers down, exposing her belly mound and placed his hand over it.

"Feel, Marc! Right here, can you feel it? Please say yes!" she cried out in hopeful anticipation.

Fingers that were used to feeling delicate arterial pulses deep in a body cavity now cupped the mound of her belly.

"My Lord," Marcus whispered, not in any blasphemy, but in true wonder and awe. He did feel it… the fluttering kicks and movements of life. He pressed on her belly lightly, and in response, he felt the fluttering kick in return and a gentle rolling. "My God, Lydia, you have a tiny human being rolling around in there!" he breathed in astonishment. He didn't even realize there were tears in his eyes.

But Lydia saw his eyes glistening in the moonbeams that made their way through the gaps of the tent. "You can feel it, can't you! I didn't just imagine it this time!" she whispered happily. "You really can!"

"I really can," he marveled. He'd never had the privilege of feeling little Marcie Nichole quickening in Suzie's belly. He'd never experienced the miracle of the first movement in a woman's womb. It was an honor that Lydia was allowing him to share this moment with her. His fingers moved over her belly gently, encouraging the tiny forming baby to respond back. "Bet it's a boy," he whispered. "Got a good kick going in there already…"

Lydia was overjoyed that her experience was now confirmed. She reached for Marc, and he put his arms around her, kissing her softly. "You are going to be the most beautiful mother in the whole world," he said quietly, and he meant it.

"Thank you for being here," she said in return… there were very complicated tears in her own eyes.

Marcus reluctantly went back to his own tent to try, with no small difficulty, to get back to sleep. *I promise to raise him… or her… right for you, Simon. I promise I'll take care of them.*

There was a change in the air. The official notice came from the French army that Simon was missing in action and presumed deceased. The fighting in the valley continued. Unofficial numbers of the hundreds of thousands of casualties, to-date, were circulating. The loss of human life was staggering, and their own graveyard had steadily grown, in the shadow of the smaller, older one, out on a distant rise, beyond the station. Lydia had planted the idea amongst the ambulance drivers that the station would welcome another visit from Father James if any of the drivers knew where he was. She wanted to see him one more time before she and Marcus left the station for good, and she knew word of mouth had already reached him, at least once, in the past.

Lydia was out in triage when a sight, over in the countryside, lifted her spirits. On the dirt road, a distance to the north, she was pretty sure she could see a slow-moving conveyance making its way toward them. Lydia ran to tell Marcus that she thought Father James might be coming the same way he had before, by mule and wagon, over the Belgian countryside. Marcus laughed and told her he hoped the good father had loaded his wagon with some heavenly wine, in addition to any other wonderful surprises he might have for them. The wagon was just a speck in the distance, so she knew it would be an hour, or more, before mules could reach the station. He did often come loaded with good things for the camp. She finished her shift in triage and then shaded her eyes to confirm it was still moving their way. Then she went in and joined the surgery.

Marcus was removing shrapnel from of a very young soldier. Lydia joined him at the table and gazed sadly at the man. "I don't think he has even learned how to shave yet," she said to Marcus as she started helping him find the shards of metal, littering the man's belly.

"He can have my stubble," Marcus replied. "It's a pain to shave every day. You might have noticed that I do skip a day, from time to time, when I get lazy... or can't find my blade—I guess I could use a scalpel, in a pinch."

"You look handsome with or without a beard," Lydia replied thoughtfully. "That's probably why Simon just grew it out, although I never asked him if he had ever not had one."

"Probably when he was twelve," Marcus chuckled. "He certainly had already grown it before you nurses arrived at the station. It was undoubtedly how you all could tell us dashing young doctors apart."

Harold cleared his throat at that, indicating he was listening to this interesting, but disreputable characterization of the doctor staff. "Your qualifications are mercifully more than your ability to keep your facial hair in check, Doctor Lovell," he announced over the tables.

Marcus looked at Lydia and winked. "Grab that..." he started.

She was already pulling out the indicated shrapnel. "Bleed," she noted, quickly reaching.

"Got it," he replied just as fast, moving a clamp into place that she had ready for him. *Like clockwork*, Marcus thought to himself.

"I wonder if that wagon—" Lydia started.

Marcus nodded. "Go look," he knew that she still searched from time to time. "Go find out. We're done with this one. Waiter? Next round, please!"

Lydia moved away from the table and went to wash the blood from her hands. She straightened her back, feeling the slight pull of the baby on her lower spine, and affectionately patted her stomach. Marcus saw the small gesture from across the surgical tables and smiled behind his mask. Soon, everyone in the station would know, whether she told them or not... it was becoming rather obvious... he enjoyed when she was tender with herself and marveled at the wonder of it all.

Lydia stepped out into the sunshine, removed her scarf for a minute and let her damp hair dry a bit, in the light wind. Abril saw her emerge and came running over. She knelt, rubbing the dog's head affectionately. "Back to work," she told the dog, and it ran off around the perimeter of the triage, keeping watch over the waiting wounded. Lydia walked over to the mess tent, got some fresh water and took a look, around the tent, down the long road. It was indeed a solitary wagon... and the mules pulling it were steadily climbing up the hill toward them, the driver not letting them slow in pace at all, despite the rise. Again, she shaded her eyes and, sure enough, it seemed once again, that Father James must have heard the heavenly summons... and was encouraging the animals not to give up. Her heart immediately cheered, remembering the priest's gift for knowing the exact right words, for everyone in need. She was certainly in need, and she wanted him to bless her baby, even if it was a little early. She waved to him eagerly and started heading down the road to meet the priest. Then, she saw Abril come bounding over the grass from behind the mess tent, also seeing her old friend. The dog ran up to the wagon and, to Lydia's surprise, leaped into the back of the wagon instead of going to the seat.

"What on earth..." Lydia said out loud, though the dog wasn't close enough to hear it.

Father James pulled the mules to a stop just short of the crest. Lydia saw Abril jump back off the wagon, followed by a tall, slender man, who started walking, in earnest, the rest of the way up the road, toward the camp.

Lydia's legs buckled, as she crumbled to the ground. Picking up his pace, Simon broke into a run to meet her. Kneeling beside her on the dirt road, he took her into his arms while Abril ran around them both, bounding in circles. Simon kissed her cheeks, her eyes, her hair, her mouth, over and over, without stopping. He buried his fingers in her hair, and she wrapped her arms around his neck as the tears streamed down her cheeks. She sought his mouth and pressed her lips against his, taking in his breath, his tongue, his scent, his feel, almost strangling him in her effort to get as close to him as possible.

Finally, he pulled back to let them each take a breath, and he laughed. She touched his face, held his bearded cheeks in her hands, and looked straight into his handsome, brown eyes. Her own had a thousand questions, none of which mattered at this very moment.

"Shall we stand?" he teased. "Or stay here in the road and block Father James from getting his wagon into the station?"

She tore her eyes from Simon just long enough to see Father James smiling down at them from the wagon seat. "We can stand," she whispered. And she wrapped her arms around Simon's neck again and pulled his lips down to her own.

"Uh, Father James," Simon said, "maybe you wouldn't mind if we just go say hello for a minute, somewhere a little less public? Before everyone else comes to greet you?"

"And to greet *you*?" Father James chuckled. "You two go on ahead and say 'hello' to each other."

Simon wrapped his arm around Lydia, and she felt how thin he was, but his color was good, and his smile was as mischievous as ever, as he took her in with those eyes. They entered the station and immediately went to their tent, where Simon pulled the sides down and tied the flap shut. He wanted no interruptions *saying hello* to his wife.

"Do you think we still know how to do this?" he teased.

"We'll figure it out," she whispered, longing for his touch. "I want to show you something."

"Let me," he said, moving in close to her. He pulled off her shirt and began kissing her neck, gently pushing her back toward their cot and lowering her down onto it while caressing her passionately. "I have dreamed of this for months on end..." he murmured, pulling off his own shirt. He bent over her, moving down her body, urgently pulling open her trousers, along with her undergarment, finally finding what he sought. Simon felt the mound of her belly and covered her with kisses where their baby grew. "Oh, God," he breathed, "thank you for keeping them safe..." He stood quickly to strip off the rest of his clothing.

Lydia reached for him. "Come take me just like you did the very first time," she whispered, still in disbelief that he was really there.

"I was afraid you were going to say that," he repeated with a smile, just as he had said on their first night together, at the inn. And he did. He started by loving every inch of her until he hovered over her and slowly reunited them while she pulled him to her. As he moved within her, she felt the tears run from her eyes. He kissed them away. "Don't cry, my beloved girl. I'm back, and we will never be parted again."

She lost herself in Simon's touch, welcoming his possession of her and rejoicing in their oneness. Lydia was whole again as he made her his own once more, and all of her fears and worries were driven away. "I love you," she whispered, over and over, until he rendered her unable to speak.

Simon laid on top of her then, his head on her breasts, and she stroked his hair and kissed the top of his head while he stroked her belly in wonder and amazement. She had not lost their baby. They were both safe, and he thanked God in a steady stream of unrehearsed litany to Divine Providence.

Lydia finally spoke. "Simon, come up here."

He did, taking her in his arms. She had seen and now traced the scar on his side. "What happened?" she asked him.

"Well, I'm not quite the man I was when I had to leave you," he admitted regretfully. "I left my right lower lung in Paris at the American Hospital there. But the surgeon was good, and I can live with the other two lobes pretty well. I really didn't think I'd make it back for a while, my love."

"Marcus kept reminding me that you would fight to come back to me adn the baby," she told him, tracing the scar with her finger. "I am so, so sorry I was not there with you. I tried everything to find you, and no one knew where you were. We got the official notice that you've been classified as 'missing in action'."

"You must've decided by now that I was gone, then. Did Marcus, was he... did he take good care of you?" Simon probed hesitantly, not sure he wanted to hear her answer. "It's okay if he did... because I asked him to, never expecting this would happen. But there it is."

She nodded. "You'll be proud of him, Simon. He's grown up a lot in the past couple of months. He's been kind and gentle and thoughtful to the baby and me. He really tried to help me believe you'd return..."

Simon cleared his throat. "Well, I just want you to know if anything did happen since you thought I wasn't coming back... that I underst—"

Lydia put her finger over his lips, leaned up, and kissed him. "Our oneness is still our oneness. That has not changed, my love."

"Really?" Simon said, astonished. "I thought Marcus would surely try... especially if you both thought..."

"He did not even try... that," she stated. "He's changing, Simon, and I'm so glad that he's our friend. I want him to be our child's godfather. In a way, he saved our baby when I didn't think I could survive without you. He got me through this terrible time of not knowing if you were dead or alive. We owe him so much."

Simon nodded and rolled over on top of her again, stroking her face, convincing himself she was really there, that he was really back at their camp. "Then I owe it to him to go find him and thank him. Besides, by now, they may be looking for you."

"Oh," she laughed, "I expect Father James took care of that already."

Simon sat up and reached for his clothes. They dressed, and he took her in his arms again and held her tight. "I can't... won't let this happen ever again," he said as much to himself as to her, as he kissed her forehead.

"Marcus is going back to the States with us in November, Simon. He asked Doctor Fortraine for all of our replacements," Lydia said, leaning against him, relishing the security of his arms.

Simon was reluctant to let her go or to leave the privacy of their tent. "I'm glad he'll go back with us... well, then, let's go find him."

They walked out of their tent, hand in hand, toward the mess. Father James was drinking tea, and Lydia sat down beside him. He saw she was radiant, and he was glad. Simon headed over to the surgery tent to find Marcus himself. He welcomed the familiar walk to the surgery and peered through the entry, putting his finger to his lips when Gretha, who was circulating, saw him and reacted in stunned surprise. Marcus had his back to the door. Simon quickly washed his hands, donned an apron and mask, and wove his way through the tables of smiling staff toward Marcus. Laura slid away, her eyes glistening over her mask at the sight of him, and he took her place.

"Is there a doctor in the house?" Simon asked quietly.

"Good Lord! Simon!" Marcus shouted. "I have a scalpel in my hand! I could've severed this poor guy's aorta... sneaking up on a man like that!"

Simon looked into the wound. "Looks like you missed, to me. I'd better give you a hand taking that bowel out. What do you say?"

Marcus looked at his friend in disbelief. "I told her you'd fight to make it back. God, it's good to see you. I'd hug you, but... open body here, you know..."

Simon's laughed across the table. "Wish we didn't have these masks, would've loved to have seen your whole expression."

Marcus shook his head. "No, you don't! Grown men don't cry, don't you know that yet?"

"Good to see you, too, Marcus," Simon replied simply. "I'm glad I made it back too."

"You find Lydia?" Marcus asked as their two sets of hands moved in a harmony forged from years of experience, and they quickly removed a section of decimated bowel from the anesthetized man in front of them.

"First thing," Simon said. "Actually, she met us on the road."

"Us?"

"Father James brought me."

"Of course. Naturally, you'd show up tagging along with the padre. Now life makes sense again."

"I heard some incredible things about you," Simon said quietly as he cut away torn tissue and sutured bleeding arteries quickly and efficiently. "I'm told that you've been a pretty terrific guy..."

"I see you haven't lost your touch here with your rather extended rest and recovery," Marcus added approvingly while brushing past Lydia's report to Simon. His emotions were all twisted in knots; he had to be careful. "Where was your little vacation? Where'd you end up? London? Brussels?"

"Paris, at the American Hospital."

"Didn't know we had one."

"It's new... I left part of my right lung there. Didn't think I was going to make it for quite a while... but I know why I did pull through," Simon said quietly while they worked side-by-side.

"Why's that? Loving wife? Baby on the way?" Marcus said lightly.

"No," Simon said softly. "Because I didn't have to go nuts wondering if she'd be cared for... and I was able to focus on just healing and getting back here... once things had finally turned around and I knew I could pull through. It's thanks to you, my friend... for taking care of her."

Marcus dropped his instruments on the tray next to them and motioned for Laura to come back and pack up the wound. The two friends made their way to the sink, all of the other personnel nodding and offering words of welcome to Simon as he passed. Simon paused by Harold, who nodded, but didn't say anything; it was good to see Simon back again.

The two friends stepped outside into the sun and walked a short way before dropping down on the dry grass. Marcus looked carefully at his friend. "How are you really, Simon? You lost a good bit of weight. Are they still rationing all the food in Paris? The cook here will have to fatten you up."

Simon sat, looking at his upper arms. "They didn't let me do push-ups after the surgery. I think I lost some muscle mass. But in answer to your question, I received excellent care. American doctors and nurses, modern equipment. They're using nitrous for anesthesia... saw my lungs, or what's left of them, on radiographs. Really good hospital prepping for the thousands of American troops arriving daily. My head was all messed up for a long time, opiates and infection and all... then they took the lobe, and it was... tough... to recover. But we'll be replaced soon, here."

Marcus looked up at the blue sky and sun overhead. "That's a relief... we can leave soon and with a clear conscience. Let the Americans finish this now. Oh, I put in for your replacement."

"Thanks." Simon fell silent, briefly. "Marcus, I uh, I know I said some things before I left about you and Lydia... about the ground rules. And I just want to say that no matter what did or didn't happen between you two, it's okay. I really mean it. I'm just grateful that you cared for her and the baby, and I wanted to say that out loud."

Marcus looked at his friend, deciding on honesty from the get-go. "Look, Simon, I told her, just recently, that I would marry her if you were actually dead. To help her raise your baby... give it, and her, a good home. And I meant every word. She's grown important to me... she gave me a chance to be one of the good guys."

"Well, I'm thankful that you rose to the occasion. Lydia loves the man you're becoming and doesn't want to lose you in her life... and neither do I," Simon stated simply.

Marcus laughed. "Well, I'm not going to marry you, Simon, so you can get that out of your head. But now that my matrimonial services are no longer required here, I think I'll try to contact Suzie, when we get back stateside."

Simon put his arm on his friend's shoulder. "Sure hope she's willing to meet with you at least. But, Marc, I would like you to consider going into practice with me. Setting up a surgical center."

"West Virginia?" Marcus asked hesitantly. "Isn't that, pretty backwoods? I don't think I'm cut out for being chased by bears and raccoons. Although this present experience has probably prepared me for that kind of life, more than I care to realize. Also, the air on top of the mountains is too thin for my lungs... maybe yours now, too. No, none of that Daniel Boone stuff for me."

Simon corrected him quickly. "No, actually, I was thinking Pittsburgh... the three rivers. It's a big city, growing fast, with teaching hospitals. It's reasonably close to Lydia's family, forty minutes or so. I hoped maybe that you'd consider staying near us... maybe just think about it."

Marcus nodded his head. A chance to be near Lydia and Simon, work with his best friends, and be part of the baby's life as it grew.

"Suzie comes first," Marcus said. "At least to try."

"Of course," Simon agreed. "And I hope she gives you another chance. If she does, there's room for everyone."

Marcus looked sad. "I missed out on everything," he admitted, his voice husky with surfacing emotion. "I realize that now, more than ever, since helping Lydia. The day-to-day things that matter in a relationship... the things that have so little to do with sexuality... or ego. Lydia has been teaching me that's not remotely what it's all about... and I had no idea that it could be so much more. I think I understand, a lot, better now. Maybe it was a good thing, for me anyway, that you had to be gone a little while. I had some growing up to do."

Simon laughed. "Sure hope you learned all that you needed to, my friend, because I'm going to do everything possible to never leave her again, which means no more life lessons."

They both laughed at that. "Where is she now?"

"Mess tent with Father James." Simon stood, followed by Marcus.

"Let's go say hello to the padre. I need to book another confession with him. I'm overdue, and those sins do pile up, don't they," Marcus admitted as Simon shook his hand, laughing again. They turned in step and went to the mess tent where Lydia and Father James were discussing the baby and their upcoming departure.

He was holding her hands and talking earnestly with her, about something, but stopped as the two men approached. Lydia marveled at the two friends together, Simon's hand on Marc's shoulder. Simon quickly went to Lydia, taking his spot behind her, resting his hands on her shoulders. She looked up at him, her eyes brimming with happiness. Carefully, she stood and went to Marcus, wrapping her arms around Marc's neck, hugging him tightly. Holding her close for a moment, Marc just breathed her in. They said nothing as Lydia pulled away and returned to Simon's arms.

Father James looked up also at the sight of Marcus beside them. "Ah, Doctor Lovell!" he exclaimed pleased. "How is my favorite prodigal son?"

"Comin' home, Father," Marcus assured him, taking a seat nearby. "Comin' home."

"Well, that's certainly good news. Anxious to hear all about it. I'll set another place at the table for you... prepare the fatted lamb and all that," the priest offered cheerfully. "This is quite a happy reunion. You know, I found Doctor Finney at the train station, looking for any sort of transportation... I do believe he would have walked the entire way, if I hadn't spotted him in the crowd. He filled me in on his half of the story on our way here, but I'm eager to hear the rest of the story."

"Later, Padre," Marcus said. "I wanted to say hello, but I can't stay too long. Still a few wounded out there waiting for me."

"I should get back to the surgery, too," Lydia said. "And I think you need to rest, Simon."

He was tired. The long trip had proven that his full capacity wasn't quite restored. "I guess you're right. Long ride from Paris."

"Come on," she told him. "I'll get you to bed."

"My nurse has spoken," he announced to the others as she stood to follow her.

Marcus and the priest watched them leave. "Two of the very finest people in the world," Marcus meant what he said.

"Agreed," Father James added. "I shall miss stopping in on your special little group."

Marcus folded his hands and looked across the table at the priest. "Got a minute, Padre?" he asked.

Father James smiled patiently. "Of course, Doctor Lovell. What's on your mind?"

Marcus looked down at the table and at his hands and quickly unfolded them, thinking it could be misinterpreted as false piety by the priest. He cleared his throat. "I, uh, I wanted to ask you a question, Father... you know, about the God thing..."

The priest's eyes twinkled. He waited patiently.

"Well, it's this way," Marcus continued. "As we were waiting... and not knowing about Simon—Doctor Finney, that is—well, I had a chance to do some soul searching of my own... with Simon entrusting Lydia into my care. And I realized that maybe I need to get acquainted, shall we say, with the God that she and Simon...

and, of course, you… it's probably the same God, actually… believe in."

The priest nodded thoughtfully. "Yes, He is one and the same, Doctor Lovell."

"Well, I just hoped that maybe before you leave us again, you could suggest some way for me to, uh, get to know Him a little better because Lydia, Nurse Finney, wants me to be the baby's godfather. And I'm not sure exactly what all that means, but it sounds like serious stuff, just like when Simon made me swear to God that I'd take care of Lydia if anything ever happened to him. And I kept that vow. I really did. And it felt really good to do it, Father. You know? It just felt right. So, I'm thinking that there might be some other aspects of this God business that might be right, too."

Father James saw the serious question in the young doctor's eyes and nodded with satisfaction. He had waited and prayed for this very moment, with this man, ever since he had met him. The priest settled himself in for the duration.

"Let's talk when you're done in the surgery," he said.

Lydia led Simon into their tent. He welcomed the chance to lay down as he felt the adrenaline from his arrival wearing off… fatigue settling in quickly. She sat beside him on the edge of the cot and placed a hand tenderly on his cheek. Simon took it and kissed her palm. He stared at her, taking in her eyes and cheeks and the way her hair escaped the scarf around her ears and forehead.

"You are so beautiful," Simon breathed. "I'm still the luckiest man alive." He was delighted when he saw that she blushed. Then, he grew very somber. "You know, I missed our anniversary. I'm sorry. I would've asked Cook to make a special dish or something for you."

Lydia leaned over and kissed him softly, her lips sensually brushing over his. "We'll have two anniversaries," she whispered against his mouth. "The second one will be today's date. The day you came back to us." She pressed his hand to her belly. Then, she took Simon's face in both hands and leaned over, kissing him fully, completely, lingering over the feel of him. "Sleep now, my love. I'll be back in a few hours when we close up in the surgery and triage." She left the tent, still half believing the turn of today's events.

Simon stared after her for a time, also absorbing this new reality, both of her presence and that he had actually made it back. He took in his surroundings, hearing an occasional thud of artillery to the east, the shelling seemed to be slowing, for the night. He reached into his pocket and retrieved the white stone, with gold flecks, that had made its way along with him: through the British CCS, the train ride, the hospital in Paris, and now back to the station.

He sat up and opened his footlocker to place it back inside and was shocked to find it, empty. Simon turned to hers and opened it, revealing his letters and small belongings had been carefully placed into the folds of her blue dress, the one she had worn on the day that the station celebrated their marriage. There were new letters from his sister, unopened, tucked away inside the folds of the fabric. He remembered watching Lydia come across the grass on that day, the dress flowing around her in the breeze, her brown hair lifting on the same air, walking toward him for the celebration that Marcus had arranged for them. So much had happened since that day when they'd all shared the French wine from Nancy, in a toast to their marriage. Simon placed the white stone on top of the dress, leaving everything else just as he found it, and shut the footlocker again. It was right that she had put everything that was theirs, together. They would take it all home with them. And someday, perhaps on another anniversary, they would open another bottle of wine, lift the lid together, and remember.

THREE RIVERS

Book II of The River Series

excerpt

With every ounce of strength he had, Simon got back onto his feet and found Marc's body again. Clenching his hands together around his friend's chest once more. Simon thought he heard shouting and tried to follow the sound through the roiling smoke. After an eternity of dragging Marcus over the fallen bricks, Simon pulled him out through the rapidly decaying entry out into the yard where firemen helped him carry Marcus to a small rise where they stretched him out on the grass. Simon bent over him, checking him for injuries, finding a gash on Marc's head where falling bricks had struck him. Assessing his friend's eyes, using the red glow of the fire, Simon saw with relief that Marc's pupils were still equal.

"Can you get him up, into better air?" Simon shouted to the firemen who nodded their confirmation. Looking back down the slope, he saw another fireman carrying out another wounded man slung over his shoulders. Running back down the slope, Simon helped him get the worker to higher ground before laying him down and also checking him quickly for injuries.

"He still alive?" the fireman shouted.

"Not by much," Simon yelled, not seeing burns. "Probably breathed in too much smoke. Get him to an ambulance."

The fireman nodded, calling for help to carry the injured away. Then Simon and the fireman looked around for more workers to emerge, but instead seeing that the outer brick wall of the building was giving way. Shoving the surgeon ahead of him up the slope, the fireman ran right behind, bricks falling hard, scattering in every direction. A huge tongue of fire split the air over their heads as they ducked. Covered in dust and smoke, they made it to the top of the slope where the hoses sprayed arcs of cold river water over them and into the conflagration. Mist from the water fell around them, streaking the dirt that covered them as they crouched down, breathing very hard, trying to fill their lungs with cooler air.

"Hey Doc," a policeman shouted. "Got one more over here…"

Wearily, Simon rose. He followed the officer to where a couple of workers sat on the ground, heads in their hands. Checking them both, Simon continued to render first aid to the injured until the fire gradually came under control and there were no more casualties requiring his attention. Then he returned to Marcus who was on the ground at a safe distance waiting, now sitting up and holding his throbbing head.

Dropping down beside him on the ground, Simon thanked God that Marc was awake again.

"Glad to see you woke up for the ending. Have you had enough fun yet?" he asked his friend. "Want to go home?"

"You mean back to the States?" Marcus asked, checking his hand for blood from his scalp.

"We're already back in the States, buddy!" Simon exclaimed, worried suddenly that his friend was disoriented from the head injury.

"Doesn't feel like it!" Marcus continued, "I thought for a minute that we were back in France, with shells dropping around us! Man, I have a headache."

Then absurdly, Simon started to laugh. Marcus was alright after all! "Good! If you feel the pain that means you're alive! Come on," he said, pulling Marcus' arm around his bare shoulders and dragging him to his feet. "You don't look so good! This time, I get to drive."

Pulling the car into the dark alley behind the house, Simon got out first and went around to help Marcus get out of the passenger side. Opening the fence to their backyard, he saw light stream out across the grass from the kitchen door which swung open for their arrival.

"Don't feel too steady yet," Marcus said quietly, still coughing up the smoke that had filled his lungs despite the make-shift bandanas they'd used, trying to filter the air. He draped his arm over Simon's shoulder and let his friend help him stumble up the walk. Flying out through the kitchen door, Susannah ran down the steps to meet them, pulling Marcus' other arm around her own shoulders as they helped him climb up the porch steps and into the kitchen. There he dropped heavily into a chair at the table while Anna and Andrew looked on, in shock.

"Got hit by a wall of falling bricks," Simon told Suzie quickly.

Immediately, Susannah grabbed a bowl of water and some towels and turned up the kitchen light to start washing the cut on

Marc's scalp. Grabbing her hand, Marcus pulled her down to kiss her and she touched his face gently.

"You're a mess," she teased tearfully.

He smiled, looking up at her. "Got a headache," he repeated.

"Okay, you can use that excuse once tonight," Suzie told him, her intense relief that he could speak coherently, clearly evident in her voice. Marcus just laughed.

Simon looked up, shocked. Lydia had somehow stumbled her way down the stairs and was now standing in the kitchen doorway, looking even more pale than she had when he saw her before he had left the house. She looked stricken with fear and he immediately went around the table to her. Despite his bare chest being covered in sweat and dirt and smoke, Simon pulled her to him and held her tight. Pressing her head against his shoulder, he stroked her hair, comforting her, kissing her forehead. As she began to sway in his arms, Simon scooped her up and carried her into the living room, placing her gently on the sofa, kneeling beside her, still caressing her face.

White as a ghost, Lydia reached up feebly and touched his beard and his lips, looking at him with her very soul reaching through her eyes, but saying nothing. Lowering his head, Simon placed his mouth gently against hers, breathing in her presence. She tasted the smoke from his lungs, and felt Simon kiss each of her eyes, her tears spilling over, though she didn't make a sound.

Simon gathered the salty wetness on his lips, regretting having caused her such dismay after having just given birth. He raised her head from the sofa just enough to wrap his arms around her and then he kissed her hard, driven by the emotions of the harrowing experience just behind him... and she, driven by how close she had come to losing him, responded. She felt too warm to his touch. Perhaps it was just a stress response from the ordeal of the fire... he hoped it was nothing more...

Acknowledgements

To the Patients

After over five decades of nursing practice, the patients must come first in any acknowledgment for this series. In the operating room, in the critical care units, in the psychiatric hospital and outpatient clinics, in home health care, and in Hospice, their perseverance, courage, and sometimes despair or defeat, have moved me repeatedly. Like Marcus in the series, they made me want to be a better person, a better nurse, a better caregiver in order to ease their suffering and to give them hope.

To My Brother-in-law

Many years ago, hearing stories of patients who had served in the world wars, my blessed brother-in-law suggested there ought to be a way to "honor their stories". Not too long after, we found my grandfather's World War I journal describing his experiences on the Western Front, featuring various locations along the Meuse River in France. It was an amazing coincidence. My brother-in-law encouraged me to write. And I am forever grateful to him for doing so.

To My Mother

Once in a lifetime, a mother comes along who lives to ninety-five with her mental acuity far surpassing her physical stamina.

A woman who happens to have been an English teacher. A woman who happens to have been an avid reader, interested in every genre from poetry, to commentary, to fiction, to biography, to the newspaper. From her recliner, with her cat on her lap (and as long as "Wheel of Fortune" and "Jeopardy" were over), she red-lined the manuscripts of The River Series, corrected grammar, untangled tenses, picked up dangling participles, and steadfastly asked where the next one hundred pages were, because she "[wasn't] getting any younger, you know!" She wanted to know how the lives of Lydia, Simon, and Marcus would come out in the end and insisted that the characters must never die. Mother passed first, unable to see the end of book six, or those that followed, but her unfailing enthusiasm for the project kept me writing even after her death. I am forever in debt to her motherly love and encouragement... may she hear it from Heaven.

To My Daughter

A gifted manager, who found resources, read and edited manuscripts, coordinated every aspect of publication tirelessly, with patience. I give heartfelt thanks to my remarkable and intrepid daughter who has given countless hours of her time and wisdom to this project.

To My Fellow Nurses and Co-workers

I want to thank the clinicians I work alongside, who have been so encouraging over the past few years, waiting for the series to come to print. Their unceasing belief in me is overwhelming. They are remarkable nurses and clinicians who share my love of patient care.

To God

My endless gratitude goes to God who gave me fingers with which to type, time with which to do it, caring people to support this work, and who does indeed hold the answer to the question: "Why?"

About the Author

Rachael Hiatt is an American author and practicing Registered Nurse for over 50 years, with Master's Degrees in both Nursing and Counseling. Her debut work, *The River Series*, is comprised of nine medical historical romance novels which follow a group of exceptional Nurses and Doctors over a 40 year period, starting in WWI. The journey plunges readers into the struggle to find courage, love, faith, and meaning in the throes of the battle between good and evil.

Rachael is a mother of two and grandmother of three. When she sets aside her pen, she finds joy in playing the piano, writing poetry, and observing the migrations of Snow Geese. With heartfelt gratitude to the patients she has had the privilege of serving as well as the practitioners she has worked alongside, to her mother—her most loyal critic—and to God, she humbly offers these novels to her readers.

Also by

Rachael Hiatt

THE RIVER SERIES
The Meuse

future releases
Three Rivers
Fishing Creek
Elk River
Six Penny Creek
Tributary
Monongahela
White Water
Frozen Falls